I0575930

A Druid's Wrath

BOOK FOUR
A Druid's Wrath

NICHOLAS SEARCY

Podium

All rights reserved. No part of this publication may be reproduced, stored in a retrieval system, or transmitted in any form or by any means electronic, mechanical, photocopying, recording, or otherwise without prior written permission from Podium Publishing.

This is a work of fiction. Names, characters, places, and incidents are either products of the author's imagination or used fictitiously. Any resemblance to actual events, locales, or persons, living, dead, or undead, is entirely coincidental.

Copyright © 2026 by Nicholas Searcy

Cover design by Nate Artuz

ISBN: 978-1-0394-7228-0

Published in 2026 by Podium Publishing
www.podiumentertainment.com

Podium

THE PATH SO FAR . . .

I like to think these journal entries help, though I'm not sure how. Maybe recording my journey is a form of catharsis, helping me to deal with past events. Or it could just be my arrogance made manifest in the belief that anyone would care about the trials I've experienced. Either way, it feels like it should be helpful, so I'll keep going with it.

When the World Tree touched Earth, the system rewrote reality. I was a dying marine biologist stranded on a deserted island, so there was absolutely no reason I should have survived. That was especially true considering that I soon found myself battling interdimensional reptiles and berserker gnomes. I even saved a dragon and, in return, earned a degree of power that I still don't fully understand.

After killing Eason Cabbot—the gnome I mentioned—and his mercenaries, I forged an alliance with Ironshore that I still hope will help see me through to the future. Yet, that was not enough. Nor was survival. I needed to find my family. So, I set out from my Grove in search of my sister, unaware that she was already dead. The journey took me through a plague-ridden city, an abandoned town where I befriended a bear guardian, and conquering another tower. When I learned that bear guardian had been killed by opportunistic hunters, I meted out nature's justice—a mistake, but one that felt right at the time.

Eventually, my journey took me to Argos, which offered friendship and a balm for my ragged soul. It also gave me the opportunity to save Isaak and Artemis—a young man and his cat—from the corruptive influence of a nearby dimensional rift.

But then came the orc horde.

It threatened not only my new allies in Ironshore, but eventually, the world itself. I had no choice but to return and fight. And fight I did. The battle nearly killed me, but we managed to eke out a victory.

Unbeknownst to me, while I fought monsters and killed hunters, my sister-in-law, Carmen, fought a tyrant and lost. She was exiled into the wilds with my nephew, Miguel. We both survived our trials, but we did so scarred and changed. We were alive, though.

That brings me to the end of my last entry. On to the next, I guess.

I keep telling myself that I'm not a hero, and to a degree, I believe that. For every person I've saved—like those people back in Norcastle—I've killed just as many others. And I fear that my days of dealing death will not soon end. But in the end, my primary goal is survival, and sometimes, that means killing.

After the battle against the orcs, I agreed to an alliance with Ironshore. After all, standing alone only sounds noble until the next crisis hits. We burned our dead, I paid my respects, and then I went back to the sort of work that felt familiar. I rebuilt myself the slow way—long days of crafting and cultivation. I also helped my new allies remake themselves by showing them the secrets of my tower, though in doing so, I opened myself up to reprisal. Thankfully, it didn't end well for my attacker, but it made dealing with Ironshore even more tense than before.

Meanwhile, Carmen walked her own road. Exile and hunger were her constant companions. She forged hope out of scrap and stubbornness, keeping Miguel and her companions alive. In the end, she learned the same lesson I'd discovered early on—no one was coming to save us. We needed to save ourselves.

While she was dealing with exile, I left my Grove and pushed deeper into the wilderness. I cleared rifts. I saved people who deserved saving, and I fought through another tower. Along the way, I felt myself growing closer to the land, to nature itself.

And all the while, family called to me, dragging me ever westward in the hopes of a reunion. Then, at last, I found Seattle—a ruinous place populated by desperate people and characterized by strife. Inadvertently, I planted myself right in the middle of that ongoing conflict.

I'm still not sure how that's going to go. Probably not well.

In any case, my exploration of Seattle told me one very important thing— my sister wasn't there. So, I once again set out—this time, through the desert— in search of Easton, the displaced suburb of Seattle where she'd once lived with her wife and son.

I didn't reach my destination.

Out of nowhere, Thor Gunderson—then the most powerful man in the world—attacked me. I still don't really know why. What I do know is that the battle nearly killed me, and it forced me to recognize that, while I had plenty of power at my disposal, I was still very much mortal.

My victory wasn't pretty. It wasn't clean. But in the end, I survived, and Thor did not. Given the circumstances, that was enough. I came away stronger, and more importantly, I gained the ability to fly via Shape of the Sky. While testing that new transformation, I was contacted by an old friend in Seattle, who informed me that my sister-in-law had arrived in the city.

I flew back as quickly as I could, hoping for the reunion I'd sought for years.

It turned out to be a bittersweet affair. Carmen and Miguel had survived, albeit not without hardship, but my sister had been dead for nearly two years. She had been betrayed by a man she'd trusted—a mentor and longtime friend.

The days after that were difficult. I didn't let myself grieve. Not really. Instead, I focused on doing something useful, on saving the only family I had left. That led me to building my next dolmen—the Circle of Spears, in honor of my sister.

Together, Carmen, Miguel, and I went back to my Grove, where they would be safe. But I knew it wouldn't last because there was only one thing on my mind—vengeance against the man who'd betrayed my sister. And I wouldn't rest until I had it.

A Druid's Wrath

1

SHOWING OFF

This is amazing," said Miguel, his mouth hanging open as he stared at the verdant landscape of Elijah's Grove. They had only just arrived, having been teleported thousands of miles in an instant via Elijah's Roots of the World Tree spell. But neither Carmen nor Miguel had any means of knowing just how vast the distance between his most recent dolmen, the Circle of Spears, and his Grove really was.

By comparison, Elijah knew precisely how far they'd come. After all, he'd spent the better part of two years trekking across the wilderness—albeit with a few distractions along the way—in an effort to reunite with his sister. However, when he'd finally found his nephew and sister-in-law, he'd been horrified to learn that Alyssa had been killed long ago.

Perhaps it had happened before he'd even left his island.

Whatever the case, that discovery had come with a healthy dose of rage, guilt, and grief.

The first came because his sister hadn't been slain by happenstance. No monster—at least not of the normal variety—had killed her. Instead, she had been murdered by a power-mad despot she'd once considered a friend. That betrayal was foremost in the most prominent facet of Elijah's Quartz Mind, though he couldn't allow himself to embark on his planned quest for vengeance.

Not yet, at least. He needed to get his family—and the other refugees who'd come to the Grove almost a week before—settled. After that, he would give himself fully to revenge.

The second emotion—guilt—was twofold. Most prominently, he'd taken his sweet time adjusting to the new world. After Earth had experienced the touch of the World Tree—and been transformed—he'd spent months simply surviving. He hadn't been driven by a need to grow stronger. Instead, he'd focused almost entirely on satisfying the necessary requirements to continue living. However, that had all changed after his protector—a powerful mist-panther guardian—had been killed, and he'd been forced to see to his own safety. A few months—and a life-altering tower run—later, and he'd become a different person.

Yet, he still wondered what might have happened if he'd taken responsibility for his own progression sooner. Would it have been enough? Maybe not. But the mere possibility that it would have let him find his sister before she was killed haunted him. The same could be said about his habit of giving in to every distraction he found in his travels. Whether it was healing the plague-stricken residents of the first human settlement he'd found or one of the superfluous tower runs he'd embarked upon, Elijah knew he'd wasted a lot of time. Certainly, he'd also grown more powerful, but he'd trade any number of levels—or strangers' lives—if he could get just a few more days with his sister.

The second facet of that guilt came from before Earth's transformation. Just before Elijah had graduated high school, he'd lost both of his parents. That had sent him down a spiral of grief where he'd pushed everyone away, and it had culminated in his jetting off to Hawaii for college, where he'd studied to become a marine biologist. And while his pursuit of a degree—and employment afterward—had been reasonably successful, it had also put thousands of miles, both figuratively as well as literally, between him and the only family he had left.

Before, he'd thought he had plenty of time to reconnect, but being diagnosed with terminal cancer had thrown those plans aside. That was how he'd ended up on his island in the first place. Knowing he was dying, Elijah had decided to live his last days with his sister—mostly at her insistence. But the world's transformation—and the subsequent crash of his plane—had seen him stranded on a deserted island.

Loneliness had taught him just how deep his regrets went. Sure, he didn't immediately set off to find his sister and her family, and even when he had, he'd taken his time. From his perspective, there had been no urgency. More, simply finding them when the entire world had been randomized and transformed made the task almost impossible. It was like finding a needle in a haystack, and it was only through coincidence—and a little planning—that he'd found Carmen and Miguel.

Or maybe he was just making excuses.

Perhaps his guilt was warranted.

Either way, there was nothing he could do to change the past. What he could do, however, was to ensure his family's safety. Carmen and Miguel weren't related to him by blood, but then again, neither was his spryggent friend, Nerthus. That didn't change the fact that all three were family.

"I thought you might like it," Elijah said to his nephew. He reached out and gripped the boy's—no, the young man's—shoulder. "It wasn't always like this. When I first got here, it was just a big meadow with the ancestral tree in the center. It looked different back then, too."

"Different how?"

"Well, it was more like a normal tree," Elijah explained. "But when Nerthus absorbed a Shard of the World Tree, it started to change. So did he, come to that."

"Indeed," said Nerthus, who had a habit of standing so still that one could almost mistake him for a tree himself, albeit an oddly shaped one with only a few leaves. Or perhaps an expertly carved sculpture. However, Nerthus was as distinct an individual as anyone else Elijah had ever met, and he was powerful in his own right. The Grove was as much his as it was Elijah's. Perhaps more so, considering how much time and effort the spryggent had spent guiding its growth.

More than that, though, Elijah owed the tree spirit his life. Without him, he'd have never embarked down the path of cultivation, and without those advantages, he had no doubt that he would have long since perished. Most recently, he'd have been slain by one of the most powerful people in the world. Even then, Elijah had been forced to use his entire tool kit to survive Thor Gunderson's ambush.

"The ethera here is so dense," Carmen said, almost as impressed as her son. She was a short woman—even compared to Elijah, who, in his more honest moments, would have admitted that he was a little below average in the height department—and even though she'd clearly lost weight during her travels, she was still quite muscular. Otherwise, she and Miguel shared the same tan skin, dark hair, and brown eyes. She asked, "How is this possible?"

"The ancestral tree is a natural treasure," Nerthus answered. "A powerful one, too. All ancestral trees are strong, influencing their environments more broadly than most treasures. My tree is far more powerful than most, especially after absorbing the Shard of the World Tree."

"Making it the center of the Grove didn't hurt, either," Elijah supplied. He and Nerthus had spoken on the subject at length, so he knew just how special his situation was. Most natural treasures didn't last long. Even if they were protected by powerful guardians, they were usually consumed by natives or even opportunistic wildlife. Not only had Elijah forgone consuming the tree, he'd also actively reinforced and empowered it. The results had been impressive, growing its influence to encompass the entire island.

Indeed, when Elijah had established his Grove—via one of the first spells his Druid archetype had granted—it had come with a Domain, inside of which was a Locus of awareness. It had since grown a little past the island's boundaries, so the result was that he could sense everything about the island, regardless of his own location.

Fortunately, he had his Quartz Mind to deal with the overwhelming amount of information.

"Do you guys want a tour?" Elijah asked.

Miguel eagerly said that he did, while Carmen's agreement was a little more subdued. So, after they gathered the other three who'd preceded them a week before—they'd been holed up in the tree house intended to become Carmen's living quarters since they'd arrived—Elijah set out to show them the highlights of his island.

Fittingly, the first location was the Grove itself. It was the beating heart of Elijah's Domain, and it was easily the most important part of the island. Everyone was suitably impressed by the varied vegetation and the stand of coffee trees Elijah had most recently planted. Nerthus had also planted a wide variety of other plants, from herbs to sunflowers and everything in between.

"Glad to see the seeds I got for you didn't go to waste," Elijah said. "Amazing work, Nerthus. Really. You've outdone yourself."

The spryggent beamed at the compliment. It was in moments like that that Elijah remembered that, though Nerthus looked like a weathered collection of twisted roots, he was, in fact, little more than an adolescent. Even since their first meeting, Nerthus's personality had developed considerably, and Elijah expected that trend to continue going forward.

After the Grove, Elijah took the group to the ruined cabin that had provided solace and protection from the elements for the first few months after the world had transformed. Then, he took the group to the beach, where he introduced them to the giant crabs that seemed to love his island so much. They didn't get close enough to get the huge crustaceans' attention, but Elijah did describe his first few encounters with the creatures.

"I woke up to them nibbling on my legs," he said. "They weren't bigger than cocker spaniels back then, but they grew to this size within a year. Thank God they leveled off. Otherwise, we might be in danger of living in a world ravaged by huge crabs," he joked.

Once they were suitably impressed by the crabs, Elijah showed off his dwindling collection of rowboats, then pointed out Ironshore across the strait. "That's where most of you are going," he said. "The people there are mostly okay. Goblins, dwarves, and gnomes. Oh, and a couple of elves. But they're nice enough, now that . . . Well, Ramik keeps them in line."

He'd almost let loose with the tale of how he'd slaughtered fifty Ironshore residents who'd attempted to invade his island, but it didn't take a genius to guess that that wouldn't have ended well. Carmen, Miguel, and Colt would be fine. But the other two? They were clearly terrified of him, and he wanted to avoid spooking them any further. Besides, they'd find out the truth soon enough, anyway. But by then, they'd be on the other side of the strait where he wouldn't have to deal with it.

The final landmark he wanted to show them was the tower, which took a couple of hours to reach. It would have taken longer, but Elijah knew the optimal path. And the others—aside from Miguel—all had a few levels under their belts. For his part, the young man didn't complain; instead, he endeavored to keep pace, and though he couldn't do so, he kept up a lot better than Elijah would have predicted.

It was impressive, and it boded well for when the young man gained access to the system and actually started gaining attribute points.

"Wow," Carmen said. "I've never actually seen a tower."

"I have," Colt said. "I was with the second group who went through the one near Easton. It was not a pleasant experience."

"They usually aren't," Elijah said. "But if you want to get stronger, Ironshore sends a group through there once a week. I'm sure they'll let you in. They have a shortage of combatants."

"I . . . may just do that," Colt stated.

"When can I do it?" asked Miguel.

"Not until you have a class," Carmen said. "And if I hear about you going anywhere close to that tower . . ."

"I know, Mom. I'm not stupid," he complained.

Carmen just shook her head. After that, Elijah led the others back to the Grove. By that point, it was time for supper, so he shared a bit of meat he had stored in his Ghoul-Hide Satchel, which they cooked in his kitchen. However, retrieving it highlighted the fact that Elijah had picked up a lot of stuff recently. So, he knew he would need to stop by Atticus's shop soon, not only to identify the items, but also to unload anything he didn't need.

After the meal, everyone but Carmen headed to the other tree house. Once they were gone, Elijah and his sister-in-law sat on his balcony, which overlooked the Grove. Both clutched steaming mugs full of the tea he'd bought back in Ironshore, and for the longest time, neither spoke.

Finally, though, Carmen said, "Thank you."

"For what?"

"For this. It's exactly what we need," she said. "When you told me about this place, I thought you were exaggerating. But now . . . I think you might have been underselling it. It's paradise."

"It wasn't always like this. My first year was incredibly difficult."

"I don't doubt it."

They both went silent for a little while longer until, once again, Carmen broke the silence and asked, "What are you going to do?"

Elijah didn't need her to elaborate. He knew what she was asking.

"I've got some things I need to take care of," he said. "Then, I'm going to Easton. I intend to kill him. That's certain. Other than that, I don't know. I still haven't decided."

For a moment, Elijah thought his sister-in-law was going to argue. But then, she just gave him a curt nod and said, "Good. If anyone in this world deserves the worst you can dish out, it's Roman Cain."

2

GETTING SETTLED

The next morning, Elijah awoke feeling refreshed, and it actually took him a few moments to remember the burden of vengeance he'd taken upon himself. The moment he settled into those thoughts, his mood darkened, but he forced the roiling emotions into their own facet, where he could ignore them at least long enough to do what needed to be done.

Because as much as he wanted to simply rush off to Easton, he knew he had a lot to accomplish before he could do so without worry. For one, he needed to finish getting Carmen and the others settled, and that meant introducing them to Ironshore. Then, he had a few other minor tasks to accomplish before he could, in good conscience, fully embrace his new mission.

And one larger task, though that would have to wait until after a visit to Ironshore.

To that end, he pushed himself out of bed, then took care of his business in the bathroom before taking a long, hot shower. To his delight, Nerthus had adjusted both the water pressure as well as the temperature, so even with his high Constitution, Elijah could feel the change. In the days before Earth's transformation, it might've felt like he was being pressure washed by near-boiling water, but now? It was soothing.

So, Elijah took a little longer than absolutely necessary before he stepped out of the shower and dressed. After that, he completely emptied his satchel, placing everything in separate piles, depending on their type. Magical items went in one section, while leftover meat went into another. The few berries he had left found their way into another section, while his clothing—which was universally soiled—was in another pile. There were bits and pieces of animal hide, a few teeth, and some wooden trinkets he'd carved during his downtime.

It was shocking how much would fit into the Ghoul-Hide Satchel, and looking at his accumulated possessions, Elijah had no choice but to come to one simple conclusion: He'd become a bit of a pack rat.

With that in mind, he set upon the items, earmarking many of them for disposal. He didn't need a half dozen poorly preserved rabbit furs, after all. Nor did he need a collection of snake fangs. The same could be said for Thor's clothing, which Elijah had looted. The cloth was nothing special, and it was all sized to fit a giant. Besides, it was all bloodstained and had been ripped to pieces by the battle. So, it went into the heap of items meant to be discarded.

The man's armor was a different story. It was mundane. Not even Crude grade. And Elijah questioned why such a powerful fighter had bothered wearing armor that was, by every metric Elijah could use, inferior to the man's bare skin. Perhaps it was meant to assuage the Thor's vanity. After all, he'd seemed to have chosen his attire to portray a specific aesthetic. Or maybe it had held sentimental value, though from what he knew of the former high ranker, that didn't seem likely.

Either way, Elijah wasn't in the habit of discarding good metal or cured leather. So, he kept that.

As for the magical items, there were a few that had yet to be identified. Like the fanged necklace. Or even Elijah's new staff. He suspected that it would help his shape-shifting in some way, but he couldn't be certain of anything until he had Atticus identify it. The Ghoul-Hide Satchel's functions were easier to discern, but Elijah wanted to get it appraised, as well.

The same was true of his Weighted Gloves.

The canteen, too.

Finally, the meat went into his cold storage. It would keep for a while in there, and though Elijah knew he wouldn't remain on the island long, he intended to leave it there for Carmen and Miguel. They couldn't hunt as easily as he could, so that seemed the most prudent course of action.

The pile of clothes—as well as his Cloak of the Iron Bear—got a generous dusting of cleansing powder. It would take a couple of hours for that to work, so he donned his lone clean pair of pants before heading out to the Grove to refamiliarize himself with everything. He could, of course, sense the entire island right down to the tiniest insect, but there was something about actually laying eyes on the flora that made all the difference.

For a while, he just walked among the bushes and flowers, delighting in the aromas as well as the fat honeybees buzzing about. Thankfully, those insects hadn't been changed by the touch of the World Tree. Upon finding his patch of lavender, he picked some so that he could get another batch of infused oil going. And of course, as he walked through the Grove, he didn't hesitate to grab a couple of berries here and there.

But eventually, his path took him to his coffee trees. Each one had reached almost twenty feet in height, which was abnormally large for that species. However, Elijah chalked that increased size up to the presence of ethera that had grown so many other things out of proportion.

The cherries were still green, which meant that they weren't yet ripe. But he could sense that it wouldn't be long before they were ready to be plucked. Then, he'd have all the coffee he could drink. And hopefully, it would have some special effects, just like his berries.

He was inspecting his trees when Carmen approached. He'd felt her awaken nearly forty-five minutes before, but he'd pointedly not paid much attention to the facet of his Mind that was dedicated to monitoring his Domain. Everyone deserved at least a little privacy, after all.

"Sleep well?" he asked, resting his hand on one of the trees' branches. He held out his other hand, asking, "Berry?"

"I did. That moss bed was probably the most comfortable place I've ever slept," she admitted, taking one of the berries. She let out an audible sigh upon popping it into her mouth. "Why does every one of these taste different?"

"I don't know," Elijah admitted. "Ethera is weird."

"You can say that again. Are these coffee trees?"

"Yeah," Elijah answered, finally looking back at her with a grin. He almost felt it, too, but he knew he was forcing it. Perhaps the day would come when every thought wasn't accompanied by pangs of loss, but for now, he would just have to fake emotions other than grief or anger. To distract himself, Elijah explained how he'd gotten the Miracle Seed. "And after that, Nerthus helped me turn one tree into a whole grove. Though when I made my calculations, I only made enough for personal use. I guess I'm lucky they're a lot bigger than I expected."

"What are we planning for today?" she asked.

"Well, I'm about to train a little," Elijah said. "About an hour or so. By the time I'm done, everyone over in Ironshore should be awake. So, we're going over there so I can get your friends settled. You and Miguel are welcome to live here on the island, but I don't want the others here." Then, his hand found the back of his neck and he added, "Uh . . . if you want to live here, I mean. Totally get it if you don't want to, what with my localized omnipotence. Well, omni-science, at least."

"What?"

"I'm not all-powerful, but I am all knowing."

"I know what the two words mean, Elijah. What are you talking about?" she asked, annoyed.

"Well, I kind of know everything that happens here on the island. Everything."

"Everything?"

"Everything."

"That's . . . disturbing," she said.

"Try living with it. Not that I'm complaining, mind you, but if I didn't have a Quartz Mind, I'd have already gone nuts, I'm sure. But Opal kind of kept it in check, too, so who knows?"

"It would be silly not to live here. For Miguel, at least—the increased ethera density has to be beneficial," she said. "And I'd love to know more about cultivation. I haven't stepped on that path yet, but I'm beginning to think that I need to remedy that. I don't intend to fight, but I'm certain that it will help me with smithing."

"Oh—yeah. Speaking of that, the town over there across the strait? They have a mine where they've found some sort of special metal," Elijah said. "I don't remember what it was called, but Carisa—she's the dwarf in charge—seemed really excited about it. So did Ramik, come to think of it."

After that, Carmen seemed a lot more excited about visiting Ironshore. However, Elijah meant to keep to his plan, not least because he didn't want to barge in on Ramik before the goblin even had a chance to properly wake up. So, after extricating himself from Carmen's interrogation on magical ores, he retreated to the beach, where he restarted the training routine he followed each time he was home.

And he was more than a little surprised to find that everything was quite a bit easier than it had ever been. To make things more productive, he found a couple of huge rocks to carry around while he swam, ran, and did various acrobatics. Still, it was only marginally taxing, at least until he went through his yoga routine in his lamellar-ape form.

That was still just as challenging as ever.

About halfway through, he felt Colt approach. The slim swordsman asked if he wanted to spar a bit, and Elijah consented. That's when he discovered just how lacking his staff-fighting technique was. Even though he knew he should have had a host of advantages on his side—regarding attributes, cultivation, and the general superiority of his chosen weapon—he found himself being soundly beaten by the one-armed man.

Of course, in a real fight, Elijah would have simply switched to one of his bestial forms and ripped Colt to shreds. But that wasn't the point, and it drove home the notion that he needed quite a lot of practice before he could ever consider himself competent with his staff.

Fortunately, Colt was willing to give him plenty of pointers, so Elijah felt that he made decent progress, even though their practice session only lasted for an hour. After that, he resolved to continue training with the man for as long as he remained on the island.

Part of that was simple necessity. He couldn't afford to be so vulnerable in his caster form, and his fight with Thor had hammered that into him. In that battle, Elijah could only retreat and hope to delay the man long enough to pounce on any weakness. Hopefully, with enough practice, he could fix that deficiency, because if Colt had proved anything, it was that attributes weren't everything. Technique counted for quite a lot.

Elijah would have been lying to himself if he didn't admit that his competitive spirit was responsible for the rest of that resolution. He'd never taken losing well. Usually, his response was to train harder, and this situation was no different.

After that, the pair returned to the Grove, where they found everyone else up and about. The spares—as Elijah referred to Theresa and Byron—remained in the tree house, obviously afraid to offend him by venturing out of bounds. Elijah hadn't gone out of his way to disabuse them of that notion, largely because he wasn't comfortable with strangers wandering around his island.

In any case, he returned to his own tree house, took a blisteringly quick shower, then dressed in his now-clean clothes. He was certain to don his normal magical kit, as well. That included his two rings—the Ring of Aquatic Travel that would let him breathe underwater and the often-useless Ring of Anonymity that would give the ability to disguise his identity. Next came his Weighted Gloves, which he willed to disappear a moment after slipping them onto his hands. After that, he tied his Sash of the Whirlwind in place before wrapping the Silver Bracer of Rage around his forearm. Finally, he slipped the Ghoul-Hide Satchel on, settled the Cloak of the Iron Bear over his shoulders, fastened it in place with the silver toggles, then took up his Dragon-Touched Staff.

Thus equipped, he descended from his tree house and joined the others before leading them to his collection of rowboats. It was then that he remembered just how much he hated rowing across the strait. At first, he was tempted to simply shift into the Shape of the Sky and fly across, but that could very well cause issues with his neighbors. On top of that, it wouldn't really save any time because Carmen and the others would still have to paddle across.

So, it was with some regret that, after everyone was on board, he shoved the rowboat into the water, leaped aboard, and began the arduous task of rowing everyone across. Of course, some of the others—including the one-armed Colt—offered to help, but he insisted he was fine with it. He even said he enjoyed it, for some indefinable reason.

Regardless, he guided the small boat across the strait with ease, and only twenty minutes later, they arrived at the dock.

Of course, suspicious glances from the residents of Ironshore soon found them. Elijah was used to that, though. So, he wasted no time in tying the boat off and helping everyone onshore.

After that, they headed to Ramik's office. For his part, the dapper goblin mayor was happy to see Elijah, and he was eager to share that they'd established trade relations with Norcastle on the other side of the mountain range.

"That's awesome," Elijah said, forcing a smile. He hadn't even remembered that they were trying to liaise with the human city, but he was glad of any success Ironshore could find. He had long suspected that their fate would be tied to his, after all. As they rose, so too would he.

Especially since humans were integrating into the town.

"There are only a few so far, but we expect more to come from Norcastle," Ramik said proudly. "We're growing, Elijah. In a few years, we may even turn a profit!"

Soon after, Elijah had made arrangements for Theresa and Byron to stay in the city. Both had a few levels under their belts, and Ramik seemed thrilled by their classes. Next, Elijah took Carmen to see the mine foreman, Carisa. The dwarven woman was even happier to meet Carmen—after discovering she was a Blacksmith—than Ramik had been about the pair of Scholars, and before long, the dwarf and his sister-in-law had forgotten he was even there.

So, Elijah, Colt, and Miguel went to the Stuck Pig, where they enjoyed a nice meal. It was a bit early for lunch, but it only took a whiff of the succulent smell of roasting meat to get the other two on board.

After that, Elijah ran some errands—buying some supplies for soapmaking, more cleansing powder, and rations—before finally going back to fetch Carmen. She had somehow found an anvil and was deep into a demonstration for Carisa.

"I'll return to the island once I'm done," Carmen said. "You go ahead."

"It's getting dark soon," Elijah responded.

"Then I'll stay the night here. I'm sure Carisa can find a place for me to bunk," Carmen stated dismissively. After the dwarven foreman eagerly agreed to that, the pair practically pushed Elijah out of the mining office.

"It wasn't so long ago that I was sneaking through town and murdering Ritualists," he mused.

"What was that, hoss?" asked Colt.

"Huh?"

"Somethin' 'bout murderin' Ritualists?"

"Nothing. I'm sure you misheard. Let's go," Elijah said, already walking toward the dock.

3

GOOD FOR THE SOUL

Normally, Elijah enjoyed the sound of birds chirping in the morning. However, after a night of heavy drinking—which didn't end until he'd blacked out—he found the cacophony to be the height of annoyance. For a long time, he just lay there, reveling in his own misery until he finally pushed himself upright and cast Soothe. It helped, though it took almost the entire run time of the spell before his headache faded and his stomach stopped roiling.

He almost regretted it.

After all, he'd consumed nearly five gallons of the potent liquor he'd gotten back in Valosta. He should have spent the entire day paying for his excess. Without those consequences hanging over his head, Elijah knew how easy it would be to turn back to the bottle.

He'd never been one to try to drown his sorrows, but then again, he'd never lost a sister, either. And now that he didn't have the dolmen's construction or getting everyone settled to distract him, he could give himself fully to the grief.

And the anger.

That was there, too—inescapable and inexorable.

Swinging his legs off the bed, Elijah bent over, resting his elbows on his knees as he stared at the floor. At least drinking the night away had given him some reprieve. But he knew he couldn't do that every time he didn't want to deal with his emotions. Not only was it unhealthy, but it was also more expensive than he could manage. Alcohol wasn't cheap in Ironshore, and his free supply was now gone.

Perhaps he could learn to ferment his berries into wine.

Shaking his head, Elijah ran his hand through his hair and let out a long sigh. Alyssa wouldn't have approved of any of it. She would have scolded him like she had when he'd gone down a similar route right after their parents had died.

She was right, too.

Elijah was an adult now. Not only did he have responsibilities, but he also had goals. More importantly, Miguel had begun to look up to him. It hadn't been long since they'd been reunited, but the young man clearly craved examples to emulate. He had Colt, and that was great. From what Elijah could tell, Miguel couldn't have picked a better man to model himself after. But he'd latched on to

Elijah, as well, which came with a responsibility to put his own self-pity aside and be there for the young man.

They all had to do that. Carmen had managed it, and so could Elijah.

With that in mind, he climbed to his feet with another sigh, but the next intake of breath nearly made him gag. Drinking himself into a stupor was messy work, and the smell of his strenuous labor hung off him like a cloak. That cemented Elijah's first order of business, and he wasted no more time before taking a shower. His homemade soap made a world of difference, picking up the slack where his spell had left off, and when he exited the bathroom, he felt like a new man.

However, he couldn't escape the reality of the night's excesses, so he spent a little time gathering bottles and cleaning the bedding. Finally, more than half an hour later, he was ready to start his day. Like always when he was home, he spent the next couple of hours training, though he wasn't afforded the opportunity of another sparring session with Colt.

That wasn't to say that the other man wasn't training on his own. He was, and Miguel was with him, but they were doing their own thing, practicing sword katas in the Grove.

So, Elijah focused on his own routine, and after the previous day's efforts, he managed to alter his regimen to push even his massive attributes to their limits. Around three hours after he'd begun, he felt a rowboat enter his Domain, and a second later, he recognized that Carmen had finally returned. He left her to her own devices for another hour, and in that time, she arrived back at the Grove, where she watched her son's training.

Elijah found her sitting on the roots of one of the trees that comprised the outer ring of his Grove, and he joined her. The first few minutes, they simply watched, but then, Elijah asked, "Did you have a productive introduction to Ironshore?"

"I did," she said. "You know they don't have a proper Blacksmith? They have some people with classes specializing in processing ore—making alloys and such—but no one to work with the final products."

"I'm guessing you're going to fill that role?"

She nodded. "I'm building my own smithy," Carmen answered. "A proper forge, like I had back in Silverado."

Elijah winced. "That name . . ."

"I know," she said with a wry smile. "I didn't name it, though."

"Do you know what happened to it?"

She shook her head, saying, "I don't know. I'm sure Roman wouldn't have abandoned it. That cold iron is too useful. Though they don't have any smiths worth a damn now. Not unless someone stepped up, and I know everyone who might've. They're all average at best. Lazy, unmotivated, and untalented at worst."

"Ouch. Tell me how you really feel."

Carmen shrugged. "You don't know how it is in a city like that," she responded. "By and large, people aren't really built to excel. They do what they have to do to get what they want. Most of the time, that means survival with a few conveniences. Some distractions. And for a crafter in Easton, the bar is incredibly low. You can get pretty rich just making run-of-the-mill equipment. The incentive to push higher just isn't there, except for personal motivation. They think they're safe. They believe the danger has passed."

"It hasn't," Elijah said. "There are more than towers out there."

He'd read a couple of guides about the progression of dimensional rifts. The most common expression of those anomalies was spontaneous manifestation. A powerful Voxx would simply tear through the membrane between universes and enter one of the planets connected to the World Tree. In a lot of ways, these were the most dangerous because they could be far more powerful than the Voxx attached to dimensional rifts and towers.

Above those were primal realms, which, as Elijah understood them, were like towers on steroids. They were bigger, more complex, and far deadlier than towers. As a result, they could accommodate up to twenty people, as opposed to the comparatively smaller groups that could challenge a tower. But even more troubling, those primal realms could exert influence on the world, transforming the terrain to fit their theme. The guide he'd read used a magmatic cave as an example, explaining that in such a scenario, the land surrounding the primal realm would take on the fiery traits of the realm.

But there were bigger threats out there, too. Ancient realms. Battle worlds. Trial planets. The list went on and on. The fact was that they'd joined an extremely dangerous multiverse, and even if the people of Easton had attained some semblance of safety, that would not remain the case for all eternity. Eventually, they would be threatened, and if they didn't have the strength to stand up to those threats, they would die.

Elijah couldn't worry about that, though. Especially considering that he had yet to decide whether or not Easton needed to share its leader's fate. His instincts told him to simply remove the city from the map, but his sense of morality—as skewed as it sometimes was—wouldn't let him do so without significant consideration.

"I'm going to be gone for a couple of weeks," he said.

"Is it . . . Is it time?"

"No," he answered. "I'm not going to Easton yet. I'll be close, but I would rather not be disturbed unless absolutely necessary."

"What are you doing?"

Elijah said, "I've been working on my Soul cultivation for a while. If I don't finalize it now, I'll have to spend a little time each day keeping it fresh. I don't want to be distracted while I do what I need to do in Easton, so I need to push through to the next step."

"Cultivation. Alyssa had started working on her Body before she passed."

"Ask Nerthus about it if you want some help. He's the one who put me on the right path," Elijah suggested. "If he can't help, I could give it a shot. I'll be honest, though—most of what I've done probably isn't replicable."

"I'll ask him. If not for me, then definitely for Miguel. He'll be getting his archetype soon, and I know how powerful cultivation can be."

"Anything that gives him a better chance of survival," Elijah agreed. "I'll help where I can, but . . . after . . . after I do what I need to do."

After that, Elijah left Carmen to her own devices as he prepared for what he intended. Once he'd left his valuables behind in the tree house, he set off across the island, and upon reaching the beach, he disrobed and waded into the cold water. Soon enough, he dived beneath the waves and was swimming toward the crevice that would lead him to the cultivation cave.

He took his time, slowly making his way as he mentally prepared. He couldn't afford to let extraneous thoughts pollute his mind, so even after he reached the cave, he spent nearly three hours forcing himself into the right headspace. He did notice that the ethera density had risen to unprecedented levels, and the flora had responded in kind. It was a practical jungle of kelp and other sea plants, with plenty of small fish, water bugs, and other marine creatures having arrived to take advantage of the thick energy.

If Elijah had to guess, the ethera in the cave was at least twice as dense as it was in the heart of his Grove. The rest of the island was even thinner, though compared to the outside world, it was an ethereal paradise. For cultivation purposes, all of which required extremely dense ethera, there probably wasn't a better location in the world. Even if there were a few places that could rival it—the world was huge now, after all—Elijah's cave was entirely sustainable. He could use it over and over again, and from what he could tell, it would just keep growing stronger.

A good thing, too, because the requirements to reach the next levels of cultivation would assuredly be quite steep.

In any case, Elijah swam to the center of the cave, then focused on his task. He didn't start the process yet. Instead, he continued to meditate as he established the right frame of mind.

Hours later, he felt he was ready.

The first step was to swirl the ethera in his Core, which wasn't particularly difficult. He'd already started cycling the energy in preparation for taking the next step in his Core cultivation, so he'd learned the basics of moving ethera. Still, it took time and the focus of all but a few of his Mind facets.

Elijah fell into a rhythm, pushing and pulling the ethera to create a whirlpool of energy that stretched his Core to its limits. The pressure continued to build until, at last, he gave it an outlet, guiding the gathered ethera to a single point that marked the genesis of his first channel—and the system of channels he intended to build.

It was like an explosion going off inside his body, and Elijah had to harness every ounce of his willpower just to keep from gasping at the sudden spike of pain. Cultivation, it seemed, required significant pain tolerance.

But that single explosion was only the beginning, and over the next few hours, he continued to swirl his ethera, then focus its pressure toward that same point. And slowly, the channel began to take shape, snaking out from his core and up his torso, forming the main trunk of the intended pattern.

Not coincidentally, the pattern he'd memorized looked very much like a tree.

That pattern was a long way off, though. He'd allocated two weeks for the process, but after excavating that single channel, he knew it would likely take even longer than his initial estimate.

Still, once begun, stopping short of completion was not an option. It was possible to resume the process, but that would affect the result. And Elijah wasn't willing to take anything but the best.

So, he leveraged his Mind as well as his considerable willpower—and tolerance for pain—to continue on. After the trunk, he used the same method to carve the branches that would take ethera throughout his body.

The first step of Soul cultivation, which he'd taken what felt like a lifetime ago, had decentralized his pathways, but that was only preparation for the second step. One had to break the system down before it could be rebuilt, better and more efficient—and more personally meaningful—than ever.

Gradually, Elijah forced the channels into being. The trunk was first, then the limbs. And finally, the branches. Later stages would build upon those efforts, creating a more elaborate system, but for now, the rudimentary design was enough.

Throughout the process, Elijah was keenly aware of the cost of any potential mistakes. He wouldn't die. Nor would he lose the ability to use ethera. Rather, the system would simply be less efficient. And given that every subsequent step built off the foundation, getting it right was an absolute necessity.

Days passed into more than a week, and eventually, he overtook the bounds of his estimated time of completion. Yet, on he went, digging the channels through his body. At some point, he stopped processing the pain. He was aware of it, but it was distant. Unimportant. However, he grew ever more exhausted until manipulating his ethera felt like trying to stir molasses.

Even so, he pushed on.

And finally, after he'd long since lost track of time, the task was done—a fact that was verified by a flash of ethera that hardened the walls of each channel. That was expected, but in his state of intense fatigue, Elijah was still startled. Suddenly, all the ethera in his body dissipated.

For a moment, he was drowning in nothingness.

Then, the apertures in his Mind opened up, and ethera flooded back in. However, unlike before, it didn't simply diffuse into his body. Rather, it followed the well-defined channels he'd spent so long carving.

And it moved so quickly that Elijah had difficulty tracking it.

The Soul wasn't some ephemeral thing. In a very real way, it connected everything about his ethereal system, and those channels concentrated the ethera, keeping it under pressure to force it to go much faster than ever before.

Elijah let out a watery gasp that sent bubbles toward the cave's air pocket above. Then, he read the notification he'd expected:

Congratulations! You have cultivated a Novice Soul!

For a while, he just floated there, satisfied with his progress. Then, he looked down to see that the process had drained the cave of most of its ethera. Fortunately, the plant life hadn't died, as it had when he'd cultivated his Body of Stone.

That was a relief, at least.

But more than anything, Elijah was glad to have taken one of the necessary steps before he could embark on his quest for revenge.

4

DOING THINGS RIGHT

T he water inside the cave was deathly still, evidence that his actions had driven the sea life away. Likely, it was a defense mechanism meant to ensure that they didn't get caught in the dangerous flows of ethera. After all, when Elijah had cultivated his Body of Stone, it had killed everything in the cave. And while death was an inevitable part of life, he didn't relish the notion of killing anything unnecessarily.

The trick was deciding when it was needed.

Regardless, after floating in the cave for a few more minutes, Elijah turned his attention to his status:

Name	Elijah Hart		
Level	76		
Archetype	Druid		
Class	Animist		
Specialization	N/A		
Alignment	N/A		
Strength	78		
Dexterity	76		
Constitution	78		
Ethera	85		
Regeneration	79		
Attunement	Nature		
Cultivation Stage: Cultivator			
Body	Core	Mind	Soul
Stone	Hatchling	Quartz	Novice

His attributes hadn't changed since he'd killed Thor, but he could feel the difference in his casting speed. The benefits were more than that, though. Initially, he'd thought the different categories of cultivation coincided with specific benefits. Back then, it had seemed so clear. The stage of his Body affected the expression of his physical attributes. It didn't raise his Strength, Dexterity, Constitution, or Regeneration. Instead, it made each point count for more. Meanwhile, his Mind gave him the ability to regenerate ethera more quickly with each higher stage. And his Soul affected the application speed of that ethera.

The Core was the odd one out, and in addition to affecting the potency of his spells, it also changed their flavor. For him, that meant his alternative shapes had taken on draconic characteristics, but for others, it would probably have quite a different effect.

In any case, Elijah now saw how nothing was quite as separate as it had once seemed. In fact, it was all intertwined in a way that meant that a step forward in any category would mean an overall benefit.

So, when he'd reached the Novice Soul stage, it had also removed something of a bottleneck for his ability to regenerate ethera. Before, his Mind was capable of pulling in far more energy than he could process. Now, though, his Soul could finally keep up. The only piece lagging behind was his Core, and he'd already begun to work on that.

Thankfully, Elijah didn't have to repopulate the cave this time. However, he did spend most of a day pulsing Nature's Bounty, and to his surprise, the spell's effective radius had nearly doubled. He could only guess that was his Novice Soul's effect at play. Once he was assured that the cave's ethera density would recover, he swam free of the cave, breaking into the ocean sometime later. After that, it only took him a few minutes to reach the shore, where he quickly dressed in the clothes he'd left there weeks before, then headed back to the Grove.

Carmen wasn't there, which he reasoned was due to her having gone to Ironshore. Idly, Elijah wondered how her forge was coming along, but he had no interest in crossing the strait to find out. She would explain everything when she returned.

Neither Miguel nor Colt was on the island, either, which felt a bit like old times. Until that moment, he hadn't really acknowledged what a lonely existence he'd led in the wake of washing ashore, but after having his family around for a few days, the lack was extremely noticeable.

But at least Nerthus was there.

Elijah busied himself by preparing for his coming trip, but there was only so much to do, so he eventually ended up wandering the Grove and inspecting all the different flora Nerthus had planted. There were so many varieties, many of which Elijah had never seen before, that he quickly lost count. In addition, there were plenty of mushrooms, hundreds of species of insects and spiders, and quite a few rodents, as well. Elijah even felt a few snakes who would inevitably feed on those rats.

It was a thriving ecosystem, though a curated one that somehow conveyed a sense of wilderness, as well. It was a unique place, and though Elijah often took it for granted, he couldn't have been more appreciative for the wondrous grove.

Eventually, he found Nerthus tending to the coffee trees, which had grown even larger in his absence.

"These were only supposed to grow to around fifteen feet tall," he remarked, resting his hand on one of the branches. It was incredibly healthy, with dense veins of ethera pulsing through it. "They've grown almost twice that height, and they're still not entirely mature."

"I suspect you are correct," said Nerthus. The spryggent had also grown a bit, too, reaching a height of around five feet. It wouldn't be long before he was taller than Elijah. "The cherries will ripen soon."

"I know. I'm very much looking forward to it," Elijah said, already imagining his first cup of coffee. "Which reminds me—sugar."

"What would you like to know about it?" asked the tree spirit.

"Well, I was wondering if I should try to grow sugarcane or sugar beets," Elijah said. He knew that the process of making granulated sugar wasn't a complicated one. Generally, the idea was to simply squeeze the liquid out of either source, then heat the product until it crystallized. After that, a centrifuge was used to separate it.

However, the problem was that sugarcane generally favored tropical environments, and sugar beets were far less efficient. More, the process was time-consuming as well as wasteful.

That's when he considered another alternative.

"What do you know about apiculture?" he asked.

"Bees?"

"For their honey," Elijah said. He preferred sugar in his coffee, and lots of it. However, he knew for a fact that his island had plenty of bees. It wouldn't take much to create an apiary that could satisfy his sweet tooth. Then, he explained the idea behind it to Nerthus, finishing with, "I'm pretty sure the honey will have the same effects as other things grown here, right?"

"I do not know," Nerthus admitted. "I can start the project if you wish. Bees are an integral part of any grove."

"I think that would be best," Elijah said, already imagining enjoying a honey-sweetened cup of coffee. "But for now . . ."

"What?" asked Nerthus when Elijah trailed off.

"Oh. Nothing. Carmen and Miguel just got back to the island."

After that, the pair waited on the others to reach the Grove, and when they did, Elijah approached. They exchanged greetings, after which he broke the news: "I managed to get to the second stage of Soul cultivation. But now,

I have a couple of errands I need to run that are going to take me at least a week."

"You like to stay busy, don't you?" Carmen responded.

Elijah shrugged. "Not usually. I mean, normally I take my time with everything. It took me almost two years before I even crossed the strait. But I can't do that now. You know why."

Miguel blurted, "You're going to kill him."

"I am," Elijah said. The young man deserved to know the truth. Besides, it would help no one if Elijah shielded him. After everything Miguel had seen, it would be pointless, too. Brutal honesty was the better path. "But not yet. I'm going to Argos first. I have a friend there who can identify my excess gear, and if it's not useful, he'll buy it. On top of that, I made a promise to another friend, and I intend to make good on it."

He'd almost forgotten to enlist Biggle's help with Konstantinos and the sickness affecting his children, but now that he had the ability to teleport to the area, he could see no reason not to get it out of the way. After all, Elijah hadn't forgotten the price he'd already paid for procrastination. Time was not promised, and every passing day meant that those children would run the risk of succumbing to their issues.

"Can I come?" asked Miguel.

Elijah was about to refuse, but then he thought better of it. Argos was the only place he'd found where he felt almost as comfortable as in his own Grove. And if Miguel wanted to see it, Elijah wasn't going to turn him down. The only question was whether or not Carmen would allow it.

"I don't have a problem with that," Elijah said. "What about you, Carmen? You want to go?"

Carmen shook her head. "No. I can't. I'm still getting the smithy set up," she said. Then, she revealed how much work had gone into the site. It seemed that Ironshore was just as eager as she was, and they'd fully committed to putting her to work. On top of that, she explained that the other two—Theresa and Byron—had found work, as well. The former was working with Biggle, while the latter had gone to work in the mines—not as a miner but, rather, utilizing his Geologist skills in some way. Elijah didn't probe further; as interesting as he found the myriad classes, he was more concerned with accomplishing his goals. "But Miggy can go."

"Seriously?" Elijah and Miguel both said at the same time.

She narrowed her eyes. "I'm not a helicopter mom," she muttered. "Miggy needs to see the world, and not just the parts that are going to try to kill him. Argos sounds like the sort of place he needs to visit."

"Oh. That makes sense," Elijah said, and it did. Miguel had been through a lot, and it was important for him to see that everything about their new world wasn't terrible. In fact, it was filled with miracles.

"You make it sound boring," Miguel mumbled under his breath. Elijah heard it just fine, though.

Elijah skated right past that, saying, "Alright, then. We're going back to Ironshore to pick up a friend. Then, we'll go to Argos."

"So soon?" asked Carmen. "Don't you need to prepare?"

Elijah slapped his Ghoul-Hide Satchel, saying, "Got everything I need right here."

Of course, Carmen had other ideas, reminding him that Miguel didn't have a magical satchel. So, after enduring her chastisement, Elijah set off for Ironshore while Miguel went to pack his clothes. He didn't have much, which was something that would soon need to change. Perhaps he could get Mari to make him a set of clothes, too.

In any case, Elijah wasn't going to sit around and wait for Miguel, so he took on the Shape of the Sky and quickly launched himself high into the air. The trip across the strait was much quicker in that form, and in only around thirty seconds, he thudded down on the path just outside of Biggle's yard.

He'd just taken on his human form when the guards arrived, reminding Elijah that he hadn't told anyone in the town about his new form. So, he spent the next few minutes assuring the pair of guards that there was no monster around. Everyone in town knew about his ability to shape-shift, so it didn't take that long to convince the two dwarves.

By that point, though, Biggle had taken notice of them.

"What in all the hells is going on out here? Elijah? What are you doing here?" the gnome demanded.

"Get packed. We're going on a trip."

"What?"

"I'll pay you. You're going to consult with another Alchemist about some sick kids," Elijah said.

"I am?"

Elijah clapped his hands. "Chop-chop, man. I want to be there before nightfall," he said.

"Where are we going?" the bushy-eyebrowed gnome asked. "And you mentioned pay? How much?"

Elijah sighed. Then, he explained the situation, ending with, "We'll be gone for no more than a week."

After that, they negotiated the price of the gnome's assistance. It was far more expensive than Elijah would have preferred, but he had no leverage in the situation. More, he wanted Biggle to just drop everything. So, a little extra was warranted, even if Elijah found it slightly irritating.

Regardless, it only took Biggle thirty minutes to pack everything he would need, and then, the pair returned to Elijah's island. This time, they took one of the rowboats he'd left behind, much to his chagrin. He'd have much preferred to fly, but he didn't think Biggle would appreciate being carried around in his talons, and Elijah certainly wasn't going to let the gnome ride on his back.

In any case, they made decent time crossing the strait, and Elijah beached the rowboat after only thirty minutes. When he noticed Biggle's hesitation to step one foot onto the shore, Elijah let out a sigh. "Nothing is going to hurt you so long as you stay on the beach," he said.

Perhaps he'd done too good of a job making the island seem dangerous. It was. Immensely so, when he was around. But the look on Biggle's face was one of abject terror.

"I've heard stories."

"And they'll tell you that everything was fine until people left the beach," Elijah said. "Remember that."

He wanted to trust the Alchemist, but his Grove was a treasure trove to someone with that class. So, he had no intention of showing Biggle anything interesting. Besides, he'd already established the rules for the people of Ironshore. They weren't permitted to travel inland. And Elijah wasn't going to change those rules for anyone but his most trusted friends.

At present, that list only contained one name from Ironshore: Kurik.

As it turned out, Elijah didn't have to worry about Biggle wandering around. The gnomish Alchemist remained in the boat while he went to fetch Miguel. When Elijah arrived in the Grove, he found Carmen fussing over her son, drilling him about behaving himself while he was with Uncle Elijah. She also grilled him about things he might've left behind.

Finally, Miguel hefted his backpack and said, "I've got everything I need, Mom. Relax."

"Don't you dare tell me to relax, mijo," she said.

He held up his hands. "Sorry, sorry. I didn't mean it. Well, I did. But you know what I mean."

Elijah cut in, saying, "Well, it's about time to hit the ol' dusty trail . . ."

Punctuating that, he grabbed Miguel by the upper arm and dragged him away, waving at Carmen as he pulled Miguel from the Grove. "We'll be back before you know it. Trust me!"

Soon enough, they'd progressed through the forest and reached the boat to find Biggle huddled in the corner. "I heard something," he said.

Elijah knew good and well that there was nothing to hear, but he just nodded sagely. "That's the guardian spirit. Extremely powerful. Eats gnomes for every meal."

"R-really?" asked the terrified Alchemist.

"No. There's nothing there. Besides, we're leaving."

Then, Elijah cast Roots of the World Tree. It completed far more quickly than it ever had before, and in only around fifteen seconds, the gate of roots and vines had formed. A moment later, the interior of the arch shimmered, then solidified into a view of the Dragon Circle.

"After you," Elijah said, gesturing to the gate.

To his credit, Miguel didn't hesitate to stride through. Biggle was a lot more circumspect. Though, at Elijah's urging, he went through, as well. Then, finally, Elijah did, too.

5

RESPONSIBILITIES

Beneath his palm, the first menhir Elijah had created pulsed with power. It was one of nine that comprised the dolmen that had unlocked so much potential, transforming Ancestral Circle into Roots of the World Tree, giving him the ability to teleport across the world, so long as he'd created a circle to receive him.

But it felt different than it had before. Stronger. The ethereal flows that coursed from one menhir to the next hadn't been nearly as obvious before, but now, Elijah felt that he could practically see the web of ethera connecting the entire thing. And in the center of that circle was a level of power Elijah hadn't seen anywhere but his Grove.

There was something beneath it, too. Something he couldn't even begin to understand.

Had the flows grown stronger? Or was Elijah simply more attuned to the ethera, now that he'd reached the second stage of Soul cultivation? He had no idea, though the guide he'd bought had suggested that progression through the stages of cultivation often came with increased perception. At the time, he'd thought that it only meant that his senses would grow sharper. That had been the case so far, with his visual acuity and hearing having progressed far past human norms, especially in his bestial shapes. Yet, he suspected that there was far more to it than that. Perhaps one day he would be able to sense ethera as clearly as he could see the leaves on a tree.

There were Scholars who specialized in studying ethera, after all. So, such a thing was almost assuredly possible. He just wasn't certain if he would ever reach that point.

"This is incredible," muttered Biggle, his mouth agape. "How far have we come? Who built this? Is it some relic of the past? I've heard about transportation networks before, but this is different than any stories I have heard."

"Transportation networks?" Elijah asked. "Like the teleportation feature associated with the Branch?"

Biggle shook his head. "No. That is often far too expensive for planetary travel. Normally, there are mages who specialize in such things," he said. "On my home world, it is still too expensive for the likes of me, but for . . . ah . . .

more prosperous people, using that network is no great burden. I have never seen such things, though. My village was too remote and far too poor to qualify for a hub."

"So, what's the point of Branch teleportation?" Elijah asked.

"Interplanetary transport," Biggle stated. "There are ships capable of moving between worlds and universes, but that is only viable on a large scale. Or if someone is obscenely wealthy. Or powerful, though the two normally come hand in hand, from my experience."

"I see," Elijah said.

"This is so cool," Miguel said, having circled the dolmen, running his hands over each heel stone. "It's like the one outside of Seattle, right? Except it's different. The rocks are different, but the carvings are, too. Why?"

"That's the nature of inspiration," Elijah stated.

"What is a Seattle?" asked Biggle, struggling to wrap his tongue around the city's name. Clearly, he had no idea what it was.

"Don't worry about it. C'mon. We're on the clock here," Elijah said. They had six days to accomplish his goals, and given that one of those goals involved trekking into a swamp, he knew they'd be pushing it to get everything done in time. So, he led his small group away from the Dragon Circle and toward Argos.

"How far have we come?" Biggle asked, struggling to keep up. His short legs were definitely a weakness when it came to trekking across the wilderness. Though it had never seemed to bother Kurik, who was only a bit taller than the gnome. So, maybe it was more that the Alchemist's class didn't give him the tools to overcome the shortcomings of his race.

"About a thousand miles? Maybe. I didn't exactly keep track when I was traveling," Elijah answered. "It could be closer to two thousand, but I don't think so. I ended up backtracking a lot in the more mountainous regions."

"Impressive," Biggle said, glancing back the way they'd come. They were well away from the Dragon Circle, so he couldn't see the dolmen. Still, Elijah thought he knew what the Alchemist was thinking.

So, he decided to cut any issues off at the pass, saying, "You will not visit one of my circles without my permission or accompaniment."

"What?"

"You heard me, Biggle. I've been told to watch out for Alchemists. I've heard that people like you can get a bit greedy. I'm not saying you're one of those sorts of Alchemists, but I am cautioning you to leave my things alone."

"I . . . see," Biggle said. "For what it's worth, I was only curious about how it all worked. I had no intention of doing whatever it is you're afraid I would do. I prefer to grow my own ingredients, not harvest them from nature."

"Good," Elijah said.

After that, the trio trekked across the terrain until, at last, they reached Argos. It had fully recovered from the tempest that had swept through the area, which only highlighted how impressive construction classes were and how quickly they could complete a project. Eventually, they would reach a point where they could easily build structures to rival anything from the old world. And they would assuredly be equipped with all the modern amenities. It was only a matter of time.

And survival.

In any case, the two guards on duty recognized Elijah, so after only a few moments' worth of polite conversation, they waved him through. Elijah found it notable that they'd barely even looked at Biggle, indicating that they had encountered nonhumans before. Soon enough, he found himself walking into Atticus's shop.

"Ah, good to see you, friend!" the tall, hawk-nosed merchant said. "I was just thinking of you. And you brought guests! Any friend of Elijah's is a friend of Atticus's. I will even give you a discount. Two percent off any weapon in my shop. Quality guaranteed, of course!"

Elijah grinned at his friend. Even with his morose tendencies of late, he couldn't help but smile when seeing Atticus. The man was so full of joy for life that it became infectious.

"I have some things I'd like appraised. And I'm sure I'll want to sell some, too."

With that, Atticus led them into the back, where they started the process of identifying each item. The first was the Ghoul-Hide Satchel, which turned out to feature a fifteen percent weight reduction and a trait called Preservation, which, true to the name, kept any perishable goods fresh for twice the duration as normal.

"A great item," Atticus said. "I would offer to purchase it, but it appears you have grown quite attached to it. A good call, my friend. One can never carry enough goods."

Next came the Weighted Gloves, which, according to Atticus, would increase his unarmed damage by twenty percent. Elijah had expected something like that, but he was impressed with the degree to which they would augment his attacks.

The canteen was, predictably, called an Endless Canteen, but to Elijah's surprise, it hadn't originated with a tower or rift. Instead, Atticus informed him that it had a creator's name attached to it: Rajesh Bedi. There was no more information, though Elijah was definitely interested in finding the maker. After all, with something like that, Seattle's water supply issues could be solved much more easily.

The spear Thor had used was called Tribal Spear, and it had an ability that allowed the wielder to recall it once thrown. Elijah had seen that in action during his fight with the Viking, so he knew precisely how useful such an ability would be. However, he still had no intention of using it himself; he'd grown accustomed to his staves, and he had no desire to change what had worked so far.

Neither had Miguel expressed any interested in the weapon—he seemed to prefer swords, from what Elijah could tell—so he intended to sell it to Atticus. Fortunately, the merchant was willing to pay good coins for the item, probably because Argos had a culture of spear use.

"I blame Delilah. All the young men want to impress her with their spear work. Most of the young women, too," Atticus said with a shake of his head. "Too bad most are too weak to use this monster. Still, I know of a few strong fighters who would pay a premium for a high-Simple-grade weapon with such a useful ability."

After that, they set it aside until they got to the negotiation part. There were still a few items left to go, and Elijah preferred to sell everything together.

There were only two other items for which Elijah had high hopes, and he wanted to save the most interesting one for last. So, he ended up having quite a few daggers and a few Crude-grade swords appraised—none of which were nice enough to pass on to Miguel, considering that his mother could make him better weapons when he came of age—before finally arriving at the penultimate item, which was the fanged necklace he'd taken from Thor.

"Interesting," Atticus said. "It's called a Wolf Totem. I'm guessing that's the origin of the teeth, though it's clearly a system reward."

"What's it do?"

"Plus three to all attributes," the merchant answered. "Powerful. But it's a Complex-grade item, so that's to be expected. The trait attached to it is even more interesting, though. Adds fifteen percent duration to all afflictions."

"Oh. Nice," Elijah said. That was as good as a fifteen percent increase to the damage of Swarm, Contagion, and Venom Strike, which meant he was definitely going to wear it. It also explained why the hunter's debuff had lasted so long. "That should help."

"Very good indeed, my friend!"

"Alright. I only have one last item to check," Elijah said, handing over his staff. He'd yet to bond it, largely because, on the off chance that it was unsuitable, binding it to himself would render it worthless. Still, he thought that unlikely, given the name.

"Dragon-Touched Staff," Atticus said. "Adds fifteen points to Strength and Dexterity, with five to Constitution. It also has a trait that increases the power of all enhancements by a flat five points. That . . . That is unheard of. Do you know how valuable this is?"

"Priceless," Elijah said.

"A less honest merchant would steal this from you," Atticus said, handing it back to Elijah without hesitation. "But they don't call me Honest Atticus for nothing."

"No one calls you that."

"They might."

"I've never heard it."

"Neither have I, but I assume that's only because they don't want to stroke my ego. Everyone knows how humble I am," Atticus said without a hint of humor.

"Right. You're the humblest man I know."

"That's what I keep telling people!"

Elijah just smiled wryly and shook his head. "Alright—so how much for the pile?" he asked. The collection of items included the nearly worthless—to Elijah, at least—weapons, as well as the Tribal Spear. Elijah also threw in Thor's armor, though Atticus confirmed that even the best piece was only low Crude grade, which meant that the set was almost useless for anything but disassembling it for parts. Still, Elijah wanted it out of his satchel, so he insisted that Atticus include it.

The bickering was a long and arduous, though good-natured, process. Every now and then, Miguel would break in to ask a question about something he'd found in Atticus's storeroom, but the merchant didn't mind it at all. Eventually, they came to an agreement, with the entire collection bringing Elijah almost fifty silver coins.

Once they exchanged the sum—via folios, which was a new addition on Atticus's part—Elijah said, "Oh. I meant to tell you this earlier. My sister-in-law is a Blacksmith, and she's going to be making some new equipment sometime soon. She's getting her forge set up right now, but I expect her to get to work within a few weeks. I might bring some of her products around, once she's up and running."

"Ah . . . I don't know, my friend. This is not a place for amateur work . . ."

"She's on the power rankings," Elijah said. "And I think she's capable of creating Complex items under the right circumstances."

"Which is why someone of her stature, skill, and no doubt beauty will be more than welcome to display her wares in my shop," the merchant said, switching gears without missing a beat. Though Miguel mouthed the word *gross* when Atticus mentioned Carmen's beauty.

"Thought that might interest you," Elijah said with a grin. "Just wanted to let you know so you'll have enough money to make some purchases. Wouldn't want you to miss out."

After that, Atticus told Elijah about Thor's visit to Argos, which elicited quite a lot of genuine laughter from everyone in the storeroom. But in the end, it was soon time for them to get going. Not only did Elijah want to introduce Miguel to the glories of Greek food, but he also wanted to visit Isaak—and maybe Delilah, if she was in town—before turning in for the night.

Because in the morning, they would set off for the swamp, where they would hopefully save some children.

6

A LOT TO LEARN

After visiting Isaak's house and catching up over a cup of tea—during which Artemis jumped in Miguel's lap, where she remained the entire time—they went to dinner, where they were served spanakopita. Everyone enjoyed it at least as much as Elijah, which was gratifying. After that, they headed to the inn, where they rented a pair of rooms—one to be shared by Elijah and Miguel, and another for Biggle—from Agatha, who seemed delighted to see Elijah.

"Everyone seems to like you here," Biggle remarked as they climbed the stairs. Fortunately, he didn't have any issues with that, despite his size. "Surprising."

"How so?"

"You don't give off the most approachable aura," the gnomish Alchemist stated. "Most people in Ironshore are terrified of you, and for good reason."

"That's only because I killed a few people."

"As I said—a good reason," the gnome stated. "In any case, I look forward to meeting this other Alchemist. I have had few opportunities to discuss my craft with someone with the same class, though that Chemist has all sorts of delightful ideas. I look forward to working with her as well. You humans are full of surprises."

After that, the group separated, and once Miguel was settled and asleep, Elijah silently left the room and headed back to Atticus's shop.

For his part, the weapons dealer seemed surprised to see Elijah. "I'm sorry, my friend. I am not up for celebrations tonight," he said.

"It's not about that. I wanted to ask for you to keep an eye out for a couple of things," Elijah said. Then, he told Atticus what he was looking for. Afterward, he said, "I don't know if you'll find what I want, but I'm throwing out a pretty wide net. Hopefully, someone will find something suitable."

"Indeed. I'll keep watch for anything that might work, my friend."

Then, seeing that Atticus was in no mood to entertain guests, Elijah said his goodbyes and headed back to the inn. He'd already found that Delilah was once again out of town—this time, running the local tower with her team—so he had nowhere else he wanted to visit.

Except maybe the tavern, though he resisted that urge. He had no wish to become an alcoholic, after all, so even if it might've felt temporarily good to once again drown his sorrows in an ocean of alcohol, he knew it was a bad idea.

Still, it was difficult.

After returning to the inn, he slept poorly, and when he rose the next morning, he felt even more anxious to get on with the task at hand. He'd spent most of the night lying awake and thinking about his sister—or, more accurately, her death—which did not put him in the best frame of mind. If the lives of children weren't at stake, he might've abandoned everything else and flown off to Easton at that very moment.

But he'd promised Konstantinos that he would help, so help he would.

Elijah rose before dawn, and he was happy to see that Miguel did the same, though he did grumble a little about how early it was. Soon enough, the pair had taken care of morning necessities, and even as the sun had begun to rise, they went to fetch Biggle. The gnome was clearly not an early riser by habit, but when he saw Elijah's no-nonsense expression, he hurried to ready himself for the day's travel.

Only a few minutes later, he joined Elijah and Miguel as they ate a breakfast of fat sausages and fluffy eggs prepared by Agatha. The meal was just as amazing as always, and all three ate with the gusto of starving men. Miguel put away enough for three people, reminding Elijah what it was like to have once been that age. Back then, he'd eaten his parents out of house and home, and he hadn't slowed down until after college.

That was the joy of a youthful metabolism.

Though, that prompted the realization that Elijah probably didn't have to worry too much about overconsumption anymore. Even if he wasn't so active, he suspected that it would take a truly impressive degree of sloth for his body to degrade on its own. And besides—he was only in his mid-thirties. With his cultivation and attributes, that meant that he was less than ten percent into his expected life span.

In any event, they finished their meal, and after Elijah paid, they set off, leaving Argos behind and heading in the direction of the swamp. In the past, Elijah had taken a roundabout path, only turning south when he hit the ravine that cut across the terrain. However, he expected that the trip would be much faster this time around, largely because they intended to travel directly toward the swamp.

The issue with that assumption soon became apparent, though.

"It's not my fault you're giants!" Biggle complained, pumping his legs to keep up. "Even with my pep-it-up potion, I can't— Wait, what are you doing? Stop that! Stop that this instant!"

"Sorry," Elijah said, having placed Biggle on his shoulders like a toddler. He could remember doing the same for his nephew when Miguel was only a couple of years old. Elijah had come home for the holidays, and they'd gone to visit the local botanical gardens that had been decorated with colorful Christmas lights. But predictably, the much younger Miguel had been incapable of keeping up, so Elijah had put the boy on his shoulders, where he'd remained for most of the outing. "I'm not going to slow down just to accommodate you. This is faster."

"It's also humiliating!"

"There's no one out here to judge you," Elijah reminded him. "I mean, we could fly, I guess. But I'm thinking you might enjoy that even less."

That shut the gnome up. He didn't want to travel in the talons of Elijah's Shape of the Sky, after all. For his part, Elijah would have preferred to avoid that, too. As convenient as flight was, he wasn't quite ready to transport passengers any meaningful distance. For one, landing was still an issue that had yet to be resolved. He could manage it, but he knew that if he didn't possess superhuman durability, he'd have already broken his legs many times over.

It would be markedly worse if he was carrying someone.

So, they strode through the wilderness, with Biggle on his shoulders. As they did, Elijah held a conversation with his nephew, and eventually, the topic turned to the boy's future. "So, have you figured out what you want to do?" he asked.

Miguel shook his head. "No. I don't even know which archetypes I'll be offered. I just don't want to be a Scholar," he said.

Surprised, Biggle asked, "Why ever not? Scholar leads to some incredibly valuable classes!"

Miguel shrugged. "But they seem so useless."

"That's untrue," Biggle stated. "Every archetype has the potential for immortality. They all perform valuable and necessary functions, as well. Warriors fight. Rangers scout. Scholars learn. Without Merchants, fair trade would be impossible. Without Administrators, our cities would not function. There is no useless archetype. Only useless people."

"How many archetypes are there?" Miguel asked.

"Twelve."

"So many?" asked Elijah. He'd only encountered a fraction of that number.

After that, Biggle listed the archetypes. Warrior, Ranger, Druid, Sorcerer, and Healer, Elijah already knew. However, there were still quite a few others. Scholars, for one. Tradesmen, who became various crafters. Merchants like Atticus. Entertainers, many of which had powerful abilities to increase the power of those who enjoyed their performances. Then there were Administrators and Explorers, as well.

"And from there, we have innumerable classes. Most are hybrids, taking bits from archetypes other than the root," Biggle explained. "My point is that there are many choices, and while the archetype is incredibly important, choosing the wrong option is something that can be rectified through progression. The class choice is one opportunity, but then there are specializations at level one hundred. After that, each time a person enters a new realm of power, they have the opportunity to evolve their class. Most will simply take a more powerful version of their own. However, there are those who choose to correct past mistakes by slowly shifting their paths to those they deem more appropriate. It is a fascinating subject, really."

"How do you know all of this?" asked Miguel.

"Ah—my mother was a Scholar. She studied classes and advised the local lord on how to guide his children in the proper direction," he admitted. "He didn't like it when his firstborn son was only offered noncombat archetypes, though. So, we were forced to flee."

"Everyone in Ironshore seems to have a similar story. Not the specifics. Just that they all seem to be running from something. It was the same with the elves."

"Elves?"

"Oh. Yeah. There's a city of elves living in a desert a little ways away. They sounded more like pioneers, though. Like, they came here for opportunity that didn't exist on their world."

"I see. That is usually the case with people who come to a newly touched world. It is the frontier, without much in the way of safety. However, there is opportunity to forge your own path, which attracts a certain type of person," Biggle explained. "Though I would be willing to wager that there are a couple of advanced settlements here. They may be talented junior members of a sect meant to fuel their progression in an unsettled world. Or they could represent various other interests. Those are the ones you need to watch out for. They'll be well equipped, knowledgeable, and driven. In a world like this, that can be a dangerous combination."

Elijah nodded, continuing on with his conversation with Miguel. The young man had no idea what direction his development might take, but Elijah didn't blame him for that. After all, he was still a child. It would have been odd if he'd known those sorts of things with any certainty, and the fact that he was still unsure meant that he was at least giving it some thought, rather than simply going for whatever sounded coolest.

Eventually, almost two days later, they reached the swamp, after which Elijah was forced to transform into a lamellar ape so that his two companions could climb atop his shoulders and avoid the many dangers of walking through the murky water. For his part, Elijah seemed to avoid the worst of it, just as he had during his first trip through the swamp.

Still, because of where they'd entered, it took an extra day for them to reach Konstantinos's compound, and when they did, they were greeted by Bessie, the guardian alligator. Elijah responded to her charge by tossing her the last hunk of desert snake stored in his satchel. She gobbled it up, returning to her position beneath the compound's largest building.

"'Lo there!" yelled Konstantinos from the deck. He was wearing a pair of overalls and nothing else, which put his incredibly skinny torso on full display. He didn't seem self-conscious about it, though. "Didn't think you'd be back!"

Elijah climbed onto the floating dock, and after Miguel and Biggle descended from his shoulders, he took on his human form. Then, he began the arduous process of cleaning the muck from his lower body while plucking any pesky leeches free. Fortunately, he'd only picked up a few small ones, and it only took a quick pulse of Soothe to get rid of the afflictions they'd carried.

Once he was done, he shook Konstantinos's hand, saying, "I said I had a friend who might be able to help." He nodded at Biggle, adding, "This is that friend. He's an Alchemist, just like you, but he might have some knowledge you don't."

After that, Biggle and Konstantinos started a conversation that lost Elijah after only a few moments. Luckily, they were quickly rescued by Marcy, who escorted them inside—after Elijah showered the rest of the muck off—where she served them mugs of tea. Then, she told the story of how a giant man had come by only a couple of months before.

"He stormed up, half dead from all the leeches," Marcy explained. "Said he was lookin' for a Druid or some such. Konnie sent him traipsing off into the swamp, but his soft heart got the better of him, so he gave 'im some potions. I wouldn't've done that. But I'm not as nice as Konnie."

"Where are the kids?" Elijah asked, looking around.

"In the other buildin'," she said. "Bryce's teachin' 'em their numbers and such. You alright in here by yourselves? I got dinner to tend to."

Elijah said that he was, while Miguel was still entranced by his surroundings. Despite everything he'd been through, he'd lived a pretty sheltered suburban life before the world had been transformed. As such, he had never been exposed to much in the way of other cultures. Sure, he'd visited some of Carmen's family, though only a couple of times because they didn't precisely approve of her sexuality. Elijah didn't know the whole story, but he did know that the resulting falling-out was why she'd left Southern California for Washington state.

Either way, Miguel certainly had never seen anything like the compound. It was cozy in a way that only a true home could be, which clearly reminded the young man of everything he'd lost.

So, Elijah decided to distract him. "So, I've been thinking," he said.

"About what?"

"About your future. I know you've been working with Colt," Elijah said. "And he speaks highly of your skills. But I think it would be a shame if you let yourself be pigeonholed like that. You need more than just the ability to swing a sword."

"I can use a spear, too. And an axe, but I'm not that good yet. I'm a good shot with a bow, too."

"I'm not talking about weapons' training. I want you to train with a friend of mine," Elijah said. "I haven't spoken to him about it, but I think I know him well enough to know what he'll say."

"What kind of friend? And training in what?"

"A dwarven friend. He's a scout for Ironshore, and he's probably the highest-level fighter they have."

"Higher than you?"

"I'm not part of Ironshore. So, no. Not even close."

"What if I want to train with you instead?"

Elijah sighed, leaning back into the couch. It was upholstered in a truly garish fabric, but it was extremely soft and comfortable. "You don't want to train with me," he said with a sigh. "Most of what I know isn't really transferable. If you end up with the Druid archetype, I won't hesitate to teach you. But I hope you don't."

"Why?" Miguel asked, a little hurt.

"Because it's not a strong archetype. Not right off, at least. It's a blend of Scholar, Healer, and Sorcerer. So, I can do a lot of things, but until I got my class, I couldn't do any of them well. Even now, strength to strength, I can't stand against someone with a more focused class. My cultivation helps, and I intend to put you on the right path with that. But being a Druid isn't about learning fancy techniques or doing sword katas. It's about connection. Instinct. It's a mindset more than an archetype. So, unless you decided to follow me down this road, there's nothing I can teach you better than someone like Kurik or Colt. Not about fighting, at least."

That wasn't what Miguel wanted to hear, and as a result, he went quiet. Elijah tried to reengage, but after a few one-word answers, he gave up. Clearly, he had a lot to learn about dealing with kids.

7

A NATURAL BALANCE

These children are remarkable," said Biggle. "I wish I had access to a Physician to understand precisely what's happening here."

The kids—who were all lined up in front of the gnome—were taller than Biggle, but they all beamed at the apparent compliment. One even threw his hands into the air in celebration. However, Elijah knew that none of them—save for Bryce, perhaps—had any clue what he was talking about.

"What's the difference between a Healer and a Physician?" asked Bryce, who looked uncomfortable at the scrutiny she'd just endured. Biggle didn't have much use for boundaries, so after feeding each of the children some concoction that he claimed would make things clearer for him, he'd leaned in close enough that his overlarge nose touched her cheek. "I thought they were the same thing."

"Ah—that's a common mistake. A Physician is a Scholar class. While a Healer specializes in fixing problems, a Physician's main purpose is diagnosis. They endeavor to understand rather than heal. Though many of them possess some ability in the latter," Biggle said. "Tell me, child—you weren't with these other children in the beginning, were you?"

"Uh . . . no. I was adopted before the apocalypse."

"Apocalypse?" Biggle asked, clearly confused. Then, his eyes widened in understanding. "Ah. I can see why you humans would see the touch of the World Tree in such a light. But this is no apocalypse. It is an opportunity. Think of it like the great forest moths. They begin life as spotted caterpillars, no larger than you are now, but then they undergo a transformation that lets them take to the skies. They grow so large that they can block the small sun."

"A caterpillar as big as me?" she gasped. "That's . . ."

"You don't have those here?" asked Biggle.

"No, we don't," Elijah said, smiling slightly. "Our caterpillars are usually smaller than a finger."

"What? That makes no sense. How would the moth grow so large, then?"

"Moths are tiny," Bryce said.

"She's right," Miguel pointed out, staring at the girl. If she'd noticed the intensity of his gaze, she might've been a bit uncomfortable. Thankfully, she hadn't recognized the young man's clear infatuation. In retrospect, it should have been predictable. They weren't far off in age, and Miguel clearly hadn't encountered many girls over the past couple of years. "Moths are really small."

Elijah nearly chuckled at Miguel's pointless contribution to the conversation but instead kept his mouth shut as Biggle said, "That . . . is troubling." He shook his head. "But never mind your oddly sized moths. My point is that you didn't endure the same transformation that blessed these children. When they come of age—provided they survive that long—they will be well on their way to the first stage of Body cultivation. I have never seen something so remarkable."

"What does it mean?" asked Konstantinos.

"Two things," Biggle said, holding up two tiny fingers. "First, you saved these children's lives. That concoction you've been feeding them is primitive but inspired. That's the difference between a passable Tradesman and an exceptional one. Creativity. It's what separates us from those less talented."

"Humility, too," Elijah pointed out.

"Bah. Humility. What use is it? If you're good, let the world know!" Biggle insisted, emphatically thrusting his finger toward the ceiling.

Elijah rolled his eyes. "What's the other thing?"

"The second is that I know how to help them," Biggle stated, puffing out his chest. He addressed Konstantinos, who still wore a pair of denim overalls with no shirt. Otherwise, he had on a straw hat, with what looked like a piece of swamp grass sticking out from between his lips. "It's a pill meant to do the same thing your little potions have done. The difference is that it'll last a lot longer."

"How much longer?" asked the other Alchemist.

"Well, you're getting a day or two out of your version, right?"

"They get dosed every day," Konstantinos answered.

"And it's yucky!" one of the children shouted. Another mimed like she was vomiting, while yet another pointed at his open mouth while he wore a grimace.

"This pill will last at least a month. Maybe two. And it uses ingredients that grow all over the place. Not just this damnable swamp," Biggle said, punctuating that statement by slapping his hand against his neck, killing a mundane mosquito. There were much bigger ones out in the swamp. "That's if you don't want me to cure them."

"Course we want you to cure 'em," said Marcy. "Why wouldn't we?"

"It's complicated, but the gist of it is that these kids' bodies are being tempered, much like what's required for Body cultivation," Biggle said. "It's a dangerous practice, but it's not entirely unheard-of. The problem is that if the mix is wrong—even by a little bit—it'll kill the subjects."

"Are they in danger?"

"Left untreated? Absolutely. They would die within a few days," Biggle said. "But because of your . . . husband's efforts, calamity has become an advantage. The conditions in the swamp struck the perfect balance, naturally creating a situation that would require an Alchemist far more skilled than me to engineer. But I can cure them. I can turn them back to normal. I know a potion that would do the trick. However, that would squander the opportunity in front of them. Bodies of Wood? Before they even begin their paths of progression? It would be an immense advantage, and one that would set them up for success."

"But we'd have to leave the poison," guessed Konstantinos. "And if they miss one dose . . ."

"It's too dangerous," said Marcy.

Konstantinos was obviously less convinced. Perhaps he knew how much of an advantage Body cultivation could prove to be. Or maybe he simply took Biggle at his word. Either way, the decision was far more complicated than it might seem. Sure, there was danger. But if that danger was properly managed, the potential rewards could be incredible.

After that, Konstantinos and Marcy sent the children away while they retreated into a back room to discuss the issue. For his part, Elijah hoped they would take the path Biggle described, but he could understand their hesitation. When a child's life hung in the balance, risks were difficult to embrace, even if logic dictated that one should do so.

In the end, they did not reach a decision before Elijah, Biggle, and Miguel— much to the last one's regret—left. However, Biggle did give Konstantinos the recipe for the pill meant to manage the poison as well as the concoction that would cure them. That gave them the tools to make whatever choice they felt most comfortable with.

Meanwhile, Miguel had mustered his courage and asked Bryce to visit him in his magical grove. The girl clearly didn't believe the following description, but she half-heartedly promised that she would try to visit if she ever got the chance. That put Miguel on cloud nine, even though, to Elijah, it seemed pretty obvious that she was just being polite.

He had no intention of telling the young man, though.

In any case, both Miguel and Biggle were in great moods as they returned the way they'd come. What made it even better was the fact that Konstantinos consented to usher them to the edge of the swamp on one of his boats. So, Elijah didn't even need to get his scales wet.

The trip back to Argos was equally uneventful, save for the fact that Elijah took the two by the ravine, where they saw one of the massive spiders ambush another bird. That delighted Miguel, but Biggle found it horrifying, prompting a discussion on how the gnomish Alchemist could find giant moths so normal, while an enormous spider terrified him.

Elijah barely listened as the pair bickered. His obligations were nearly satisfied, which meant that he was on the verge of setting out for Easton. When he got there, he would exact his revenge. At present, the only question was whether or not he intended to hold the whole city accountable for his sister's death—and Carmen's as well as Miguel's exile—or if he would only take vengeance on Roman.

He had yet to decide, but Elijah knew the time would come when the choice was forced upon him, one way or another.

In any case, they arrived in Argos a couple of days later, which meant that they had a free day. So, Elijah allowed Miguel to wander the town alone while he stopped by Atticus's shop to see if the merchant had had any luck filling his requests.

"No luck, my friend. I have some items that would fit," Atticus answered with a shake of his head. "But they're nothing special. I feel certain that I will have a chance to obtain the equipment you require in a month or so. There are a few scheduled tower runs upcoming, which usually results in an influx of inventory. We have also been getting more traders of late."

"Really?"

"Yes. From a wide variety of places, too. I'm told there is a tribe of nomadic hunters who reside on the plains past the swamp to the south. Some of my products come from their forays into that region's towers. We've seen quite a few traveling merchants, as well," Atticus explained. "I only wish Argos had more dedicated crafters. We've a few decent Leatherworkers, Builders, and quite a lot of Farmers. No Blacksmiths or Tailors, though."

"Once Carmen gets settled, hopefully we can figure something out," Elijah said.

"If she's as good as you say, we will all get very rich!" he exclaimed.

Elijah shrugged. "I'm told she's good, but I've never seen her products," he said honestly. "In any case, I'll be heading back home tomorrow, but I'll try to stop by here sometime soon."

With that, Elijah returned to his hotel room, where he got started on the next phase of his cultivation. He knew the basics of how to take the next step with his Core, but he'd only spent a little time practicing the technique. It required him to take in as much ethera as he could—enough to make him feel like he was going to burst—then swirl it around before expelling it as slowly as possible. To Elijah, it was a little like taking a long, deep breath, then holding it in, though with the added difficulty of doing some calisthenics along the way. It wasn't a perfect analogy, but it described the process well enough for him.

Regardless, he quickly found the first issue.

The ethera density in Argos was severely lacking, and as a result, it took almost ten minutes for his Core to reach complete saturation. Then, another ten to push it to its uncomfortable limit. But even then, it felt hollow. Like he should have been filling a balloon with water, but all he had was air.

It was the best he could do, though, and he spent the next half hour swirling the ethera around until he could hold it no longer. Then, he let it out.

Almost an hour, and he'd done very little good. He couldn't even notice any difference, even though he knew it should have expanded ever so slightly. To him, the activity seemed a lot like working out. It was meant to be a long process, and he wouldn't notice improvement for a while.

He kept going, though, repeating the cycle a few more times before he started to lose focus. He probably would have continued, but Miguel's return was distracting enough to throw a wrench into those plans. So, after his nephew excitedly described his foray into Argos, Elijah broached the subject they'd begun to discuss on the way to the swamp.

"Would you like to train with Kurik? If so, I can set it up when we get back," Elijah said. "Don't feel obligated to agree, though. If you have no interest in learning the skills he can teach, then it would just be a waste of time."

Miguel narrowed his eyes. "Why wouldn't I want to do it? I would have given anything to have those skills after we were exiled," he said.

"Alright, then. I guess that settles that," Elijah said. He glanced at the window, seeing that darkness had completely settled over Argos. "Get some sleep. We're going to leave early in the morning."

Miguel quickly agreed, but even after the lights were extinguished, sleep was elusive, and for both of them. Miguel was clearly too excited for slumber, but Elijah had other things on his mind.

Because now that he'd met his obligations with Konstantinos, he only had one more task to accomplish before setting off for Easton. Once he'd introduced Miguel to Kurik—whom he still hadn't asked to mentor the kid—there would be nothing else, aside from a few preparations for the journey, to delay his departure.

And now that it was so close, Elijah was eager to get started. Excitement wasn't the right word. Nor was anxiety. Instead, it was a mixture of both, with a healthy dose of dread thrown in. Some righteous indignation, too. A sense of serving justice, as well. To put it mildly, he was beset by a snarl of varied emotions that were extremely difficult to identify. The end result, though, was that he looked forward to looking his sister's murderer in the face and watching the light leave his eyes.

That, at least, was a comforting thought that ushered him into sleep.

8

FINAL PREPARATIONS

Elijah awoke a little before dawn, but he didn't immediately rise. For one, he didn't want to wake Miguel, but for another, he wanted to spend an hour cycling ethera through his Core. He wanted to create a routine that would, over time, better prepare him for success. So, he pushed himself to a seated position, crossed his legs, and closed his eyes before getting down to the task at hand. This time, it took him a little longer to saturate his Core, which he took as a good sign, but he cut himself off after only one cycle.

The rising sun told him that it was time to get on with the primary objective. With that in mind, he woke Miguel, who rose and turned an accusatory, bleary-eyed gaze in Elijah's direction. "What's the rush? We could sleep in," he complained.

"Sleeping in is how everyone else gets ahead of you," Elijah cautioned. "That's what my dad used to tell me. When I was your age, I didn't really believe him, but now, I realize he was a lot smarter than I ever gave him credit for back then."

Miguel asked, "What was he like?"

"Old and wise."

"C'mon. Be serious."

"Ouch," Elijah muttered, running his hand through his hair. Having a pre-teen chastise him for not being serious was a bit of a blow to the concept of his own maturity. "Fine. He was about my height. Maybe a little taller. And he had the kind of tan you only get from spending years outside. He never wanted to be indoors. Whenever he wasn't working, he wanted to be camping. Or fishing. Hunting, maybe. Sometimes, he just went hiking. Your mom and I used to go with him all the time. So did our mom. She liked to gather herbs and stuff. Mushrooms, too. Those were good times."

"They got in a car wreck, right?" Miguel asked, his voice small.

Elijah nodded. "Yeah. One day, they were there. Happy. Healthy. Like two monuments that I thought would never disappear. But then, the next day, I was standing outside as your mom identified their bodies," Elijah said. "It didn't feel real. Not to me. Not until the funeral. But even after that, for years, I would turn around and half expect them to be there."

That was why he ran away after high school. Sure, he usually categorized it as going off to college, but in reality, he'd done it to escape the memory of his dead parents. It hadn't really worked. Only time could do that. But he'd been a stupid kid with equally dumb ideas.

"But without the things they taught me, I never would have survived the touch of the World Tree," Elijah said, surprised that, even after all this time, no tears came. Usually, they did when he really thought about his parents. "Though I thought I was a better campfire cook before everything happened. I mean, I wasn't good. I used to joke that I could burn water. But it wasn't—"

"That's because you don't have a cooking skill," Miguel said. "Right?"

"What? A cooking skill?"

"Yeah. Lots of people have them," his nephew explained. "It's part of one of the archetypes. Maybe a couple of them. But without it, food just kind of tastes bland. Before . . . everything happened with Mom, we went to school, and my teacher, Mr. Gary, said that it was because of ethera. Like, our bodies need it, so if food doesn't have enough of it or something, it ends up tasting bland. That's where the different cooking skills come in. They inject ethera into normal food."

Elijah just stared at him.

It explained so much. Maybe the problem wasn't that the crabs on his island didn't taste good. The issue was with him and his lack of cooking skills. Perhaps those same crabs, cooked by someone with actual ability, would taste amazing. It also put some of his other experiences into perspective. Like how every time he visited a new town, he found someone whose cooking was even better than what one would expect in a five-star restaurant.

"Are you okay?" asked Miguel.

"You just blew my mind."

"Huh?"

"I need to hire someone that can cook," Elijah said, his mind already going to his coffee project. What would happen if he roasted the beans himself? Would the product be inferior? He hoped not, but he wasn't willing to take that chance. Sure, now that the trees were approaching maturity, they would bear fruit far more often, but he didn't want to waste his precious coffee cherries on a failed endeavor.

After all, the whole point was to make delicious coffee that had beneficial properties like his Grove berries. If he ruined that by roasting his own beans, he'd never forgive himself.

He shook his head. "You just added an item to my to-do list," Elijah said. "Thankfully, it can wait."

"Until after you kill Roman?"

"Yes."

"He saved my life, you know. Why would he do that? He barely knew me. When that other guy took me, I thought I was going to die. Then, when he gave me to Roman, I thought he'd use me against Mom. But he didn't. He was furious. Killed the kidnapper in, like, a second. And I still don't know why," Miguel said.

Elijah didn't know either, and he said as much. However, he added, "But it doesn't matter. From the situation your mom described, I think it's safe to say that he's at least deluded. Maybe he had a psychotic break. Or he might've just always been an asshole that draws the line at messing with kids. I really don't know. He is going to die, though. Probably painfully."

He'd considered sugarcoating the reality of what was coming, but he figured Miguel deserved to know the unfettered truth. To that end, he'd vowed to be completely honest with his nephew.

But that didn't mean he reveled in that conversation, so it wasn't long after that statement before he rose and headed to the bathroom. Less than an hour later, he, Miguel, and Biggle were marching toward Argos's gate. Elijah had hoped that a visit to the city would help him to deal with his sister's death—and the anger that had come with it—but if anything, it had only made things worse.

It only took a few hours to reach the Dragon Circle, so they were forced to sit around for another hour before Elijah's cooldown ran out. When it did, he opened a gate, and everyone stepped through and into Elijah's Grove.

That was when he realized the issue.

Biggle stumbled, staring around the Grove, wide-eyed.

"Shit," Elijah muttered.

"What is this place? The ethera density . . . Those berries . . ."

Elijah grabbed the Alchemist by the collar before he could run off. Then, he knelt beside the gnome and said, "This is my Grove, Biggle. I like you. I think we're on the verge of being friends. But if you come to this Grove without my permission, I won't hesitate to kill you. The same goes for anyone else in Ironshore."

"I would never!" Biggle insisted, struggling to free himself. It didn't work.

"Sure. I know that. I'm just letting you know the rules. You're the only Ironshore resident other than Kurik and the human refugees who've seen this Grove," Elijah said. "I'll caution you not to spread any information about what you've seen here. I don't want to have to kill a bunch of people just to make a point."

"Do you have any idea what you have here?" Biggle asked, looking around. "This grove could fuel the progression of a hundred fighters. Maybe a thousand. The potions I could make . . . The pills I could create . . ."

He trailed off, then sighed. "Ah, it's for the best. I don't have the expertise to utilize ingredients of this quality," he admitted. "I can't even identify most of these things."

"Even if you could . . ."

"Hands off," Biggle said, raising his tiny hands. "You have my word."

"I knew I could count on you," Elijah stated. "And if it turns out I can't . . . Well, it wouldn't be the first time I've killed a gnome."

Biggle swallowed hard, then said, "You truly are a violent person. You know that?"

"I'm whatever I need to be," Elijah countered, releasing the gnome.

Biggle straightened his collar, but he didn't respond. Instead, he seemed eager to leave the Grove behind, which Elijah thought was for the best. In truth, he had never seen himself as a violent person. However, some things were worth protecting, and sometimes, that meant letting the more feral side of himself out. Besides, a few threats were preferable to having to slaughter a bunch of unwelcome visitors, which he would unhesitatingly do if they invaded his Grove.

Or threatened his family.

In any case, he led Biggle to the beach, then used one of the rowboats to return him to Ironshore. Meanwhile, Miguel went to train near the old cabin. He only paid attention to the young man for long enough to know that he was in no danger before turning his attention to other matters.

While he was in Ironshore, Elijah spent some time topping off his supplies before returning to his island. He hated using the rowboat, but if he didn't take it back, no one else would pick up the slack. So, he got to rowing, and when he reached the island, he retrieved his old jars, filled them with a scentless oil he'd bought in Ironshore, then stuffed a bunch of lavender into each one.

By the time he finished taking his revenge, the infused oil would be ready for another batch of soap.

He'd just finished that task when Carmen returned to the island. He'd considered stopping by her new smithy, but he hadn't wanted to disturb her. So, he waited until she got back to the Grove before heading out to meet her.

"It's time, isn't it?" she guessed.

Elijah nodded. "I'm leaving in the morning."

Then, he described his plan. His intention was to use the individual teleportation function of Roots of the World Tree, which worked on a different cooldown than the gate portion, to travel to the Circle of Spears outside of Seattle. Then, he would use Shape of the Sky to fly to Easton.

Hopefully, he could reach the city in a day or two.

"I don't know how long I'll stay there. It depends on if I want to destroy the city," he remarked.

"You think you can do that?" she asked, her face smudged with soot.

Elijah shrugged. "Maybe. Not quickly, though," he said. Calamity could do a lot of damage, and in a wide area, but it was not strong enough to tear down buildings. "It would take a while."

He expected Carmen to argue on behalf of Easton, but she didn't. Instead, she said, "Make him suffer."

"I will," Elijah promised.

Indeed, that was one of the reasons he was even considering the city's total destruction. From what Carmen had said, Roman valued that city more than anything, so its destruction would assuredly cause him more pain than anything else Elijah could do.

"But more than anything, I need you to survive," Carmen stated, reaching out to grip his arm. "Miguel is safe here. It's been so long since we had that. And without you, that all disappears. So, survive."

Elijah intended to do that, too. But if it came down to a choice between taking his revenge and his own death, Elijah wasn't certain which route he would choose. Hopefully, it wouldn't end up with that choice.

"I talked to a friend while I was in Ironshore. Kurik. He's a scout," Elijah said. "He's coming by tomorrow to pick Miguel up. It's not quite an apprenticeship—that won't come unless Miggy gets the right archetype and class. But it's training. Kurik's going to show him woodcraft, trapping, and hunting. I told him that it was all subject to your approval, though, so if you don't want it to happen, just tell Kurik when he comes by."

"You're willing to let him into the Grove?" asked Carmen.

Elijah nodded. "He's a friend," he said. "I trust him."

"Then so do I," Carmen stated, adding that the plan had her approval.

"Well, since I'm not leaving until the morning, do you and Miggy want to go have a last meal at the Stuck Pig? Hopefully, they're not still serving orc ribs," he said.

9

A NEW PERSPECTIVE

After saying his goodbyes and cautioning Miguel to heed Kurik's commands, Elijah gathered his things, double-checked that he had everything he would need, then used Shape of the Sky. The transformation came much more quickly, barely taking a second when, before, it had taken a couple. Soon enough, he'd launched himself toward the sky. He beat his powerful wings, rising above the Grove as he quickly gained altitude.

There was something undeniably addictive about flight, about defying gravity to soar through the air. Not only was it a much quicker means of travel than going on foot, but it represented a degree of freedom that few humans had ever enjoyed. In his flight form, he could go almost anywhere, do almost anything. And that was a heady notion, especially given the breadth of miracles waiting to be discovered.

He'd seen a few such miracles since Earth had been touched by the World Tree. Some were large, like the presence of a skyscraper in the middle of an untouched and pristine valley. Or the deep ravine that rivaled—or perhaps even exceeded—the Grand Canyon in scope. But there were plenty of small miracles, as well. The peaceful glades, the curious wildlife, the streams and waterfalls—the whole world was magical and miraculous, and though Elijah was wholeheartedly committed to his quest for vengeance, he couldn't deny that a good part of him desperately wanted to fly off toward the horizon on a different sort of quest—one of discovery.

Elijah circled his island at an altitude of thousands of feet, and from that vantage, the entire landscape was laid out before him. He could see his island, small compared to the massive mainland. Ironshore looked tiny, as well. A fairly well-contained collection of buildings that seemed far too small to house the few thousand people Elijah knew lived there.

Then there were the looming mountains just beyond the town. The range stretched as far as Elijah could see, jutting much higher than his current altitude. At present, the peaks were wreathed in clouds and blanketed in white snow, making him feel even smaller than he really was.

Elijah had become powerful. According to the power rankings, he was the strongest person on Earth. However, when he looked upon those mountains, he knew just how little that title counted.

Before experiencing the touch of the World Tree and being transformed, Earth had seemed a lot smaller than it really was. Elijah blamed global communication, the ease of travel, and the internet for that perception. However, the moment all of that quit working, that view had shifted. Suddenly, a few hundred miles was a long way to travel—let alone thousands. Before, Elijah could have gone on the internet to see what was happening on the other side of the world. Now, he didn't even know what was going on in Ironshore unless he physically went there and asked around.

And that wasn't even considering the world's transformation. According to everything he'd heard, Earth was now rumored to be as large as Saturn. Elijah had barely paid attention during lessons that covered astronomy, but he had some idea of the scope that size represented. The planet was at least ten times its former size, and filled with wonders and dangers to match its new stature.

Those thoughts flitted through Elijah's mind as he circled his island. Then, he turned his attention to the ocean. From so high up, he could see dozens of miles, and when he used Eyes of the Eagle, he could see much, much farther. And under the effects of that augmentation, he could see darkness on the horizon. It was hundreds of miles away, he knew, but he could see enough to suspect that that smudge in the distance represented an enormous storm.

Was it coming toward his island?

Elijah couldn't know. However, despite the rain-soaked climate of his region, the island had never experienced hurricanes or the like. So, he felt reasonably certain that they were safe from truly inclement weather. Besides, he also expected that the Grove would survive any storm the world could throw its way. Sure, there would almost assuredly be damage. Maybe his coffee trees would be uprooted. But the ancestral tree would be fine. So would his and his sister's tree houses.

For a while, he continued to circle until, at last, he decided to get a move on. Initially, he'd intended to use Roots of the World Tree to instantly teleport to Seattle, but overnight, he'd decided against that tactic. The ability to immediately jump thousands of miles was too valuable to use it just to save a couple of days. The last thing he wanted was for the spell to be on cooldown when he needed it most—like if he needed a quick escape. Another part of the choice to forgo the use of Roots of the World Tree was based on his burgeoning skill at flying. He hadn't used the form nearly enough for flight to feel instinctive, so he intended to use the trip to simultaneously work on his skills while also putting himself in the right mindset for the coming trials.

Because Elijah didn't think getting revenge on Roman would be easy.

Perhaps from a physical standpoint, he could manage it well enough. After all, he was the strongest person in the world, according to the power ladder. That had to mean something. On top of that, he had a wealth of combat experience, and in a wide variety of situations, to draw upon. He'd recently killed one of the top three most powerful people in the world, too. So, Elijah knew he had the ability to do what needed to be done.

But killing someone in cold blood required a different frame of mind. That was especially true if he intended to bring down the city, too. Which was still up in the air, if he was honest with himself. On the one hand, from what Carmen had described, the entire city of Easton was rotten to the core, and the world would be a better place if that city no longer existed. However, on the other hand, Elijah knew that Carmen's perception was tainted by her own mindset. Inevitably, there were still innocent people in that city. And even if there weren't, there were degrees of guilt. Some people doubtless deserved execution. But others, even if they were in some way complicit in Alyssa's murder, hadn't earned that fate.

It was a complex situation, and one Elijah intended to ponder as he flew toward the city in question.

He beat his wings against the air, climbing ever higher until he passed through the clouds and into an entirely new world. Via One with Nature, he could feel things he couldn't identify in and above the clouds. However, he saw nothing but a few shimmers in the air. It reminded him of what he thought of as the Predator effect, derived from the titular movie alien who could camouflage itself almost completely. However, when it moved, it created a barely visible shimmer.

The same was true of the things Elijah sensed through One with Nature. They represented a wide variety of shapes. There were things that felt like serpents, a few amorphous blobs, and humanoid variants, among many others. It took Elijah a few minutes to recognize that they were made of air, putting him in mind of spirits. Or elementals, perhaps.

Fortunately, they were not aggressive. Indeed, they ignored him altogether, even when he came close. Still, it was an interesting discovery, and one Elijah would have studied closer if he didn't have his mission to worry about. As it was, he quickly left the clouds behind as he soared toward the mountains.

As he drew closer, he recognized many other flying creatures. Some were recognizable species of birds, though they were typically much larger than they had been before Earth's transformation. Yet, there were other beasts that could only be described as magical in nature. Elijah saw a flock of winged serpents in the distance, as well as an animal that looked strikingly like a griffin, though he couldn't be sure, considering that it dived into the forested mountainside before he had a chance to study it.

Eventually, Elijah found the path through the mountains. He didn't try to fly over them, instead targeting the pass he'd used before. As he flew through it, he saw that the remnants of the spiders had begun to fade. At last, the gossamer webs that had once coated the entire area had started to dissolve. There were other animals about, too, which boded well for the ecosystem's recovery from the invasive monster's presence.

He covered ground much more quickly than he had in his first few trips, and after only a few hours—some of which he spent practicing flying through narrow valleys—he began his descent into the foothills. On a whim, Elijah decided to stop by Norcastle.

Mostly, he wanted to check on Jess and Essex, but he also wanted to make certain that Ironshore's interests were protected. After all, they were his allies, and their fate affected his own. The stronger they were, the better they would be able to protect their territory, which was a good thing for him.

So long as they didn't get any ideas about invading his island, that is.

But they'd stayed away so far, and Elijah could only hope that that pattern would continue.

After a while, he saw Norcastle in the distance, so he landed—badly—and, after using Touch of Nature to heal the resulting injuries, he shifted into his draconid form and continued on to the tree line closest to the city.

Once there, he settled down to study the situation.

The city itself looked much the same as it always had. The gate was guarded, but not by either of the people Elijah remembered. That didn't mean anything, though. Perhaps it was just a different shift. Either way, Elijah couldn't tell much from afar, so he embraced Guise of the Unseen before padding across the large, open field until he reached the wall.

Once there, he launched himself upward, using his claws to grab hold of the uneven stones so he could climb to the top. He reached his goal unseen, then crossed the four-foot-wide wall walk before leaping down to the ground on the other side.

And just like that, he was inside Norcastle.

After looking around a bit, Elijah could confirm that not much had really changed. Some of the people seemed to have higher levels, and the stench of corruption was gone. There also weren't any corpse wagons to be found, so he felt confident that the plague had not returned. That meant that Essex and his people—or perhaps the mayor's men—were doing their duty by periodically running the tower. Hopefully, Reaver's Citadel hadn't resulted in too many deaths, though Elijah expected that there would be a few, regardless of his efforts.

He'd detailed the tower's layout—at least what he'd seen—for Essex before leaving the first time, but even then, people would still have to do the work. And with the unforgiving nature of each tower's challenges, it was inevitable that some casualties would occur.

Regardless, Elijah was satisfied that his efforts hadn't been wasted, so he moved on with the first task, which was to ensure that Essex was still around. A quick trip to the man's office told Elijah that he was fine—if a little overworked—but he didn't bother emerging from stealth. That would only cause the man problems.

So, he moved on to the next—and more important—task.

The hospital was a lot less crowded this time around, so it didn't take Elijah long to find Jess. She looked much the same as always, wearing purple scrubs and a pair of sneakers, though she felt a little stronger than before. That was probably inevitable. After all, she gained experience through healing, which was her job.

Elijah followed her for about an hour until she went to an office that would provide a bit of privacy. Once inside, he dropped Shape of the Predator and, even as he resumed his human form, asked, "Miss me?"

She gave a start, nearly falling out of her chair. Then, she patted her chest, saying, "Jesus—you scared the hell out of me, Elijah!"

"Sorry. I was trying to be spontaneous and romantic."

"By popping up out of nowhere? You have a weird idea of romance."

"Mostly derived from romantic comedies. So . . . yeah. You're probably right. But I was just kidding. Sort of," he said. "I didn't leave under the best of circumstances, so I figured it wasn't a great idea to just come strolling in here. Hence the stealth."

She let out a deep breath. "That was probably a good idea. There was someone looking for you a couple of months back," she said. "Big guy. Really strong. I don't think you want to let him find you."

"Oh, him? I crushed his skull," Elijah said, picking up a knickknack off the desk. It was a little bobblehead of a baseball player. "But in my defense, he didn't give me much choice. He stabbed me in the heart. And in the back. A couple of times, if I remember right. Plus, he was all like, 'I'm a mighty Viking hunter, and you are my prey! Raa!' Or something like that. He wasn't a nice guy is what I'm saying. Had a nice water bottle, though. Really useful."

"What?" Jess asked, clearly struggling to follow Elijah's interpretation of the fight. After only a second, she just shook her head and said, "You haven't changed."

"More than it seems," Elijah said, his tone suddenly serious. "Probably not as much as I should, though."

Indeed, most of the time, Elijah felt like the same person he'd been the last time he'd visited Norcastle. But so much had changed that he knew that wasn't the case. Even his conversation with Jess felt forced, and not in his normal nervous way.

"Are you okay?" she asked, reaching out to touch his arm.

Elijah shrugged. "I don't know, honestly," he admitted. "I found out my sister died. It . . . I haven't taken it well. It happened years ago. But . . . I still feel guilty that I wasn't there for her."

"It's not your fault."

Elijah gave her a small, sad smile. "You don't know that. Neither do I. Chances are, I'd have ended up the same as her, even if I had been there. But the not knowing—that's the worst," he said, shaking his head. "I'm fine, though. I just thought I'd stop by to see if everything was okay here."

After that, Jess explained that Essex had made a deal with the mayor to send joint teams into the tower. That had proved a success, and since then, the captain of the guard had worked to gradually gain more freedoms for the people. The mayor had acquiesced, especially when Kurik had appeared and offered an ongoing trade deal. After that, his attitude had shifted, and the corruption that had been so prevalent the last time Elijah had visited had faded into the background.

"I mean, he's still a shady figure, but it's a lot better now," Jess stated. "We all have full access to the Branch, too. So long as we pay a few copper etherium, we can use it as much as we want."

"That's great, Jess. I'm glad I didn't kill him last time," Elijah said. He'd considered it after the man had sent some thugs to his inn. Back then, he hadn't known if their intention was to simply collect him, rob him, or murder him, but he'd chosen to interpret it in the worst way. As such, the only reason he hadn't gone to teach the mayor a lesson was because Jess had asked him not to.

Plus, back then, he'd maintained an aversion to kill humans. That still persisted to a certain extent, but if Elijah felt justified, he wouldn't hesitate.

"Either way, I'm glad you're okay. That's a load off my mind," he said. "But I'm going to be on my way."

"You don't want to stick around? Maybe have a meal?" she asked, hopeful.

Elijah was tempted to take her up on it, but he shook his head and said, "No. Rain check, maybe."

Then, he left the room, shifting into his draconid form the moment he entered the hall. Once he was out of sight, he once again adopted Guise of the Unseen before heading toward the wall.

10

MIGRATION

Elijah sat cross-legged on a boulder, his eyes closed and focused almost entirely on One with Nature. During his previous attempts at cycling his ethera in an effort to begin the process of advancing his Core to the next stage, he had begun to feel something that he'd never felt before.

Or, rather, that he'd only experienced it a single time, when he'd first tried his hand at cultivation and very nearly succumbed to what Nerthus had referred to as the Call. Back then, the spryggent had described it as giving himself completely to the Mother. Or to nature itself. Though, Elijah hadn't understood it at the time.

Now, he was beginning to.

Because nature wasn't just some ephemeral concept. Certainly, it could be referred to in that way, but there was an underlying structure. Not an awareness, per se, but a desire. A need. An influence that Elijah couldn't quite categorize or understand. But it was powerful, he knew, and he expected that it was partially responsible for some of his more questionable decisions.

Like when he'd killed those hunters. Or when he'd nearly lost himself to his animalistic instincts during his first tower run. As he sat there, he traced that influence back to the very first time he'd laid eyes on Ironshore. Back then, he'd felt outraged at the deforestation and the billowing clouds of smoke that had come from the budding town. It wasn't until later that he'd moved away from that snap judgment and to something more reasonable.

But he hadn't forgotten his initial anger.

That he attributed to his connection to nature making itself known. It should have been obvious that his class would influence the way he saw the world. Or maybe it was his attunement. After all, nature was listed right there on his status.

Regardless of the origin, Elijah felt that he couldn't truly progress until he understood the influences working to dictate his actions. In a few years, he didn't want to look back and realize that he'd begun to walk the path of some lunatic ecoterrorist. Nor did he want to lose his connection with something so powerful, largely because he felt it would prove necessary in the future.

He didn't know how.

Nor did he know why he believed it to be true. Yet, he did believe it, and that meant that he needed to understand what was going on. So, he meditated, focusing his attention on One with Nature.

He felt every last detail of his surroundings, and for a fifty-foot radius. When he truly concentrated on that deluge of information, Elijah felt overwhelmed by the sheer scope. Billions of microbes. Thousands of insects. A few animals. A host of vegetation. The list went on and on. However, beneath it all was what Elijah was looking for.

There was an order to things. It felt cliché to think of it in such a way, but it felt like a circle of subsistence. An ongoing battle for survival that somehow fit perfectly together in a way where every individual organism got what it needed.

Where did he fit into that?

He felt simultaneously like an outsider, a part of the ecosystem, and a steward. A guardian of the delicate balance of life that was accepted, but never truly a part of that world. Unless he gave in.

He felt the pull. The Call.

He could leave everything behind and join with nature. Like that, he wouldn't need to worry about things like vengeance. Instead, he would merely become part of the cycle, and when his time came, he would die, only to fuel someone else's survival. In that way, he would live on.

It was beautiful.

But it was also antithetical to everything it meant to be sapient. That subversion of the self was entirely unnatural, which was ironic, given that it would allow him to truly become One with Nature.

Elijah sighed, then opened his eyes to see a sun-dappled glen. He was a few hours away from Norcastle, where he'd stopped for the night. His morning cycling practice had somehow turned into a meditation on nature, but he didn't regret the loss of a few cycles of Core cultivation. On the contrary, he felt that he'd made progress on a path he'd yet to truly recognize.

Still, he'd already spent enough time idling in the dell. So, he unfolded his legs and reached into his satchel, retrieving a hunk of dried meat. As he chewed on that, he hefted his Endless Canteen to wash it down.

After breaking his fast, Elijah spent a few minutes stretching stiff muscles before using Shape of the Sky and launching himself upward. His takeoff was much better than it had been only a couple of days before, and he hoped his improvement would continue, at least until he could land without risk of breaking his bones.

He flapped his wings, gaining a little altitude before speeding on his way. Elijah was tempted to stop by Argos, but he'd just left the city a few days before. So, it wasn't that difficult to ignore that temptation. Instead, he flew toward the ravine, hoping to cut the swamp out of his journey. Yet, when he reached the area, he discovered that those large birds that were the frequent prey of the canyon spiders were quite territorial. They didn't appreciate his intrusion, and Elijah had no intention of fighting an aerial battle—after all, his current form wasn't meant for fighting—so he reluctantly veered south.

Soon after, he found himself flying over the swamp.

Even at an altitude of a few hundred feet, the insects were maddening. But at least he didn't have to wade through tepid, waist-deep water. It took Elijah the rest of the day to reach the outer edge of the swamp, but as night fell, he landed on one of the infrequent islands, where he spent a fitful night sleeping. He'd done the same during previous trips into the swamp, but that didn't mean it was any less nerve-racking.

Still, Elijah endured the rigors of swamp life for the span of a night, and the next morning, he left it entirely behind. If he kept his pace, he would reach Easton in only a few days. A week and a half, at most.

No sooner had that thought entered his mind than he noticed a dark splotch on the horizon. At first, Elijah thought it was another storm, but if that was the case, it was even larger than the one off the coast of his island. As Elijah continued to fly north, the cloud resolved itself into thousands—maybe hundreds of thousands—of tiny shapes.

It was only when he got much closer and used Eyes of the Eagle that he got a good look at the creatures, confirming that they weren't tiny at all.

They were also nightmarish.

With bodies that mostly resembled birds, they had all the requisite pieces. Wings. Feathers. Enormous talons that were larger even than Elijah's own. But instead of the expected raptor's heads, they had the faces of women. However, they weren't ordinary women. Nor were they beautiful. They were, instead, horrifying mixtures of bird and woman that sent a shiver of unease coursing up Elijah's spine.

Instantly, he knew these were no natural beasts. They weren't guardians, either. Rather, they were monsters—those unfortunate creatures that had been snatched up almost by accident and deposited in an unfamiliar world. They did not belong, and yet, there they were—an affront to nature that Elijah was loath to let stand.

But good sense won out over his outrage, and he recognized that he couldn't fight tens of thousands of migrating harpies. That mythological moniker was the only way Elijah could describe them, and it felt appropriate, even if it was more than a little unnerving.

He dived, hoping to avoid the swarm.

Yet, he'd gotten close enough that the monsters had seen him, so a few hundred of the creatures mirrored his move. He crashed down into the lowland forest, shifting into his draconid form before he hit the ground. That softened the blow, though the impact still rattled his teeth.

But Elijah didn't have time to consider that because the first of the harpies arrived only a few seconds later. And they were even more grotesque than he'd first thought, with huge fleshy noses that resembled beaks. The first to attack was enormous—at least as big as his predator form, which was the size of a tiger—and with a wingspan to match. It crashed into him before he could dodge, though he used Flicker Step before the momentum could take him more than a few inches.

He disappeared, reappearing behind the monster, and after the single instant it took to reorient himself, Elijah pounced, using Venom Strike for good measure. Fortunately, the monster possessed no great defensive abilities, and Elijah's claws bit deep, ripping into its delicate wings with ease.

The creature screeched in pain, the sound cutting through every facet of Elijah's Mind and stunning him. He staggered, recovering after a second or two. However, by that point, it was too late.

A dozen more harpies had arrived.

And one of them had latched on to his back with its enormous talons. In only a moment, it was dragging him into the sky.

He shifted into his largest shape, transforming into a lamellar ape. The sudden influx of weight threw the harpy slightly off, which was enough for Elijah to latch on to the creature's talons—one in each hand—and wrench them apart. He put everything he had into the move, and it was more successful than he expected, going far past the point of pulling them apart and into the territory of breaking the bones.

Once again, Elijah was assailed by the monster's debilitating screeches, but that was only a minor concern, considering that he was falling directly into a mass of hungry harpies. With the instincts of the lamellar ape raging through him, Elijah let out a challenging roar as he fell.

He hit with a thunderous impact that broke the unlucky harpy that was directly beneath him, but Elijah gave that monster's fate no thought. Instead, he lashed out with a backhanded blow that sent another harpy flying backward until it hit a nearby tree trunk. The sound of broken bones joined the cacophony of birdcalls that had accompanied the flock of harpies.

Elijah loped after it, leaping in to ensure that it was dead. As he did, he used his upgraded Soul to fuel another transformation, this time back into his draconid shape. He hissed before clamping his jaws around the monster's body, crushing it even further. Though, he didn't stick around to finish it. Instead, he raced along, dodging talons and, to his surprise, barbed tails, along the way. In his draconid form, he had the Dexterity to manage the feat, though even then, he knew that the mass of harpies would eventually overwhelm him.

So, the goal wasn't to kill them. Rather, he only wanted to escape long enough to engage Guise of the Unseen.

With that in mind, Elijah raced along, taking the hits he couldn't avoid. He could have easily endured them in the lamellar-ape shape, but it was ill-suited for escape. Certainly, in that form, Elijah could move incredibly quickly, but if he tried that in the middle of a forest, he would have hit so many trees that any extra speed he could put on would have been completely negated.

No—the draconid form was his best shot, even if it left his scales in tatters. Never was that clearer than when he sensed even more harpies hovering just overhead. Some descended through the trees, turning hundreds into thousands as the ferocious monsters continued to hunt him.

Elijah ran, bounding over the terrain with well-practiced agility. It took almost an hour, during which he was further injured, before he managed to lose them for long enough to engage Guise of the Unseen. Still, even though he was cloaked in stealth, Elijah didn't slow down. Instead, he kept running for hours more until he stumbled upon an abandoned convenience store.

Such buildings were not uncommon, but this one was mostly intact, so he hoped it would provide him shelter until the flock of harpies moved on. So, he padded inside, and even though his wounds screamed at him for attention, he took the time to ensure that no other creatures had claimed the location as their own den. Even with his natural affinity for animals, no creature would take an invasion of their home lightly.

Thankfully, the building was empty, so Elijah found his way to a back office, where he finally shifted into his human form and saw to his wounds. They were extensive, with bits and pieces of his skin hanging off in ribbons. Blood coated his clothes, and half his scalp had been torn away.

Even more distressingly, the moment he stopped moving, he let himself acknowledge the debilitating venom coursing through his veins. Those barbed tails hadn't simply been for show. Instead, they'd delivered one injection of venom after another. It wasn't as deadly as his own Venom Strike, and it didn't have anything on the afflictions delivered by Swarm. Yet, it was still enough to muddle his thoughts and make him cough up blood.

Or maybe that was the result of numerous internal injuries.

Regardless, Elijah quickly got to work healing, stacking Healing Rain, Soothe, and multiple casts of Touch of Nature. He only got the first cycle out before his injuries—blood loss and a debilitating venom among them—took their toll. He didn't pass out, but he might as well have, for all he was able to move. Or think. Instead, he sank into a foggy, mostly paralyzed state where he could do nothing but wait for Healing Rain and Soothe to counteract his conditions.

11

THE IMPORTANCE OF DENTAL HYGIENE

Even as Elijah drifted in and out of semiconsciousness, his mind seemed determined to settle on his past and how it might affect his future. At times, he'd find himself daydreaming about growing up with Alyssa, and only minutes later, his thoughts would turn to what he intended to do to Roman. Back and forth, over and over, seeming to go on for an eternity.

It was not a pleasant way to spend the couple of days it took him to recover from the harpies' attacks and their insidious venom that stubbornly resisted his efforts at curing himself. In the end, Elijah wasn't sure if he'd simply outlasted it or if he'd finally overwhelmed it. Either way, though, he returned to complete lucidity after a long two days, during which he used every ounce of ethera in his Core, and multiple times.

By the time he regained his wits, Elijah knew well enough to recognize how lucky he'd gotten. Individually, the harpies weren't terribly strong. He could kill them easily enough. However, when their flock numbered in the many tens of thousands, and with the potent venom they could inject, their lethality was nearly absolute. Few people would have managed to survive such an onslaught.

Even two days later, Elijah could sense that they were still in the area. Every now and again, he would feel one of them swoop into range of One with Nature. Fortunately, though, they seemed unwilling to land for more than a second or two, so his hiding place remained as viable as it had been when he'd found the abandoned convenience store.

That meant that he didn't dare take to the skies for now.

Still, he decided to take shelter in the old gas station for another day, at least. As he did, he alternated his time between healing—his wounds had proved extremely stubborn, so long as the venom remained in his system—and cycling his Core. He still hadn't made much progress, but Elijah expected that his failure was due to the low ethera density. After all, Nerthus had told him multiple times that even reaching the first stage of Core cultivation was incredibly difficult— to the point that it would require outside assistance—on Earth. And it would remain that way until the density of the planet's ethera reached a certain point.

It had definitely risen over the past couple of years, but Elijah expected that it still had a long way yet to go. However, he also had a bit of a secret weapon in the form of his Grove and, more importantly, his cultivation cave. With the advantage that those spots' high ethera density represented, he hoped to make some strides in Core cultivation once he returned home.

His stomach twisted at the thought.

For some reason, it felt almost like a betrayal to think of anything other than avenging Alyssa's death. And it was even worse to make plans for the future, as if his current quest was just an item to be checked off a list. It was so much more than that, and rationally, he knew that fact, but his grief and guilt had no need for logic.

So, it was with renewed focus that, three days after first taking shelter in the convenience store, Elijah shifted into his draconid form, then adopted Guise of the Unseen before leaving it behind. Sure enough, his suspicions about the harpies proved correct, and the entire area was lousy with them. Most nested high in the tops of trees, but Elijah caught sight of a few as they swooped down to kill some unsuspecting beast. When they did, every harpy in the area would descend upon the slain animal, where the entire group would rip and tear the poor creature to shreds. Sometimes, the more volatile harpies would take things too far and attack one another, resulting in a bloodbath.

Elijah kept a close eye on every monster he could sense, either with his mundane senses or via One with Nature. He didn't think they could see through his ability's camouflage—especially in the forest—but he also didn't want to take any chances, either. After all, he'd seen what those creatures could do to their chosen prey, and he wanted nothing to do with them.

Or the nasty venom they could inflict upon him.

With that in mind, Elijah padded through the forest, careful and hidden beneath Guise of the Unseen. It was slow, but it was safe. Like that, he gradually covered ground. Miles melted before him until night began to fall, and he found shelter in an old, abandoned mobile home. There were a dozen more in the area, suggesting that the region had once been a trailer park, but most of the other structures had fallen before the rigors of time. After all, those sorts of homes had never been built to last.

Still, the one where Elijah sheltered was mostly intact, though he did get a bit of a surprise when he found the previous owner's remains. The bones had been picked clean of any flesh, so only a skeleton was left. A woman, from what Elijah could tell from the pelvis. In the next room, he found a few much smaller skeletons.

Children.

Humanity had been hit hard by what many referred to as the apocalypse. Billions had died. But the hardest hit had been the children who didn't even have the benefit of the system to ease the transition. All around them, creatures—and monsters in human skin, like Roman—developed unnatural abilities, and they had no way to defend themselves. It was a miracle any had survived.

Though there was some hope. Miguel had made it. So had plenty of children in Norcastle and Argos—more in the latter than the former, but there was no shortage of young people in either. Elijah felt some optimism at that thought. Even as he stared at the remains of the children who'd once called the trailer home, he could find some room for hope.

Though it was tempered by reality. Humanity had suffered many losses, and Elijah suspected that more were to come. It was while he was clearing another of the rooms of any debris that a notification flashed before Elijah's mind's eye:

Four years have passed since your planet (Earth) felt the transformative touch of the World Tree. In one year, the top five thousand (5,000) humans and top five hundred (500) settlers will be afforded the opportunity to endure the Trial of Primacy.

Participation is not mandatory, though it is encouraged. In one (1) year, present yourself at any Branch of the World Tree and you will be teleported to the Trial Grounds.

Prepare yourselves accordingly.

"The Trial of Primacy?" Elijah muttered aloud. His voice was barely a whisper, largely because the harpies were still about. "What the hell is that?"

But as always, there was no answer. The system seemed hell-bent on forcing everyone to consult the Knowledge Base for answers. When he went back to the elven city of Arvandor, he intended to use the Librarian to get at least one answer. Maybe he would ask about the Trial of Primacy.

More than that, though, Elijah was surprised that his estimate of time had been a little off. Until that point, he'd thought that they'd passed the four-year mark months past. However, unless the system used some other calendar, he'd been mistaken. Still, four years was a long time, and it felt even longer than it really was.

Simultaneously, though, it was like he'd washed ashore on the island only recently. Much had happened since then. He was an entirely different person, and not just because he'd beaten cancer that should have been terminal. Not only were his priorities completely different now, but he was also the most powerful person in the world.

That came with responsibilities.

Expectations.

He sighed, shaking his head as he sat in the corner of the room. He leaned against the wall and tilted his head toward the half-rotted ceiling.

He wasn't as strong as he seemed. Elijah knew that better than most. Despite having a head start on almost everyone in the world—in the form of his cultivation, which was assuredly more advanced than almost anyone else's—he had struggled in his fight against Thor. Certainly, he'd won—and that was what ultimately mattered—but it had highlighted the issues he would face going forward.

On paper, he was strong.

But his archetype, which was a hybrid that took pieces from a bunch of different disciplines, was never meant to be a front-line combatant. Sure, his class helped. So did his cultivation. But it wasn't enough to let him stand toe-to-toe with true combatants of similar level.

He could do wondrous things. As far as he knew, nobody else had the ability to teleport across thousands of miles. He could create his own equipment, at least to a certain extent, and he could grow some truly remarkable things in his gardens. Yet, those things didn't help in a fight.

Not for the first time, Elijah thought back to K'hana's shock when she'd discovered that he was a Druid. It was warranted, too. From the guide he'd recently read, the archetype was heavily implied to be a mostly noncombat class that focused on nurturing a grove.

That wasn't Elijah's path, though. He liked fighting. He enjoyed exploration. And while he also liked tending to his Grove, the reality was that he would go insane if that was the entire scope of his future. So, he had no choice but to push ahead with his cultivation, and hopefully, when it came time to choose his specialization, he could further adapt his archetype to his purposes.

After that, there was an evolution to anticipate, too. Equipment would help, as well.

No—Elijah's path was clear. He needed to scratch and claw for every advantage he could find, lest he be held back by his archetype's noncombat nature. In the meantime, he would lean on his versatility as he continued to gain levels.

With that in mind, he settled in to rest as he ate a couple of Grove berries. Without those little fruits, his recovery would have taken much longer, which just solidified another one of Elijah's advantages. Everything grown in his Grove was infused with dense ethera. As such, it often had special properties, like the restorative traits of his Grove berries. Hopefully, his coffee would be even better. And he still intended to make another staff once he finished his quest. The Dragon-Touched Staff was great. Better than he could have expected. Yet, it still didn't feel as natural as either of his other two staves had.

His mind whirled with plans for the future as he rested, and eventually, he settled in to sleep. Thankfully, his dreams were of the normal, nonsensical variety, so he ended up resting well before rising the next morning and continuing on his way.

Gradually, he made his way across the landscape. He was tempted to take the same path he'd taken on his way to Seattle—after all, he could swing by Arvandor to use his question—but ultimately, he chose not to do so. Largely, that decision was based on simple expedience. Easton was located to the north-east, while Seattle was almost due north. So, it made sense to cut diagonally across the terrain, even if it meant exploring new territory.

Eventually, Elijah's path took him by a ruined commercial park located on either side of a three-mile stretch of interstate. The highway was packed with abandoned automobiles, most of which bore some degree of damage. Some looked like they'd been stripped for parts, but judging by the rust, that had occurred some time ago. There were no signs that the region was populated.

As Elijah progressed along the highway, he saw a few car dealerships, then a couple of big-box stores—the sort that sold everything in ridiculous bulk, like gallon jugs of mayonnaise. Elijah inspected a couple of those, but other than picking up a couple of computers, a few giant packages of underwear, and a dozen tubes of toothpaste, he found nothing of worth. He knew the last would've already passed their expiration date, which meant that the paste inside would be a little less effective. However, Elijah was counting on the fact that the tubes were unopened to have extended their shelf life a bit. Besides, even then, it would be better than the charcoal he normally used to clean his teeth.

He also grabbed a box full of toothbrushes.

With ethera and healing, he didn't think he needed to worry about cavities. However, those two factors did nothing for bad breath.

Whatever the case, his scouring of the big-box stores took half a day before he decided to move on. Even then, the harpies were still around, which meant that he would need to continue on foot.

So, that's what he did, shifting back into his draconid form and using his stealth ability to remain undetected as he drew ever closer to Easton, where he would exact his revenge.

12

AVOIDING DISTRACTIONS

A gentle rain fell, each drop flowing off Elijah's sleek scales as he leaped from one rock to the next. Beneath him, a river raged, spraying a mist into the air as the swift-moving water crashed into the boulders. Elijah had spent hours trying to find a crossing—the current was far too strong to safely swim across the wide river—and not for the first time, he cursed the harpies that prevented him from taking flight.

Their numbers had begun to thin, but he couldn't help but liken them to a swarm of locusts. Except these particular pests were as large as lions, and with wingspans to match, rather than the size of thumbs. Regardless, so long as he was careful, they didn't pose much of a threat. That would change if he failed to use Guise of the Unseen, though, so he remained cloaked in his camouflaging skill.

Still, despite the relative safety he enjoyed, Elijah couldn't help but lament the slow pace of travel. When he'd set out, he'd hoped to be in Easton in a couple of days. And that would have been a viable expectation, given the speed he could achieve with Shape of the Sky. However, traveling overland was much slower, especially when he had to do so under the effect of Guise of the Unseen. It didn't prevent him from running flat out, but moving that quickly would strain the ability, which would chance exposing him to the harpies.

So, as frustrating as it was, Elijah exercised every ounce of his patience to maintain his pace.

He leaped from the final boulder and to the riverbank, then left the river behind. Elijah wasn't certain if the river had originated with Earth, but he doubted it. The thing was half a mile wide, a size that wasn't usually conducive to such a rapid current, but he didn't know enough about rivers to say for certain if such a body of water had existed before Earth's transformation.

What certainly hadn't existed back then were the creatures that called the river home. They could only be described as monsters, though for once, Elijah chose discretion rather than confrontation. Not only would a fight bring the harpies down on his head, but he also had no interest in letting himself get distracted by one side quest or another, as he had throughout his travels before discovering his sister's fate.

With that in mind, he continued on, crossing a few other, smaller rivers along the way. He also saw a couple of settlements in various states of development. One had high walls and seemed well protected, while another was open to attack and was barely holding on. The residents of the latter looked like they could use Elijah's help, but as was the case with the river monsters, he chose to ignore them.

Perhaps that made him selfish, but with every step closer to Easton, his mindset focused on the conflict to come. He refused to dilute that by getting sidetracked.

Days passed until, at last, he left the harpies behind. Or put more accurately, they chose to continue on, launching themselves into the sky and flying off as one ridiculously huge flock.

In the beginning, he'd estimated that they numbered in the tens of thousands, but after traveling beneath them for more than a week, Elijah amended that estimate to millions. One day, that might prove to be an issue, especially for any settlements in their path. Fortunately, the harpies seemed willing to avoid the populated towns and villages Elijah had passed along the way, which engendered hope that harmony was possible.

If not, then someone would have their hands full with dealing with the monsters.

But not him. Not now.

Elijah didn't immediately take to the skies. Instead, he remained with his feet planted firmly on the ground, though he did abandon Guise of the Unseen. After a day of traveling out in the open, he judged it safe and used Shape of the Sky and, once again, flew high above the landscape.

From that vantage point, he saw the terrain far more clearly. It wasn't particularly mountainous, but it wasn't flat, either. More importantly, the area was absolutely littered with remnants of Earth's fallen civilization. He saw overgrown subdivisions, stores, and even a couple of complexes that looked like they'd once served as schools.

He also saw people.

Not a lot of them, but there were enough small groups out and about that Elijah expected he was getting close to a sizable population center. Still, it wasn't until he saw the tall wall brimming with ethera that he realized that he'd arrived in Easton. Carmen had spent some time describing it, so he knew precisely what he was looking at.

Still, Elijah didn't immediately head into the city. Instead, he circled for a couple of hours until he saw a familiar sight.

He landed in the center of the street that cut through his sister's old neighborhood. The surrounding homes looked little different than any other place Elijah had visited. A few of the houses remained intact, but most had been subjected to catastrophic damage. That had been exacerbated by time and the weather, which had collapsed most of the structures.

Elijah remembered the last time he'd visited. Back then, Miguel had only been four or five years old. Just about to start kindergarten. Carmen had been working on her dissertation, while Alyssa had just started her career as a police officer a couple of years before. For his part, Elijah had just gotten a job after finishing his doctorate, and he'd decided to visit his sister before starting.

In those days, the apathy concerning his chosen field hadn't truly set in, and he'd been eager to do important research that he'd hoped would change the world.

"I was so naive," he muttered to himself, having shifted back to his human form.

They all were. Alyssa thought she was going to help her community and change police practices for the better. She'd tried. For a while. But eventually, she'd come to realize that there was only so much a single police officer could do, and she'd shifted her focus toward the pursuit of a law degree.

Carmen might've been the most realistic of them. She knew her chosen field wasn't particularly important, but she was no less enthusiastic for it. Who could have predicted that she would use those skills to become one of the strongest crafters in the world? Certainly not Elijah.

For what felt like the thousandth time, Elijah wished he'd chosen to come back home sooner. If he'd taken a flight even a day earlier, he would have been in Easton when the world had transformed.

But would that have helped?

Without Nerthus's guidance in cultivating his Body, the cancer would have remained. And he'd been close enough to death that there was almost no chance that he would have discovered the means to cure himself without the spryggent's help. So, as easy as it was to second-guess the past, Elijah knew that it wouldn't have mattered. There was nothing he could have done to prevent Alyssa's death. In fact, his presence would have been a hindrance.

With that in mind, Elijah continued down the street, the iron cap on the butt of his staff clicking against the pavement. Most of the street was covered by a layer of dirt or vegetation, but there were still a few bare patches. There were animals all around, many of them having created nests inside the houses, but none of them bothered Elijah as he strode toward his sister's house.

His path unimpeded, he reached the site only a few minutes later.

The low-slung, single-story house was just as overgrown as all the rest, and half of it had been entirely destroyed. The other half remained strikingly intact, though, so Elijah hoped that his reasons for visiting the house would bear fruit.

He stepped forward, and an audible flapping sound announced the sudden ascent of a giant bird that had nested atop the house. Flashing back to his ordeal with the harpies, Elijah immediately shifted into his lamellar-ape form. His heart pounding, he wheeled around, ready to fight. However, the bird was just a normal, if overgrown, crow. It circled a couple of times, cawing loudly, but it clearly had no intention of picking a fight.

His heart beating out of his chest, Elijah steadied himself before shifting back to his human form. The experience with the harpies had clearly taken its toll.

It took a few moments for his heartbeat to normalize, and when it did, he continued forward. The door had been knocked from its hinges, and it lay to the side, half on the porch and the other half tangled in the overgrown topiary that hid most of the house's facade.

Elijah stepped inside.

The sun was still high in the sky, but the interior of the house was mired in darkness. As a result, it took a few moments for Elijah's eyesight to adjust to the gloom. While he waited, he focused on One with Nature, cataloging the various organisms in the house. There were a few rodents, plenty of reptiles like lizards and snakes, and more insects than Elijah wanted to count. He did make note of a large colony of termites that reminded him of his experiences in the Magister's Estate.

But there was nothing inside that would threaten his life. So, when his eyes adjusted, Elijah set about his task without fear. The first place he visited was the kitchen, where he found a bunch of rusted pots and a host of empty cabinets. After the world's transformation, Easton's residents had survived in no small part due to extensive scavenging efforts. So, the fact that the house had been picked clean of immediately useful things—which included the cabinets' contents—wasn't particularly surprising.

Still, Elijah did find a huge cast-iron pan that he thought would be useful. It was marred by a patina of rust, but he knew that wasn't enough to ruin such a sturdy pan.

Not that he could use it for its intended purpose. After all, he didn't have a cooking skill, which meant that anything he prepared would be bland and tasteless. Maybe he could gift it to someone. Or perhaps his pack rat tendencies were making themselves known.

In any case, it didn't take him long to move on from his sister's kitchen.

The next stop was the living room, where he'd hoped to find some photos. However, that hope was quickly dashed when he saw that anything that hadn't been taken was rotted, probably due to the area's humid climate.

Still, Elijah spent a while sifting through the ruins, hoping to get lucky.

He did not.

And after some time, he moved on to what had to be Miguel's room. There, he found much of the same. The bed had been stripped of its mattress, and the chest of drawers was entirely empty. The television remained, as well as an old gaming system. However, Elijah knew that neither would work, even if he managed to provide electricity. In its ruined state, the house offered minimal protection against the elements, which didn't mix well with electronics.

Elijah did find a few shirts hanging in the closet, though they were far too small for the current Miguel. So, it wasn't long before he moved to the master bedroom, where he found more of the same. Decayed photos. Inactive electronics. And rotted clothes. However, he did find a pistol in a case under the bed.

"Useless hunk of metal," he said aloud, tossing it back to the floor. The other discovery was in that same case, and for a long moment, Elijah stared at the wad of cash. He knew it was an emergency fund, intended for use if the electrical grid went offline and cards stopped working. A reasonable thing to have, but ultimately, it had proved entirely useless. What use was a few bills when monsters were trying to rip your face off?

The rest of Elijah's search bore no fruit, so when he found the basement, he didn't have high hopes. He descended the steps, his shoulders slumping in both fatigue and frustration. Yet, that all disappeared when he laid eyes on an item in the corner.

13

MEMORIES AND TEARS

Tiny clouds of dust kicked up with each of Elijah's steps as he shuffled forward, lost amid the roiling memories of days long past. Just like the rest of the house, the basement had been ransacked. Boxes had been overturned to spill their contents over the concrete floor. Most of it was useless. One had contained old winter wear; another had been filled with tangled Christmas lights. There was a disassembled fake Christmas tree as well as a few old festive wreaths. Elijah saw a couple of bicycles, their tires having dry-rotted. And a host of other bits and pieces that were all that remained of the lives Alyssa and her family had once led.

But Elijah only had eyes for one item, as well as the wooden crate beside it.

He approached, then laid his hand on the old record player. The facade was brushed aluminum, with sides of laminated particle board and a clear plastic hood that had been so discolored by age that it obscured the inner workings of the player itself. On either side of the machine were matching speakers, maybe six or seven inches tall.

With bated breath, Elijah reached out and touched the plastic hood, feeling the rough surface that had been through so much over the years. Like everything else in the basement, it was covered in a thick layer of dust, which took a couple of swipes from Elijah's hand to remove. And there on the top was the Nirvana sticker he expected. He stared at the simple black-and-yellow decal as he remembered the day his sister had gotten it.

She hadn't even been a teenager when she went through her grunge phase. Of course, they were both at least a decade too young to have lived through the genre's heyday, but Alyssa had never cared about following trends. Indeed—she'd reveled in eschewing the sorts of things all her peers seemed to hold in such high esteem.

And because Elijah had idolized his older sister, he had, as well.

At least when it came to entertainment.

The sticker was surrounded by a dozen others, all representing various bands. In a lot of ways, it was a timeline of her evolving tastes. She had never cared about consistency, putting hip-hop artists right next to death metal, and with everything in between.

It was a perfect representation of who Alyssa had been in her youth. A girl searching for something—anything—that spoke to her. And when she found it, she latched on with both hands. It didn't matter if it matched her perceived persona. She'd never cared about fitting in. Instead, as cliché as it was to think of it in such terms, she had always walked to the beat of her own drum.

And she'd paid for it, too. On top of being tall, awkward, and lesbian, she'd made no efforts to be like all the other girls. That had made her something of a loner. Sure—she'd had a few friends, but they were relationships of circumstance rather than true affection.

But Elijah had always been there, a few years younger, but still, they were incredibly close.

And now she was gone.

Forever.

He would never listen to music with her again. He'd never hear her talk about the girls she liked. The obscure movies she always overanalyzed. Her plans to lead the way in changing law enforcement. The list went on and on. If there was one word that could describe Alyssa, it was that she was committed. It didn't matter the subject. If she latched on to something, she embraced it completely, and to a nearly obsessive degree.

And Elijah missed that.

Tears carving a path down his cheeks, he opened the record player's lid, exposing the interior. It all looked to be in good order. No missing pieces, and the hood had protected it from the dust. It was a shame, then, that there was no electricity.

Still, Elijah hefted it and slipped it into his satchel. It was almost too wide to fit, but he managed it. And once it was inside the bag, it settled in next to all his other supplies. The speakers came next, after he'd wrapped the wires around them. Finally, Elijah turned his attention to the wooden crate.

Leaning forward, he pursed his lips and blew. With his Strength, it was like using a can of compressed air, and the dust billowed before him. Not having expected that, Elijah pulled away, coughing as he waved his hand in front of his face. Once the dust settled, though, he saw the crate's contents.

His sister's collection of records had never been large. Often, she traded them in at a local secondhand store so she could satisfy the terms of whatever her latest obsession might have been. Her fixations were powerful but flighty, and when she was done with something, she moved on quickly.

Even so, like the stickers, the crate's contents were akin to a timeline of her tastes. The first record was, predictably, Nirvana's *Nevermind*—the one with the underwater baby on the cover—and though the iconic photo was faded with age, it was still more than recognizable. Elijah flipped to the next, which was a record by Aerosmith. The next after that was Blind Melon. And then things took a hard left turn when he found a record from the eighties.

The cover featured a simple portrait of a pretty teenage girl with red hair and a single word. *Tiffany*.

It was the pop star's first album, and the one that launched her to stardom in the late eighties. Of course, if Nirvana was before Alyssa's and Elijah's time, then that album—which was the sort of vapid teen pop of the era—certainly was. However, it also featured some themes that resonated with Alyssa in a way that none of the current music of the time ever did.

More than that, though, it was special because it was the album Alyssa had been listening to the night she had come out to Elijah.

That year, Elijah had just started to get serious about boxing, and he'd spent most afternoons after school at the gym. So, he didn't get home until a few hours after his sister, and when he did, he arrived to find her crying in bed while listening to "I Think We're Alone Now."

He remembered it so vividly. Almost twenty years had passed since that day, but the memory was still so fresh in his mind. He sat on the end of her bed and awkwardly patted her on the foot, telling her that it would be okay. At the time, he'd had no clue what had made her so distraught, but he knew enough to offer whatever comfort he could muster.

Of course, Alyssa had insisted that it wouldn't. That's when Elijah asked what had happened, and she'd just blurted out that she was a freak. She'd practically screamed that everyone at school was going to find out about it, too. And in true dramatic teenager fashion, she'd collapsed onto the bed in a fit of tears.

Elijah had continued to try to comfort her, but he had no clue what was really the matter. Alyssa had never cared about fitting in, after all. So, if someone thought she was a freak, she'd have borne that label with pride.

Finally, she'd let the proverbial cat out of the bag, revealing that she was, in fact, a lesbian. More, she'd confessed her love to one of the other girls on her track team.

Those feelings were not reciprocated, and Alyssa had retreated in horror, leaving track practice early.

At the time, Elijah had had no idea how to respond. He didn't really understand the gravity of her revelation until much later, but he definitely understood that Alyssa was hurting. So, he did his best to comfort her.

It didn't really work, though.

Still, she eventually got over the rejection, and when Elijah finally realized what it really meant that she'd chosen to come out to him before she'd even done so with their parents, it brought them closer than ever before.

And since that day, Elijah had always associated that song with his relationship with his sister. There were other songs they enjoyed together, too. Lots of other albums, many of which were represented in that crate. As Elijah flipped through them, his grief continued to mount with every memory they brought to the forefront of his mind.

The time she'd helped him get ready for his junior prom. The day of her graduation. The night she got home from her first real date with a girl. Long conversations about their plans for the future.

The night their parents had died.

The day Elijah had left for Hawaii.

Alyssa's old music had even been playing in the background when Elijah had let her know—in a phone call—that he had been diagnosed with cancer. She hadn't believed him not initially. Denial was often the first phase in those sorts of situations. For a while, she had even insisted on coming to Hawaii to support him.

Elijah wished he'd let her.

He wished he'd done so many things. Made so many changes. Those feelings of grief and guilt wrapped even more tightly around his heart, constricting his mind and soul to the point where he could scarcely think.

And then there was the rage burning everything else for fuel.

He would never again see his sister. Never hear her voice. They would never sit and listen to music again. They wouldn't watch movies together. They wouldn't reconnect after Elijah's ill-conceived flight to Hawaii.

She would never see her son grow into a man.

She would never get to grow old with the love of her life.

She would never see the miracles Elijah sometimes took for granted.

And it was all because of one deluded and self-absorbed man. Elijah wanted to lash out, then and there. He needed to destroy something. To tear the house down. Yet, he kept himself under control, slipping the records—one by one—into his Ghoul-Hide Satchel for safekeeping.

He spent a little more time looking through the basement, but he found nothing else of sentimental value. So, a couple of hours later, he regretfully climbed the stairs and traversed the interior of the house until he'd left it behind.

After a single look back, Elijah adopted the Shape of the Sky, transforming over the course of a second or two, then launched himself toward the blanket of gloomy clouds above. Only a few minutes later, he landed in a copse of trees just outside Easton, then used Shape of the Predator.

As was the case in Norcastle, Elijah had no interest in announcing his presence to the residents—or, more importantly, the guards—of Easton. Instead, he chose to enter under Guise of the Unseen. However, when he found his way to the wall, he discovered that it was far too sheer to climb the hundred-foot edifice. So, after seeing that, Elijah slowly padded along the length of the wall until he reached a gate.

It was guarded by a half dozen men wearing blue-and-white uniforms. Each one felt reasonably strong, though Elijah had no notion of their levels. But judging by the ethera wafting off of them, they were at least high enough to give him pause. More importantly, when he came into view, one of the guards' eyes settled on him for the briefest of seconds before moving on.

Elijah didn't know if the man had seen him. Probably not, or he would have attacked. After all, he was in his terrifying draconid form, which would certainly elicit some reaction. More likely, the guard had only noticed something out of the ordinary. Or he'd gotten a feeling. And Elijah suspected that if he tried to walk through the gate in broad daylight, he'd be detected.

So, without further hesitation, Elijah retreated a few hundred yards and settled behind a tree, where he intended to wait until nightfall to enter the city. Impatience gripped him, but he pushed past it, focusing on the impending task.

14

THE LAY OF THE LAND

Flickering ethereal lights cast the gate in wavering shadows, which proved to be perfect cover for Elijah's ingress. He slipped past one of the guards, narrowly avoiding her by a scant handful of inches. She started, looking around in shock, but when she saw nothing, she muttered, "Must've been the wind."

Her partner said, "Storm's comin', I think. Saw it on the horizon earlier."

The woman shook her head. "What I wouldn't give to still be able to check my phone for the forecast," she sighed. "The things we miss, huh?"

"Netflix."

"Huh?"

"I miss Netflix," the man elaborated. "Not just the good stuff, either. Those cheap, cash-grab, one-big-star movies they used to pump out. I would get some beer and pizza and just turn one of those silly things on."

"If they were silly, then why did you watch them?" she asked.

He shrugged. "Guess we all need a little silliness sometimes," he answered. "Call it a release. I don't know. But I miss it."

"I guess that makes sense. I liked . . ."

Elijah passed out of earshot as he stepped into the city, completely unnoticed by the guards. Even when he was well out of sight, he didn't bother shifting back to his human form. He knew his appearance was distinct, and his experiences in Seattle told him that he only had a vague idea of what kind of identification abilities people could aim at him. Isaiah had known his whole status, and Elijah couldn't chance someone with similar abilities recognizing who he was and interfering with his plans for Easton.

Or, as he discovered a few minutes later, Valoria. He'd overheard that bit of information by eavesdropping on a conversation between two pedestrians who were more than a little critical of the name change. Unbeknownst to them, not only did Elijah overhear them, but their conversation didn't go unnoticed by a few other pedestrians. Most notably, there was a man with shifty eyes who seemed extremely interested, and he followed the pair as they turned a corner.

Elijah let them be, but he suspected that he'd just discovered the presence of the secret police Carmen had described. How fascist had the government become if people couldn't even criticize something as innocuous as a name change without incurring the city-state's wrath?

Shaking his draconic head, Elijah moved on, wandering through the city. A couple of times, he bumped into one of the many pedestrians, but there were enough people in the area that no one suspected that an invisible predator moved among them. However, as the night wore on, the traffic slowly dwindled, and Elijah let himself truly take everything in.

And he had to admit that the city represented an impressive achievement.

It was clean, orderly, and far more structurally advanced than places like Seattle. There was no obvious crime, and certainly, it didn't feel like every alley might be the site of a murder. There were blue-and-white-clad guards on nearly every corner, though, and plenty of plainclothes watchers were out and about, too. Elijah recognized them easily enough, and he suspected that the citizens did, as well. However, the residents clearly chose to ignore the obvious.

Still, Elijah couldn't help but offer his begrudging respect for what Roman had accomplished. Sure, it was built on a foundation of evil, but there was no denying that the city was a safe place to live.

Eventually, Elijah passed through a large square. At first, he didn't understand the purpose of the platform in its center, but after inspecting it more closely, he smelled the unmistakable scent of blood. Then, recognition dawned in his mind, and he saw it for what it was.

A stage for execution.

A series of blocks—ten—stood in a line on the stage. Each one was missing a rounded chunk, and the resulting divot was stained with the blood Elijah smelled. Seeing that, it wasn't difficult to imagine a row of prisoners strapped to the blocks and being beheaded by an axe-wielding executioner.

And given the prevalence of the iron-rich scent that pervaded everything, the edifice had seen quite a lot of use.

Elijah moved on, his anger mounting. Sometimes, executions were necessary, especially in a situation where you couldn't afford to jail a dangerous prisoner. When you were struggling to provide for law-abiding citizens, it was an easy decision to rid yourself of that sort of burden.

Yet, that situation didn't describe Valoria.

More, from Elijah's perspective, that sort of circumstance was, by definition, rare. The fact that executions in Valoria clearly weren't uncommon told Elijah that there was more at play than simple expedience or the public good.

Moving on from the square did nothing to assuage Elijah's outrage, especially when he wandered into a less affluent portion of the city. There was a clear line of demarcation, beyond which were simple, unadorned, and unimaginative buildings that looked like cubes made of lifeless brick. A few bore graffiti, some of which were messages that insulted Roman or his government, and the residents were poorly fed, dirty, and cloaked in rags.

Obviously, all was not well in Valoria.

Over time, Elijah overheard enough to recognize that the majority of the poorest caste were Scholars, which, because of Carmen's descriptions, he knew were second-class citizens in the city. Roman didn't value their potential contributions, and as such, even being permitted to live in Valoria was a relatively new development. For the first couple of years, they were routinely turned away unless they could prove themselves immediately valuable.

Most couldn't.

Elijah wondered how many had died because Roman saw no value in Scholars. Thousands, at the very least. Certainly, overextending the city's resources might have destroyed everything they had built. But Elijah found it distasteful that they hadn't even tried to find a solution that didn't involve turning a bunch of people away to survive in the hostile wilderness.

But at the end of the day, Elijah hadn't come to Valoria to judge the city based on its policies. Instead, as distressing as the situation was, he only really cared about holding Roman—and his comrades—accountable. And that meant he needed to gather some information. So, he found his way to the back of a secluded alley, where he assumed his human form.

Regrettably, he donned a pair of boots, largely because, for once, he didn't want to stand out. In addition, he focused on his Ring of Anonymity:

Ring of Anonymity Equipped. Choose Mode:
Anonymous
Robert Thane—Level 41 Warrior (Currently Active)
Deactivated

Hopefully, no one would be able to see through the subterfuge. Often, he forgot about the Ring of Anonymity, but in this instance, he was totally focused, and he had no room for mistakes. So, once he'd hidden his Sash of the Whirlwind under his shirt, he checked himself over. His disguise wasn't perfect, but he expected it would be enough. The only issue was that, while wearing the boots, One with Nature winked out.

That left Elijah feeling a little blind, but he'd expected it, so he didn't panic.

Regardless, he applied his various buffs, took a deep breath, then headed out of the alley. He kept his staff out, mostly because there were few people who traveled the city completely unarmed. It would have been stranger if he was one of those few. Besides, he didn't have far to go.

He joined the sparse flow of pedestrians, keeping his head down as he made his way to his destination, which turned out to be a tavern called the Swift Hiccup. It was a rowdy place—not quite low-class, but not exactly swanky, either—which was perfect for what Elijah had planned.

He stepped into the building, and he was immediately assaulted by a wall of noise. Raucous laughter mingled with a bawdy song sung by a scantily clad woman on the other side of the room, and an undercurrent of conversation filled the air. Elijah staggered a bit as he crossed to the bar, then unsteadily sat on a stool.

"What's your poison?" asked a gaunt-faced barman.

"Whiskey, if ya got it," Elijah slurred dramatically.

The bartender nodded, then went to fetch the drink. By the time he returned with a shot glass and a bottle, another man sidled up to sit next to Elijah. The barman filled the glass, then slid it toward Elijah.

"You new here, buddy?"

Elijah downed the drink. "Newish," he admitted. "Been out in Silverado for the past few months. Just got back this afternoon."

"Ah, you work for the government?" the man asked.

Elijah glanced at the fellow. He was average height, with only a bit of fringe on his head and quite a large paunch around his middle. Elijah nodded, saying, "That obvious?"

"Not really, in that getup. But most everybody with your level works for the government in some way or the other. Especially Warriors."

Elijah saw an opportunity. "Ain't that the truth," he said, tapping the bar. As the barman refilled his shot glass, Elijah said, "How're things round 'ere?"

The man spit on the floor. "That jumped-up thug is causin' trouble again," he said. "Actin' like he runs the joint. He's holed up in that hotel over on the other side of Justice Square. Some folks say he's on the verge of rebellion. Uppity asshole. His kind should know their place. King Roman will deal with that, though. Everybody knows what happens to anybody who messes with the king."

Elijah raised his glass, "Long live the king."

That, more than anything, loosened the man's lips, and he went on to describe the situation in great detail. Laramie, the warlord who'd betrayed Carmen, had been rewarded with a very important position within the city. At present, he was Roman's most senior general, and he'd spent the past year fighting Easton's—or Valoria's—wars. The rumor was that, as a result of his success, he'd begun to get ideas about his place in everything.

"Ain't like he's gonna actually rebel, though. He's just posturin' so the king'll give him somethin' or 'nother," Elijah's new friend said. "You know how it is. He wants etherium, probably. Natural treasures. That sorta thing."

"The rich get richer," Elijah said sagely.

"If that ain't the truth, I don't know what is!" the paunchy man exclaimed before clapping Elijah on the shoulder. "You're built like a brick shithouse, kid. How high is your Strength?"

Elijah shrugged. "High enough to survive, not high enough to thrive."

That brought a laugh from the increasingly drunk man. For his part, Elijah had already gotten what he wanted. The Swift Hiccup had been chosen for a reason. From what he'd overheard while exploring the city, it was frequented by low-level guards and other government officials. And in Elijah's experience, those were the sorts of people with the loosest lips. They had enough authority to take pride in it, but they were weak enough to feel a need to prove themselves to strangers.

And in a bar, that usually meant spreading gossip and rumors.

It just so happened that Elijah had found exactly what he sought from the first person he met. He'd expected to spend most of the night hanging out in the bar, but now, he felt that he had everything he needed to do what was necessary.

"Well, it's gettin' late," slurred Elijah. "I think I'm gonna get home and see my wife. Maybe we'll meet again, friend."

Elijah followed that up by gripping the drunken man's shoulder. For his part, the bald fellow asked Elijah to stick around for another drink, but Elijah wasn't having that. Instead, he paid his bill, then headed out.

He didn't intend to hit Laramie yet. It was too late to start that kind of mission, and he was tired—both mentally and physically—after the day's travails. So, after wandering around a little more, he found a mid-tier hotel where he rented a bed for the night.

Once inside the third-story room, he removed his shoes with a long sigh of relief. He could function without One with Nature, but not having it was disconcerting in a way he hadn't expected. Perhaps he needed to work on that because he expected it wouldn't be the last time he'd be forced to travel incognito.

Regardless, Elijah cast Soothe on himself, then found the basin on the nightstand. There was no bathroom, so he used the contents of the ceramic bowl to wash his face. He'd just finished rinsing the soap away when he felt someone in the hall.

No—not one someone. Many people. Ten, to be exact.

Elijah calmly crossed to the window, then looked outside. There were dozens of men standing in the street, but he only had eyes for one of them. Pacing back and forth was a tall, athletic, and armored man who wore his hair in thick dreadlocks.

"Laramie," Elijah whispered.

Then, he made a decision. He was tired of sneaking around and asking questions like he was some sort of spy. He wanted to get on with the task he'd come to Valoria to accomplish. And the first step was to rid the world of the man who'd betrayed his sister-in-law.

So, with fury dancing in his heart, Elijah grabbed his staff, took a deep breath, then strode toward the door.

15

PREY

For the first time in his human form, Elijah let his fury truly envelope every facet of his Mind. It sharpened his focus to a knife's edge, and as he arranged his enhancements appropriately—using his attribute enhancements and forgoing Essence of the Lion for Shield of Brambles—his grip tightened on his Dragon-Touched Staff.

There were two men on the other side of the door, then eight more arrayed across the hall. However, while they had numbers on their side—ten on one was definitely an advantage—they didn't feel all that strong. Indeed, Elijah had gotten used to inferring people's attributes by monitoring their movements. And these men were nothing special.

So, Elijah didn't even bother shifting, largely because he didn't think he needed it. Instead, he wanted to keep that in his back pocket, just in case someone else was watching. With that in mind, he reached out and opened the door. The would-be assailant's eyes widened in shock, but Elijah didn't let him react.

His hand shot out, faster and more accurately than the man could even track. And in an instant, Elijah's fingers wrapped around his target's exposed throat, clamped down, and ripped the man's windpipe free.

Blood spurted as he tried to react, but by that point, it was too late. He hit Elijah with his sword, but the blow lacked the power necessary to bypass his enhanced Constitution. Because, with the Dragon-Touched Staff, his buffs had grown by an extra five points each. With that, plus the extra five points in the attribute he'd gained just by using the weapon, his Constitution had been inflated even further than normal.

But Elijah wasn't worried about that. Instead, before the first man even fell, he was already swinging his staff in a wide arc that took the other nearby foe in the hip. When it connected, it did so with the sound of crunching bone. The man howled in agony as his leg collapsed beneath him, and he tipped over. Elijah stomped down on his head. When that didn't kill him, he did it again, which did the trick by shattering the fellow's skull.

That's when the other eight people finally reacted.

Fortunately, the hall was narrow, only allowing two people to attack him at once. Unfortunately, even that was more than Elijah could handle. His staff work hadn't had the chance to improve, and so, even with his advantage in attributes, he quickly found himself on the back foot as he desperately attempted to parry one attack after another.

The guards were all dressed identically, in blue-and-white uniforms and sturdy chain mail armor. More, they each wielded swords, and they obviously knew how to use them. Yet, Elijah was surprised that he'd managed to hold his own for as long as he had. They weren't weaklings, but they didn't fight like powerful Warriors, either. The fact that they hadn't used any real skills or spells was a good indication that they really didn't know what they were doing.

It was almost as if they'd spent all their time drilling with their weapons rather than incorporating their class-given abilities into a coherent fighting style.

Still, Elijah's own relative incompetence as well as the sheer disadvantage of numbers eventually bore out, and he felt a blade bite deep into his stomach, only to erupt out the other side.

Elijah coughed, coating his bearded chin in bright-red blood.

The guard who'd managed to impale him seemed almost surprised at the development. He was even more shocked when Elijah grinned, then pushed him away. The sword slid free, and another spurt of blood came with it.

Elijah used Soothe. Then Healing Rain. Finally, he pulsed Touch of Nature. The sequence played out over the course of only a few seconds—far more quickly than he'd ever cast them before. As he cast, the guards stared at him in horror.

That was a mistake.

Elijah grinned, his teeth coated in blood as his wound healed.

"Nice shot," he growled, his voice low and raspy.

Then, he initiated the transformation into the lamellar ape.

Laramie paced back and forth, resisting the urge to adjust his restrictive uniform. He'd worn it almost every day for the past year, and he still wasn't accustomed to the way it fit. He had never been much for formality—before or after the apocalypse—but his station required a certain image. And given that he wanted to keep his position as general of Valoria's army, he would do whatever was required.

Even wear an ill-fitting uniform.

"Are you certain he was in there?" he demanded, affecting the same sort of speech pattern used by Roman. Ever since he'd altered his manner of speaking, he'd noticed that people gave him the benefit of the doubt. His uniform helped, but his demeanor truly sold the fact that he was a man of power.

Eugene—one of the secret police—was a balding, overweight man and a talented actor. No one ever suspected that he was gathering information on everyone he met. Most recently, that included the stranger who'd come into town asking pointed questions about people far beyond him.

People like Laramie himself.

More importantly, the stranger was strong. Even Eugene's skills were incapable of measuring precisely how powerful he was, which was a red flag in and of itself. That was why Laramie had sent ten men into the hotel to detain the man.

"He's in there. Saw him go in my own self," the spy said, his words slurred. It was an act, Laramie knew, but a convincing one. "And the clerk was keepin' a lookout for if he left. He didn't."

"I don't like this," Laramie muttered.

Just then, the building shook. And given that it was four stories tall, that was quite a feat. A moment later, something came crashing through the wall, scattering bricks and dust into the air.

A body thudded into the ground only a few feet from Laramie.

He danced backward, but he couldn't avoid the blood and viscera as it splattered him.

"What the—"

A roar cut him off, and then Laramie heard the screams of terror. He looked up to see a shape flash past the brand-new hole in the wall, and he got the impression of scales and immense size before it disappeared.

Even as more screams assailed his ears, Laramie demanded, "What the hell was that?!"

No one had any answers. So, he turned to Eugene, only to see the fat man sprinting away. Laramie very much considered joining him. Whatever was in there, it was dangerous. Perhaps a powerful Voxx had bypassed the wall's defenses.

Or maybe the man inside had some sort of demonic pet to do his bidding.

Even as those thoughts skated through Laramie's mind, the screams abruptly ceased. For a brief moment, his men stared at the hole in the wall, unsure of what to do. This was his time to step up, to take command. Just like he'd done after the apocalypse when everyone else was gripped by panic. He'd led his people to survival.

When he was about to do just that, a huge, hulking, and black-scaled creature stepped up to the gaping hole. In the scant light, it was barely visible, but what Laramie saw was enough to send a tremor of fear up his spine.

And then it leaped free.

People shouted. A few screamed in abject terror.

But most stood their ground as the thing landed amid them, cracking the stone street upon impact. It shot forward, raking its thick, stubby claws across a man's territory. His armor proved entirely useless against the attack, and chain mail parted before spurts of blood filled the air.

The man never even got the chance to scream before the monster snapped out, decapitating him with a single bite.

A moment of silence followed the ghastly act before one of the guards let out a roar and attacked. The other forty-plus men followed, burying the creature beneath dozens of hacking attacks. The sound of metal on metal filled the air, accompanied by shouts of surprise.

Laramie had no idea what was happening until he added his own attacks to the mix. He thrust his sword forward, but when the tip made contact, it felt like he'd tried to stab a brick wall. The clang of metal assaulted his ears before he felt a sting in his arm. He looked down to see a thick thorn buried in his forearm.

When he stabbed again, he felt another.

Meanwhile, the creature was not idle. With every passing second, it lashed out with one sweeping attack after another. And where those claws landed, men were torn to bloody tatters.

It was a massacre.

And what was worse, when Laramie got a look at the creature, he saw that it was entirely unhurt. Even more disturbingly, it seemed to take pleasure in the slaughter. One after another, the men fell before its wrath.

Laramie backed away.

He couldn't fight something like that.

If he did, he'd end up just like his friends. And then, where would everyone be? His people needed him. It was better if he ran, sacrificing the few for the good of the many. Yes—that was the only answer.

It didn't take him long to convince himself before he was sprinting away, his footsteps accompanied by the sound of dying guards.

He turned the corner, continuing to sprint down the center of the street. People watched, perplexed to see one of their defenders—especially one as recognizable as him—running as though his life depended on it. Part of him wanted to warn the residents of the danger the monster's presence represented, but something in the back of his mind kept him from doing so.

Because if he truly wanted to escape, any delay would be beneficial. Even if it meant that each of the residents he passed needed to be sacrificed.

So, he ran.

He wasn't certain how long his flight lasted, but eventually, he slowed to a walk. His head whipped back and forth as he searched for any indication that the monster had followed, but there was nothing there. However, in his panicked state, he'd gotten turned around. Valoria was quite large, and though much of the city was laid out in a perfect and easily navigable grid, that wasn't the case in the less affluent districts like the one in which he'd found himself.

That was how he ended up at a dead end.

And when he turned, he saw something horrifying walking toward him. It was a reptile, but one that moved like a hunting cat. With black scales and a long snout filled with razor-sharp teeth, the creature looked even more intimidating than the scaled horror that had killed his men.

It was coming right at him, too. Slowly, and with deadly grace, it padded forward.

Laramie drew his sword and held it before him. Belatedly, he remembered to cast his spells, but they were only useful for enhancement. That was part of his class, Fighter. He had a couple of attack skills, but to use them, he needed to satisfy certain requirements that just weren't possible before the fight began.

"Come on, you fucking monster!" he growled, waving his sword like he was trying to fend off an aggressive dog.

The monster laughed.

It actually laughed!

The sound was like a chuckling hiss, but it was unmistakable. "Are you . . . Are you aware?"

"Are you?" it rasped, stopping ten feet away.

Then, it struck.

Laramie tried to react, but he was far too slow. His sword clanged against the ground as he missed the retreating creature. It actually took him a moment before he realized that it had wounded him. He didn't dare take his eyes off his enemy, but he could feel a tiny nick—barely more than a paper cut—on his thigh. Was that the extent of its power?

It struck again, raking its claws against the other leg, retreating before he could counterattack.

Once it reached the ten-foot mark, it sank down to its haunches. Then, it hissed, "You feel it, don't you? I've never asked if it's painful, but I suspect it is."

"What?"

"The afflictions," it answered, staring at him with cold reptilian eyes. "Contagion is pure rot, but Venom Strike causes necrosis. Two instances of each are probably enough to incapacitate you."

"I don't—"

Laramie fell to his knees as one of his legs gave out. Then the next followed. "W-what do you want?" he spit.

"I want to know everything about your . . . king," the monster said. "Give me what I want, and I will spare you quite a lot of pain."

With his legs having already become useless, it didn't take much to convince Laramie to talk. He was a survivor, after all, and he would latch on to any hope that might see him through to another day. So, he spilled his guts, telling the monster everything it wanted to know.

When he was done, he coughed, "Now, spare me. I did what you asked!"

The monster disappeared. And then, an immense pressure gripped his skull from behind before everything went dark.

16

CONSEQUENCES

Fiona strode through the lobby of her apartment building, her heels clicking against the marble tile. She hardly noticed the grand entryway or the stunning artwork. Instead, she took it all for granted, as if it was no less than someone like her deserved. After all, she was the king's closest adviser and—if she had her way—his soon-to-be lover. Perhaps his queen.

That very day, she had taken the first steps along that path by visiting a woman with a very interesting class. Once a plastic surgeon, she'd taken the Healer archetype. However, instead of becoming a Cleric or a Priest like so many others, she had taken a completely different approach by taking a class dependent on her very specific background.

Fiona didn't know the name of the class. Nor did she need to, really. All she needed to know was that the woman could solve her issue. And after seeing a demonstration, Fiona was certain that she could do just that. Similar to her old profession, the woman's new class was focused on fixing imperfections. She could mold flesh, shaping it to her desires.

Of course, judging by the patient's screams, it was quite painful, but Fiona could endure that if she could make herself more attractive to the subject of her infatuation. It would have been much easier if Roman's tastes hadn't been so specific. His late wife had been a perfect example of what he preferred. The woman had looked like a suburban version of a Playboy Bunny, with all the plastic parts that would imply.

Fiona, by contrast, had always been petite.

But that was going to change, and soon. The doctor would give her the bait she needed to get Roman on the hook. Then, she would reel him in. From there, they would rule Valoria and create an empire that would stand for millennia. It was practically foretold, a fact that had been revealed when Roman had told her about the quest the system had given him.

And he'd completed it, cementing her belief that he was special. Certainly, she didn't believe he was destined to be humanity's savior, as he often claimed. However, she couldn't really think of anyone better, either. And besides, savior or not, he was one of the most powerful men in the world.

That was all that really mattered.

Because she never wanted to feel weak again. If she couldn't have the power herself—and she didn't really believe she ever would—she would find someone strong to protect her. She refused to get into another situation like she'd experienced in the wake of the apocalypse. Back then, her husband had shown his true colors, proving himself too weak to be anything but monster fodder.

Sure, David had tried to protect her. He'd fought. And he had died on the very first day, leaving her alone and at the mercy of the world. How she'd managed to claw her way to safety was still a source of bewilderment.

But that was the past. Now, she had a real man to protect her. To keep her safe no matter what happened. She just needed him to realize that she was the best partner he could ever find.

Thus, the visit to the doctor.

Those thoughts occupied her mind as she made her way through the lobby and into the elevator. It was an ingenious contraption powered by ethera rather than electricity, but she took it for granted. So long as it went up and down without too much fuss, she was content to let the marvel of ethereal engineering fade into the background.

It rose from one floor to the next until, at last, she reached the penthouse. The doors opened, and she stepped inside. The moment she was alone and out of the potential public eye, she sighed, removing one shoe after another and padding toward her kitchen, where she poured herself a huge glass of wine.

However, she never got to enjoy it because, when she turned around, she saw something truly disturbing. The glass fell from her hand as she reached to her hip, grabbing at the wand at her waist.

She was too slow, though.

Even as the glass hit the floor, splattering the burgundy liquid across the rug, the stranger in the corner flashed forward. He didn't use an ability. Instead, he moved under the influence of his attributes. Before she could bring her wand to bear, his hand clamped around her wrist.

He squeezed.

And her wrist broke.

The wand—a twisted rod of some unidentifiable metal—clattered to the floor, and she let out a scream that was cut off when he slapped his other hand over her mouth and shoved her against the wall.

"Don't," he said. "I don't want to have to kill you."

She tried to scream again, but the sound was muffled by his hand. As tears traced lines of mascara down her cheeks, she stopped struggling. Then, she forced a nod.

He cocked his head to the side, studying her face before suddenly removing his hands and backing away. She slumped to the floor with a whimper.

Fiona had thought herself accustomed to pain. She'd been through quite a lot of it since the apocalypse. However, her broken wrist had proved that she wasn't quite as used to it as she'd thought.

"W-what do you want?" she sobbed.

"I want to show you something," the man said, reaching into the gray purse at his side. That gave her an opportunity to memorize her attacker's features. He was a short man—maybe an inch or so shy of average—but somewhat stocky. His face was handsome enough, in an unrefined sort of way, though his looks weren't helped by the scraggly beard and unruly blond hair. Still, there was something about him that she could at least acknowledge might attract a certain type of woman.

Not her, though.

The man wore anachronistic and oddly cut clothing, including a large fur coat. In truth, that wasn't really out of the ordinary in a city like Valoria, which was on the cutting edge of craftsmanship. Those sorts of people were always trying new things, which meant that plenty of strange fashion trends had swept through the city over the past year.

However, Fiona's eyes were drawn to two features more than anything else.

First, the man's feet were unshod, with his pants ending a bit above his ankles. Strange, that, and more than a little remarkable.

The second thing—or things, really—that stood out were the scars marring his body. One of his hands bore the evidence of a long-healed burn, while there were plenty of other scars decorating his neck and disappearing beneath his shirt.

By the time Fiona had cataloged those features, he'd retrieved something from his bag. And it wasn't until it thudded onto the floor, then rolled to a stop next to her that she realized what it was.

Of course, she screamed.

Because that was the only logical reaction to seeing a severed head, especially when it had belonged to someone she knew. Laramie's long dreadlocks were unmistakable, and when she looked down into the dead general's cold, lifeless eyes, she couldn't contain her shock.

The intruder slapped her with enough force to nearly dislocate her jaw.

"Sorry," he muttered, not seeming as if he meant it as he loomed over her. He straightened to his full height. "Don't scream."

"What do you want?" she demanded again, forcing some degree of defiance into her voice.

"I want to know how to get into the palace," he said simply. "I'm told you can do that."

"Told by whom?"

The man's eyes flicked toward the severed head. "He was very talkative there in the end," the intruder said.

"Why do you want to get into the palace?" she asked, mustering some of her courage. Her wrist was still useless, but if she could get the man talking, perhaps she could hit him with one of her spells. She hadn't been keeping up with her leveling of late, but that didn't mean she was completely helpless.

"Stop."

"What?"

"Gathering ethera. If you keep going, I'm going to rip your arms off," he said calmly.

"If you do that, you won't get the information you want."

He shrugged. "It won't kill you. I've thought about it a lot. I can't regrow limbs, but I can stop bleeding pretty easily. Especially for someone as low level as you," he said, his voice almost conversational. "And that means you won't die. I don't think it would do much for the pain, though."

"Y-you would—"

"Stop stalling," he said. "Your security people are already dead. You will be soon, too."

"Unless I give you a way into the palace?"

He didn't answer, but she didn't need him to, either. Fiona could read the situation. The man was dangerous. A killer. He wouldn't hesitate to murder her if she didn't provide what he wanted.

She took a deep breath, knowing how big of a betrayal she was about to commit. Would Roman forgive her? Maybe. He understood survival better than most. And there was a chance that she could warn him once the intruder left. She had an ethereal construct for just such an occasion. It ran on silver coins, but that was nothing considering the situation.

So, Fiona reached up to the delicate chain around her neck, then dragged it over her head. The pendant was a simple ruby in a silver setting, but that necklace was the most meaningful gift she had ever received. Not because it was valuable. It was, but Fiona was more concerned with what it represented— Roman's trust. With that pendant, she could bypass most of the palace's security features. The implications of that weren't lost on her, so she valued the pendant quite highly.

She tossed it to the man, who deftly caught it.

That's when Fiona struck, aiming a Greater Ethereal Bolt at his chest.

Spell: Greater Ethereal Bolt	Conjure a large ball of destructive ethera, casting it at a target. Splashes in a three-yard radius. Briefly stuns on impact. Duration of stun dependent on Ethera attribute. Current duration: 1.2 seconds. Victim's Ethera and Constitution attributes determine resistance.

The blue ball of roiling ethera snapped into being instantly. Then, it was sailing through the air in the intruder's direction. Fiona was already casting another when it hit him. She knew she would need to pile on the damage if she wanted to defeat the man, and that meant casting as many times as she could before the stun ran its course.

However, before she could complete her second spell, the man was only inches away, his clothes smoking but otherwise unharmed.

He did look angry, though.

His hand snapped out, his fingers wrapping around her throat. Before Fiona could react, he had lifted her off the ground, pinning her against the wall. "I wish you wouldn't have done that," he said. "I wasn't going to kill you. I really wasn't. I was just going to tie you up, leaving you for someone else to find. But now . . ."

"N-no!" she croaked, trying to cast a spell—anything would do. But as panicked as she was by the situation, she couldn't focus well enough to do so.

She kicked and scratched, writhing as she tried to escape. Eventually, she managed to utter a single word. "Why?" she rasped.

"Because you helped kill an innocent woman!" he spit.

Before she could really process it, she muttered, "Which one?"

It was barely more than a whisper, but it seemed to work. The man's fingers loosened. Then, he shook his head, echoing her own question: "Which one? Which one?"

He gave a harsh laugh, then shook his head. "Rotten to the core," he muttered.

Then, he reached back, and before Fiona knew what was happening, she saw a fist descending toward her face. It connected with skull-shattering force. The wall cracked behind her, but she was high enough of a level that the blow didn't kill her.

The second one did.

Limp, she fell to the floor, unthinking and unseeing.

17

INFILTRATION

Shame mingled with guilt to create a confusing miasma of emotions that Elijah struggled to reconcile with the bonfire of rage still blazing within his heart. He hadn't set out to kill Fiona. Instead, when he'd infiltrated her apartment, he'd only intended to intimidate her into giving him access to the palace. Once that was done, his plan was to tie her up and imprison her within her own home. By the time she worked her way free, his mission would have been finished.

But then she had revealed the depths of her own depravity. Of her own complicity in the cesspool that was Easton. Or Valoria, as the locals called it.

"Which one?" she'd blurted.

Which one.

Elijah had snapped, letting his rage overwhelm him, and by the time he'd regained control, she was dead. However, as shameful as the act of killing a prisoner was, he didn't regret it. She had earned her punishment. But even that fact—and it was an indisputable reality—did nothing to assuage his guilt.

That emotional confusion accompanied Elijah as he padded out of the apartment building and into the street beyond. There were few pedestrians about, and the ones that were around wore expensive clothing and copious jewelry. To Elijah, they looked like they were cosplaying aristocrats from a bygone era, and after some of what he'd seen in the less affluent areas, he couldn't help but feel a note of irritation.

The wealth inequality was disgusting.

Even more infuriating was the regressive attitude that pervaded much of Valoria's population. They considered Scholars to be second-class citizens, and those people were treated accordingly. Many were not even afforded an opportunity to work in their own fields. Instead, they were used as manual laborers, paid a pittance to do the jobs the other citizens deemed beneath them.

That was Roman's other sin. Certainly, Elijah had come to punish the man for killing Alyssa. Without that act, he would never have considered holding the man accountable. However, now that he was committed to taking his vengeance, everything Elijah saw seemed to support it.

Was there ever a situation where murder—or assassination, he supposed—was moral? Maybe. Maybe not. But Elijah was sure of one thing—the world would be a much better place without Roman taking up space.

So, despite the swirl of guilt and shame—and rage—circling his mind, Elijah's commitment never wavered. In fact, with every person he passed, it felt stronger than ever before.

In his draconid form and cloaked in Guise of the Unseen, he continued down the street, completely undetected by the pedestrians or the blue-and-white-clad guards. A few of the latter seemed to have some inkling of his presence, recognizable when Elijah's passage elicited an attentive scan of their surroundings. However, it was just as obvious that, despite their suspicions, they couldn't see him.

So, Elijah progressed through the city unmolested, eventually arriving at the palace grounds. They were expansive, with a perfectly coifed lawn, manicured trees, and burbling fountains. However, to Elijah, it was all hollow. The trees felt like they'd been enslaved and pruned into specific and unnatural shapes that had nothing to do with their true forms. They were treated like accessories rather than living things.

Which just added fuel to the fire of Elijah's fury.

He struggled to ignore it as he stalked through the grounds. The palace itself was a ridiculously over-the-top exaggeration of Gothic architecture that reminded Elijah of the Magister's Estate. Which was saying something, considering that the entire vibe of that tower had been meant to be creepy.

Tall, aggressive spires, flying buttresses, and pointed arches were in abundance, and Elijah saw dozens of guards patrolling the grounds. The first group he passed gave him a bit of a start, though.

"You don't feel that?" asked one of the men.

A woman who'd been walking beside him answered, "Yeah. My Guard Sense is going crazy, but I don't see anything."

Elijah quickly vacated the area, interpreting the mentioned Guard Sense to be an ability like One with Nature that would give them extrasensory perception. It wasn't perfect, but then again, neither was One with Nature. When someone was using some sort of obscuring skill—like the vampire back in the tower—he couldn't precisely sense them. Instead, he could sense something of an absence that took a certain mindset to notice. The same was probably true of the soldiers' Guard Sense.

And Elijah didn't want to push his luck by sticking too close to the guards.

Gradually, he padded through the grounds, staying to the shadows as often as possible. Only a few times was he forced to veer close to the patrolling guards, and each time, the sentries went on alert. Fortunately, he moved quickly enough that they never had an opportunity to figure out what was going on.

Eventually, Elijah found his way to an open door that led beneath the palace. At first, he thought he'd found the outside entrance to a storeroom, but the smells assaulting his nose quickly disabused him of that notion. It was the unmistakable odor of unwashed humanity. Pungent body odor, the acrid scent of human waste, and the smell of blood grew stronger with every step.

But there was more to it, too.

A scent Elijah could only call rot, almost like roadkill, flowed beneath the other smells, hinting that something was amiss. Perhaps they buried their dead beneath the palace, he guessed. But that made no sense. Nobody would design their home to include that sort of thing. A mausoleum or crypt, perhaps, but those usually featured embalmed bodies, so they weren't pervaded by the smell of rot.

Elijah didn't know what was going on.

So, he kept going, looking for a means of ingress into the palace. The other doors he'd found had been guarded by many powerful-feeling sentries. If it came down to a fight, he felt like he could take them, but not without kicking up a fuss. He wasn't ready to engage in all-out battle, though. If he did, he'd bring the entirety of Valoria's defenses down upon his head.

That wouldn't work for what he had planned, so stealth remained the best way forward.

The passage continued to slope downward at an easy decline, doubling back and forth as it progressed ever deeper. Then, it leveled out, ending in a large chamber lit by wall-mounted sconces filled with flickering torches. There were three guards on duty, and they stood sentry before a massive iron-bound door.

Elijah considered simply going back.

There had to be another entrance.

Yet, he suspected that he would need to kill if he wanted to enter the palace. And given the isolated nature of the chamber—as well as the light guard presence—he expected that this would be the best chance he would get. So, without further hesitation, Elijah slithered forward, circling around the edge of the room until he found himself facing the back of one of the guards.

He stood before the door, while the other two sat on a pair of stools nearby, where they were playing cards. Even as the pair bantered back and forth, Elijah embraced Predator Strike and pounced, decapitating the upright guard with a single bite of his powerful jaws.

Then, he used Flicker Step, disappearing and reappearing behind one of the other guards. He struck again. This time, there was more resistance—without Predator Strike to augment his attack, he only had his Strength on his side—but it wasn't enough. The man's skull shattered beneath his forceful bite.

Before he fell, Elijah launched himself forward, attempting to rip into the third man's face. The sentry scrambled backward, tipping over his stool and letting out a scream that was cut short by Elijah's attack. The guard used some sort of shield skill, fouling Elijah's initial strike. However, the second attack—a swipe from his claws—shattered the plane of ethera, allowing Elijah free access to the man's delicate throat. He ripped it out with a second swipe of his claws, sending an arc of blood to splatter across the wall.

Only three seconds had passed, and the guards were all dead.

Elijah stood over his final kill, looking down at the man with no emotion. It wasn't so different a mindset from what he usually adopted in towers. They weren't people. Just enemies. Obstacles that needed to be overcome.

It was a dangerous frame of mind.

And he rejected it.

They were people. They probably had families. Friends. Hopes and dreams.

But they had chosen the wrong side. They had supported Roman. There was an argument that they'd only done what they needed to do to survive, and while accurate, that didn't excuse the horrors in which they had engaged. Because the guards had done plenty of horrible things, too.

During his exploration of the city and the conversation with the man in the tavern, Elijah had learned a bit about the men and women who wore the blue-and-white uniforms. And what he'd learned was enough to assuage any guilt he might've felt. They'd engaged in wholesale slaughter during the failed rebellion, an act that most citizens considered excessive.

But they hadn't stopped there, either.

They never missed an opportunity to bully the population—especially those whom the city's leaders deemed expendable. Or worthless. As a result, some truly despicable acts—ranging from sexual assault to extortion and mur-der—had been swept under the table.

No—Elijah might've felt guilty about killing Fiona, but that was as much to do with the fact that she was a mostly helpless woman as anything else. The soldiers couldn't claim innocence. The moment they'd donned their uniforms, they'd established themselves as combatants.

And with them, anything would go.

Elijah shifted into his human form, then searched the guards. Their armor was nothing special, so he didn't bother taking it. His Ghoul-Hide Satchel held far more than its appearance would suggest, but its capacity wasn't infinite. So, he needed to be selective about what he looted, and given that the armor didn't seem valuable, Elijah left it on their bodies.

However, he did take a couple of decent daggers that felt more power-ful than normal. Both were cool to the touch, suggesting that they had been made from the cold iron Carmen had mentioned. Still, they seemed poorly constructed, which probably affected their grades. Whatever the case, he could never have enough knives, and they didn't take up much room.

He also found a ring of keys, which he expected would unlock the gate—and any others past it. So, once he'd ensured that they had nothing else of value, he piled the corpses near the door, unlocked it, then pushed it open, revealing another corridor.

However, this one was slightly different in that, only a dozen feet in, there were two doors—one on either side of the hall. Elijah stalked forward, then checked inside the first. It was empty, which gave him a perfect location to stash the bodies. It only took a couple of minutes to carry them to what looked like a jail cell, then deposit them inside before moving on.

He did so after having switched back to his draconid form under Guise of the Unseen. Like that, he continued on until, at last, the torch-lit tunnel terminated in a huge chamber. It was hundreds of yards across and just as deep.

But Elijah wasn't concerned with the dimensions.

Instead, he was only concerned with the cages, each one containing naked people, that lined the walls. Stacked three high, there must've been hundreds of them, and they all held at least a few prisoners. They were all dirty, emaciated, and on the edge of death.

That left Elijah with a choice.

He could free them, taking precious time to heal them. Given their condition, that might take a while.

Or he could ignore the issue and continue on with his task.

He glanced toward the center of the room, where he saw a raised circle decorated with chains and a series of square plinths. Each one was stained with blood, telling Elijah that he'd found another execution site.

The fires of his rage reignited.

Elijah stalked through the prison, ignoring the pitiful people in the cages. He still hadn't decided what to do with them, but whichever path he chose, he needed to scout things out. After all, who knew what horrors the dungeon held?

The answer to that question came soon after, when he found another room. It was much smaller, and inside there was a corpulent man who Elijah's instincts told him was someone important.

Not that it mattered.

With what he saw, Elijah's conscience wouldn't allow him to ignore the monster in human form. So, without further ado, he stepped through the open door and prepared for battle.

18

THE WARDEN'S DOMAIN

Don't struggle," growled Waldo, unbuckling his belt. "You want your parents freed, don't you?"

The girl shrank against the wall—as if he was some sort of despicable monster. After everything he'd done for her, she had the audacity to look at him like he was beneath her? The girl—he didn't even remember her name—was the daughter of one of the prisoners outside. If he remembered correctly, they had been executed a few days before—but that didn't matter. The girl didn't know, which was all that was important.

He stepped forward, intending to grab her by the hair and show her precisely who was in charge. She needed to be put back in her place. She needed to understand who she was dealing with.

So many people regarded the apocalypse as some terrible calamity that had befallen humanity. But Waldo McArthur wasn't one of them. Before, he'd been a powerless security guard. A loser who couldn't even be trusted to carry a gun on the job. Now, though? He was a man of consequence and power. He was important. The king himself had said so, and his word was law.

Everywhere but in Waldo's prison, at least. In there, he was the warden. It was his domain, which meant that, in that expansive facility, even the king couldn't rival his authority. Which made the little slip of a girl—barely more than sixteen years old—and her revulsion so much more irritating.

But that was fine.

He would show her.

He would show them all.

Or that was the plan right up until a monster out of nightmares erupted out of the shadows, burying its claws in his shoulder and aiming a horrifyingly swift bite at Waldo's head.

He shifted far more quickly than a man of his size should've been capable of moving, narrowly avoiding the creature's razor-sharp teeth as they snapped shut with the force of finality. Only then did Waldo remember that, in the prison, his authority was absolute.

After all, he was the Jailer. The Divine System had given him that class, and he'd used it as it was intended to be used. Utilizing Strength of the Jailer, he wrapped his meaty hands around the monster, then levered it free. It left more than a few wounds behind, but he had potions for that. Ignoring his blood-soaked shirt, he heaved the monster across the room.

It hit with bone-crunching force, collapsing to the ground a second later.

Waldo advanced, intending to finish the creature off. But then, it shifted, transforming before his very eyes. The thing's scales melted away, and its body morphed into the last thing he expected.

"You're human?" he muttered. Then, as a short, bearded man with blond hair pushed himself to his feet, Waldo grinned. "You're human."

"Good eye, asshole," the man growled, ethera swirling all around him.

That would not do at all.

Waldo used Warden's Shackles:

Spell: Warden's Shackles	Create an affliction that rapidly drains a prisoner's store of ethera. Only usable inside the Warden's jail. Rate of drain based on caster's level, Core cultivation, and Ethera attribute.

The man gasped, and Waldo's grin widened. "You don't like that one little bit, do you?" he taunted. "I'm told it's quite painful, having the magic sucked right out of you."

That's when someone whacked him in the back of the head. It wasn't enough to even stagger Waldo, but it did elicit quite a response. He whipped around, aiming a backhanded blow at the girl who dared to attack him. She held a candlestick like a weapon, as if she expected it to do any good. She didn't even have a class yet.

Which meant that, because of Waldo's enhanced Strength, the chances the girl would survive were precisely zero. Oh well—he would find another one soon enough. He had a lot of prisoners, after all. And many of them had family that were desperate enough to do anything to save them.

But then something stopped his hand.

He glanced in that direction to see that the man's fingers wrapped around his wrist. Waldo tried to yank his arm free, but the disheveled man's grip was like iron. Well, he had something to deal with that, too.

He used Fetters of Domination.

Spell: Fetters of Domination	Create an affliction that weakens a prisoner by 75%. Only usable inside the Warden's Jail. Affliction is less effective on those with higher effective attributes than the caster. Resistance based on relative Strength.

The moment the ability fell upon the interloper, Waldo yanked his arm free. Even then, it was difficult, and it threw him off-balance. He tripped and fell, bouncing a little because of his girth. It didn't hurt, but the embarrassment of it sent him into a rage. He wheeled around, growling, "You're going to pay for that! I'll—"

Something bit him, cutting off his tirade.

He looked down to see a tiny millipede latched on to his ankle. Its pincers had gone right through his trousers, drawing blood. More distressingly, it was not alone. A hundred of the little monsters had come from nowhere, and they seemed hell-bent on swarming him.

He screamed, slapping the little creatures and splattering their guts across the floor. He got most of them fairly easily—they couldn't stand before his enhanced attributes—but there were so many that he still picked up a few bites. That was fine, though. Once he was done with the intruder and the girl, he would take a potion—made by the best alchemist in the city, no less—and he would be fine.

It was his ace in the hole. For all his powers, especially within his domain, accidents still happened. And he'd never been afforded the use of a Healer. So, he'd made do by contracting the local Alchemist. It had saved him no less than three times already, and he expected it would prove to be just as useful in the future.

But first, he needed to deal with the man who'd barged into his office and assaulted him. Now that Fetters of Domination was active, it shouldn't be difficult. He only . . .

He tried to rise, but a wave of dizziness washed over him.

Elijah spared one facet of his Quartz Mind to look at his status, and he didn't like what he saw. His physical attributes had been reduced by more than half, which was a debilitating level of weakness that even exceeded what he'd experienced at the hands of Thor. Without that, though, Elijah would never have been prepared for whatever ability the disgusting warden had cast on him.

So, even though he was much weaker, he didn't let it completely incapacitate him. Instead, he focused on what he could do rather than what he couldn't. That had led him to casting Swarm.

It was only barely possible. Another of the man's abilities had drained Elijah's ethera so quickly that he could only use Soothe and a single cast of Touch of Nature before his Core had been drained. However, even as his body healed, his Quartz Mind and his newly upgraded Novice Soul went to work, restoring what had been lost.

It had drained almost as quickly as he could recover ethera, but he'd managed to build just enough to cast Swarm.

He couldn't keep that up, though. So, he knew he'd need to finish the warden without the advantage of most of his physical attributes or spells.

Fortunately, he wasn't entirely weakened. So, as the fat man struggled to rise, Elijah leveled his staff in his foe's direction. At the same time, he side-stepped to put himself between the warden and his victim. The girl was young. Very, very young. She wore a simple white dress and was clearly terrified. Still, she'd distracted the warden for a precious few seconds that had allowed Elijah to adjust.

Not that he was keeping score. The moment he'd recognized the situation, he'd resolved to save her. And that resolution hadn't changed.

The warden reached into his pocket, though his fingers didn't seem to work as well as they should, which made him fumble the task. The delay was only a couple of seconds, but that allowed Elijah to close on him just as he pulled a small bottle free. It looked like it would only hold about eight ounces, and it was filled with vibrant green liquid.

To Elijah, it felt both full of life and somehow fake, at the same time. Sort of like artificial sweetener, though far fouler. Regardless, he could read the situation —and the warden's desperation—well enough to recognize that he didn't want the man to drink it. Likely, it was a potion not dissimilar from the one Thor had used to prolong their fight. So, Elijah acted quickly, aiming the butt of his staff at the warden's wrist.

He connected, but as weakened as he was, it did little good, other than once again delaying the man's relief. So, Elijah hit it again. This time, the warden tried to avoid the blow, but if Elijah was weakened, then the fat man was on his last leg. Elijah intended to keep him there as he continued to aim one blow after another at the bottle.

And eventually, he succeeded in loosening the warden's grip. However, when the bottle crashed to the ground, cracking at the point of impact and spilling its contents all over the floor, the warden turned his attention on Elijah. Even in his afflicted state, the man was powerful enough to muster a spell.

Immediately, thick ethereal chains erupted from his bulbous stomach and darted at Elijah. He tried to dodge, but his low attributes failed him. He stumbled, which was all the opening the warden's chains needed to wrap around him. They continued to grow, one link after another as they encircled him a half dozen times.

The man coughed, clenching his fist. The chains tightened. Elijah struggled, but there was nothing he could do. He could feel his bones creaking under the pressure. He wriggled, straining every muscle in his body. It was useless, though.

A hundred thoughts raced through Elijah's mind, but none was more prevalent than regret. For everything he'd done wrong, for all the times he'd lost track of his priorities—because, in that moment, he knew he was going to die. The warden had robbed him of his attributes as well as his ability to heal. There was no chance he would survive.

And yet, there was some solace in knowing that the grotesque man would soon perish, as well. Already, the afflictions from Swarm and the Contagion from Elijah's flurry of attacks that had also been laced with Venom Strike had nearly killed the man. He still had some ways to go, but it was only a matter of time before he succumbed.

That was good to know.

Elijah's vision began to darken as the warden continued his unhinged and panicked demands. And all his thoughts coalesced into a single one. He was sorry that he hadn't avenged his sister's death, but at least he'd fallen trying to save someone else. She would have approved of that.

Abruptly, the grip of the chains weakened.

Then, they fell away, dissipating into ethereal motes. Elijah collapsed, more than a few of his bones broken. It certainly wasn't as bad as it had been after his fight with Thor—they were all clean breaks, as far as he could tell—but there was nothing good about having multiple fractures.

He gasped for breath, but soon, his recovery was interrupted by a thumping sound. Elijah looked up to see the girl repeatedly beating the warden over the head with the candlestick. He was already dead, a good portion of his skull having been caved in. And yet, the girl—weeping profusely—continued her assault.

That's when Elijah felt the weakening afflictions—the one that reduced his attributes as well as the one that constantly drained his ethera—fall away. Flexing every aperture in his Mind, Elijah dragged as much ethera through the channels of his Novice Soul and into his Core, keeping going until he had enough energy to fuel Soothe.

Then, he kept going until he could use Touch of Nature.

And Healing Rain, which affected the girl, as well. She'd had quite a few bruises and scratches—the man clearly hadn't been gentle with her—so the nourishing precipitation had some work to do.

Finally, Elijah tried to speak to the girl, but she clearly couldn't hear him. Instead, she'd collapsed atop the man, and even though she'd exhausted her strength, she continued to weakly rap the candlestick against his skull.

Once he was healed, Elijah pushed himself to his feet, then grabbed ahold of her arm. She whipped her head around, glaring at him with wild eyes, and he said, "It's okay. He's dead now. You're safe."

"N-nobody is safe in this city," she breathed, her voice hoarse.

"They will be," Elijah said with no small degree of resolve. "They will be."

19

THE CURSE OF EMPATHY

$\mathbf{A}$re you hurt?" Elijah asked, releasing the girl's wrist.

"I . . . I twisted my ankle," she mumbled between sobs. "But . . . But it's fine now. How is it fine now?"

Elijah pointed to the ceiling, where clouds had gathered, dumping Healing Rain on them both. "Spell," he said.

"But how?" she asked. "He drains ethera. That's why nobody can resist once they're in here."

Elijah had certainly felt the bite of that ability, but he'd overcome it—at least temporarily—via his cultivation. However, even that wasn't enough to resist for long, and he'd only managed a few casts before he'd lost access to his own spells. However, since the warden had been slain, the detrimental effect had faded away. The same was true of the one that limited his attributes.

"I'm special," he said.

"Are you here to save us?" the girl asked, her eyes wide with hope.

The answer to that question was a definitive no. He had come to the city to kill Roman and anyone else who'd had a hand in his sister's death. However, he couldn't ignore the plight of so many. He didn't know if the people in the cages he'd seen were there for legitimate reasons, but he suspected that that wasn't the case. Valoria was a cesspool of corruption, inequality, and oppression, which didn't give Elijah any confidence concerning the legitimacy of their actions.

And the presence of the disgusting warden had only sullied Elijah's opinion of the city even further. It took a truly horrible person to do what that man had intended, so Elijah didn't feel even remotely guilty about his death.

"That wasn't why I came here, but yes," he said. "I'll help you escape."

"And what about the guards? What about the rest of the army?" she asked.

"I intend to kill them all," Elijah stated. "And the leader, as well as anyone who else tries to stop me. You're welcome to help. Or you can sit it out. It makes no difference in what I'm going to do, though."

"Who are you?"

"Just a person who has a bone to pick with Roman Cain," Elijah answered. Then, he sighed, before kneeling beside the warden's body. He began to rummage through the man's pockets. "What's your name?"

"Leslie," the girl answered. "Leslie Manning. M-my parents are out there. Are you going to free them?"

At first, Elijah didn't answer. Instead, he continued looking through the warden's pockets. He found a folio, but when he tried to access it, he got no response. Other than that, the warden only had some mundane clothing, a flask full of some truly foul-smelling alcohol, and a Rolex watch that no longer kept time. Elijah took it all, moving to another pocket.

"Jackpot," he said when he found what he was looking for. He hefted the key ring, saying, "I'm pretty sure this will open the cages." He tossed it to Leslie, who caught it after a brief fumble. "Go start unlocking them. If people are hurt, send them in here. I'll heal them."

After that, Elijah settled in to wait, summoning Healing Rain the second one of the naked prisoners stumbled in. There were no clothes around, and it seemed that the man was accustomed to his own nudity. He didn't seem self-conscious, which was probably due as much to his poor condition as his mental state. Still, as soon as the regenerative precipitation hit him, the man let out a sigh of relief and gave Elijah a nod.

Over the next hour, more people came into the room. When one was healed, another would take their place until, at last, Elijah had healed nearly a thousand people. And to his surprise, he gained another level, bringing him to seventy-eight. That, more than anything, told him just how close to death the prisoners had been.

Finally, a man and a woman approached, introducing themselves. Elijah barely registered their names, but he did notice that they had scrounged up some rags to cover their nudity. Many others had, as well.

"Thank you," the woman said. "What are you going to do?"

"Our daughter said you intend to kill the guards. We want to help," the man said before Elijah could answer.

"No."

"What?"

"I don't need your help," Elijah stated. He'd thought about it long and hard, eventually coming to the conclusion that bringing a thousand half-starved prisoners with him would do more harm than good. "But I do intend to kill the guards. And anyone else in my way. Once I'm finished, you can take their gear. In fact, there are three bodies down the hall over that way." Elijah pointed in the direction he'd arrived. "Take their armor and weapons."

"What else should we do? If we go back out there, we'll be captured and imprisoned. The warden is dead, but they have other means of keeping us powerless."

Elijah answered, "I don't really care what you do. Like I said, I'm here on my own mission. I've already deviated by freeing you. I've wasted more than an hour healing you. I don't regret those actions, but if I do anything else, it will interrupt my task. At best, it'll make it more difficult. At worst, it'll mean they're ready for me."

With that, he stood. He'd completely healed from the injuries he'd incurred, so he was back to full strength. However, when he made to leave, he felt a wave of guilt. He couldn't leave them like this. No matter what he said, his empathy wouldn't allow him to ignore their plight.

So, before he left, Elijah reached into his bag and retrieved a handful of berries. Each one was around the size of a strawberry, but more importantly, he knew that even a quarter of a Grove berry would do wonders for the prisoners' state. So, he retrieved one of his knives, then started cutting the berries into pieces. It would take almost his entire supply, but that was a small price to pay to help the innocent people.

"Here," Elijah said, handing the woman one of the quarter slices. "Eat this. It'll help."

She took it into her dirty fingers, then hesitantly popped it into her mouth. A moment later, she gasped, "What is that?"

"Grove berry," Elijah answered. "I have enough for everyone to get a slice like that. So, get people organized while I cut them up."

The woman was quick to respond, and Elijah got to work. With his high Dexterity, he accomplished his task quickly, and before he knew it, he was handing out a slice of Grove berry to each of the prisoners. Within moments of ingesting the magical fruit, each of the prisoners started to look healthier. Color bloomed in their cheeks, and they noticeably filled out. They were all still clearly malnourished, but it helped. More importantly, the Grove berries gave a sorely needed burst of energy.

Seeing the prisoners smiling was almost enough to distract Elijah from his mission. However, all he had to do was focus on the facet of his Quartz Mind where he'd quarantined his seething anger to reaffirm his attention. Still, he made certain that everyone was as well recovered as they could be before he told the two leaders that he was moving on.

"We don't know how to thank you," said the man.

"We don't even know your name," the woman added.

"I know," Elijah said. Then, he turned and left, taking the only other exit he'd found. It sloped upward, so he expected that it would lead to the palace. Once he was out of sight, he shifted into his draconid form and let Guise of the Unseen envelop him. As soon as it did, he let out a subtle sigh of relief.

He liked helping people. Probably a little too much, if he was honest. And it had taken every ounce of his willpower to abandon the prisoners. He'd aided them enough that there was some hope for survival, but it was far from guaranteed. That was especially true given the situation in the city.

Without armor or weapons, there was every chance that they would only be recaptured or killed.

Elijah pushed those thoughts from his mind as he continued upward, eventually reaching an intersection manned by another trio of guards. Using a similar tactic to the one he'd used against the previous guards, he snuck up behind one, used Predator Strike to ensure an easy kill, then Flicker Step to take out another before they had a chance to react. The final kill came easily enough, largely because the remaining guard never got past fumbling with his sword. It was all the delay Elijah needed to gain the advantage and kill him with a swipe of his claws across the man's throat.

Once they were dead, he dragged the bodies back the way he'd come, depositing them inside the prison. The former captives quickly fell upon the guards looting their gear. But Elijah didn't see anything else because he moved on without a word.

Four more times, he repeated the actions. At one intersection, he did find something interesting, though. That same odd smell of death wafted out of one passage. Elijah wanted to investigate, but he pulled himself up short. That would almost assuredly prove to be one more distraction that he couldn't afford. It wouldn't be long before the missing guards would be discovered, so he needed to get a move on, lest he run the chance of being found.

So, as much as his instincts screamed at him to investigate, he refused to acknowledge them.

With that in mind, he continued on, climbing ever higher until, at last, he reached the palace proper. The tunnel ended in a heavy door, beyond which was a much more opulent hall. So, Elijah slaughtered the two soldiers on guard, dragged them back to the prison, then returned to the palace entrance.

Shifting back to his human form, he opened the door and slipped through it before once again adopting his stealthy draconid shape. After pulling the door closed, he continued on. Vaguely, Elijah acknowledged the rich decor. The dungeons had featured bare, utilitarian walls and flickering torches, but the palace corridors were the exact opposite. Everywhere he looked, there was marble, gold, and silver. Masterful paintings decorated the walls, and statues were displayed in alcoves.

It was as if someone had seen examples of aristocratic wealth on television and endeavored to copy what they had seen on-screen. As a result, everything looked incredibly impressive, so long as it was beheld at a distance. Anyone familiar with the aped styles on display would know the difference the moment they noticed the sloppy details.

Elijah was no expert. Nor was he some great appreciator of art. However, he knew enough and cared enough to recognize the mockery such blatantly poor facsimiles represented.

If his opinion of Roman could get any worse, it would have at that point.

Keeping going, Elijah found a multitude of guards barring his way. However, instead of using his previous strategy, which would leave plenty of evidence behind, he chose a more subtle tactic.

Soon enough, he'd found his way to a side room that was close enough that he could sense the collection of men and women guarding what Elijah thought was the entrance to Roman's personal quarters. He resumed his human form, then cast Swarm, targeting it via One with Nature.

The spell manifested in the form of a thousand fleas. They descended upon the guards, completely undetected before they started biting. Even then, the guards' reactions were subdued, and the fleas disappeared before they grew truly distressed.

Elijah waited a few minutes, then used Swarm again.

And again after that.

Without the enhancement provided by his old Staff of Natural Harmony, the afflictions they delivered weren't nearly as overwhelming as they once had been. That situation was further exacerbated by the fact that the guards had a decent number of levels under their belt.

However, they weren't invulnerable. And three casts of Swarm meant that the sheer weight of afflictions eventually showed their worth.

The first guard abruptly fell to her knees. The next followed soon after. By the time the first had fallen to all fours, another three had collapsed. The leader—who was, presumably, the highest level—maintained his feet the longest. While his comrades collapsed all around him, he panicked, demanding to know what was wrong. The others were in no condition to answer, and now that the afflictions had reached a crescendo, there was no stopping what was coming.

By the time he finally collapsed, the first two had fallen unconscious. They died only thirty seconds later. The rest followed soon enough until, at last, they were all dead.

After that, Elijah took a few minutes to stash the bodies in the side room. He gathered anything he thought was useful, including a few pouches full of etherium. Most of the coins were copper, but there were a few silver ones in there, as well. And one gold etherium, which was quite a haul, all things considered. He also added a few knives and a sword to his collection, but the armor didn't seem very high-quality, so he left that.

Once all of that was finished, he shifted back into his draconid form, used Guise of the Unseen, and entered what he suspected was Roman's quarters. At last, he'd reached his goal. Soon enough, he would kill the man who'd murdered his sister.

That thought, while somewhat disturbing, comforted Elijah in a way nothing else had since he'd discovered Alyssa's fate.

20

AMBUSH

The moment Elijah stepped into the room, his instincts went wild. Without thought, he threw himself to the side. Still, he felt something pierce his scales, embedding in his back hip. He refused to let a single sound emerge from his mouth. Instead, he skidded to a stop, slipping a little on the now-bloody tile floor before turning to face his attacker.

He'd been exploring the wing for what felt like hours, and the whole time, he'd found no inhabitants. So, he was more than a little surprised to see four men on the other side of the room. Each one was wearing black fatigues, reminding Elijah of Isaiah's men back in Seattle. However, Elijah could tell from their stances alone that these new foes were far more capable than those men and women.

More, he suspected that they were all former military.

Living in Hawaii, Elijah had encountered plenty of navy personnel, so he'd learned to identify them just by their bearing. It was similar to how some people could recognize police, even when they were off duty. Regardless, Elijah felt almost certain that he was facing a quartet of hardened soldiers.

One held a crossbow, telling him what he had embedded in his hip. Another had a sword and shield. The third carried a staff. And the fourth was armed with a mace. Elijah didn't need to see them use any abilities to recognize their identities. The shield bearer was a protector, the staff-wielder was a Sorcerer, and the man with the mace was probably the Healer. The soldier with the crossbow was a Ranger.

As Elijah had learned from the elves as well as his dealings in Seattle and Argos, it was the preferred party composition for those who made a living running towers.

"Reloading," the man with the crossbow said, dragging another bolt out of the quiver at his waist.

"Advancing," said the defender, stepping forward, his shield held in front of him. Then, he let out a shout that cut right through every facet of Elijah's Mind. Suddenly, all he could think about was attacking the man with the shield. It wasn't until a second later, when he instinctively shunted that anger to its own facet, where he quarantined it, that he realized what had happened.

The man had tried to force him to attack the least vulnerable among them, which was the absolute worst strategy for anyone who wanted to win. Still, it represented an opportunity. So, he stepped toward the man, a low growl emitting from his throat.

He could sense the others preparing attacks.

Still, Elijah didn't alter course.

Ethera swirled around the Sorcerer, while the Ranger finished reloading. Meanwhile, the protector prepared to meet Elijah. Just as everything reached a crescendo, he used Flicker Step, disappearing at the same moment a ball of fire and another crossbow bolt tore across the room.

But Elijah was gone, and less than an instant later, he appeared behind the Healer. Using Venom Strike, he launched himself at the man. He didn't go for the head, though. Instead, he raked his claws across the man's leg, amputating it in a single swipe. Then, he bounded away, and it was just in time, too, because the defender hadn't been idle.

Even as the Healer collapsed, the shield bearer charged. But he was too slow because Elijah had already changed direction, darting at the Sorcerer. The man swung his staff, but Elijah ducked low, avoiding the attack before throwing himself at the man's chest. He hit with enough force to knock the Sorcerer from his feet.

Elijah ripped through an ethereal shield—all Sorcerers seemed to have that spell—and into his chest, eviscerating his flesh with a half dozen gouging attacks, each one delivering Contagion and Venom Strike. The defender followed Elijah, though his movements were too clumsy. He let out another shout, but it was just as useless as before.

Leaping high into the air, Elijah kicked off the wall to change direction, then descended upon the Ranger. To his credit, the man reacted quickly, throwing out his hand and producing an ethereal net. However, Elijah had the benefit of high Dexterity as well as the Haste from the Sash of the Whirlwind, so it wasn't difficult to dodge the skill. He hit the ground, then pounced on the Ranger, treating him much the same as he had the Sorcerer.

Yet, the new target was much stronger than the spellcaster, and he only staggered a bit rather than being knocked to his back. Elijah didn't care; he only needed to scratch the man a few times, and when he did, he kicked away, returning to the door.

The defender didn't follow.

That's when Elijah heard the screams.

"Heal me!" growled the Ranger through gritted teeth. His face was pale, and it was already wet with sweat.

The Healer was worse, but then again, he'd had a leg amputated, and he was trying to reattach it to the stump. Ethera swirled around him as he desperately tried to heal the damage well enough that the loss wasn't permanent.

Because of that, he was too distracted to heal the Ranger or the Sorcerer, both of whom were in dire straits.

The defender stomped on the ground, and to Elijah's surprise, a dome of pure ethera bloomed into being. He swiped at it, but he was shocked to find that it remained entirely solid.

The defender shouted, "See to the others, Mark!"

"Trying to reattach my goddamn leg, Bill!"

"And they're dying, and my Barrier won't last forever!"

"Fine!"

Mark waved his mace, and immediately, the Sorcerer started to look a bit better. He repeated the motion, and the Ranger began to recover, too. However, Elijah knew from experience that a simple healing spell wouldn't do much for those afflictions. As far as he'd seen, it was incredibly difficult to remove them. Sure, he'd read a few guides that suggested that such afflictions were removable via specific spells, but otherwise, they would have to run their course.

The Sorcerer vomited, spewing blood on the floor.

"What's going on with them?!" demanded the defender, still facing Elijah. "I thought you could heal anything!"

"I don't fucking know! What the hell is that thing?"

Elijah sighed, then shifted into his human form. That drew a few gasps, but before any of them could say anything, he stated, "I'm not a thing. I'm human, same as you."

"What? Is that some kind of shape-shifter?" spit the defender.

"Something like that," Elijah said, pacing back and forth. He was ready to switch to his lamellar-ape form the moment the shield went down. "Why are you dressed differently than all the other guards I've killed?"

"We're not guards," the defender said. He turned his head, checking the others out of the corner of his eye. The Healer still hadn't been successful in reattaching his leg, and though he'd continued to heal the others, the afflictions continued unabated. "Why are you here?"

"This and that."

"You killed the other guards?" the defender asked.

Elijah nodded.

"Why?"

"They deserved it. So do you," Elijah said. "The second this shield drops, I'm going to rip you all to pieces. Your Healer's running low on ethera, right? He won't have enough to keep you alive through what I'm about to do."

"Why? We've done nothing to you!"

"Not directly. But the man in charge of this city took someone very dear to me," Elijah explained. "He's going to die. And so is everyone who—"

"Are you talking about that putz who keeps calling himself a king?"

"I am."

"Kill him, then! We don't care! We're just mercenaries, man. He hired us to help him run through some towers. That's all we've done. We haven't killed any people. We don't participate in his little schemes. We haven't fought in his wars. We've only killed monsters, man—I swear!"

To Elijah, that had the ring of truth, but he knew that desperation could drive people to be very convincing in their lies. More, from everything he knew about Roman, it tracked. The stories he'd heard had painted the man as a hands-off sort of leader. A lead-from-the-back type. The only reason it had worked was because of the results. From the very beginning, Easton had been a safe haven for the survivors. People would ignore a lot of character flaws if it meant they were safe from the literal monsters roaming the wilderness.

"You attacked me."

"We thought you were a Voxx!"

That took Elijah aback. "How could you think that?"

"You're big, scary, and scaly. That sounds like Voxx to me, man."

Elijah was about to respond, but he thought better of it. Sure, the Voxx were easily recognizable to him, but much of that was due to the fact that he could sense the wrongness within them. It wasn't so different from when he encountered monsters, though it was far stronger. However, without that to clue him in, he had to admit that, at a glance, his bestial forms could be mistaken for Voxx.

And that irritated him.

Still, Elijah took control of himself, asking, "What do you propose?"

"Let us go. We'll be out of this city before sunrise. Never looking back. Just gone. You can do what you need to do," Bill, the defender stated.

"And I'm just supposed to trust you?" Elijah asked.

The man cocked his head to the side and raised his hand with two fingers extended. "Scout's honor?"

"Wrong salute, Bill," coughed the Ranger.

"It's the thought that counts," Bill insisted. Then, he looked at Elijah, venturing, "Right?"

It was probably smarter to just kill them. However, Elijah was brought up short by two things. First, they'd actually put up a decent fight, and now that they'd had a chance to regroup, there was a good chance that they'd be even more difficult to dispatch. Second, he actually believed the defender's story. They weren't wearing the same gear as all the rest of the guards, which suggested they were outsiders like Bill had claimed.

And in the back of Elijah's mind, there was a thought he didn't really want to acknowledge. He'd already killed a lot of people. Adding to that body count was inevitable. In addition to killing Roman—which was nonnegotiable—he would almost assuredly be forced to fight on his way out. He accepted that, and he'd already painted the blue-and-white-clad guards with the same brush he'd used with Roman and his closest allies.

But he didn't want to be the sort of person who'd slaughter people just for being in the wrong place at the wrong time. There had to be a line.

It was only when he examined those thoughts that he realized that he'd already made his choice. Perhaps it would come back to bite him, but that was a risk he intended to accept. Besides, they'd already tried to ambush him and failed miserably. If they tried again, he'd do what was necessary.

"Fine."

"Fine?"

"I won't kill you," Elijah said. "Not now. But if you get in my way . . ."

The man held up his hand, saying, "I get it. Believe me, we just want out of here. Been wanting that for a while, actually. That guy is insane."

"How so?"

"He's a believer," said Bill. "A true believer. He thinks he's going to save the world or some shit."

"Fucking lunatic," added the Ranger. "Good goddamn riddance."

The others voiced their agreement.

Elijah asked, "Where is he?"

Bill shrugged. "Not sure. But here's how you get to his rooms," the defender answered. Then, he described the path Elijah would need to take. It was a good thing, too, because it would have taken a while for Elijah to figure it out. The route featured more than a few switchbacks and a couple of half-hidden passages. "He's paranoid as shit, man. Thinks everyone's out to get him. They probably are, but still . . ."

Elijah gave the man a nod of thanks, then said, "Don't get in my way."

Without another word, he shifted back into his draconid form and left the room. The moment he was out of sight, he used Guise of the Unseen. He could still sense the men behind him, so he watched them for long enough to establish that they were going to make good on their promise. As soon as the shield dropped, they started to pack. Or Bill did. The others were too busy trying to counteract Elijah's ongoing afflictions.

With the Wolf Totem, they lasted quite a long time, after all.

Satisfied that they would do as they'd said, Elijah followed the man's directions through the wing until, at last, he arrived in a well-appointed suite. It reminded him a little of the Reaver's quarters in the second tower he'd conquered, though there were a few modern conveniences that set it apart. In addition, it featured a wide balcony that overlooked the city.

That's where Elijah waited for Roman.

It took almost an hour before the man showed up. Elijah watched his sister's murderer, idly cataloging his features. He was a tall man, broad shouldered and with salt-and-pepper hair. He wore the armor Carmen had made, and at his hip was the sword she'd been forced to create.

False Dragon's Fang it was called.

That both annoyed and amused him. The former because he hated the notion of associating dragons with someone as despicable as Roman. However, his amusement came because the system had intended the name mockingly. Or that was how Elijah saw it, at least.

But Elijah wasn't concerned with the man's equipment, especially once he removed it, hanging the armor on a dressing mannequin in the closet and propping the still-sheathed sword by the bed.

Elijah watched as his sister's murderer entered the bathroom, emerging only twenty minutes later, wearing nothing but a towel around his waist. Then, Roman enjoyed a glass of some sort of liquor before, at last, climbing into bed. Elijah waited until, via One with Nature, he sensed that the man's breathing had evened out, indicating that he was asleep.

His first instinct was to kill Roman slowly. To dismember him piece by piece, all the while ignoring the inevitable pleas for mercy. Yet, Elijah pushed that desire aside in favor of expedience. He just wanted Roman dead. He wanted it to be over. Perhaps then he could move on, secure in the knowledge that he'd avenged Alyssa's murder.

Did Roman deserve a clean death?

No.

Emphatically.

However, Elijah knew that, if he went down that road, there was a good chance that he'd regret staining his soul in such a way. Better to simply kill the man and be done.

So, he padded into the room, used Venom Strike as well as Predator Strike, then pounced.

21

COMPLICATIONS

As Elijah descended upon the sleeping man, a thousand emotions flashed through his mind. Guilt. Shame. Regret. But overwhelming them all was the rage that had been simmering within him for weeks since discovering his sister's fate.

He hit the unconscious figure with predictable fury, his jaws clamping down on the man's head. He squeezed, and it burst like a watermelon. However, Elijah's first clue that things were not as they seemed came from the taste. For better or worse, he'd become quite acclimated to the way blood played across his tongue. Yet, when Roman's skull burst, he wasn't rewarded with the iron-rich taste he expected. Instead, it was a flavorless gel that threw Elijah's mind into turmoil.

A second later, he felt a projectile moving toward him with the speed of a bullet. He leaped, kicking off the nearby wall and landing on the other side of the bed. The projectile had clipped him, but it had done no real damage.

Not at first, at least.

That didn't last, though. The moment he landed, he felt a searing pain shooting through his leg, rendering his back claw useless. Elijah responded by crouching behind the bed, shifting into his human form, and casting Soothe before using Touch of Nature. The shooting pain slowed, but it didn't stop. So, Elijah used Healing Rain as well before chaining Touch of Nature as many times as he could over the course of the next ten seconds.

Meanwhile, via another facet of his Mind, Elijah felt his attacker cautiously approaching from the other side of the room. By the time he'd managed to corral the venom coursing through his body, the man had winked out of sight. Yet, Elijah could still feel tiny organisms clinging to his skin. More, he could detect his footfalls, as well. If he hadn't had so much experience with illusions—his fight against Thor and the battle against the vampire in the Magister's Estate—he never would have noticed. But now? He'd trained himself to recognize it.

So, when the man finally rounded the corner of the enormous four-poster bed, Elijah met him with a sweeping staff strike that knocked him from his feet.

Elijah then followed it up with an overhand attack that should have crushed his attacker's skull. Yet, when the staff descended, it found no target to receive the blow. Instead, it crashed into the floor, the metal cap clapping against the tiles. Then, Elijah felt someone behind him, and he dived forward.

Another attack nicked him, and like the other, it delivered another dose of venom. Fortunately, Soothe and Healing Rain persisted, so it was healed before it had the chance to get going.

Elijah rolled to his feet, facing his opponent.

Predictably, it was Roman. The man looked identical to the one from the bed, save that he was fully dressed and wearing all his equipment. In addition to the sword in his hand, Roman carried a dagger at his belt. There was a bow nearby, as well, explaining the origin of that first projectile.

"Good," Elijah said, leveling his staff at the man. "When I hit your clone, I thought you might run. I'm glad you stayed to fight."

"Who are you?" growled the self-styled king.

"My name is Elijah Hart."

"Is that supposed to mean something to me?" Roman asked. Then, recognition dawned in the expression on his face. "You're number one."

"I am."

"I . . . I'll give you anything," he said, taking a step back. "What do you want? Money? I have thousands of etherium. I have equipment, too. The best in the empire. Girls, as well. As many as you want. Boys, if that's your preference. I can give you anything you want."

"I want my sister back."

For the first time since becoming a system-sanctioned lord, Roman regretted his chosen path of conquest. Not only had it robbed him of the Seal of Authority, which would have doubtless come in handy against the powerful enemy before him, but his choice had also shifted his power away from the city and into his armies. Now, even in his own city, he was only a little more powerful than a normal person of his level.

Hart.

The name was etched into Roman's mind. It represented the turning point where he'd gone from a man who was simply reacting to the world's transformation to one that stood a chance of saving what was left of humanity.

"Alyssa," he whispered.

But the odd man who'd invaded his bedroom did not respond. Instead, he leveled his staff at Roman, and a second later, a bolt of lightning descended from the ceiling, striking Roman in the chest. It sent him flying across the room, but fortunately, he had Assassin's Calm to keep him from losing consciousness.

Ability: Assassin's Calm	A passive enhancement that allows the caster to maintain cognitive ability even when enduring attacks that would otherwise render them unconscious. Number of charges based on Ethera attribute. Current charges: Three (3).

When he'd first received the ability, he'd considered it a waste. However, it had since proved to be the difference between life and death, and on more than one occasion. Unfortunately, while Assassin's Calm kept him conscious, it did nothing to combat the involuntary contractions of his muscles that came with the intense electrical current he'd just endured.

So, Roman hit the wall a second later, cracking the plaster and knocking one of the paintings loose. He only remained there for a split second before he saw a beast out of nightmare rushing in his direction. It was like someone had crossed a sasquatch with a dinosaur, then packed on a ton of muscle to boot. The monster covered the ground in an instant, and when it came into range, it swung its long arms like siege weapons tipped with massive claws.

But by that point, Roman had regained control of his body, and he used Predation again.

Ability: Predation	Disappear from sight, teleporting behind your foe. Charge based on Dexterity. Current charges: Two (2). Cooldown based on Dexterity. Current cooldown: Seven (7) minutes.

He only had two charges, and he'd already wasted one of them after the assassin had destroyed his Decoy. Still, as he teleported behind the monster, he hoped it would be enough. The moment he reappeared, Roman dragged the Stiletto of Sundering from its sheath at his belt and used Weaken:

Spell: Weaken	Inflict your opponent with crippling weakness, cutting their attributes by 60%. Duration based on Dexterity. Current duration: 3.3 seconds.

The creature tried to respond to the attack, but Roman had surprised it. So, the blade flashed forward. Yet, to his surprise, it didn't slice through the monster's thick scales. Instead, the sound of metal on metal echoed through the room, and he was rewarded with only a single scratch.

But the ability—both his own as well as the one attached to the Stiletto of Sundering—worked. Roman saw the monster stumble as its attributes were ripped away. He permitted himself a grin as he followed it up with his finisher:

Ability: Murder	Instantly slay anyone weaker than you. Viability based on total power. Cooldown based on cultivation level. Current cooldown: Seven (7) weeks.

It was fortunate that he hadn't had to use it for some time. Otherwise, it wouldn't have been available. If it hadn't been, he suspected that he'd have no chance of defeating the hulking brute of a monster.

Roman's sword flashed forward in a one-handed attack, biting deep into the off-balance monster's shoulder. However, instead of the expected influx of kill energy, he received nothing but a backhanded attack that sent him sprawling across the room.

Because of Assassin's Calm, he didn't lose consciousness when his head hit one of the posts, snapping it in two from the sheer force of his flight. He looked up to see the creature turning to face him. The Stiletto of Sundering—the very weapon that had allowed him to kill Alyssa—was sticking out of his side.

The monster yanked it free with a spurt of blood. Then, it growled, "Nice try."

After that, the ethera in the room swirled, and the monster's wound completely closed.

Elijah felt Guardian's Renewal fight a war against the raging energy inside him. It was aided by Healing Rain as well as Soothe, but still, it felt like it was on the verge of failure. He had no idea what kind of ability Roman had used on him, but he suspected that it was contingent on the weakness he'd felt at the end of the dagger attack. The moment it had scratched him, his attributes had dropped precipitously, leveling off at only forty percent of their normal values.

He knew that if he hadn't immediately activated Guardian's Renewal, he would have been slain by the follow-up. But because of the powerful healing spell—as well as his other two spells—he'd barely managed to last long enough for his attributes to return to normal. Then, Guardian's Renewal had finished its job, returning him to perfect health.

He stepped forward, and Roman tried to scramble away. Elijah didn't rush. He didn't need to. He felt certain that he'd just taken the man's best shot and survived. Likely, Roman didn't have anything left.

Of course, the man wasn't going to simply surrender. Instead, he finally pushed himself to his feet and aimed his sword at Elijah. As he did, he exasperatedly spit, "What are you?"

"An angry brother," Elijah growled, stepping toward Roman. He didn't intend to finish the fight just yet, so he didn't throw himself at his foe. Instead, he approached slowly. Almost gently.

And Roman responded by trying to skewer him with his sword.

The weapon moved blisteringly fast, suggesting that it was under the influence of some other ability. And its edge glistened with red light, confirming the presence of another. However, Elijah didn't bother trying to dodge. Instead, he only embraced Iron Scales, which resulted in the satisfying clink of metal against metal. The attack also elicited a response from Shield of Brambles, piercing Roman's chest with a sharp thorn.

The man danced back, then attempted to flee.

Elijah wasn't going to allow that, though. So, he rushed sideways, planting himself in front of the door. Roman surprised him by diving onto the bed, where he'd dropped his bow, and in less than a second, he'd conjured an arrow from nothing and fired it at Elijah. It hit him in the shoulder, digging through Elijah's scales despite his active ability.

But it was no real use.

It didn't bear any afflictions. Nor did it go deeper than the muscle. It was a flesh wound, nothing more. Elijah continued toward his sister's murderer, vengeance gripping his heart and mind. He saw the fear dancing on Roman's face. The terror. The knowledge that he couldn't escape what was coming.

Elijah drank it in, savoring the man's psychological turmoil.

Roman tried to dart around Elijah, but his attributes were too low, and he was caught in mid-stride as Elijah clamped his giant claw around the man's neck. Then, he raised him high into the air. Roman's legs kicked like he was in the middle of a child's tantrum, which Elijah thought was appropriate.

From everything he had seen, Roman was a small, selfish man. A child who could only see things from his own distorted perspective. A nuisance that needed to be destroyed.

Roman tried to speak, but it only came out in an unintelligible rasp as Elijah calmly strode toward the balcony. Once they were there, he let his transformation drop away. For what he was going to do, he wanted to be in his human form. He'd taken the man's measure, and he knew that his natural shape was more than enough to deal with Roman.

In a way, it was slightly disappointing.

He'd come into the palace expecting a grand fight. A true battle to shake the heavens. But, aside from that one sequence, all Elijah had gotten was the weak attacks of an overconfident man who thought his position and authority could save him.

But it couldn't.

Not from Elijah. Not from a brother's fury.

22

CLOSING A DOOR

The night air was pleasant, playing against Elijah's skin with the cool breath of impending autumn. Yet, he didn't really allow himself to feel it. Instead, he focused on the city laid out before him. Even in the depths of night, there were plenty of people out and about. The city itself was lit by a thousand torches and ethereal lamps. But there were a few other fires, too. Great blazes that swept across the city, devouring everything Roman had built.

"You know it's all doomed, don't you?" Elijah whispered. "This whole city is going to burn, and everyone who ever pledged loyalty to you will fall."

"I . . . am . . . humanity's only . . . hope . . ."

It took Elijah a moment to comprehend what the man had said, but when he finally wrapped his mind around it, he barked a harsh laugh. "You?" he spit with no small degree of incredulity. "You're barely in the top ten, and it doesn't feel like you spent any time working on your cultivation. You're too weak to be anyone's hope."

Roman tried to argue, but Elijah had no interest in hearing it. So, he squeezed Roman's throat with a little more force, then, at last, slammed him against the ground. The force shook the balcony, and Elijah knelt atop the self-styled king. He leaned close, whispering, "You are a small, pathetic, little man who murdered his only friend for nothing. If there is a hell, that's where you're going. No one will ever remember you, and if they do, it will only be to curse your name. I promise you that much."

Then, Elijah picked the man up by his neck before once again slamming him against the floor. He did it again after that. And another four times. By that point, the back of Roman's head was a mass of blood and shattered skull, but that didn't stop Elijah from keeping going. Again and again, he bashed Roman's head against the ground, not even stopping when he felt the experience from the man's death entering his body.

Over and over, he continued to batter the skull of his sister's murderer against the ground until, at last, he was holding nothing but a handful of skin. He hadn't just decapitated the man. He'd removed his head by way of blunt-force trauma.

For a long moment, Elijah just stared ahead, and for once, his mind was blank.

He was empty.

Exhausted.

He'd achieved his goal, but rather than feeling a sense of accomplishment, he just felt nothing. Then, suddenly, there came an onslaught of grief and anger. Frustration. Guilt. A thousand other, subtler emotions contributed to his state of mind, and before he could get ahold of himself, he had begun to weep.

He knew he was behind enemy lines and that he should leave the area. However, in his current mindset, he couldn't force himself to move. He'd expected to feel better about it all once he killed Roman. But he didn't. The pain he'd felt upon hearing the news of Alyssa's death was even stronger now.

And Elijah couldn't take it.

He wanted to lash out, to go on a rampage that wouldn't be sated until he'd killed everyone and everything. Or retreat to a cave in the middle of nowhere. Or return to the Grove and take comfort in his family's presence. A hundred other plans flitted through his mind, but he knew that none would help.

Only time would do that.

After a few minutes, he mechanically pushed himself to his feet and took notice of his latest notification. He'd gained another level. Not surprising, given that Roman had been in the top ten. That, plus all the others he'd killed since coming into Valoria, had been quite a boon to his levels, pushing him to seventy-nine.

One more, and he'd get a new spell.

But at the moment, he didn't really care about that. Indeed, he found it difficult to care about anything, with all the emotions flowing through him. Still, he went about the process of collecting loot with all the efficiency he could muster. He gave Roman's dignity no consideration, stripping him down to his underwear and shoving anything that seemed worthwhile into his Ghoul-Hide Satchel.

That included his armor as well as his sword and dagger. But there were also a couple of rings and a curious pendant that seemed to emit a decent amount of ethera. When Elijah touched it, he received a notification:

> **You have slain a sanctioned city lord (Valoria). Bond the Seal of Authority to embark on a quest to replace him.**

Elijah stared down at the item in his hand. But it didn't take even a moment for him to reject the offer. The last thing he wanted was to rule over a city, and even if the position did appeal to him, he certainly wouldn't have chosen Valoria. So, without giving it any more thought, he shoved it into his satchel next to all the rest of his loot.

Beyond that, the former lord had nothing of consequence, so Elijah moved to the rest of the room, looking for something very specific. It wasn't long before he found a display case featuring a half dozen weapons. Each one had a plaque, identifying them as belonging to warriors Roman had conquered. And then, there was the one at the top. An elaborately carved spear that he recognized from Carmen's descriptions. He didn't need to read the plaque beneath it, but he did.

"Spear of the Dragon Lancer, wielded by the hero Alyssa Hart," it said.

Elijah broke the glass door, shattering it with a single blow. Then, he threw the other weapons into his Ghoul-Hide Satchel before hefting his sister's weapon. It was light, but then again, it had been made for someone without the benefit of his cultivation or levels. Still, he felt a connection to it, and not one based on the system. Instead, it was like looking upon the last remnant of his sister.

He stared at it, taking in each detail as he studied every inch of the spear. It was a good weapon, and he knew Alyssa had used it well. She'd tried to save people. She'd stood up for innocents. And it had gotten her killed.

Perhaps there was a lesson there, but it was one Elijah refused to learn. After all, he and Alyssa had come from the same place. They'd been raised by the same parents. And they were more alike—at least regarding morals—than they weren't. As a result, Elijah knew that, if they had switched places, he would have made many of the same choices. Perhaps, in that case, Alyssa would have been the one avenging him.

But that wasn't how things had worked out.

Elijah sighed, then pushed the spear into his satchel, as well. It had gotten quite full, so he was glad that he'd be going home soon. Still, as he stood there in Roman's quarters, Elijah couldn't help but feel that he hadn't done enough, that his vengeance had been cut short. He'd accomplished his mission, but it had just felt so unsatisfying. More of an extermination than a dispensation of justice.

Then, he remembered the fires he'd seen in the city, and it didn't take him long to connect their presence with the people he'd set free. Maybe they had chosen to rebel against their former captors. If that was the case, then they would need help.

The thought only had to cross Elijah's mind before he shifted into his draconid form, adopted Guise of the Unseen, then left Roman's rooms behind. As he moved through the palace, he found that, like an anthill that had been kicked, it had erupted into activity. Guards and governmental officials raced through the halls. Some were clearly on their way into the city, but many others had begun to muster inside a large chamber.

Elijah saw his opportunity.

So, once he'd found his way to an adjacent and abandoned hall, he once again embraced Swarm, aiming it with One with Nature. Because of how the ability worked, it could easily bypass walls. That meant that Elijah could remain in relative safety while he inflicted his Swarm upon the gathered soldiers.

Biting flies flew across the chamber, delivering their afflictions unto the unsuspecting crowd, and when those flies dissipated into motes of ethera, Elijah summoned another set. And another after that. By the third, half the guards had already begun to show signs of sickness, but Elijah refused to stop.

Indeed, he kept going until his entire store of ethera had been used. By that point, everyone inside had felt the effects of his afflictions. Of course, they'd begun to panic, as well. But they'd already grown too weak. In fact, they were already dead—they just didn't know it yet.

Elijah focused on recovering his ethera as he watched the soldiers die. None of them managed to resist for long. They were laughably weak, and Swarm, when used properly, was incredibly powerful—so long as it had plenty of time to work. Still, it left Elijah with a bad taste in his mouth.

Killing needed to be more difficult than that.

But then again, would the result have been any different if he'd gone in there in his guardian form? No. With his attributes alone, he was all but untouchable against people like that.

Regardless, he couldn't let that stop him from doing what was necessary. These soldiers were tools of oppression, and even though he hadn't, until that very moment, realized that he'd committed himself to freeing the city from their clutches, he'd already chosen not to disregard the citizens' plight.

So, the moment Elijah recovered his ethera, he moved on to the next gathering point, where he repeated his actions from before. As he did, he paced himself better, letting Swarm's afflictions work rather than rushing to pile them on as quickly as possible. It was much more efficient, and by the time they succumbed, he had only used half of his ethera.

Over the course of the rest of the night, Elijah kept going, killing thousands of people. Along the way, he gained level eighty, but he didn't bother checking his notifications. Even though he knew he had gotten another spell, he didn't intend to use it yet. After all, trying out a new ability without testing it extensively was a good way to get killed. Besides, what he was doing was working.

By the time morning came around, Elijah had slaughtered everyone in the palace. Some might have been relatively innocent. He couldn't know one way or the other. However, the moment he had chosen a side, they had all become enemy combatants. And there was only one way to deal with those.

Elijah wasn't interested in keeping his enemies alive, after all.

Once he'd finished his deadly trek through the palace, he progressed into the grounds. Along the way, he killed any guards he found, though it was much more difficult because, out in the open, he couldn't rely entirely on Swarm. Instead, he was forced to use his bestial forms, which were just as effective but required more effort. With his battle experience, high attributes, advanced cultivation, and powerful spells, he was never in any true danger, though.

Not unless he made some serious mistakes, which he did not.

Eventually he reached the city proper, where he had an even easier time. Troops were everywhere, arranged in groups of five. Most had the benefit of a Healer, defender, and a trio of damage-dealing classes including Sorcerers and Rangers. But so long as Elijah took out the Healers quickly, the rest went down without much difficulty.

Each of the archetypes were good at what they did. The defenders were difficult to permanently put down, the Rangers and Sorcerers could output quite a lot of damage, and the Healers could keep a group alive through all manner of attacks. Yet, they were incapable of dealing with someone like Elijah—an intelligent and superior opponent who could fill all roles at once.

The results were predictable.

And Elijah slowly made his way through the city until he was brought up short by a surprising development. He stopped in his tracks as he studied the scene, the anger and grief that had faded into the background returning tenfold.

23

CROSSING LINES

A bonfire blazed, casting the entire square in flickering light as the amassed people—each attired in high-quality clothing that marked them as members of the upper class—roared their approval. In the center of the plaza were a group of soldiers, each clad in blue and white, and at their feet were dozens of corpses. The autumn predawn morning was cool enough that Elijah could see steam rising from their still-warm bodies.

"The traitor does not deserve a statue!" yelled a man in a slightly more elaborate uniform. "She fostered rebellion in our midst, undermining the king and putting us all in danger!"

That brought another cheer from the gathered aristocrats and soldiers. Each and every one of them bore the signs of battle. Or slaughter, given the clear number disparity. It wasn't surprising. As Elijah had made his way through the city, he'd seen guards and their wealthy supporters ganging up on much weaker and less numerous groups of people they clearly marked as inferior. Though he'd noticed that they only did so when they had an advantage, either in power or numbers. In any even battle—which were rare, given the soldiers' obviously higher level of progression—they were far less aggressive, often fleeing to join one of the larger groups.

Retreat was not a bad strategy. Indeed, it was intelligent. Still, it struck Elijah as cowardly, though that could have been the result of the opinions he'd formed in his short time within the city.

Of course, he'd killed many such groups, but he couldn't get them all.

None of that was on his mind, though. Instead, he only had eyes for the situation at the center of the square. Dozens of guards had thrown ropes over the statue of a heroic woman clad in heavy armor and carrying a spear. It wasn't a perfect likeness, but the artist had been talented enough to capture Alyssa's spirit. So, Elijah had no trouble recognizing his sister.

More, Carmen had told him of the existence of such a statue, which had been built after she'd heroically sacrificed her life in the tower. Or at least that was the story Roman and his flunkies had told the population. Carmen had a different impression, though. Once she'd learned the truth, she had come to the opinion that the monument's construction had been rooted in Roman's guilt. Elijah wasn't so sure that was the case. For a man who could murder his own friend, and for no reason but to increase his own power, guilt was assuredly an alien concept.

Either way, Elijah didn't care about the origin of the statue. Instead, he was far more concerned with the fact that the aristocrats and guards seemed hell-bent on tearing it down. In the corner of one facet of Elijah's Quartz Mind, he could see the logic that had led them to that action. Before her death, Alyssa had been a rallying point for those who didn't like the way Roman had run the city, and afterward, she had become a martyr. Even though most never knew the truth of how she'd died, her opinions had continued to hold sway among the downtrodden, and she had become a symbol of the rebellion. Even putting that insurrection down hadn't changed how they saw her.

That was why the aristocrats and guards wanted to destroy the statue. The action was as much a symbol as a representation of aristocratic frustration that had come to a head in the ongoing unrest Elijah had begun by freeing the prisoners. He'd seen plenty of familiar faces during the fighting, so it was no secret what had started the latest revolt.

But all of that meant nothing to Elijah when he saw what those people were going to do to his sister.

His mind went white with rage, and before he knew what he was doing, he'd dropped his draconid form—it was terrible for dealing with multiple opponents, anyway—and resumed his natural shape. Then, he cast Calamity.

The spell was unique in that, originally, he'd thought it had a cooldown. However, as his store of ethera grew, he discovered the truth. That was reflected in the spell's description:

Spell: Calamity	Bury your enemies beneath the power of nature. Conjure a natural disaster appropriate to your environment. Only usable in caster form. Each cast requires more ethera than the last. Reset based on Regeneration attribute. Current reset: 2.3 hours.

When he had first gotten access to the spell, it had taken more than half of his ethera, so he could only use it a single time. However, as his pool of energy grew, the system's description had elaborated on the soft cooldown. The end result was that, now that he had the ethera to support it, Elijah could cast the spell a handful of times before he ran dry of energy.

It was a little frustrating that the system had waited so long to reveal that to him, but in retrospect, it didn't matter that much. By the time it became relevant back in Reaver's Citadel, he'd already seen the difference, and he'd long since adjusted his expectations.

All of that flitted through one isolated facet of Elijah's Mind as he leveled his most devastating spell at the crowd. There were no innocents there. To him, they all deserved precisely what was coming to them.

And given that most of them were low level, what was coming was a degree of destruction they'd never experienced and were ill-equipped to endure. Even over the howling winds and thunder, Elijah could hear their collected screams. That only spurred him on, and the moment the spell played out, he cast it again.

Then, a third time, draining his ethera by a significant amount.

One part of Elijah simply didn't care about those sorts of things. With so much anger coursing through him, he couldn't be bothered with simple details like the amount of ethera in his Core. However, he retained enough capability for rational thought that he cut himself off from casting a fourth instance of the spell.

By that point, the guards had mustered their response. Some had fallen, but they possessed enough Constitution to endure Calamity, albeit not without some injuries. There were a few Healers that had begun the recovery process, though. The healthy guards quickly sighted in on Elijah as the originator of their suffering, and they charged—defenders in the front, with the melee damage dealers following soon after. Only a few Sorcerers had made it through the barrage of Calamity unscathed, but they were the most powerful among the group. And they quickly leveled their power at Elijah.

He welcomed the challenge by shifting into his lamellar-ape form.

The transformation caught the charging defenders by surprise, and a few stumbled to a stop. That only stoked the fires of Elijah's bestial instincts, and he let loose with a massive roar that shook every loose stone in the square. Then, he charged, catching them by surprise.

The first swipe of Elijah's claws was rebuffed by stalwart armor that, upon impact, sent a jolt of cold up his arm. It was uncomfortable, but it did very little damage. More importantly, while the armor negated the slicing attack of his claws, it did nothing for the immense momentum he could bring to bear. The impact sent his first victim rocketing into another guard, and the pair ended up getting tangled with a third.

Elijah leaped upon them, smashing his fists against their armored forms. That armor protected them for a few moments, but eventually, Elijah's assault found the limits of whatever protection it could provide. First, it only dented, but soon enough, those dents became cracks. And before long, Elijah had completely destroyed the metal plates.

Once that happened, the guards were defenseless before his fury.

In only a handful of seconds, he crushed them beneath his fists, shattering bones and rupturing organs.

That's when the others finally fell upon him, pelting him with a hundred different attacks. A few managed to bypass the defenses offered by his thick scales.

Fireballs burned him; ice missiles tore into him, as did arrows and blades. Most were rebuffed by Iron Scales, which cut their damage by ninety percent.

Still, the sheer volume of attacks meant that some were going to get through, and even the ones that didn't bypass his defenses added to the aggregate damage he was forced to endure. But Elijah had been through it all before. If nothing else, he could withstand pain like few others on Earth.

And even as he was buried beneath a barrage of attacks, Elijah didn't remain still. Instead, he marked his first target with Brand of the Stalker before gathering himself and leaping across the square.

Ability: Brand of the Stalker	Sear a brand on an enemy, preventing all forms of stealth and increasing your damage against them by 14%.

Often, he used the ability without thought, marking his foes simply to get the boost to his damage. However, there were also times when he used it to keep tabs on his intended prey. Most recently, he'd done so while tracking Laramie. Otherwise, he would never have found the man.

In the middle of a battle, it served a similar—albeit still different—purpose, letting him keep tabs on a single individual who needed to die before all the others.

Elijah landed atop the woman, crushing her to the ground. She'd used some sort of shielding ability at the last second, but the plane of ethera had shattered under Elijah's massive weight. That exposed her to his ensuing attacks.

She died after only two swipes of his claws. The first ripped into her face, but the second tore out her throat. A few healing spells landed upon her after the first, but Elijah knew she would bleed out before they could finish the job. Still, he took a moment to crush her skull, just to make sure.

Then, he turned his attention to the other Healers.

What followed was a massacre, both bloody and horrifying, as Elijah let the full weight of his savage instincts take over. Usually, he kept them in check, shunting them off to their own facet. Yet, that was impossible when every part of his Mind shuddered under the effects of his unbridled rage.

He leaned into it, letting it envelope him as it never had before.

No longer was he a man inhabiting the body of a beast. Instead, he was fully an enraged animal. Suddenly, his body moved with coordination it had never before possessed, his attacks becoming both more brutal and graceful at the same time.

Elijah reveled in the bloodlust as well as the power, creating a level of carnage most people could scarcely imagine, much less endure.

It wasn't enough, though.

His ire could not be sated. His hunger for death could never be satisfied. Yet, he kept going, moving from the Healers to the Sorcerers and Rangers in turn. The defenders attempted to redirect him, using a few skills and abilities to hem him in and block his efforts. Elijah barely noticed them, barreling through each attempt with unfathomable fury.

A few times, they managed to draw his focus via one ability or another. Some were similar to the one the mercenary had used in the palace, but others were more subtle. The most effective was an ability that incited an obsession within Elijah. His every thought centered on one man, and everything else seemed inconsequential.

As a result, Elijah rushed him, feeling as if there was no one else on the battlefield. Even as a hundred other attacks fell upon his back, Elijah kept going. He never escaped that ability. Instead, it only ended when he killed the defender. If Elijah hadn't already killed all the Healers, he might've been in trouble, but without their influence, the defender couldn't keep up with the level of damage Elijah could bring to bear.

After Elijah broke free of that ability, his fury mounted to unprecedented levels, and any subsequent attempts to manipulate him broke upon the bulwark of his unfettered rage.

In the end, he found himself alone amid a sea of corpses.

With his breath coming in ragged gasps, Elijah took a few minutes to regain his tenuous grip on his sanity. When he did, he saw that his hide had been torn to tatters. Even with copious use of Iron Scales, he'd taken enough damage that, without significant healing, he would be incapable of going on.

But he wasn't concerned with that at the moment.

Instead, he only had eyes for the state of his sister's statue. Because the efforts to topple it had been successful. Alyssa's stone form had fallen, and upon impact, it had shattered into four distinct pieces.

Elijah let the form of the lamellar ape fall away, and he knelt beside her dislodged head, tears of frustration, pain, and grief once again falling down his cheeks.

24

DEMON CORE

The smell of rot pervaded Benedict's nostrils, cloaking him in a blanket of death from which there was no escape. It was difficult to remember a time when that smell didn't cling to everything he touched. Even before the world had transformed, he was familiar with it, and he'd become even more so since everything had changed. However, there was a part of him that tired of that cloying, sickly sweet smell, making him regret the class he'd chosen.

It gave him power, and it had allowed him to steadily progress, especially since that lunatic king had locked him in the dungeon that had been his home for more than a year. It may have been even longer; time was difficult to gauge when one never saw the sun, after all.

Benedict could have escaped. His minions were strong enough to rip his shackles from their anchors on the wall. But then what? The men who routinely slaughtered his minions were strong enough to give him trouble, which was an untenable risk that he refused to take. After all, why would he, aside from the ability to live somewhere more comfortable? He had everything he needed in the labyrinthine dungeon, and he'd reaped the benefits of his situation, progressing to level fifty-nine, which had put him into the top ten.

It was during his most recent inspection of the power rankings that he'd discovered something incredibly interesting, though:

Planetary Power Rankings (Earth)
Elijah Hart—Level 81
Oscar Ramirez—Level 77
Sadie Song—Level 75
Hu Shui—Level 73
Niko Song—Level 72
Davu Adebowale—Level 68
Anupriya Pandey—Level 65
Benedict Emerson—Level 59
Ram Khandu—Level 59
Gunnar Lindstrom—Level 59
. . .
. . .

In a raspy voice, he croaked, "It seems our dear king has run afoul of something he couldn't handle."

His chains clinked as he reached out to stroke the cheek of his latest creation—a mostly intact woman whose only real flaw was a deeply bruised throat. "What do you think, my beauty?" he asked. "Is it time?"

Predictably, she didn't answer. But then again, she never did. Even though she had a body, there was nothing in her mind. He controlled her every movement. Not down to the last twitch, but rather the general shape of her actions. It was the same with all his other minions, and he had the ability to either macro- or micromanage them.

Even as he considered it, two things happened.

First, he achieved level sixty, but before he could check his new ability, another notification shifted before his inner eye:

A powerful entity has offered you a task:
Objective:
Escape.
Reward:
Blessing of the Archdemon Thakon Kilzean
Do you accept?

"What?" rasped Benedict, his throat raw from lack of use.

Then, something flickered into being a second later. Before the image coalesced into anything recognizable, a silky voice echoed in Benedict's ears. "Apologies," it said. "Normally, there is an order to these sorts of things, but your world is so weak that my projection was delayed. I hope you can find it in your heart to forgive me."

By the time the voice finished, the shimmering flicker had resolved itself into a tall, slim man. He wore a simple black toga that had been clasped into place by a golden pin in the shape of a fist. On his feet were delicate sandals that laced up to his knees, but there was nothing else to his outfit.

Not that he needed clothing to be impressive.

The man was nearly six and a half feet tall, with glistening black curls and a pale complexion unmarred by a single blemish. The only oddity—aside from his striking beauty—was a pair of glittering green horns standing out from his forehead. And despite the incongruity they represented, Benedict couldn't help but feel that they only added to the man's—no, the creature's—perfect appearance.

"You are a demon?" Benedict asked, marshaling his composure.

"Archdemon. But yes, I am a member of the demonic race. As you can become, as well," the demon said, turning and giving Benedict a view of the leathery wings folded against his back. "Your low birth need not hold you back. All elder races can induct worthy candidates."

"And you wish to . . . induct me? Why?" asked Benedict.

"Why else? War."

"With whom?"

"The angels, of course," said Thakon Kilzean as he circled the room. He reached out, running a finger along the shoulder of one of Benedict's minions. And to the Warlock's surprise, he felt it. That meant that the demon was no mere illusion. Nor was he a figment of Benedict's imagination. It had been some time since he'd experienced hallucinations, but even in the depths of his . . . delusions, he'd never once felt their touch.

"May I ask why?" he asked.

"They are self-righteous hypocrites who deserve to be wiped from memory," Thakon said with a note of amusement. "More importantly, they have chosen to meddle in this world. As have the dragons. Even the mechaniques have their eyes on this unremarkable place. So, of course we demons must have our piece of the pie, as well." He cocked his head to the side. "That is an expression here, correct? Piece of the pie."

Benedict had no idea what the archdemon was talking about, though he could infer that angels, dragons, and mechaniques were powerful races of people. Demons, as well.

"What does . . . becoming a demon entail?"

"Do you accept the quest?"

"Not until I get an explanation."

"Smart. Very demonic of you. Cunning and unfettered self-reliance. That is why I chose you," Thakon stated. "And ruthlessness, of course. That is a trait held in high esteem by all the elder races, though. Even those self-righteous hypocrites, the angels. They may pretend otherwise. The dragons go on and on about the balance, while the mechaniques only care for their self-mutilation. And the angels pretend they are driven by morality. It's all a smoke screen, though. A disguise for their true motivations. They are no better than us, even if they pretend otherwise."

"That does not answer my question," Benedict stated evenly. His voice was still raspy, but even that small amount of speaking had loosened his vocal cords. "What does becoming a demon entail?"

"Nothing, as of now. You get a fancy new Core that's better than anything you could achieve on your own. There are only a handful of people on this world who could rival its power," said Thakon. "Other than increasing your potential, you will see no real transformation until you reach the fourth stage."

"And after that?"

"You will grow closer to the ideal form until you attain perfection in the seventh stage."

"By perfection, you mean . . ."

"Wings, tail, horns—I believe your legends are quite clear on what to expect," the archdemon stated. "Of course, you can suppress those features if you wish, though I can't fathom why anyone would."

"What are the detriments?"

"Why would those exist?"

"Nothing is free. If something seems too good to be true, then it is likely a lie."

Thakon rolled his eyes, then let out a dramatic sigh. "I'm trying to pull you up from the mud, and you keep slapping my hand away. Do you want to play with corpses for the rest of your life? If so, refuse. If not, then I offer you the means to change your circumstances. Make no mistake—I will not beg. I have other candidates. Do not test my patience, mortal."

"So there are detriments."

"I did not say that!" Thakon rumbled. The dungeon shook, albeit barely noticeably and for only an instant. In addition, Thakon's form flickered until he closed his eyes, took a deep breath, and said, "Apologies. It has been an eternity since I've had to control my power so firmly. The only detriment is that you will make an enemy of the angels. Traveling to their worlds will prove deadly for anyone with a Demon Core. But you don't want to go there, anyway. So boring. Sure, it's technically paradise, but at what cost? They have plenty of skeletons in their closets, as well. Oh, that's a delightful turn of phrase. It loses a bit of impact when translated to my native tongue, but it's still quite colorful."

The archdemon pointedly looked Benedict up and down, then said, "It will also do wonders for your complexion."

Benedict frowned. He tried not to think about it, but because his Regeneration had been so terribly affected by maintaining such a large horde of minions, he had struggled to maintain his health. Most of the damage was cosmetic, but he currently had seeping sores all over his body. At times, he could ignore it, but at others, he thought that he had begun to look like his unliving minions.

He was not a particularly vain man. Indeed, he'd rarely given much thought to his appearance, other than to make certain that he was at least presentable. However, he couldn't ignore his plague-stricken skin.

That, as well as the promise of power, made his choice an easy one. To date, he'd not seen any information on how to increase his Core cultivation, so the value of the demon's offer was undeniable.

With that in mind, Benedict mentally gave his confirmation of the quest. Then, without further discussion, he directed his strongest minions to break his chains free. The moment they succeeded, he received a notification that he'd completed the quest:

> **Congratulations! You have completed a task. Stand by for reward . . .**

He tapped his foot impatiently, which elicited another dramatic roll of Thakon's eyes. A moment later, he received another notification:

> **Blessing of the Archdemon Thakon Kilzean received. Please choose**
> **which form it takes:**
> **Core Advancement**
> **Item (Heart of the Demon)**
> **Spell (Hell's Fury)**

"Pick the Core advancement," Thakon stated. "The other options are powerful. They had to be to be included as a reward for completing the task. However, as strong as they are, none will bear the continued power of advancing your Core."

Benedict was of a mind to agree, though he was intrigued by the other two options. Any item that could rival Core advancement in power would surely be useful. By that same logic, the spell would surely be formidable, as well.

Still, not only would Core advancement impact every other facet of his power, but it also had the potential to continue growing stronger. So, he followed the archdemon's advice and chose the first option without any regret.

The moment he made the choice, power erupted inside him. He was used to pain—after all, he felt every blow leveled against his minions—but even he couldn't stand before the onslaught of agony that came with his Core advancement.

"It actually isn't the advancement that you're feeling. Everyone receives a rudimentary Core when they choose an archetype, but it is a tiny, pitiful thing," said Thakon, suddenly looming over Benedict. "This is a proper Core. But forming such a thing does not come without pain. Normally, that would be spread across years. We don't have time for that, though. The only solace I can offer you is to grant you unconsciousness until the process completes."

"No . . ."

"What?"

"Leave me be," Benedict growled, having fallen to his knees. His fingers dug into the dirty floor as power raged through him. He could feel his Core shattering, then reforming, then shattering once again. At the center of it burned an everlasting flame that constantly pulsed, over and over. Pain didn't begin to describe it. Not adequately, at least. But Benedict was set on enduring the process without succumbing to unconsciousness.

He wanted to feel it.

He wanted to know what was happening.

All so, when the time came, he could replicate it.

So, he held on through the agony until, what felt like an eternity later, it settled. A notification soon followed:

> **Congratulations! You have cultivated a Demon Core! Current stage: Imp.**

As sweat dripped from his forehead to puddle beneath him, he let out a sigh of relief. Another notification followed the last:

> **You have reached the first threshold. Current stage: Cultivator.**

Then, Thakon's silky voice echoed in his ears: "Rise, brother. Welcome to the Legion."

Benedict felt a smile spread across his face as he looked up to see the arch-demon's extended hand. He took it, once again surprised to feel that Thakon was not an illusion, and allowed himself to be dragged to his feet. Already, he could feel the power coursing through him. However, he was disturbed to note that his minions—every last one—had fallen. He could no longer feel them, either.

"My minions . . ."

Thakon said, "Your class remains the same, but the expression of it has now been altered. Warlock you remain, but you no longer need to muck about with corpses. Let me show you . . ."

25

EXODUS

Tears fell upon the upturned stone face, then traced lines down the mis-shapen cheeks to disappear from Elijah's sight. He knew it wasn't his sister. In truth, it barely even resembled her. But in his fragile state, it felt like he was holding the real thing. Like he'd never left home. Like he'd never let her die.

"It should have been me," he muttered, guilt washing over him. With grief—fresh and hot—twisting his thoughts, it felt like he'd traded his death for hers, all those months ago. And he desperately wished it were otherwise. She was the better person. She was stronger, more empathetic. She'd tried to change the world for the better. Meanwhile, Elijah had spent years playing with fish.

Perhaps it would have been different if he'd done so in an effort to achieve some goal, but with the benefit of hindsight, he knew that was never the case. Back then, he was just passing the time, riding the wave of momentum as he waited for something to happen. For something to change.

And it had.

He'd managed to not only survive, but also thrive. But at the same time, Alyssa had done what she'd always done—stand up for people who couldn't stand up for themselves. And she'd been killed for it.

It just wasn't fair.

For a long time, those thoughts gripped Elijah as he knelt in the center of that square, surrounded by the ghastly fruits of his labor. Dead bodies—ripped and torn and dismembered—carpeted the paving stones, proof of his lost restraint. He'd always intended to kill them. They deserved it, as far as he was concerned. However, he hadn't meant to lose himself in the process. But with his roiling emotions, his savage instincts had taken over, and he hadn't even tried to hold them back.

The results were obvious.

Finally, Elijah picked himself up. Suddenly, he didn't care about Valoria's fate. Even as dawn approached, the battle still raged. Despite his efforts, thousands of soldiers remained at large, and they were stronger and better equipped than the rebels. More, they were accompanied by the aristocratic sycophants who'd enabled the entire government.

Maybe they would fend off the rebels.

Or perhaps those insurrectionists would win the day.

Elijah simply didn't care anymore. His battle lust had been sated, and now, he only wanted to leave the cesspool that represented everything that was wrong with humanity behind. But he didn't intend to abandon his sister.

So, he gathered the ropes that had been used to topple the statue, then spent a little more than an hour weaving together a net. He'd done much the same hundreds of times back on his island, both with nets and baskets, so he had plenty of experience to see him through to the end. And with his high Dexterity, the task was trivial.

Once he'd finished the process, he laid it out and lined it with clothes he stripped from the bodies all around him. All were soaked in blood, but Elijah didn't care.

As he worked, plenty of people stumbled upon the site, but they kept their distance. No one—be they rebels or soldiers—wanted anything to do with what had happened in that square. There was nothing to suggest that Elijah was the author of so much carnage, but none were willing to chance it. So, he was left alone to finish his work.

After the net had been lined with clothes, Elijah embarked upon the task of gathering the remains of the statue and loading the pieces onto the net. Then, when that was finished, he tied it all together before hefting it onto his shoulder.

The entire thing weighed more than a ton, which wouldn't have been so arduous a weight in his guardian form. Yet, he refused to shift. Partially, that was because he was afraid of revisiting the savage fury that had engulfed him, but it was also a self-imposed penance. Deserved or not, Elijah still felt guilty for everything that had happened, and in the back of his mind, he felt that the hardship represented by remaining in his human form would somehow atone for his perceived failures.

Of course, Elijah knew—somewhere deep down—that it was not warranted. Yet, he was in no frame of mind to acknowledge that reality. So, once he'd hefted the makeshift bundle onto his back, he began his journey out of the city.

As he walked the streets, he passed many ongoing battles. Most ignored him, but every now and then, someone would try to attack. Elijah was ruthless in his responses, aiming Storm's Fury at anyone who drew close. It was the very first attack spell he'd ever gotten, and often, he neglected its use because, against anything that was near his level, the damage it could do was negligible. But when aimed at people less than half his level, and without the benefit of strong cultivation? It was deadly.

More importantly, he could cast it hundreds of times before running low on ethera, and even then, he could nearly keep up with that strain if he flexed his Mind.

So, as he traversed the streets of the city, Elijah became a walking thunderstorm of death. Often, he took hits, but he ignored them as he used Healing

Rain and Soothe to mend his injuries. That, as much as the lightning, deterred most would-be assailants. Elijah knew from experience how disorienting it was to see someone's mortal wounds mend in seconds.

All the while, he never stopped moving forward.

At some point, he left the city behind. He wasn't certain when he'd made the choice not to use any of his unique advantages, but he was more than five miles outside of Valoria when he realized that he had no intention of flying, teleporting, or shifting into his other forms that might ease the burden of travel.

Instead, Elijah's penance had become something of a pilgrimage. An exodus meant to assuage his guilt while honoring his sister. More of the former than the latter, if he was honest with himself. Alyssa would have likely called him a dramatic idiot.

She was always more levelheaded than he was, anyway. Practical in a way that he could never match. And the world was a worse place now that she was gone.

As Elijah trudged through the wilderness, he ignored all distractions. He also refused to stop, even for a moment, to rest. Instead, he continued to put one foot in front of the other, and when he grew too fatigued to take another step, he ate one of his Grove berries to recover his energy.

With every footfall, Elijah conjured a new memory of his sister. Some were good, like when she'd helped him choose an outfit for his first date with Lucy. He'd never been particularly adept when it came to style, so she'd taken pity on him, ensuring that he put his best foot forward in his first forays into love. Some were bad, like one of the many times they'd argued over some triviality that, in retrospect, hadn't mattered at all.

But they were all part of who Alyssa had been. A part of the relationship they'd shared. For most of their childhood, they'd been close, and Elijah had a wealth of memories to draw upon.

And as he strode across the wilderness, he sank into an almost meditative trance, remembering everything in the most vivid details. As the days went by, he often found tears streaming down his cheeks.

They seemed appropriate.

At times, he encountered a few Voxx trails that he expected would either lead to spontaneously manifesting invaders or even interdimensional rifts. Yet, for the first time ever, he ignored them. As usual, the wildlife left him alone. He even sensed a few nearby monsters at one point, but they were content to let him continue on his way.

Days turned into a week, and eventually, Elijah lost track of time. The days blended together until he could barely discern one from the next. He never stopped—even at night—and, more than once, he was forced to cross rivers or canyons. Those were difficult, though with his high attributes and equipment like the Ring of Aquatic Travel, he managed it just the same.

Until, at last, he reached the destination he didn't even know he was traveling toward.

The Circle of Spears loomed before him, surrounding a verdant oasis that teemed with the sense of nature. He'd been in the desert for a while, though he barely took notice of the arid landscape. The only concession he made to the terrain was that he was forced to slake his thirst a little more often. Fortunately, the Endless Canteen held hundreds of gallons of water, which meant that he had plenty.

When he reached the dolmen, passing between the trilithon he'd built, he finally let his burden fall away. It thudded to the ground, and Elijah fell soon after.

After weeks on his feet, he could no longer stand. Even with his inflated attributes, his body had distinct limits, and he'd far exceeded them. Now that he'd found his destination, though, he let the impact of the journey fall upon his shoulders. He didn't precisely pass into unconsciousness. Instead, for the longest time, his state stood somewhere between wakefulness and sleep, day-dreaming about the memories he'd examined along the way.

In addition, an idea began to take shape. A way to honor his sister's memory and her intent at the same time. It was only the seed of a notion, but as Elijah lay there, it began to sprout into something far more substantial. In a lot of ways, it was a fever dream brought on by extreme exhaustion and borderline malnutrition.

But there was inspiration there, too.

A desire to get things right.

To make up for all the things he'd gotten wrong in his life.

For a while, he dipped in and out of unconsciousness. In a lot of ways, he was lucky he hadn't collapsed sooner. If he had, he probably would not have survived. However, the thick ethera—and vitality—of the oasis nourished him. It didn't precisely heal him, but it was distinctly better than anywhere else outside of his island.

At one point, he imagined Alyssa there with him, comforting him as she always had. He tried to return the favor, but she dissipated the moment he attempted to focus on her. Even at the height of his exhaustion-based delusion, Elijah knew it wasn't real. But there was a chance, wasn't there? Magic existed. So, why couldn't ghosts?

Perhaps she had even ended up as one of the tower denizens? What if she could earn her way to resurrection?

A thousand possibilities—each less likely than the next—flitted through Elijah's mind. And even though he knew none of them were real—dead was dead, even with the existence of magic; every guide he'd read was adamant about that reality—he clung to those dreams.

Then, at last, he regained his full faculties.

Sitting up, he looked around the oasis. It was even more verdant than it had been when he and Carmen had built the dolmen, and it was packed full of so much life that it almost seemed a tangible thing. That had attracted plenty of animals, as well. From fat insects to reptiles, and everything in between.

And of course, Snappy remained in the pond at its center, happily living his life, completely uncomprehending of the internal crisis Elijah had just experienced. In a way, it was comforting, knowing that no matter what hardships or tragedies he went through, nature would continue on.

Over the next few minutes, Elijah took stock of his body. He'd lost weight. Maybe fifteen pounds, which didn't seem like a lot, but considering that he hadn't exactly been heavy to begin with, it made quite a difference in his body. More, he was covered in the consequences of his trek across hundreds of miles, with half-healed wounds from his time in Valoria marring his form. There were sores along his shoulders where the ropes had dug into his flesh, too.

So, Elijah cast Soothe on himself before summoning Healing Rain. Then, for good measure, he flared Touch of Nature as he undressed. The clothes were ruined. Despite being Simple grade, their materials weren't up to the rigors he'd endured, so he'd decided to exchange them for a different set.

After that, he retrieved his homemade restorative soap from his satchel and began to bathe. Where the soap went, healthy skin followed until, nearly twenty minutes later, Elijah was more refreshed than he'd been since leaving his Grove.

Once he was clean and in much better condition, Elijah once again took up his burden, then used Roots of the World Tree to teleport to the Dragon Circle. Of all the cities he'd visited, Argos was the only place that deserved what he had planned.

Elijah knew that he could have simply teleported straight from Valoria to his ultimate destination. However, the journey had been important. A necessary thing meant for self-reflection and remembrance.

And penance.

It was a pilgrimage, though not in service of any god. Instead, it was meant to honor the sister he'd lost. Now, he intended to create a more lasting monument to the person she had been.

So, after adjusting the awkward burden he'd carried for countless miles, he set off for Argos, hoping that he could find what he needed in the city.

26

EASING THE BURDEN

The last few miles of Elijah's journey were the most difficult. Despite having traveled beneath his burden for weeks, once again resuming the weight of the statue left his back bent. Still, as he had from the very beginning, Elijah continued to put one foot in front of the other without delay or dissent.

But he didn't go into that same trance that had carried him so far. Instead, he was painfully aware of his surroundings. During his self-imposed pilgrimage, autumn had tightened its grip on the region. The leaves had begun to change colors, painting the forest in deep browns and vivid oranges. In addition, the wildlife had started preparing for winter, hoarding food and storing fat for hibernation. Finally, the air had taken on a chilly bite, hinting that a frigid winter was just around the corner.

Hopefully, Argos was ready for what was coming because Elijah suspected it would be far colder than normal.

Still, despite his task, now that Elijah had submersed himself in nature's influence, he couldn't deny that it was comforting in a way nothing else could be. He basked in it, letting it soothe his soul.

After a few hours, he arrived at the city's gates. The two guards recognized him, and what's more, they could see the size of his burden. So, they didn't delay him. Instead, they just waved him through, and from there, Elijah made his way to Atticus's shop. As he walked through the city, he saw a host of familiar sights. They were almost as comforting as being inundated by the aura of nature that had accompanied him from the Dragon Circle.

It only took Elijah about twenty minutes to reach Atticus's shop, and when he did, he gently dropped his burden. Then, he stepped inside.

Atticus looked up from where he'd been cleaning one of the glass cases, and when he saw Elijah, his smiling face turned serious. "What happened to you, my friend?" he asked.

"Is it that bad?" Elijah asked in response. He'd known that the journey had taken its toll, but he had thought his experience in the oasis had reversed some of that damage. Clearly, that wasn't the case.

"You look like you haven't eaten in weeks," Atticus said, rushing over. "What happened?"

As the merchant asked the question, he reached out as if he intended to help steady Elijah. But it was unnecessary, which he quickly made clear. "I'm fine," he said, backing away. "Just had a long journey."

"Do you want to talk about it?"

Elijah shook his head. "Not really. Not yet," he admitted. "I really came here for two reasons. First, I have a lot of equipment I need identified. I'll probably sell some of it, assuming you're buying."

Despite his obvious concern, Atticus flashed a bright smile. It was forced, and they both knew it, but Elijah appreciated that his friend had chosen to approach the situation like it was a normal transaction. That helped. Atticus spread his long arms, saying, "Of course, my friend. Atticus's Arsenal is always in the market for high-quality items."

With that, he led Elijah to the back where they commenced with the appraisal process. Atticus's particular ability required the use of the table, so Elijah first placed the series of weapons he'd taken from the various guards in Valoria atop the surface.

"Nothing special. Mostly middle Crude grade. One is high Crude," Atticus said. "The materials are good, though. Poorly constructed. If I sell these, it will be to someone who has a disassembly skill. The materials are worth more than the weapons, I'm sorry to say."

"Disassembly skill?" Elijah asked.

"Yes. Some Tradesmen have an ability where they can salvage the materials from crafted items. Some of the efficacy of those materials is lost in the process, and there are conditions that must be met, but it is a very useful skill for those who wish to waste as little as possible."

"Do you think my sister-in-law might have that kind of skill? She's a Blacksmith."

"And on the power rankings, if I remember correctly?"

Elijah nodded. "She is."

"Then almost definitely. I don't know any real Blacksmiths. Just a couple of Tinkerers. But if they have that kind of skill, then she will, as well."

"Then I probably shouldn't sell these," Elijah said.

"That would be my advice. However, if she cannot use the materials, then I will buy them, of course."

"Thanks."

Even so, Elijah did end up selling the few higher-grade pieces to Atticus. Those he judged were worth more in their current forms than they would be after being broken down into their base parts. After that, Elijah got to the pieces he'd taken from Roman's display case.

Those were all a little disappointing. Each piece was at least Simple grade, but their traits and abilities were nothing useful for Elijah. Besides, he liked using staves, and as far as he could tell, the swords weren't in the style Colt or Miguel preferred. So, he was better served just selling them.

However, he did keep the suit of armor—which was composed of multiple pieces that included a long duster with built-in bracers, a chain mail coat, and greaves. After all, it had been created for Colt, and as far as Elijah was concerned, it would be most useful in the Samurai's possession.

Next, they moved on to Roman's bow, which was called Blind Eye.

"Adds five to Dexterity and Strength," Atticus explained. "The trait increases the effectiveness of all ambush skills by five percent. It also has an ability called Conjure Arrow, which is pretty self-explanatory. A very good weapon, my friend. I know of a dozen Rangers who would kill for such a weapon."

"I think I'll keep that one," Elijah said. "Miguel hasn't gotten his archetype yet, so if he gets Ranger, this would come in handy."

"That's a lot of weapon for someone without a class," Atticus stated. "Heavy draw. I suspect it takes at least thirty Strength just to pull it back."

"He'll grow into it," Elijah responded. "But if he doesn't, I'll be back."

"Fair enough, my friend. Anything else?"

"A sword," Elijah said, reaching into his Ghoul-Hide Satchel and retrieving the False Dragon's Fang. He set it on Atticus's table, which immediately drew a reaction. Yet, it was not the one Elijah had expected.

Instead of being awed by the admittedly impressive weapon, Atticus took a step back, demanding, "You haven't bonded that thing, have you?"

Elijah shook his head. "I don't use swords."

"Good. Very good."

"What's wrong? It's almost Complex-grade. My sister-in-law made it."

"Did she do so under duress?"

Elijah shrugged. "I guess. Why does that matter?" he asked. Carmen had created the weapon in order to avoid having her people killed. If that didn't count as duress, he didn't know what would.

"It is cursed."

"Cursed? What does that mean?" Elijah asked. "I mean, I understand the definition of the word. But what does it mean in the context of this item?"

"A cursed item has a hidden ability. In this case, it's called Arrogance of the False Dragon. Here," Atticus said, waving his hand. Above the table, a box similar to the ones containing the notifications appeared:

Ability: Arrogance of the False Dragon	Positive: Assert influence over a captive population more easily. Negative: Become overconfident to the point of ruin. May include delusions of grandeur.

"Every curse will have two sides," Atticus explained. "A positive and a nega-tive. Normally, the negative will outweigh the positive, but from what I've read, that is not always the case. Some cursed items are so powerful that people will-ingly accept the cost. That normally only happens with much higher-grade items, though. The example I read about in the guide was a scepter taken up by a temple priestess. Its ability was an aura that ensured prosperity for those in the city surrounding her. However, the negative aspect was that it caused rapid aging. She accepted it willingly, and over the millennia, her successors have, as well."

Elijah said, "I see."

But even as he spoke, he wondered if the curse was the cause of the state of Valoria. Perhaps, but he reminded himself that Roman's crimes preceded the creation of the False Dragon's Fang. That assuaged any crisis of conscience he might have experienced.

"I would destroy it," Atticus advised. "The weapon is a nice piece, but that curse will doubtless prove to be insidious, my friend. You are lucky that you had it appraised before using it. Otherwise, you might never have known."

"I don't use swords," Elijah reiterated. However, in the past, he had bonded items before getting them appraised. That would have to stop.

Regardless, now that he'd had all his loot appraised, Elijah could get to the true reason he'd come to Argos. So, he asked, "Do you know any Architects? Perhaps a Sculptor?"

"For what purpose, my friend?"

Elijah told him what he had in mind, then said, "I'm willing to pay whatever it takes. I guess I also need to finally meet whoever's in charge of this town so I can work out where to put it. My first instinct is to put it near the statue of Heracles, but . . . I don't know. I don't think it matters so much where it is. I just want it to be accessible."

After that, Atticus explained that Argos was ruled by a council, and as it turned out, Elijah was actually acquainted with one of the six members. "Agatha's a councilor?" he asked, thinking of the once-surly innkeeper who'd eventually taken a liking to Elijah.

"Likely the most important member," Atticus revealed. "She tends to brow-beat anyone who doesn't get in line behind her."

"Interesting. Do you think she'll have an issue with my plans?"

Atticus was adamant that no one would have a problem with it, which was reassuring. After that came a whirlwind of activity. First, Atticus led Elijah to a woman he claimed was the best Architect in town. It only took a few minutes to get her on board, largely because Elijah didn't haggle on the price.

Next, Elijah was introduced to Argos's highest-level Builder. Because of his efforts during Argos's rebuild in the wake of the tempest that had swept through the area months before, Elijah already knew of the great bear of a man.

However, he'd never met him. As it turned out, Dion—which was the Builder's name—took to the idea with great fervor, promising to put his best crew on the project the moment everything was ready.

The following step was to get the project approved by the council, which turned out to be even easier than Elijah could have expected. When he told Agatha what he wanted to do, she said, "Then we will accommodate you. There is a plot only three blocks away that will be perfect."

As it turned out, the plot, which stood atop a low hill overlooking the city, had once held a large mosque that had collapsed soon after the world's transformation. Since then, it had been empty, save for the foundations. Elijah first thought it would be a little too big, but Atticus insisted, "Larger is better, my friend. Remember that always."

Once Elijah had bought the lot from the city, the final item on his to-do list was to meet with a Sculptor. Oddly enough, the best artist in town was not a single person, but rather a pair of siblings—Penelope and Iason—who worked in tandem. Unfortunately, they didn't seem to like one another very much, so, even though they had enthusiastically embraced the project, talking to them proved to be quite a labor.

Yet, Elijah endured, and after leaving Alyssa's statue with them and explaining what he wanted, he set off toward the mountains. For one, he had a few days before the plans could be finalized, and for another, he had a very specific material he wanted to use for the project.

So, Elijah once again found himself trekking across the wilderness. However, his psychological burden felt much lighter than it had during his previous travels, largely because he felt secure in the knowledge that he was finally doing something worthwhile. And he was eager to complete the project that he hoped would adequately honor his sister's memory.

27

FIRST STEPS

A cool rain fell upon Elijah's shoulders as he trekked toward the mountains. Without the multiton burden of his sister's statue on his back, he felt physically unburdened. However, the weight of his own expectations for his chosen task still weighed heavily upon him. He wasn't certain when he had chosen to remain in his human form, but it felt appropriate. After all, using his bestial forms, he could have satisfied the terms of his self-imposed quest much more quickly and far more easily. Yet, that facilitation would have robbed it of much of its meaning.

Or that was his justification.

In reality, Elijah could acknowledge that part of his reasoning came down to a simple fact. He thought he needed to suffer in order to give the act more significance. In a lot of ways, it truly was a self-inflicted penance.

But by that point, Elijah had grown accustomed to it, so he let purpose fuel his journey as he trudged through the forest. As he did, he refused to let himself slip back into the trancelike state that had seen him through from Valoria to the Circle of Spears. Instead, he focused on three things.

First, he continuously pushed his cultivation exercises, constantly cycling ethera through his Core in order to expand his capacity. It wasn't very effective, but he felt it was good—and necessary—practice. After all, he couldn't afford to just sit around his Grove, or in his cultivation cave, for months while he worked on the process. Nor could he let himself neglect his progression. The battles in Valoria had pushed him past level eighty, but he knew that levels were not the only facet of progression.

The next subject of his focus concerned his plans for his sister's memorial. The Architect would take care of the building, and the Sculptor siblings would do their part, as well. But Elijah was more concerned with what came after the project was completed.

And finally, he let himself feel his surroundings in a deep and meaningful way. Every tiny organism. Every rock and tree. Every animal, small and large. He immersed himself in nature, once again letting it soothe him. It didn't banish his grief. It did nothing to rid him of the guilt he still carried. Nor did it assuage his pain. However, it did bolster his ability to deal with all the issues he'd taken upon his shoulders.

Every now and again, Elijah would check his Domain, as well. He observed as Colt continued to train Miguel, incorporating grueling physical activities as well as constant weapons instruction. But it didn't end there. Every other day saw Kurik landing on the island and taking Miguel with him, presumably to venture out into the wilderness and train him as a scout.

On those days, the boy's enthusiasm was difficult to miss.

Elijah also saw something that had initially worried him. At long last, Miguel had finally met the island's other guardians, stumbling onto the family of deer during one of his forest runs. It was alarming enough that Elijah almost abandoned his task altogether and returned to the island. After all, those deer were incredibly dangerous. If he made the wrong move, the stag would disintegrate him with those powerful beams of light it could create.

Yet, Elijah's alarm seemed unwarranted. The two adult deer were a bit skittish around him, but the pair of juveniles—they'd grown slightly larger—were more than eager to approach. It wasn't long before they were chasing one another through the meadow where the deer had made their home.

It reminded Elijah of how easily Miguel had befriended the giant turtle, Snappy. Or how quickly Artemis had taken to him. Perhaps the young man had a gift for such things. Or maybe the creatures could sense that he was no threat to them. One way or another, it was nice to see that, after everything Miguel had been through, he was still capable of having fun.

The other facets of Elijah's Mind drifted through his memories. Most centered around his sister, but he also thought of other people he'd lost. Like his parents. Or his ex-girlfriend back in Hawaii. He rarely thought of Nora anymore, largely because, with the benefit of space, he'd come to realize that their relationship had never been anything truly special. Just a pair of people who'd gotten together out of shared loneliness, then stayed together because they actually enjoyed one another's company. But it wasn't love. There had never been a spark.

Not like with Lucy.

More than once, Elijah had regretted how his first real relationship had ended. And he was ashamed of how he'd treated Lucy back then. In the summer after their breakup, he'd found comfort with other women—a few of whom had treated him extremely poorly—so it was a miracle that she would even tolerate his presence anymore. Yet, when they'd reunited only a few months past, she'd given her support without hesitation.

Perhaps he needed to take that relationship—be it friendship or something more—more seriously. That reminded him of his obligation regarding Seattle. He still intended to help, just on his own terms and timeline.

Eventually, Elijah reached the mountains, where he embarked on a quest to find the perfect stone. He'd felt it once before—or its aura of ethera, at least—but back then, he'd had no need or ability to quarry it. This time, though, he was prepared.

Slowly, Elijah scoured the mountains until, after three more days, he found what he was looking for.

The cliff face was tall. Perhaps two hundred feet, and extending for a quarter of a mile in either direction. The size of the cliff was immaterial, though. What truly drew Elijah's eye was the composition. In most ways, it looked like marble, predominantly white, but with highlights of deep green. Even just looking at it, Elijah knew it was special—a supposition supported by the dense aura of ethera it emitted, as well. It was almost as strong as a natural treasure, though without the sense of vitality that came with them. It reminded Elijah of the ore that came from Ironshore's mine.

That prompted a thread of thought questioning what really made natural treasures. Was it the life they tended to emit? Or was it something else? Elijah could feel the difference, though he wasn't capable of pinpointing exactly what separated natural treasures from other powerful resources.

In any case, while Elijah wouldn't have harvested a natural treasure, he had no issues with taking the stone. So, without further hesitation, he drew a large pickax from his Ghoul-Hide Satchel, climbed to the top of the cliff, and got to work. He'd acquired the tool from Dion, the Builder he'd contracted, and it was reputed to be a Simple-grade item. However, when Elijah swung the pickax at the cliff, he was surprised to find that it didn't even chip the durable stone.

So, after a few more attempts, Elijah shifted into his lamellar-ape form and brought his claws to bear. That was better, giving him some insight into how his claws compared to high-grade items.

Over the next few hours, Elijah worked to carve a huge block from the stone. Then, once it had been cut completely free, he laboriously wrapped it in rope he'd bought in Argos before lowering it to the ground. There were complications, of course. The process was awkward, made even more difficult by the fact that Elijah really didn't know much about quarrying stone. Yet, he was a quick study with incredible attributes that were perfectly suited to the task. So, he pushed through, managing to set the stone at the bottom of the cliff before moving on to the next block.

That one went much more quickly, and after that, Elijah settled into a groove. The process was labor-intensive, but by that point, Elijah was well accustomed to such hardship. So, he persisted, and over the next few days, he harvested nearly a hundred such blocks.

On the trip back to Argos, by necessity, he was forced to abandon his previous decision to remain in his human form. Instead, he used his lamellar-ape form, balancing one block on each shoulder as he set off toward Argos. It was still a ridiculous amount of weight to carry, far exceeding that of the heel stones he'd used in his dolmens. However, because his Strength had increased—both by virtue of his levels and because of his equipment—he managed it.

Still, when he reached Argos and deposited the blocks just outside the city, he was exhausted. But he didn't stop to rest. Instead, he shifted to the Shape of the Sky and set off toward his makeshift quarry. When he landed, he ate one of his few remaining Grove berries, slept for a couple of hours, then continued his task. Each trip took about twelve hours, which meant that he could only make a couple a day. Thankfully, he wasn't forced to do everything himself because, on the fifth such day, Dion and his crew arrived with a pair of huge wagons.

The barrel-chested Builder and his team quickly got to work, stacking twenty blocks onto each wagon. Once they were fully loaded, Elijah asked, "Is that going to hold? It looks like it's going to topple over."

Dion clapped Elijah on his shoulder and let out an abrupt laugh. "Ah, so you have never worked with a true Builder, eh?" the man asked. "It is a skill called Teamster's Balance. We'll keep those blocks in the wagons, don't you worry."

Elijah took the man at his word, though he still eyed the precariously piled blocks with some unease. Even so, he chose to trust Dion, largely because he'd come so highly recommended by Atticus.

In either case, the addition of the Builders' efforts turned a project that should have taken six weeks into one that they managed to complete in only two. Even as they drove their wagons—which were pulled by the crew—across the terrain, Elijah continued with his own efforts, trudging across the landscape and carrying two blocks at a time.

When they finally finished, Elijah once again met with the people he'd contracted. The two Sculptors had finalized their plans, while the Architect gave Elijah three options from which to choose. To him, the decision seemed obvious, and he picked the one that called to him most strongly.

Then, at last, everyone got to work.

As they did, Elijah finally took the time to rest, though he didn't head to an inn to sleep. Instead, he planted himself in the center of the build site, where he continuously flared Nature's Bounty as well as One with Nature. However, because there were no plants around, the former ability didn't really result in much in the way of growth. That wasn't Elijah's purpose. Instead, he wanted to suffuse the intended memorial with his power.

Because, if the construction of the dolmens had proved anything, it was that construction wasn't just about piling materials into a recognizable shape. There was far more to it than that. Ethera changed everything, after all.

More days passed, and the workers continued with their task. Often, they took advantage of Elijah's healing abilities, as well, and after that first day, he'd resigned himself to continuously keeping Healing Rain active. That attracted many of Argos's residents, too. There were quite a few Healers in the city, though they were often overworked. So, most people only visited a Healer when their lives were in danger. That was where Healing Rain came in. It was an easy spell to maintain, and it worked wonders on minor ailments. So, most days saw Elijah surrounded by a dozen or so people.

That was fine with him, too. He didn't get much in the way of experience for healing them, but they often brought him food, which seemed a good trade.

More importantly, doing good and helping people nourished him in an entirely different way. That was the first of many steps toward healing his wounded psyche. It would be a long journey, but to Elijah, it felt that the first part of any voyage was always the most difficult.

In any case, it took a little more than a week before the building started to come together. There was still quite a lot of detail work to be done, but Elijah was more than happy with the results so far.

And now that he had verified that everything was coming together, he felt free to embark on the final addition for the project. So, after letting everyone know that he would be back in a couple of weeks, Elijah used Roots of the World Tree and, for the first time in more than two months, returned to his Grove.

28

THE NATURE OF RESTRAINT

The dense ethera of the Grove washed over Elijah as he reappeared on his island. Sometimes, it was easy to forget just how thick it was compared to the rest of the world. When he was elsewhere, he barely even noticed the lack. However, the moment he returned to the Grove, it was like swimming in a soothing ocean of vital energy. He let out a sigh as he looked around the Grove.

Much of it was the same, though his eyes were drawn to the area dedicated to his coffee trees. They'd continued to grow, reaching a height of almost fifty feet, which was enormous for that species of tree. That didn't seem out of the ordinary, though. Elijah's Grove berries had started off as bunchberries, but the thick ethera and both his and Nerthus's ministrations had transformed them into something else entirely. The same was true of all the other plants in the Grove, as well. Some had simply grown much larger than normal, but others had mutated even more than the berries.

Either way, it all felt appropriate. Natural. And that was what truly mattered.

Sensing Nerthus on the other side of the Grove, Elijah crossed the intervening space to find the spryggent tending to a dozen artificial beehives. They resembled the hives he'd seen before Earth's transformation, though instead of being made of unimaginative particle board or the like, these new hives had been grown much like Elijah's tree house. Shaped like acorns, they looked like functional works of art, especially with tens of thousands of fat honeybees swarming the area.

One landed on Elijah's outstretched hand, and he was surprised to see that it was around fifty percent larger than a normal honeybee, which meant it was about an inch and a half long. In fact, with its fuzzy body and curious nature, it looked almost like a cartoon version of the familiar insects.

"They are quite friendly," Nerthus said without looking up. "I chose these hives specifically for that reason."

"Nerthus, this is amazing," Elijah responded with no small degree of awe. "You've outdone yourself. Really."

"The child likes the bees, as well," Nerthus said. "He has an incredible affinity for animals."

"I've noticed that they tolerate him a lot more than they do most people," Elijah admitted. "I thought it had to do with him not having an archetype yet. Maybe they can sense that he isn't a threat to them or something."

"Perhaps," Nerthus conceded. "Yet, I think it is more than that. It will be interesting to see which archetypes and classes he is offered. He may even have the chance to become a Druid, as well."

"Do you think that would be wise?"

"Of course," Nerthus said, finally looking back at Elijah. "Druid is the most powerful archetype in existence."

"Uh . . . Not everybody thinks that," Elijah said, rubbing the back of his neck. "In fact, I've met a few people who think the opposite. Well, that's not exactly true. Nobody thinks Druids aren't strong. It's just that I get the impression that most Druids are borderline noncombatants."

"Ah. That is true. Strength comes in many forms, though. There are whole worlds tended to by Druids. Beautiful places where everything exists in perfect harmony. Anything that threatens that balance is eradicated. Is that not power?"

Elijah nodded. He knew that his archetype was not meant to be the strongest in combat. Even his attribute bonuses were not on par with some others, and his repertoire of spells lacked focus. That wasn't difficult to understand, given that a good portion of the archetype seemed focused on noncombat abilities like healing, Nature's Bounty, or One with Nature. Though the third had some combat applications, it was clearly meant to help a Druid to connect with the source of his power. Or the balance he was meant to protect.

Regardless, Elijah had circumvented many of those inadequacies by choosing a distinctly combat-focused class. And he'd managed to shore up his attribute deficiencies with cultivation. However, he did realize that those were only Band-Aids that didn't truly fix the problem.

So, he asked, "What does progression look like for me? I know that I'll have a chance for specialization in a few levels. Then, I'll get to evolve my class, too. But what does that mean?"

"It means that you will be able to correct your path to better align with your goals," Nerthus stated. "If you wish for more combat power, that will be available via an evolution. Or if you want to focus more on the Grove, that will be possible, as well. The system will provide options based on your actions as well as how it interprets your suitability."

"Will I lose any of my current abilities?"

"No. When those abilities evolve, the options will align with your new direction, though. For instance, if you were to choose to focus on healing, then some of your combat spells might develop additional effects that assist in that function," Nerthus explained. "Though it should be said that no spell, even after many evolutions, will completely change its nature. A damaging spell will always be a damaging spell."

"Sounds complicated."

"Of course. The system was created by the twelve most powerful beings to have ever existed, all working in concert to ease the burden of progression. It is not self-aware, but it is reactive and complex beyond our comprehension," Nerthus stated.

"What was it like before?"

"Those days are lost in darkness. Only vague stories remain, and the truth is obscured by time."

Elijah nodded. Even humanity lacked a true vision of the past, and that history was far shorter than the scale of what Nerthus had described. Elijah asked, "And this system is benevolent?"

"It is neutral. It does not judge. Instead, it only guides. The purpose is benevolent, though."

"I see," Elijah said, though he had difficulty wrapping his thoughts around the sheer scope of it all. Regardless, he didn't have the free time to spend contemplating the nature of the multiverse or the system. Instead, he had more grounded issues to worry about. So, after only a few more minutes, during which he let Nerthus explain the progress of the rest of the Grove, Elijah described what he wanted from Nerthus.

"Has the tree produced any other seeds?" he asked.

"Three others. Though more should grow over the next few years," Nerthus answered. "Why?"

"I need one."

Then, Elijah explained why he wanted one of the ancestral tree's seeds. Once he understood what Elijah had planned, Nerthus gave his approval and gathered the seed in question.

After that, Elijah set off for Ironshore, using Shape of the Sky to cover the distance in a little more than a minute. He landed in Druid's Park, startling a few children. Oddly enough, though, they did not fear him. Rather, they were simply shocked by his sudden landing. Apparently, news of his new form had spread through the town.

Elijah took a few minutes to ensure that the tree was healthy, and once he was satisfied, he started toward Carmen's forge, arriving after only a few more minutes. When he stepped inside, he saw her hammering away at a bar of glowing metal. For the first time since their reunion, she wore a genuine smile upon her face.

There were a few other people around. Most were dwarves, but Elijah saw a couple of gnomes and a single goblin, as well. The smithy itself was quite impressive, with enough room to accommodate a few dozen Blacksmiths. However, Elijah quickly noticed a couple of things about the workers. First, they were all incredibly young, probably having only attained their archetypes recently. Second, none of them were actually forging anything. Instead, they were helping with the smelting process, working bellows, or doing other grunt work.

"You can't be in here, fella," said one of the dwarves. His red beard was only an inch long, but his shoulders were wide and muscular. "If you're wantin' ta commission somethin', you'll have to talk to Miss Corie down at the shop."

Elijah just stared at the young dwarf, then shook his head before continuing into the building.

"Hey! I said you can't—"

Someone reached over to grab the would-be smith, whispering something rendered unintelligible by the activity within the smithy. Elijah was both pleased and a little saddened when the dwarf's face paled before he took a step back. Apparently, Elijah's reputation had preceded him.

With a sigh, he continued on until he reached Carmen. "Whatcha makin'?" he asked, leaning forward.

She started, clearly surprised to find Elijah standing next to her. Patting her chest, she breathed, "You scared the hell out of me. What are you doing here? Is it done?"

Elijah nodded. "It's done. Do you want to hear the whole story?" he asked.

Carmen said that she did, and after that, they retreated to the small office she'd attached to the smithy. Once there, Elijah laid out the entire tale, including running into the harpies, finding the records, and killing both Laramie and Fiona. When he described the fight with Roman, he only hit the high points, ending with, "After that, I . . . I went on a rampage. I killed hundreds of guards."

That was a bit of a lie. In reality, he'd slaughtered more than a thousand. But Carmen didn't need to know that.

"When I left the city, the battle was still going on. I don't know who won."

"Nobody," Carmen said with a shake of her head. She slumped in her chair, adding, "So, it's over?"

"Not yet," Elijah said. "I'm done killing, but there's one more thing we need to do."

Then, he told her about the project he'd begun. For the most part, Carmen took to the idea pretty well, though it clearly made her a little uncomfortable. Still, when Elijah asked her to come with him back to Argos, she agreed.

"I need to go find Miguel," Elijah said. "Do you know where he is?"

"Off in the wilderness with Kurik," Carmen answered. "Colt's with them, too. He said he wanted to shore up his own woodcraft, but I think he just wants to make sure Miguel doesn't forget his sword training. If you ask me, he and the dwarf are competing to see who can pass more knowledge on to my son."

"That's a good thing, right?"

Carmen shrugged. "I don't know. I worry about him being stretched too thin. But he enjoys all of it. You should hear him going on and on about all the things he's seen," she said. "Or about sword forms. God. If I have to hear him explain the minute differences between stances one more time . . ."

Elijah forced a laugh. That was one of the more relatable aspects of Miguel's training. "When I used to box, I'd talk my dad's ear off about everything I learned," he said. "It's a good thing. It means he's engaged."

"I hope so. I still don't know what to think about all of this," she admitted. "I know he needs to be able to take care of himself. I know he wants power. And I know why. But every time I see him learning how to kill, I feel like a failure as a parent. I mean, it really wasn't that long ago that we were telling him that violence never solved anything. So naive."

"It was a different world, Carmen," Elijah said, reaching out to grip her shoulder. She flinched a little at his touch, evidence that she hadn't completely recovered from her own ordeal. "But just because he can kill doesn't mean he will. Restraint is what separates the good ones from the bad."

"Is it?" she asked. "Does that apply to you?"

"It does," Elijah answered.

"Which side do you fall on?" she persisted. Clearly, she thought she knew the answer. "You didn't practice much restraint in Easton, did you?"

"I asked myself that same question," Elijah admitted, pulling away and pacing to the other side of the room. "And the only answer I came up with was that yes, I restrained myself. Do you know how I know that?"

Carmen shook her head.

"Because there were survivors," Elijah stated. Indeed, he'd wanted to kill every person in the city. His instincts screamed at him to do so. And failing that, at least everyone associated with the corrupt government Roman had created. But he hadn't. Sure, he'd killed thousands, but if he'd given in to his instincts, that number would have been in the tens of thousands. To him, that felt like restraint. Still, that did nothing to assuage his guilt. So, he said, "I'm going to find Miguel. I hope to leave tomorrow morning, if that's okay with you."

Then, without another word, he strode toward the door. He could feel Carmen's gaze following him the whole way, though.

29

A FITTING MEMORIAL

That night, Elijah didn't sleep much. Instead, he lay awake in his incredibly comfortable bed of moss, just staring up at the gently glowing flowers on his ceiling. Bioluminescence had always fascinated Elijah, but he knew that these particular flowers were powered not by a biological process but, rather, by ethera. Still, they were an interesting case that reminded him of just how magical his world had become.

But he wasn't thinking about that.

Instead, he found himself contemplating the future. Soon, he would completely lay Alyssa to rest. Her memory would remain with him always, but he expected that the project's completion would feel like shutting a door. After that, he would need to move on, both because he had other obligations as well as for his own mental well-being. It wouldn't do to dwell any longer.

What did the future hold, though?

Would he immediately set off for Seattle to uphold his end of the bargain he'd struck with Isaiah? Perhaps. Already, he'd delayed it for months, so there was no telling what he'd find when he returned to the embattled city. Hopefully, Lucy wouldn't pay the price for his procrastination.

In addition, he had other goals on his mind. First, he'd already resolved to investigate the storm that still persisted far out to sea. Something told him that it was important, though he didn't know precisely what form that importance might take. Then, he also needed to take care of his coffee, the cherries of which would ripen soon enough. That was probably the project he most looked forward to, but he also wanted to begin work on a new staff sometime in the near future. The Dragon-Touched Staff was a powerful piece of equipment, but it was incredibly one-dimensional. He expected he could do better, so long as he approached the project with the right attitude.

After that, he needed to test out his latest ability:

Ability: Debilitating Roar	Let out an enraged bellow that sends all nearby targets fleeing in fear, decreasing their damage by 15%. Increases caster's foot speed by 10%. Only usable when caster is under the influence of Shape of the Guardian. Duration based on Ethera attribute. Current duration: 9.2 seconds. Resistance based on target's Constitution attribute.

It was the ability he'd received at level eighty, and if Elijah was honest, he found the description a little disappointing. It was easy to conjure situations where it would be useful, but he'd hoped for something direct. Perhaps that would come at level eighty-five. He also hoped to start receiving some upgrades to his current spells sometime soon because abilities like Calamity and Storm's Fury had started to lose some of their efficacy, especially against anything his level. Even the attribute bonuses of his bestial transformations had begun to feel underwhelming.

Whatever the case, he needed a low-danger situation in which to test the new ability.

Finally, he knew that Miguel was quickly approaching the point where he would need to choose an archetype. When his nephew reached that stage, Elijah intended to make certain that the young man had every advantage he could provide, including help with his cultivation, high-grade equipment, and whatever guidance he could offer.

But underlying everything else was the knowledge that he needed to continue to progress. Lying in bed, he looked at his status:

Name	Elijah Hart
Level	81
Archetype	Druid
Class	Animist
Specialization	N/A
Alignment	N/A
Strength	85
Dexterity	81
Constitution	85
Ethera	90

Regeneration	84		
Attunement	Nature		
Cultivation Stage: Cultivator			
Body	Core	Mind	Soul
Stone	Hatchling	Quartz	Novice

In addition to the normal attributes he gained with each level, Elijah's arduous journey had also resulted in an additional two-point gain in both Strength and Constitution. That was a testament to what he'd put himself through. Given his already-high attributes, gaining anything outside of his automatic level allocation was incredibly difficult.

"Carrying tons of rock across hundreds of miles has its benefits, I guess," he muttered to himself before checking the power rankings:

Planetary Power Rankings (Earth)

Elijah Hart—Level 81
Oscar Ramirez—Level 79
Sadie Song—Level 76
Hu Shui—Level 74
Niko Song—Level 74
Davu Adebowale—Level 69
Anupriya Pandey—Level 67
Benedict Emerson—Level 61
Ram Khandu—Level 60
Gunnar Lindstrom—Level 59

. . .

. . .

. . .

Khadija Yatib—Level 51

Already, the other people at the top of the list had begun to close in on him, but that wasn't unexpected. They were all clearly driven, and just as obviously, they'd found favorable circumstances for leveling. However, what worried Elijah was the rest of the list. The person at the hundredth spot was level fifty-one, which was only eight levels from the top ten. Over the past couple of months, the average level of the top one hundred had risen quite a bit, indicating that the gap was beginning to close between those at the top and the ones at the bottom.

If Elijah didn't continue to progress, he could easily find himself in the bottom half of the list by the time the Trial of Primacy came. He still didn't know much about what it represented, but, given that name, he suspected it would be competitive. As such, he needed to take his own progression seriously, lest he pay for it when—or if—he participated in that event.

He made a mental note to investigate the Trial of Primacy as soon as he found an available Librarian who could guide his research. It joined a few other questions he intended to ask at some point. With everything going on, he didn't know when he'd get the opportunity to do what needed to be done. He was owed questions in Seattle and the elven city of Arvandor, so he just needed to take the time to travel to those locations and ask.

Another item to add to his list, he supposed.

Regardless, he had a full plate, and that wouldn't soon change. So, with that in mind, Elijah rose before the sun had even peaked over the horizon and went through his normal training routine. By the time he'd finished, morning had dawned, and he returned to the Grove to find that Miguel, Carmen, and Colt were already prepared for the coming day. All three wore packs not dissimilar from the first one he'd gotten back in Ironshore.

"All packed?" Elijah asked, using his staff as a walking stick as he approached.

"How long do you expect we'll be gone?" asked Carmen.

"At least a week. Probably closer to a month," he admitted. "You're all free to skip this part, but I thought it would be best if Carmen and Miguel had a hand in it."

Nobody even questioned why Colt would come along. He rarely ventured far from either Carmen's or Miguel's side. Likely, part of that was for protection, but Elijah could tell that the man considered them family.

"We're going," Carmen said.

"Alright. Give me a few minutes to shower and change. Then, we'll head out," he said.

After that, he did as he'd said, going to his tree house to shower, change, and grab everything he thought he might need. Once he'd stuffed it all into his Ghoul-Hide Satchel, he called out for Nerthus.

"You have those seeds we talked about earlier?" he asked.

Nerthus handed over a pouch, saying, "There is no guarantee that these will take root. The vines are a finicky sort."

"All I can do is try. This is important, though."

And it was. When one of the seeds was nestled safely in his satchel, Elijah returned to collect his family before once again asking if they were ready to go. Of course, Miguel had forgotten something, which he rushed off to gather, eliciting a groan from Carmen. When he returned, Elijah used Roots of the World Tree, opening a gate to the Dragon Circle outside of Argos.

After that, they made their way to the city. Miguel and Colt were both familiar enough with Argos, but Carmen had never been. As a result, she was suitably impressed by what she saw.

"Everyone here is so friendly . . ."

"Part of that is because of me," Elijah said. "I've spent a lot of time here, so most everyone recognizes me. But I also think it's because they're just good people."

"I was beginning to think that places like this couldn't survive in this new world," she said as they walked through the city.

"I don't think that's true. I visited another couple of places that were mostly okay," Elijah said. "I think that, for the most part, people are good. It's just that sometimes they run into a bad apple like Roman. Or those rich water-hoarding assholes in Seattle."

"So you think those places are the exception to the rule? Or is this the exception?"

"I don't know," Elijah admitted, running his hand through his hair. "Maybe the answer is that there isn't a rule. Maybe it's just a take-it-as-you-find-it sort of situation. Either way, Argos is a good place full of good people. That's why I chose to put the memorial here."

"Why not Ironshore?"

"We're human. Alyssa deserves to be remembered in a human settlement."

"It's not because they tried to kill you?" asked Carmen.

Elijah stopped. "You heard about that, huh?" he asked. "Which time?"

"Both. I'm surprised you didn't burn it all down," she said. "So were most of the people who live there."

"I thought about it," Elijah admitted. "But both times it was an isolated thing. I trust Ramik, but I still wonder what will happen when they figure out what's on my island. It's a tempting target."

"It is. But for what it's worth, I don't think any of them will invade your Grove anytime soon. They're terrified."

"They should be."

After that, they continued on, and after Elijah rented rooms for them at Agatha's hotel, they headed to the site of the monument. And it looked much as it had when Elijah had left it.

"It's huge," Carmen breathed.

Indeed, it was the size of a full-blown mansion, and it was made almost entirely from the stone Elijah had quarried. To him, it looked a lot like the Temple of Athena Nike in Athens, though with a few caveats. For one, the columns were carved in a spiral shape, with unadorned capitals. That would change as Elijah, Carmen, and the twin Sculptors went to work, but even now, the effect was elegant and straightforward in its simplicity.

The other major difference was the statue at the top of the building. Based on and incorporating pieces of the statue Elijah had carried out of Valoria, it was meant to depict an idealized version of Alyssa. The figure stood in a heroic pose, with her spear raised high and pointing toward the sky.

The final difference between the monument to Alyssa's memory and the ancient Athenian temple was that the new version had an expansive, open-air courtyard in its center. That was where Elijah intended to plant the ancestral-tree seed.

"Are you ready to get to work?" Elijah asked.

Carmen nodded. "I am."

To Miguel and Colt, Elijah said, "You're welcome to stick around, but you may get bored. Maybe explore the town a little. Meet some people. Eat some good food. I'm sure if you ask nicely, Isaak would show you around."

"I want to watch," Miguel said. "At least for today."

"Fine by me," Elijah said.

Then, he and the others climbed the steps—also made of that same white-and-green marble—to the monument. Once inside, Elijah spoke to Dion, the Builder, who told him that everything went exactly as planned. He eagerly took Elijah on a short tour, narrating as he went. "The temple is a true marvel. Do you feel the ethera wafting off the dragonstone?"

"Is that what it's called?" Elijah asked, surprised.

"Indeed. Very rare, the guides say. That we have a vein nearby bodes well for the city's future prosperity," Dion answered. "Ah—here are the rooms you asked for."

There were seven rooms in the building, all meant for housing. Other than that, there was another large chamber that played host to the unused remnants of Alyssa's statue. But Elijah didn't need to see that again, so he forwent visiting. Instead, he made his way to the central courtyard, where he planted the ancestral-tree seed.

Once he'd covered it up and summoned Healing Rain, he used Nature's Bounty. Then, to Carmen, he said, "You should go find the Sculptors. Penelope and Iason. Just look for two siblings who won't stop arguing and you'll find them."

"What are you going to do?"

"Grow a very special tree," Elijah said. "Then, we're going to have a party."

30

THE IMPORTANCE OF A GOOD HAT

Come on! Why can't I go with you?" demanded Miguel. "You always said that having someone to watch your back is important."

"This ain't that kinda city, kid," Colt said, running his hand through his short hair. He'd had the barber back in Ironshore cut it down to little more than a fringe, which was his preferred style. Easier to handle that way. "You heard your uncle. It's 'bout as safe a spot as there is. 'Sides—you need to venture out on your own a bit. Havin' me or your uncle hoverin' over your shoulder won't do you a bit of good. A boy needs his independence as much as he needs guidance."

Miguel looked like he was going to argue, but then the boy thought better of it. That was as expected. When Colt had first taken the young man under his wing, he'd been a bit unruly and very undisciplined. But he'd latched on to the structure Colt provided, his grip tightening even more after their exile.

That wasn't to say that Miguel never acted like the teenage boy he was. He certainly did, and often. But he'd learned that when Colt gave instructions, he expected them to be followed, and without complaint.

"Fine. Whatever," Miguel said. "Maybe Isaak can show me around."

"Maybe," Colt allowed. "But that ain't much different than havin' me or your uncle round."

Miguel glared at him.

Colt didn't waver, though. "And don't leave the city."

"But—"

"No buts, kid. It's dangerous out there. I heard stories about some kinda man-eater from a while back. Nobody ever killed it, either. It ain't hit nobody in a while, but that don't mean it ain't still out there. And somebody like you? Without levels? You make a juicy target for a monster like that."

"We should go back to the swamp," Miguel said. His cheeks reddened. "To check on the kids. You know, to make sure they're okay."

"The kids, huh?"

"Yeah. I thought we should've stayed until they had everything they needed. But Uncle Elijah said that he didn't want to influence their decision," the young man persisted. "By now, they had to've made a choice, though."

"That's the only reason you wanna go? To check on the kids."

"Uh . . . No. I think the swamp is . . . uh . . . cool. With all the mud and . . . leeches . . ."

"Right. Leeches. That's what all the kids're into these days, eh?"

"I'm not a kid," Miguel insisted. "I'll get my archetype any day now."

"Well, till you do, you're a kid," he said. Then, he shook his head and said, "Now go on. Git. Don't wanna see you till sunset at least. Go get into some trouble. Have a rock fight. Explore. Just be a kid. You ain't had much opportunity for that kinda thing since . . . well, since forever."

"Fine," Miguel huffed. "Can I at least take a sword, though?"

"Spear."

"But I don't like the spear!"

"That's all you get till you prove you can handle the sword," Colt said. In truth, Miguel had progressed exceedingly well with his swordsmanship, but Colt had high standards that the young man had yet to meet.

After that, Miguel only argued for a little longer before taking up the spear they'd brought with them, then leaving the hotel's common room behind. For his part, Colt glanced at the innkeeper, Agatha, and shrugged, saying, "Kids, right?"

"Don't have to tell me. My boys were a lot worse. At least he listens."

"Most of the time," Colt said with a chuckle as he leaned against the bar. Then, he reached up, intending to tip his hat to the elderly woman, but brought himself up short when he remembered that he still hadn't replaced the one he'd lost back in Easton. "Say, you don't know of a decent haberdasher round here, do you?"

"Haberdasher?"

"Hat maker," Colt explained. He gave her a tight smile, adding, "I seem to've misplaced my bonnet."

She answered, "Old Markakis is your best bet. He's got a fair few hats. Not sure if he makes them, but he's a Tailor."

After she gave him directions, Colt said, "Much obliged, ma'am."

Then, he departed from the hotel. Vaguely, he was aware of Miguel following him for a bit, but eventually, he left the boy behind. As he walked through the town, Colt was amazed at how normal it all seemed. There were plenty of cultural differences from any other place he'd ever been, but aside from those, it was remarkably similar to his hometown back in Oklahoma. Or, presumably, hundreds of other midsize towns throughout the world.

Argos was too big to be considered a town, though. If he'd had to guess, he would have said that it played host to at least a hundred thousand people. Maybe more. That was how most settlements were, from what he could tell. Anywhere that offered a modicum of safety attracted refugees like moths to a flame. The settlements that didn't grow usually ended up getting overrun.

Colt had seen plenty of evidence of that during their exile. And he sus-pected that more would fall everyday until everything normalized. But one thing was certain—the world wasn't getting any safer, and humanity needed to take its own progression seriously or there would be another culling not dis-similar from what had happened directly after Earth experienced the touch of the World Tree.

For his part, Colt was lucky. He'd always been a man of action. As a former soldier, he felt he was well suited to the new world, and his lifelong fascination with the art of Bushido had served him well with his Warrior archetype and the Samurai class that had followed.

However, he hadn't had a purpose until he'd reached Easton and found Alyssa. She'd shown him the good people were capable of, and he'd followed her willingly. After her death, he'd pledged himself to Carmen. And now, she'd become something of a little sister to him. After everything they'd experienced together, they were practically family.

But Colt knew that he needed to keep pushing forward. He was just outside the top one hundred, but that could be said for thousands of people. Maybe tens of thousands. It was especially necessary because, like everyone else, he'd gotten a notification a couple of months before:

> **Four years have passed since your planet (Earth) felt the transformative touch of the World Tree. In one year, the top five thousand (5,000) humans and top five hundred (500) settlers will be afforded the opportunity to endure the Trial of Primacy.**
>
> **Participation is not mandatory, though it is encouraged. In one (1) year, present yourself at any Branch of the World Tree and you will be teleported to the Trial Grounds.**
>
> **Prepare yourselves accordingly.**

He had a little less than ten more months to ensure that he would be eligible to go, and he intended to use every day to accomplish that goal. But first, he needed a proper hat. So, he followed Agatha's directions, eventually arriving at a small shop faced by large windows that displayed a series of mannequins dressed in all the latest fashions. Colt wasn't in the market for clothes, but he could admire the cut of the two suits on display.

He adjusted his coat, then stepped inside, his entry announced by the tin-kling of a bell. The interior of the shop was much as he would have expected. There were dozens of mannequins lining the wall, each one displaying the Tai-lor's wares. Colt also saw a few tables upon which were folded cheaper, less formal clothing like tee-shirts and blue jeans. Though his senses told him that, despite their modern appearance, the pieces were not mundane.

"How might I help you?" came a nasally voice from the back of the room. Colt's eyes quickly found the owner, who was a short, thin, and bespectacled man with a mop of brown hair.

"I'd be much obliged if you'd point me to your finest hats," Colt said with a crooked smile that he hoped was charming.

"Hats? I don't sell hats. Do you see any hats?"

"I do not," Colt admitted. "Bit new in town, if I'm honest. I was told you were my best bet."

"Well, I don't have any hats. Please leave."

"Surely the finest Tailor in the city could make one measly hat."

"I said I don't . . . Wait, who said I was the finest Tailor in the city?"

"Everyone says so," Colt stated.

"Perhaps I could be persuaded to take on a custom job," Markakis said.

Colt gave the man his warmest smile. Then, he retrieved a few silver coins from his pouch, saying, "Will this be persuasion enough?"

Markakis cleared his throat, then said, "Yes. I believe it will. Tell me, Mr. . . ."

"Colt."

"Mr. Colt, tell me—"

"It's just Colt. Ain't no *mister* attached."

"Right. Colt. Tell me what you require."

Miguel sat on the stoop, idly petting Artemis. The cat had found him the moment he'd left the inn, and she had followed him all the way to Isaak's house. Of course, the other young man wasn't around, which had thrown a bit of a wet blanket on Miguel's plans to enlist Isaak's help in finding something interesting to do. So, without any other ideas, Miguel had sat on the stoop in an effort to figure things out.

"He lost me on purpose," he said to the purring cat. The thing was the size of a Siberian husky, which made it the biggest cat Miguel had ever seen. However, the beast acted just like every other cat he'd ever met. "I know he did."

The cat purred in solidarity.

Or probably because she enjoyed the attention.

"He wouldn't have been able to if I had an archetype," he went on. "I saw the stuff Uncle Elijah could do, too. If I had those kinds of abilities, nobody would stop me from doing what I wanted."

But what did he want?

That was a question that had plagued him ever since he had met his uncle. Sure—Elijah had visited years ago, but those memories were hazy. By contrast, everything that had happened since Seattle was extremely vivid. Elijah was one of the most powerful people in the world. Everyone said that he was at the top of the power rankings that Miguel had never seen.

And he'd gone to Easton and killed Roman.

Nobody had said it outright, but Miguel could read between the lines. Elijah had set out to get revenge, and when he'd returned, the results were obvious.

That had robbed Miguel of purpose. For the entirety of their voyage across the wilderness, he'd imagined himself making Roman pay for what he'd done. He had dreamed of doing so in a thousand different ways, too. But now? That door was closed to him.

So, where did that leave him?

What purpose did he have?

Colt always said that a man needed a purpose, and now, Miguel had none.

He sighed, leaning back on the stoop, propping himself up with one elbow as he looked at the spear he held in his other hand. It wasn't even a Crude-grade weapon, which meant that it was next to useless against anything with any degree of power. However, it did have a durability enchantment on it, so at least it wouldn't snap at the first sign of strain.

"Mom used a spear," he said to the cat. "I mean, it's a good weapon. That's what Colt says. Better reach than a sword. Easier to use, too. It's what most armies used before guns and stuff. But it just doesn't feel right."

Or not completely right, he had to amend. He enjoyed training with all sorts of weapons, but none of them had really grabbed ahold of him. Miguel was at least self-aware enough to recognize that much of the reason he wanted to use a sword was because Colt used one. Otherwise, he felt no real connection to the weapon. The same was true of spears and axes, daggers and bows.

But he needed to learn to focus. Otherwise, he would never become a master with any particular weapon.

Just as he was starting to get lost in thought, he heard a scream from nearby. Instinctively, he shot to his feet and looked around for the source. He saw nothing, but another shout gave him some direction. So, without further thought, he grabbed his spear and sprinted toward the sound.

31

ALYSSA'S SON

Miguel raced down the empty street, spear in hand, as he heard another scream emanate from within the alley ahead. He skidded to a stop, turning to see three burly young men surrounding a small figure curled on the ground. The largest of the attackers aimed a kick at the victim, but he never had the chance to connect. Instead, Miguel barreled into him.

To Miguel, it felt like he'd just collided with a brick wall, but he was moving fast enough that he managed to send the unsuspecting young man stumbling into a nearby trash can. The impact sent garbage scattering across the alley. The would-be attacker tripped over the can, ending up sprawled on the trash-strewn ground.

Meanwhile, Miguel planted, then swept his spear around to trip the next nearest young man. Once again, it felt like he'd hit a telephone pole, but the inertia of his swing knocked the feet out from under the enemy. Finally, Miguel aimed a front kick at the last assailant, who turned out to be a tall, rangy girl. The blow took her in the stomach, and she stumbled backward, gasping for air.

Miguel set his feet over the fallen figure, then leveled his spear, shifting it from one opponent to the next.

"Don't," he spit, the deadly blade hovering only a few inches from the first bully's face. "I swear to God, if you do what I think you're about to do, I'll rip out your throat. You're a Warrior, right? That means you probably have Heavy Blow active. That means you're getting ready to activate Shock Wave. Don't. I'll kill you before it charges up."

"You won't get us all," said the girl. "I'll roast you before you—"

"That makes you a Sorcerer, then. Ethereal Bolt, right? You know how quickly I can impale you with this spear? Less than a second. I know because it wouldn't be my first time. Your little spell won't mean much when you've got a foot of steel in your belly," Miguel stated, his voice calm despite the hammering of his heartbeat.

He flicked his eyes toward the young man who'd been his second victim. He'd landed hard, banging his head on the ground. It hadn't knocked him unconscious, but it had clearly dazed him. That meant he was a low-Constitution archetype. Probably a Ranger, but he could just as easily have been a noncombatant. Maybe one of the rare ones. Miguel didn't think he was a Healer, though. If he was, then he'd have already mended his budding concussion.

"This doesn't have anything to do with you!" growled the Warrior.

"Seems like it has plenty to do with me," Miguel said, staying on the balls of his feet, just like he'd been taught. It wasn't so different from when he'd played soccer before Earth had been touched by the World Tree. He needed to be ready to move at the slightest provocation. "I can't stand by and let you beat someone up three on one."

"We got a hero over here," said the girl with a snort. "You think you're some kind of fairy-tale knight? Prince Charming, maybe?"

Miguel didn't rise to the taunt, instead keeping himself ready for battle. He didn't want to kill anyone, but if it came down to it, he wouldn't hesitate. While some of his sharp edges had been filed down over the past few months of relative peace, the mindset that had seen him through the journey across the wilderness wasn't buried so deep that it wouldn't return at the slightest provocation.

"Just leave," he said after a moment. "Call it a draw. You go your way, I'll go mine."

"That little bitch deserves to—"

Just then, a loud meow came from the head of the alley. Miguel's eyes flicked in that direction, and he almost grinned when he saw Artemis standing there. She didn't look particularly intimidating—not to Miguel at least—but he knew she was a deadly predator. Clearly, the trio of bullies knew that, as well, because the moment they laid eyes on the giant Maine coon, they paled.

"W-what . . . the . . . Is that your cat?"

"She's a friend," Miguel said. "Just leave. She won't attack. Not unless she has to."

That did the trick. The three bullies quickly regained their feet and raced out of the alley. Miguel found it amusing how they pressed their backs against the wall so they wouldn't have to get any closer to Artemis than absolutely necessary. Once they were gone, the cat sat and started grooming herself. She'd never even made a threatening move, but the danger she represented was enough to send those bullies running.

Elijah could do the same when he wanted. Sure—he usually didn't, instead preferring to wear a friendly mask. But Miguel had seen a few flashes of the man beneath.

The same was true of Colt.

And his mother. Both of them, really. Carmen was only a Blacksmith, but she was made of sterner stuff than most Warriors.

That was what Miguel wanted. Not because he intended to bully people into submission but, rather, because he knew he'd need the power it represented. If he was strong enough, then nobody would dare mess with him or his family.

Once he was sure the bullies were gone, Miguel finally turned around to get a good look at the person he'd saved. She was tiny—well under a hundred pounds—and looked like she was made of skin and bones. What's more, a good chunk of her black hair had been ripped out, leaving only a bloody scalp behind, and most of the skin Miguel could see was purpled with bruising.

He knelt beside her, saying, "It's okay. They're gone."

Suddenly, her eyes opened, and she lunged at him. Miguel managed to fend her off, mostly because her outburst only lasted a second before her strength gave out. But even as she collapsed to the ground, he knew he needed to help her. So, he tossed his spear aside, scooped her in his arms, and lifted.

After that, Miguel turned and strode out of the alley. His burden wasn't particularly heavy, so he managed a decent enough pace as he headed toward the temple—or monument—Elijah had built for Alyssa.

As he did, he got more than a few odd looks from the people he passed along the way. He had no idea why none of them bothered to help, but he couldn't let that distract him.

With her eyes closed, Carmen ran her hand over the surface of the column, feeling for any imperfections. She didn't particularly care for working with stone, but she'd taken to the project with gusto. After all, the entire building was meant to honor her wife. What sort of person would she be if she didn't give it her all?

Idly, she glanced toward the courtyard. There, Elijah sat cross-legged beside a sapling. It looked little different from any other juvenile oak tree she'd ever seen. However, even she could feel the deeply powerful ethera coursing through its thin branches. Would it end up being a natural treasure? Or was it something else entirely? She had seen the other tree in Druid's Park, and she was very familiar with their progenitor in Elijah's Grove. Yet, she still had difficulty understanding how they were all connected.

But she knew they were.

She could feel it as well as she could feel the enchantments in her own creations. And then there was the stone Elijah had found. Fittingly, given his Core, it was called dragonstone, and it seemed just as perfect for a monument meant to commemorate Alyssa's life.

Sighing, she focused on the structure itself. The inner courtyard was lined with columns, which she had spent the past day carving. The two Sculptors, Penelope and Iason, had initially objected to her participation, but then they had discovered her level. They'd come around pretty quickly after that, and Carmen had endeavored to justify their acquiescence ever since.

She leaned in with her summoned chisel, continuing her work. The design was simple enough, meant to represent a dragon coiled around each column, but that simplicity didn't make it any easier to carve. Everything needed to be perfect, which necessitated a certain degree of focus. On top of that, she had to continuously flare her technique Imbue Enchantment the entire time. Otherwise, the product would suffer.

More than once, she'd wished the columns had been made of some sort of high-quality metal. It would have made for an inferior building, but it would have been much easier for her to work.

"Can't have everything, I suppose," she mumbled to herself, continuing her exhausting labor.

Just as she'd finished carving the scales on one coil, Carmen heard a disturbance near the entrance of the temple. Immediately, she cut off the ability and summoned her hammer. It wasn't meant to be a weapon of war, but her summoned blacksmithing hammer did the job well enough that she hadn't bothered creating another weapon. After it manifested, she used Augment Weapons, and it burst into flame.

"Just let me through!" she heard Miguel's voice. "Uncle Elijah! I need your help!"

Before Carmen could even respond, Elijah was moving. He raced across the courtyard, and when he hit the steps leading to the exit, his feet slapped against the dragonstone floor. Carmen followed close behind him, and when she saw her son, she let out a sigh of relief.

"What's going on here?" Carmen demanded as she closed in on the young man. He was holding a child in his arms.

"Set her down," Elijah said, noticing what it took Carmen another moment to recognize. The child was battered and malnourished, and to a degree that pulled at Carmen's heartstrings.

Elijah knelt beside her, then laid his hand on her shoulder. A second later, she gasped, bolting upright. Or she tried to. Elijah's hand kept her in place as he said, "Stay still. I'm not done healing you."

"W-what . . . Where am I? What is this place?" she gasped in a surprisingly deep voice. It was still feminine, but the raspy sound didn't fit such a young girl.

"Never mind that. How about you tell me what happened?" Elijah coaxed.

"She was getting beaten up by three people who had archetypes," Miguel provided. "I saw . . . and . . . well, I couldn't just let them keep going."

"I see," Elijah said.

Carmen focused on the girl and asked, "Why did they attack you?"

"It's nothing," the girl said, trying to rise. "I just—"

"Answer the question," Elijah stated. He reached into his satchel and retrieved one of his miraculous berries. "And I'll give you one of these."

"But don't eat it all at once or it'll knock you out," Miguel supplied.

"Right. Low attributes," Elijah muttered. "Better make it a half, then. That should be enough."

The girl clearly didn't know what to do, and her eyes flicked back and forth from Elijah to Miguel, then to Carmen and the pair of men who'd been tasked with standing guard at the entrance. They were part of Dion's Builder crew, and they were meant to prevent any of the local population from walking off with the valuable dragonstone.

"I . . . I tried to take . . . uh . . . something that wasn't quite mine," the girl admitted with a defeated sigh. "But it wasn't my fault. They took it first."

"Took what?" asked Elijah.

"My dad's ring. I told them it wasn't valuable, but they didn't care. They took everything else, too," the girl breathed. "It wasn't much. But if it's gone when my brother gets back . . ."

"Where is your brother?"

"Running the tower," she said. "He's an adventurer. He keeps saying that he's going to strike it rich, but I think he's just looking for a way out of Argos. He wants to get strong enough to go to a bigger city and . . . and . . . every time he leaves, people like Nikolas and Gabby come around. I tried to fight them, but . . . but I don't have an archetype yet. And . . . And . . ."

By that point, she'd started sobbing.

Elijah awkwardly patted her on the head, saying, "There, there."

"Elijah."

"What?"

Carmen shook her head, saying, "You're terrible at this. Are you done healing her?"

"Sure. She's pretty malnourished, though."

"Well, give her the berry," Carmen said. "Then let me take over."

Elijah shrugged, saying, "Be my guest. I have a tree to tend to anyway." Then, he muttered something about trees being easier. Whatever the case, he handed the berry over, then left the area.

"What's your name?" Carmen asked, helping the girl to her feet. She was skin and bones, evidence of the hard life she had led. Whoever her brother was, he had failed to do his job of providing for his sister. "And where are your parents?"

"Dead."

"Oh. I'm sorry," Carmen said with a shake of her head.

"Happened a while ago," the girl answered, her shoulders drooping dramatically.

Then, without warning, she disappeared. It actually took Carmen a moment to recognize that she'd used some sort of ability. And that the coin purse she kept tied to her belt was missing.

"What the . . . What the hell just happened?" she muttered.

"That was so cool," Miguel breathed, looking around as if he was going to find the girl. But Carmen felt certain that she was long gone. How she'd done it was a bit of a mystery—clearly, she was a little more developed than she seemed—but, beyond that, Carmen had no idea what had happened.

She sighed.

"That was definitely not cool," she said. "Not cool at all."

32

COMPLETION

Better hope he doesn't find that little girl," Elijah said with a shake of his head. "That's trouble if I've ever seen it."

"Not really a little girl, is she? She's old enough to have an archetype. And a class. None of the archetypes I know of have skills that help people steal," Carmen said.

"She couldn't have been more than fourteen or fifteen," Elijah countered. "Plus, you saw her, right? I think *little girl* is an appropriate description."

After the thief had disappeared, Miguel had left the build site to hunt the girl down. Elijah wasn't sure if he was driven by admiration, attraction, or anger—all three were valid emotions for the boy—but he could tell that Miguel wasn't going to give up until he'd searched every corner of Argos. It was almost endearing how enthusiastically he'd taken to his chosen task.

"Do you think there's a Thief class?" Carmen asked, standing beside Elijah and staring down the small hill upon which the would-be temple sat. "That's kind of scary, if you think about it. People who specialize in taking things that don't belong to them? What if someone chose that class just because it was the best they had available? Are they doomed to go down that path?"

Elijah shook his head. "No. Everything I've heard says that we get multiple chances to correct our progression," he said. "Like you, for instance. I'd be willing to bet that you'll get a chance to evolve your Blacksmith class into something else. Maybe a more generic crafter. You don't have to take it. There'll be more direct evolutions, too. But those are all meant to help you refine and customize your class to something that fits what you want to become."

"Interesting. You know, when we first started, I thought this system was kind of simple. But then I started to see just how many classes there were," Carmen mused. "Now, even those seemingly infinite classes will have multiple offshoots. And I'm guessing even more than that the higher people go."

"And that's not even considering specializations," Elijah said. "I don't really know much about them, but I think that's what I'm going to ask about the next time I get to a Branch."

"There's one here," Carmen reminded him.

"But no Librarian. Looking for information in that Knowledge Base without any guidance is like . . ."

"Finding a needle in a haystack while blindfolded."

"And wearing gloves," Elijah added.

"With a time limit."

"Something like that," he said with a chuckle. It felt good just having a regular conversation that didn't revolve around Alyssa's death or what he'd done in Valoria. It was almost normal. But in the back of his mind, his guilt continued to roil. Hopefully, completing the temple—because that was what it had turned out to be, regardless of his initial intention—would help him move on.

Because he knew just how unhealthy it was to constantly dwell on the past.

"Do you think he'll be okay?" Carmen asked.

Elijah didn't need her to specify the subject. In truth, he didn't know the answer to her question. The world was a dangerous place, and one where even the competent could fall at any given moment. Elijah intended to give his nephew every opportunity he could, though.

"I hope so," he answered. "I've already talked to Nerthus about guiding Miggy's cultivation, at least for the first step. It'll take a lot of energy, especially if he's not nature attuned. But he'll reach the first step in Body, Mind, and Soul cultivation before he gets a single level. The Core will be more difficult, and it'll take a lot of time."

Indeed, Elijah had skipped a step by having his Core advanced by the quest to rescue Sara the dragon. Most people had to engage in some variant of his current cycling. The first step was much easier than the second, but it was still a process that usually took months. On top of that, its efficacy would be much lower than his own Dragon Core's—unless a member of some other elder race descended and gave Miguel a similar opportunity, which didn't seem likely.

He asked, "How are you doing with cultivation?"

Carmen shook her head. "Poorly. My attunement is creation. I haven't found an appropriate environment yet."

"Have you thought about making one?" asked Elijah.

"What?"

"I mean, take this temple, for instance," he said. "You feel how thick the ethera is in here, don't you?"

"Yeah. It feels a lot like your island. Or more like Druid's Park."

"But what if it didn't?"

"Not following."

"Imagine this. You get a bunch of this dragonstone. Like, enough to build a whole smithy. You gather a ton of that metal Carisa and her dwarves are pulling out of that mine," Elijah said. "Then, you refine it all before building that forge. Something big and impressive, with all the best materials you can find. Put your stamp on everything. Enchant every block. Make it yours. I'm willing to bet that will give you the environment you need to advance your cultivation."

Then, he added, "Probably your apprentices, too." He gestured to the half-finished building behind them. "This place is meant to be a monument to Alyssa. But what if it was dedicated to smithing? Crafting? I've thought a lot about this, and I think that's how people normally do it. Like, if your attunement is conflict, maybe you go to a battlefield. If it's nature, you go to a natural treasure or something like my Grove. That sort of thing."

Carmen was silent for a moment before she said, "That makes a lot of sense."

Elijah grinned. "I do that sometimes. Make sense, I mean. It's not just all crazy ramblings all the time for me," he said. "I can be serious, too. Once upon a time, I was a scientist, you know."

"A bad one, from what I hear."

"Well, yes. But I did do science. That has to count for something."

She shook her head. "Do science? I don't think that's the right way to say it."

He shrugged. "It gets the point across. Anyway—I need to get back to the tree. It's not quite at the point where it can thrive on its own," he said. "Plus, I want to make sure everything grows the way I want it to grow."

"Can you guide it like that?" Carmen asked.

Elijah shrugged. "Sort of. I'm getting better at controlling things," he said. Indeed, his time in the courtyard hadn't been idly spent. In the past, he'd simply sat in the middle of his Grove and flared Nature's Bounty as well as One with Nature. However, with the temple courtyard, he'd chosen to experiment a little while he tried to encourage some aspects of growth while discouraging others.

His inspiration was, of course, Nerthus. The spyrggent could guide growth in the Grove right down to the last detail. It wasn't artificial like a man-made garden, but it certainly wasn't wild, either. Elijah felt that figuring all of that out was the key to understanding the nurturing aspect of his archetype.

So far, his efforts in the temple had felt clumsy, but they had borne some small fruit, as well. Of course, he knew he still had a long way to go, but so long as he made some progress, he was happy.

With that in mind, he completed his conversation with Carmen and returned to the courtyard. It looked very different than it had in the beginning. Instead of bare ground, it now sported thick grass, juvenile bushes, and vines—which had sprouted from the seeds Elijah had gotten from Nerthus—that had begun to snake around the finished columns. However, instead of hiding the results of Carmen's efforts, those vines accentuated the serpentine nature of her carved dragons, making them look alive.

But that was only the beginning.

Elijah had taken more than a few cues from Nerthus's design sensibilities, and he'd incorporated them into the project. Hopefully, it would turn out like the picture he held in his imagination. Or failing that, at least it would come close.

The tree in the center of the courtyard was only a sapling, but he knew from experience just how quickly it could grow to maturity. Eventually, it would tower above the building, covering the roof with its branches.

But that would take months.

Perhaps years.

The ancestral tree in his Grove hadn't reached that point until after he'd made contact with Ironshore, and that was with the benefit of the thick ethera in the Grove. The offshoots would take longer.

That was okay, though. Trees functioned on their own timelines, after all.

So, Elijah paced around the courtyard, constantly flaring his abilities as he physically guided the growth of the vines. In the past, he might have considered it tedious, but there was a certain comfort in gardening that he'd never before felt. Perhaps that was his archetype at work. Or his attunement. But it could just as easily be the personality changes he'd experienced over the past few years. Some of that was prompted by Earth's transformation, but a lot could be chalked up to simple maturity.

Back in Hawaii, he'd yet to fully embrace adulthood. But he'd grown quite a lot since then.

"Over thirty years old, and I'm just now considering myself an adult," he muttered to himself with a shake of his head.

Like that, days passed. When he needed rest, Elijah slept. When he needed to eat, he descended into the city and found something delicious. At times, he reminisced with Carmen or spoke with Miguel about his future. He even got to know Colt, who seemed to have, at some point, picked up a truly impressive cowboy hat. It fit him well, especially with the armor Elijah had returned to him.

But most of all, Elijah focused on guiding the courtyard's and the tree's growth. Meanwhile, Carmen bent the whole of her focus toward carving each of the columns. Sometimes, Elijah heard her muttering about enchantments and intent, but he only understood about half of what she said. And even that didn't make a lot of sense to him. Regardless, she seemed completely engrossed in the project, which he considered a very good thing.

And finally, Miguel continued to search for the little thief. A few times, Elijah noticed that the young man had picked up a few scrapes or bruises, but he'd pointedly looked the other way on those occasions. So did Carmen, recognizing that Miguel wasn't truly injured. More, she clearly knew that the search was good for him, even if she and Elijah both knew that it would likely end in frustration.

Still, Elijah would only worry about that if it proved necessary. For now, Miguel wasn't in any real danger, so Elijah focused on his task.

And slowly, things took shape. Even as Elijah and Carmen worked on the courtyard, the Builders and Sculptors hammered the rest of the temple into shape. Once the structure itself was finished, they started working on the hill, creating a terraced slope through which a set of broad steps were cut.

Those terraces bore more flora, though not of the sort that Elijah would grow. Instead, the landscaping was mostly mundane, though Elijah did take a day or two to ensure that everything took root before returning to his true project.

And after almost three weeks of work, once Carmen had finished her carvings, Elijah deemed the courtyard to be finished. With a sigh, he took a step back and looked everything over.

"Do you think it's done?" asked Carmen, standing next to him.

Elijah closed his eyes and felt the ambient ethera. It was thick, though not nearly as dense as what he'd find even in Ironshore. But that was predictable. Once the ancestral-tree sapling connected to its progenitor, the ethera would grow denser. Either way, Elijah was more concerned with how it felt.

There was plenty of nature there. But there was something else that he couldn't quite identify. Something that felt, for lack of a better way to put it, like Alyssa. He couldn't put his finger on exactly what that meant, but he knew it to be true.

"I think so," he said, opening his eyes.

The moment the words left his mouth, a new notification flashed before his inner eye. When he read it, he couldn't stop the sad smile from turning up the corners of his mouth.

"You got it, too, didn't you?" Carmen asked.

"I did."

"This is what you had in mind, isn't it?"

"It is. She deserves it," Elijah said. "There's more to it, though. Now that the temple is finished, I intend to make an announcement to the people of Argos."

"We should throw a party," Carmen said. "A feast. A huge banquet."

"That was kind of what I had in mind," Elijah said. "Alyssa always hated parties, though."

Carmen shook her head. "You didn't know her as well as you thought you did. Or maybe she just grew up."

"That's . . . fair. I wish I had spent more time with her. But—"

"This isn't the time for regrets," Carmen said. "This is a time for celebration. Of her life. Of what she stood for. That's what this is all about, right? Honoring the person she was. Don't let your regrets stain it."

Elijah wanted to argue that he had every right to give voice to his issues. However, it only took one look at the notification for him to swallow his selfish words. Instead, he just said, "You're right. A party would be nice."

33

DEDICATION

Elijah stepped up to the edge of the stairs and looked down at the crowd that had gathered at the base of the terraced hill. There were more than a thousand people present, many of whom were Argos's most influential leaders. The council was there, as were the most prominent merchants, tradespeople, and farmers. He cleared his throat, then once again glanced at the notification he'd received upon the temple's completion:

Congratulations! You have created a unique structure, Temple of Virtue.
Overall Grade: Complex
Enchantment Grade: D

Temple of Virtue. A fitting name if Elijah had ever seen one. Certainly, that exemplified the life Alyssa had tried to lead. She was as moral a person as any Elijah had ever met, and she'd died because she had refused to remain quiet while others suffered. She had stood for justice and compassion, which made the monument they'd created in her honor feel appropriate.

Finally, Elijah raised his voice, using his immense attributes to augment the volume: "Thank you all for coming. It means a lot to see so many people here." He took a deep breath. "I know none of you knew Alyssa, but I chose Argos for this temple because, in my experience, the people of this city exemplify the same traits she held dear. You treated me well even though I was a stranger, and when disaster struck, you banded together to help one another. My sister would have felt at home here, and so do I."

He looked from one face to another. Each and every person there had lost people. Everyone on Earth had. Whether they'd lost family, friends, neighbors, or coworkers, few had managed to pass through the crucible that was Earth's transformation unscathed. So, they could all sympathize with his loss. As such, Elijah saw more than a few wet cheeks.

"But this temple isn't just about Alyssa. It's about everyone we've lost. A celebration of their lives that will endure long after we're all gone," Elijah went on.

"For now, though, let it be a place of healing. From now on, I'll do everything I can to visit every four weeks, and I'll remain here for a day while I heal anyone who comes to this temple. I invite other Healers to do the same. There will be no charge. No donations accepted. This is a service provided so that we can honor the friends and family we've all lost."

Elijah pointed to the temple, adding, "In there, we're all equal. I don't care about status, strength, or social standing. I won't ask questions how you were injured. I will simply heal you, and with a smile on my face.

"But for now, I will be hosting a celebration of my sister's life. Food. Music. A good time," he went on. "That's it. Let's have a party."

For a moment, no one responded, but thankfully, someone took pity on him and started clapping. That turned into a smattering of applause, which in turn fostered cheers. For his part, Elijah just sighed and glanced at Carmen.

"Good speech," she said. "Up until the end, at least. How did you screw up telling people that you were paying for an enormous banquet? Usually, announcing that you're giving away food and alcohol for free gets a better response."

Elijah shrugged. "I don't like public speaking," he said, which was true. The only reason he'd agreed to speak at all was because he felt that he owed it to his sister. And because the people of Argos knew him. "Was it really that bad?"

"It wasn't good," she said with a smile. "But it's fine. By the time people get into that alcohol you brought, nobody will remember your horrible speech."

"Horrible? I thought you said it just wasn't good."

"Horrible isn't good."

"Yeah, but it's implied that—"

"It was acceptable. Just leave it at that, Elijah."

Elijah sighed, but he chose not to press the point. Instead, he scanned the crowd. A few people had stepped forward to be healed, so he wasted no time before tending to them. Meanwhile, the rest of the crowd descended upon the town's central square, where all the food and alcohol Elijah had furnished had been set up.

The food wasn't difficult. All he'd had to do was spend a couple of days hunting, and he had enough meat to feed the entire town. It was amazing just how efficiently he could stalk and kill large prey animals, and in fact, it was so easy that he almost felt guilty about the act. The only solace was that he knew that nothing would go to waste.

The alcohol had been a bit more difficult to source, and it had required him to teleport to the Moon Glade and meet with the Distiller in Valosta. He'd proceeded to overpay for the man's entire stock of beer and whiskey. It had cost Elijah far more than he wanted to think about, but he knew better than most just how essential a little booze was for a decent party.

Even with those efforts, it hadn't been enough, so he'd also bought everything he could from Argos's local Brewers. They were low level, and their products weren't great, but Elijah didn't think anyone would care so much, considering it was free.

In addition, the locals chose to pitch in with a host of vegetables that rounded out the food offerings. A handful of people with cooking skills had offered their services, as well, which held no small degree of importance. After all, without those skills, even the highest-quality ingredients would be largely tasteless to anyone with a class.

Finally, Elijah had hired some people with Entertainer archetypes to play music in the square. It wasn't really to his taste, trending more toward twangy acoustic sets, but the upbeat music definitely gave the event a festive atmosphere.

After healing the petitioners, Elijah and Carmen led a few of Argos's leaders through the temple, showing them the highlights. The first one they saw was the building itself, which still bore the signs of its inspiration. At the most basic level, it looked like an enlarged version of the Temple of Athena Nike, though the exterior columns had been decorated with fanciful carvings of noble warrior women. In addition, the pediment bore a relief sculpture of a winged angel fighting against a host of demons.

The exterior carvings were all the products of Iason and Penelope, and though they'd gone in a different direction than Elijah would have chosen, he couldn't argue with the effectiveness of their work. Bringing it all together was the huge statue at the peak of the roof.

In a lot of ways, it looked like Alyssa. Or perhaps the idealized version of her that Elijah remembered. It had been based on the broken statue he'd brought back from Valoria, though every aspect had been improved. From the material—it was made of dragonstone—to the workmanship itself, it was a far superior piece, depicting an armored woman, armed with a spear and standing vigil over everything beneath her.

"It doesn't really look like her," Carmen said. "But it still feels like her."

"I know. I was just thinking the same thing," Elijah said, looking up at the statue. "Do you think she would have approved?"

Carmen snorted. "God, no. She would have been embarrassed by the kind of adulation that statue implies."

Elijah's heart briefly jumped into his throat, but then he let out a chuckle himself. "Yeah. She would have been, wouldn't she?" he agreed.

After that, they continued into the building, showing the Argos natives the series of rooms arranged throughout the temple. They were intended for housing and healing, but they could be used for other purposes, as well. Elijah hadn't thought too much about what those other purposes might end up being, but thankfully, no one put him on the spot by asking that most obvious of questions.

Finally, they reached the open-air courtyard, which drew quite a few gasps.

That was definitely satisfying, especially given how much work had gone into the project. The centerpiece was the ancestral tree, which had grown to a little over ten feet tall. It was barely more than a sapling, but even then, it radiated a sense of calm and power that could not be denied. Even if that was the end of the wonders, it would have been quite effective. However, it was only the beginning.

Surrounding that juvenile tree was a carpet of clovers, broken up by periodic bushes from which blossomed aromatic flowers that gave the whole courtyard an exceedingly sweet smell.

Elijah had intended to put a fountain in, but he hadn't really thought about it until the Builders had already finalized the structure. So, instead of forcing them to redo their work, he'd adjusted his plans. And the results were just as stunning as he'd hoped, with the courtyard radiating unmatched serenity.

However, what made the whole thing seem truly magical were the columns lining the square space. They were around twenty feet tall, and Carmen had carved each one with subtly different coiling dragons. More, Elijah had guided a series of vines to grow along the same pattern, giving the columns depth they otherwise would have lacked. The final detail, though, was the one that pushed it to another level.

From those vines sprouted gently glowing flowers—the same kind that provided illumination in his and his sister-in-law's tree houses—casting the whole courtyard in ethereal light that made the dragonstone columns look alive.

"This is unlike anything I have ever witnessed, my friend," said Atticus.

"Beautiful," agreed Agatha, and a chorus of similar comments followed.

"Thank you. The Temple of Virtue will be open to anyone who wants to use it," Elijah stated. "But I'll say this—if I come back here and find that it has been vandalized in any way, I won't spare the perpetrators my wrath. I don't want to have to do that, so please, try to protect this place when I'm not here."

Afterwards, the group of leaders all agreed to do just that. Elijah wasn't sure how they all knew just how dangerous he was, but they seemed to take his words very seriously. Either way, it wasn't long after that that everyone descended from the temple and headed to the town's large square to take part in the party.

For a while, Elijah walked among them. He ate a little, drank a bit, and even danced. But as much as he wanted the festival to be a celebration of his sister's life—and it was—his heart wasn't really in it. He wanted to be happy, to remember all the good times he'd shared with his sister, but the reality of it was that grief didn't always cooperate with those sorts of desires.

So, he eventually found himself sitting on an isolated bench, well away from all the rowdy merrymakers, and thinking about the past, the present, and the future.

Until, via One with Nature, he felt a familiar presence nearby.

He didn't even look up as he said, "Hey there, Delilah."

She didn't immediately respond. Instead, she just sat beside him and, for a while, remained silent. Out of the corner of his eye, Elijah saw that she'd forgone her normal armor. Instead, she wore a simple pair of blue jeans and a tee-shirt. He wasn't sure which one he preferred. Perhaps the answer was that it didn't matter what she was wearing. She made anything look good.

"Are you okay?" she asked.

Elijah considered making a joke. Or going off on some tangent-laden response. But for once, he marshaled his self-control and said, "I don't know. Maybe. Probably not."

"Do you want to talk about it?"

Elijah leaned against the bench, tilting his head back with a sigh. "Not really," he admitted. "There's not much to say. I'm sad, and I don't think there's anything I can do to change that. And I don't really want to, either. That's normal, right? I should be upset that my sister's dead."

The last word was difficult to force out. It was like saying it aloud made it feel more real. Of course, he knew Alyssa wasn't just going to magically show up and tell everyone that she'd never really been dead. That wasn't how the world worked. Dead was dead.

But grief and reason didn't always play well together.

"Being sad is normal, yes," Delilah said. "But you don't have to go through it alone."

"You know—I kind of hoped that building that temple would make me feel better," he said. "Like, it would let me turn a corner and go back to normal. That's not how it works, though. I look at that thing, and even though I still believe in its purpose, it's just a reminder of what I've lost. Of what Carmen has lost. And Miggy."

"What's even worse is that I've been through all of this before," he went on, finally turning to face Delilah. "Like, I lost my parents a while back. I didn't react well to that, either. I hoped that maybe I learned my lesson. Practice is supposed to make perfect, right? I guess it just doesn't work that way with grief."

For her part, Delilah could read the situation well enough that she didn't respond. Elijah didn't want someone to rationalize his feelings. He didn't want someone to make it better. He just needed someone to listen to it all.

And Delilah did.

For more than an hour, Elijah just let off a stream-of-consciousness-style rundown of everything on his mind. It ranged from grief to depression and back to hope, with everything in between. And to her credit, Delilah listened.

Eventually, Elijah pushed himself to his feet and said, "I think I'm going to go for a long walk."

"You don't want to come back to my place?" she asked.

Elijah shook his head. "Not that kind of night," he said. Then, he flashed a smile and added, "Rain check, though. If you're lucky, I might even take you back to my magic island one day."

Without another word, he padded away, his thoughts swirling with a myriad of emotions he didn't know what to do with.

34

BECOME USEFUL

Miguel slipped between two revelers, keeping his hand on his dagger. He really wished he'd brought his spear, but according to his mother, that wasn't appropriate for a festival. As if half the people in the square weren't armed. Even Colt had his sword in the scabbard at his hip, and nobody had tried to convince him to leave the weapon back in the hotel room.

As those thoughts shifted through his mind, Miguel's eyes flicked back and forth at the merrymakers. Most of Argos had turned out for the festival, which wasn't surprising, given the fact that there was free food available. And alcohol, though Miguel didn't care about that. He'd tasted beer a couple of times, and the taste had left him wondering why adults seemed so enamored with the stuff.

The food did smell amazing, though, and Miguel's feet followed his nose to a table where a bunch of skewers were on offer. He took one, thanking the woman behind the table, and wandered away before she could make conversation. However, after taking his first bite, he very nearly turned around and went back for seconds. The skewer featured roasted pork and peppers, and it was one of the tastiest things he'd ever eaten. The meat was juicy, the peppers were crisp, and everything had that something extra that Miguel could identify as the result of someone's use of a cooking skill.

Still, he kept going, eating his meal as he went. Along the way, he watched the crowd of Argos residents. They all looked so happy. So content. Meanwhile, Miguel felt the opposite. He'd thought that he'd gotten over his mother's death, but the reality was that he'd simply distracted himself from those feelings. Now, though, he had plenty of opportunity to examine his emotions, and that act had pushed him into a melancholy mood.

He had to admit that part of it was due to the revelers themselves. He was old enough to recognize his mother's and uncle's intent. They wanted to celebrate Alyssa's life. Yet, Miguel found the party somewhat offensive, and he felt—erroneously, he knew—that the people were celebrating his mother's death. That was a big distinction, and one he couldn't really ignore, even if he knew it was an unfair assessment.

After he'd finished the skewer, Miguel found another table manned by the old innkeeper, Agatha. She waved him over and said, "I have something special for you. Just wait."

Then, she reached under the table—which was laden with fruit—and retrieved a small wrapped package. She handed it to Miguel.

"What is it?" he asked.

"Open," Agatha answered with an impatient gesture. She grinned. "It is good."

Miguel did as she asked, revealing a small rectangular pastry. Upon inspection, he saw that it featured many flaky layers, and it smelled of chocolate. "This looks amazing. What is it called?" he asked, genuinely interested. He hadn't had many opportunities lately to eat sweets, so he wasn't going to waste one that presented itself so willingly.

"Chocolate mascarpone baklava," she answered with a grin. "Very rich. Very good. Eat."

Miguel nodded, then took a bite. Immediately, flavors he thought he'd forgotten burst in his mouth. It had been years since he'd had chocolate, but even then, he'd never had anything like the baklava. "Oh my God," he mumbled around the mouthful of flaky goodness. "So good."

"Yes. Very good," she said, her grin widening. "Send your uncle to me. I have more."

Miguel promised that he would, though he had no idea where Elijah was. Even if he did know of his uncle's whereabouts, he wasn't willing to go hunt him down—largely because, as he ate the baklava, he saw a familiar figure slipping through the crowd.

She was even shorter than him, and because of how thin she was, the girl looked even younger than he was. But she already had access to her archetype, which meant that she was probably at least a year or so older. More importantly, Miguel had become a little obsessed with her, mostly due to the fact that he'd saved her from being beaten, and she'd repaid that kindness by stealing his mother's coin purse and disappearing.

At the very least, Miguel thought he deserved an explanation. So, he bade farewell to Agatha, then started following the girl. As he did, he was careful to stay well back so as to keep her from noticing his presence. A few times, she glanced in his direction, but he'd managed to avoid her searching gaze by slipping behind one reveler or another. In the chaos of the festival, remaining unseen wasn't that difficult.

So, over the next few minutes, he watched the girl as she made her way through the crowd, bumping into people every few steps. At first, Miguel didn't recognize what she was doing, but then he caught sight of a darting hand, and it dawned on him. She was working the crowd, stealing from people even as they celebrated his mother's life.

It was galling.

But it was also a little impressive. She was stealing from people, and right out in the open. That had to be difficult.

A few times, Miguel thought he noticed her use a skill or spell, but he couldn't be sure. He had no idea what archetype she was, and it was obvious that she had a class he'd never encountered, as well. Still, it was clear that she was using something to remain undetected.

It was fascinating watching her.

And before he realized what he was doing, he'd followed her from the square. The surrounding streets had plenty of traffic, which he used to his advantage as he continued to tail the girl. However, after around fifteen minutes, she led him into what was plainly a bad part of town.

Nowhere in Argos could truly be classified as a slum. Yet, human nature seemed to dictate that some people would have it better than others, and those prosperous few didn't like to live next to the ones who struggled a little more. In Argos, the poorer part of town was characterized by less elaborate buildings that were far closer together. The streets were a little narrower, and the pedestrians were more shabbily dressed. Still, no one looked malnourished or overly dirty.

Well, nobody but the girl Miguel was following.

However, he'd begun to suspect that she looked the way she did by design. Maybe she used her small stature to make people believe she was younger—and less powerful—than she was.

Either way, Miguel continued to follow her until, at last, she entered an old warehouse that looked long abandoned. The building abutted the town's wall, and it was around fifty yards wide. Perhaps it had once been a true warehouse or a department store. Miguel had no idea because it bore no signage or any other indication as to its nature, current or former.

As Miguel leaned out from behind a building, studying the warehouse, he felt something press against his back.

"Don't move, kid," came a gruff voice.

Of course, Miguel moved.

He dived forward, yanking his dagger from its sheath at his waist as he rolled to his feet. That's when he realized he was surrounded. Three figures, all of which were larger than he was, encircled him. Each one had a weapon drawn. One wielded a sword, another a staff, and a third had leveled a wand in his direction.

"What do you want?" Miguel demanded.

"What are you doing here?"

"Is this private property? I didn't see any signs."

"Signs?"

"Like 'Beware of petty thugs' or something," Miguel said.

It took the sword wielder a moment to wrap his mind around the obvious insult, and when he did, he snarled and stepped forward.

"Stop!" said the girl with the wand. "We're not here to beat up little kids, no matter how smart their mouths are."

"What do you want to do?" asked the fellow with the staff.

"Not our call. Let Zoe decide."

"Zoe's not our leader," said the one with the sword.

"You could just let me go."

"Shut up."

"I'm just saying. Nobody's crossed any lines yet," Miguel stated with some degree of false bravado. If it came down to a fight, he intended to put everything into an all-out attack so he might have a shot at escape. Because from the way these three moved, they had the benefit of enhanced attributes. That meant he had no chance in a fair fight.

"Come with us. I promise, nobody will hurt you, kid," said the girl.

Miguel bristled at being referred to as if he was a child, but he suppressed his anger. Did they know what he'd been through? That he'd killed monsters? That he had crossed the wilderness? No. If they did, they wouldn't dismiss him so easily.

He held up his hands. "Fine," he said with forced affability. "But I'll warn you right now. If you do anything to me, someone will make sure you pay."

"Think you're some kind of big shot?" snorted the young man with the sword. He stepped forward, and before Miguel could react, he'd snatched the dagger away. The sword wielder only looked to be a couple of years older than Miguel, but those were important years. He was at least a foot taller, with a wispy mustache decorating his upper lip.

Miguel glanced at the other two. The one with the staff was a little shorter, though he looked to be at least fifty pounds heavier. And not with muscle. The girl was somewhere in between, though with a pleasant look about her. Whatever the case, they didn't look like hardened criminals.

Hopefully, that impression would prove accurate.

Soon enough, they were escorting Miguel into the warehouse. Once inside, he saw that it was a large open space, though there were a few crates piled on the other side of the expansive room. There, a familiar figure sat next to an ethereal lamp. As the trio guided Miguel closer, he saw a pile of coins scattered across a makeshift table made from an old door that stood atop a barrel.

She looked up, then frowned. "Seriously? Him? What are you doing here, kid?" she demanded.

"You know him?" asked the wand-wielding girl.

"He's the one who saved me from those idiots that jumped me the other day," she answered.

"Him? He doesn't even have an archetype."

"I don't know how he did it, but—"

"Attributes aren't everything," Miguel said. "And you just disappeared. Are you a thief? Why did those guys attack you?"

"Just get him out of here," said the thief. At her order, the two boys grabbed Miguel's arms.

"What? After I saved you? Come on!" Miguel demanded, fruitlessly attempting to escape. But their attributes were too high.

"I'll tell you what," she said, standing. "Get an archetype. Maybe a class. Then come back here and I'll tell you everything you want to know. But until then, you're just an annoying kid who happened to be in the right place at the wrong time."

"I saved you," he spit.

"Thanks for that. But every good deed doesn't deserve a reward," she said. Then, she nodded toward the door.

As the two boys dragged Miguel away, he shouted, "At least tell me your name!"

"Stop."

The two did.

The girl approached. She still looked painfully thin, but at least she wasn't covered in bruises. "Name's Zoe. Best thief in Argos. Probably the world," she boasted. Then, she kissed her fingers before placing them on his lips. "Come back and see me when you're useful."

Without another word, she turned on her heel and returned to her seat. As she did, the two boys dragged Miguel away. He'd stopped resisting, stunned by her brazen actions. Even when they pushed him out the door and told him not to come back, he just stood there, staring forward.

Eventually, he let out a long sigh and returned to the square. As he traversed the city, though, he could only think of the fact that he now had a goal.

"Become useful," she'd said.

And Miguel intended to do just that.

35

MOVING ON

Elijah lay on his back atop the temple, his head resting against the statue of his sister as he stared up at the night sky. When he'd set the festival into motion, he'd hoped it would help him move on. A celebration of Alyssa's life had seemed like such a good idea at the time. Yet, when the time came to actually participate in the party, the situation had left him sick to his stomach.

The conversation with Delilah had helped a little, but he'd been in no mood to be comforted. So, he'd spent the last few hours wandering through the town. Most of the residents recognized him, so he'd been forced to endure condolences, well-wishes, and overzealous invitations alike. It had gotten so onerous that he'd had no choice but to return to the temple and retreat to where nobody else would find him.

That was how he'd found himself next to Alyssa's statue.

Up close, it didn't really look like her. Without any real examples, the Sculptors had done what they could. The resemblance was limited, though to Elijah, the tone of the piece was what was truly important. It felt like Alyssa, which was all he really cared about.

As he lay there, he felt someone standing below. When he realized who it was, Elijah levered himself upright, then leaped down to the ground. His attributes were high enough that such a fall wouldn't permanently hurt him, but the sudden stop he experienced upon landing was still a little jarring.

He played it off, asking, "Why aren't you down there celebrating? I saw a few girls your age when I was walking through town. I'm sure one of them would agree to dance if you asked."

Miguel didn't respond.

"What's going on?" Elijah asked.

The boy shrugged. "I don't know. I'm just ready to get my archetype, I guess," he admitted. That surprised Elijah. He'd expected the issue to revolve around Alyssa's death, so the answer offered by Miguel left him a little disconcerted.

"What happened?"

"Nothing," Miguel badly lied. "I'm just tired of being weak. If a level five attacked me right now, I couldn't do anything to stop them. I don't like that."

"I think you'd be surprised. You could probably hold your own."

"You know what I mean," Miguel said, sitting on the top step of the stairs leading down to the town. "Nobody messes with you. You walk around like you own the whole world. You can go places even Colt is afraid to go. Like that swamp. Or the desert. Do you know how often we were attacked before we got to Seattle? Every day. Sometimes, every hour. But you just walk around without a care in the world."

"That's not because I'm strong. It's because . . ."

Elijah trailed off. He'd rarely considered how his archetype—or perhaps his attunement—affected his surroundings. But looking back, it was so obvious that being attuned to nature made the wildlife more amenable to his presence. Most of the time, they ignored him.

Others clearly didn't have that benefit.

"I want to be like you," Miguel said.

"No, you don't."

"You said that before. You said that your archetype is weak. But do you know how crazy that sounds? You're the strongest person in the world, and—"

"I have the highest level. That doesn't make me the strongest," Elijah said.

"What's the difference?"

"Levels aren't a gauge of power. They're a mark of progression, and not even the only one," Elijah pointed out. "There are three pillars of power. The first is levels. The second is cultivation. And the third is equipment. One isn't more important than the others."

"So, a level one with great gear could beat you?"

"No."

"But you said—"

"Great gear is a part of the equation. I have good equipment. I have better cultivation than most. And I have high levels. You can't neglect one if you expect to be the best you can be."

That was a reminder that Elijah had done just that. He had a few good items, but he knew he could have been more diligent with his equipment. He didn't even have any proper armor. And while he didn't think he would ever run around in a full set of plate armor, he knew that his oversight had put him at a disadvantage.

The same was true with his staff, which was decent, but not ideal. He would have preferred to use something he'd made himself, but that was a time-consuming process that he'd neglected because his priority was to kill Roman as quickly as possible. Now that his sister's murderer had paid for his crimes, Elijah needed to rethink his strategy.

But first, he wanted to do something else.

So, he reached out, offering his hand to Miguel. The young man took it, and Elijah helped his nephew to his feet. "Come on. I want to show you something," he said.

"Right now? At night?"

"Night isn't so scary, so long as you know what to expect," Elijah said. Indeed, there was a certain peace that could only be experienced in the deepest part of the night. For Elijah, the darkness held no mystery. He could feel everything around him. But for others who had to worry about nocturnal predators—of which there were plenty—it was probably horrifying. "Just trust me."

Then, Elijah led his nephew down the steps and through the city. Soon enough, they'd passed through the gate and entered the forest. Elijah continued on for more than an hour until he reached a familiar spot.

"Here it is."

"What?" asked Miguel, his voice low.

"You don't have to whisper."

"O-oh. Yeah. So . . . uh . . . what is this place?" he asked.

Elijah looked around. The area didn't look much different than anywhere else in the forest. However, for Elijah, it held special meaning. It was there that he'd chosen to help Isaak.

It felt like a turning point for him. At the time, he'd been warring with his actions against the hunters, and he knew that if he'd taken a different route, if he hadn't healed Isaak and helped him in the rift, he likely would have gone down a completely different road. It was one he didn't want to consider.

Still, he explained what had happened, pulling no punches. He didn't sugarcoat what he'd done to those hunters. Nor did he downplay how conflicted he was about helping Isaak.

"I think I would've become a monster," he mused. "I would have killed people without thought, and for no other reason than because they violated my personal code of ethics. I still might. That's what being me is like. I don't know if it was always in me, that violence. Or maybe it's my archetype influencing me. I think that's something that happens, but it could just as easily be my personality. My point is that once you get power, you need to use it responsibly. You can't just kill everyone you disagree with."

"You do."

"I really don't. I've restrained my instincts more often than you could know."

"Why are you telling me this?" asked Miguel.

"Honestly? Because you're a good listener who can't run away," Elijah admitted with a chuckle. "Plus, I think we're more alike than either of us knows. You feel it, don't you? That connection? It's why animals like you so much. I'd be surprised if you didn't have a nature attunement, just like me."

"You think so? Could I be a Druid, too?"

"Maybe. If that's what you want. But I'll only say this one more time—most Druids aren't fighters. They tend to their groves, kind of like Nerthus. Or they heal people. Some help Farmers. I'm the black sheep of Druids, I think," Elijah said. "But I'm constantly working against that unsuitability for combat. My class helps. And I'll keep shifting my path toward battle. But it's a long journey, and if you're the fighter I think you are, you may want to consider a different route."

"I see," Miguel said, incapable of hiding his disappointment.

"You know what? How about I get a guide about classes available for people with nature attunements?" he suggested. There were a thousand other things he would have preferred to research, but they were of much less importance compared to preparing Miguel for the most important decision in his life. "We could figure out what to expect. That way, you can go into it with your eyes wide-open."

"I . . . I would like that," Miguel said.

"That settles it. I'll fly to Arvandor soon. They owe me a question," he said.

After that, he and Miguel continued to discuss the topic, and though it was entirely speculative in nature, it was an interesting conversation. Finally, Miguel asked, "What are you going to do now?"

"I need to get some more levels," Elijah answered. "And I need to familiarize myself with an ability I got recently. The Trial of Primacy is coming up, and I feel pretty sure that I'll need to be at my best if I want to survive."

"What then?"

Elijah shrugged. "I have no idea. I want to keep exploring the world. Helping people is nice, too," he said. "I want to keep progressing. Maybe visit other worlds." He let out a small chuckle and shook his head. "Visit other worlds. That would've sounded crazy even a few years ago. But now? It's a real possibility. Did you know there's a place called the Empire of Scale? It's ruled by dragons. Do you realize how insane that is?"

"You can transform into a giant scaled sasquatch monster. Dragons doesn't seem that weird."

Elijah was about to refute that claim, but then he realized that Miguel was right. He'd internalized his ability to transform to such an extent that it didn't even seem odd anymore. However, upon a few seconds' worth of introspection, he recognized just how magical it must have seemed from everyone else's perspective. After all, he'd yet to find anyone else who could shape-shift. That didn't mean they weren't out there, but it did suggest that it was an uncommon ability, at least at their current stage. Perhaps it would grow more common in the future, though.

"What about us?" asked Miguel.

"What do you mean?"

"Are you just going to leave us behind?"

"What? No!" Elijah insisted. "I intend to help you find your path. And your mom and I have been talking about her next project. She's about to set down roots in Ironshore. I don't know what comes next, but whatever it is, we'll confront it as a family."

"Except for the Trial of Primacy. That requires you to leave, right? I heard Mom talking about it . . ."

"Nerthus will be here to take care of you and your mom."

Elijah had already spoken to Carmen about it, and she had been adamant that, despite the fact that she'd earned a spot, she had no intention of participating in the Trial. She'd had enough adventure for two lifetimes.

"I guess," Miguel said.

"Well, let's get started, then," Elijah said. "Sit down."

"Here?" asked Miguel, looking around nervously. He clearly wasn't comfortable in the woods at night. That was probably a good attitude to have, given the inherently dangerous wilderness.

"Yes, here. Sit."

Miguel did, crossing his legs.

"Now, close your eyes. Good. Listen. Feel. Have you ever meditated before?" Elijah asked.

"Colt's been teaching me a little."

"That's good. Focus on that, then," Elijah said. As he sat in front of his nephew, he flared One with Nature and Nature's Bounty. "Do you feel anything different?"

Miguel didn't speak for a moment, but then, he let out a disappointed sigh. "No. Nothing. Just a little cold."

"Keep trying," Elijah ordered. He had no idea if it was even possible for someone without an archetype to sense the underlying structure of nature, but if it was, he intended for Miguel to do it. Perhaps then he'd be a step ahead once he began the path of his own progression.

36

THE TOWER

Elijah ducked under the long arm of the sasquatch, following that up with a vicious uppercut from his staff. The blow connected with the monster's chin, and the impact sent the huge creature flipping backward. Elijah spun, and before the first sasquatch hit the ground, he'd already aimed Storm's Fury at the last monster in the pack. It was busy trying to extricate itself from the thorny vines that had encased its legs, so it never got the chance to react to the thick bolt of blue lightning that descended from above. It hit the monster square in the chest, sending it into convulsions.

Meanwhile, Elijah could sense the first creature picking itself up from the ground, so he wheeled around, leaped high into the air, and brought the Dragon-Touched Staff down on the thing's overlarge head. The sound of cracking bone filled the air as Elijah brough his enhanced Strength to bear, shattering the monster's skull. It spasmed, but it didn't immediately die. Instead, a seizure gripped the creature, and it windmilled its arms. That took Elijah by surprise, and one of its thick limbs knocked his feet out from under him.

As he fell, he tried to right himself, but it was useless. He ended up collapsing atop the monster's bulging chest, and the smell of wet fur filled his nostrils. But more distressingly, the other sasquatch had recovered from the lightning-induced spasm and was well on its way to freeing itself from Elijah's Snaring Roots.

He rolled free of the dying sasquatch just in time to see the other dashing in his direction. Elijah had very little leverage, but still, he managed to throw himself across the ground and avoid the worst of the monster's charge. Even so, he took a vicious kick in the leg that sent him spinning around like a top. His motion only ceased when he rammed into the maze's wall with a thud.

His head spun, but he kept his wits about him enough to remember to cast Soothe.

Then, as his thoughts sharpened, he kicked off the wall and charged the remaining sasquatch. Once again, his staff arced out, this time, colliding with the monster's shin. The creature saw it coming, so the blow didn't sweep its leg out from under it, but it still elicited a slight stumble. Elijah pounced on that small opening, jabbing the other end of his staff into the monster's stomach, then following that up with a blisteringly fast combo that cracked bones in its ribcage.

The monster howled in pain, lashing out. However, with Soothe coursing through him, Elijah didn't bother playing it safe. Instead, he bulled his way into the sasquatch, knocking it further off-balance with a shoulder tackle. Then, he stomped on the thing's instep before dipping low, grabbing its plant leg, then lifting. The move sent the monster toppling over his back, where it landed in a heaping sprawl of too-long arms and legs.

Elijah leaped upon the opportunity that represented, pelting the creature with one attack after another until he landed a series of attacks on its skull, cracking it just like he had the previous creature's.

Then, at last, the area went quiet, save for Elijah's panting breaths.

Despite his success, it had not gone nearly as well as he'd hoped. For one, he'd been forced to heal, which was one of the restrictions he'd imposed upon himself. For another, his staff work was sloppy, and he still failed to truly incorporate his spells into his fighting style. His casting speed was just too slow to be instant, which meant that each time he wanted to use a spell, he was forced to pause for at least a second or two.

"Still a long way to go," he muttered to himself, looking around at the fallen sasquatches. He'd been in the tower for a little more than a week, and in that time, he'd quickly discovered that it offered very little in the way of challenge. The first level had been easy enough the first time through, and it was even easier now that he knew precisely how to get the most out of it. Even killing the goblins hadn't taxed him, though he'd noticed that they were a far higher level than the last time he'd come through the tower.

The Sea of Sorrows had been the most challenging, but it wasn't even as difficult as his first time through. However, traversing the seafloor had given him an idea of how to make things even more difficult. A handicap meant to even the odds and push him to his limits.

So, since then, he'd remained in his human form, only using his healing spells when absolutely necessary. And his growth had been incredible. Not in terms of levels, though he'd made some progress there, as well. Rather, his true gains had to do with his fighting style. For some time, he'd made a concerted effort in learning to use his staves properly, but that had just been training. Real fighting had forced those lessons to coalesce into a practical fighting style. Yet, as he'd just said, he still had a long way to go.

That was one of the reasons he'd entered the tower in the first place, and in that endeavor, it had been a success. The other reason was less productive. He had hoped that challenging the tower would give him an opportunity to determine his path going forward, but he still had no idea what to do next.

After spending another week in Argos, he and his family had returned to the island. There, Elijah had spent a few days doing next to nothing before finally deciding to enter the tower. He told himself it was so that he could continue to progress, but in reality, it was a stalling tactic.

He had plenty on his plate. He knew that. But after Valoria and Argos, he was having difficulty mustering the motivation to do any of the things he knew he needed to do. It was easy enough to say that he wanted to prepare for the Trial of Primacy, but it was something else altogether to actually do so. He'd hoped the run through the Keledge Tower would put him on the right track.

But now that he was close to completing it—he'd already killed the root raptors, and after taking care of the sasquatch camp, there was nothing really left—he was back at square one.

At least he'd gotten a few rewards along the way. The first was a wicked-looking axe called a Polished-Obsidian Hatchet that felt like it was at least Simple grade. The second was a pair of Sealskin Slippers that were decently graded, as well. He hoped that his performance would net him something good when he finally left the tower behind.

However, the most overtly beneficial aspect of the tower run was the fact that he'd gained two more levels, pushing him to level eighty-three. He knew it should have been more, but apparently, running the same towers over and over again netted less experience each time. Eventually, the amount of experience would level out—at least according to Kurik—but that wasn't until at least the twentieth run.

That told Elijah just how difficult leveling was going to be. The whole system seemed to reward exploration, and it was easy to imagine going from one tower to another just to keep the experience rewards high. Perhaps that would be an advantage for him. After all, he was more mobile than most, what with Shape of the Sky as well as his ability to teleport across great distances.

With that in mind, Elijah progressed through the maze. The various tower challengers from Ironshore had gone to great lengths in order to map it out, and Elijah had acquired one of those maps before heading inside. It was invaluable, and it had made the level much easier than either of the other two times he'd challenged it. Still, there were a few stray root raptors out and about, so Elijah dealt with them along the way. Eventually, though, he reached the exit.

Congratulations! You have completed Level Three of the Keledge Tower.
Grade: A.
To exit the tower, step through the portal.

Satisfied with his grade, he reached down and retrieved his reward from the silver box that had manifested at his feet. And for a long moment, he just stared at the item, which turned out to be a slab of rough wood. He glanced at the notification:

Reward for completing Level Three of the Keledge Tower: Bark of the Mother Tree

---

Unsure of what to do with it, Elijah shoved it into his Ghoul-Hide Satchel and stepped through the exit. A moment later, he found himself swimming toward the surface. When he crested the waves, he leaped free, transforming via Shape of the Sky, and flew toward the Grove. He still hadn't quite gotten the hang of landing, but at least he didn't break anything this time.

Predictably, no one else was around.

Miguel was off traipsing through the wilderness with Kurik, while Carmen and Colt were in Ironshore. That left him all alone in the Grove.

Except for Nerthus, of course.

So, Elijah crossed the Grove and found the spryggent tending to a stand of bushes. Once he reached Nerthus, Elijah asked, "What's up?"

That elicited an excited explanation from the spryggent about how those particular bushes would increase the ethera density in the Grove by as much as three-tenths of a percent while also emitting a pleasant smell. It was nice to see Nerthus so happy, and it almost made Elijah forget his own issues.

Finally, he retrieved the slab of wood from his satchel and showed it to his friend. "Any idea what this is for? It's called Bark of the Mother Tree."

"Where did you get this?" demanded Nerthus.

"Uh . . . reward from the tower. Why?"

"Mother trees are nearly as sacred as ancestral trees," Nerthus answered. "They grow much larger, though they are not nearly as spiritual. Their bark is prized for its durability, though. In most places, that piece of bark is as good as a natural treasure. Perhaps better, for some applications."

"Hmm."

Elijah looked at the piece. It was perhaps three feet wide, and maybe a foot longer than that. So, he couldn't use it for a staff. And even if he could, it just felt wrong in a way he couldn't quite articulate. Perhaps it was because it hadn't come from his Grove. Whatever the case, he expected that Carmen could give him some advice on what to do with it.

Next, he showed Nerthus the other rewards he'd gotten, but the spryggent wasn't terribly interested in them. If it didn't have to do with the Grove or trees, Nerthus just couldn't be bothered to care.

So, once he'd finished catching up with the keeper of his Grove, Elijah once again adopted Shape of the Sky, then launched himself toward the clouds above. In seconds, he was hundreds of feet into the air and staring toward the open ocean. Without Eyes of the Eagle active, he could only barely see the dark smudge on the horizon, but he knew it was there all the same.

For a moment, he circled his island, hesitant to give in to his adventurous spirit. He had so many other things he should have been doing that simple exploration felt like a bit of a waste. However, most of his best memories had come on the heels of wanderlust, and he was desperately curious what sort of storm would be visible from so far away.

So, without further hesitation, he flapped his wings and sped toward the tempest.

He raced across the sky, keeping an eye on his destination as well as the waves below. Down there, he could see shadows of enormous sea creatures, though their true nature was obscured by the ocean water. Were they whales? Sea monsters from myth? Perhaps there was even a kraken down there.

But for now, Elijah was more concerned with what was in front of him. As he sped toward the storm, he became increasingly worried. The clouds roiled, dark and ominous, and lightning flashed. The height of the waves beneath him steadily increased until it was like Elijah was looking down at an oceanic mountain range with towering peaks and deep valleys.

And by his estimation, the storm was still more than a hundred miles away.

He pushed on, both eager and more than a little frightened. And in his mental state, where he'd felt more than a little apathetic ever since he'd left Argos, that jolt of adrenaline only served to spur him forward.

37

THE STORM

Wind whipped against Elijah's wings, threatening to send him plummeting to the roiling sea below. However, he'd spent enough time practicing flight to adjust accordingly. Still, he knew that if he got much closer, he'd be in danger of being tossed from the sky.

But he kept going.

The enormous storm was still at least fifty miles away, but it stretched from one end of the horizon to another, looking like an enormous black wall. Periodically, lightning arced through it, illuminating those swirling clouds, but that only made the sight that much more ominous.

Because there were things in there.

Elijah could only see shapes and shadows, but what he could see was enough to make any sane person turn around. Huge forms slithered from one end to another, putting him in mind of flying serpents. But there were other, much smaller shapes, as well—and those were even more concerning because they didn't confine their movements to the clouds. More importantly, as Elijah drew closer, he recognized them.

It had been more than four years since his plane had been ripped to pieces by some sort of giant bird, but Elijah knew he'd never forget that brief glimpse he'd experienced as he fell toward the ocean. And that memory confirmed that he now beheld the same species.

And there were hundreds of them, all riding the wind like fish swimming through the ocean. Elijah could only hope that, one day, he could emulate their grace.

At least that was the most pervasive thought in his mind right up until he felt something rocket into range of One with Nature. That brief warning was barely enough to allow him to tuck his wings close to his body and begin a dive that narrowly let him avoid the outstretched talons of one of those immense birds.

Elijah glanced up to see a mass of slate gray feathers. The thing's wingspan was more than twice Elijah's own, and its talons were larger than his entire torso. More importantly, he could see light glinting off those feathers, implying that they were metallic. So were its claws and beak, though that was as much as Elijah saw before the thing wheeled around and began another attack.

He dived, gaining speed with every foot of lost altitude, but the huge raptor had gravity on its side, as well. The towering waves drew ever closer, and the wind threatened to rip Elijah to pieces. Yet, he waited until the very last second—when he was only a few feet above the water—to throw his wings wide and level out. He glided through the trough between two waves, and over the wind he heard a loud splash as his pursuer hit the water.

But Elijah's victory was short-lived, as a moment later, with a few furious flaps of its great wings, the creature threw itself back into the air. Thankfully, though, Elijah's maneuver had bought him a little time, and he used that to great advantage as he stuck dangerously close to the sea's surface.

He kept just ahead of the giant bird, though the thing was clearly bigger, faster, and more coordinated than he was, so it was only a matter of time before it caught him. Elijah reluctantly pushed his adventurous spirit aside and turned his thoughts toward escape.

He'd just begun to speed back toward his island when another bird appeared. Then another.

Before Elijah knew what was going on, he was surrounded by a flock of those feathery monsters. Desperately, he dodged one while flapping his wings to gain altitude in order to avoid another darting attack that would have ripped him to pieces. He used every point of his Dexterity attribute to his advantage, and for the first time, he truly let his instincts take over.

And it was glorious.

For a few scant seconds, Elijah was untouchable. Even as a dozen birds the size of fighter jets attacked, he twirled, climbed, and dodged.

But it couldn't last.

There were too many. And they were far too skilled.

Elijah knew that, but he was too caught up in the high brought on by his avian instincts to heed the warning in his mind. And in the end, it cost him. It was a small mistake—barely a few inches off in one of his maneuvers—but it was enough to allow one of the raptors to clip Elijah's wing. That, in turn, slowed him just enough that he couldn't avoid the next attack.

Or the next one after that.

Even as they ripped him to shreds, Elijah shifted back into his human form, intending to use Roots of the World Tree to teleport back to his island. However, two things prevented that. First, the concentration necessary to cast that spell was impossible in his current situation. And second, he didn't have time because, the moment his body completed the transformation, he was whisked away by a strong gust of wind.

Then another took him in the opposite direction. Over and over, the swirling winds pushed him back and forth. The erratic nature of his fall was the only thing that saved him from the birds, though they still got in a few good hits, even if they failed to snatch him up into their enormous talons.

The wind also served to slow his fall just enough that when he hit the water, he didn't do so with terminal velocity. It still hurt, but he managed to avoid breaking anything terribly important. Only a few ribs and what felt like a small fracture in his ankle. More distressingly, just because he'd fallen into the sea didn't mean he was out of the proverbial woods.

Indeed, there were three issues with his current predicament.

First, the birds had already proved they had precisely zero problems with diving into the ocean to get to their prey, and it was only a matter of seconds before they resumed their assault. Second, the rolling waves were the size of skyscrapers, which was enough to strike fear into even his heart. Facing down monsters was one thing. But looking up at a wall of seawater was something else entirely.

And finally, he could sense gargantuan beasts swimming beneath him, as well. Elijah didn't think he was lucky enough that they would prove peaceful.

So, he furiously cast Roots of the World Tree, hoping to complete it before the myriad dangers of his circumstances asserted their claim on his life. But as he'd expected, he just didn't have enough time to finish the cast before one of the birds came screaming down out of the sky. Elijah dived, twisting and pushing himself through the water as quickly as he could manage.

It wasn't enough, though. The bird hit the water like a missile, the shock wave alone enough to stun him. And when its talons wrapped around his waist, Elijah knew he had no choice but to act, and decisively so. He initiated the much quicker transformation into the lamellar-ape form, and the second it completed, he let out a roar and slammed his fists into the bird's talons.

It screeched, and by reflex—or perhaps because Elijah's blow had broken some bones—it released him. By that point, the creature had already climbed dozens of feet into the air, and when Elijah fell, he did so in such a way that he was slammed by one of the massive waves as it rolled past.

It was like getting hit by a moving brick wall, and for a moment, Elijah was disoriented. However, because he still had the Ring of Aquatic Travel equipped, at least he didn't have to breathe.

More importantly, the birds seemed to have either written him off or decided he wasn't worth the trouble because, when he finally surfaced, they'd begun to fly away. For Elijah's part, he had more important issues on his mind.

Because there was something speeding toward him from the depths. And it was enormous.

Elijah braced himself for another fight, but it was one that never manifested. A dolphin the size of a minivan burst through the water, did a somersault, then dived back into the side of the wave. Then, it returned and, before Elijah could react, started nudging him away from the storm.

It wasn't until a few moments later that Elijah made the connection. There were many instances of dolphins having saved humans in the pre–World Tree past, and it seemed that this mutated version hadn't completely discarded those instincts. On top of that, Elijah's experiences suggested an explanation for how he'd survived the plane crash four-plus years before.

After all, he'd fallen from an altitude of thousands of feet. There was no way that, in his condition at the time, he should have lived through such a fall. Yet he had. That led him to believe that, perhaps, his fall had been arrested by the chaotic gusts of wind. Then, maybe he'd been saved by a dolphin or some other helpful beast.

Strange things had happened, and given his nature attunement, that seemed a far better explanation than a one-in-a-billion chance that he'd fallen in just such a way to avoid having all his bones broken and then miraculously drifted hundreds of miles to the island.

Or maybe he was just grasping at straws.

Either way, the explanation was good enough for him. Not that it mattered overmuch. The past was the past, and though he was grateful for his own survival, he didn't have the leeway to give it much thought.

Once the dolphin had guided him a couple of miles away from where he'd been attacked, Elijah managed to say, "You probably can't even understand me, can you? Well, on the off chance that you can, thank you."

The dolphin did not answer.

Because it was a dolphin.

In any case, the creature seemed to sense that Elijah was out of danger, so it gave him one last nudge, then dived beneath the waves. After that, Elijah finally completed his cast of Roots of the World Tree, teleporting back to his Grove.

Once he was back on solid ground, he fell to his knees and vomited a gallon of seawater. Of course, that brought Nerthus's ire as well as an explanation for how bad saltwater was for plants. Elijah didn't need the spryggent's admonishment, but as he collapsed onto his back, he gratefully endured it.

Because his brush with death had banished the thread of apathy from his heart. He had a lot to do before the Trial of Primacy, and he couldn't afford to waste more time challenging the tower.

So, after lying there for a few minutes, Elijah pushed himself to a sitting position and looked inward. For the past months, each time he'd had a few extra minutes, he'd spent it cycling his Core. However, just because he had plenty of practice didn't make the process any easier. At times in the past, he'd likened it to having his spirit waterboarded.

But he persisted, and he managed three cycles—each one like trying to stir molasses—before he felt Carmen arrive on the island. More and more, she spent her nights in Ironshore, presumably working.

When she returned to the Grove, Elijah opened his eyes and said, "You're quite a workaholic. Working on a new project?"

"Sort of," she admitted, holding out her hand. Elijah took it, and she hauled him to his feet. "I'm preparing to start that project you suggested back in Argos. Right now, I'm just calling it the Forge. A bit early to start naming things, considering we haven't even laid the foundation yet. But it feels right."

"What kind of preparations do you have to make?" Elijah asked.

To answer that question, Carmen eagerly explained that they were currently gathering enough blood tin—which was the ore they'd found in the mines—for the structure, but also for any tools they might need.

"It's all going to work together," Carmen said. "It has to. I'm also going to need some help getting enough of that dragonstone back here. It's the most powerful stone I've ever seen."

"Just let me know when and I'll help. It just needs to be done soon because I have a promise to keep back in Seattle," he said. Then, after a second, he reached into his Ghoul-Hide Satchel and pulled the Bark of the Mother Tree out. As he did, he said, "Oh—I also got this from the tower."

"Whoa."

"That good?" he asked as Carmen took it.

"Can I buy this from you?" she asked without answering his question.

"You can have it. What do you have planned?" he asked.

"I'm not sure," she answered. "Something for Miggy, though. It feels like him. Like you, too, but you don't need anything I can make."

Elijah said, "That's probably true."

He'd rather Miguel have something special than to take it for himself. After that, he discussed his plans with Carmen. She only made a few comments, but she did ask a couple of poignant questions that helped him solidify his intentions. So, once the conversation was over, Elijah felt a lot better about the future.

38

AN ISSUE OF TRANSPORTATION

For the first time since completing the Temple of Virtue in Argos, Elijah awoke with a sense of purpose. Nearly dying to a few overgrown birds was enough to cement his need to grow stronger. After all, if he couldn't protect his family and his Grove—or guide Miguel—then what did his position atop the power rankings really mean? It was just a number on a list. Power was meaningless if it didn't have a purpose.

So, Elijah pushed himself out of his mossy bed and thrust his arms toward the flowery ceiling as he stretched. He didn't really need it. His Regeneration was so high that his every muscle was in peak condition at all times. Yet, old habits tended to die a slow death, and he'd yet to move so far from his humanity that he could neglect something as simple as loosening tight muscles.

Nor could he neglect his bladder, so after he took care of that, he headed to his kitchen and gathered the ingredients for tea. As he did, he turned his attention to the coffee trees within his Grove. They were finally ready for harvest, but there were many steps he needed to take before he could enjoy the fruits of their growth. At the same time, he was aware that Carmen had risen, as well, so he gathered enough ingredients for a second mug of tea. By the time it was ready, Carmen had descended from her own tree house and was crossing the Grove.

That's where Elijah met her. As he offered her the steaming mug, he said, "Good morning."

She let out a sigh, then shook her head. "Sometimes I wonder how we made it," she admitted. "It wasn't so long ago that we were being picked off, one by one, by those sidhe monsters. And now I'm in paradise enjoying a cup of tea that has no business being this good. I have friends again. A job. It almost feels like all that horribleness never even happened."

She took a sip, then continued, "But I know better. Just because this place is safe, it doesn't mean everywhere is."

Elijah didn't know how to respond to that, save to assure her that he would do everything he could to protect her. That just elicited a small smile as she said, "You're a lot like Alyssa. She wanted to protect everyone, too."

"I don't care about everyone. I care about you and Miggy. A few others, too. But everybody else can—"

"That's a lie, and you know it," Carmen definitively stated. "From everything you've said, and based on what I saw in Argos, you care as much as anyone can. You're pathologically incapable of not helping people. Like I said—just like Alyssa. The difference is that you don't trust as easily as she did."

Elijah didn't bother disputing that assertion. Instead, he changed the subject, saying, "I'm going to investigate ways to get the dragonstone you need back here. I'm not sure what the answer is, but I intend to ask Ramik. If he doesn't know—or if there's no easy way to do it—I'll just tote it myself. It'll take a few trips, but I'll do what needs to be done."

"You don't have to do that. There's some decent stone nearby. I can make do."

"It's not as good as dragonstone, though."

"It's not."

"Then it's settled. Like you just said, I'm incapable of not helping, right? You and Miggy deserve the best. Otherwise, what's the point of having the most powerful person in the world as your patron?" he asked.

"Patron? Ugh. Don't ever refer to yourself that way again."

"Sponsor?"

"No."

"Benefactor?"

"Still no," she said with a tight smile.

"Well, there's just no pleasing you," he replied with a grin of his own. After that, the pair drank their tea and discussed less serious things. Carmen spoke of her plans for her forge, while Elijah talked about his coffee. It was a decidedly normal conversation, given the circumstances, and as such, Elijah found it extremely comforting.

Still, all good things inevitably come to an end, and so it was with his pleasant conversation with Carmen. She needed to get to Ironshore for work, while Elijah needed to speak to Ramik. The only difference was that Carmen had a bit of a commute ahead of her, while Elijah simply had to shift into Shape of the Sky and launch himself into the air. Only a couple of minutes later, he landed just outside of town and strode past the wall. As he did so, he gave the guards a small wave, which they nervously returned.

Upon entering the city, it became immediately apparent that Ironshore was growing. He'd been back a few times in the previous few months, but he'd not paid much attention to the state of the city. Now, though, he let himself take it all in, and he was incredibly impressed by the progress on display. The overall tone of the architecture remained the same as always, reminding Elijah of Victorian London, but everything was bigger, grander, and more solid. In addition, Elijah saw a few humans here and there, none of which he recognized. Clearly, the trade alliance with Norcastle had continued to bear fruit.

A good thing, so long as Ramik and his people kept an eye on the newcomers. Elijah was well acquainted with human curiosity, and ignorance was no excuse for anyone trespassing on his island.

He took his time as he strode through the city, greeting those he knew while politely nodding at those he didn't. The residents of the city seemed a lot less overtly hostile, but there were still plenty of nervous glances following him around. Perhaps that was a good thing, though. After all, if they were frightened, then they wouldn't dare invade his Grove.

Soon, Elijah reached his destination, which had received quite an upgrade over the past few months. The government building had been completely overhauled, and it looked more like a palace than it resembled the old mostly unadorned building that had been its previous incarnation. Looking upon it, Elijah got the impression of wealth, power, and most of all, authority. Hopefully, that would keep any newcomers under control.

Elijah climbed the steps that ran along the entire front of the building, entering through a pair of enormous brass double doors. The two guards—a goblin and a dwarf—watched him, but they didn't even consider barring his way. Upon entering the building, Elijah was confronted with a huge lobby that wouldn't have been out of place in the Imperium. In the center was a massive desk manned by a trio of figures. A goblin, a gnome, and a dwarf—each one wore the sort of clothes Elijah usually associated with Ramik, which meant that they were dressed in dark tailored suits.

Elijah approached. "Looks like you've done some renovations," he remarked. "Is Ramik around?"

"Do you have an appointment?" asked the goblin, her voice conveying both boredom and annoyance.

"Nope!" Elijah said cheerfully.

"Then the mayor is unavailable."

"It's fine. I'll find him myself," Elijah said, still smiling as he walked past the kiosk. The goblin tried to object, but her coworkers quickly stepped in, whispering his identity. Her green skin went pale, but by that point, Elijah was already a few feet away. He wasn't sure where Ramik's office was, but given the layout of the building, he expected that the huge set of stairs in the center of the lobby probably led in the right direction. So, that's where he went, his bare feet slapping against the cold tile of the floor.

Upon mounting the steps, Elijah became aware of a panting figure running in his direction. At first, he thought the little gnome meant to attack, but his true intention became apparent as he slowed to a stop. "Let me lead you to the mayor's office, honored Druid," he said, still trying to catch his breath.

Elijah glanced at him, taking in his appearance in the space of an instant.

And he was more than a little unimpressed. The gnome was a little taller than normal—almost dwarf sized—but he had quite a paunch around his middle. More importantly, he looked incredibly young.

"Alright," Elijah said.

Then, the young gnome led him up the stairs—laboring the whole way—before circling along a balcony toward what looked like a normal and nondescript office door. He knocked, and Ramik's familiar voice bade him enter. The office on the other side was neither opulent nor unadorned, though there were a few nods to Ramik's preferences. A few tasteful paintings decorated the walls, and the same monstrosity of a desk dominated the room. A few leather chairs completed the decor.

"Hey, Ramik," Elijah said. "What's new?"

Ramik smiled, saying, "Good to see you, Elijah. The city is booming, just like I predicted."

After that, he dismissed the young gnome before excitedly detailing Ironshore's progress. The trade alliance with Norcastle had brought in a nice trickle of wealth, and there were even plans to branch out to other cities like Argos. More importantly, the increased ethera density had given his people quite a boon in terms of cultivation, which allowed them to take advantage of Biggle's powerful potions. That, combined with the influx of levels they'd received after the failed orc invasion, and they were in much better shape than they could have reasonably expected.

"And Carisa's people are strong enough to push deeper into the earth," he finished. "That mine could be our ticket to true prosperity."

"That's awesome, Ramik. I'm glad everything is going well," he said. "But there are two things I wanted to discuss. The first is just that I feel the need to reiterate that no one should set foot on my island without my permission. I know there are some new people here. I trust that you've let them all know the rules."

"It is part of our orientation," Ramik stated. "Combined with the stories of what happened to Cabbot and his people, that's enough to keep them all away. Most people aren't terribly brave when certain death is on offer."

"Good," Elijah said. "Now—the real issue is that I need a way to transport a few dozen tons of rock."

Then, he described his issue, letting Ramik know that the stone was intended for Carmen's forge. "Do you know a way around the problem?" he asked.

Ramik tapped his pointed chin. After a moment, he answered, "There are two options. The first is to commission one of our Carpenters—we have three that could manage the job—to create a series of crates. So long as they are limited to stone, they will accommodate up to five times their normal volume. However, weight would only be cut in half, which could prove to be an issue, even with your Strength."

Elijah had tested it extensively, and he was only capable of carrying two blocks at a time. That meant that, regardless of the crates' capacity, his limitations would dictate that he could only carry four. In turn, that would necessitate multiple trips, so that was not an ideal solution.

"What's the other option?"

"It is extremely expensive."

"I have money," Elijah said. Indeed, he barely used his funds anyway, so he'd amassed a small fortune in coins. He knew that wouldn't count much in the wider multiverse, but on Earth, he was considered quite wealthy, even after the expenditure with the Temple of Virtue.

After that, Ramik explained the other solution. It was actually a system that, due to its cost, was not very popular except in very specific circumstances. The first part was a ring that acted as a key to an interdimensional space that could hold a vast volume of goods. However, the only way to withdraw those goods was to combine the ring with the second part, which was a stationary anchor.

"So, what makes it so expensive?"

"The rings are single-use," Ramik explained. "They become useless after that. Even the materials are impossible to recycle. But the ring-storage system can hold more than ten times what the crates can hold."

He went on to explain that even the anchor had limitations—chiefly that it could only be used once a month.

"It's almost as expensive as transporting goods via the Branch," Ramik said. "Most people just use one of the Teamsters guilds. That is not an option here, though."

In the end, Elijah's decision was an easy one. After all, what was money for if not to be spent? So, armed with Ramik's explanation, he headed to the Branch and bought the system for fifteen gold etherium, which was nearly three-quarters of his total wealth. The only solace to such an expenditure was that if he wanted to purchase another ring, he could do so for a little less than five gold.

However, even then, he could easily see why it wasn't a popular method of transporting goods.

Still, he felt good about the purchase. Before he teleported to the Dragon Circle, though, he had a couple more tasks to complete.

39

SUN COPPER

I need a wok," Elijah said.

"What?" asked Carmen, looking up from her anvil. She'd spent the past hour trying to hammer a piece of armor into shape, and despite her best efforts, the sheet of metal was not cooperating. Part of the problem was that it was mundane steel, and as such, it could only be pushed so far, but the bigger issue was that her attention kept wandering to much more interesting projects.

Like the forge she was going to build, which was such a huge project that, anytime she thought about it, she felt more than a little overwhelmed. Or the armor she wanted to forge for when Miguel finally gained his archetype. She also wanted to do something special for Elijah, though she'd yet to think of anything he might need.

Either way, by comparison, her normal work that would end up being sold to people in Norcastle or equipping Ironshore's fighters was downright boring. Still, she endeavored to give each piece the entirety of her focus. That was one of the things she'd learned during her exile. Every project deserved her best efforts. It didn't matter if she was working with mundane steel or some magical alloy—none of her creations would be shortchanged.

Easier said than done, but she was determined to do her best.

"A wok. Like, this big around," Elijah said, holding his hands around two feet apart. "Maybe smaller. I don't know. The point is that I need a wok."

"And why do you need a wok?"

"I feel like we're saying *wok* a lot," he said, rubbing the back of his neck. "But it's for my coffee."

"You can't make coffee in a wok."

"No—the wok is for the roasting. I shoplifted a French press in a Walmart I visited a couple of months ago. I also got, like, an entire buggy full of underwear. And toothpaste. My breath is minty fresh now," Elijah explained. He clapped his hand over his mouth and exhaled, sniffing the result a second later. "Well, sort of. Did you know that toothpaste has an expiration date? It doesn't, like, become poisonous or anything, but it loses quite a lot of its minty goodness. I should probably make my own. You wouldn't know how to make toothpaste, would you?"

"Baking soda, salt, essential oils, and water."

"Wait, really? That seems easy."

Carmen shrugged. "That's the basic recipe. You could add other things like turmeric or—"

"Never mind. I'm sure somebody else has figured it out," Elijah said. "Plus, you're getting off topic. The wok. I want it to be made from as high-quality a material as you can find. I can pay whatever."

"I'm not going to charge you, and you know it," Carmen said, shaking her head at his slightly manic demeanor. She'd heard enough stories from Alyssa to know that meant that he had latched on to something he thought was important. Maybe multiple things. But that didn't matter for the time being because his request had sparked her imagination. A wok wasn't particularly difficult to make, and it didn't require a lot of material. That opened up a lot of possibilities, but one in particular was more exciting than all the rest. "I think I have an idea. When do you need this wok?"

"Uh . . . as soon as possible? I still need to pick the cherries and begin the process of separating the pulp from the bean," he said. "I'm going to use the wet method, which involves . . ."

Carmen only half listened to Elijah's explanation of the practice. She was already vaguely familiar with it, and much less excited about the process than he clearly was. Regardless, it would take at least a week, and probably a bit more than that, before the beans were ready to be roasted. So, Carmen had plenty of time for her own part, which was to forge a wok.

"So, can you do it?" he asked.

"Way ahead of you," she answered. Then, she tapped her temple, saying, "Already planning it. It'll be ready in a couple of days."

"Really? What are you going to use as the base? And—"

"You'll see. But I do need some wood from the Grove. I'm sure Nerthus could find something," she said. "Now go. You're in the way."

"Wow. Rude," Elijah muttered in a dramatic stage whisper that he certainly meant for her to hear. Carmen ignored it because she was already wholly focused on the new project.

The first step was to gather materials, and for that, she needed to visit Carisa. So, she left the now-temporary smithy behind and headed toward the offices on the outskirts of town. It was the middle of the day, so the mine was a hive of activity, and rightly so. Not only had they tapped into a large vein of blood tin, but they'd also found a few other decent-quality sources of ore. However, Carmen was only really interested in one.

So, with that in mind, she found her way to Carisa's office. The door was open, but Carmen still knocked, eliciting a grunted, "Come in."

Carmen did just that, stepping inside to see the dwarven foreman hunched over her desk and studying a map of the mine. It was far more elaborate than the one in Silverado, and it was already almost a mile deep in some places. But Carisa had plans for expansion.

"How's it going?" Carmen asked. She and the dwarven woman had become quite friendly over the past few months, largely because they shared a love of all things metal.

"Follow the ore," Carisa said, looking up. "That's what my pa used ta tell me. Always follow the ore. Meant to remind me ta keep my mind focused on what's important, but in this case, it's literal. Got to follow that ore, no matter where it goes. And it's goin' deep, too. Gettin' thicker as we go. I think we're on the verge of findin' somethin' big."

"Watch out for critters," Carmen said.

"What in the hells are critters?"

Carmen explained what she meant, describing the monsters she and the other people from Silverado had fought in its mine. "We called them critters because they looked like movie monsters. Movies are—"

"I know what movies are. Got me a player a few weeks ago from one of them Norcastle lads. It's interestin', that's for sure. Not too certain what the purple lizard monster is meant to represent, but I find it very unsettlin'."

"Purple lizard . . . Oh. That," Carmen said, realizing that Carisa had been watching programs intended for children. It was all she could do not to chuckle. "Anyway. I want some of that sun copper you found last week."

"There ain't much of it."

"I know. I don't need much. I intend to mix it with that blood tin. Before the World Tree, copper and tin made bronze. I'm hoping for something like that."

"Interesting. I think I can spare a few pounds, provided you can make a coupla more of them pickaxes you made for me last week. They're better 'n anything we have," Carisa said.

"Deal. I'll get on that as soon as I'm done with the project for Elijah," Carmen said with a grin.

"For . . . Elijah . . . You know what, no charge. Just—"

"It's fine, Carisa. He's not as scary as you think he is," she pointed out.

"Tell that to the fifty people he killed. Or the orcs he slaughtered."

Carmen had heard the story already, and from both sides. Elijah had revealed his sins as some sort of self-imposed penance—or maybe he just wanted Carmen to know what she was dealing with. Meanwhile, Carisa hadn't spoken of it until she'd gotten drunk a few nights after Carmen had gotten to Ironshore.

"Fair enough," she said. Sometimes, it was hard to reconcile the Elijah she knew with the sort of man who could so easily kill people. But everyone had changed after the world's transformation, and he was no exception.

After that, she collected the ore and headed back to the forge. Technically, the ore wasn't called sun copper. It was solar malachite. However, it was colloquially referred to as the former. Carmen didn't care one way or the other, so she quickly got down to the business at hand.

The first part was to crush the ore into a powder—the finer the better—which she accomplished by running it through a crusher she'd gotten from the mining operation. They had plenty of people who specialized in smelting, so they had all the proper equipment. That meant that Carmen did, as well.

Once the ore had been crushed into powder, she poured it into a giant crucible along with a load of infused charcoal she'd already prepared. Then, it was a simple process of heating the crucible. Normally, copper melted at around a thousand degrees, but apparently, sun copper was a different story altogether, and it took quite a bit more before it melted. Once it did, Carmen dumped the crucible into a nearby pan before separating the copper from the charcoal.

Then, it went back into the crucible to be rendered into a liquid. That took infused coal as well as Carmen's ability, Melt, and even then, it was only barely enough. Still, she managed it, then poured the contents of the crucible into a series of molds.

If she was working with normal copper, without the addition of ethera, she would've skipped that step, jumping right to the final mold. However, she had plans for the ingots.

Once they'd cooled, she did the same with a much smaller amount of blood tin. The ratio was meant to be around ninety percent copper and ten percent tin, a formula to which she intended to adhere as closely as possible.

Finally, she had her ingots ready. It was at that point that Elijah returned with a large branch that he said came from his Grove, but aside from waving him to put it aside, she couldn't afford to pay him any attention. Instead, she was entirely focused on using her various abilities to reduce impurities and infuse the resulting ingots with as much ethera as they could handle.

It was a long and tedious process, but one that Carmen refused to short-change. She knew precisely how important it was to the final product, so she swallowed her frustrations and committed to the work. Eventually, she finished.

That was when she threw all the copper ingots into the crucible and melted them. Once they had liquefied, she added the tin, and when it had all mixed together, she poured it into a different, much larger mold. As it cooled, she took a short break, during which she went to a nearby restaurant, where she ate a meal that she barely paid attention to. Instead, her mind was entirely on the project.

Perhaps Elijah wasn't the only one to get a little manic when he was working on something he cared about.

In any case, Carmen finished her meal, then returned to the smithy. Once there, she inspected the cooled bar, and once she found nothing amiss, used Refine Material as well as Decontaminate, reducing the bar as she removed impurities. It wasn't strictly necessary—surely, a wok made of that material would suffice to roast a few coffee beans—but Carmen had always believed that if something was worth doing, it was worth doing to the best of her abilities. And in this case, that meant refining the metal until it was absolutely pure.

Of course, that meant that she had a lot less to work with, which in turn necessitated the creation of another few bars. At each juncture, she used Ethereal Infusion to ensure that the material was absolutely saturated with energy.

And after two days, she had achieved a product as close to perfection as her skills and the materials allowed. That was supported by the notification she received:

Faythium Ingot
Overall Grade: Complex (Low)

"Yes!" she shouted, only then realizing that she was absolutely alone in the smithy. She glanced at the nearby window, seeing that it was the dead of night. Perhaps she'd grown a little too focused on the project.

At least she hadn't neglected Miguel, though. He was traipsing through the wilderness with Colt and Kurik, so he wouldn't even know that she was pushing herself so hard.

For a moment, she considered returning to the Grove—or at least to the bed she kept in her office near the forge—but she ultimately decided against it. After her success, there was almost no chance that she could sleep anyway. Not until the project was finished, at least.

So, Carmen looked down at the ingot. It looked like bronze, but there was a blue shimmer to it that marked it as magical. Plus, she could feel the energy coursing through it. That was as befitted a Complex-grade material.

She reluctantly set it aside, knowing that the metal behaved similarly to bronze. That meant it wasn't meant to be forged. Instead, it was more suited to casting. So, Carmen found a piece of wood meant for the creation of molds, then got to work carving the basic shape of a wok. The idea was to create a wooden facsimile of the intended product, then place that piece into a receptacle filled with packed sand. Once the wooden piece was removed, then the resulting cavity would be in the appropriate shape. After that, molten metal would be poured into the cast, and when it cooled, a rough piece would be created.

Or that was what was supposed to happen.

In reality, the process was finicky, and Carmen found it even more tedious than it really was. Getting the sand packed just right was the worst part, and it made her long for the moments when she could simply pound metal into shape. Yet, she persisted, adjusting along the way until she got the result she wanted.

It took nearly ten tries before that happened, and by that point, she was absolutely exhausted.

Even so, she couldn't help but smile as she held the rough version of the wok aloft. It was a little more than two feet across, with steeply sloped sides and a rounded bottom. She hadn't affixed a handle yet—that was what the Grove wood was for—and the piece needed a lot of refinement. But the hours' worth of tedious work had pushed her past the mania associated with success and into exhaustion.

So, she set the wok aside and retreated to her office, where she collapsed onto the cot she kept for just that purpose. When she fell asleep, she dreamed of uncooperative sand and blended metals.

40

WOK

"Okay, so this is a problem," Elijah said, looking at the spatial anchor, then across the Grove and to the dense forest surrounding it. The anchor itself was just a rod that had been driven into the ground, though now that it had been activated, it was impossible to move without ruining his previous efforts.

He'd spent the past few days loading the ring with fifty multiton rocks. Hopefully, that would be enough for Carmen's project. However, his current issue was that he couldn't unload the ring without crushing a quarter of his Grove. It just highlighted the fact that he hadn't quite thought things through when he'd placed the anchor, but if he deactivated and tried to move it now, he'd lose the attached interdimensional space and all the stone in it.

"Uh . . . Nerthus? Little help here?" he called. "You around, man?"

"I am not a man," Nerthus stated, having climbed out of a nearby tree. He leaped down. "I am a spryggent."

"Right. It's a colloquialism. So, here's the deal," Elijah started before explaining the situation. He ended it with, "And now I need to get the blocks from here to at least the beach without tearing anything up."

"You have two issues. First, you need a path."

"But what about emptying the ring?"

"One at a time."

Elijah started to say something, then stopped. "I'm so stupid," he muttered. Indeed, he'd lost the forest for the trees as he focused on the problem. He'd never even considered not emptying the ring all at once. But there was nothing stopping him from withdrawing each stone individually and carrying it to where it was supposed to go. As Nerthus had said, though, he needed a path through the forest. So, that was task number one on his list.

"What's the second thing?" he asked.

"Getting the blocks across the strait," Nerthus said. "The people of Ironshore have ships, but you have no apparatus through which to load them. The shallows cannot accommodate such large ships, either. So, you need to build a dock."

"Ugh."

That was something Elijah very much wanted to avoid. However, he didn't really see any way around it. That didn't mean he needed to build it himself, though, so without emptying the ring, Elijah shifted into the Shape of the Sky and flew to Ironshore, where he met with Ramik and enlisted the goblin's help to hire a couple of Builders who would be willing to construct a dock.

As it turned out, the process was easy enough, and before long, the group of goblins, gnomes, and dwarves had sailed across the strait armed with a bevy of materials from which they began to build the requested dock. Elijah didn't miss the fact that they were all terrified, but that was unavoidable. So long as they did the job, he wouldn't interfere.

Meanwhile, he left them to their task and got to work clearing a viable path through the forest. At first, he tried to work with the landscape, but soon enough, he grew too frustrated with the process and just started ripping trees out of the ground. It wasn't exactly druidic of him, but it was his island. He would do what he wanted, regardless of how loudly his instincts screamed at him to stop.

Eventually, he'd ripped his way across the island until, at last, he reached the beach, where he saw that the Builder crew had nearly completed his new dock. It was an impressive wooden structure that jutted out from the beach for nearly two hundred feet.

"Maybe I need to get a yacht," Elijah said to himself. Or at least something better than a rowboat so that Miguel and Carmen could cross the strait more easily. Whatever the case, he only had to wait another hour before the Builder foreman approached and announced that they were finished.

As Elijah paid the goblin, he couldn't help but marvel at how productive people could be, given the right skills. In addition to the dock, the Builders had cleared a large area of the beach that would serve perfectly for his blocks. So, once they were gone, Elijah wasted no more time before returning to the Grove, where he began the process of transporting the blocks to the dock, one giant hunk of stone at a time.

Even though Elijah's attributes were more than up to the task, the whole ordeal took far longer than he would have liked, and it was well into night before he'd finished. Still, he was no stranger to work, and there was a certain satisfaction he experienced upon seeing the white-and-green dragonstone stacked upon his beach.

But he didn't intend to move it until morning. While he had no issues personally crossing the strait at night, something told him that it would be inadvisable for Ironshore's boats. So, with that in mind, he retreated to his Grove, where he checked on his coffee. The cherries were currently soaking in a vat of water, where they would ferment over the course of the next week before he removed the pulp and set the beans out to dry.

It was one of two methods of processing coffee cherries, but from what he understood from his limited knowledge of coffee, it was the one that resulted in the highest-quality coffee beans. It also took advantage of the dense ethera in his Grove, which created all sorts of interesting situations when it came to bacterial growth.

Regardless, it would be another couple of days before it was ready for the next step, so Elijah spent the next few hours cycling the ethera in his Core. Then, he went to bed, where, for the first time in a while, he slept completely soundly all through the night. The next morning, he awoke feeling refreshed and ready for the coming day. So, after engaging in his normal morning routine, he flew across the strait and hired one of the ships to bring the dragonstone across.

Once he'd taken care of that, he headed to Carmen's forge, hoping that she had completed work on his wok. When he reached the building, he was a little surprised to find that Miguel was there, and he was actually engaged in an argument with his mother.

"You can't keep doing this, Mom," he said.

"I'm your mother. You don't get to tell me—"

"What's going on, guys?" Elijah asked on approach. That earned him a glare from Carmen and a pleading expression from Miguel.

His nephew said, "You need to tell her to stop, Uncle Elijah. She hasn't been home in three days. I don't think she's slept more than a few hours in that time, either."

"I slept," she argued with a roll of her eyes.

"Please, Mom—"

As they continued their discussion, Elijah backed away and pretended he couldn't hear them. The last thing he wanted was to get involved in that sort of argument, so he busied himself by engaging in a thorough inspection of a nearby furnace. His head was deep inside the apparatus when he heard Carmen clear her throat behind him.

"Uh . . . Sorry? I'm just really into furnaces," Elijah said.

"You have soot on your face."

"That's . . . how I like it?"

Carmen shook her head. "Go ahead. Say it."

"Say what? You have a nice furnace. A little cold right now, but I'm sure it gets really hot when you—"

"You're going to tell me that Miggy is right and that I'm working too hard," she said. "Well, you're right. I get so obsessed when I get into a project that I sort of just lose track of time."

"What project?" Elijah asked, neglecting to point out that he hadn't actually said anything about her work habits. In his experience, it was better to just stay out of it.

"Your wok, of course."

"You've been working on the wok for four days?" he asked.

"Sort of," she said with a slight shrug. "Most of the first day was spent creating the alloy. It's called faythium, by the way."

"Sounds fancy."

"Fancy?"

"Yes?"

She shook her head. "But it has to be cast instead of forged. No beating it with a hammer, you know? Instead, it works off molds. Anyway, I don't have as much experience with that, so I screwed up the first try. I thought it was pretty good when I first saw it, but . . . well, it wasn't. I was half asleep at the time, and I made a lot of mistakes. So, I had to melt it all down, make a new mold, then try again. And another ten times after that."

"It's just a wok."

"It's never just a wok," Carmen said. "If I'm going to make something, I'm going to do it to the best of my abilities. Nobody tells you how to tend to your Grove, right? So, I'd appreciate it if you didn't remark on my process."

Elijah nodded earnestly, knowing that he had no interest in getting on Carmen's bad side. So, he said, "Sure. But you're finished?"

"Just," she admitted. "I was just polishing it when Miggy came by."

After that, she headed to the back of the smithy. Elijah followed, his eyes locking onto what looked like a bundle of rags. Carmen reached it, then uncovered a huge wok. It was bronze in color, though with an azure shimmer. There were two wooden handles—one on each side—as well.

"Looks nice," Elijah said. "May I?"

Carmen handed it to him, and he nearly dropped it. "Wow. Heavy."

"Yeah. That's the issue I've been working on. The first attempt was at least five times as heavy, and each version after that was the result of me trying to lighten the load," Carmen said. "It's way thinner than any normal wok, but that material is functionally indestructible unless you're trying to wear it as armor. Even then, it would take quite a shot to even scratch it."

"Are you thinking of making armor out of it? For Miggy, maybe?"

Carmen shook her head again. "Not a chance. He's getting something better than this," she said. "Plus, a full set of this stuff would be too heavy for him until he gained quite a few attributes. And I hate working with it."

"That bad?"

She shrugged. "It was a fun experiment, but it's not my thing," she said. "I prefer banging metals with my hammer, not creating casts and molds."

"Fair enough," Elijah said. "So, what's the end result? Is it Simple grade, at least?"

"Mid-Complex."

"What? Seriously?" Elijah asked, looking at the wok in a new light.

"The alloy alone was low Complex. The end result is actually a little disappointing, given that. But I'm going to chalk it up to my inexperience with the process," she said. "I bet if I started over, I could get it to high Complex."

"No need," Elijah said, stepping back when he saw the gleam in Carmen's eye. Her perfectionist nature was probably why she'd had so many sleepless nights since he'd given her the project. "What's it do?"

"Other than being almost indestructible? It has a trait called Savory. Helps preserve flavors and provides a constant stream of ethera to anything cooked in that little pan," she said.

"Amazing. This is exactly what I was hoping for. But it does bring to mind something I forgot," he said, setting the wok down. Then, he reached into his Ghoul-Hide Satchel and, over the next minute or so, retrieved the collection of low-quality weapons he'd looted back in Valoria. "Atticus said that some crafters have a skill that lets them disassemble finished products. So, as the highest-level crafter I know, these are probably best in your hands."

Carmen let him know that she had access to just such an ability, but added, "It's not as good as it would be for someone who specializes in that kind of thing, but I can get something out of these, assuming you don't want to just sell them or give them away."

Elijah said, "Do what you want with them. Also, I have this."

Then, he pulled the cursed False Dragon's Fang out of his satchel. He hadn't forgotten about it. Rather, he'd hesitated to give it back to Carmen because he knew it would elicit an emotional reaction. And he was right to expect that. Carmen's eyes went wide, and he could see her muscles trembling as she said, "I'd hoped to never see that again."

"It's cursed, you know," Elijah said. "Anyone who binds it will experience delusions of grandeur, according to Atticus's appraisal."

Then, he went on to explain that curses were something of a safeguard against forcing crafters into servitude against their will. "If you do that, you might get a cursed item," he finished. "Kind of keeps people from being taken advantage of."

"What are you going to do with it?" Carmen asked.

"That's up to you. It's yours, as far as I'm concerned."

"Get rid of it."

"You don't want to—"

"Just bury it. Or toss it into the ocean. Or a volcano. I never want to see it again," she said.

Elijah agreed, shoving the sword back into his satchel. Finally, in an attempt to change the subject, he said, "I got the dragonstone back. I hired a boat to bring it over from the island. They're going to deposit it near the town, so you can do what you want with it."

"Thank you," she said, her voice subdued. Clearly, she was still wrestling with what had happened.

"I . . . uh . . . I was thinking. I have a couple of days before my coffee is ready for roasting," Elijah said. "Do you mind if I take Miguel somewhere? Just out into the wilderness a little. I think he's got a nature attunement, just like me, and I think it'll be good for him to connect, you know? I wanted to show him something."

"That's . . . That's fine," she said. "Just . . . be careful."

"Are you okay? I didn't mean to upset you . . ."

"I'm fine. Just a lot of emotions right now. But go ahead. Miguel would probably love to go on an adventure with you," she said.

After that, Elijah backed out of the forge and went in search of his nephew.

41

CLASSES

Where are we going?" asked Miguel, following Elijah through the woods outside Ironshore.

"Does it matter? The journey is more important than the destination," Elijah said, doing his best to seem wise. "Worry less about where we're going and more about how we're going to get there. Or why we continue on."

Miguel rolled his eyes, and Elijah's aura of stoic pseudo-intellectualism broke as he gave a little chuckle. "Seriously, though—where are we going?" the young man asked.

"A place called Arvandor," Elijah answered. "It's a city populated by elves. Then, we're going to cross the desert to the Circle of Spears."

"Why?"

"Because I said so."

That elicited a narrowing of Miguel's eyes. "C'mon. Be serious."

"Fine," Elijah said with a long-suffering sigh. "What do you know about the Branches of the World Tree? Or the Knowledge Base, more specifically."

"Uh . . . it has guides. Kind of like Wikipedia."

"Except there's no way to really search it," Elijah stated. "All the information in the multiverse, but no way to find what you're really looking for. Sometimes, it's easy to hunt answers down. I think that's one of the benefits of being recently touched by the World Tree. We need to know the basics, so it puts those front and center. But what do you think we do when we need to find more specific information?"

"Somebody could search it. Make a job out of it, like a professor or something."

"Kind of. But it's more than that. There's a class called Librarian that can find things. They're like personified search engines. You give them a question, and they find the answer via one of their abilities. But like a lot of abilities and spells, those skills have cooldowns. So, they can only answer questions so often, which makes it valuable."

"Supply and demand. We learned about it in school," Miguel revealed.

"In school? You were in, what? Fourth grade? Seems a little early to learn about that kind of thing."

That's when Miguel revealed that he'd been enrolled in something of a special school meant for advanced students.

"Your mom was a gifted student, too," Elijah said. "Both of them, I expect. But our parents wanted Alyssa to skip grades she was so smart."

"What about you?"

Elijah chuckled. "I was above average," he said. "Never really had a drive for academics, if I'm honest. I liked the idea of learning all those wonderful things, but the reality turned out to be too tedious for my taste. Probably why I made for a terrible biologist."

"What does that have to do with this place we're going?"

"They have a Librarian there that owes me a question," Elijah said. "And I'm going to use it for you. Also, elves."

"Elves? Like, real elves? Kurik said there was one in Ironshore, but—"

"I've met her. Nice lady. But no—these are sand elves. I helped them out once before, so like I said, they owe me. Plus, I'm on a bit of a diplomatic mission," he said. Then, he explained what he meant to Miguel. The young man had already latched on to the idea of a city filled with elves, which meant he only barely listened to Elijah's explanation.

In any case, when Elijah asked him if he wanted to come, Miguel gave an enthusiastic agreement. So, only a couple of hours later, they returned to the Grove, where Elijah made sure his nephew had everything he needed—including his weapons—before opening a gate to the Moon Well. The two stepped through a moment later.

The pond, the dolmen, and the surrounding glade was much the same as the last time Elijah had been there, though he did notice that the ambient ethera had experienced an uptick in density. It wasn't as noticeable as in the areas where he'd planted the ancestral-tree saplings, but it was still hard to miss.

"This is where Trevor and his family lived?"

"Trevor?"

"The moon deer. There's Trevor and Susan, then their parents Bubba and Annabelle," Miguel said.

"Those are some . . . interesting names."

"They like them," Miguel said with a shrug.

"Right. But yes, this is where I found them," Elijah said. Then, he explained that the deer had been injured. "I healed them, and then when I saw they were still in danger, I brought them back to the island."

"You should do that more. We could have a whole bunch of powerful animals living there," Miguel suggested.

"The island is too small for that," Elijah replied. "The ecosystem won't handle it. Besides, most guardians are predators. It wouldn't be long before they started fighting one another."

"Oh. Yeah. That makes sense, I guess. But can you imagine a lion guardian? Or a walrus?"

Elijah chuckled. "I met a bear guardian once," he said, leading Miguel away from the dolmen. The undergrowth wasn't very dense, so the way was easy enough. "Really surly character. Only reason he tolerated me was because I fed him a ton of fish."

As they traveled, Elijah recounted a few more of his adventures. He tried to veer away from the more harrowing parts, instead focusing on his connection with nature and the miraculous things he'd seen. There were plenty, so he didn't have any issues finding appropriate topics.

For his part, Miguel proved an attentive and enthusiastic listener, asking poignant questions that would have been more appropriate coming from someone much older. It prompted some interesting discussions, mostly about the nature of the world, but also about things Miguel found interesting. Unsurprisingly, most of it had to do with nature.

Curiously, though, Miguel didn't really care much about plant life. Instead, he latched on to animals, growing excited when they saw anything furry, feathery, or scaly.

"I think you might've ended up as a zoologist or something," Elijah said. "Maybe a veterinarian."

Miguel said, "I like animals, so maybe. But I once read on the internet that a lot of veterinarians ended up having to put a bunch of animals down. I don't know if I could handle that."

"Everything dies eventually," Elijah said. "That's part of life."

After a while, they reached the end of the forest and started across the plains. If it was just Elijah, he would have kept going—or probably have flown—but he wanted Miguel to see the world from a different perspective. His experience during their exodus had not been pleasant, and Elijah thought it was important for the young man to see that their new world wasn't all danger and death. There was beauty there, too.

That seemed like an important distinction, given the shape Elijah expected for Miguel's development to take.

In any case, they continued on, and the landscape slowly transformed from a lowland forest to a prairie, and then to a desert. It wasn't as arid as the one surrounding Seattle, but aside from a few scrubby bushes and some hardy grass, it was almost entirely devoid of vegetation. There was plenty of animal life, though, and as they trekked through the area, Elijah kept a running commentary on what he sensed via One with Nature. Overall, it took almost three days of travel—stopping each night—before they reached the Twilight Clefts.

There, they were met by a troop of elves, one of which was familiar.

"Long time no see, Syka," Elijah said, grinning at the Golemancer. She was flanked by a pair of other elves on one side and her earth golem on the other.

Syka returned his smile with one of her own, saying, "Welcome back! Are you here to challenge the tower again? And who's this? He's cute!"

"He's twelve."

"Almost thirteen," Miguel interjected, though he did so with a bit of a stammer.

"Which is still twelve," Elijah insisted. "Miguel, this is Syka. And her bouldery buddy there is Gbartik."

"Uh . . . actually, this is Jibann. Gbartik was destroyed," Syka said with a shake of her head.

"Weird names," Miguel remarked.

"Miggy. That's rude."

"They are!"

"Think nothing of it. They're randomly named," Syka said. "They're not real. No souls. No minds. Just hunks of rock."

Jibann shifted slightly.

After that, Syka introduced the other two elves, then offered to take them to Arvandor. Elijah agreed, and after that, they were led through the huge canyons and to the elven city. Along the way, Miguel kept his eyes firmly trained on Syka, and it wasn't difficult to see why. The Golemancer was possessed of the same ethereal beauty characteristic of every other elf, which, for a relatively sheltered young man like Miguel, was too much to ignore.

Elijah tried to drag the boy's attention to other sights, but it just didn't seem to be in the cards. So, he was glad when they finally reached the city, which finally dragged Miguel out of his infatuated stupor.

"Wow," he said as they passed through the first tunnel. "You didn't say it was all underground."

In fact, Elijah had. Miguel was just too distracted by elven beauty to hear it. But he didn't make a big deal out of it, and eventually, they were escorted to the Branch chamber. There, K'hana awaited alongside her little brother the Librarian.

"Greetings, Druid," she said with a bow.

"Oh, we don't have to stand on ceremony," Elijah said. "We're friends, right? Let's get to the question because I have a proposition I want to discuss with you."

"I see."

After that, Elijah asked her brother—whose name he'd actually forgotten—his question: "I'm looking for information on potential classes for people with nature attunements."

The young elf nodded, then closed his eyes before placing his hand against the Branch. Nearby, the Envoy's eyes narrowed. From what Elijah understood, the relationship between Envoys and the area around their Branches was something like what existed between the Jailer and his jail. They were supposed to be the ultimate power, so long as they remained in that clearly defined area.

Of course, as Elijah had proved with the warden, that wasn't exactly foolproof, so he didn't know how the limits were determined. He'd only guessed the nature of the warden's power based on a discussion with Nerthus. Either way, he didn't have any intention of testing those limits with the Envoy.

As those thoughts flitted through Elijah's mind, the Librarian used his skill, resulting in the Branch lighting up with ethereal power. Next, a leaf appeared in his hand. He handed it over to Elijah, saying, "This is called 'Nature Classes—a Sample.' I hope it's what you wanted."

After thanking the Librarian, Elijah set up a meeting with K'hana in a couple of hours, then dragged Miguel back to a set of rooms they were provided. He settled down to read the guide. That's when he discovered that, because he'd yet to receive an archetype, Miguel couldn't read the guide.

"I didn't expect that, if I'm honest. A little frustrating," Elijah admitted.

"Tell me about it. That's why I can't wait to get my archetype."

So, Elijah settled in to interpret the information for his nephew. And to his surprise, there were hundreds of class options for each archetype.

"How about we narrow it down. Which archetypes interest you the most?" Elijah asked.

"Um . . . mostly Warrior, Ranger, and . . . uh . . . Druid," he said. "Maybe Sorcerer, but I don't know."

"So, mostly combat archetypes," Elijah said. "Let's start with the Warrior stuff right now, then we'll progress through the others."

After that, they went through the options associated with the stated archetype. Many were not dependent on attunements, and they fell into three categories. The defender-style classes, which were suited for durability and were often used for protection, were the most numerous. But then, there were the melee-focused damage dealers—one of which was the Berserker class that he recognized from his fight with Cabbot. And finally, there were the hybrids that traded suitability in a single purpose for versatility. Elijah was familiar with that.

However, there were dozens of ways each purpose was achieved. Some used a wide variety of weapons, while others focused on a single tool. It was easy to dismiss those differences as mere flavor, but one line stuck out to Elijah more than any other.

He read it aloud, "At first glance, class choices may not seem impactful. A Fighter seems little different from a Knight. Yet, despite overlap, progression will always mean differentiation. The gaps between classes grow wider as one gains levels, engages in cultivation, chooses specializations, and evolves. So, choose wisely."

"This doesn't help at all," Miguel said.

"I know," was Elijah's response as he sat on the bed beside his nephew. "Ramik once told me that established societies usually have Scholars that specialize in class information. They're meant to help people make the perfect choices. We don't have any of that."

"So, what am I supposed to do?" Miguel asked, looking over at his uncle.

"I don't know," Elijah admitted. "I didn't even choose my archetype. The system chose for me."

"What? Really?"

"Yeah. I was on a plane, remember? The lights went out, and before I could wrap my head around what was going on, a giant bird ripped a hole in the fuselage," he explained. "I fell into the ocean, and I didn't wake up until a while later. By that point, the choice had been made for me. But it was a good thing. If I'd have gotten anything but Druid, I probably wouldn't have survived. And besides—I had a ridiculous compatibility with the archetype, so it seems pretty clear that I was destined for it."

"Is that what I should do? Just pick the one with the best compatibility?"

"Maybe. Do you trust the system?"

"I don't know."

"Yeah, me, neither. It seems like it wants to help, but I like the idea of having choice, too," Elijah explained. "Like, what if it told me I was suited to be a trash collector? Would I have picked whatever archetype led to the Trash Man class?"

"Is that a thing?"

Elijah shrugged. "No clue. My point is that you should take the system's compatibility rating into account, but ultimately, I think you should go with your heart. I've told you that you don't want to be a Druid, but if that's where your heart leads you, I'll do everything I can to help you be the best Druid you can be."

"Really?"

"Of course. Now, here's what I'm going to do—during my meeting with K'hana, I'm going to ask if she has anyone who can transcribe the information in this guide to a book or something. That way, you can look through it yourself. Sound good?" Elijah asked.

"Yeah."

"Alright then. Don't get into any trouble while I'm gone," Elijah said before pushing himself to his feet and heading out of the room. Hopefully, his conversation with K'hana would be more definitively fruitful than the guide had been.

42

A WHOLE NEW WARLOCK

Benedict Emerson leaned forward, checking his reflection in the shattered mirror. Even though cracks marred the silvery surface, he could still see his features clearly enough.

And the sight was pleasing.

In the past, Benedict had never been referred to as handsome. His skin was too sallow, his body was thin to the point of looking malnourished, and his complexion had long been marred by acne scars. Now, though, when he looked upon his own reflection, he could see none of that. His skin was still pale, but rather than looking like a waxy corpse, he resembled a vampire—the sexy sort usually played by a teen heartthrob. That impression was supported by his glistening black hair and sharp cheekbones.

Of his acne scars there was nothing left. Just smooth skin. And his body had filled out quite a bit since he'd escaped that dungeon beneath Easton.

Apparently, getting a Demon Core did the body good.

He took a step back, adjusting his long leather coat. Beneath it, he wore a plain white shirt and a pair of black pants—all Simple grade, if he had to guess, and elegantly cut. They were the sort of clothes worn by a young and eligible aristocrat.

Like Mr. Darcy in the *Pride and Prejudice* movie, though without all that English reserve.

"Looking good, master," hissed a voice beside him. "Very dapper."

Benedict took a deep breath through his nose, then glanced at the imp. It was tiny—barely bigger than a hare—with huge bat-like ears, a forked tail, and wickedly sharp teeth. At first, Benedict had considered it a poor substitute for the hordes of undead minions he'd once possessed. However, there were two key differences that had convinced him otherwise.

First, and perhaps most importantly, the imp didn't lower his Regeneration. Instead, summoning it and binding it to his service had required certain reagents and reserved a defined portion of his Ethera. One was barely even noticeable, but the more imps—or other demonic entities—he bound to his service, the more onerous the burden would become.

The other difference was the talking. Rarely did a moment go by when the stupid thing didn't have some comment or other. Most were sycophantic, but in the sort of way that Benedict just knew the imp was being sarcastic. Other times, it gave backhanded compliments. Or whispered insults under its breath that were only loud enough for Benedict to hear a word here or there. But what he did hear was enough that he'd actually kicked the little creature across the room on more than one occasion.

"Shut up," Benedict said. "Or I'll kick you again."

"Master is the best at kicking," the imp said. "Truly a prodigy of the foot."

Benedict kicked the thing, sending it sailing across the room before it hit a mannequin. It toppled over with a clatter, and despite the noise, he smiled with no small degree of satisfaction.

Until the stupid imp climbed out of the wreckage and gave him a thumbs-up.

After that, Benedict had to take a deep breath to keep himself from crossing the room and kicking it again. Once he'd calmed himself, he turned his attention from the imp and looked over the shop. It had once been one of Easton's most prestigious, and the wares were truly impressive. Or they had been before all the looting. Now, ball gowns, tuxedos, and expensive hats lay trampled on the floor. Most had been burned in the fire that had gutted the place, too.

That his current outfit had survived was a minor miracle.

So, Benedict straightened his coat, then stepped through the shattered window and into the street beyond. He glanced up at the night sky, and in the moonlight, he could see circling carrion birds. They were high enough level that if their intended prey had yet to die, they were more than capable of correcting that issue. More than once, Benedict had been forced to exercise his power to drive them off.

Fortunately, they seemed to have learned to leave him be. The same couldn't be said for the other survivors.

There weren't many left.

Apparently, when people had the power of superheroes—even if they were C- and D-team superheroes—mortality rates of any conflict went through the roof. Especially for the noncombatants who had so few protections against those with martial classes. Benedict had missed the worst of the fighting, but even what he'd seen had been brutal.

Of course, he'd added his own brand of chaos to the mix, using abilities like Heat Blood and Infection to whittle enemies down. By the time they recognized the issue, they were too far gone to recover.

That was Benedict's preference. For all that he was a willing killer, he didn't like direct confrontation. That was the advantage of his minions. He could send a horde of undead at the problem and never be forced to get his own hands dirty. Yet, with his new Demon Core, that tactic had been taken from him.

And he'd gotten an imp instead.

Despite the other advantages, he wasn't certain if it was a good trade. Sure, he was stronger, faster, and more durable than ever before. In addition, his spells were far more potent, as well. Yet, the loss of what he considered his class-defining ability was difficult to see as a net positive.

According to the demon Thakon, a single imp was more powerful than a hundred undead minions. And it was only the beginning. Eventually, not only would he be able to summon multiple imps, but he would also be able to add other, more powerful demonic creatures to his budding army.

For now, though, he was vulnerable.

So, when he set out from the ruined clothing shop, he did so with no small degree of caution. As he walked through the city, he was absolutely aghast at how quickly it had fallen. It had been some time since he'd walked the streets of Easton—and even then, it was under guard—but he still remembered the majestic palace, the orderly streets, and the well-built structures.

Most of those had fallen. Many had burned, and plenty of others had been torn to pieces by battles between powerful combatants. Even the wall had been breached, and any protections it offered had been sundered.

Every now and then, Benedict saw hints that there were survivors, but he knew that they would be few and far between. Because when the wall had fallen, it had let in the monsters. Without the guards or hunters keeping them at bay, the wildlife had quickly come to reclaim the city as their own. It had been a slaughter of many sides.

Some people had made it, but most had already abandoned the city after taking whatever they could. He didn't know where they intended to go. Nor did Bendict really care. He just wasn't in the habit of helping the same sort of people who would have bullied him in the past. No—they could fend for themselves.

"Well, well, well," a rough voice echoed from behind him. "What's a pretty boy like you doing in a place like this? Don't you know it's dangerous?"

Benedict stopped in his tracks and turned—just his head—to see a burly man wearing a charred blue-and-white tabard over chain mail armor. He carried a shining silvery halberd. Bendict's eyes flicked across the street, where he saw a slender man with a bow. Footsteps from the other direction told him that at least two others had joined them.

"You think I'm pretty?" he asked. "How kind."

"Not a compliment, man," said the thug. "Go on now. Take that coat off. Give us whatever else you got on you and we'll let you go."

"But boss, you said we would get to—"

"Shut up, Jerry."

"But—"

"I said to shut your mouth!" growled the leader, gesturing angrily at the archer. "Or I'll shut it for you!"

"Fine. Whatever."

"I swear to God, Jerry—if you weren't my brother-in-law . . ."

The man took a deep breath, then said, "Your stuff, man. Give it over and you get to go on your merry way. If you—"

Suddenly a massive column of roiling fire engulfed the man. For a long few seconds, it burned, hot and bright enough to illuminate the entire road. Then, as abruptly as it had appeared, the fire winked out, leaving only a human-shaped pile of ashes behind. A cool breeze swept through, scattering the ashes across the street.

Then, someone screamed.

"It burns!" the imp shouted in glee, clapping its hands like a child. "Did I do good, master? Do you like the fire?"

"Yes. I believe I do," Benedict admitted.

That was the other benefit of the imp. While it was no more durable than a child, the creature had an innate talent for fire that manifested in the form of an ability called Pyre. The results of said ability were obvious as Benedict watched the remainder of the ashes scatter across the cobblestones.

"What did you do?!" demanded Jerry, aiming an arrow in Benedict's direction.

"I did nothing to him. But you? That is a different story altogether. Do you feel it, Jerry? That burning in your veins? It will get worse," Benedict promised. Then, he finally glanced at the other two bandits. One had already fallen. "Oh, dear. I do believe it's too late for her."

The other fell a second later.

That only left Jerry.

"Can I burn him, master? Please? I will be good!"

Benedict glanced at the imp. "No. I have a use for him," he said.

By that point, poor Jerry had already collapsed. However, Heat Blood alone didn't work nearly as quickly as when it was combined with Infection and Empowered Affliction, which he'd used on the other two would-be bandits. So, even if Jerry was on the verge of incapacitation, he would last a while longer. Hopefully, it would be enough time to accomplish his goal.

Benedict approached the agonized man, whose entire body had locked up. He knelt beside the trembling figure, then tapped him on the head. "I know it hurts. I can stop it. I can make it end. Do you want that?"

Jerry summoned his courage and spit, "Fuck you!"

"No, thank you," he said politely. The very idea of letting anyone touch him in that way was abhorrent. "You will suffer for quite some time. Hours, at least. Your death will not be quick. As I said, I can end it. I can give you solace. I only need your permission."

To his credit, Jerry lasted for nearly five minutes before he was begging for mercy. Soon after that, Benedict cast Demonic Pact and thrust the deal upon the man. "Do you, of free will and without dishonesty, accept my terms?" he asked. "The terms being that I will take your spirit in exchange for ending your suffering."

Jerry screamed something unintelligible. Apparently, having one's blood on the verge of boiling was quite painful, even when one took enhanced Constitution and Regeneration into account.

"I need your agreement, Jerry. Please. I want to help you."

Finally, Jerry shouted, "Yes!"

"Good, good," Benedict breathed, smiling as he felt the spell complete its cast. The moment it did, a blinding light erupted from Jerry's chest. Benedict blinked, and when his vision cleared, he saw a tiny purple crystal hovering a few inches above the now-dead bandit. Benedict grabbed it, and when his fingers wrapped around the crystal, he felt a torrent of energy envelope him.

He struggled against the power of Jerry's spirit, using every ounce of willpower he possessed to keep it contained in the gem. His struggle only lasted a few seconds, but to him, it felt like an eternity. Once he'd forced it under his control, he used another ability:

Spell: Summon Ritual Dagger	Manifest a dagger used in demonic rituals.

It was a simple but necessary spell because, without it, he would be incapable of casting the second-most-important spell in his repertoire:

Spell: Empower Summoning Circle	Use a contracted spirit to empower a ritual circle drawn with the blood of an enemy.

He could have used a normal blade to cut into Jerry's corpse, but according to Thakon, the ritual circle would be far more powerful—and more likely to be successful—if he used the summoned Ritual Dagger. Not one to gainsay a clear expert in all things demonic, Benedict had taken the archdemon at his word.

Over the next few minutes, Benedict hacked into Jerry's corpse, eliciting a spurt of blood that he used to draw a very precise rune upon the ground. Thakon had cautioned him against making any mistakes, so he drew the circle as perfectly as possible. Fortunately, he had enough Dexterity to steady his hands to a supernatural degree.

Once he was finished with the circle, Benedict placed the spirit gem in the center and cast Empower Summoning Circle. The purple crystal once again blazed with light, but it only took a second for that glow to transfer to the circle itself.

That's when he finally cast the final spell:

Spell: Summon Demonling	Using an empowered summoning circle, summon a tier-1 fel servant and bind the creature to your will. Cooldown based on Ethera attribute. Current cooldown: 18.6 days.

The circle erupted into flames, and the imp clapped in glee. Then, abruptly, the flames petered out, revealing another imp.

"Master," it said in its rough but high-pitched voice. "I serve."

"I serve, too!" said the first imp.

And so, Benedict's demonic army had begun to take shape. The only question was what he intended to do with it. For now, he only wanted to leave Easton behind. But the future? He wasn't sure. He supposed he would have to take that as it came. So, he rose to his feet, motioned for the imps to follow him, then strode down the street, silently hoping that someone else might try to rob him.

43

ALLIANCES

Why would I do that?" asked K'hana, sitting primly on an elaborately colored cushion.

"Because you need people," Elijah answered. "Your city here is not as isolated as you think. You can't even run your tower, can you? Or did something change while I was gone?"

"We feel confident that, with your notes, we can overcome our deficiencies," she claimed. But even Elijah, who sometimes missed social cues, could tell that she was exaggerating.

He said as much, which elicited a frown from the beautiful elf before he added, "But if you ally yourselves with Seattle, you will have all the help you could want."

"And in return, I will help them find water," she said.

To Elijah, it seemed like a perfectly good deal. She had an ability that the people of Seattle sorely needed, and the elves of Arvandor had a need that Seattle's much larger population could help fill. So, he was a little confused as to why K'hana would object to the proposed alliance.

"I don't get what the issue is," he admitted, leaning back on his own cushion. He looked around. There were a few other elves there, each one sitting on their own unique cushion, but they all clearly deferred to K'hana. Elijah reached down and took a loud, slurping sip of the tea he'd been provided. It was flavorful, with a hint of something fruity, but he couldn't identify it. "Good tea. Seriously, though—what's going on? Why wouldn't you want to form an alliance?"

"We have heard of this city," she answered with a sigh. "It is a place of chaos. War. Their laws are not followed, and they do not care for their people. It is a shameful place, and I do not wish to associate with the people who would create such a city."

"Ouch. Tell me how you really feel," Elijah muttered to himself. "Would it help if I told you that the man I want you to meet is a good guy?"

"If he was a good person, he would have put a stop to the injustice so prevalent in his city," K'hana pointed out.

"That's kind of what I'm trying to facilitate," Elijah stated. "Water is the problem. It's complicated, but for most people in Seattle, there's not enough of it. If you can help them solve that issue, it will save a lot of lives. And it will give Isaiah the leverage he needs to take firmer control. Peace is what's at stake here. You can help with that."

There was a chance it would prevent Elijah from having to kill a lot of people on Mercer Mesa, too. After Valoria, his bloodlust had been sated. He would kill if he had to, but if he could avoid it, he would.

"More importantly, it helps you," Elijah said. "How long until the tower surges? A month? Maybe two? You'll be overrun by Voxx."

"You could help us conquer it," she suggested.

"I have other things to do," Elijah said. "And even if I didn't, relying on me is not a viable long-term solution. I won't always be around."

"You could be," came a voice from nearby.

Elijah glanced in that direction, and he saw that the sentence had originated with an older elf. The only real nods to age were a couple of lines at the corners of her eyes and gray hair, but Elijah could tell she was much older than she appeared.

"What do you mean?" Elijah asked.

"You are young, fit, and powerful. I propose a joining with our Water Witch," she said.

For a second, Elijah struggled to wrap his mind around what the elf had said, but when he did, his eyes flicked toward K'hana. Her expression was stoic, but there was a blush of embarrassment on her cheeks.

He coughed.

"Uh . . . No, thanks," he said.

K'hana blurted, "What?"

"Why?" asked the older elf at the same time.

"Um . . . Right. That probably sounded rude. In my culture, people . . . um . . . join together as a couple because they're in love. Not to cement an alliance."

Of course, that wasn't necessarily true. Throughout history, marriage—which was what he assumed they were talking about—had been used as a diplomatic tool. Yet, that had fallen out of favor long ago, and Elijah was anything but comfortable with it. In addition, despite K'hana's obvious beauty, he just didn't find her all that appealing. Perhaps it was her personality, which was a little too reserved for his taste, or the alien nature of her looks, but when he looked at her, he just didn't feel those sorts of feelings.

Or maybe he just preferred humans.

He didn't think of himself as that picky regarding appearance. However, there was a cultural gulf between them that would almost assuredly be difficult to bridge. But maybe that was just his excuse. Regardless, he couldn't help his tastes. And that was only considering it from a personal standpoint. It was even less appealing from a political perspective. The elves just didn't have much that he wanted, so even if he was willing to leave his Grove—which he definitely was not—there wasn't a lot of reason for him to latch himself to Arvandor.

"Well, this is awkward," he muttered as the elves stared at him in disbelief. Clearly, they thought he would fall all over himself to take them up on the offer. He massaged the back of his neck, saying, "It's . . . um . . . It's not you. It's totally me."

By that point, they were all staring daggers at him.

"Did I just commit a social faux pas? If it makes any difference, I kind of do that a lot. I spent a long time alone, and I still haven't really recovered my social graces," he babbled. "God. Social graces. I sound like a Southern beauty queen or something. My point is that I'm not good with these kinds of things. But I really do think this alliance between Arvandor and Seattle is a good idea. That said, I can see that I've overstayed my welcome. So . . . um . . . Bye, I guess? Catch you on the flip side."

Then, he gave them an awkward finger-gun salute, which he immediately regretted. Either way, he pushed himself to his feet and backed away, mumbling to himself, "Finger gun? When is it ever a good idea to unironically give someone the finger gun? And the flip side? Ugh."

Thankfully, the elves only stared at him like he'd grown horns. That was better than the alternative, which involved attacking him for his affront to good manners. He didn't think they were particularly violent, but he also suspected that even elves would react poorly to such a blunt rejection.

For better or worse, none of them tried to stop him, and Elijah decided that it was high time he and Miguel left the elven city behind. So, he quickly returned to the rooms they had been given and told his nephew, "Time to go. Get your stuff together, big guy. We need to vámonos."

"What did you do?" Miguel asked.

"Huh? Who said I did anything? It's just time to leave," Elijah said.

"It's the middle of the night."

"Night walks are the best. Stars and moons and all of that. Plus, the best predators come out at night."

"That doesn't sound—"

There was a knock at the door, which cut Miguel off. Elijah sighed. "Okay, so whatever happens here, just don't freak out," he said. Then, before Miguel could respond, Elijah opened the door to see K'hana standing there. "Hey. Long time no see."

"You saw me ten minutes ago," she said, cocking her head to the side.

"Right. Just an expression. What's up? Please tell me you're not going to make another marriage proposal. I'm flattered, but—"

"I am coming with you," she said.

Elijah narrowed his eyes. "I'm not going to change my mind," he said.

"Nor would I want you to. Elder Hama did not ask for my input before suggesting that . . . partnership," K'hana stated. "If she had, I would have refused."

"Huh? I'm not good enough for you, then?" Elijah asked, slightly offended.

"You just said the same thing about me."

"I know, but . . . Wow. So, that doesn't feel so great. I know it's silly, but I still kind of go through life thinking everyone loves me."

"They don't," Miguel said. "In Ironshore especially. Most of them . . . Well, hate is a strong word, but—"

"Zip it."

"What does *zip it* mean?" asked K'hana.

"That my uncle likes to ignore things he doesn't like," Miguel supplied cheerfully. With a grin, he added, "I'm Miggy, by the way."

"I am K'hana."

"Great. We're all acquainted. Now, what changed?" Elijah asked. "Because back there, you were all like, 'No, I won't ally with a bunch of backward thugs who can't keep the peace in their own city.' And now you're begging me to take you with me? I need a bit of an explanation here."

"Very well. I was always going to go," she said. "The alliance makes sense. My people wished for me to extract more benefits before I agreed. I do not wish to do so."

"What sort of benefits?"

"You are a Druid. Your abilities could assist our farming efforts," she said. "We have no food shortages now, but our population has seen a significant increase over the past few years. Soon, our farms will not be enough."

"I think I need to introduce you to a friend," Elijah said. Then, he explained how Lucy's greenhouse worked, finishing with, "I'm sure that if you help them, she'll be willing to help you. Maybe she could even help you set up a greenhouse of your own. I don't want to speak for her, but just knowing what's possible could help. And if not, I'd be happy to assist. You could have just asked, though. No need for the subterfuge."

"I see," she said. "I apologize if I offended you."

Then, she bowed.

Elijah let out another sigh. "Oh, c'mon. Don't do that. Let's just . . . Let's just go," he said. "We've got a lot of ground to cover, and we're on a timer."

Indeed, Elijah hadn't really thought his little excursion through. For one, while he thought his own presence was necessary, he had no intention of taking Miguel back into Seattle. The whole point was to help the young man to commune with nature, and that part of the journey would be finished once they reached the Circle of Spears, where Elijah intended to send Miguel back home.

But he'd forgotten one major thing before setting out.

His coffee. The cherries were assuredly ready to be separated from the beans by now, which meant that he needed to do that as soon as possible or he would lose the whole batch. After that, he only needed to wait a day or so for them to dry, then enlist the help of a Cook to roast them.

Regardless—the point was that he needed to head back to the island for a few days before continuing on to Seattle. Which presented a problem, if K'hana wanted to tag along. It had been his idea, but one he'd barely thought through.

"Also, and don't freak out, but I'm going to take you to my island for a couple of days. We'll be back on track soon after that," he said.

"How?"

"Magic."

"That's his answer to everything," Miguel said. "You get used to it."

"I don't understand," K'hana said.

"It's simple. Do you trust me?"

"No."

"Oh."

"Didn't expect that answer, did you?" Miguel laughed.

"I did not," Elijah admitted. "But I guess we've got a few days. Hopefully, I will have earned her trust by then. And if not . . . Well, we'll figure it out. Onward and upward, I always say."

"I've never heard you say that," Miguel pointed out.

"Shut up. And respect your elders," Elijah said. "Now finish packing. We're on the clock here."

To drive the point home, he tapped his finger against his wrist. Clearly, K'hana didn't understand the gesture, which just as obviously had her rethinking her decision to accompany him to Seattle. But at least Miguel made the connection because he spent the next couple of minutes thrusting his belongings into his pack.

"Why did you take all of that out?" Elijah asked.

"Because you said we were going to be here for a little while."

"Don't do that. Keep things in your pack until you need them," Elijah said. "You should write that down."

"I don't have a pen or paper."

"Then remember it."

"I probably won't," Miguel admitted.

Elijah sighed, then glanced at K'hana. "Young people, right? So disrespectful."

She didn't answer, which Elijah chose to take as agreement. In any case, once Miguel was packed, the trio set off through the city, eventually exiting into the Twilight Clefts and beginning their journey to the Circle of Spears.

44

VISITOR

He's a cute little guy, right?" asked Elijah, which caused K'hana to recoil. That certainly wasn't the reaction he'd intended to elicit. Though, that was probably due to the creature he held in his hands.

"I don't think she likes Lizard Face," Miguel remarked, scratching the creature's scaly ribs.

"They are incredibly venomous!" she hissed, taking a step back to put some distance between herself and the giant sand monitor Elijah held in his arms. The thing was as large as a Komodo dragon, so without his enhanced Strength, he never would've been capable of holding it aloft. Or at least not easily.

"Lizard Face?" asked Elijah.

Miguel shrugged. "He needed a name."

"That's worse than Snappy."

"Snappy is a good name!" Miguel insisted.

"And Trevor? What about Susan, Annabelle, and Bubba?" Elijah asked with a small smirk. As he spoke, the sand monitor tasted the air, then closed its eyes and rested its head on Elijah's shoulder.

"Those are good names, too!"

"Giving animals people names is weird," Elijah stated.

"Whatever. Talking to you is like talking to a brick wall," Miguel muttered. "Nobody else is ever right."

"In this case, I am objectively right."

"That's not what *objectively* means."

"It is if I say so," Elijah stated. "Respect your elders."

"Is . . . that thing coming with us?" asked K'hana, cutting in. Elijah suspected she'd done so to put a stop to the bickering. Both he and Miguel knew it didn't mean anything. It was good-natured. But it was clear that K'hana's culture didn't really include things like that. Or perhaps she was just as uptight as she seemed.

"Oh, no. I just thought you'd want to meet him," Elijah said. "You know, a lot of people in Seattle eat these fellows. They taste a bit like chicken, especially when they're fried."

With that, he set the monitor down, and it waddled off. Normally, they moved pretty slowly, but when they were threatened, the lizards could move like lightning. Elijah watched it with some admiration as it dipped behind a low rise and disappeared. It wasn't a skill or anything. Their hides were simply perfect for camouflaging them in the desert.

"I guess we'll get moving again," Elijah said, setting off. The other two followed, with Miguel hurrying to catch up.

"You think we'll get there today?" he asked.

Elijah shrugged. "Probably," he said. Only a few days before, they'd passed the copse of Joshua trees he'd planted the first time he'd been in the desert. And to his horror, he'd found that most of them had been chopped down. That had infuriated and saddened Elijah to the point where he'd spent a couple of days replanting the trees and helping them take root.

But now, they were closing in on the Circle of Spears, which meant he had a choice to make. To that end, he asked K'hana, "Can I trust you?"

"Perhaps," she said without hesitation.

Elijah stopped, and the other two stopped, as well. "That wasn't the answer I expected."

"I suspected as much," she admitted. "But I feel that I must be honest. If breaking your trust will help my people survive, then I will do so without hesitation. They are my first priority. However, I will not break your trust unless it is absolutely necessary."

That elaboration made Elijah feel a little better, but it wasn't really what he'd wanted to hear. It meant that it would be a little irresponsible to take K'hana to his island. So, that left him with a few choices, none of which were ideal. First, he could simply go straight to Seattle and drop the elf off with Lucy or Isaiah. That ran the risk of taking longer than he could afford, but it was probably the safest option.

Yet, it would also necessitate taking Miguel into the city, which he had no intention of doing. It wasn't the cesspool that Valoria had been, but it was perhaps much more dangerous. And given that Miguel didn't have an archetype yet, it would be even worse for him.

So, he wanted to avoid that route if possible.

The other option was to take Miguel home while leaving K'hana in the oasis. But that was just as dangerous for her because, without Elijah around, the wildlife would prove much deadlier. There was every chance that Snappy might react poorly to the intrusion into his territory, and if that happened, either the turtle or K'hana would end up gravely injured.

Finally, there was the option that made the most sense, but also played host to the most risk. Taking K'hana back to the island would only delay him a little, but it would be much safer for everyone involved. Yet, it did come with the risk involved in showing anyone—especially someone like K'hana, who knew the value of a place like the Grove—his island.

It seemed like a lose-lose sort of situation, and not for the first time, Elijah wished he'd thought things through before setting off. But the past was the past, and as such, he couldn't change his circumstances. So, he needed to work with what he had.

And looking at his options, everything pointed to taking K'hana to the island. Hopefully, the fact that it was thousands of miles away from her home would keep her from being able to determine the location of his Grove.

Besides, he knew he couldn't keep it a secret indefinitely. Eventually, the people of Ironshore would let it be known that something interesting was on his island. Perhaps they already had. The only answer to that sort of threat was to simply be stronger than anyone who might try to invade his Domain.

So, he said, "I've got two choices for you, K'hana."

"Does one of them involve killing me?" she asked, and Elijah felt ethera swirling around her.

"What? No! Jesus . . ."

"I don't think she knows who Jesus was," supplied Miguel.

"No. The choice is more of an invitation. I was going to ask if you wanted to come back to my island," he said. "The alternative is to hang out in an oasis with an ornery turtle. So . . . up to you."

"Snappy isn't ornery," Miguel said. "He's just a little shy around strangers."

"He tried to eat Colt the first time he wandered near the pond," Elijah pointed out. "And there's a reason birds don't land there anymore."

"Just shy, like I said. And he didn't eat Colt. That has to count for something."

Elijah rolled his eyes, then turned his focus back to K'hana, who was clearly having second thoughts about her decision to accompany him. "So, what's it going to be? We'll be gone for about a week, then we'll come back here," he said. "I promise you'll be unharmed."

She took a deep breath, then said, "I will accompany you to this . . . island."

Letting out a sigh of relief, Elijah said, "Awesome. Then, on we go as we try to forget this awkward interaction ever happened."

After that, he did just as he'd described, marching off across the desert. The other two struggled to keep up at first—he often forgot that others weren't equipped with his level of physical attributes—so he slowed to what felt like a glacial pace. To distract himself, he occupied one facet of his Mind with cycling his Core while with another he focused on maintaining a steady conversation with Miguel. Throughout their journey, he'd endeavored to help the young man connect with nature, and one of the best ways of doing that was to describe all the different forms of life. And even in the desert, there were plenty of living creatures ranging from spiders to reptiles to large worms that lived below the surface. It may have looked desolate, but that appearance was far from reality.

For his part, Miguel soaked in the information like a sponge. He had his mothers' intellectual curiosity, which told Elijah that his nephew would probably make a fair Scholar, if that was the route he chose.

Finally, though, they reached the Circle of Spears. While Miguel dashed toward the pond to reacquaint himself with his favorite turtle, Elijah watched K'hana's reaction as she circled the dolmen.

"Who made this?" she asked at last.

"Me and my sister-in-law. Pretty awesome, right? Getting those monuments just right was a pain, but the carvings turned out really well, I think," Elijah said. Then, he went on to describe the process, explaining where he'd gotten the stones and how he and Carmen had put everything together. "But it's more than just a monument. It's tied to one of my spells. I won't go into how it all works, but from here, I can open a gate to a few different places. One of those is my island, which is where we're headed."

After that, Elijah yelled for Miguel. Predictably, the boy was loath to leave the turtle behind, but he came anyway. And then, Elijah used Roots of the World Tree, creating a gate made of vines that snaked up from the ground. The air inside shimmered into a portal to the Grove.

Elijah gestured, "After you."

Miguel was the first to step through. K'hana hesitantly followed. And finally, Elijah brought up the rear, letting the gate fade away the moment he was through. The dense ethera of the island enveloped him like a warm blanket, and he took a deep, relaxing breath before saying, "Ah. That feels good."

"W-what is this place?" K'hana whispered, looking around in obvious wonder.

"My island," Elijah said. "Well, my Grove to be more accurate. But the Grove is on my island, so I guess I was right the first time. Regardless, welcome—let me show you to where you'll be staying for the next few days."

Elijah had considered sending K'hana to Ironshore, but he'd thought better of letting her wander too far. Instead, he wanted to keep her on the island where he could keep an eye on her. So, with that in mind, he escorted her to his tree house and showed her to the guest room. Once she was on her way to getting settled in, Elijah turned his attention to the biggest reason he'd returned to the island.

His coffee cherries were ready to be removed from the water, then separated from their beans. So, he headed to the large trough where he'd submerged them and got to work plucking them from the liquid. Once that was done, he removed the beans from the flesh, tossing them into a separate basket.

It was a tedious process, but Elijah found that it was strangely calming. More, it gave him an opportunity to continue his Core cultivation. And at last, he felt that he was finally starting to make progress. Though, even as his Core felt like it was expanding, he couldn't deny that cycling had become even more difficult. However, that was as expected, based on everything he'd learned. So, he kept at it, and over the next eight hours, he finished his task.

Once the beans had been separated, Nerthus took the discarded flesh away, saying that it would make a great addition to his compost heap. Meanwhile, Elijah laid the beans out to dry. Night had already fallen, but he hoped the process would be complete by the middle of the next day.

As he worked, Elijah also kept one facet of his Mind trained on K'hana. She didn't stray far from the tree house, instead confining her movements to the Grove. Yet, it was clear that she was impressed—and a little frightened—by what she saw. Never was that more apparent than when she spent an entire hour standing at the base of the ancestral tree and just staring up at its branches.

That's where Elijah joined her.

"This tree is not normal," she said after a few moments.

"It's not. Even among others of its species, it's special," Elijah said. "I think you can understand why I was hesitant to bring you here. If the wrong sort of person sees this tree—or the rest of this Grove—everything will be in danger. I hope you're not that kind of person."

"I would never violate a Druid's Grove," she said. "Those of us who came to this planet are not as well learned as some, but we hold nature's protectors in high esteem."

"Didn't feel like it before when you first found out I was a Druid," Elijah remarked.

She glanced at him, saying, "I was merely surprised. Druids are not normally combatants."

"Well, I am," Elijah said. "But I'm still a Druid, and this Grove is everything to me. So, please respect it while you're here. And I'll ask that you not reveal anything about this place when you return to your people."

"I will not. You have my word."

"Good," Elijah said. Then, he clapped his hands together and asked, "So, how would you like to see the ocean?"

45

Dappled sunlight fell upon Elijah's face, eliciting a feeling of peace that he'd so seldom experienced. Sometimes, it felt like he was being pulled in a thousand different directions. In most cases, it was his own fault. He'd taken so many things onto his shoulders that the combined weight of his responsibilities—self-imposed or externally motivated—was almost enough to crush him.

But he endeavored to persevere, continuing on to the best of his abilities.

That wasn't to say that he hadn't made mistakes. He had, and plenty of them. So many, in fact, that he had no interest in enumerating them. The most recent was the apathy that had enveloped him after completing the Temple of Virtue, an attitude that had wasted precious time that he couldn't get back. But there were smaller mistakes, as well, like his failure in scheduling that had cost him more time. Now, though, he was on the verge of getting everything back on track.

But first, he wanted to taste the fruits of his labor.

To that end, he'd spent part of the previous day hiring a Chef in Ironshore to roast his coffee beans. The haughty goblin—Moag was his name—hadn't come cheap, but according to Ramik, he was the most effective cook in the city. Luckily, the goblin was as efficient as he was expensive to hire, and he'd finished the project in only a couple of hours. Before Earth had been touched by the World Tree, roasting coffee beans typically took no more than fifteen minutes, but apparently, things changed once ethera was added to the mix.

Elijah wasn't so bold as to try to tell a Chef how to do his job. He'd resolved to trust the goblin to do the task he'd been hired to do. And the moment Elijah had smelled the product—which Moag had ground for him, as well—he knew that the goblin had hit a home run. Even a whiff of the stuff gave him a jolt of energy and vitality, which boded well for the future effects.

Still, Elijah had forced himself to wait until the next morning to sample it, largely because he wanted to share the experience with Carmen and K'hana, who remained on the island. After gathering the pair and boiling some water in his kitchen, Elijah put his looted French press to good use.

He'd never used one before—all his coffee had come from electric coffee makers in the past—but it wasn't a terribly complicated apparatus. Regardless, it wasn't long before he'd managed to make three cups, which he'd liberally sweetened with honey provided by Nerthus's apiary.

Thus armed, he'd headed out to the balcony, where the two women waited. Carmen and K'hana had taken to one another quite well, which was nice, considering how Elijah had basically ignored the elf since returning to the island. He hadn't meant to, but he'd been a little preoccupied with his Core cultivation, getting his coffee taken care of, and training with Miguel.

As it turned out, both Colt and Kurik had entered the tower the day before Elijah returned to the Grove, so he'd taken it upon himself to keep his nephew occupied. He wasn't the outdoorsman that Kurik was, and he certainly couldn't hold a candle to Colt's expertise with weaponry. However, Elijah was light-years beyond either one when it came to cultivation. So, with Nerthus's help, he'd begun to train Miguel so the young man would be ready to take the leap with his Body, Mind, and Soul as soon as he gained his archetype. The spryggent had even offered to help in a similar—if less powerful—way to how he'd assisted Elijah.

Apparently, doing so required Nerthus to sacrifice some of his own power. It was a temporary impairment, and when Elijah found out about it, he'd told Nerthus to save his strength. However, the spryggent had insisted, saying that his power was meant to be used in such a way. Doing so would only be possible if Miguel ended up with a nature attunement, though.

Even so, Elijah's lessons would help his nephew regardless of his attunement, so the instruction persisted—despite Miguel's disdain. He was an active young man, and at present, he didn't have the temperament to enjoy sitting in a glade for hours on end. He'd have much preferred to be practicing his sword skills, traipsing about the wilderness, or playing with whichever animal he'd happened upon that day. Still, he was his mothers' son, and he possessed the willpower to move past his personal feelings and commit to doing what was necessary.

Miguel's attitude reminded Elijah of Alyssa.

At present, the young man was sitting next to the ancestral tree as he attempted to meditate. But Elijah could tell that it wasn't really working. He was too twitchy.

Elijah sighed. He knew it wasn't the process of a day teaching Miguel to connect with nature. For his part, Elijah had something of a cheat with One with Nature, which, in addition to letting him feel everything in the effect's radius, also allowed him to connect with that ephemeral structure that underlay everything.

For Elijah, it was like looking at a lake. Most people only ever saw the surface and, even if they appreciated it, didn't truly perceive everything below. Elijah's own perception didn't extend to the bottom—in the analogy, he could barely see a foot past the surface—but even that was impactful on his psyche to the point where he sometimes questioned if he would have taken the same actions if he hadn't felt that influence.

In any case, when Elijah found his way to the balcony, he said, "Ladies. Coffee is served."

Then, he handed the steaming mugs to their recipients. K'hana asked, "This coffee—is it like tea? We do not have it on my world."

"Better," Carmen said with a grin as she sniffed the mug. Elijah had done the same, verifying that there just wasn't anything like the smell of freshly brewed coffee. Perhaps it was a learned response, but the smell always brought a smile to his face. "Plus, I'm pretty sure this is going to be special. What quality did Moag say it was?"

"He said, and I quote, 'Food and drink is not meant to be graded, only enjoyed.' I pressed him, too. He wouldn't give it up," Elijah stated. "Don't you have an identification skill?"

"Only works to full effect on things I've made myself," Carmen answered. "I can usually get a name from stuff related to blacksmithing, but with this? I get nothing."

"Pity," Elijah said. "Well, we'll just have to wing it. Cheers."

Elijah brought the cup to his lips, then took a sip. Flavor erupted across his tongue. The normal tastes were all there. It was a bit nutty. Bitter, too. But it was more than that, and in a similar way to how his Grove berries differed from normal berries. He took another sip, enjoying the way the flavors played across his tongue.

"Yep. That's the best coffee I've ever tasted," he said. The honey gave it a slightly different flavor than if he'd used sugar, but even that was somehow more—and in every way—than typical honey. He took another sip, then asked Carmen, "What do you think? It's good, right?"

"You have no idea how much I've missed this," she answered.

Elijah then asked K'hana the same question. But the elf didn't have the same reaction. She said, "It is . . . good."

"Ouch," Elijah said, clutching at a mock wound in his chest. "That bad, huh?"

"Ah . . . No . . ."

"It's okay if you don't like it," Carmen said. "Coffee isn't for everyone. I wasn't an immediate convert, but Alyssa . . . Well, she always loved the stuff. So, eventually, I did, too."

Over the next quarter hour, Elijah and Carmen finished their coffee. So did K'hana, who'd asked for more honey so she could choke it down. But it was only after they'd finished the contents of their mugs that they got a shock.

"You're seeing this, right?" Elijah breathed, looking at his notification.

> You have consumed a Complex-grade beverage. The following benefits
> will be applied:
> +5 Strength, Dexterity, Constitution, and Ethera. +10 Regeneration.
> Duration: 24.2 hours.

"That's incredible," Carmen muttered. "I never . . . I thought it would be like your Grove berries. But this is so much better."

Elijah couldn't disagree. And even K'hana was impressed, claiming that attribute-enhancing food and drink was incredibly rare. She'd never consumed anything with those effects, and she admitted, "I have always thought the stories of such foods were myths. This is a great boon."

"I wonder what the limits are. Like, could I feed this to Miggy?" Elijah asked.

"Maybe once he gets his archetype," Carmen said. "But I suspect it's similar to equipment. He can barely even lift Crude-grade gear right now. Anything higher, and it's too much for him. The same is probably true for this coffee."

"Do you think I could make something with my berries, then?" Elijah asked. "And what happens if you drink two different types in a row? Do you get two buffs? I assume that if you drink a second cup of coffee, it'll just reset the timer or something."

"One drink and one food enhancement at a time," K'hana said. "That is how it was in the stories we were told."

"Ah. I'll have to test it out at some point," Elijah said. Though he knew that, with the amount of effort that had gone into his coffee, there was little chance of stumbling across something similar, at least in the short term. Perhaps as the ambient ethera on Earth continued to climb and those with appropriate skills gained levels, it would become more common. Either way, he was more than satisfied with his choice to use the Miracle Seed to satisfy his long-gestating caffeine addiction.

After a little while longer—during which he enjoyed a second cup of coffee, claiming that he wanted to test the resulting buff—he said, "Well, I think this little vacation is done. My spell is going to reset in a couple of hours, so get your things together. I'm going to say goodbye to Miguel, and as soon as the spell's off cooldown, we're headed back to the Circle of Spears and then to Seattle."

The next two hours went by without incident, except that Miguel expressed—and in quite a fervent manner—that he wished to accompany Elijah to Seattle. However, Elijah's reasoning remained just as valid as ever, and he refused to take his nephew into such a dangerous city. For all he knew, the situation there had devolved into open warfare, and no matter Miguel's skills with weapons, he still didn't have an archetype. As such, he was incredibly vulnerable. Despite that flawless reasoning, Miguel wasn't happy about Elijah's refusal, and he stormed off into the woods.

"He'll get over it," Carmen said when Elijah expressed some concern over the exchange. "He's a kid. I know he's been through a lot, and most of the time, he acts more mature than his age. But he's still a child in a lot of ways."

"I know," Elijah said. But he didn't enjoy being cast as the bad guy in anyone's story, much less his nephew's.

Soon, his cooldown was up, and he once again cast Roots of the World Tree. After the gate manifested, he and K'hana stepped through and into the oasis. The heat of the desert hit them both like a solid wall, and in seconds, Elijah felt sweat trickling down his back.

"Let's go," he said.

The two covered the distance between the Circle of Spears and Seattle much more quickly than they would have if Miguel had come along. K'hana didn't have high Strength or Dexterity, but she had enough of both to allow her to move through the desert at superhuman speeds. So, it was only half a day before Seattle came into view.

As they passed the landlocked ships, K'hana stared at them in awe. She'd only gotten a brief glimpse of the ocean back on Elijah's island, but even that had been enough to elicit no small degree of anxiety in the elf. And seeing the ships—along with Elijah's explanation of how they worked—brought some of that back to the fore. She said, "My world has no oceans. Even that oasis would have been considered a great treasure. To see such large vessels that can cross thousands of miles of ocean . . . It is hard to imagine such a world."

They only paused for a few minutes so the curious—and anxious—elf could inspect the hulking derelicts before they moved on. As they drew closer to Seattle's gates, Elijah suggested that K'hana wear a headscarf so that her ears were hidden. Her incredible beauty would still be on display, but without the tapered ears of her race being visible, the hope was that she could avoid undue notice. K'hana consented to follow Elijah's lead, so when they finally reached the city, she'd covered her head and ears. In addition, she'd wrapped the same scarf around the lower half of her face.

However, that proved unnecessary because the gates were entirely unguarded. Even as they cautiously passed through, Elijah heard a massive explosion coming from the area on the other side of Mercer Mesa.

Clearly, the tentative peace of Seattle had already been broken.

46

MAKING AN EXAMPLE

Whating's going on?" asked Elijah, grabbing a pedestrian's arm. The man tried to jerk free, but he was entirely unsuccessful. "I don't want any trouble. I just want to know what to expect."

"War," the man spit. "Those assholes on Mercer Mesa allied with the Lake City Adventurers and attacked the government. Or what's left of it. They won't last long, though. They don't have the power."

"Shit," Elijah breathed, releasing the man. As the fellow ran off, joining the flow of other pedestrians, Elijah turned to K'hana and said, "This visit might be short-lived. If it comes down to it, we're just going to leave, alright? I don't want to fight a war if there's no chance of our side winning."

"I understand," she said, though Elijah felt ethera whirling around her. It was subtle, but it was there, nonetheless.

After that, the pair traversed the city. Along the way, Elijah saw that, in a lot of ways, Seattle was exactly as he'd left it. Most of the residents were clearly trying to go about their lives, the same as always. But periodic explosions from the other side of the city had put everyone on edge. They didn't know what would happen when the fighting was finished, and they were obviously nervous about what the future might hold.

K'hana tried not to gape at the technology on display, but her efforts yielded mixed results. Most of the time, she remained stoic and stone-faced, though there were a few bits of technology—like phones and computers—that elicited wide-eyed gasps once Elijah explained their nature.

"These devices allowed you to access information so easily?" she wondered.

"Yeah," Elijah answered. "They were very useful tools, but most of us took them for granted. More often than not, we used them for entertainment, usually the silly sort."

Because of how steep the cost of targeted research was in the new world, Elijah had come to value information a lot more than in the past. On quite a few occasions, he'd found himself wishing the internet still worked. If it did, finding information about classes, cultivation, and just about everything else would have been much easier. Even his search for his family would have ended much more quickly.

But that was a useless lamentation. The world was the way it was, and all they could do was adjust accordingly to the changed reality.

With that in mind, Elijah and K'hana trekked across the city. A few times, they passed old battlegrounds where the local buildings bore the brunt of the destruction. Husks of cars and piles of near-molten slag were in abundance, as well.

And then there were the bodies.

They weren't that common, but a couple of times, Elijah looked down an alley to see dozens of corpses heaped into large piles. They were all naked, having been stripped of anything even remotely valuable, and they'd been treated with absolutely no dignity. In the past, such blatant disregard for the dead would have transformed Seattle into a hotbed of disease. Yet, most people were hardy enough to withstand those sorts of sicknesses.

Elijah did wonder what would happen if microbes started to evolve. Would that result in superinfections? Viruses that even healing spells couldn't combat? It was a troubling thought, especially when he considered how incredibly deadly some diseases had been even before the world had been transformed. Hopefully, he would never have to deal with that sort of thing.

Regardless, they made their way through the eastern half of the city without much issue. It wasn't until they had passed Mercer Mesa, which acted as something of a dividing line between the peaceful portion and the war zone, that they began to have issues. At first, they were merely watched—and by both sides of the conflict—but inevitably, they found a squad barring their path.

There were two men and three women, all wearing an eclectic collection of gear that marked them as Lake City Adventurers. The leader, who was a tall, dark-skinned woman with short hair, called out, "You two are going to want to stop right there."

Elijah considered simply taking on the Shape of the Guardian and massacring the people. Something told him that route would end up being easier. However, after losing control in Valoria, he'd resolved to avoid killing unless it proved absolutely necessary. It wasn't guilt, precisely but, rather, an acknowledgment that there was usually a better way to solve issues. Besides, even as misguided as they might be, they were still people. And without his grief-induced rage obscuring his good sense, he held that human life was worth a little inconvenience.

So, he slowed to a stop, then leaned on his staff as he asked, "What's up? Is this area off-limits or something?"

"For you? Absolutely," she answered.

Elijah sighed. "Guess we'll just turn back, then," he said, glancing around. There were a few bodies nearby, most of which wore the black Kevlar armor of the local government. Elijah hadn't exactly committed to fighting a war, but he had agreed to help Isaiah. That made them, at the very least, temporary allies.

Which meant that the people in front of him were probably his enemies.

"Not so fast, friend," the woman said. She held a long, wicked-bladed spear and wore chain mail armor that clinked when she stepped forward. "Our time is valuable, you see. And the war effort requires funding. Our soldiers need food. Equipment. Surely, you'd like to donate a bit to a good cause. Etherium or equipment—it'll all go to good use."

Elijah asked, "And if we don't?"

"Ah, you don't want to go down that road," she answered with a shake of her head. "Nothing good in that direction. You're not so stingy as to deny us what's fair, are you?"

"Seems like what's fair to you might feel a bit like a boot on my neck," Elijah remarked.

"You're looking at this all wrong."

"Oh?" Elijah asked, shifting slightly. He'd already dedicated one facet of his Quartz Mind to casting Soothe, while another was occupied by an impending transformation into his lamellar-ape form. "Enlighten me, then. How should I be looking at this? Because it looks a bit like a shakedown to me."

"Ah. Well, I can't really deny that. A girl's got to eat, if you know what I mean," she said with an affable smile. "So, since we're both on the same page here, let's cut right to it. You hand over your valuables, and we'll let you leave. Can't let you come this way, though. Not safe for noncombatants."

"Who said we're noncombatants?" asked Elijah, realizing that the woman didn't intend to let them leave. Even if they paid, they would be attacked. Elijah wasn't certain how he knew that, but he was certain it was the truth.

The cast of Soothe he'd held on the cusp of completion finished, and he immediately moved to Shape of the Guardian. Having obviously felt Elijah's cast, K'hana erupted into motion, summoning her Water Whip. At the same time, she enveloped herself in a thin layer of water that slightly distorted her appearance.

Elijah raced forward, transforming a little with each step. It only took a moment or two for the shift to complete, but in that time, he'd already covered most of the ground between him and the woman. She recoiled but otherwise reacted quickly, stomping on the ground and manifesting a large metal shield.

Elijah crashed into it, but to his surprise, the thing didn't shatter. Nor did it move. Instead, it merely dented. At the same time, the rest of the woman's squad closed in, two of them aiming sword blows at his side. When they connected, they did so with metallic clangs as Elijah used Iron Scales. As their blades rebounded, a roiling ball of shadow slammed into him, splashing across his torso like a wave of tar that restricted his movements, though only slightly.

He hit the shield again, deepening the dent.

"Take it out!" shouted the woman, clearly straining.

"We're trying!" came an answering call as an arrow glanced off of Elijah's scales.

Elijah was about to hit the shield again when he recognized that he'd once again been manipulated by a protector-style class. He'd encountered such an ability when he'd fought the team of mercenaries in Valoria, but that variety had been far less subtle. Perhaps it was an inferior version. Or maybe the woman was higher level. Yet, Elijah couldn't be bothered to care. Now that he knew what was going on, he had no difficulty ripping his attention away from the shield and bounding toward one of the less protected members of the group.

"Resist!" the shielded woman barked.

"Adjust—"

The next man never got the chance to finish his statement, as Elijah barreled into him before he could get the words out. He was a melee fighter, armored in chain mail, but he clearly didn't have the benefit of much in the way of Constitution. As a result, he practically exploded from Elijah's charge. Bones crunched, and blood erupted from his every orifice before he went tumbling across the street and into a pile of rubble.

He was dead before his momentum was spent.

At the same time, K'hana's Water Whip arced out, severing the arm of a woman who looked like a Sorcerer. The disarmed mage screamed in pain, but it cut off only a second later when Elijah used his newest ability.

Ability: Debilitating Roar	Let out an enraged bellow that sends all nearby targets fleeing in fear, decreasing their damage by 15%. Increases caster's foot speed by 10%. Only usable when caster is under the influence of Shape of the Guardian. Duration based on Ethera attribute. Current duration: 9.2 seconds. Resistance based on target's Constitution attribute.

He'd tried it out a few times in the tower, so he knew what to expect. Still, he'd only used it against nonsapient creatures, so when he opened his mouth and let out a primal shout, he was a little surprised at the remaining combatants' reactions.

The now-one-armed woman cut her agonized scream off, turned, and ran away. The other just stared at Elijah in horror, his face pale, as he dropped his weapon. Then, he too fled, scrambling into the ruins of a building without looking back. The only one who managed to resist was the leader, and Elijah saw that her resistance wasn't complete. A puddle of urine collected beneath her feet, and she shook in abject terror.

But she held her ground.

It only lasted a moment before K'hana's Water Whip slashed out, decapitating her. She had been frozen in fear, and even though she'd managed to regain control just before the serpentine stream of water connected with her neck, it was far too late to erect any defenses.

Her head tumbled free, and as she collapsed, the world went silent, but for the clatter of her chain-mail-clad body hitting the ground.

"Damn it," Elijah said, shifting back into his human form. "I didn't want to have to kill them."

"They attempted to rob us," K'hana said. "They deserved to die."

Elijah wanted to argue, but he held his tongue. Not only did he suspect that it would do little good—cultural differences being what they were—but he also didn't really disagree. While he wished he could have ended the situation non-violently, the reality was that if he'd done things differently, there was a chance that he or K'hana would have been injured.

Or killed.

For better or worse, the world had turned ruthless. There was room for peace, but when someone broke it, the response needed to be swift and merciless.

"Check the bodies," he said. "Take anything useful. We'll get the items appraised later."

K'hana knelt beside the leader's corpse while Elijah searched the rubble for the one he'd crushed. As it turned out, their armor was of decent quality, but their weapons were nothing special. Elijah did find a few vials that K'hana said looked like healing potions. So, he pocketed everything.

Fortunately, the ones who'd run off hadn't come back, even though the effects of Debilitating Roar had faded after only a handful of seconds. But that didn't mean they wouldn't return, so Elijah and K'hana quickly moved on. As they traversed the city, Elijah sensed that they were being watched, but no one accosted them, and it wasn't long before they arrived at their destination—the capitol building.

And it was in much worse shape than it had been during Elijah's last visit.

The grounds had been ripped to shreds, and the dry fountain at the center had been reduced to rubble. The building itself was still intact, but there were plenty of signs that it had endured a number of powerful attacks. In all, it looked as if a battle had been fought on Isaiah's doorstep. The whole area was encircled by a makeshift wall of sandbags and piled rubble, with rough towers jutting above the man-made edifice.

Elijah's and K'hana's arrival didn't go unnoticed, either, and he could see that plenty of ranged weapons—from bows to wands—were aimed in their direction. Seeing that, he didn't bother with a stealthy approach. Instead, he led K'hana to the only gap in the wall, which was manned by a squad of men and women in black fatigues.

"Stop there. What do you want?" asked a man in the back. He was stocky, with salt-and-pepper hair that had been cut into a military style.

"I'm here to see Isaiah. I owe him a favor."

"Is that so? I'll—"

"Let him in," came a voice over the man's radio. That reminded Elijah that he still had the radio Isaiah had given him in his pocket. He just hadn't thought to use it.

"Yes, sir," said the guard. After that, his underlings parted, letting Elijah through. However, the man still sent one of the others to escort them to the capitol.

47

SEATTLE'S PLIGHT

I'm Elijah, by the way," he said to the woman who'd been assigned to escort them. She was pretty, maybe twenty years old if he had to guess. But Elijah acknowledged that his perception of age might be a little off. After all, with high attributes and a Body of Wood, the effects of aging really took a back seat. Even he looked a few years younger than he really was, though much of it was hidden by his lacking grooming habits and scraggly appearance. Perhaps he should have gotten a haircut before heading out on what amounted to a diplomatic mission. When the woman didn't respond, he said, "Nice to meet you. Hot day today, isn't it? Oh, yeah—I'm very much enjoying my time in Seattle, thank you for asking."

"Abigail," she muttered.

"What was that?"

"My name is Abigail. And I have a boyfriend," she said.

"Uh . . . Good for you?" he responded. Then, he realized what she must've thought, and he shook his head. Why did everyone always think the worst of his intentions? "This is K'hana. I don't know if she has a boyfriend or not."

"I do not have a life partner."

"Samesies," Elijah said. "It's rough going out there, you know? Not like it used to be. But I'll be completely honest—I'm glad the dating apps are a thing of the past. I didn't have a lot of experience with Tinder and the like, but what I saw was not good. You're lucky you didn't have to go through that, K'hana. Back me up here, Abby. It was terrible, right?"

"Um . . ."

"But then again, I don't think K'hana would've had much trouble, all things considered. The pointed ears might turn some people the other way, but I'm sure most would be more than willing to ignore that. Of course, there's no accounting for cultural differences. I don't know much about the mating habits of elves."

"You're an elf?" asked Abigail. Then, she told Elijah, "And my name is Abigail. Not Abby."

"Fair enough."

At the same time, K'hana unfurled her scarf, revealing the rest of her face as well as her tapered ears. That elicited a gasp from their escort, who actually

stumbled as she climbed a set of steps leading to the front doors of the capitol building. She caught herself on a handrail, but her cheeks reddened in
embarrassment.

"I've never seen an elf before. There was a gnome that came through here a
few months back, and I've heard of dwarves. But no elves."

"If all goes well, you'll see some more in the coming months," Elijah said.
"But don't tell anyone. I'm sure Isaiah will want to take credit."

After that, they went silent as they were led through the building and to
Isaiah's office. The interior of the capitol didn't look any different than it had
the last time Elijah had visited, which was a little surprising, given the degree
of damage outside. Perhaps the attackers had been rebuffed before reaching the
building itself.

Regardless, they arrived at the office a few minutes later, where they were
handed off to another set of guards—both of which were burly men who
seemed a little stronger than the average riffraff—who let them inside. There,
Isaiah was sitting behind his desk.

"About time," he said. "I was beginning to think you weren't going to hold
up your end of our bargain."

Elijah frowned. "I never said when I would help. Just that I would," he
stated. "Any assumption otherwise was your fault."

"It was implied. Our situation is dire. People died while you were galivant-
ing around doing whatever it is you do. I—"

"Be careful what you say next. I'm here to help, and in more ways than
you expect. But I'm not going to stand here and let you browbeat me because
I refuse to operate on your schedule," Elijah said, his tone suddenly icy. And
given that he was the highest-level person among humanity's remaining population, his ire was best avoided.

It wasn't as if Elijah could rip the building down around Isaiah—especially
when the man had some levels under his belt—but he could cause a lot of damage if so inclined. Valoria was evidence of that.

To his credit, Isaiah took a deep breath and said, "Fine. Tell me what you
have in mind."

Isaiah tightened his fist as he sat behind his desk. He was already dealing with
a crisis that could tear everything down, and now he had to deal with a prima
donna like Elijah Hart? The man acted as if the entire world revolved around
him. Meanwhile, Isaiah had been fighting tooth and nail to try to preserve as
much of Seattle as he could manage. Even while multiple groups had risen to
oppose him, he'd kept order, negotiated peace deals, and prevented the weak
from succumbing to the dangers of the new world. So, seeing someone like
Elijah, who only seemed to care about himself, was galling—a situation that
was exacerbated by the fact that Isaiah needed the man's help. Otherwise, the

militants of Lake City and the water hoarders of Mercer Mesa would slowly overwhelm him and his allies.

But he didn't have enough power.

For what felt like the thousandth time, he wished he'd chosen a different option when he'd achieved Lordship. The quest to do so had been onerous, requiring him to consolidate his power and reach a specific spot on the power rankings. That hadn't lasted much past attaining his title as a lord, but it still represented a sizable accomplishment. More, the path he had chosen—that of the Watcher—had worked hand in glove with his class's power set, allowing him to keep an eye on everything in his city.

Yet, as powerful as information often was, it usually proved useless in a direct confrontation. The reality of Isaiah's path was that it was never meant for fighting. He'd hoped to field a force of powerful combatants to fill that void, but Bruce Garret had used his access to the tower to pull most of the truly promising fighters into the Lake City faction.

It wasn't difficult to see why they'd gone that way, either. The tower offered a chance to grow stronger via a mostly set path. There were whole books that had been written about the best ways to challenge it. So, there wasn't much in the way of danger, so long as the challenging party didn't make any egregious mistakes in their group composition or within the tower itself.

So, the strong kept getting stronger, and they'd begun to wonder why they allowed someone like Isaiah to maintain power. And then, the Mercers had stepped in, promising unfettered access to their water source. From there, the two factions had slowly begun to overwhelm Isaiah and his tentative allies, the Hunters of Rainier. The tensions had grown even more onerous until, at last, open battle had erupted. Hundreds had already died, and more deaths would follow unless Isaiah put an end to the conflict.

If he could guarantee that it would work, he would have already surrendered his position. He didn't care about being in charge. However, he'd seen the way the Mercers treated their underlings. He'd watched as the so-called Lake City Adventurers took what they wanted, daring anyone to oppose them. No— if he surrendered, not only would he be giving up his own life, but also the lives of many others who depended on him to protect them.

Even so, Isaiah had sought a truce, which had been summarily rejected. Bruce had responded with a simple question: "Why would we negotiate with you when we're winning?"

It was a good question, and one to which Isaiah had no answers. But now that Elijah Hart had returned to Seattle, there was a chance of turning things around. Isaiah might have once doubted the man's power, but only that day, he'd watched via one of his drones as Elijah had ripped a group of Adventurers to pieces. It was as horrifying as it was hope inducing.

"So, I think I might have a fix for your water problem that doesn't involve me flying up to Mercer Mesa and slaughtering a bunch of rich assholes," Elijah said.

"Fly?"

"Yeah. I can fly. The point is that this woman is the answer to your problems," Elijah said, gesturing to the woman who'd accompanied him into Seattle. Isaiah had watched her decapitate a seasoned Adventurer with a whip that looked like it was made of semisolid water, so he knew she was dangerous. More, he also knew that she was an elf.

Seattle had played host to a few nonhumans over the years, and there was even a small community of dwarves—only about two dozen of them—who ran a traveling caravan that passed through every month or so. But Isaiah had never seen an elf before, and he was unsurprised to see that the myths had gotten it mostly right. The woman—her name was K'hana Tamira—was a level fifty Water Witch, according to Isaiah's All-Seeing Eye skill, and she was an absolute vision of perfection.

"I'm going to need more than that if you expect me to understand what you're talking about," Isaiah said to the infuriating man. "She's strong, but she won't make much of a difference in a pitched battle. Lake City has a hundred people that are close to her level. No offense, ma'am."

"None taken, my lord."

Elijah rolled his eyes at that, which only irritated Isaiah even further. Then, he said, "She's not here to fight. She's here to help you find water."

Then, the elven woman explained that she came from a world even more arid than the Seattle desert, and as such, her people had long leaned on those with classes that could find water in even the driest deserts. K'hana was one of those people, and she said that, via a series of skills, she could locate enough water to support even a city the size of Seattle.

"And you would do this out of the goodness of your heart?" he asked in disbelief.

"No," she said. "I will not. I wish to ally my people with yours. You gain access to water, while we use your people to help us keep our tower from overflowing. In addition, we would like to create a trade alliance as well as an agreement for mutual defense. Our people do not have a history of battle. We come from a peaceful world. As such, we have only a few combatants."

"Pending the details, I think that sounds reasonable," Isaiah said, struggling to believe his good fortune. In one fell swoop, the elf's arrival had given him hope that the city's most pressing needs would be solved. However, that still left the issue of the ongoing war. "But it won't mean anything if Mercer and Lake City have their way. They've already expanded their territories, and they threaten to take the whole city."

"Perhaps we should be talking to one of them, then," suggested the elf. "I thought you were the lord of this city."

Isaiah didn't rise to that comment. Instead, he focused on Elijah, saying, "You agreed to assist."

"I did."

"Are you backing out of that agreement? This helps. I won't deny that. And I'm grateful. However, you agreed to help us take care of Mercer and Lake City," Isaiah stated evenly. "I took you to be a man of honor."

Elijah laughed at that. "Honor? Not much use for that. I do what I can for people that need it. I protect what I care about," he said. "And I try to maintain the balance of nature. Honor doesn't come into that equation. But I still intend to help. You seem better than the Mercers, at least. And given that I've already been attacked by those others, you're our best bet."

"Good," he said. "Because one of those things—or people, I suppose—that you care about is about to be attacked by Lake City. My information tells me that they intend to take the Garden in three days."

48

RAID

Elijah's heart nearly stopped as the memory of a hundred little delays came rushing to mind. Perhaps his reaction to Alyssa's death was understandable, but he'd wasted a lot of time pointlessly trekking across the wilderness. In the aftermath, he'd spent weeks wallowing in apathy that still hadn't entirely lifted. And as a result, he'd put one of the few people he actually cared about in danger.

Lucy wasn't usually at the forefront of his mind. She wasn't family. But he'd loved her once, and those feelings hadn't completely faded. At worst, she was a friend, and at best, she might one day be something more. However, over the years, he'd adopted the habit of pushing her from his thoughts, and because of that, her situation—and that of Seattle—was the last thing on his mind.

Now, he was going to have to deal with the consequences. Even as he pushed himself to his feet, his thoughts drifted into a dark place that he'd most recently visited in Valoria. If something had happened to Lucy, he was going to tear the ones responsible to pieces.

Isaiah rose, urgently saying, "She's fine. I should have led with that. They haven't attacked yet."

"But they will, right? How do we stop it? When are they doing it? And—"

"Right now, they're holed up in their headquarters," Isaiah answered. "Or the important ones are, at least. They call it the Adventurer's Guild."

"If you know where they are, then why haven't you already taken care of it?"

"They're too strong," the man answered, standing and placing his hands on the edge of the desk. He leaned forward, continuing, "We're not all as powerful as you are. We can't just walk into a city and destroy a group of seasoned Adventurers. My people had all they could handle just defending this place. Assaulting their headquarters will be much more difficult."

"You know their levels? Do they have anyone on the ladder?" asked Elijah.

"No. The core group—five people, plus the leader, Bruce Garret—are only a level away, though. They've each cultivated their bodies to the first stage, as well. Bruce has everything but the Core at the first stage," Isaiah explained.

"You sure do know a lot about them," Elijah noted. Although, that should not have been terribly surprising. After all, Isaiah had already demonstrated that he could read Elijah's status like a book. It stood to reason that he could do the same with the other people in the city.

"My entire class revolves around information gathering," Isaiah responded. "I have very limited combat capability."

"I see."

Elijah's initial reaction was to simply head to this Adventurer's Guild head-quarters and start killing people. However, if Isaiah was as good at gathering information as he claimed, perhaps there was an advantage there. So, he asked, "What's the plan, then? Do you have a layout of the building? What about defenses? Detailed information about the enemies?"

As it turned out, Isaiah had all of that and more. He produced a list of the fighters inside the building—most were in their forties, but there were a few on the verge of entering the power rankings—as well as a map, which detailed poten-tial points of ingress. On top of that, he said, "I can disable their defenses, too."

"What kind of defenses are we talking about?"

"They call it an array," Isaiah explained. "It's like an artificial Domain. If you have the key—one of the pendants they give to members once they satisfy certain requirements—you'll be unaffected. However, if you don't, it'll decrease your physical attributes by as much as twenty-five percent. Less based on the Ethera attribute."

That didn't seem so bad, but Elijah had no interest in losing that many attri-butes. So, he was more than willing to let Isaiah do his thing.

"More importantly, I can guide you," Isaiah stated. "Make sure you don't step into a situation you can't control. They have a few stealth operators, and some of their guards can avoid detection, as well."

"But not from you?"

"I see everything," Isaiah responded.

To Elijah, that sounded a bit like his Domain. Perhaps that was the benefit of Isaiah's class, like he'd claimed, but Elijah expected that there was something else at work. After all, it had taken quite a lot of effort before Elijah's Domain had taken hold. Regardless, with what he'd seen, he didn't have any trouble believing Isaiah's claims.

"Here," Isaiah said, pulling a small device from his pocket. "Put that in your ear and I'll be able to talk to you."

"Uh . . . There might be a problem with that," Elijah said, noting that, in his bestial forms, he didn't really have ears—at least not in the shape that could accommodate the tiny earwig Isaiah had offered. Instead, in his draconid form, his ears were nothing more than small pits on the side of his head. In his lamellar-ape form, they were much larger. He'd not noticed the orientation of his ears in his Shape of the Sky form.

But then again, perhaps it would work like his clothing or other equipment and transform with him, so he just took the earwig and said, "But let's hope not."

Then, he slipped it into his ear.

"Would you like my assistance?" asked K'hana.

Elijah shook his head. "No. The alliance is too important," he said. "I don't want to risk you getting injured."

That was only part of the reason. Elijah intended to use Guise of the Unseen, which would be impossible if K'hana was tagging along. Also, when he was inevitably discovered, he didn't want to have to worry about keeping her safe. For better or worse, he didn't really fit into most groups. Instead, he was far more comfortable fighting alone.

One day, he'd have to work on changing that. At some point, he knew he'd encounter a situation he couldn't tackle alone. The issue was that his class was built on versatility. What made him special was the fact that he could fill multiple roles at once. Groups, though, were built to take advantage of highly specialized combatants. So, if he ended up in one of those parties, he'd be relegated to being a worse version of whichever role he was assigned. It would take time and training to overcome those issues.

But it was neither the time nor the place for that.

After getting a brief rundown from Isaiah—and refusing to let one of his teams accompany him—Elijah set off. Most of the journey was undertaken in his human form, but when he approached the territory claimed by the Lake City Adventurers, he ducked into an abandoned building, ensured that no one was looking, and shifted into his draconid form.

He'd considered simply flying in and dropping onto the roof of the building, but he chose the less bombastic path. As satisfying as it would have been to take that route, stealth was both safer and more tactically sound.

Once he was cloaked in Guise of the Unseen, Elijah crept out of the abandoned building and crossed the block or so to the territory controlled by the Adventurers. Once, the region had been on the waterfront, but now that everything was desert, new buildings spilled out into the area that had once been Puget Sound. Encircling the territory was a concrete wall that reached fifteen feet in height.

That was new. Elijah had only seen the area from afar, but he felt certain that he would have noticed such an obstacle. Regardless, with his attributes, it was easy enough to vault to the top of the edifice, though he did feel a slight tingle as he crossed the wall walk and leaped down to the other side.

That was the defensive array, he knew. Thankfully, he was immune to its effects due to the pendant he'd gotten from Isaiah. So, he continued forward, passing between buildings and keeping to the shadows as much as possible. He knew that wasn't strictly necessary—Guise of the Unseen was more than enough to hide him from most people—but old habits died hard.

Like that, he slowly made his way through the district, noticing that there were quite a few noncombatants in the area. Night had already fallen, but it wasn't so late that the streets had emptied. There were children about, as well, suggesting that at least some of the so-called Adventurers had families. What about the men and women he intended to kill? Did they have husbands and wives waiting for them at home? Children? Brothers and sisters?

Often, Elijah skated past the implications of all the deaths he'd caused. It was easy to cast those people as faceless enemies. But the reality was that the impact of those deaths didn't end when Elijah had moved on. They all had people that cared about them. People who depended on them. Their lives would be changed, and probably for the worse, because of Elijah's actions.

It cemented the notion that he needed to be more judicious with his power. Killing people was easy. Sometimes incredibly so. Restraining himself would be much more difficult, especially when he felt justified.

Of course, reality didn't care about moral quandaries, and the fact of the matter was that if he didn't do something about Bruce Garret and his Adventurers—and the people of Mercer Mesa—they would hurt someone he cared about. And Elijah's brand of doing something usually involved copious violence. He simply wasn't equipped for political maneuvering or the like, and even if he was, that had already proved ineffective. After all, that was supposed to be Isaiah's area of expertise, and he'd already admitted that he couldn't do what needed to be done.

No—Elijah knew he was going to have to kill a lot of people. And as a result, he would create widows, widowers, and orphans. It was an unavoidable aspect of any battle, and as unpalatable as it was to consider, Elijah knew it was necessary.

So, it was with a murky conscience that he arrived at the Adventurer's Guild headquarters. It was a large, squarish building that was a few blocks away from the old shoreline. At five stories tall, and constructed of brick, it was a remnant of the old world that had somehow survived events that had torn most of the other buildings within the city down. More importantly, it was guarded by dozens of combatants, all arranged in groups of five, with most of them patrolling the surrounding area.

Elijah watched from the shadows, observing the patterns. All the while, Isaiah spoke in his ear: "There are two points of ingress you can use. The first is the side door. It is guarded, but only lightly. It's the riskier of the two options. The second entrance is on the roof, and it would require you to climb the fire escape. That route has been rigged with traps that I can't deactivate from afar."

"What kind of traps?" Elijah asked.

"They're called ethereal claymores. Just like claymores from the old world, they explode, sending shrapnel to tear the victim to pieces. However, instead of being powered by combustion, they're powered by ethera. We think someone in there has a skill to make them deadlier, too," Isaiah explained.

"What about the walls?" Elijah hissed. He didn't even know where the device's microphone was, but Isaiah had already proved that he could hear him just fine.

"What about them?"

"What if I climb them?" Elijah asked.

"Uh . . . One second. Yeah. That should work," Isaiah said. "If you can do it."

"It'll be fine," Elijah said. Like his old mist-panther form, the draconid shape was made for climbing, but even as a human, he wouldn't have had any difficulty. That was the benefit of his high attributes.

With that plan in mind, he stalked forward and, with the assistance of Isaiah's constant input, was able to avoid the patrols. According to him, they each had at least one member with a skill similar to the Guard Sense referenced by the soldiers in Valoria. It wasn't enough to see through Guise of the Unseen—so long as he was careful, at least—but he didn't want to push his luck.

As a result, covering those hundred or so yards took about twenty minutes, but eventually, Elijah reached the building's far wall. The night was overcast, so it stood in dark shadow that he hoped would keep him concealed. So, without further ado, he leaped, digging his claws into the brick and vaulting from one handhold to the next as he climbed the building. Unfortunately, it made a little noise, but he'd timed his climb so that no one was close enough to hear it.

And just like that, he reached the top and climbed onto the flat roof.

There were four guards up there, too. Positioned one to a side, they were armed with binoculars and heavy crossbows, but their attention was entirely focused on the area around the building.

Elijah stalked forward, and when he approached the first, he used Predator Strike before attacking. However, he didn't use his normal skull-bite attack. Instead, his claws found the woman's throat, silently ripping through the tender flesh. He caught her as she fell, then lowered her to the ground before going after the second. That man fell, just like the first sentry. It was the same with the remaining two, though with the last, he indulged his instincts and crushed the man's skull.

"Alright. I'm going in," Elijah said, approaching the door that would lead him into the building below. But just as he opened the door, Isaiah shouted something that was quickly lost in the sound of an explosion. Elijah's vision turned white as he was hit by a shock wave that sent him tumbling across the roof.

49

COOLER HEADS WILL PREVAIL

Elijah cartwheeled, skipping across the roof as his scales melted from the intense heat of the explosion. However, at least one facet of his Quartz Mind remained aware enough that he initiated a transformation into the Shape of the Sky, which completed as he went over the edge and began a plummet to the ground below. He beat his wings, pain arcing through him with every motion. The membranous material that comprised the appendages was ripped in places, scattering blood across the ground below, but they were still capable of holding him aloft.

And in his state, if he'd let himself fall from that roof, he might never have risen.

Still, flight was only barely possible, and he ended up expending far more energy than normal before he crashed into another nearby building. The moment he was back on solid ground, he initiated another transformation into his human form. Only then did he look at the state of his body.

Groaning, he took in what looked like third-degree burns that covered most of his skin. On top of that, he could feel multiple broken bones as well as what he took to be some sort of affliction coursing through his body and weakening him.

But it wasn't the first time he'd been so grievously injured, and one facet of his Mind had already begun to cast Soothe, Healing Rain, and Touch of Nature. Completely healing would not be a quick process, but he felt confident that he could regain functionality in short order.

It wouldn't be pretty, though.

"Elijah!" shouted Isaiah through the earpiece. That was when Elijah realized that the man had been yelling for some time. He just hadn't quite heard it because his eardrums had burst from the cacophonous explosion.

"You don't have to shout."

"Are you okay? Do you need an extraction?"

"I'm fine," Elijah said, having already healed most of the fractures. A few still persisted, but they weren't so serious that they'd slow him down. More concerning were the burns. And the affliction, which had stubbornly hung on, weakening him. "Just need to heal for a second."

"You may not have that long," Isaiah stated. "Every Adventurer in Lake City is converging on your location."

"What hit me?" Elijah asked.

"One of the claymores."

"And what happened to 'I see everything,' huh?" Elijah asked.

"I missed it. I don't know how," Isaiah admitted. "Are you sure you're okay? You look . . ."

"Yeah, I'm fine. This isn't as bad as getting digested by a whale," Elijah muttered. Already, the burns had begun to scab over. It would take a few more minutes before they were completely healed, though. "Honestly, it looks worse than it is. And how do you know how I look, anyway?"

Then, he focused on a gap in his awareness. It was only about six inches wide, but he'd encountered stealth skills on enough occasions that he knew what that absence meant. "Oh. Drones, right? How long do I have?"

"Six minutes," Isaiah said. "Based on their normal response times, at least. They're being careful as they surround the building you're in."

"Should be enough," Elijah mumbled to himself. He could have used Guardian's Renewal to instantly recover, but he wanted to keep that in reserve. It was too powerful, with too long of a cooldown, to use when his normal healing spells would suffice. "Just keep me updated on their movements."

After that, Elijah focused on healing, flooding his body with Touch of Nature as often as he could. The spell had once been quite powerful, but of late, he'd noticed that its relative potency had really begun to lag behind. As a result, it took more casts to heal from similar amounts of damage. From what he understood, that was normal. Healing spells typically restored a static amount of life—or vitality, as the guides referred to it—but each person gained a larger pool of that life force as they progressed through levels and benefited from increased attributes. Because of that, people were harder to injure, but they were also more difficult to heal, requiring evolved spells to heal the same amount of relative damage. Or, in Elijah's case, more casts.

Fortunately, his pool of available ethera had grown quite a bit larger than it had been when he'd first acquired the spell, so he could effectively cast it without ceasing. His potent Regeneration could easily keep pace with any ethera he used.

The only issue was that it took more time.

Either way, he kept at it until almost ten minutes later, Isaiah said, "They're coming in. I tried to delay them a little with a couple of my drones, but they didn't last long."

"It's alright," Elijah said, standing. He wished his Serpent Healer's Crook hadn't been damaged. Otherwise, his healing spells would have been far more potent. As it was, his skin was still beet red where the damaged skin had flaked away, but there were a few spots that were still scabbed over. His bones were in better shape, having mended almost completely. His right forearm still bore a fracture, and he suspected that the orbital bone below his right eye was chipped. However, neither injury was so severe that he couldn't ignore it. He stretched a bit, then said, "Just keep me updated on what to expect. My detection radius is around fifty feet. So, let me know about whatever's going on outside of that."

With that, Elijah went silent and, once again, adopted the Shape of the Predator. Then, he let Guise of the Unseen settle upon him, and he disappeared into stealth. Before he'd transformed, he'd checked his buffs, and for one of the first times ever, he used Ward of the Seasons in a combat situation. There were Sorcerers among the Adventurers, and he wanted as much protection as possible from their spells. To make room, he forwent Aura of Renewal, largely because he intended to remain in his bestial forms, where the enhanced Regeneration attribute was only marginally effective.

He stalked forward, ready to slaughter everyone who'd come after him.

The building itself was the sort of office complex that was so common in any American city of sufficient size. Ten stories tall, mostly metal and glass, and completely unimaginative in its architecture. Just a giant rectangle that could efficiently and cheaply house all sorts of offices.

Elijah had ended up on the sixth floor, which turned out to be the sort of cubicle farm in which he'd never wanted to find himself. The idea of slaving away in that kind of environment was one of his worst nightmares. The partitions were partially rotted away, and many had fallen, but the overall layout remained in place. All the electronics were gone, presumably having been scrapped for materials or sold in one of Seattle's many markets.

But the combination of features made the cubicle farm a perfect setting for Elijah's preferred style of fighting. As much as he liked Shape of the Guardian or his natural form, Shape of the Predator would always have a special place in his heart. Some of that was due to his relationship with the mist panther that had inspired his class, but it was also because it was the safest way for him to fight.

Until it wasn't.

That was where the lamellar-ape form came into play, though.

In any case, Elijah crept through the area, staying low to the ground like the stalking predator he was. So, when he sensed someone reach the floor, he was ready to pounce.

There were five of them—a mostly full group, from what he understood. Six was the maximum that could enter a tower, but most people considered five to be the core of any good group, with the final member being considered extra—at least in Seattle and Argos. Perhaps things were different in other parts of the world.

Their roles were easily identifiable. The defender wore thick plate armor the color of blood and carried a large shield that looked like a repurposed car door.

There was a robed Sorcerer carrying a staff, a pair of men in leather armor and wielding daggers, and a woman who lagged behind the rest. That final member carried a scepter made of twisted silver and topped with a giant emerald. Her armor was chain mail, and by process of elimination, Elijah marked her as the group's Healer.

And his first target.

"See anything?" asked the Sorcerer.

The defender said, "Negative. Stay frosty."

It was only after she spoke that Elijah could identify her as a woman. Apparently, real armor didn't make many allowances for feminine shape, and her head was encased by a large helmet that looked like a metal bucket.

"What do you think it is?" asked one of the dagger wielders.

"No idea. Somebody said it looked like a dragon," answered the other.

"Dragons aren't real."

"They are so. I read about 'em in a guide. Supposed to be really strong, too. God, I hope we're not fighting a dragon."

It was at that moment that Elijah pounced, barreling into the Healer, the momentum enough to throw her back through the door and knock it from its hinges. Even as it splintered, Elijah bit, though his attack was stymied by a thick, golden, spell-wrought barrier that encased the woman's entire body.

She screamed as his claws raked the plane of solid light, the sound of his talons against the spell like scratching glass. But it didn't immediately shatter, which told Elijah that she had some power under her belt. That was okay, though, because he wasted no time before biting it again.

And when that failed, again after that.

Over and over, his jaws snapped shut with enough force to shatter stone. And after only a few seconds, the shield ran out of energy, exposing the woman to his natural weapons. By that point, the others had responded, rushing back through the door. Elijah bit down on her hastily raised arms, crushing the bone before he was forced to flee into the shadows.

A second later, the defender lumbered into the hall to stand over the fallen Healer. She shouted, asking the woman if she was okay, but the answer to that question was obvious, considering that both of her arms were only hanging on by a few strips of sinew. Without her shield spell, she'd stood no chance of resisting the power of Elijah's jaws.

She made her discomfort known by screaming in agony.

The defender yelled out orders, but Elijah had already rushed around a corner, avoiding a clump of roiling earth that hit the wall with the force of a cannonball. No one immediately followed, which, after a couple of moments, allowed him to slip into a different room and adopt Guise of the Unseen.

Then, when he spied a missing ceiling tile, he got the idea to use that to his advantage. After all, people rarely looked up. So, he shifted into his human form—there was no way the flimsy ceiling could accommodate his huge draco-nid shape—and pulled himself into the crawl space above the tiles. Once there, it didn't take him long to creep forward until he felt the five fighters directly below him.

That's when he used Swarm.

A bunch of tiny gnats manifested, landing on the men and women who were hunting him. The conjured insects were so small and their bites were so light that no one in the group even knew they were being loaded with afflictions. Of course, the Healer was still whimpering about her nearly missing arms. She was trying to heal herself, but apparently, the spell took concentration she could not muster. So, it kept fizzling out.

Then, the Sorcerer coughed, spitting up blood.

One of the melee fighters did the same, while the Healer wept.

"Disease! Cure us!" shouted the defender.

"My arms . . ."

"Concentrate, woman! If you don't, we're going to die!"

That snapped the Healer out of her misery, and Elijah felt her cast a spell. A golden globe manifested, pulsing once every second. Each pulse sent a ripple of ethera through their surroundings. It only extended for about ten feet, but that was enough to encompass the entire group. When Elijah saw the Sorcer-er's change in posture, it was confirmation that the Healer had cured Swarm's afflictions.

So, when the globe winked out, he cast the spell again.

For now, that was his limit. He had enough ethera to cast it again—a few more times, actually—but he couldn't afford to use the entire contents of his Core on one group. Because there were more out there.

Besides—he had a plan to finish them off.

To that end, the moment the group began to once again manifest symp-toms, Elijah made his move, shifting into his draconid form, then using Guise of the Unseen before embracing Predator Strike and Venom Strike. Before the ceiling could collapse, he launched himself through the flimsy tiles and hit the Healer like a runaway train. She'd used her shield again, which was as expected. So, the moment he hit, he used Flicker Step, teleporting behind the next-most-vulnerable person.

The Sorcerer never saw him coming, and his ethereal shield was far thin-ner than the Healer's. More importantly, he was already under the effects of Swarm's afflictions, which meant that he was slow to respond. And finally, the Healer had proved that she was prone to panic, so whatever abilities she might've brought to bear in defense of her companion were forgotten after being knocked to the floor.

So, Elijah bit through the Sorcerer's ethereal shield, then clamped his jaws around the man's head and squeezed. His skull popped like a melon, which only elicited more panic from the Healer. She tried to cast a heal on the Sorcerer, but there was no spell that could regrow a head.

Her frantic efforts gave Elijah the opportunity to dart toward one of the melee fighters and rake his claws across the man's leg, delivering Venom Strike as well as Contagion before, once again, rushing down the hall. The frustrated defender followed, shouting for the others to join her, but she was too slow to catch him.

Or that's what Elijah thought until she used some sort of ability and leaped in his direction. He tried to dodge, but his feet were suddenly rooted in place, so he couldn't avoid her descending shield slam as it crashed into him.

What he could do was initiate a transformation into his lamellar-ape form, though. It took a second, which meant that the shield hit him mid-transformation, but as he was knocked down the hall, he finished shifting.

And when he rose, the defender took an involuntary step back.

Elijah could feel that a couple more of his bones had nearly been broken by the attack, but it was nothing vital. He could still exert the majority of his Strength. And now that he was in his guardian form, the pain only fueled his instinctive rage. He didn't give himself over to it—not completely—but he did use that to numb the effect of the pain on his mind.

With a roar, he threw himself at the defender, ready to rip her limb from limb.

50

TERRIFYING

Fluorescent lights flickered as Elijah charged down the hall, intent on tearing through the defender. She held her ground, setting her feet and raising her shield.

It did no good.

He hit with the force of a speeding truck, eliciting a loud clang as the shield split in two. However, Elijah kept his wits about him enough to recognize that she was not his primary target. Instead, unless he was forced to act otherwise, he would focus on that woman last. Others in the group were simultaneously more dangerous and far more vulnerable, and he wanted to take them out before they had a chance to bring their full abilities to bear.

So, Elijah continued his charge, using his immense Strength to power a backhand that sent the woman stumbling to the side. The impact dazed the woman, but he didn't stop to finish her off. No matter how much he overpowered her, she would be a tough nut to crack. The others were far easier targets.

With the rage of the Shape of the Guardian rushing through him, Elijah didn't even think about his comparative lack of Dexterity, so when he reached the corner, he couldn't stop himself from skidding into the wall and breaking through the drywall. It didn't slow him down much, though, and soon enough, he launched himself at the pair of melee combatants.

The first leather-clad man raised his swords and used some sort of ability, though Elijah didn't hesitate before crashing into him. He quickly discovered that he should have been far more cautious, though. The fighter's blades moved like lightning, knocking Elijah's claws aside and returning a riposte that would have gored him if he hadn't had Iron Scales active. As it was, he still took a deep gouge that spurted blood.

"Riposte down!" the man shouted, backpedaling. He turned that into a somersault that played out far more quickly than should have been possible, given his suspected attributes. Clearly, it was another ability.

"Heart Seeker!" shouted the other, throwing a dagger in his direction. The blade glinted with black energy, and before Elijah could react, it hit him in the chest. Once again, Iron Scales saved him, but the weapon still embedded itself more than an inch deep in his hide.

"Shit! It didn't work!"

"What do we—"

Elijah finally reached his target. He wrapped his claws around the man's arms and pulled them in opposite directions. The fighter kicked and screamed as he tried to resist, but his Strength was far inferior to Elijah's. The results were predictable.

Elijah roared as he tore the man's arms off. They came free with a shower of blood and meat, and the fighter fell to the ground where Elijah stomped on his head with all the might he could muster. That's when the remaining fighter realized just how outmatched he was.

He used some ability, disappearing from Elijah's sight.

But that didn't matter because he was still visible via One with Nature. Elijah kicked the dead body near his feet, sending it spinning through the air to collide with the man who'd suddenly gone invisible. That interrupted the ability, and he flickered back into view just in time for Elijah to use Brand of the Stalker and pounce on him.

It was just as Elijah snapped out, wrapping his jaws around the unfortunate man's shoulder, that the defender finally returned. More importantly, the Healer had made it, too, though her arms were still ruined. She cast a heal on Elijah's current opponent, but there was no way she could keep up with the damage he caused. The man dropped dead a moment later, his chest caved in and his heart destroyed.

Just as Elijah whipped around to confront the defender, the woman rammed her shield into his side, sending him skidding backward. When he lashed out a counterattack, he found himself hitting only a familiar golden plane of ethera. It even dissipated the momentum of his attack, allowing the defender to use her sword to strike with absolute impunity. In response, Elijah jerked his attention away from the nearly impervious defender and threw himself at the Healer.

Or at least that was what he tried to do.

In reality, his feet remained stuck to the ground, obviously under the effect of some sort of spell.

"I can't hold it long!" screamed the Healer. "Immobilize only lasts thirty seconds, and that's if it's not partially resisted!"

"Run!" screamed the defender.

"I won't leave you—"

Elijah let out a roar of frustration as he tried to jerk his feet from the floor. It didn't work, but the tiles began to break, which spurred on his efforts.

"The other team is down a floor!" shouted the defender. "I'll be fine! Just go!"

Elijah backhanded the defender, and he was rewarded with a slight crack in the ethereal shield. However, the defender remained upright and alive, a fact that infuriated Elijah.

Finally convinced, the Healer turned and ran. Her gait was unbalanced—likely because of her useless arms, which were hanging by a few ligaments and a couple of strips of skin—and she stumbled into the wall. Still, she kept going, turning a corner just as Elijah felt the tiles at his feet break free.

That was all he needed, and he threw himself down the hall.

Yet, he once again found himself stymied when he hit another plane of force. This one shimmered with silver energy, and though he smashed through it only a couple of seconds later, he knew the delay was enough of a head start to ensure the Healer's escape.

"Just you and me, monster."

Elijah turned, his frustration having long since turned to rage. "Monster? Do you want to see how monstrous I can be? Do you? Fine."

Then, he used the Silver Bracer of Rage, augmenting his already-monstrous Strength as he bounded toward the defender. So far, he'd only tried to bypass the woman because she didn't really pose much of a threat. But now? She was the only one left, and so, she drew the entirety of his attention.

She took the first blow on her shield, counterattacking with a low sweep of her sword. The blade hit Elijah in the shin, but he ignored it. She didn't have much in the way of offensive power. Only defense. In a lot of ways, she was similar to what he expected his lamellar-ape form should have been. The only difference was that he had quite a few more levels, better cultivation, and much higher Strength.

The results of that combination were predictable.

His first attack dented her shield, and his second ripped it from her grip. She continued to back away as he pummeled her, but she couldn't escape his wrath. She also activated one ability after another. Most were variations of shields, but there were a few attacks in there, as well. None of them were capable of inflicting serious harm upon Elijah, though one caused a persistent bleeding effect even though it barely pierced his scales.

It didn't matter.

Elijah pummeled the woman until she was battered and broken. He wanted to kill her. With so much rage coursing through him, there was a part of him that actually needed it. But at the last moment, he pulled back and forced himself to return to his human form.

Breathing hard—and not because of exertion—Elijah stared at the woman's twisted form. She had multiple broken bones, more than a few dislocated joints, and she was barely conscious. In short—she was no threat. Not anymore.

He didn't need to kill her.

Sure, someone could heal her later. And they probably would. But for now? In order to accomplish his goals? It just wasn't necessary. And besides, he didn't want to be the sort of person who resorted to murder at every turn. Often, it was warranted. But in this instance? There was no reason to take that next step.

So, without further thought, he turned, shifted into his draconid form, and disappeared around the corner. The moment he did, he used Guise of the Unseen and found the staircase he needed to descend to the next floor down.

Bruce Garret paced back and forth, staring at the old office building. Nobody had bothered to disconnect it from the electrical grid, so there were a few flickering lights shining through the windows. Most of it was dark, though.

Three full groups of his Adventurers surrounded him, each member nearly high enough level to place themselves on the power ladder. He'd sent three more such groups into the building to find and kill the monster that had set off the Adventurer's Guild's defenses.

"Lost contact with blue team," said his second-in-command, Mariah. She was much stronger than he was in combat, but she lacked his vision. And besides, his archetype and class weren't intended to personally fight any battles. He was a Tactician by archetype and a Guild Leader by class. As such, nearly every aspect of his power set was devoted to leading, managing, and augmenting the members of the guild. Certainly, they had to swear an oath to his organization, but for what he had to offer, many were willing to do whatever it took. "Three dead. Two are alive, but one unconscious."

Bruce glanced at Mariah, who was looking at a tablet. She had a Warrior archetype, with the War Captain class. It had combat abilities—and solid attribute bonuses, as well—but the true value of the class was that it gave her skills that eased the burden of managing battles. She could keep track of up to six teams at once, and each of those was given a buff that increased their Constitutions by a significant amount. That, combined with Bruce's own buffs, had given them a distinct advantage in any conflict.

Until now.

"What—"

"Red team disabled. Two dead. Three unconscious."

"What the hell is in there?!" demanded Bruce.

"Unclear," Mariah answered in her characteristically monotone voice. The woman was invaluable, but a people person she was not.

Just then, a figure came running out of the front door, her arms flapping at her sides. It took Bruce a moment to recognize her as the blue-team Healer, though he couldn't remember her name. Only when she drew closer and he saw the severity of her wounds as well as the sheer panic on her face did he snap back to attention.

When she reached the group of men and women, she fell to her knees as she sobbed uncontrollably. "M-monster. Worse than anything I saw in the tower. I . . . I don't know . . . I don't know what it is . . . It's . . . the devil . . ."

Just then, something crashed through the sixth-floor window, landing only a dozen feet in front of the building's front door. It was a body.

"Green team has engaged," Mariah said as two other Healers collapsed onto the fallen woman. But one look was all it took for Bruce to write her off. The damage to her arms was too severe, but even worse was her demeanor. He'd seen it before. She would never willingly fight again. "One dead. Two still fighting. One missing. The last is unconscious."

"Stabilize her. We need answers," Bruce said. At that moment, he wished he had more abilities to keep track of his people, but that wasn't the focus of his class. He could augment them, so long as they were in range, and he could even offer quests, though they were limited both in scope and reward. But it was that ability that had given him so much power.

After all, running towers was already lucrative. Doing so with a quest resulted in even more wealth. The same was true for mundane tasks associated with running the guild. If someone wanted to hire them as guards, he could offer a quest to his people in order to augment their pay. Or if some monster needed to be hunted. Bruce knew he'd only scratched the surface of what was possible, and he envisioned a day when he had a global network of Adventurers working for him. Not only would it help keep the world free from tower surges, but it would be incredibly lucrative for him, too—both in terms of etherium and as experience.

Because the larger his guild, the more experience he got.

If he kept going like he was, he would be at the top of the power ladder in no time.

But none of that would happen if he couldn't take the city. Or if all his people died at the hands—or claws—of whatever monster had tried to invade the headquarters.

The two Healers did as they'd been asked, and though the girl was still crippled, she was at least coherent. So, he knelt beside her and asked, "What happened? What was it?"

"Monster. Man. I don't know," she said. Then, she went on to describe being attacked by some sort of lizard creature, then another, much larger scaled monster. There was a human somewhere in the mix, as well.

Bruce didn't know what to make of it, and he didn't have time to think it through before Mariah announced, "Green team is down. All dead. Purple team down, as well."

"Someone's coming out!" shouted one member of the team.

Bruce looked up to see a man push through the front door. From a distance, his features were difficult to make out, but Bruce could see the basics well enough. He was short—maybe five and a half feet all—and wiry, with a mop of curly blond hair and a full beard to match. He carried a staff that was about the same length as he was tall, and his clothes were unremarkable, though he wore a bright-red sash, a magnificent fur cloak, and a gray leather purse at his waist.

All in all, Bruce recognized the eclectic attire for what it was. The man was wearing a treasure trove of high-quality equipment that had clearly originated in a tower. That meant he was dangerous.

"Stop!" Bruce shouted.

To his surprise, the man did just that. "I guess you're the big man in charge, huh?" came a slightly raspy voice. "I'm going to have to request that you surrender immediately. Otherwise, I'll end up killing everyone here. I'm trying to be less of a murder hobo lately, but people keep attacking me, which makes it a lot more difficult. I never was good at self-improvement. But it's not a quick journey, right? The goal is to be a little less murder-hobo-y each day. And given that I killed a city only a couple of months ago, I think I'm making progress."

"Killed a city . . ."

"Oh, right. You all probably don't know about that. Forget I said anything. Now, are you going to surrender? Or am I going to have to backslide on the murder-hobo thing?"

"Kill this clown," Bruce said, embracing Strength in Numbers:

Ability: Strength in Numbers	Empower your official guild members, increasing each of their physical attributes by twenty (20) points. Range dependent on Ethera attribute. Current range: One hundred (100) yards. Out-of-range guild members will be unaffected.

He also used Haste of the Guild:

Ability: Haste of the Guild	Empower your official guild members, increasing their haste by 3%. Range dependent on Ethera attribute. Current range: One hundred (100) yards. Out-of-range guild members will be unaffected.

Finally, he used Tactical Superiority, which was actually an ability from his archetype, rather than his class:

Ability: Tactical Superiority	Empower your army, lessening damage taken by 5%. Also increases their damage by 3%. Range dependent on Ethera attribute. Current range: Fifty (50) yards.

Thus empowered, three groups of Adventurers attacked the lone figure. And though they had the advantage of numbers, Bruce backed away, ready to use the ace up his sleeve if it looked like they were going to lose.

51

SACRIFICE

Silvery light shone down on the street between the guild headquarters and the abandoned building as Bruce eagerly watched three groups of seasoned Adventurers rush toward the lone figure. Their defenders led the way—two of which held shields, while the other was armed only with a massive sword—while the melee fighters fanned out to surround the man. All three Sorcerers began the process of casting their most potent spells, while the Healers lagged behind. Finally, the two Rangers were the farthest away, ready to pepper the man with arrows the moment the defenders engaged.

It was a standard formation for fighting through the tower, and even if it wasn't ideal against an intelligent opponent, it had become habit for the members of the Adventurer's Guild. Meanwhile, Bruce and Mariah stayed far enough behind that they would be able to avoid any stray attacks.

And if it came down to it, Bruce would have time to do what needed to be done. But he wouldn't commit to that path just yet. He had faith in his people, especially against a singular opponent. Often, he'd claimed that his Adventurers could hold up even against those monsters at the top of the power rankings, so he had every reason to believe they could hold their own against the man standing so nonchalantly in front of the building.

"Murder-hoboing it is, then," the fellow said. Then, Bruce felt the ambient ethera swirl.

"Shields!" he shouted.

The defenders responded to his order with drilled quickness, and a series of shields sprang up around the Healers. Then, another set enveloped the Sorcerers, who were the second-most-vulnerable members of the force. The next target would be the Rangers, though they never got the chance for that before the sky opened and lightning forked down from suddenly manifested clouds. Blades of wind cut through his people, kicking up dust and debris even as the earth roiled and broke beneath them.

Shouts of panic filled the air, but Bruce was happy to see that his people kept their wits about them.

A fly bit him on the neck, and he slapped the tiny insect, killing it. "What do you think—"

Another bite. Then another. It was only after the fourth that he looked inward and shouted, "Watch for afflictions!"

As the Healers responded, blanketing the area with curing spells, he drank a potion. Mariah did the same, though she still seemed as calm as ever. "The affliction is not initially life-threatening for anyone above fifty Constitution," she intoned, still reading from the tablet she'd somehow linked to her powers. Luckily, they were far enough from the localized storm that she didn't have to shout. "But it compounds. Each instance will do five percent more damage and be slightly more difficult to cure."

"Monstrous flies?"

"Conjured," Mariah answered. "More powerful than they should be."

"Equipment?"

"Perhaps," she acknowledged. "It is difficult to say for sure."

Bruce shook his head and focused on the battle. He was horrified to see that the man was gone, and in his place was some sort of scaled monstrosity that looked like someone had crossed a lizard and a sasquatch, with a little bit of gorilla thrown in for good measure. The monster was enormous, and judging by the way it sent his highest-level tanks staggering with every blow, it was ridiculously strong.

More distressingly, when the Rangers' arrows hit its hide—along with the melee fighters' weapons—they resulted in very little damage. "What is going on there? Is that some sort of pet? Where did it come from?"

"That is the man," Mariah said. "He has a transformation ability, likely associated with his class. By my calculations, he is capable of mitigating up to ninety percent of all incoming physical damage—less if his Constitution is lower than his opponent's highest attribute—at the cost of stamina." A fireball from one of the Sorcerers hit him. "And the damage from elemental spells seems to have been cut significantly, as well. That I believe is due to a buff of some sort, though without further observation, I cannot say for certain."

"Damn it," growled Bruce, watching the man creature leap over one of the tanks and grab hold of a Healer. Before anyone could react, the foe spun like a hammer thrower, then launched the Healer down the street. The woman flew for nearly fifty yards before hitting the pavement, bouncing a couple of times, and then rolling to a stop. She didn't move after that.

"What are your orders, sir?" asked Mariah. "There is time to retreat. We can bunker down in the headquarters. Thad's traps are still active."

"The one on the roof was the strongest he could create," Bruce said. Indeed, the Trapper was one of the highest-level members of the guild, and his traps were legendary for their potency. "If that couldn't take this guy out, then what makes you think any of the others will?"

"We could engage in a fighting retreat," she suggested. "Perhaps we can exhaust him. Stamina is a finite resource, even if it is not as quantifiable as ethera."

Bruce ignored her.

Instead, he was doing the calculations in his head. Even if they managed to defeat the creature, what good would it do? The guild's most powerful members would be killed, which would make the guild vulnerable to a takeover by that idealist idiot Isaiah and his lackeys from Rainier. And they would win, too. Sure, the Adventurers had the advantage now, but it was tenuous. Any losses would affect their ability to maintain control.

But losses didn't seem avoidable in this instance.

Was it time?

If he took the final step, he'd lose everything. However, he would survive. More, he would kill the man who'd ruined everything. And Isaiah, too, if he was lucky. Maybe that stubborn Gardener, as well. All of that raced through Bruce's mind as he watched yet another one of his guild members die—this time, a Sorcerer was crushed to paste by a series of pounding blows that looked strikingly like a gorilla attack.

He glanced at Mariah, saying, "For what it's worth, I didn't want to do this."

"What was that, sir?" she asked, not looking up from her tablet.

"Nothing."

Then, he used Dissolution.

Ability: Dissolution	Sacrifice your entire guild, gaining power according to the number of underlings killed. +5 Strength, Dexterity, and Constitution for every sacrifice. Bonuses increase by 35% for every minute active. Maximum effect based on Ethera attribute. Current maximum effect: 196 attribute points in each category. Duration based on Regeneration attribute. Current duration: 6.2 minutes.

Bruce had more than five thousand guild members—most of which were comparatively low level—under him, but he would only gain power from twenty of them. Yet, the ability had no degrees. It was all or nothing. Either he sacrificed every member of the guild, all at once, or none of them. There was no in-between. No half measures. And while so many of those deaths would be wasted, the ones who did count toward the buff would give him the power to overcome the enemy.

All around him, his people fell. Dissolution didn't instantly kill, so the monster man finished a few off before the rest lost their lives. As they did, Bruce stepped forward, an influx of attributes crashing into him like a runaway truck. He staggered under the increased power, but more distressingly, he felt his muscles bulge to ridiculous proportions. His clothes ripped to pieces as he grew, both in bulk and height, until he was even larger than his chosen enemy.

He flexed his fist. "I could get used to this," he rumbled as his tattered clothing fell away. Then, naked as the day he was born, he stepped forward, his footfall loud in the suddenly silent street.

Elijah stared in horror at the transformed man. He was enormous—at least fifteen feet tall, and as muscular as any bodybuilder—but his body was asymmetrical. One arm was almost a foot longer and far bulkier than the other, and he moved with a limp because his legs followed the same pattern. A huge lump of muscle grew from his back, looking like a tumor and giving him the appearance of a hunchback.

He was also quite hirsute, putting Elijah in mind of the missing link between humanity and its prehistoric predecessors.

But Elijah was more concerned with the fact that the entire group of Adventurers—eleven that were left—had simply keeled over and died. He knew it wasn't the effect of his Swarm, either. As powerful as his afflictions were, there was no evidence that they'd had a chance to build so effectively.

That meant something else had happened.

"He used an ability," came Isaiah's voice. "We knew Bruce had it, but I never thought . . ."

The man stepped forward, and Elijah asked, "What does it do?"

"Increases his attributes . . . by . . . a lot. According to my surveillance, he sacrificed every single guild member for a temporary boost in power. They're all dead. Almost five thousand Adventurers," Elijah heard through the earpiece. "You should probably run."

Elijah had no intention of doing that. He'd fought people with high attributes before, and he knew he'd have to do so again. So, without further hesitation, he charged the transformed man.

He hit the monstrosity with a shoulder tackle that knocked him back a few feet. However, for Elijah, it felt like he'd just rammed an immovable rampart. Despite his momentum, size, and incredible Strength, the maneuver was completely ineffective. Bruce shouted something unintelligible, then snapped out a punch that sent Elijah skidding backward. Because he'd had Iron Scales active, it was only marginally effective. Yet, Elijah had discovered a few things about the ability.

It was incredible against piercing and slashing attacks, but it was less effective against blunt force. It still stopped plenty of damage, but some of that momentum still went through his hide to wreak havoc on the more vulnerable bits beneath his scales.

Regardless, Elijah took the blow in stride, then leaped back into the fray. As he did, he saw that a thorn had pierced Bruce's forearm. It hadn't gone more than a quarter of an inch deep, which told him that Bruce's Constitution was at least as high as his Strength.

For the next minute, they traded blows, and Elijah felt confident that they were fairly equal in terms of power—which was frightening enough—but just as the fight passed the one-minute mark, Elijah started to get the worst of each exchange. The fight continued, and the thunderous punches began to take a toll.

Finally, a hit landed that sent him tumbling backward into the remnants of a wall. When he crashed into it, he was buried in dislodged bricks and mortar.

"What the hell?" he muttered, climbing free from the pile of rubble. "Is he getting stronger?"

"I think so," Isaiah said. "Like I already told you—you should've just run."

"I think you're right," Elijah said, already initiating a shift into Shape of the Sky. The man was strong, but he couldn't fly. That gave Elijah the escape route he needed. Once Bruce saw Elijah's transformation, he charged, but the metamorphosis completed before the giant misshapen man arrived. So, without hesitation, Elijah leaped into the air.

Bruce roared, picked up a giant hunk of cement, and threw it at Elijah. By that point, he was a few dozen feet above the ground, but he was incapable of dodging the boulder that moved at the speed of a bullet. It hit him in the leg, throwing him off-balance and sending him plummeting back toward the ground.

Where Bruce waited.

Elijah knew he had no chance of survival if the monstrous man managed to get his grubby hands on him while he was using Shape of the Sky. It had no real defenses, and given that even when using Iron Scales in the Shape of the Guardian he'd taken damage, he knew precisely what would happen.

So, he beat his wings to slow his fall, then initiated another shift.

Not into the lamellar-ape form. Nor did he adopt the draconid form. Instead, he returned to his human shape and cast Storm's Fury. The lightning bolt descended, hitting the giant man directly in the forehead. It didn't do much, but it stunned Bruce for just long enough to keep him from latching on to Elijah.

He hit the ground hard, his already-injured leg crumpling under him. But he didn't let that stop him. Using one facet of his Quartz Mind to cast Soothe, he used another to prepare Snaring Roots. One cast followed the other, and even as blessed relief flowed through him, his other spell erupted into being, manifesting a tangle of thorny vines that wrapped around Bruce's legs.

Elijah leaped away—mostly one-legged—and cast Healing Rain. But Bruce was already ripping free. Snaring Roots had rarely functioned as more than a delaying tactic, and with the man's augmented power, it was barely even that. But it did give Elijah the chance to cast two more spells.

Touch of Nature added its effect to Soothe and Healing Rain, while Shape of the Predator transformed him into a draconid. If he couldn't outmuscle the man, then he hoped to outmaneuver him. Nothing was better for that than Shape of the Predator.

Once it took hold, he darted to the side, ready to fight the battle on completely different terms.

52

THE WEIGHT OF REALITY

Elijah dashed to the side, then immediately changed directions. The transformed Bruce thundered past him, incapable of changing directions so quickly. He tripped over a pile of rubble, and though he managed to right himself only a moment later, it gave Elijah just enough time to dart in, slash his claws across the man's calf, then retreat. To his horror, though, he barely even made a scratch.

By that point, they'd been going back and forth for a couple of minutes, and Elijah could tell that he was outclassed in terms of sheer power. It was an unfamiliar experience—even against Thor, the two had fought on mostly even terms regarding attributes—and it nullified many of Elijah's normal strategies. However, he'd discovered a couple of things that had kept him from succumbing.

First, running was useless. He'd tried on multiple occasions, but Bruce had more than enough Strength to catch him. So, his only real option was to stand and fight—which wasn't going well—but at least he hadn't taken more than a few grazing blows along the way.

The second thing he'd figured out was that Bruce was incredibly clumsy. That was almost assuredly due to the fact that he was new to his increased attributes. According to Carmen, that was common. After she'd tossed all her starting attributes into Strength, it had taken her a few minutes to adjust to all the extra power. And that was only couple of handfuls of points. Bruce's situation was much more extreme.

That was the only factor that kept Elijah from being overwhelmed. He was weaker, slower, and far more vulnerable than the transformed man. But he'd come upon his attributes the natural way, and as such, he was far more accustomed to how everything worked.

By Isaiah's estimate, Bruce could only display about seventy percent of his attributes. It would have been higher, but it seemed that each passing minute increased his power, which in turn negated his efforts at adjustment. Still, throwing himself at Elijah wasn't so difficult, even if controlling that charge was.

So, for the past couple of minutes, Elijah had been playing a game of cat and mouse as he attempted to build afflictions in the man. Fortunately, his Soothe and Healing Rain had already mended his damaged leg, so he wasn't hobbled by any injuries. If he had been, he'd have already lost the battle and his life.

Bruce let out a roar, leaping to his feet and throwing an old car door at Elijah. He leaped over it, but even that temporary distraction gave Bruce the opening he needed to hit Elijah with a vicious backhand that sent him bouncing across the road. He came to a rest in a pile of bodies that had once been a group of Adventurers. He tried to rise, but his leg collapsed beneath him.

It wasn't broken, but it had been twisted out of joint.

And with Bruce bearing down on him, he only had one choice.

Elijah shifted back to his human form and cast Soothe, then Touch of Nature. He barely had a chance to shove his dislocated knee back into place before Bruce reached him. The man reached down with one enormous hand. Elijah tried to knock those grabbing fingers away, but they were undeniable.

Suddenly, Bruce had his hand around Elijah's waist. He lifted him. And Elijah shoved his staff into the man's eye.

Garret reeled, loosening his grip only slightly, which Elijah used to wriggle his way free. But his escape was only temporary because, almost as soon as he hit the ground, he felt a large foot connect with his ribs. Abruptly, Elijah found himself sailing through the air like a punted football, and a moment later, he thudded into the side of a building.

The impact cracked a couple of ribs and at least one of his vertebrae, but Elijah was more concerned with the upcoming fall. He thrust his hand out, grabbing a metal windowsill, arresting his descent. But his respite only lasted a split second before he felt something rushing in his direction. He turned to see that Bruce had leaped toward him, likely thinking he could finally finish Elijah off.

So, Elijah let go.

As he did, he shifted back into his Shape of the Sky, and before he hit the ground, the transformation had completed. He beat his wings, leveling off and gliding away. Bruce kicked off the building and rocketed in Elijah's direction. To counter, Elijah tried to gain altitude, but he was too slow.

Bruce clipped his wing, cracking the delicate bones and sending Elijah twirling back toward the ground. He hit, cartwheeling over a pile of rubble and coming to a rest only a moment later. About thirty yards away, Bruce landed, cracking the pavement with the impact. Then, he picked up another rock and threw it in Elijah's direction.

The Shape of the Sky wasn't meant for ground travel, so he only barely managed to skitter out of the way. As he did, he initiated another transformation into his human form so he could heal. He never got the chance because, by the time he'd completely shifted, Bruce was back on top of him. His enormous fist fell with inevitability, and though Elijah tried to escape its path, he was hemmed in by the rubble and his injured arm. Even so, every facet of his Quartz Mind was working on his situation. One was casting Soothe again. Another held Healing

Rain just on the edge of activation. And still another was ready to use Touch of Nature. Finally, he had Shape of the Guardian queued up, though he didn't think he'd ever get the chance to use it.

His Constitution was high, but against the monstrous man's ever-rising Strength, it was nothing. Even so, Elijah lashed out with his staff, and he was lucky enough to clip Bruce's most vulnerable bits. It was little more than a graze, but as any man could attest, that was enough to at least foster a distraction. And as it happened, that tiny hitch in Bruce's attack gave Elijah the time he needed to complete the cast of Soothe. More importantly, it allowed him to scramble backward over the rubble and escape the descending fist.

It thundered into the pile of cement, crushing it to dust as Elijah rolled free. Healing Rain completed casting at that moment, bathing him in rejuvenating precipitation. And finally, he managed to channel Touch of Nature, mending his wounded arm enough that, when he sprang to his feet, he did so with much more verve and plenty of vigor.

That's when he caught a front kick to the chest that nearly caved his ribs in. It threw him backward like he'd been launched from the world's largest sling-shot, and he didn't land for almost an entire second. When he did, he skipped across the ground, narrowly managing to complete the cast of Shape of the Guardian before coming to a stop nearly a hundred and fifty yards away from where he'd started.

He picked himself up. Even with Soothe and Touch of Nature, he was still very injured. And he was well out of range of Healing Rain. But with every passing second, Soothe helped mend his wounds. The problem was that, with all his shape-shifting and casting, he knew he was on the verge of being out of ethera.

More troubling, he had no idea how to win the fight.

And given how quickly Bruce was covering the ground between them, he couldn't escape, either. Because not only had the man gotten even stronger and faster, but he seemed to be adjusting to his attributes, too. Soon, Elijah would be outclassed in every department.

His mind raced as he tried to think of a plan. He'd tried to fly away, and to no avail. Every time he'd launched himself into the sky, Bruce had brought him down with thrown boulders. He'd tried to escape on foot, but that had been even less effective. And fighting seemed to be a dead end, as well.

But there had to be a way.

Elijah braced for impact, seeing that his Silver Bracer of Rage had come off cooldown. He used the ability, adding more Strength to his total. Then, he met the enraged and enlarged man, Strength to Strength, and he was horrified to find that he wasn't even close to a match.

He was thrown to the ground as if he was nothing more than a child's toy, and then Bruce started to get serious. Elijah tried to fight back, using his boxing background to parry punches and block kicks. But he was so far outclassed that even those efforts resulted in injuries. In moments, he'd felt more bones break, and he knew he would be forced to use Guardian's Renewal soon if he wanted to survive.

But then what?

He couldn't keep up. And the man was getting stronger all the time. Each facet of Elijah's Mind whirled as it tried to find an answer, but in the end, there was none to be found. Against such superior power, none of his versatility mattered. He just didn't have the ability to win the fight.

He couldn't give up, though. So, he fought on, eventually using Guardian's Renewal as a last-ditch gambit to escape. His body mended, and he kicked out. Miraculously, his foot connected with Bruce's knee, buckling it slightly. That was the opening Elijah needed, and he threw himself to his feet, bowling the off-balance man to the ground.

In the past, he would have fallen upon his enemy with a flurry of powerful blows. But in this case, he knew it would do no good. Even catching the man completely off guard, he'd done no lasting damage. He was too durable. His Constitution was too high. So, Elijah ran.

He poured every ounce of Strength he could muster into a straightway sprint, and he accelerated with the speed of a sports car. Yet, he could feel the recovered guild leader hot on his heels. Elijah tried to corner, kicking off a destroyed semitruck to facilitate a turn.

That's when Bruce caught up, hitting him with a shoulder tackle that knocked him back into the truck. The vehicle flipped three times, and Elijah barely managed to avoid being crushed beneath the thing.

Bruce caught him by the neck and lifted him off his feet.

"You cost me everything!" he rumbled, his voice distorted and cracking.

Elijah didn't answer. Instead, he scratched and clawed, but he knew it would do no good. His efforts only left a few red marks on the man's hirsute skin. But he refused to give in. He refused to go down without fighting to the last moment.

One blow after another rained down on Elijah, and eventually, he stopped blocking. Not by choice. But because each one fell with the weight of an industrial power hammer, pushing him to the verge of unconsciousness.

Then, just before Elijah's body reached the end of its endurance, something changed.

The sound of gunshots echoed in his ears, but it took a moment for Elijah's head to clear. When it did, he saw that a swarm of drones hovered nearby, and each one sported a cannon beneath its fuselage. However, instead of shooting bullets, they fired balls of ethera that reminded Elijah of Ethereal Bolt. When they hit Bruce's giant form, they elicited a brief instant of a stun.

Normally, that wouldn't have mattered. But with more than a hundred of the things firing one after another, it chained into something effective. Elijah stared, dumbfounded by the situation until Isaiah screamed in his ear, "Run! I can't keep this up much longer! I'm almost out of ethera!"

Elijah shook his head.

"Whaa . . ."

Then, the weight of Isaiah's words hit him, and he awkwardly crawled to his feet. After that, with the backdrop of all those blue ethereal bolts, he staggered away. His entire body was in agony, but still, he pushed on.

Until the drones went quiet.

It didn't take Bruce long to recover after that, and when he did, he let out a roar and quickly caught up to Elijah, knocking him over and sending him skidding across the ground on his stomach.

He screamed something Elijah didn't hear, then rolled him over. Elijah tried to resist, but his body was limp. His energy was gone. And his consciousness was barely hanging on.

Bruce towered over him, a menacing glare twisting his misshapen features as he announced his superiority. Then, he reached back, preparing to deliver what they both knew would be the final blow.

Elijah closed his eyes, waiting for the proverbial hammer to fall.

It never did.

But a second later, something else fell atop him. It writhed for a second, then went still. Elijah opened his eyes to see Bruce's naked body—which had gone back to his normal size—lying on top of him. He pushed it away. The man tried to fend him off, but his hands were weak. Barely better than someone without an archetype.

After shifting into the Shape of the Guardian, Elijah awkwardly reached out, his claws wrapping around Bruce's head. The man screamed. Elijah ignored it. And then, at last, he squeezed with all the strength he had left. It wasn't much, but it was enough that he soon felt brains and skull oozing between his fingers.

Then, he fell backward, his breath coming in ragged gasps as he struggled to remain conscious.

53

ONE DOWN, ONE TO GO

Elijah lay there, staring up at the twinkling stars. One thing he'd noticed about the desert was just how clear the nights were. He could see so much, which elicited so many questions about the larger universe. How many of those stars hosted planets? Was K'hana's home planet up there? What about Ramik's? Kurik's? Would he one day visit those places?

Not if he ran into another monster like the guild master, Bruce Garret. The man had been much more powerful than Elijah had been led to believe, and because of that, he'd been completely outclassed. If the man's transformation hadn't run its course, the battle would have ended much differently.

He sighed.

It had been a while since he'd been made to feel so weak. So ineffectual. It was like he'd gone back to his first days after washing ashore on his island, when even the crabs were capable of killing him. Despite all the work he'd put into his cultivation, all the levels he'd gained, he was not invincible. Even someone like Garret, in the right situation, could defeat him.

It was a lesson he should have learned after his fight with the Warden, but back then, he'd been a little too preoccupied to properly internalize anything of the sort. Now, though, he had that luxury.

And the lesson was a simple one: Context was important. The world wasn't simple. Levels mattered—and so did cultivation—but neither was a guarantee of victory. The most powerful person didn't always win. There were other factors that contributed to every set of circumstances. One of those was equipment—with the right set of gear, a person could far outperform his level—but even more impactful was context.

In a vacuum, Garret couldn't hold a candle to Elijah. But after whatever ability he'd used? He displayed a level of power that far exceeded anything Elijah had ever fought.

That meant that Elijah couldn't keep going through the world like he was unassailable. He'd gotten a bit cocky after attaining the top spot on the power rankings. But while that was quite an achievement, it wasn't the guarantee of superiority he'd once thought it would be. After all, there weren't that many levels separating the ones at the top of the ladder from the people who weren't even on it.

On top of that, he often punched above his weight, and that meant that others could do so, as well. All they needed was the right circumstance. It seemed obvious in retrospect, but Elijah had been riding high off of his own successes, and he'd ignored common sense. Just because he had power, it didn't mean that he was omnipotent. And he would do well to remember that, or he would end up biting off more than he could chew.

Again.

As those thoughts gripped him, Elijah heard Isaiah's voice through his earpiece asking, "Do you require a Healer? We don't have many, but—"

"I'm fine. Just give me a minute," Elijah groaned, sitting up. He'd let his bestial form fall away, and he could see just how much damage he'd taken. It wasn't pretty, either. Multiple broken bones, but fortunately, none were severe. Many lacerations. A body that was already turning black and blue from all the contusions. A slight concussion that he'd isolated into one facet of his Mind. And he felt certain that there was at least a little internal bleeding.

But the most serious issue was that his sternum had been cracked, which made breathing difficult—to say the least. So, that was his first target for healing.

As soon as he'd gained enough ethera to cast, he used Soothe and Healing Rain before channeling Touch of Nature. After his sternum was healed, Elijah stopped focusing on any particular injury. Instead, he let the healing suffuse his entire body. It was slower for specific wounds, but it would bring him to full health much more quickly.

In the end, he managed to get back on his feet after only an hour. During that time, he noticed Isaiah's drones buzzing around and looting the bodies of the Adventurers. At first, Elijah had hoped that they'd only been knocked unconscious, but it quickly became clear that Garret's ability—whatever it was called—had killed them.

"Such a waste," he muttered. And it was. All those people dead because they couldn't coexist with their neighbors. It was more complicated than that—because it always was—but that was the underlying theme. They wanted power and control, and they were willing to take it by force. "Do you know how he did it?"

"I have my suspicions," Isaiah answered. Then, he described the situation as he understood it. Garret had sacrificed everyone in his guild for temporary power. "I think most of that sacrifice went to waste, or you wouldn't have survived as long as you did."

Elijah sighed. There were an infinite number of abilities out there that he didn't understand, and he suspected that, one day, his lack of knowledge would come back and bite him. In the fight against Garret, it almost had.

"You know I'm entitled to that gear," Elijah said. "My kills, my loot."

"I am aware," Isaiah stated. "Perhaps we can work out a deal where I can purchase everything. And I think it is fair to split the contents of the guild hall."

Elijah didn't like that idea. He'd done most of the work, after all. But he wasn't so greedy that he intended to cut Isaiah off altogether. "Seems more like a seventy-thirty kind of thing."

After that, they began their negotiations. It didn't take long, largely because Elijah wasn't really all that interested, aside from a desire not to roll over. His funds had taken quite a hit after his most recent expenditures, but he knew he could always earn more etherium. By the time they were finished, he just said, "How about you just pay me for anything I don't want to personally use? Give me fifty gold, and you can have it all."

"Deal."

By that point, Elijah had finished recuperating to the point where he felt confident in flying back to the capitol, where he intended to pick K'hana up and head to Lucy's. So, he used Shape of the Sky, then launched himself into the air. After flapping his wings a few times, he gained enough altitude that he could glide to his destination. However, even that small amount of movement told him that he wasn't quite as healed as he'd thought. He would need a little more time before he was back to normal.

So, as gingerly as he could, he landed near the capitol's makeshift wall. He'd made sure not to drop down on top of the guards, but he was still close enough that they were forced to react. Thankfully, Isaiah had already let them know what was going on, so they didn't launch any attacks, and after Elijah shifted back to his human form, they allowed him inside, albeit with an escort that led him across the grounds and into the building.

He didn't end up back in Isaiah's office, though. Instead, he was led deeper into the capitol building and to a large chamber that looked like every military command center he'd seen in movies. Large screens decorated the walls, while dozens of people in black fatigues worked at various computers. Isaiah stood in the center, with K'hana primly seated nearby.

Elijah approached.

"So, this is the heart of your operation, huh?" he asked.

Hands clutched behind his back, Isaiah didn't even glance away from the screen as he said, "Not at all. I'm the heart of the operation. Everything here is so others can do their jobs."

"I see. So, what's the plan? I took care of your Adventurer problem, and I'm guessing you still want me to do something about Mercer Mesa," Elijah guessed.

"I do. A frontal assault on the Mesa is suicide. They have multiple people with classes meant for defense," Isaiah explained as a map of the plateau flashed on the screen. "Anyone who tries to climb those cliffs is going to get a deadly surprise. I've seen it happen, and it's not pretty."

"Nature of the defenses?"

"Traps, mostly. But they also have a small army to protect the settlement," Isaiah said. "They are controlled by someone you know."

A photograph of an older man with blindingly white teeth and a boater's tan replaced the map of Mercer Mesa.

"Barry?"

"He took Administrator as an archetype," Isaiah explained. "That became a class called Demagogue. The people who work for him are loyal to a fault."

"He manipulates them with a skill?"

"It's more like his arguments are more persuasive," Isaiah answered. "He also has an ability called Incite that will whip them into a frenzy, increasing their attributes."

"That doesn't make sense," Elijah said. "Why was he stealing when I ran into him my first time in town? Those people had him cornered. They were going to kill him."

"Were they?"

"Yes. They were. I was there."

"But did you see what you thought you saw? This man's stock in trade is manipulation. He was doing it decades before the world changed, and he certainly didn't stop afterward," Isaiah said.

That's when Elijah figured it out. "Those men were never going to hurt him," he guessed. "They probably worked for him. It was all a setup to get me onto the Mesa so he could try to rope me in by dangling his daughter in front of me."

"That is my suspicion."

"Why didn't you say anything before?" Elijah asked.

Isaiah answered, "Because it didn't matter then. It does now."

Elijah gritted his teeth, growling, "I'm going to kill him."

"That's the plan."

After that, Elijah listened as Isaiah went over his proposal for assaulting the Mesa. It wasn't complex, but it required precise timing and a giant distraction. When they were finished, Elijah excused himself and left the capitol. K'hana stayed behind to work out the details of Arvandor's alliance with Seattle, though she would join him at Lucy's when she was done.

He didn't fly to Lucy's apartment building. Rather, he just walked, which gave him plenty of time to continue healing. So, when he finally reached her building, he was feeling much better than before.

Not perfect, but still better. Hopefully, he would be completely healed by morning because that was when they planned to attack.

Still, he hesitated before approaching the building. There were a couple of guards out front—both of whom were wearing crafted gear—so he couldn't just walk in and knock on the door. But that wasn't why he hesitated. Instead, he was worried about what Lucy would think of him.

For one, despite knowing of Seattle's situation, he'd ignored it for months. And he'd only barely arrived in time to keep her from being attacked. If the shoe was on the other foot, he'd at least be irritated about that.

More than anything, though, he couldn't help but feel anxious that Lucy would look at him differently once she knew what he'd done in Valoria. Once she knew how many people he'd killed. Would she judge him? Almost certainly. But how harshly was a different question altogether.

Oddly, he never considered simply keeping it to himself. He and Lucy had never lied to one another, and he didn't intend to start now. If that meant she was disgusted by his actions, then so be it.

So, with a sigh, he stepped forward, and after getting cleared by the guards, he found his way to Lucy's apartment. He hesitated for only a few moments before knocking on the door. Lucy—wearing a pair of cotton shorts and a tee-shirt—answered a second later. Her hair was a mess, and her glasses had fallen halfway down her nose, but she still looked just as attractive as ever.

"Hey," he said with a forced smile. "I'm back."

"What happened?"

"Nothing. Well, not nothing. The Adventurers are kind of gone now. But—"

"I already knew that. Isaiah told me. I'm talking about the other thing."

"What other thing?" Elijah asked.

"Even after all these years, I know you and your looks. And this one," she said, gesturing to his face. "That's the same as after your parents died. So, what happened?"

He shook his head. "Can I just come in? It's kind of a long story."

She acquiesced, and after he insisted upon brewing her a cup of his coffee, they settled in. Then, Elijah told her everything.

54

DIVE BOMB

I couldn't stop myself," Elijah said, staring at his cup of coffee. He hadn't taken a single sip, and by now, it had gone completely cold. "I was just so angry. Everywhere I looked, I saw a reminder of how broken that city was. It looked nice. It kept people safe. But it was a cesspool that fed all of humanity's worst instincts."

He looked up. "I killed hundreds of them, Lucy. Thousands, probably. And the worst part of it is that I don't really regret it," he admitted. "I mean, I feel guilty about losing control. But that guilt—it's not really strong enough to make me regret it. What I do feel guilty about is that I didn't do it sooner, that I spent all that time doing nothing, wandering around the world and getting distracted by things that didn't really matter. I know it wouldn't have made a difference. If I'd have set out from my island sooner, I probably would have died before I ever got to Easton. And I saved a lot of lives by giving in to those distractions. But still . . . I'd give them all up if it meant I could have saved Alyssa.

"Does that make me a bad person? I think that makes me a bad person."

"It makes you human," Lucy said, leaning forward as she gripped her own mug in two hands. She'd long since finished her cup of coffee. That wasn't surprising, though—Elijah had spent the past forty-five minutes rambling about what he'd done after leaving Seattle the last time. Unsurprisingly, the bulk of that had centered on his actions in Valoria, though he did spend a fair amount of time reminiscing with Lucy about fond memories they'd both shared with Alyssa.

Elijah had done the same with Carmen, but with Lucy, it was different. Like Elijah, she'd grown up around Alyssa. They had both seen her at her best, at her teenage worst, and everything in between. By comparison, Carmen had only seen the finished product. A fully formed adult woman who knew who she was and what she wanted from the world.

"Sometimes, I don't feel so human anymore," Elijah admitted. "I mean, I spend a lot of my time running around on four legs. Or flying. I can do that now, by the way. I can actually fly. Do you realize how crazy that sounds?"

She shook her head, saying, "It wasn't that long ago that I saw an alligator the size of a passenger plane. In the desert, which doesn't make sense at all.

Oh, and Seattle is now a desert. The world is a crazy place. You flying is the least of it."

"I can see down your shirt, by the way. Nice."

She sighed, then gave him a small smile. "You always do that."

"Look down your shirt? In my defense, it's, like, right there. And I happen to like—"

"You know that's not what I mean," she interrupted. "You undercut any emotional moment by diverting the conversation into something else, then make a joke."

"What I'm looking at is no joke," Elijah insisted.

"Do you want to have a real discussion? Or are you going to keep doing this?" she asked, obviously frustrated as she set her mug down on the coffee table. Then, she leaned back. "Because if you don't want to talk about it, all you have to do is say so. I'm not going to push. You don't have to divert."

Elijah let out a long breath, then said, "Honestly? I don't want to talk about it. I know I probably need to, but . . ."

"But you're not ready."

"Something like that. I'm still working through some things."

And he was. It wasn't at the forefront of his mind, but Elijah did worry about what all the killing was doing to him. It felt easier every time he did it, which was more than a little troubling. As he'd noted in the fight against the Adventurers, he was trying to move away from killing as his first response to any conflict, but it seemed that the world was conspiring against that endeavor. Perhaps that was the nature of the multiverse. Maybe killing was just how problems got solved.

But he had no intention of letting those thoughts take over his mind. He had other things that needed his attention. So, he moved the conversation along, explaining what had happened at the guild hall. "He was strong, Lucy. It cost him, though. It's terrifying, thinking of all the possibilities with certain classes," Elijah said. "I mean, I still don't know how all of that worked, but he sacrificed those people for a temporary boost in power."

"Oaths."

"What?"

"Every member of his Adventurers' guild had to give an oath. It's why they didn't have more people," Lucy said. "Lots of the hunters had opportunities to join, but they chose not to because Garret made everyone give some sort of oath. It was backed up by ethera, too. They made a big ceremony out of it, as well. I'm willing to bet that part of that oath was an agreement to be sacrificed."

"That . . . That makes it a little less frightening," Elijah admitted. If people had to consent to something like that, then its power was limited. However, it wasn't difficult to imagine that, in some places, someone with a similar class might force the issue. Roman certainly would have if such a thing had been available to him. But it was good that there were limits. "But we don't need to worry about them anymore. The entire guild is dead. Now, I just have to deal with Mercer Mesa."

"How are you going to do it?" she asked.

"Violently."

"You just said—"

"Those people are trash," Elijah said. "If they were hoarding a luxury, it would be different. But they're monopolizing a necessity. Without that water, people die. They already have, from what I understand. This whole thing can be laid at their feet. Am I wrong about that?"

He'd thought about it a lot, and as far as he could tell, the people of Mercer Mesa were responsible for Seattle's instability. Perhaps there still would have been issues between Isaiah and the Adventurers, but Elijah expected that the situation would have been far less volatile if water shortages wouldn't have been part of the equation. On top of that, he'd learned that the people of Mercer Mesa had refused to help with the attack of the giant alligator monster that had destroyed part of the city. They were selfish, and their goals ran counter to a productive, safe society.

"You're not wrong," Lucy said. "I just wish it was better. I wish people were better."

"Some are. It's not like this everywhere."

"Really?" she asked.

"Argos is mostly peaceful. There's a place on the other side of the Twilight Clefts that is, too. Same with the elves of Arvandor," he explained. "The town near my island is peaceful, as well. Even Norcastle is better now, and it's governed by a bit of a dick. I think it's because, even when there is a power disparity, this system gives people the ability to fight back against oppression if they want to. I mean, if someone tries to mess with my friend in his shop, they're going to lose. I think a lot of noncombatants are going to get abilities like that."

"Is that a rational conclusion? Or just hope?"

"Maybe a little of both."

After that, the two lapsed into silence, but it only lasted a few minutes before K'hana arrived. Elijah introduced the two to one another, and they almost immediately started to discuss all the ways they could help one another. He had little interest in that, so he excused himself and went to the apartment's guest bedroom. There, he concentrated on healing himself and cycling his Core. More of the former than the latter, but he'd taken to working on his cultivation as often as possible. Outside of when he was fighting, he kept it going at all times, and he'd slowly made progress. He still felt that he was a long way from his efforts bearing fruit, but the fact that he had made verifiable improvement was encouraging.

That night, he didn't sleep. Instead, he focused entirely on preparing himself for what he expected to be a difficult battle. Part of that was getting himself back to peak condition, but he also pulled out his long-ignored laptop, plugged in a USB drive containing all the information Isaiah had given him, and memorized the map as well as everything else that seemed useful.

With his Quartz Mind, it wasn't even difficult, which prompted him to wish he'd had access to cultivation back in college. It would have trivialized all the rote memorization required by any advanced degree. But if he'd had those advantages back then, there was no way he'd have followed the path of an academic, so it was a bit of a moot point. Besides, it wasn't like anyone could change the past.

The rest of the night and most of the following morning was busy but tedious, though by midafternoon, he felt as prepared as he could be. By that point, K'hana and Lucy had reached an agreement, though Elijah didn't really concern himself with the details. All he cared about was that they would help one another, and given how friendly they were acting, that seemed to be the case.

"Do you wish for me to help?" asked K'hana when Elijah let them know that he would be leaving on his mission as soon as the sun set. "If I had been there before, you might not have been so grievously injured."

"You'd have probably died," Elijah said.

"I am no helpless damsel."

"Never said you were. But the fact of the matter is that I'm more durable than you," Elijah explained. "And that guild leader seemed like the kind of guy who'd target the most vulnerable first. Maybe that would have given me the chance to take him out before he grew so strong, but I don't think you would have survived. With how strong he was . . ."

"Is that kind of thing common?" Lucy asked K'hana.

The elven woman didn't look terribly happy to have her own weakness pointed out. It was an unassailable fact, though, and Elijah didn't regret saying it, especially if it kept her alive. Tersely, she said, "I do not know. I have heard of classes that form symbiotic relationships with their people. Most are Tacticians or Administrators. The Noble class is the most common. They increase productivity and experience for noncombat classes, but they have abilities that can enhance their own power at the expense of their citizens'. Some variants even have the ability to control the way their people see them, though that is rare from what I understand. I am no expert, though. On my world, we were too isolated for those sorts of classes to manifest."

"Interesting," said Elijah.

He knew that each archetype had its own purpose, but he'd never really thought about what kind of abilities they might have. Sure, Tacticians would probably get abilities that would help them organize and empower armies, but beyond that, Elijah had never thought about what else they could do. The same was true of Administrators like Barry. Isaiah had given him some information on the man's suspected capabilities, but Elijah knew that there was a chance that he was walking into another very dangerous set of circumstances.

Whatever the case, it was a situation he couldn't ignore. Even if he didn't feel a moral obligation to do something about their water hoarding—which he definitely felt—he'd also made a promise to Isaiah, and he intended to keep his word.

So, when the sun set, Elijah went to the roof of Lucy's building, transformed into the Shape of the Sky, then flew to the capitol. He landed inside the walls, then made his way toward Isaiah's command center. Once he arrived, he was surprised to find that Isaiah had gathered a group of soldiers.

"What's with these guys?" he asked. Each of the men wore black fatigues, just like everyone else in Isaiah's army. However, these soldiers felt far more powerful. If they weren't on the verge of entering the ranks of the top one hundred, Elijah would have been surprised.

"Former SEALs," Isaiah said.

"In training, sir," said one of the men. "We never finished."

Elijah was aware that the SEALs had a history of training in Washington state parks, but that had supposedly ended when a judge banned them from doing so. Apparently, they had ignored that ban. Before the world's transformation, Elijah might've found that unconscionable, but right now, he was grateful for their presence.

Perhaps there was a lesson there, but it was one Elijah didn't have time to examine.

Isaiah then explained that the former SEALs in training were his special-operations team. Elijah didn't know how effective they would be, but he expected that their pre–World Tree training would serve them well. After all, it took quite a lot of grit and determination to become a navy SEAL, and that would translate well to the new world.

Regardless, the plan was for Elijah to attack from the air while the team scaled the cliff. Meanwhile, Isaiah would send his drones to disarm the traps. He knew he wouldn't get them all, and without the distraction provided by Elijah and the SEALs, it would be a useless endeavor. They would just replace the traps before anyone could take advantage of the vulnerability. Yet, having to deal with an attack would hopefully prevent that.

Elijah agreed to the plan, and once everyone was ready, the SEALs left. An hour later, they were in position.

"You're up. Good luck," Isaiah said.

"Yeah. Sure."

Then, Elijah left the building, adopted the Shape of the Sky, and took off. He didn't bother hiding his presence. Instead, when he reached Mercer Mesa, he flew around for a few minutes, ensuring that everyone who lived there saw his rainbow scales. Predictably, they panicked, gathering to deal with what they thought was a monster attack.

"Now," Isaiah said through the earpiece Elijah had once again donned.

Elijah dived, and when he came within a few hundred yards of the plateau's surface, he initiated the transformation into Shape of the Guardian. The gathered crowd aimed various spells and projectiles in his direction, but their aim was terrible. Only a few hit him, and those were rendered ineffective by his high Constitution, Ward of the Seasons, and Iron Scales. He hit the crowd with thunderous impact, the shock wave sending three people flying away to land on their backs.

"I want to speak to Barry," he growled. "Right now. Or everyone here is going to die a horrible, horrible death."

55

DEMAGOGUE

Elijah's knees were killing him.

It was understandable, too. After falling for a few hundred feet and landing in the middle of Mercer Mesa, he was a little surprised that he hadn't broken anything. By comparison, a couple of sore joints was a small price to pay for his bombastic entrance. Still, he was continuously surprised by how durable his body was. Sure, he could look at the numbers in his status and recognize that they were high. But that didn't tell the same story that lifting tons of rock, outrunning a car, or remaining mostly unharmed by a fall that would have easily killed him before the World Tree had transformed Earth.

"Barry," he growled again at the stunned crowd. "Now."

"You can talk?" asked one of the men. To his credit, he'd positioned himself in front of a woman, clearly ready to protect her. It was a reminder that, despite their evil actions, not everyone who lived on the Mesa was irredeemable. They were just people, albeit greedy ones whose actions had resulted in a multitude of deaths. Did that make them evil? Or was that just one bad tally mark on the ledger of their actions? Surely, they had good traits, as well. Perhaps they'd spent their lives feeding the homeless. Or volunteering at hospitals. Maybe some had even donated organs. There was also the chance that they'd been manipulated. Or they might have chosen to go along in order to protect themselves and their families from the retribution that would surely follow any resistance.

But regardless of the philosophy surrounding the perception of good and evil, Elijah knew that his mission was just. The people of Mercer Mesa needed to be stopped.

"Of course I can talk. And I want to exercise that ability by speaking to Barry. Now. Or I start killing," Elijah growled. As conflicted as he was, he wouldn't hesitate to do what was necessary.

Besides—if he didn't, the team creeping up the sides of the plateau would. According to Isaiah's voice in his ear, the traps had all been deactivated, and the team of SEALs was already near the top. It wouldn't be long before they arrived. So, Elijah needed to make his offer before they got there, and for that, he needed to speak to the leader, Barry.

"What do you want?" asked the man in question, shouldering his way through the crowd. "Come to take your pound of flesh, monster? We know what you did to the Adventurer's Guild. Killing all those poor people, and for no other reason than to put the rest of us beneath your boot! Thug, I call you. Criminal! Tyrant!"

It was almost like looking at—and hearing—a different man, and for a brief moment, Elijah even questioned his own actions. Had he been justified in attacking the guild? He'd thought so. After all, he'd seen evidence that they were preparing to mount an attack on the Garden. And yet, a seed of doubt blossomed into a flower of hesitation.

"Speechless!" Barry bellowed. He wore white linen pants and a colorful shirt that made him look like an upper-class man on vacation in the Caribbean. "Proof of his guilt! Begone, monster! Begone and never return!"

At that moment, Elijah realized that Barry was using some sort of ability. He had no idea what it was called or how it worked, but he knew that he was being manipulated. So, with all but two facets of his Quartz Mind, he searched for answers. With that much brainpower—or perhaps because of his attributes— he quickly discovered a thread of ethera in his Mind. He isolated it, then quarantined it in one facet of his Mind.

It all happened in the blink of an eye, but to Elijah, it was like suddenly opening a door and letting fresh air into a smoky kitchen. His thoughts focused, and he saw Barry as the man he was. A small and pitiful person who lorded himself over anyone he could dominate. And by virtue of his Demagogue class, that meant everyone on the Mesa. Did that mean they couldn't be held accountable for their actions? After what Elijah had just felt, he wasn't so sure.

Thankfully, his Mind cultivation helped to mitigate the ability.

But what would happen if he met someone who could overcome that defense? Suddenly, Elijah felt very vulnerable.

And angry.

It was one thing to attack him physically, but trying to manipulate his thoughts was crossing a line he'd never expected anyone to be able to pass. So, without further debate, he leaped forward, shouldering the remaining Mercer Mesa residents out of the way before grabbing Barry around the waist.

Everyone gasped.

Barry tried to resist, using some sort of ability that created a hazy gray shield around him, but it only took a slight flex of Elijah's fist to shatter it. Then came Barry's bones. The man screamed in agony, "You can't do this! Do you know who I am?!"

Elijah growled, "I do."

Then, he bashed Barry against the ground. The first blow killed the man, showing just how weak he really was, but Elijah slammed him down again for good measure. Then, he reached back and threw Barry's corpse as far as he could. And given his Strength as well as the man's comparatively minuscule weight, the throw ended up sending that body arcing over the surrounding mansions and past the edge of the plateau. Where he landed Elijah had no idea.

Nor did he really care.

He turned to the people and said, "You will open the Mesa up to—"

It was at that point that the SEALs arrived, though they didn't hit with a hail of gunfire, as they might've in the old world. Instead, they had adapted just like everyone else. There was a protector, a Sorcerer, a Healer, a melee combatant, and a Ranger. But that was where the similarities between them and any other group Elijah had seen ended. They moved with efficiency and precision, killing four people before anyone could even react.

That had always been the plan. As far as Isaiah and the other residents of Seattle were concerned, the people of Mercer Mesa had long since established themselves as the enemy. And for better or worse, military men and women only had one reaction to finding themselves in the company of an enemy. That was what drove Isaiah, and it was definitely the attitude held by the SEALs.

They executed three more people before everyone threw their hands up in surrender. To their credit, the SEALs stopped at that point. They weren't interested in needless slaughter, especially when the enemy had given up.

After that, Elijah let himself return to his human form.

"You!" came a feminine voice. Elijah glanced over to see Victoria kneeling on the ground in all her plastic glory. Her hands were on her head, but if looks could have killed, Elijah would have already been dead. "How could you?! We welcomed you into our home, and this is how you repay us? Trash!"

"You did this to yourself," Elijah said with a shake of his head. "Hoarding water while the city dies of thirst? What did you think would happen? You call me trash? I say you're worse than that. You're actively evil."

"We didn't . . . I don't know anything about that," she insisted.

"Your ignorance is not an excuse," Elijah said with a tired sigh. He'd recovered from the previous night's ordeal, but he was still exhausted. As much as he felt for the people of Seattle, he couldn't help but realize that he hated the place. There was no sense of community and little in the way of law and order, and everyone in the city felt like they were on edge. That, in turn, left Elijah feeling like an exposed nerve.

He watched as the SEALs restrained the gathered people. By the time they'd finished, more of Isaiah's people had arrived, and they were currently moving from house to house, looking for stragglers. They found a few, but the majority of the residents were already in custody.

Some shouted about who they were—or who they used to be. Others offered largely worthless bribes. And still others tried to escape. Yet, none won free. A few fights broke out—there were enough combatants on the Mesa to put up a decent resistance—but they were quickly overcome. Without Barry to incite them, their will quickly broke.

To Elijah, it felt like he was watching the death of an era. The former elites of the world were finally giving way to new power structures. Would anything really change, though? New wealth would rise. And inevitably, they would eventually come to treat poorer people as lesser.

He sighed.

Those sorts of issues were beyond him. He just wanted to go back to his Grove and rest for a couple of days. After that? He wasn't sure. All he really knew was that he didn't want to be in Seattle anymore.

First, though, he had a few things to take care of. So, after he made certain that everything was in hand, he used Shape of the Sky, then launched himself into the air. A few moments later, he was flying toward the capitol, where he landed soon after. After that, he made his way to Isaiah's command center. Notably, no one tried to stop him.

Either word of what he'd done the night before had already gotten around, or the fact that he'd arrived in a form that looked curiously like a dragon forced the government employees to keep their distance. For his part, Elijah was happy with that arrangement. He was in no mood to deal with people.

However, he couldn't avoid Isaiah. So, when he reached the command center and found the man, Elijah asked, "Does that satisfy my part of the agreement?"

"It does," Isaiah said. "And for what it's worth, you did a good thing. Those people would have run Seattle into the ground."

"And you won't?" Elijah asked.

"My goal is to make this place into a utopia. With ethera, I think we can do it, too. You'll see," Isaiah said. "In a couple of years, you won't be able to recognize this city. Everyone will be safe. They'll all have what they need. It'll be paradise."

"That's a noble goal," Elijah said. "I hope you reach it."

"You could help."

Elijah shook his head. "Not my place," he stated. "But before I go, I think you owe me a couple of questions at the Branch. It's time for you to pay up."

"I can't convince you to stick around?" Isaiah asked again.

"Not a chance. This place makes me feel dirty," Elijah said. "I wouldn't have come back if it wasn't for Lucy. Or our agreement, I suppose."

"I see," Isaiah said. And it looked for a moment like he was going to say something further. Elijah didn't miss the fact that everyone in the room was looking at him. But then, the lord of Seattle let out a sigh. "This world can be so much more than it is. We just need to get over the hump of survival, and we can have paradise on Earth. But I understand." He signaled to one of the guards, saying, "Lead Mr. Hart to the Branch. He is entitled to our Librarian's help with two topics. And fifty gold from the city's coffers."

"Yes, sir," the woman said with a salute.

After shaking Isaiah's hand, Elijah was escorted to the other side of the building, where he saw the city's Branch. It was slightly larger than the other Branches he'd seen, and it looked like a small sapling with expansive crystalline limbs. There were three people nearby. One was clearly the Envoy attached to the Branch, but the other two were introduced as Librarians. After that, he asked his questions.

First, he requested information on specializations. He knew he was coming up on one, and he wanted to be as prepared as possible for whatever choices he was given. Next, he asked about class evolutions for Animists. The first question yielded results after only a few seconds, but the second took almost five minutes, during which the Librarian—a plump young woman who wore round spectacles—was forced to expend quite a bit of effort. Elijah suspected that she had to use her entire repertoire of abilities to finally get an answer.

When the leaf grew, she let out a sigh of relief before handing it to Elijah. "Sorry," she said. "That was difficult to find."

"I see," Elijah said. "I thought it was as simple as just asking a question and getting an answer."

"Some topics are far beyond us," she said. "We get a lot of skills, just like everybody else, but some questions require higher-level attributes and evolved skills. That was almost more than I could handle. But I got a ton of experience!"

"That's great. And—"

"Oh, did you get the free leaf?" she asked.

"Uh . . . Not sure what you mean," Elijah said.

"About the Trial of Primacy. Everyone who qualifies gets a free information packet explaining what it is, how it works, and what you're supposed to do when the day comes," she said. "Just touch the Branch and you'll get it."

Elijah looked at the Branch Envoy questioningly, then got a nod to go ahead. He touched the Branch, and immediately, another leaf grew. He took it, adding it to his collection, and after that, he had no more reason to remain in the capitol. So, he thanked them, bade them farewell, and left to return to Lucy's so he could see the fruits of the Librarians' labor.

56

KNOWLEDGE

Elijah lay on the bed and, for a long while, stared at the ceiling. A fan twirled lazily above him, but otherwise, the surface above him was blank. It was such a stark difference from the places he usually slept. There were no stars twinkling above him. No subtle sounds of nature. No glowing flowers. Just blank drywall.

He sighed, already wishing he was back home. Or out in the forest. Even a tower would have felt more normal, if only because he wouldn't have time to sit around and think about the unnaturalness of human habitation. People did everything they could to separate themselves from nature, to surround themselves with concrete and steel, all in the pursuit of comfort and safety. They achieved those goals, and yet, they lost something, as well. Some ineffable connection with the natural world whose absence few even noticed, let alone lamented.

But Elijah felt it, and right down to his bones, and he could only feel that humanity was worse off for how firmly they'd embraced civilization.

To distract himself from that depressive feeling, he focused on the first of his guides:

Official Notice:
The Trial of Primacy

The Trial of Primacy is a benefit and challenge offered on newly touched worlds. The number of participants depends on the population of the world in question, but it has rarely exceeded ten thousand (10,000) participants. Normally, it is much lower.

The Trial itself can be compared to a tower or primal realm. However, it differs in a number of ways. The most obvious is that the space where the Trial takes place is only temporarily connected to these newly touched worlds. In addition, the Trial of Primacy can be held in an ancestral realm, trial planet, battle world, or even an excised world.

These are much larger than towers or primal realms, and they often have unique histories.

However, the primary goal of a Trial of Primacy is to help establish a hierarchy on newly touched planets. Secondarily, it will allow for some unique benefits, including prime cultivation environments, leveling opportunities, equipment, and feats of Strength to be added to your Legacy.

Third, at the completion of the Trial of Primacy, many of the system's latent features, including the World Tree's full Communications Apparatus, Market, and long-distance (but still global) teleportation network will be unlocked.

And finally, when the Trial of Primacy is completed and everyone has returned to their world, ambient levels of ethera will receive a boost, reaching the density necessary for Core cultivation.

Please note that if, at any time, participants wish to leave, they will be provided the means to do so. All tower surges and primal-realm advancement will be halted during this time, though they will remain open for anyone who wishes to challenge them.

Good luck and may you take advantage of this opportunity.

Even though it was not terribly complicated, Elijah took the time to read the guide—or notice—thrice. Yet, he saw that he'd missed nothing on the first read-through. The idea was simple, he supposed. Anyone who qualified for the Trial of Primacy would be transferred to a special space—not dissimilar from a tower—where they would face challenges. The completion of those challenges would result in advancement.

Yet, there were a few new pieces of information that stood out to Elijah. The first was the mention of Feats of Strength, which would be added to his Legacy. When he'd evolved Ancestral Circle into Roots of the World Tree, Feats of Strength had been mentioned, though at the time, Elijah hadn't considered them to be anything official. However, the notice he'd just read seemed to imply that it was an official—if hidden—aspect of the system. And the Trial of Primacy offered an opportunity to add to that.

The second bit of information that seemed important was that, at the conclusion of the Trial, more Branch features would be unlocked, including communication and worldwide teleportation. While searching for his family, Elijah had checked on the latter, but he'd been disappointed to find that, while the teleportation network was technically available, most settlements were out of range from one another. Yet, Elijah wasn't that excited about that feature, largely because he'd already been told that it was far too pricey to use except in emergencies.

But for Elijah, it might be worth it. He could use that system once, then create a dolmen on the other side of the world. That way, he could expand his own network much farther than would normally be possible. From what he'd been told, Earth was now the size of Saturn, which meant that, even though its diameter was only ten times its old size, the surface area was almost a hundred times larger than before the planet had been touched by the World Tree. Covering that much ground, even in his flight form, was not feasible, at least in the short term.

It was something to think about, for sure.

The most important part of that section concerned the world's ambient ethera. Elijah had felt its rise over the past four and a half years, and he'd always expected it to eventually reach the point where it could support Core cultivation. His Grove and especially his cave had long since gotten to that level, but the rest of the world lagged far behind. It was one of the reasons he'd had so much trouble pushing himself to the next stage. Yet, the fact that the system would enhance Earth's ethera density meant that it wouldn't be long before others caught up to him.

In turn, that meant that if he wanted to maintain his advantages, he had something of a time limit. As he thought about it, Elijah decided to set himself a goal. He would do everything he could to advance his Core to the second stage before the Trial of Primacy.

Finally, Elijah took note of the last paragraph. If people wanted to leave the Trial of Primacy, they could. However, even as he reread that statement, he felt that doing so would result in some sort of detriment that exceeded the loss of benefits. The system didn't like failure, and he expected that wouldn't cease to be the case in the Trial of Primacy. If there were Feats of Strength attached to his official Legacy, then were there Feats of Weakness, as well?

Maybe.

In any case, the notice about the Trial of Primacy held quite a lot of useful information. Some of it was explicit, but there was plenty between the lines, as well. Hopefully, the other two guides Elijah had gotten would prove just as helpful. He moved on to the first, which was called "A Primer on Specializations":

Guide: A Primer on Specializations
Specializations are available at levels 100, 225, 450, and 900. There are rumors about further specializations that may be developed in the Transcendent Realm, but they are unconfirmed. Generally, each specialization opportunity results in three choices, each intended to enhance an aspect of a class's abilities. For example, a War Master may be given the following three choices: Defense—Enhances the War Master's defensive abilities by a percentage based on Legacy. Damage—Enhances the War Master's damage abilities by a percentage based on Legacy. Balance—Gives a smaller enhancement to all the War Master's abilities. Also based on Legacy. It should be noted that not all War Masters will receive the same specialization choices. Much is determined by Legacy, yet most will see similar options.

After that, the guide gave a few more examples, but they all followed the same pattern. Then, there were hundreds of pages containing other known specializations for various classes. And while Animist was not represented, there were a few for other Druid classes. The first one Elijah saw was called Preserver:

Archetype: Druid Class: Preserver		
Common Specialization Options (Increases represent the average. Individual results will vary based on Legacy.)		
Growth	Healing	Connection
Increase the potency of abilities that affect plant growth by 5%.	Increase the potency of healing abilities by 10%.	Transform One with Nature into a more powerful variant. Future evolutions will be reflected.

Another variant of the Druid archetype seemed to focus on various forms of damage spells, with one branch increasing damage-over-time abilities, another affecting direct damage spells like Storm's Fury, and the final focusing on slaying unnatural entities with spells like Nature's Rebuke.

It was one of the spells that Elijah often neglected, largely because it wasn't that damaging against anything the system considered natural. And he'd discovered that that definition was extremely narrow. So far, the only creatures he'd seen that qualified were the vampires—and, presumably, the ghouls—in the Magister's Estate and Voxx.

Either way, it was a relatively cheap spell to cast, and he knew he needed to get into the habit of using it as often as possible. Perhaps it would have helped against the monster Bruce Garret had become.

It was just another reminder that he was far from perfect. Like most people, he developed habits, and because his class tended to focus on his animal forms, he sometimes neglected his other spells. That needed to change, and soon.

He spent another couple of hours perusing "A Primer on Specializations," but eventually, he moved on to the final guide he'd acquired, which was called "Evolutions of the Animist":

Guide: Evolutions of the Animist

The Animist is a rare class associated with the Druid archetype, and it focuses on shape-shifting into bestial forms. Shape of the Predator specializes in stealth and assassination, Shape of the Guardian is a fair defender and melee combatant, and Shape of the Sky allows for rapid travel. Shape of Mastery is the final form before evolution, and it focuses on single combat.

The evolutions associated with the class generally follow this theme, though most focus on making one form more powerful than the others. In addition, there are evolutions meant to adjust the Animist's path to one more appropriate for a traditional Druid. Finally, there are evolutions that will permanently transform the Animist into a more powerful bestial form.

Availability of evolutions is based on Legacy.

After that, Elijah read a list of fifteen possible class evolutions. As the blurb had suggested, they each had a very specific concentration that would shift his class into a narrower focus. Some would enhance his lamellar-ape form. Others, his predator shape. There was even one that would augment Shape of the Sky. But as interesting as they were, Elijah quickly realized that there was too much variation based on his Legacy for him to make any plans.

However, that didn't mean that the guide was useless. Far from it. It established a pattern for the choices he might be given. Like the specializations, evolutions served to narrow the focus of his class. Yet, unlike specializations, there were a few that would change his direction altogether.

Like the evolutions that would effectively turn him into a beast. Or a guardian, more accurately. What would drive an Animist in that direction? He knew from experience just how easily one could be overwhelmed by the instincts that came with their bestial forms. It had almost happened to him. Elijah knew he'd never allow himself to go down that road, but perhaps others wouldn't be so reticent.

The biggest benefit of that guide also highlighted another oversight. Spells and abilities in the Mortal Realm—which was from level one to one twenty-five—followed a set path. That meant that his future abilities were predetermined. Every Animist would get the same spells. As such, it would have made sense for Elijah to find a guide that would let him know what was coming.

But he was out of questions.

Thankfully, "Evolutions of the Animist" did reveal the existence of one: Shape of Mastery. He had no idea what form it would take, but it was said to focus on one-on-one combat. That was interesting, and it would definitely fill a niche. Yet, that wouldn't come until the peak of the realm, so it would likely be some time before he would know more.

Unless he could enlist the services of another Librarian, which didn't seem likely.

Finally, Elijah checked his status:

Name	Elijah Hart
Level	84
Archetype	Druid
Class	Animist
Specialization	N/A
Alignment	N/A
Strength	90
Dexterity	85
Constitution	89

Ethera	93		
Regeneration	88		
Attunement	Nature		
Cultivation Stage: Cultivator			
Body	Core	Mind	Soul
Stone	Hatchling	Quartz	Novice

He'd only gained one level from the fighting in Seattle, largely because he hadn't really killed that many people. Most of the Adventurers had been sacrificed by Bruce, and the leader himself wasn't actually that high of a level. Instead, his incredible power had been temporarily boosted by that sacrifice ability. So, he hadn't awarded much in the way of experience. The same could be said for killing Barry.

He hung his head.

He hated thinking of killing people in those terms. They were more than just bags of experience. They were living, breathing human beings, complete with hopes and dreams and people who cared about them. Even Barry, as detestable as he was, had had a family. Elijah needed to remember that, or he'd end up going to an extremely dark place.

In any case, he focused on his gains, which exceeded the one point per attribute he was awarded for each level. He'd gained extra points in everything but Ethera. Some had come from his efforts constructing the temple. Toting enormous stone blocks was great for building Strength and Constitution, apparently. But he'd also gained a couple of points from other activities, like fighting and cycling his Core.

Although, Elijah was less interested in the individual points than he was in the fact that he had a couple of attributes that were on the verge of crossing the one-hundred-point threshold. It was an important mark, and not just because he suspected it would be more impactful than normal. Rather, it was a mark of how far Elijah had come. After all, he hadn't forgotten that, only a little more than four years before, his physical attributes had been pathetic. Back then, his body had been ravaged by chemotherapy and cancer, which had left his Strength at a mere three points. His Constitution had been even lower. And now, he was close to reaching triple digits.

It was a good reminder of just how far he'd come.

And how far he had yet to go.

With that in mind, he settled back into the bed and, for once, fell asleep quickly and slept soundly.

57

OTHER PRIORITIES

He had won.

As Isaiah stared at the huge screen, which was divided into a dozen squares, that simple fact was abundantly apparent. Everywhere he looked, he saw dead bodies. Most of the corpses belonged to members of the Lake City Adventurers. Apparently, Bruce Garret had an ability associated with his Guild Leader class that allowed him to magically enforce certain conditions upon people who'd sworn oaths to his guild. One of the requirements to join had been a pledge to defend it unto death, which gave Garet all the leeway he needed to sacrifice everyone in the guild.

From what Isaiah could tell, most of the resultant energy had gone to waste. And as inefficient as the act was, it was also the only reason Elijah Hart had managed to survive. If Garret had absorbed all the energy, he wouldn't have simply been unstoppable. He could have squashed the Druid like a bug.

But Isaiah couldn't concern himself with Garret any longer. He and his guild were dead. Mercer Mesa was under control, with some of the worst residents having been confined to jail. It wasn't a lasting solution, but Isaiah hoped something more permanent would present itself soon. Because the alternative was to execute them, and that was a step he didn't want to take.

It was a slippery slope, after all. If he could justify killing imprisoned enemies, where would it stop? He had very few checks on his power now. And he knew that, if he allowed himself to solve his problems that way, he would end up doing so for every issue he encountered. Before long, he would start killing people for disagreeing with him too vehemently, which would turn him into a tyrant.

Isaiah wouldn't allow himself to descend to those depths, so he'd long since vowed to find other ways. That wasn't to say that he wouldn't engage in violence if necessary. It only meant that he would try everything else—as he had with both the Lake City Adventurers as well as Mercer Mesa—before going down that road.

He took a deep breath, then turned to his people. Everyone in the room had the Scholar archetype, which meant they were perfectly suited for gathering and parsing information. But none of them were fighters, and he could see how much the battles had affected them.

"We have won a great victory," he said. "Because of the people in this room, Seattle has a chance to once again become the great city it used to be. People will no longer have to worry about whether or not they'll get a cup of water for the day. Our gardens will flourish, and our people will survive. That's the first step before we can regain all that we've lost, and due to the sacrifices of the people in this room—and our soldiers out there—we have that opportunity.

"You should all be proud of what we accomplished. You've saved lives today," he said. Someone clapped, but it was clearly premature because nobody else joined in. Finally, Isaiah said, "Thank you and keep up the good work."

After that, he turned away from the screen and fled the command center. Not long after, he reached his office. Only after the door had closed did he let out a long sigh and collapse into his chair. Absently, he rubbed his chest. A wound he'd received shortly after the world had been transformed continued to bother him. Back then, he'd taken a spear to the chest—courtesy of a would-be bandit—and the injury had never fully healed. Even now, years later, his heart regularly skipped a beat, and he sometimes had trouble breathing.

Of course, he hid the infirmity from everyone else. A leader needed to project strength. Any perceived weakness would invite challenge and suggest to his followers that he wasn't the man for the job. The only person who knew of the injury was the Healer he saw once a week, and according to her, it would be years before she progressed to the point where she could completely rid him of the aftereffects.

So, Isaiah had resolved himself to simply dealing with it. Increased attributes helped. So did reaching the Body of Wood stage of his cultivation. And yet, there were times when it felt like he was having a heart attack.

Stress made it worse, too. Which meant that his chest currently felt like he had an elephant sitting on it. Perhaps it was time to call for the Healer again. That usually alleviated the symptoms for a few days, at least.

But before he could do so, Isaiah abruptly realized that he was not alone. There was a statue of a rabbit sitting on his desk. Or he assumed it was a rabbit. The thing was nearly two feet tall, with giant ears that stood straight up, and a body that seemed somewhat sturdier than any hare Isaiah had ever seen.

And it was made of what looked like faceted diamond.

Not a series of gems, either. Instead, it looked as if it had been carved from a single stone. So, when it moved, turning its head toward Isaiah, he couldn't help but flinch.

It flickered and then, an instant later, projected a beam of light onto the surface of the desk. Over the next few moments, a figure slowly appeared. To Isaiah, it looked a lot like something being 3D printed, but with light instead of plastic. As he watched, Isaiah slowly embraced the couple of combat skills he possessed, and he mentally activated his most powerful combat drone. It was strong, but because it required a ridiculous amount of ethera to operate, he usually kept it in reserve as his personal guard.

"There's no need for that," said the figure, which looked like a man made of the same diamond as the bunny. "Do not waste your ethera, young man."

"What is going on?" Isaiah asked, embracing Placid Mind to divorce himself from his emotions. Clearly, the figure didn't mean him harm. And judging by the amount of ethera wafting off the bunny, it could hurt him if it chose to do so.

"Good. Straight to business. No point in dealing with superfluous emotions and details. I am here to offer you an opportunity, my boy," the figure said, gesturing animatedly. "Here. One second. I think I remember how to do this . . . Ah. There it is."

At that moment, a notification appeared before Isaiah's inner eye:

A powerful entity has offered you a task:
Objective:
Replace a major organ with an artificial version.
Reward:
Blessing of the Mechanique Delp Dariq
Do you accept?

Isaiah read the notification, then asked, "How did you know?"

"I've been watching you, my boy. Ingenious, what you've done with so little ethera. That leg of yours is quite an impressive feat of engineering, if I do say so myself! And the heart? You've a little way to go before it's usable, but you are on the right track. It takes me back to when I first started replacing my organic bits. Ah—good times," Delp said.

Of course, Isaiah knew about the mechaniques. They were one of the few surviving elder races, though the most reclusive. The guide he'd read said that they were living golems who cared for nothing but their machines and replacing bits of their bodies. When he'd read the description, Isaiah had assumed they would all be emotionless robots, and yet, Delp was quite animated.

"Your blessing. What does it entail?"

"Ah—that. I'm supposed to tell you that you will get three options of equal value," the mechanique said via his projection. "Hogwash! Oh, I like that word. We had a similar word in my original language. No one left who speaks it, though. Just me . . ."

After a moment of silence, during which the projection hung his head, Isaiah asked, "Three options?"

"Oh. Right. Only one is worth taking. Core advancement. Not possible on this planet yet, except in very special circumstances. If you had a nature attunement, perhaps you could take advantage of those, but you don't. In any case, this is no ordinary core. You'll have a Mechanique Core. Far more powerful than anything you'd get through natural cultivation."

Isaiah didn't need to be told about special Cores. He'd already met three people with such advantages. Elijah Hart was one, and according to everything he'd seen, the Druid's Dragon Core was the most powerful. However, the two visitors he'd received a little more than a month before had both possessed Angel Cores that could, in most ways, rival Elijah's.

"And all I need to do is finish my project," Isaiah stated. The artificial heart he'd been building was not really his project alone. Instead, it was a cooperative effort between him, a former heart surgeon turned Healer, and an Engineer who'd once built robots for a living. Between them, they'd almost finished the prototype, which used all sorts of rare and powerful materials, though Isaiah was still hesitant to shove that thing into his chest.

"If it makes any difference, you won't live more than six more months without it," the mechanique said via his projection. "There are no Healers on this planet with high enough levels to repair a heart that has been damaged so severely. If you'd had access to a high-level Healer with the right class, perhaps they could have fixed it at the time. But by now, too long has passed. Healing an old injury is far different than mending a fresh one. It should have been a death sentence."

"Kind of sounds like that's exactly what it is," Isaiah said. "Just a delayed one."

Delp Dariq let out a booming laugh that rattled the desk. "That it is, my boy. That it is. But as I said, this is an opportunity. Take it," he said. "Implant that heart and all your problems will be solved."

"All of them?"

"Well, most. Some, probably. One, at the very least!"

Isaiah didn't hesitate before accepting the task. In a lot of ways, he didn't have much choice in the matter, but he also knew that it was an opportunity that most people would not receive. He knew about special Cores, and he recognized just how powerful they could be. For instance, Elijah Hart had an archetype that wasn't exactly suited for combat, and even though his class worked to correct that, he still should have been weaker than even-level foes. Yet, because of his Core cultivation, he could not only hold his own, but also defeat enemies that would have otherwise killed him with little trouble.

Isaiah hoped for similar benefits.

"Good!" said the mechanique after Isaiah accepted the task. "I'll see you again when you start to advance your Core!"

Then, without any warning, the rabbit turned and hopped away. It disappeared into a rift in space before it hit the ground, which left Isaiah with a host of questions that he knew wouldn't soon be answered. In any case, he had a goal now. All he needed was to shove an artificial heart into his chest—and some-how survive—and he'd gain a significant boon.

He was tempted to leave his office right at that moment, but he knew that would be a mistake. Not only did he have a hundred tasks pulling him in as many directions, but he could sense a visitor coming his way. So, he took a few minutes to compose himself before Elijah Hart knocked on his door.

"Enter," he announced, standing as he adjusted his shirt. He wore the same black fatigues as his underlings, though his had been made from sterner stuff than the standard issue uniform. There were increased dangers to being the leader, and so, he needed increased protections, too.

The door opened, admitting the Druid. The man hadn't made any conces-sions to civility. His beard was still wild and untrimmed, his hair was shaggy, and his clothes—while high-quality—looked unremarkable. Most of all, though, Isaiah found himself annoyed by the man's bare feet. He didn't care if it was, as his information suggested, tied to an ability. It was just bad manners.

Of course, he didn't expect more from someone like Elijah Hart. The man was powerful, but he was reckless, selfish, and worst of all, unpredictable. One day, those traits would get the Druid killed, and Isaiah wasn't certain if he would celebrate or mourn the man's passing.

"What can I do for you?" Isaiah asked.

"I'm only here to let you know that I'll be leaving tomorrow," he said, uncharacteristically thinking of how his actions might affect other people. "Just wanted to make sure we're square before I leave. K'hana is going to stay behind. I guess she wants to get started on the exchange of services."

"There's no reason to wait," Isaiah admitted. Indeed, the elven woman had already started the process of finding water, and the initial results were promis-ing. When she left, she would lead a team of his fighters to her tower.

"Right. So, is there anything else we need to discuss? Because I'll admit that I'm tired of city life."

"There's one more thing," Isaiah said after only a moment's hesitation. "There's a situation in Hong Kong. I promised I would spread the word to any powerful people I might encounter. You qualify."

"Alright? Lay it on me."

58

STRUCTURE

As he left Isaiah's office, Elijah had no idea what to do. The situation in Hong Kong sounded dire, but Elijah was in no position to help. He only had six months before the Trial of Primacy, and he had a lot of work to do before he would feel ready for whatever challenges it would present. On top of that, he only had a vague direction—east—to go on, meaning that finding the city would be incredibly difficult.

Perhaps things would be different if he'd personally met the two emissaries, but that just wasn't the case. They'd left Seattle over a month before he'd arrived, and there was no telling where they'd ended up. Even Isaiah wasn't sure. So, as concerned as Elijah was—the way it was described, the undead were a grave threat—there wasn't much he could do about it.

The rest of the meeting had been productive. Elijah had looked through a report on the items looted from the Adventurer's Guild, and he'd seen nothing that fit him. There were a couple of unarmed weapons, but neither were better than his Weighted Gloves. He saw a couple of Rings of Anonymity, too. And a few pieces of armor that gave minor attribute increases. However, nothing really caught his eye. Besides—Isaiah's people would need all the help they could get. And while Elijah wasn't particularly selfless, he felt that it was best if he left that low-quality gear to Isaiah and his army. So, he collected his payment—fifty gold was no small sum—and told Isaiah that he'd return sometime in the future before heading out of the capitol, shifting into Shape of the Sky, and taking off.

A few minutes later, he landed outside the giant greenhouse that was the Garden, shifted back to his human form, and headed inside. He found Lucy not long after, where she was busy showing K'hana around.

"This place is quite impressive," the elf was saying as Elijah approached.

Lucy responded, "And we're planning an expansion soon, too. Seattle's population is mostly stable, but we still get a trickle of refugees each month. My dream is to grow enough food that nobody ever has to go without."

"You think you can do that?" asked Elijah as he approached, his tone a bit skeptical. "There are a lot of people who live here."

Lucy gave him a small smile before she answered, "I think so. Eventually. Isaiah's agreed to subsidize my costs. He wants the same thing I want."

"Easier to control people if you're the one handing out food," Elijah stated. He still didn't trust Isaiah—not completely. Maybe the man's heart was in the right place, but from Elijah's perspective, people in power usually only cared about keeping it. And on top of that, the notion that Isaiah could easily spy on the entire city made him feel violated in a way he couldn't really explain. Benevolent or not, Isaiah's abilities made Elijah uncomfortable.

"He's a good man, Elijah," Lucy said.

"Good men can be corrupted," Elijah said with a shrug. "Lots of dictators start off with the best of intentions."

That much was certainly true. History was full of people who'd gained power with the hopes of changing things for the better. But bit by bit, they were corrupted by that power until its pursuit was all that was left. Sure, they had excuses. They believed that whatever moral sacrifices they had to make were justified. Even someone like Roman, who'd killed hundreds—if not thousands—of his citizens, had clearly felt that he was doing the right thing.

So, how long would it be before Isaiah succumbed to that same way of thinking? The path to hell was paved with good intentions, after all. When utopia was at stake, was there anything a leader wouldn't do? If he could remove that one bad apple to save the bunch, would he hesitate? What if there were two bad apples? A hundred? A thousand? Where was the line when perfection was seen as an achievable goal?

Elijah shook his head, saying, "I hope he's as good of a person as you say. And I hope he maintains perspective. If he doesn't . . . Well, you can always come and live in my island paradise."

"Did you just invite me to move in?"

Elijah shrugged. "Maybe. As friends," he said with a grin. "Open invitation and all of that. Did I mention it was an island paradise? I mean, my beaches are infested with giant crabs, but they're not that strong. I like to think of them as mascots."

"You know I'm not going with you, right?" Lucy answered. "I have my Garden. There are people here I care about. I can't just abandon my home."

"Oh. Right," Elijah said, running his hand through his hair. "I was only joking."

He hadn't been. If he'd had his way, he would've moved everyone he cared about—which was a short list—to his island. Or at least to Ironshore. The rest of the world just seemed far too dangerous, and not just because of the wildlife. Monsters being monsters Elijah understood, but when people descended into despotism, it just felt worse. Hopefully, Isaiah would prove immune to the temptation of tyranny, but Elijah wasn't going to bet on it. After all, there was a very famous saying about power and corruption that seemed very appropriate to Elijah's experiences with civilization in the new version of Earth.

"You weren't, but that's okay," Lucy said, reaching out to put her hand on his. "Maybe I can visit someday. You've made it sound like a wonderful place."

Her familiar touch brought up a host of memories Elijah wasn't really prepared to confront. Once upon a time, he'd loved Lucy. He still did, even though it had faded from a teenager's fiery obsession to something far more sustainable. He wasn't even sure if it was a romantic love anymore. Perhaps they were only meant to be friends.

Elijah sighed and said, "It's probably not as great as I make it seem. Like I said, it is infested with giant crabs. And it rains a lot. Plus, we're kind of isolated. But my tree house is pretty cool, if I say so myself."

"I'd like to see it someday."

"It's a date," Elijah said with a smile.

After that, there really wasn't much else to say. So, after a couple of goodbyes, Elijah left the Garden behind. He didn't immediately take to the air, but instead walked through Seattle for what he hoped would be the last time for a long while. He didn't outright hate civilization, but spending any time in a place like Seattle—or Valoria before it—left him feeling like he was coated in slime. He would be glad to leave it behind.

But still, he forced himself to walk through some of the more populated areas, just to ensure that things were better than when he'd arrived. That was when he finally caught sight of the city's tower. It was a twisted structure that looked like a fun-house-mirror version of a castle's parapet.

Isaiah had given him a USB drive with all the information they'd gathered on the tower, which was quite a lot, all things considered. With only a few days' worth of study, he would know everything there was to know about it. From enemies to strategies and layouts, it was everything he would need to challenge the tower in relative safety. On top of that, as part of the deal he'd made with Isaiah, he had the right to do so, even if he'd have to wait until a slot opened up. And yet, he had no interest in running through a tower at the moment. Not only did he have other things he wanted to do, but risking his life for a couple of levels and a few trinkets just wasn't appealing so soon after everything that had happened in Seattle.

For better or worse, Elijah had begun to sour on towers. They were a good way to advance, and he knew he'd have to run them if he wanted to keep up with everyone else. However, they also seemed so pointless—assuming that there were others around who could keep them from overflowing. Using his power to fight in the real world was much more preferable, as far as he was concerned.

In any case, he had no intention of challenging the tower at this point. Perhaps he would have time for it later. So, after he'd wandered around Seattle for another couple of hours, he threw himself into the air and flew to the Circle of Spears. His passage didn't go unnoticed—a huge rainbow-colored reptile flying across the sky was unignorable—but he was gone before he could cause too much commotion. As soon as he reached the dolmen, he opened a gate to the Dragon Circle and stepped through.

Not long after, he returned to Argos—or, more specifically, to the Temple of Virtue—to keep his promise of healing. To let everyone know that he was around, he climbed to the roof, then channeled a little ethera into the statue atop the temple. The spear in the warrior's hand lit up, becoming a beacon that could be seen throughout the town.

It was the agreed-upon signal that he was around, and soon enough, injured and sick people had begun to climb the steps toward the temple. By the time they reached the top, Elijah had already summoned Healing Rain, and the first person to step into the rejuvenating cascade of precipitation let out a gasp. The same—or similar—scenes presented themselves each time someone arrived.

Only a few injuries were bad enough that Elijah needed to use Soothe or Touch of Nature, but one was particularly serious. The woman in question had a wound on her arm that had been so thoroughly infected that, in the old world, it would have necessitated amputation. It fell before nearly a dozen casts of Touch of Nature, and the woman dropped to her knees and thanked him profusely.

Elijah didn't much care for that attention, but he knew it came with the territory. If he was going to help people, then he needed to grow accustomed to praise.

He stayed at the temple for the next twelve hours, and in that time, he lost count of how many people he'd healed. It was almost as cathartic for him as it was for his patients. If everything else went to hell, at least Elijah could always take solace in the act of healing.

Finally, he healed the last of them, and once he sent the man on his way, Elijah deactivated the beacon and, at last, headed home via the Roots of the World Tree. Thankfully, using it to teleport himself back to the Grove could be activated from anywhere, though it still took quite some time to activate the spell. Regardless, he soon arrived back in his Grove, and when he did, he couldn't help but take a deep breath and bask in the dense ethera of his island.

After speaking to Nerthus for a few minutes—the spryggent was quite proud of some of his gardening accomplishments—Elijah retired to his tree house, where he took a long, scalding shower. Even as he relaxed, and his muscles unkinked, he found himself pondering the future.

He only had about six months to go before the Trial of Primacy. Six months to push himself as high as he could go. He needed to train, as well. To take his equipment more seriously, too. And he needed to prepare Carmen and Miguel for his absence. Thankfully, six months was a decent span of time, so he felt sure that he could accomplish his goals.

After his shower, he pulled his laptop out of his satchel and started making plans. He was capable of keeping it all in his head, but there was something about putting it all down in a word processor that made things so much more concrete. Fortunately, he didn't have to worry too much about power. With the converter he'd bought in Seattle, as well as the high density of ambient ethera, the laptop had all the electricity it would need.

Perhaps that meant he could power all sorts of electronics. Maybe a giant television. Or an electric coffee maker. Any number of small appliances would come in handy. He suspected that obtaining those would require a trip back to Seattle, though, and he didn't really have any desire to return to that place.

So, he focused on the task at hand, making plans not just for himself but for Miguel, too. After all, the boy's training had been a bit haphazard of late. Elijah aimed to fix that. The key to improvement was consistency, which was a lesson Miguel needed to learn.

59

BRICK BY BRICK

Carmen's file scraped against the block of dragonstone, removing only the tiniest bit of material. In a lot of cases, it would have been frustrating, but Carmen had long since fallen into what she referred to as a worker's trance. It wasn't a skill or anything—just a tendency to dive so deeply into a task that everything else sort of faded away. She'd done it often enough before the world's transformation, and it had become more common in the wake of the World Tree's touch.

She could have used her abilities to make it easier, but that would take attention away from Ethereal Infusion, which she'd resolved to maintain at all times while working on what she'd begun referring to as the Great Forge. Even one lapse, and she felt that she'd create a weak link. And while that might not completely ruin the final product—or even be noticeable to most people—when she had taken on the project, she had told herself that she would cut no corners. So, Carmen kept to the original plan, regardless of how tedious it was.

Gradually, the carving began to take shape. She'd roughed it out with a chisel, but refining it required a much defter tool, which was where the file came into play. It had been made with sun copper and enchanted to be much harder than even the magical metal would normally be. As a result, it was on the verge of being Complex grade, and like all the other tools she'd made over the past few months, it possessed an ability.

Ability: Crafter's Imbuement	Using this tool upon raw materials imbues them with a small trickle of ethera.

When she'd created the first tool in the set—which was a hammer—Carmen had been ecstatic. Until that point, she hadn't been able to focus the ability of any items she'd created. Instead, the system seemed to assign them at random. However, while helping Elijah with the Circle of Spears and creating the Temple of Virtue, she had learned that her intent while crafting could guide the final product in certain ways. It wasn't foolproof, and there was still some variance—especially with weapons and armor—but tools were simple enough that she could get the result she wanted.

It wasn't easy, though. One stray thought while crafting, and she might've ruined it. Still, throughout all her experiences, Carmen had learned to focus, and the results were precisely what she'd intended.

But those were just the tools. A means to an end. The real work came when she'd started to work on the dragonstone. She was no stonemason, but like every other crafter—aside from people like Elijah, whose abilities in the field were very limited—she'd begun her journey as a Tradesman. As such, she could achieve passable results with a wide variety of materials.

So, Carmen had spent days carving the huge dragonstone blocks into large bricks. Then, she'd begun the purification cycle, which included using Decontaminate and Refine Material. Over and over, a dozen times for each brick, she broke those pieces down until they were completely uncontaminated by anything that wasn't dragonstone.

Thankfully, she'd had plenty of help with that—mostly from the town's Stonemason, who was a dwarf named Boryn. Otherwise, Carmen wouldn't have completed more than one of the blocks a week. But with Boryn's—and his apprentices'—help, they'd managed to purify and shape a third of the dragonstone into usable bricks. The rest was up to Carmen.

She could have pawned the carving off on someone else, but she felt in her soul that doing so would weaken the personalized effect of the Great Forge. She'd thought a lot about her conversation with Elijah, about how to create a cultivation environment dedicated to her attunement of creation. And she'd gotten it into her head that, in order for it to resonate most strongly with her, she needed to be the one to do the bulk of the work. Carmen wasn't certain why she felt that way, but she did all the same. And she'd learned to trust those instincts.

Finally, she finished the carving, then leaned forward to blow the dust away. One of her helpers would come in and sweep the detritus up. It was still useful for other crafters, after all, though Carmen wasn't sure where it would end up.

In any case, the carving was only one more step. There was one more stage to complete before she'd count the brick finished. So, without further hesitation, Carmen retrieved a long rod of blood tin. It was silver, but with a slight red shimmer. More importantly, it too had been through multiple rounds of purification, so it practically glowed with ethereal potential. Carmen set the thin rod on the first carving, then placed her finger on the end before activating Smolder. The blood tin melted, filling the carved recess and spilling over the edge. That was perfectly normal, so she ignored it as she slowly moved the rod along, inlaying the ethereal metal into the brick.

Without her abilities, it would have been useless. The moment the tin cooled, it would detach from the brick. However, once she'd completed the process, which took almost half the rod, she used Bind to fuse the two materials. It took an incredible amount of ethera, which nearly drained her. However, that was expected.

The next step was a lot touchier, and it would require every point of her Dexterity attribute. Thankfully, her class had enhanced it quite a bit, but more importantly, she'd already completed the process a dozen times. So, by that point, she was an expert. Still, it required a steady hand and as much focus as she could manage.

Brick in hand, she approached the grinder. It was a contraption she'd built herself, though the belt had been created by a local Tinkerer. Carmen didn't know what he'd used for the abrasive belt, but it worked well enough to grind even the excess tin—which was unnaturally durable—from the surface of the brick. The only issue was that it would also cut into the dragonstone if Carmen wasn't careful.

And given that the bricks needed to be absolutely identical, any variance created by the grinder would render the brick unusable. Too much effort and too many expensive materials had been used for her to let that happen.

The good thing was that using the grinder, which consisted of a series of wheels, around which the belt had been strung, was almost meditative. Sure, she had to operate the thing with a pedal, but with her stamina—and Crafter's Stamina—it was no great strain. Indeed, it was extremely satisfying, seeing the rough belt grind the metal away, bit by bit.

It was time-consuming, though. So, it was hours later before, at last, Carmen had finished. She held the brick out, inspecting it closely. The designs—which were all symbols associated with enchantments meant to condense ethera. She hoped it would result in much thicker ethera inside the forge, which would simultaneously enhance any item created within and provide an appropriate setting for cultivation.

Congratulations! You have created a unique component, Enchanted Dragonstone Brick.
Overall Grade: Complex (Low)
Enchantment Grade: D

"Yes!" she breathed, pumping her fist in celebration. It was the thirteenth time she'd created one of the enchanted bricks, but each success came with a burst of experience as well as satisfaction. When she turned to set the block aside, she saw that someone had invaded her smithy and gave a start. "What are you doing here?! How long have you been sitting there?"

"Huh?" Elijah asked from where he was sitting on the pile of other raw blocks that were waiting to be enchanted. "Oh, about two hours or so? I don't know. I'm guessing you decided to take my advice and run with it, huh? Doing everything yourself?"

She nodded. "It's easier for combat classes," she said. "All they need to do is find a battlefield or something. Maybe a dojo? I don't know. But with crafters, it's harder. Nerthus's advice has been helpful."

In truth, she probably could have cultivated in her current smithy. It would just take a while, and it would have dubious usefulness after she reached the first stage. Of course, Core cultivation was still largely impossible on Earth—except for people like Elijah, she amended. Perhaps she would be able to clear that hurdle once she'd finished the Great Forge.

"You sure you don't need any help?" he asked.

Setting the completed brick down next to its identical siblings, she answered, "No. I need to do as much of this as possible myself. Otherwise, it'll be diluted. I think." She wiped the sweat from her brow. "I'm kind of just playing it by ear right now, but my instincts tell me that the more help I get with this, the less it will help me with my cultivation."

"Fair enough."

Carmen crossed to where Elijah was sitting, then joined him atop the stacked bricks. With her legs dangling, she asked, "What's up? Are you back? Or is this temporary?"

Elijah answered, "I don't know. With the Trial of Primacy coming up, I know I have a lot of preparation ahead of me. This can't just be like a tower run. If I go in unprepared, I'll end up dead."

"What do you need?"

"Levels. Cultivation. Equipment. I've been thinking about armor. I mean, when I'm in my bestial forms, I have scales, but I can't help but think that I'm missing the boat with armor. Even if it doesn't make me more durable, a lot of it still has abilities that would help me, right? I don't know. I have Atticus keeping an eye out for a good Leatherworker, but he hasn't found anyone yet. So, I might just use that gnome that works across town. I can't remember his name."

"Rikin," Carmen provided. She'd met most of the higher-level crafters in Ironshore, largely because most worthwhile projects required cooperation between a wide variety of professions. For instance, when she made armor, it would turn out better if the padding was made by someone used to working with textiles or leather.

"Yeah. Him. Is he any good?" Elijah asked.

"He's in his forties," she answered, referring to the gnome's level. It wasn't as impressive as it sounded. He was more than sixty years old, and he looked it, too. The only reason he'd come to Earth in the first place was because he wanted to help his daughter—who was a Farmer—develop. However, his advanced age as well as his low level, which had been under twenty-five before coming to Earth, showed that he wasn't terribly talented. But he was the highest-level leatherworker in the city. "Personally, I'd use Gavina. She's lower level, but she's not even twenty years old yet. Much more talented. I don't know if that would translate into the final product, but it'd pay off by helping her gain some levels so that, next time you need her, she can do something even better."

Elijah nodded. "Not sure if I can afford to make a choice based on developing someone I don't even know," he admitted. "This trial is going to be extremely dangerous."

"Even for you?"

"I'm not invincible, Carmen. I almost died only a few days ago," he admitted, which surprised her. Then, he told her what had happened in Seattle, ending with, "It just highlights that we can't rest on our laurels. Even if people are lower level, there are so many different abilities out there that could make them even more dangerous. I mean, I've spent most of the past four years punching up. There's nothing to say that other people can't do the same thing. Which brings me to Miggy."

"What about him?" she asked.

"I came up with a training program for him," Elijah answered.

"He already trains every day."

"He does," her brother-in-law agreed. "But it's not focused. I know he doesn't have an archetype yet, but it's coming any day now. He needs to decide what he wants to do. For instance, if he's going to be a Warrior, then all his training with Kurik will be useless. And if he wants to be a Druid—"

"I thought you said that was a bad idea."

"It is. Probably. It's not an archetype meant for fighting. Maybe that's a good thing, but I think we both know that Miggy will never be happy sitting in the Grove and gardening with Nerthus," Elijah stated.

"That's true," she agreed. Even if she wished it were otherwise, Carmen knew her son well enough to recognize that the life Elijah described would be hell for Miguel. "What do you suggest?"

"I'm going to talk to him. Ask him what he really wants."

"Good luck with that."

Carmen had tried to talk to her son about his impending archetype choice, and on dozens of occasions. To date, he'd been noncommittal.

"But maybe you can get through to him," she conceded. "I'm guessing you're going to structure his training based on what he says?"

"I have a generic schedule, but that's the plan," Elijah answered. "Plus, I think Nerthus might have some methods to prepare him for cultivation. But I didn't want to overstep, so I thought I'd ask you before I did anything."

"Of course," she said. With anyone else—except maybe Colt—she might have refused. But she trusted Elijah, and what's more, she knew that he had Miguel's best interests at heart. Besides, he was the most powerful person in the world. If he wasn't an expert, then nobody was.

"Alright then," Elijah said. "What about you? Are you okay?"

She answered honestly, saying, "This is the most at peace I've been since Alyssa died. Maybe since before that. I'm not saying Ironshore is perfect. It's not. There are still people here who don't trust humans. But it's so much better than what I left behind. I think I've found a place here."

"Good," he said, reaching around and wrapping his arm around her shoulder. He pulled her close, saying, "You and Miggy are the only family I have left. And Nerthus, but he can take care of himself. I need you two to be okay."

"You know that goes both ways, right? You're all we have, too. So don't go and do anything to get yourself killed. It would break Miggy."

"Just Miggy?"

"Me, too, idiot," she said with a smile. Her own family—from before she'd met Alyssa, at least—had mostly abandoned her after she'd come out. Partially as a result of that, she'd latched on to Elijah as something of a little brother. And though her instincts told her to protect him, she knew that he was so far beyond her in terms of power that such efforts would be useless. All she could do was offer her support, which she wholeheartedly did. Then, she said, "You want to get a drink? Talk things out?"

"Wish I could," he said, sliding off of the stacked bricks. "But I've got a lot to do. Plus, Miggy just got back to the island, and I want to get that done. Tomorrow's going to be the start of something important, I think."

With that, Carmen said goodbye, and he left the smithy behind. After, Carmen went back to work. She'd completed thirteen bricks, and she had thousands more ahead of her.

60

TRAINING

With the light of a gibbous moon shining down on him, Elijah landed in a clearing near the Grove. When he hit the ground, it still sent a shock through his legs and up his spine, but the impact was far less severe than it had been even six weeks before. All his practice, it seemed, had come in handy. Still, he knew he had a long way to go before he could approach the natural grace of a true avian predator like the birds who inhabited the storm to the west of his island. But where they had reached the peak, Elijah had only begun to glimpse what was possible with Shape of the Sky, so he hoped to one day surpass them.

For now, though, he had other things on his mind. Without hesitation, he resumed his human shape, then used Soothe to mend any damage he might have incurred before setting off toward the coast where he knew he'd find Miguel.

When the young man had returned to the island, he hadn't gone straight back to the Grove. Instead, he'd meandered through the island's forest, ending up on the very same promontory where Elijah had first encountered the Voxx. The sight of that rock jutting out over a deep and protected fishing hole brought back quite a few memories. Some of them—like catching fish that were then confiscated by the panther—were good. Others, like the aforementioned encounter with the Voxxian monster that had nearly killed him and the island's guardian, were decidedly less so.

With a sigh, he leaped over a fallen tree, then climbed the angled rock to the flat peak. There, he found Miguel sitting with his legs dangling over the edge. The young man tossed a loose stone into the water.

"You know," Elijah said, sitting beside his nephew. "I almost died here once."

"Really?"

"Yeah. You know about the Voxx, right?" Elijah asked. Miguel nodded, and he went on, "Well, this was my favorite fishing spot for the first six months after the world transformed. There are some huge steelhead trout down there. A lot bigger than they were before everything changed. More dangerous, too. I almost lost a finger on more than one occasion.

"But there I was, just minding my own business with this huge Voxxian monster—it was bigger than my lamellar-ape form—burst out of the water,"

Elijah explained. "I was only level two at the time, so I knew there was no chance I could take it."

"Only level two? Six months in? How?"

Elijah shrugged. "When I first washed ashore, I was barely alive," he said. "Cancer, you know? And chemotherapy. I think my Strength attribute was only at three points. And my Constitution was a one. So, it was all I could do to just survive. Even then, I probably wouldn't have made it with my buddy."

"The guardian."

"Yep. He was a mist panther. Or I think that's what he was called. Either way, I think he took pity on me. So, I gave him some of my food, and he looked out for me," Elijah said. "That's how I survived the Voxx attack. I managed to delay it for a few seconds, which gave me a chance to run away. Just as it caught up, the panther found me. They fought, going back and forth until, at last, the panther won. I'll never forget that. No matter what else happens, I'll always remember that day because it was then that I fully realized how much the world had changed. There's no room for weakness in this world. Maybe if we'd been born someplace that was touched by the World Tree centuries ago, we could afford a little weakness. I don't know. But Earth? Right now, it's a battlefield out there. I think you understand that better than most, after everything you've been through.

"But that panther saved me. He gave me a chance to survive, and I took it. I've been fighting—off and on—ever since then," Elijah stated.

"Why are you telling me this?" asked Miguel.

Elijah shrugged. "I don't know. Maybe to give you context," he said. "I almost died a few days ago. I was strutting around like I was Earth's top dog, and I almost got killed by someone thirty levels lower than me."

"How?"

"Doesn't matter. I don't think it's unique," Elijah answered. "His class was rare, I'm sure. But something I've come to realize is that we're all vulnerable. Even when we're stronger than everyone else, we can't stop. We can't hold back. If we do, we'll end up in the ground."

"I know," Miguel said.

Elijah didn't doubt it. The young man had been through so much that there was no way he wasn't just as aware of the world's dangers as Elijah was. Still, it bore mentioning, if only because returning to the scene of his first brush with the Voxx had brought it to mind.

"Have you had a chance to look through the nature-attuned classes?" Elijah asked. He'd been gone for a while, which should have given Miguel plenty of opportunity to study the guide.

"Yeah. A bunch of times," Miguel answered.

"And?"

"There are a lot of them that sound good," he hedged. "Colt says the class doesn't matter. It's the man behind the class that makes the difference."

Elijah nodded. "That's true enough," he agreed. "But let me tell you another story."

Then, he recounted his encounter with Thor. Elijah knew that the other high ranker hadn't approached his cultivation level—which had been confirmed by Isaiah, who'd scanned him when he passed through Seattle—but due to his high-grade, combat-focused class, he was able to stand toe-to-toe with Elijah.

"Our classes matter," he said. "So does cultivation. Our abilities. Our Cores. It's all part of it. If you want to fight, then you need to pick a class meant for it."

"I don't think my mom wants that."

"Probably not," Elijah allowed. "But it's not her life. It's yours. So, I'll ask you this—who are you? Are you the type of man who can sit in the back and craft? Are you the sort who can spend his life tending to a garden? Can you spend your days running a shop? If so, that's great. Be the best damned shopkeeper you can be. Or crafter. Or gardener. We will support your choices no matter what."

"I . . . I don't want that," Miguel said. "I want to fight."

"There you have it, then. This is about you. Not me. Not your mom. Not Colt. You. Going through life making your choices based on whether or not you'll please everyone else is a good way to end up with a lot of regrets," Elijah advised. "Next question—how do you want to fight? With magic, maybe? Do you want to—"

"No," Miguel answered. "I . . . I'm going to be a Warrior like mom. Or a Ranger."

"Explain why."

Without hesitation, Miguel said, "I feel like Sorcerers are too limited. They can do a lot of damage, but the second somebody breaks through their shields, they're vulnerable."

"That's mostly true. But you remember Isaak, right? You met him in Argos," Elijah said. Miguel nodded. "He has this skill where he basically gets a second life. It has a cooldown, and he's vulnerable while it's active. But it'll let him survive a fatal wound."

"Are you supposed to be telling people that?"

Most people liked to keep the details of their abilities to themselves, so it was a bit of a faux pas to reveal Isaak's secrets. That was unimportant next to guiding Miguel forward, though. Elijah shrugged. "Probably not. You won't tell on me, will you?"

"No," Miguel said quickly. Then, he went on, "But it's more than survivability. I just . . . I like fighting with weapons. They're more solid. They're dependable. And I want to be able to take a hit if everything goes wrong."

"You're not just saying that because your mom was a Warrior, right?"

"I'm not," he insisted. "I doubt I'd get her class anyway. I asked Nerthus about it, and he'd never even heard of a Dragon Lancer. I think it was pretty rare."

"Maybe. But Nerthus isn't much older than you, relatively speaking. He doesn't know everything."

"Really?"

"That's what he said. When I first met him, he was barely more than a foot tall," Elijah said, glancing at his nephew. The young man had continued to grow, and he expected that it wouldn't be that long before Miguel was taller than him. Not that that was a huge accomplishment. Elijah was a lot of things, but he'd never been blessed with great height. "If you took Warrior, what kind of class would you hope for?"

"Some kind of hybrid," Miguel answered, again without hesitation. "I don't want to be a protector. I want to have options."

"You know that versatility comes at a cost, right? If you go that route, you'll never be as good at a particular task as someone who specialized," Elijah explained.

"I know. Like I said, I want options. And I want something that will take advantage of my attunement."

"What if it isn't nature?"

"It is."

"You seem sure."

"I am," Miguel said. "I feel it sometimes. It took a while before I recognized what it was, but now that Nerthus told me what to look for, I can feel it. Especially when I'm around animals like Trevor and his family."

"And if you become a Ranger?"

"I don't know. Same thoughts, I guess. Is that wrong?"

Elijah shook his head. "It's fine. But now that we're sure you want to be a fighter of some sort, we need to start taking your training seriously," he said. "What I have in mind is more geared toward after you get your archetype, but it'll be fine to get started before."

Then, he explained what he'd planned. At first, Miguel seemed eager, but as Elijah went on, detailing every minute of every day, his enthusiasm waned a little. Still, by the time Elijah finished, Miguel maintained the same steely-eyed determination he'd worn like a cloak since the beginning.

The next morning, they began his training. For the most part, Elijah accompanied him, but he also enlisted Colt's help, especially for the weapons training. Finally, he'd asked Nerthus to do everything he could to prepare Miguel to step into the world of cultivation as soon as he obtained an archetype.

The training itself was nothing groundbreaking. Lots of running, swimming, and lifting heavy things. The difference was that, with Elijah there, Miguel's recovery time was cut down to almost nothing. He could train longer and harder before exhaustion finally pushed him over the edge. That was where Nerthus came in, guiding Miguel through hours of meditation that seemed far more effective than Elijah's attempts at teaching his nephew to connect with nature.

Finally, at the end of each day, Elijah gave Miguel a quarter of one of his Grove berries. According to Nerthus, they were pseudo natural treasures, and as such, they were capable of—over time—creating a buildup of ethera that would help in Body cultivation. Elijah was counting on the berries helping when the time came to push himself to the next stage, and he hoped that their addition to his nephew's diet would work toward preparing Miguel for what came next.

It was an absolutely brutal regimen, and one that Miguel had no chance of maintaining without Elijah's help. However, he got quite a surprise when Nerthus revealed that he had limited healing capabilities within the Grove. Those abilities manifested similarly to Elijah's Healing Rain, though Nerthus insisted, "The rain itself is not capable of healing. It is just rain. The interaction between it and the high density of ethera within the Grove creates a rejuvenating effect that is approximately a quarter as powerful as your unenhanced spell."

That meant that Elijah could afford to leave the island without completely derailing Miguel's training. That was a definitely a relief because, after a week, he'd begun to grow restless. His natural wanderlust was part of it, but Elijah also had a host of tasks begging for his attention.

With one of those tasks, he'd already begun to work toward completion. Though it would be some time before those efforts reached fruition. The rest would require some travel. Still, he put it off, watching as Miguel benefited from the copious training. He'd gained two months' worth of benefits in only ten days, and they were just getting started.

But finally, with the clock steadily ticking down until the Trial of Primacy, Elijah knew he could delay no longer. So, even as he watched Miguel meditate with Nerthus, he decided that the time had come for him to leave.

61

PREPARATION

Elijah awoke to the feeling of someone climbing the steps to his tree house. Even in his drowsy state, it only took a moment for him to focus on that facet of his Quartz Mind and identify Carmen. And she didn't seem happy, judging by the set of her shoulders and the scowl on her face.

"Damn," he muttered, throwing his blanket aside. He pushed himself upright and ran his hand through his hair before swinging his legs over the side. Then, he staggered across the room and into the short hall, arriving in the entryway as Carmen knocked on the door. He opened it with a smile. "Good morning. Want some coffee?"

"Sure," she said, pushing past him. "Plus, you can explain to me where you're going."

Elijah didn't immediately launch into an explanation. Instead, he made good on his promise of glorious caffeine, boiling some water in the kitchen before using his French press to make the coffee. Idly, he wondered if he was losing some of the beverage's efficacy by preparing the coffee himself. Without any cooking abilities, he knew that some of the ethera would be lost, so it made sense that it would be less powerful than if an actual Cook—or maybe someone who had a Barista class—prepared it.

In any case, he didn't have a Barista handy, so he resolved himself to making do with what he could produce himself. That wasn't so bad, considering that it was still quite effective.

After brewing the coffee, then dousing both cups in honey, he crossed the kitchen and handed Carmen a steaming mug. She took a sip, then let out a sigh of contentment, some of the tension draining out of her. "You could probably sell this," she remarked. "I bet people would pay silvers for it."

"And share my coffee? No, thanks," Elijah said with a shudder. "It's all mine. Except when I have guests, I guess. Besides, it's not like I need money. I made, like, fifty gold in Seattle."

"Seriously? Just like that?"

"Yeah. I . . . uh . . . I defeated a lot of enemies," he muttered, preferring not to go into details. It would just upset her. "So, what's up? You came storming in here like you're on a mission."

"I didn't storm."

"Tell that to your face," he said.

She rolled her eyes. "You're leaving," Carmen stated.

"I have to," he responded, sitting in one of the chairs. "The Trial of Primacy is coming up, and I'm not even close to prepared. I need supplies. Armor, too. And I need to get stronger. The people in there will be no joke, and that's not even considering whatever challenges the system's going to throw at us. It's going to be more difficult than a tower. Maybe worse than a primal realm, which is still more than I can handle. If I'm going to survive that, much less pass the Trial, I'm going to need to be at my best."

"You don't have to participate in the Trial, though. Miggy could use your help. Now that he's got it in his head that he's going to take one of the direct-combat archetypes, he needs to be as strong as possible. His training is a lot more effective when you're around," she said.

Carmen was no stranger to physical training. She hadn't been a true body-builder before the World Tree's touch, but she'd been a habitual weight lifter since college. As such, she knew just how helpful Elijah's healing spells really were when it came to recovery.

"I know. Nerthus is going to pick up the slack while I'm gone," he said. "His spell isn't quite as potent, but it's good enough to maximize Miggy's gains. But even if that wasn't the case, I have to go. I recently had a fight that didn't really go my way. It was a good reminder that being at the top of the power rankings doesn't really guarantee anything. If we want to be safe—"

"This isn't about our safety," Carmen interrupted. She pointed at him, continuing, "This is about you. Alyssa was the same way. She didn't admit it, but she was driven to be the best. The strongest. And look how that turned out."

"I'm not her."

"You may as well be," Carmen argued. "You hide it behind all your personality quirks, but you can't stand coming in second. Which you are, by the way."

"Huh?"

"Look at the power rankings," Carmen replied.

Elijah did.

Planetary Power Rankings (Earth)

Oscar Ramirez—Level 85
Elijah Hart—Level 84
Sadie Song—Level 79
Hu Shui—Level 76
Niko Song—Level 76
Davu Adebowale—Level 70
Anupriya Pandey—Level 69
Benedict Emerson—Level 66
Ram Khandu—Level 63
Gunnar Lindstrom—Level 61

. . .

. . .

. . .

"What the hell? Last I looked, he was a few levels behind," Elijah said. Admittedly, he didn't typically keep a close eye on the power rankings, but he hadn't expected Oscar Ramirez—wherever he was—to have jumped him. After all, Elijah hadn't been idle. Certainly, he hadn't been actively looking for levels, but he'd still gained a few over the past months. "What is he doing to level so fast?"

"That's not my point," Carmen stated. "You're not going to stay on top forever. You can't define yourself by being the strongest person in the world."

"Highest level."

She narrowed her eyes. "What?"

"It's not really a ranking of the most powerful people," he said. "It's just levels. That's only a part of what makes someone strong."

"Don't be pedantic. The point is that you're needed here. This grove is a treasure trove. If you're not around, who's going to protect it?"

"I will," Nerthus stated, stepping out of one of the branches that made up the wall. "I apologize for eavesdropping, but it is difficult for me not to hear everything in the Grove. Normally, I ignore it. However, I felt inclined to offer my input. I am now capable of protecting the Grove—and the island—from all but the most powerful of intruders. In addition, the family of guardian deer have taken this as their home, and they will defend it. This island is no fortress, but for now, we are more than able to protect it and anyone who resides here. In addition, I am eager to help young master Miguel however I can."

"Why?" asked Carmen.

"Because he's my nephew, right?" Elijah guessed.

"No. He has the seed of a nature attunement. That is not so common that it should be ignored," Nerthus answered. "It is my duty to nurture that seed just as I tend to the rest of the Grove."

"Oh. See?" Elijah said. "Miggy will be fine."

Carmen sighed, then took another sip of her coffee. "Maybe I'm not going to be fine," she said. "I know this is all just a normal day for you, but I can't help but draw some parallels between Alyssa going to that tower and you participating in this Trial of Primacy."

Elijah didn't immediately answer. Instead, he just stared at her for a moment, dumbfounded that he hadn't made the connection. Of course Carmen would be concerned. Her family had been torn apart by that tower run. And now that she and Miguel were just getting settled, Elijah was going to leave on a similar task. How could she not have reservations?

"I'll be fine," he said, reaching out to put his hand on hers. She flinched at his touch, but it only lasted a moment. "You know that, right? I've run multiple towers. I can handle myself."

"You just said that you recently lost a fight," Carmen pointed out. "And there are going to be five thousand people in this trial."

"More than that, actually. That's just the humans. There are spots for the nonhumans, too," Elijah corrected her. Then, he saw her face and said, "Which is a totally not the point."

"Good save," she said sarcastically.

"You know I consistently put my foot in my mouth. It's part of my charm," Elijah said. "But seriously, Carmen. The whole point of me taking off is so that I can be as prepared as possible for the trial. And besides—this isn't like a tower. If things get too hairy, I can just leave. That's what the notice said, at least, and I don't think the system needs to lie to us."

"Just promise you'll be careful. In your preparations and in the Trial."

"I promise," he said, though he wasn't necessarily sure he could commit to that. Progression required a certain amount of risk, so he knew he'd be forced to put his life on the line. Hopefully, he could manage it, though.

"What are you going to do? Run some towers?" Carmen asked.

"I don't know. Probably," he answered. "I need to do some other stuff first, though. I need to talk to Atticus about some of my plans, plus I want to find out if anyone from Argos is planning on participating in the Trial. What about you? How is your project coming along?"

"Slowly," she sighed. "I'm enchanting every single brick, which you can guess is a bit time-consuming."

Once Carmen explained the process, Elijah admitted, "Sounds tedious."

"It can be, but it's also satisfying. I'm learning a lot, too. Getting a little experience, as well," she said. "But I'll be glad when it's finished. Then I can start working on my cultivation. I think it'll really help me once I start pushing for quality again."

After that, their conversation turned to more mundane subjects, like the gossip in Ironshore. Carmen hadn't been there long, but her knowledge of the goings-on in the town was light-years beyond Elijah's. When he pointed that out, she just frowned and said, "Well, you have a habit of threatening everyone every time you come into town. Of course they wouldn't be comfortable around you. Plus, you're never around."

"That's fair."

Then, Carmen went on to explain that the trade alliance with Norcastle had been even more successful than expected, which had brought a flood of etherium into the town. More, there was a small community of humans that had migrated to Ironshore. Most were Miners, but their families had come, as well.

"And don't worry. They know this island is off-limits. Everyone in Ironshore is quick to tell any visitors that everyone who comes here ends up dead," Carmen stated. "It's a bit silly, honestly. I thought they should downplay the uniqueness, but I was overruled."

By the time they finished their second cups of coffee, they'd exhausted most topics of conversation. More, Elijah didn't think he could put off his departure much longer. So, he bade Carmen goodbye and went to find Miguel. The young man was already deep into his training, which met with Elijah's approval. After telling Miguel that he'd be checking back in soon, he used Roots of the World Tree and teleported to Argos.

A few minutes later, he arrived at the gates, then made his way to Atticus's shop. As soon as he entered, the merchant looked up from where he was studying a pair of metal greaves, and when he recognized Elijah, a smile spread across his face. "Welcome back, my friend! I did not expect you so soon," he said.

Elijah shrugged. "Time's ticking away," he said. "I'm starting to prepare for the Trial of Primacy, and I hoped you'd have some good news for me. Any luck with the search?"

While building the Temple of Virtue, Elijah had asked Atticus to remain on the lookout for talented Leatherworkers and a Bowyer. At the time, he'd intended to find gear for Miguel, but now it seemed that he might find uses for those crafters himself.

"Regrettably, no," Atticus admitted. "But if you're just looking for armor, I have some decent options."

"Only leather," Elijah stated. Indeed, he'd given it a lot of thought, and the idea of using anything else just didn't feel right to him. Perhaps it was that metal armor was inorganic, or maybe it was all in his head, but he didn't think he'd get the most out of it unless he confined his choices to leather or cloth—and the latter only if he couldn't find the former.

"In that case, I have nothing worthwhile," Atticus said. "However, I do have good news!"

"Yeah?"

"There is an Artificer in Argos. He's low level. Just got his class a couple of weeks ago. But I've seen some of his work, and I'm very impressed," Atticus explained.

"What does an Artificer do, exactly?"

"Think of a Tinkerer, but with a bit more focus on ethereal contraptions. As soon as I heard about young Lars, I looked it up in a guide I bought months ago," he said. Then, he went on: "An Artificer can enchant tools that mimic class abilities. For instance, he made an engraving tool for me that allows me to empower very basic enchantments. I still need to study the designs, and even if I get it right, it will be quite limited. However, it will allow me to do a fair imitation of an Enchanter, which is far more than I would've been able to do without that tool."

"Interesting."

Atticus laughed. "That is an understatement, my friend! I heard that his most popular tools are cooking implements," he stated. "Imagine being able to cook your own food again—and actually enjoy the product! It's revolutionary."

Elijah scratched his chin. "That could be helpful," he said. Indeed, he'd long lamented his inability to cook anything properly, but he was more concerned with coffee at the moment. If his coffee already gave such a fantastic buff, then what would it give if it was brewed by someone with a cooking skill? Or, in this case, by someone with a French press enchanted to mimic one of those skills?

The idea was more than intriguing.

"Just keep an eye out for a high-level Leatherworker," Elijah said. "The level to beat is thirty-five."

That was the level of the girl back in Ironshore. Elijah would use her if necessary, but he wanted something better.

"Will do, my friend."

"What about the nearby tower? Is there anyone running it right now?" Elijah asked.

That was the problem with the towers to which Elijah had access. With the exception of the Magister's Estate near Arvandor, they were all in a constant rotation as the local forces took advantage of the leveling opportunities they represented. So, if Elijah wanted to run them, he needed to get in line.

"Regrettably, Delilah led her team inside only this morning. They won't return for a few days," Atticus answered. "But I do know of one that might be abandoned. Here—let me get a map."

He did just that, then showed Elijah where it was said to be. The tower was to the south, well past the swamp, and Atticus's knowledge was based on hearsay. But it seemed like as good an opportunity as any. So, Elijah decided that, once he found the Artificer and commissioned a French press, he would go check it out.

62

ARTIFICER'S GOODS

The city of Argos looked much the same as it always did, though Elijah still felt warmed by the general aura of acceptance he felt while walking its streets. Everywhere else he went, it seemed as if everyone was waiting for him to snap and start killing people. They either walked on eggshells around him—as they did in Ironshore—or responded with outright hostility, like in Seattle. He had passed through other places where the population was neutral, but those never really sprang to mind when he thought about his reception in the various locales he'd visited. Either way, every smile he saw, every wave thrown in his direction, and each time he saw a group of elderly women excitedly gossiping about him filled Elijah with much-needed joy.

It was telling that he'd had to travel hundreds of miles from his home just to be accepted.

Of course, the reactions of Ironshore's residents weren't unjustified. They'd seen just what he could do if pushed in the wrong direction—not only with the invaders he'd killed, but also in the battle against the orcs. So, their fear was as understandable as it was disappointing. Would the people of Argos react similarly if they saw what he could do?

Perhaps.

Elijah hoped he'd never find out, though.

A gentle but cold rain began to fall as he made his way through the streets. Many of the city's residents dashed inside at the first few drops, but Elijah enjoyed it. With his Cloak of the Iron Bear, he didn't have to worry about the temperature. So, he had few reasons not to bask in the impromptu shower. Whatever the case, by the time he reached the Artificer's shop, his clothes were soaked through—which suggested he should have probably been a bit more cognizant of the weather. He pushed through the door, which resulted in a deafening whistle that echoed through the shop.

Elijah clapped his hands over his ears, letting out a gasp. The sound was so loud and shrill that it was physically painful, and with the ringing in his ears that followed in its wake, it took him a moment to recognize that the sound had stopped. He pulled his hands away, half expecting them to be bloody.

"Sorry," came a voice from nearby. "I'm still working on the bell."

Elijah looked toward the voice, seeing a slight, pale-skinned young man. His face was dusted with freckles, and he wore his hair with the sides shaved clean but a mop of curls on top. Otherwise, the most curious thing about him was that he wore what looked like a pair of welder's goggles atop his head.

"Lars?" Elijah asked, glancing around the room. To him, it looked like a pawnshop, with all sorts of items—some of which were recognizable, but others that weren't—piled onto shelves. Apparently, organization wasn't Lars's strongest suit because there didn't appear to be any rhyme or reason to how everything had been arranged. Next to an old microwave was a Swiss Army knife, and next to that was a leather apron. There were gloves, various other articles of clothing, and plenty of appliances, as well.

"I am," said the young man. He certainly didn't look or sound Greek. "What can I do for you?"

"I've heard you're an Artificer. What exactly is that?" Elijah asked, picking up an old Game Boy. He flipped the switch, and surprisingly, a surge of ethera passed through it. However, instead of a video game, the screen showed a top-down map that it only took Elijah a second to recognize as the surrounding area. "This is a map . . ."

"It is!" Lars exclaimed. "One of a kind, too. I think the Game Boy screen gives it a kind of retro look that you won't find anywhere else! Barely requires any charging, either. Superefficient. I'm calling it a Map Boy."

Elijah didn't find the device nearly as exciting as Lars clearly did—largely because, with the size of the screen, it was difficult to make anything out. "How does it work?" he asked, turning it over. There was a silver plate covering the back side.

"It's how my class works," Lars answered. "I copy skills—that one is based on an Explorer skill, and it not only maps the area, but also shows points of interest. Then, I add them to devices. The trick is finding the right skills for the job. And getting people to let me copy them. And I guess it's not so easy making them interface with the item, either. The whole thing is difficult is what I'm getting at. But my prices are very reasonable considering how much work goes into each item!"

"Interesting," Elijah said, setting the item down. He liked the notion of the skill, but he didn't think the Game Boy screen was best suited for it. In any case, he had a couple of other ideas for equipment. The first was obvious. He reached into his Ghoul-Hide Satchel, retrieving his French press. Upon pulling it out, he asked, "Can you put a cooking skill on this? Nothing fancy. Just make it maintain ethera or something when I'm brewing."

"Hmm. Give me a second," Lars said, tapping his sharp chin. Then, he held up his finger and said, "Be right back." He turned to rush to the other end of the shop, but before he dipped into the back room, he said, "If you're going to shoplift, let me know."

Before Elijah could respond—he felt like he'd heard that line before—Lars was gone. That left Elijah to peruse the goods, but the problem was that he had no idea where to begin. The items were all clearly enchanted—judging by the ethera wafting off of them, at least—but there was no indication as to what any of them actually did. Did that chain saw have a log-cutting skill? Or was it meant for dismemberment? Or something else entirely? What about that television? Or the vacuum cleaner? To say the selection was eclectic was an understatement, though from Lars's description of the Game Boy, the possibilities of getting something useful were nearly endless.

By the time those thoughts had flitted through Elijah's head, Lars returned carrying a giant three-ring binder. It was decorated with a bunch of semi-anthropomorphic cartoon horses.

"Uh . . . My Little Pony?" asked Elijah.

Lars blushed. "It was the only notebook I could find when I got the Skill Catalog skill," he said. "Belonged to my little sister. I tried covering it up with something else, but . . . it won't work. It's a magical item, so it resists damage. And apparently covering those ponies up with duct tape or marker counts as damage."

"Ah," Elijah breathed, not willing to extend that topic of conversation. The characteristics of the skill were interesting, but he didn't want to broach the subject of the young man's sister. With everything that had happened, talking about people's loved ones was a touchy subject, largely because so many of them were no longer among the living. It was much safer not to ask questions about that kind of thing.

Lars flipped open the book, turning to a page somewhere in the middle before he said, "Aha! Here it is. Percolate. Tradesman archetype. Cook class. Allows for the infusion of ethera while filtering a liquid through a porous substance or surface. Should work for your little coffee thingy."

"French press."

"Yeah, that's what I meant. So, let's talk about cost. One skill or spell ought to do it," Lars said, stepping forward. "Just put your hand on this and— Urk—"

Elijah had reacted on instinct, his hand snapping out to wrap around the Artificer's neck. In his defense, he'd felt a swirl of foreign ethera like Lars was activating an ability. Usually—at least in his experience—that meant someone was about to attack him. And given how dangerous people could be, Elijah wasn't going to take any chances.

It was only after he saw the horrified look on Lars's face that he realized that he'd made an error. He released the young man, but he also took a step back. Just in case. "Sorry," he said. "I've been . . . attacked a lot recently."

Lars bent over and coughed a couple of times, and then, with one hand resting on his knee, held up one finger. "Can't imagine why people would attack you. You seem so nice . . ."

His binder had completely disappeared.

Finally, Lars caught his breath and straightened to his full height. "It's my fault. I should have warned you," he said. "My price for doing commissions is that I need you to donate one skill."

"I'd rather pay etherium."

"No thanks. Only skills."

"But—"

"My class doesn't advance unless I make stuff. Now, I could keep making the same things over and over again, which is super boring. Or I could make new stuff. But to do that, I need new skills to add to my Skill Catalog. I'd rather have that than a few extra coins."

"Damn," Elijah said with a shake of his head. "How does it work?"

"You put your hand in the book, I activate a skill, then you consent to having an ability of your choice copied," he said. "It's not really a big deal."

Elijah scratched his chin. "Three items," he said. "I'll give you two skills."

"Deal!"

Elijah almost groaned at how quickly Lars had agreed. It was just further evidence that negotiation was not one of his strengths. But he'd known that since he'd bought his first car, when the saleswoman had beguiled him with a pretty face, a little flirting, and a whole lot of lying. He'd ended up overpaying by thousands of dollars. His second time buying a car hadn't gone any better, even if instead of being hoodwinked by a good-looking woman he'd been ripped off by a fast-talking grifter of a used-car salesman.

And he hadn't gotten any better at it in the years since. The transformation of the world hadn't changed that, either.

Whatever the case, he felt certain that he could have gotten all three items for one skill, but it was a little late to change the terms. So, he followed Lars's instructions and laid his hand on the suddenly reappeared binder. Even though he knew it was coming, when Lars used his skill, Elijah flinched, but he maintained contact with the binder. Then, a notification flashed before his inner eye:

Lars Aaland would like to copy one of your abilities. Do you consent?

Elijah selected the affirmative option, which resulted in another notification.

Please choose an ability to be copied.

After that, his spell book opened. It was much longer than the last time he'd looked at the entire thing, but that was to be expected. He hadn't opened it in years, preferring instead to look at his individual spell descriptions. In any case, he didn't need to look at it long before he found the one he wished to offer.

Spell: Nature's Bounty	Encourage the growth of plants.

"This one makes plants grow more quickly," Elijah said. "I figure you could make something that they can put in farms and the like."

"Ah, yes. Interesting," Lars said as his ethera surged. Elijah felt nothing, but a moment later, he received confirmation that his spell had been copied.

After that, he offered Eyes of the Eagle, which Lars seemed very excited about. "How about I give you one more ability and you use it for an item specifically for me?" he asked. It wasn't really part of his original plan, but the possibilities of Lars's abilities were so broad that he kept getting ideas.

"That is acceptable," Lars said.

Then, Elijah let him copy Healing Rain. The idea was that he could heal himself and others with it if, for whatever reason, he ran out of ethera. It would be like having a free but low-powered heal.

"I think I can put that on a sprinkler," Lars stated after studying the spell in his binder. When Elijah got a peek at it, he just saw unintelligible scribbles that looked like they were the product of an unmedicated schizophrenic. If he hadn't already seen some of the products of Lars's skills, that might've scared him off. "Should work at around half power compared to the spell. Now, what else do you want? You have three more items."

Elijah told him. The first was the enchanted French press that he hoped would make his coffee better, but he also wanted an enchanted pan—he'd left the wok back home because he couldn't really make use of its special properties—that would make his cooking more edible. Then, he wanted a version of the mapping enchantment he'd seen on the Game Boy, but with a larger screen. Finally, he bought a checkered flag, complete with a pole that was meant to be stuck into the ground, that would increase his Regeneration attribute for a few hours. The buff wasn't huge—only fifteen points—but it didn't conflict with his own buffs, so it would be a net benefit.

In addition, Elijah's perusal of the shop gave him a couple more useful items. The first was a skinning knife that borrowed a Hunter's skill to dress animals more efficiently. The next was a fire starter that would work even underwater. And finally, he bought a small A-frame tent that would discourage detection.

"It's based on a skill I got from an elf that was passing through town a few months ago," Lars stated. "He called the skill Tracker's Protection." Then, he read the description from his book, "Discourages detection from hostile entities. I thought it fit the tent idea, and it uses so little ethera that it'll last all night on one charge."

"Perfect. How much do I owe you?" he asked.

That's when the dickering started. This time, Elijah felt that he got the better of Lars, but he had no real idea of what the enchanted items were worth. If they'd been normal items, he'd have had more of an idea, but Lars's products differed from those of other Tradesmen in a couple of key ways. First, the copied skills were far less powerful than the originals, and as such, the items Lars could create weren't on the same tier as something someone like the weapons and armor Carmen could make. The trade-off was that Lars didn't have to build anything from scratch. He didn't need special materials or weeks of work. He just had to have the right copied skill, which he could slap onto an appropriate item.

The second issue was that they would need to be recharged. Some lasted longer than others, but they would all run out of ethera after a while.

And finally, they were temporary. After a while, they would start to lose efficacy until they stopped working altogether. That wasn't ideal, but Lars assured Elijah that they would last at least a couple of months' worth of heavy use.

So, once Lars had the details of Elijah's order, he said, "I can have this done by tomorrow midday."

That worked for Elijah, so he left the young man behind and headed toward Agatha's inn, where he hoped to get a good meal.

63

KHOTONT

Elijah soared through the air above the swamp, his thoughts centered on the items he'd gotten from Lars. To most people, a pan, a mapping tablet, a flag of Regeneration, and an enchanted French press wouldn't be that huge of a deal, but for him, they were absolute game changers. The pan would allow him to cook his meals without losing any of the ethera that gave it taste, and the French press would give his coffee a little—or perhaps a lot of—extra kick. He hadn't used it yet, but he hoped that it would manifest in a more potent buff. And the mapping tablet would prove invaluable once he was in the Trial of Primacy. To test it out, he'd taken it out into the wilderness around Argos, and to his surprise, it not only gave him a moderately detailed map of an area in a half-mile radius of his location, but for about half that distance, it actually highlighted points of interest. He'd used it to find a weak natural treasure. Even though he'd left the fern where he'd found it, the fact that the map showed it was a great sign of things to come.

The fire starter he had bought, which was a converted laser pointer, was less impressive but no less effective. Elijah had tried it underwater, and it had worked fantastically well. The fire it conjured only lasted a couple of minutes, but that was probably enough for his purposes. The memories of dozens of cold, wet nights were enough to make him appreciate the little device.

Elijah had yet to try the tent, skinning knife, or flag out, but the other items had performed their functions well enough that he didn't think it necessary. He trusted that, when the time came, each would play its role as well as the others.

The only issue with Lars's products was that they required recharging. That meant that Elijah would need to push his ethera into a small rune the Artificer had drawn on each item, channeling his energy for at least a few minutes for each item. If he completely used their stored ethera, it would take much longer to recharge them.

They also didn't have fancy names like the Cloak of the Iron Bear or any of his other equipment. That highlighted their temporary nature, at least to Elijah. Perhaps as Lars gained levels, he would be able to make longer-lasting items. For now, though, Elijah was glad that he'd stuck around for the extra day, even if he could feel his available time ticking down.

Fortunately, there hadn't been any aerial predators to hinder his path, so as he flew over the swamp, he did so at the speed of a Cessna. He couldn't quite rival passenger jets or fighter planes, but he expected that, as his attributes grew, so too would his top speed. The only thing that slowed him down was the occasional updraft, which would throw him off course if he wasn't careful.

Gradually, he crossed the immense swamp, and as he did so, he couldn't help but marvel at the sheer scope of the area. Distance was a little hard to judge without much context, but he suspected that the swamp could rival a state like Texas in size—which meant that it was absolutely enormous.

However, it only took a day and a half before he found the edge, and when he did, he observed the reemergence of the ruins that dotted the rest of the region. It was so difficult to think of the remnants of pretransformation-Earth's civilization as such, but given that they were abandoned and crumbling, there really was no other viable term.

Still, each time Elijah saw a half-destroyed suburban neighborhood or crumbling store, he couldn't help but feel a pang of sadness. Accompanying that was a note of satisfaction, though. While he took no joy in the knowledge that so many people had died, nature's ongoing reclamation of those areas elicited some degree of serenity. Was that his attunement at work? Or was it the simple result of knowing that Earth had been on a collision course with disaster, all at the hands of industrialization?

Maybe it was both.

Whatever the case, the touch of the World Tree had brought that to a halt, and the wild places of the world had begun to resume their rightful stature.

After another day, Elijah spotted something troubling down below, and he landed just outside of what looked like a destroyed town. Unlike the other ruins he'd seen, these fallen buildings had been constructed much more recently. Elijah resumed his human form and strode forward, his Dragon-Touched Staff thudding against the ground with every step.

Three large buildings—huge yurts, he thought—had comprised the village, and they looked like they'd been trampled by a herd of elephants. The wood from which they'd been made had been snapped like bundles of twigs, and people's belongings were scattered across the whole village. Elijah saw old clothes—ripped and torn—leather harnesses, and even a few makeshift children's dolls in the ruins, but he found no bodies, which garnered hope that the people who'd lived there had managed to survive.

However, as he looked at the remains of the settlement, he couldn't help but wonder what had managed to destroy it so thoroughly. A monster, perhaps. It didn't look like the work of people, largely because nothing had been taken. The leather, at the very least, was valuable enough that it wouldn't have been left behind.

Still, even though Elijah spent a couple of hours investigating the scene, he found no evidence to suggest the cause of the destruction. So, after checking his map tablet and finding nothing of note, he set off in the direction of the tower Atticus had mentioned. The merchant's directions hadn't been perfect, but Elijah hoped that they would at least put him in the right area. Finding it after that wouldn't be terribly difficult.

Because of his resolution not to spend too much time in any of his bestial forms, Elijah set off on foot. As he did so, he observed the territory. The swamp had long since given way to an expansive prairie. Parts of the plains were verdant with lush grasses, but the region through which he now passed was more like a savanna with thick clumps of yellow grass, the stark and unforgiving landscape periodically broken up by multicolored flowers and other vegetation.

More than once, Elijah just stopped to appreciate the scenery. It was so different from the forests to which he'd grown so accustomed, but there was certainly something about the vast savanna that spoke to him. With all the open space and huge blue sky, it felt like freedom.

As Elijah progressed through the savanna, he saw a half dozen other trampled settlements, some of which would qualify as small cities. If he'd had to guess, some of them would have held at least a few thousand people, though when Elijah passed through, they were all deserted. Most of those were surrounded by fields that had once held crops, but those too had been trampled, and any evidence of what produce had once grown there was gone amid the turned earth.

Finally, Elijah caught sight of a plume of smoke on the horizon. It was miles away, but after taking off at a light jog, he covered enough distance that, before nightfall, he saw the source. It was another town, though this one was the largest he'd yet seen in the steppes. As he drew closer, he saw that it was surrounded by a large, sturdy wall that practically glowed with ethera. Otherwise, it looked extremely primitive—more of a huge berm of piled dirt than a wall—and behind that earthen bulwark peeked a few stout buildings.

Atticus hadn't known much about the people who lived on the plains, so Elijah didn't know what to expect as he approached a small opening—it was barely a few feet wide—in the berm. He was greeted by a pair of men, and to his surprise, they were both shorter than him. Moreover, they wore leather armor trimmed in fur and wielded short recurve bows. Both men were of East Asian descent.

"Where'd you come from?" demanded one, fingering an axe at his waist. "Why are you here? Did you lead the monster to us?"

"Uh . . . no?"

"Do you see a monster, Baatar?" asked the other, gesturing with his bow. The other man squinted into the dusky evening. "No?"

"Believe me—you'd see it if it was here," said the smarter of the two.

"Oh. Yeah. Doesn't mean it's not tracking him, though!"

"It doesn't track. It just tramples."

"I didn't see any monster," Elijah said. "I come from Argos, past the swamp. What's going on here?"

"Past the swamp? Nobody crosses the swamp," said Baatar.

"I did," Elijah said.

"People used to cross. But that was before the monster came," said the smart one. "Why did you travel here?"

"Exploring. I'm a Cartographer. I get experience for seeing new things and mapping them," he said.

"Ouch," said the guard. "You have my sympathies."

Elijah had had the presence of mind to use the Ring of Anonymity to create a new identity. This time, he was Abraham Sykes, a level forty-one Explorer. Cartographer was one of the most common classes associated with the archetype, a fact that completed his disguise.

"Yeah," Elijah said. "When I chose it, I didn't expect travel to be so difficult. I have a few abilities that make me less conspicuous in the wilderness, but I've had more close calls than I'd like. Still, someone needs to map the world, right? People will thank me one day!"

"Sure, bud" was the reply to Elijah's enthusiasm. Left unsaid was the caveat that he needed to survive first, which for most people was a dubious prospect.

"Can I enter? I was kind of looking forward to sleeping in a bed tonight," Elijah said.

Baatar quickly answered, "No entry. The town's full, what with all the refugees from the monster."

"Oh. Then, a meal? I have money."

"Damn it, Baatar," said the other guard. "Just keep your lips together, will you?" Then, to Elijah, he said, "Of course you can enter. There probably aren't any beds, but I'm sure somebody'll let you sleep in the stables."

"That's fine. Just want to get a roof over my head. Plus, some decent food. Sometimes, I wish I'd have taken a Cook class."

"Don't I know it," Baatar said, his first reasonable contribution to the conversation.

After that, the helpful guard directed Elijah toward a large building at the center of the settlement. He also discovered that the town had once been in Mongolia, and it was called Khotont. That explained the steppes, at least.

The first thing Elijah noticed upon entering the town was that there were horses inside. Lots and lots of horses. In fact, he suspected that there were more horses than people, which was a little disconcerting, especially considering that Elijah could feel the power wafting off of the beasts. Clearly, many of them had leveled at least as much as the people of Khotont.

The residents wore simple clothing, though in a wide variety of colors ranging from various shades of red to blues and greens and everything in between. Most of the people were of Asian descent, but there were a couple of darker- and lighter-skinned folks around, as well.

The architecture was fairly simple, and like Argos, it was a blend of old and new, though there was very little wood in evidence. Instead, they preferred stone and brick, which didn't surprise Elijah, considering that he'd only seen a few scattered trees since he'd left the swamp behind.

Finally, he reached the building that was his destination. It was large—probably fifty yards across—and circular, looking like the world's biggest yurt. However, it was made of stone, and when Elijah stepped inside, he saw dozens of long tables occupied by hundreds of people.

Elijah followed a line of people to what looked like a cafeteria-style serving table, where he helped himself to as much food as he could heap upon a plate he picked up along the way. In addition, someone that looked like they must've worked there shoved a mug of beer into his hand, then demanded two copper. Elijah paid it gladly, then retreated to one of the tables.

He got more than a few looks from the locals, but they were far more interested in their food and their own conversations to care about him too much. So, when he sat and started to dig in, he overheard a bit of gossip.

"Wait, did you say the monster is a boar?" Elijah asked around a mouthful of red meat.

The local looked at him and said, "Of course. Have you been living under a rock? My team and I are going to hunt it tomorrow morning."

Elijah asked a few more questions of the man, who was happy to brag about how he and his friends were going to slay the great monster and bring peace to the steppes. And he learned that the monster in question was no ordinary pig. Instead, it was a giant boar that was said to be larger than an African elephant. When he asked why they hadn't killed it yet, he learned that the beast's hide was said to be impenetrable.

"But I just got a new skill," the man boasted. "Armor Piercing. With that on my side, I'll get through. Might have to hit it a few times, but it'll eventually bleed out."

"I hope so," Elijah said, genuinely hoping the man would survive. He hadn't even learned the hunter's name, but he was an affable sort who was easy to root for. "If you need help, let me know. I don't have a lot of combat skills, but I can heal a bit."

"Ha! Thank you, but no. Our Healer is more than up to the task," he said with utmost confidence. Elijah hoped he was right. "I have to say, you're much better than the other stranger who came here the other day. He racked up a huge gambling debt that he couldn't pay. Poor sap. He'll be lucky if he isn't executed."

Elijah nodded, barely listening. Instead, he decided to say, "I'm told you have a tower around here. Can you point me in the right direction? I want to add it to my map."

"Of course. Northwest. But don't think about going in there."

"Why? Is it more dangerous than normal towers?"

"No. It's just that the waiting list is a mile long. My team and I are scheduled for three months from now. That's why we're hunting the monster. It'll give us a chance to level a bit without the tower."

"I see," Elijah said, disappointed. Perhaps he should just go back to Seattle and hope that Isaiah could squeeze him in. With the Adventurers dead, there had to be a few open slots. But then again, he didn't want to do that, largely because he didn't like the idea of being watched every time he set foot into the city. He believed that Isaiah had Seattle's best interests at heart, but that didn't make the Big Brother aspect of the man's powers any easier to endure.

But it seemed that he might not have much choice.

Elijah finished his meal, said goodbye to his new acquaintance, then headed to find somewhere to sleep. Hopefully, tomorrow would be a little more fruitful.

64

THE HUNT

Elijah awoke to a wet nose in his face. For a brief instant, he panicked. Suddenly, the instincts he'd developed living in the wilderness and running towers came to the fore, and he scrambled backward through the hay that had been his bed for the night. As he did so, his ethera swirled with Soothe, the preemptive cast having become a necessary habit. However, after only a moment, he realized that he was in no danger.

The horse cocked its head to the side, looking at him like he'd grown horns.

Elijah let out a nervous chuckle. The black stallion was a beautiful animal, though it differed from most horses he'd ever seen. That was characteristic of the Mongolian breed. They were stocky compared to other equine variants, and rarely exceeded five feet in height. The breed was interesting in that it had largely remained unchanged since the time of Genghis Khan, when they had enabled the Mongolian hordes to conquer much of the known world.

During the previous day, Elijah had learned that part of the reason the city of Khotont was so crowded was that they'd had to make room for vast herds of horses. Normally, Mongolian horses were left outdoors, where they were expected to fend for themselves—within reason, at least. But with the stampeding boar trampling everything in its path, the residents had brought their valuable herds within the city's walls, constructing large paddocks and stables to house them.

That was lucky for Elijah because, otherwise, he'd have been forced to bed down under the stars. It was not a new experience for him, but he'd been looking forward to getting out of the weather, which had turned to snow and biting wind. With his Cloak of the Iron Bear, the cold didn't bother him—in fact, he'd gained a couple of attribute points due to the ability attached to it—but the wet was annoying.

In any case, he hadn't expected to wake up with a snout in his face.

He reached out, laying his hand on the animal's nose. It accepted his touch without issue, and Elijah felt the beast's strength at his fingertips. He'd known since entering Khotont that the horses were no ordinary creatures. They'd progressed quite a lot, with many reaching levels high enough that they would have been on the power rankings if they'd been human.

Or that was what his senses told him. In truth, Elijah wasn't even sure if beasts had levels. Logic suggested they did, but nonsapient creatures could have completely different systems of progression than their sapient counterparts. Not that it really mattered. Power was power, regardless of how it was quantified, and these horses definitely had plenty.

The people of the steppes—who were mostly Mongolian, but included a few African and South American settlements, as well—depended on the horses for so much. They not only used them for battle and transportation and as beasts of burden, but they also milked the mares and, at times, slaughtered them for their meat. The entire Mongolian culture had once revolved around horses, and the touch of the World Tree—or, more appropriately, the decline in modernity that came with it—had brought the creatures back to prominence.

Elijah couldn't help but wonder if there were classes that revolved around having companion beasts. Did the horses have any say in the matter? Or would such a bond be forced upon them? The stallion that had woken him up didn't seem unhappy, but Elijah couldn't be certain if that was the result of the creature's actual feelings or whether it was a state forced upon the beast by the system.

Maybe it didn't really matter when dealing with nonsapient animals.

Elijah sighed. No—it definitely mattered. His instincts told him that much. The only real question was whether he'd let those feelings influence him. That was the danger of his attunement, especially considering that he kept One with Nature active at all times. It wasn't uncommon for him to wonder if his emotions were his or if he'd been influenced by an outside force he didn't truly understand.

Nerthus had referred to it as the Mother, warning against letting the Call overwhelm him. At the time, Elijah had resisted, giving himself a false sense of security. However, since then, he'd learned that he'd only managed to overcome the first wave. Now, the Call was more subtle but no less dangerous, and Elijah needed to be cognizant of the danger it posed to his personality.

Being around people helped with that.

So, without further ado, Elijah pushed himself to his feet and cast Healing Rain before tilting his head to the stable's ceiling and letting the rejuvenating shower envelope him. He wasn't injured, but it did wonders to loosen tight muscles and, most importantly, wash away the stink of sleeping in a stable. On top of that, the water would disappear only a few minutes after the Healing Rain ceased, so he didn't even have to worry about getting his clothes wet.

Once he was fully awake and dry, Elijah ate one of his Grove berries, receiving a jolt of energy as soon as he swallowed the miraculous fruit. Then, he gathered his satchel and staff and left the stable behind. When he stepped outside, he saw that the city was even busier than it had been the day before, which meant that the streets were crowded with people and horses. The pedestrians were so tightly packed that the closeness made Elijah uncomfortable.

He wasn't claustrophobic or antisocial, but this crowd was on an entirely different level from anything he'd experienced in the past few years. So, he had to stop himself from shifting into Shape of the Sky and flying away. Thankfully, the pack of pedestrians thinned a bit as he left the city behind.

Originally, he'd intended to wander the town and learn more about it—while perhaps seeing if they had anything worthwhile to purchase—but the crowd had cemented his desire to leave. Still, it had taken almost two hours to cross from the stable to the exit, so by that point, midmorning had come and gone.

There were plenty of other people who were leaving the city, as well, though none of them looked like they were prepared for a long journey. Instead, they were heading out to farm, hunt, or gather. With the monstrous boar out there, it was dangerous, but starvation didn't make any concessions to that sort of thing. People needed to eat, and the presence of a monster wasn't going to change that simple fact of life.

Elijah separated from the group and wandered away. Some people noticed, but they were far too focused on their own tasks to care much about one stranger heading off alone. In any case, he only continued for an hour or so before he settled down to think of his next move.

The tower was out for now, which meant that if Elijah wanted to progress, he needed to find another. Perhaps the one next to his island would have to suffice. Or maybe he should return to Seattle and work his way into the rotation. Regardless, it was a disappointing turn of events that cemented the towers as strategic resources that could determine the viability of Earth's future leaders. Without them, gaining experience was difficult. Certainly, people could just wander off into the wilderness looking for dimensional rifts or powerful beasts—be they guardians, monsters, or just normal animals who'd gained a few levels—but that brought with it significant danger. Unlike towers, the wilderness was unregulated. As such, people never knew what they would encounter. Maybe they'd find a creature like the hydra that would easily kill them. Or they might find nothing but weak beasts that gave minuscule levels of experience.

That was the true benefit of the towers. Because they scaled with the levels of the challengers, they always offered an appropriate challenge that would give noticeable levels of experience. To a lesser extent, rifts were the same way, but because they were random—and limited, as they disappeared once conquered—they didn't offer a viable leveling strategy.

As he sat there, Elijah realized why people desperate to progress might pick up everything and head to a newly touched world like Earth. Sure, noncombat classes could gain experience by doing their jobs, but the system didn't reward repetitive tasks very well. Without danger or novelty, progress was extraordinarily slow. For instance, if a Blacksmith wanted to gain levels, they would need to constantly innovate, either via using rare materials or new methods. They could progress by making the same things over and over, but it would take exponentially longer to do so.

But a planet like Earth offered incredible opportunities for novelty and danger, which made it a great environment for progression—at least compared to other, more established worlds where opportunities were closely guarded resources.

It wouldn't last, though. As humanity continued to tame the planet, progression would become more and more difficult. Perhaps it would take a century or more, but eventually, it would be no different than the planets left behind by the dwarves, gnomes, and elves Elijah had met.

Elijah was still giving it some thought when he felt a subtle rumble in the earth. At first, it skated past his notice, but he started to pay attention when the wildlife in the area—ranging from snakes to insects to small varmints—started running. That's when Elijah looked up and saw a cloud of dust in the distance. After close to a minute, he saw the culprit.

Or culprits.

There were dozens of people on horseback, each one armed with a bow or spear. The mounted archers kept up a steady stream of arrows as they raced across the grassland, while the spearmen sliced toward their prey like lancers. It was an impressive display of horsemanship and skill, but Elijah only barely noticed. Instead, his attention was on the creature that had drawn their ire.

In the city, Elijah had heard that the monster was a boar the size of an elephant. However, those rumors paled before reality. The creature was a wild pig, with short, bristly fur and sharp tusks, but the reported size was clearly the result of an obvious underestimation.

The thing wasn't the size of an elephant.

Instead, it was at least twice that size. The distance obscured exact measurements, but based on the comparison between the horses and the creature in question, he estimated that it was at least twenty feet at the shoulder. Maybe even a little bigger.

For a long few moments, Elijah just stared at the scene, and he only broke out of his reverie when the great boar swept its head to the side, connecting with a hunter who failed to react in time. The nimble horse attempted to dance aside, but it was too slow. The larger beast's enormous tusk pierced its side before the momentum of its attack sent the smaller animal—and its rider—rocketing away to tumble across the prairie.

It was too much to hope either man or animal had survived.

To their credit, the hunters didn't panic. Instead, they encircled the creature, continuing to pepper it with attacks that, from Elijah's perspective, did almost no good. Arrows glanced off of its hide, and even the spears—which had the momentum of a horseman's charge behind them—failed to do any damage. The beast snorted and bucked, never slowing its mad dash.

When it drew closer, Elijah saw that the boar was even larger than he'd first thought. More, its wild, shaggy hide glistened with ethera, and its tusks gleamed with a deadly aura. Foam spewed forth from its gaping maw, and its beady eyes twitched with terror and madness.

That was all Elijah saw before disaster once again struck. Despite their clear skill, the hunters were no match for the beast. And on top of that, they had just as obviously been taxed by the pursuit to the point where a mistake was inevitable. When it happened, three more hunters fell. Two of them were ripped to pieces by the boar's sharp tusks, but the other only took a glancing blow. Even that was enough to send the two—rider and mount—to ragdoll across the grassland.

He ran forward, watching in horror as the creature wheeled on the other hunters and charged. Another two got trampled, and by the time Elijah reached the scene, panic suffused their ranks. So, he shouted, "Scatter!"

Then, without further thought, he cast Storm's Fury at the enraged beast. Lightning arced down from the cloudless sky, slapping the boar in the head. Despite the fact that the bolt came from above, the beast quickly zeroed in on Elijah and charged him.

Getting the creature's attention had been the goal, but now, Elijah found himself on the wrong end of a furious multiton living tank.

65

UNASSAILABLE TRUTH

A thousand insects manifested by Swarm descended upon the boar, but to Elijah's horror, their bites proved entirely incapable of penetrating the creature's hide. However, he didn't have the chance to lament the conjured insects' impotency before he was forced to flee its thundering charge. As he turned to flee, he used Snaring Roots, then Brand of the Stalker and Nature's Rebuke. The results were mixed.

Brand of the Stalker landed, and the creature's location blossomed in his mind. However, Nature's Rebuke was entirely resisted, refusing to take hold. Was that because it was a natural beast? Or was it simply too powerful? Perhaps a countering skill was at work. Whatever the case, Snaring Roots was at least effective, the resulting vines snaking out from the earth and wrapping around its hooves. The delay caused by the spell was only temporary, though, and the creature quickly ripped itself free to continue its charge.

By that point, Elijah was already running.

He could have shifted into Shape of the Sky, but that wouldn't have accomplished the goal. The moment he lost the creature's attention, it would turn on the fallen hunters, trampling them beneath its hooves.

They couldn't kill it. And if they were forced to outrun it, they would leave their fallen brethren behind. No—they needed time, and Elijah was the only one who could provide them with the room they required to survive. So, when he was a little less than a hundred yards away, he once again used Storm's Fury. The spell wasn't very effective, but it certainly maintained the creature's attention, which was the overall goal.

Could Elijah have fought the beast?

Perhaps. But while he didn't have access to an inspection ability like so many others seemed to possess, he had developed some ability to recognize a foe's relative power. At the most basic level, he confined those instincts into four categories. First, there were those who were so far below him that their power was trivial to him. Second came the category into which most people fit—strong enough that they could pose a threat, but still below him. Then, there were those who were of a level with—or slightly above—him. And finally, he could recognize when something was so far beyond him that fighting the threat would put him at an extreme disadvantage.

The boar fell into the final category.

He knew it was stronger than him, which meant that fighting it wasn't really an option—at least not until he got it away from the fallen hunters. So, for now, Elijah only needed to lead it on a chase. For that, he intended to utilize a similar strategy to what he'd employed in the Sea of Sorrows when he'd led the giant isopod into a trap.

This time, though, the chase was much more harrowing. Even though his attributes had increased quite a bit, and he had plenty of abilities to help him, the boar was many times stronger than him. The isopod had been, as well, but not to the same degree. It was a grim reminder that the world was filled with a wide range of dangers, many of which could stomp him into oblivion.

Those thoughts flitted through Elijah's mind as he ran, leading the enormous boar away from the hunters. As he did so, he felt the ethera shift as the creature engaged another ability. Instead of swirling all around it like a protective coat, it coalesced around the monster's legs, spurring it forward in an incredible charge. It barreled toward him with the speed of a bullet train, and Elijah was forced to dodge to the side, narrowly avoiding the monster's razor-sharp tusks and thudding hooves.

As he dived aside, he shifted into his draconid form. The increased Dexterity let him quickly regain his feet, and the added Strength that came with the predator shape gave him the power he needed to put some distance between himself and the enraged boar. He raced away, finally outpacing the monster. However, he never let it get so far behind that it would lose interest.

Like that, he traveled for dozens of miles until he reached one of the destroyed towns. Once there, he decided to try his luck against the powerful creature. So, he dipped behind a pile of rubble, then used that to hide his retreat. The moment he left combat, Elijah slipped into Guise of the Unseen before doubling back.

The boar, having lost track of him, had decided to take out its frustrations on the fallen town, attacking rubble and trampling any structures that remained standing. Not for the first time, Elijah watched it in awe. The creature was incredibly powerful—stronger even than the hydra, if he had to guess—and explosions of debris followed it wherever it went.

It was no wonder it had made such easy work of the hunters.

However, as Elijah observed the creature, he couldn't help but feel a sense of loss. This was no monster. He was certain of it. Nor was it an ordinary beast. It was a guardian, not so different from the bear or the panther—or even Snappy the tortoise. And yet, it was clearly mad.

There was only one thing that could have driven it to that state. Elijah had long known that guardians were inextricably tied to their natural treasures, and in a way that he couldn't really understand. When Bessy—the alligator guardian back in the swamp—had lost her natural treasure, she'd been lucky to latch on to Konstantinos, Marcy, and their family of adopted children. Was madness what would have awaited if she hadn't found something to replace her treasure?

The more Elijah thought about it, the more he settled into the idea. The boar was a menace. It had killed hundreds of people and destroyed a dozen towns—an act that would likely result in even more deaths before everything was said and done. Yet, could it be held accountable when it had clearly been driven insane?

But more importantly, could Elijah save it?

He knew it was a lost cause, but still, he had to try. He wouldn't have been much of a Druid if he didn't. The problem was that the boar hadn't stopped, not even for a second. Instead, it seemed hell-bent on causing as much destruction as possible. Like a child throwing a tantrum.

Or a psychopath who only wanted to watch the world burn, to tear apart the world that had failed them.

Elijah continued to watch, waiting for an opening until, finally, he saw an opportunity. The creature had gotten one of its tusks hung in the rubble of a large building, and though Elijah knew it wouldn't last long, he chose to use that brief moment of idle distraction to his advantage. He pounced—not to kill but, rather, to simply let him get closer.

He leaped upon the monster's back, and the moment he landed, the thing went wild. Fortunately, with his Dexterity, remaining atop the beast was possible, even with its wild bucking. He shifted into his human form and grabbed hold of the monster's bristly fur. It felt like it would have been at home on a wire brush, and if Elijah hadn't possessed significant Constitution, he was certain that his hands would have been cut to pieces. However, as it stood, he only felt a mild discomfort.

In any case, he channeled Soothe, then Touch of Nature while flaring One with Nature and Nature's Bounty. He had no ability to commune with animals, so he used everything at his disposal. At first, it did nothing, but after a moment, Elijah felt everything click together.

And a world of madness opened up to him.

Loss. Grief. Confusion. A hundred emotions, each one powerful enough to bring tears to Elijah's eyes, roiled. But over everything else was the fury of one who had been wronged. The impotent rage of someone who'd lost everything they held dear. The potent frustration of a creature who didn't know what else to do.

Elijah had felt such a connection once before, but the mist panther who'd guarded his island had been serene. Accepting. It had known it was dying, and it had made its choice. The boar was the opposite. It would have preferred to die. Perhaps there was a part of it—the only sliver of sanity that remained—that hoped someone would put it out of its misery.

When the connection broke only a few seconds later, Elijah nearly fell from the boar's broad back. But at the last second, he reaffirmed his grip.

Tears in his eyes, Elijah knew the guardian was too far gone to save. He could heal physical injuries, but none of his spells could do anything for psychological trauma. Even if they could, he questioned whether or not they would prove effective. The wounds went so deep that they'd destroyed large swaths of the boar's mind.

The guardian was gone.

Only a monster remained.

And Elijah knew what to do with those.

With a sad sigh, he shifted back into his draconid form, then tested the creature's defenses. To his shock, his claws did no damage at all to the monster's hide. Just like when he'd used Swarm, they were entirely ineffective. The same was true even when he used Venom Strike; without penetration, the necrotic venom had no way of getting into the beast's system.

Elijah tried a few other attacks, even switching to his lamellar-ape form to test blunt force, but the boar was entirely unassailable. However, his attacks were obviously irritating, and with each blow, the monster's wild bucking grew more pronounced until, at last, Elijah's grip started to loosen.

It was then that he realized he had no other choice but to flee. This time, though, he didn't need to lead the creature on a chase. So, he shifted into the Shape of the Sky, then launched himself into the air. The boar didn't like that, and it whipped around with far more quickness than a beast of its size should have possessed. As Elijah flapped his wings, the monster leaped, aiming to impale him with its sharp tusks.

He furiously climbed, but the boar's Strength was immense, and it shot through the air like a rocket. Elijah beat his wings against the air, climbing higher and higher until, after almost two hundred feet, the boar reached the apex of its leap. Then, even as Elijah continued to climb, it fell to the ground with the force of a meteor. When it hit, a shock wave spread through the area, destroying anything the monster's rampage hadn't already claimed.

Elijah felt the impact even hundreds of feet toward the sky, and the updraft threw him off course, sending him spinning through the air until he regained control a few seconds later. By that point, the boar had already recovered, and its fury reached new heights. Thankfully, its path took it in the opposite direction of Khotont, which meant that disaster had been averted.

Because even with its enchanted earthen wall, the city could not stand before the boar's fury. It was too strong. Too durable. The people of Khotont had no chance against such a foe.

From hundreds of feet in the air, Elijah followed the creature, watching it for any signs of weakness. For a long time, he saw nothing, but after a few more hours, it slowed to a trot, showing that it was not entirely inexhaustible. The beast still randomly tore large furrows in the plains, though its ire had clearly waned.

So, after following it for a couple more hours, Elijah decided to head back to the site of the battle. Many of the hunters had been injured, and though it would ruin his disguise as a Cartographer, he was willing to make that sacrifice in the name of saving a few lives.

Once he was within a mile or two, he landed and shifted back to his human form before taking off at a trot. He arrived to find that the hunters had established a temporary camp a mile or two away from the scene of the battle. There, they were busy tending to their wounded—who were clearly too injured to move.

When Elijah approached, he got more than a few surprised looks, but after he explained that he could heal, they put their shock on the back burner. Not surprisingly, Elijah recognized one of the injured men as the one who'd boasted about his new Armor Piercing ability. He'd lost an arm in the battle.

Without delay, Elijah went to work healing the injured, but the whole time, his mind whirled with the events of the day. Not only was it impossible to get the ruined state of the guardian's mind out of his thoughts, but he couldn't escape the unassailable fact that something needed to be done about the rampaging creature. Left to its own devices, it would continue to kill, growing stronger with every person—or beast—it trampled.

It needed to be put down. Elijah knew that down to his very core. But the question that dominated his thoughts more than any other was how he was going to kill such an invulnerable beast.

66

WILHELM

We can't thank you enough," said Tömörbaatar, passing Elijah a cup.

One whiff was all it took for him to identify the milky-white liquid as something alcoholic, but it was unlike anything Elijah had ever seen before. So, he asked, "What's this?"

"Airag. Fermented mare's milk," the short leader of the hunters said. He'd been one of Elijah's first patients, and though he'd received the most healing, he still had a long scar across his face. There was another one that stretched from his right shoulder to his left hip, though that was hidden beneath his rough tunic. Tömörbaatar had been the most injured among the survivors, but three men and one woman had died in the battle.

Six horses—including Tömörbaatar's own mount—had fallen, as well. Not wanting the animals' sacrifices to go to waste, the remaining hunters had quickly processed the beasts, and Elijah had already eaten some of their flesh. Consuming horsemeat had never been on his bucket list, but he'd expected that if he'd refused, it would have been considered rude.

The meat itself wasn't terrible. A little like extremely lean beef, though with a bit of a sweet undercurrent. Elijah had expected the Mongolian group to accompany the meal with some sort of ceremony—they practically revered their horses—but nothing of the sort happened. They mourned the loss of their companions—both bestial and human—but they hadn't attached any extra significance to consuming the meat of their mounts. It was just another meal.

Elijah brought the cup to his lips and took a sip. The first thing he noticed was the texture, which was surprisingly fizzy. And when it hit his tongue, he was immediately reminded of yogurt, though with a slight sweetness to it. He could also taste the alcohol, though it wasn't overwhelming. There was a sourness to it, as well, but as with the alcohol, it wasn't enough to overpower the rest of the flavor.

In short, it was unlike anything he'd ever had, and after taking another sip, Elijah decided it would certainly never make it on his list of favorite beverages. It wasn't bad, but it definitely wasn't something he intended to seek out in the future.

"Good," he lied.

Tömörbaatar laughed heartily, then slapped Elijah's shoulder. The blow was much more solid than the small man should've been capable of producing, which told Elijah that the hunter was a little higher level than most. He'd checked, and Tömörbaatar wasn't on the power rankings, but Elijah expected that he wasn't far off.

The other hunters gathered around the fire weren't much lower, either, which meant that the team had been quite a formidable one. And yet, they hadn't stood a chance against the boar. If Elijah had needed a reminder of just how dangerous the world was, the existence of the boar definitely satisfied that requirement.

"It's a bit of an acquired taste," admitted Tömörbaatar, echoing Elijah's sentiments concerning the beverage.

"It's not bad. Just . . . different," Elijah maintained, forcing himself to take another sip. It was worse than the first, and he nearly choked on the stuff. He gave his new friend a thumbs-up. "Tasty. But I don't want to take it all for myself . . ."

Tömörbaatar laughed again as Elijah offered to return the cup. Then, the hunter downed the entire thing in one huge gulp. It stained his voluminous mustache white. Elijah chuckled, as well, resting his forearms on his knees as he glanced at the fire. The camp wasn't large, but it was protected by one of Tömörbaatar's skills. The hunter hadn't revealed the ability's name, but he had described its effects, which were similar to the one Lars had used to enchant Elijah's new tent. The basic idea was that it would discourage the wildlife from coming within range of the camp, much like the array around Ironshore that did the same.

The difference was that Tömörbaatar's skill was completely mobile. If he could build a fire, then he was mostly protected, at least from anything within a certain attribute range. The array around Ironshore was stronger and less dependent on attributes, but it was also stationary.

Regardless, the Mongolian hunter seemed to take its efficacy for granted, so Elijah chose to follow his lead. It wasn't as if he had much to fear from the wilderness, anyway. Over the past few years, he'd slept outdoors more often than he'd had a roof over his head, and he'd had few difficulties.

He glanced around at the surviving hunters. Only a couple had been uninjured by the fight, so Elijah had had his work cut out for him when it came to healing. Luckily, Soothe and Healing Rain were both incredibly efficient, and Touch of Nature was good at filling in the gaps. However, he couldn't help once again notice that his healing spells were far less effective than they'd once been. It took more casts to get the same results he'd once taken for granted.

Hopefully, he would get an upgrade sometime soon.

If he got the chance to enlist the services of a Librarian, he fully intended to get a complete spell list for his class. It would be useless after he reached the first threshold, but for now, it would be nice to know what he could expect. Would he get the chance to upgrade his spells like he had with Ancestral Circle? Or would he just keep getting more abilities? He already struggled to use all the spells he had available, so even if he wanted new toys with which to play, he recognized that more wasn't necessarily better. It would probably be more beneficial to focus on the spells he already had, empowering them so that they were even more useful.

Even if he didn't receive the opportunity to evolve his spells, Elijah still had another chance to strengthen them. His ongoing Core cultivation had continued to show results, and he suspected that it would only be a couple more months before he reached the point where he would need to make the final push. For that, he had his cultivation cave, which, according to his Locus, had grown even stronger than before he'd progressed to the Novice tier of Soul cultivation.

Still, even as he sat by that campfire, sharing small talk with Tömörbaatar, Elijah continued to cycle his core, pushing his boundaries with every rotation.

Eventually, though, the others retired for the night. In the morning, they would trek back to Khotont and report their failure. For his part, Elijah couldn't sleep. He was tired, but with his high attributes—and the addition of one of his berries—he had no trouble staying awake. Instead, as he watched over the camp, he continued to cycle his Core. More importantly, he thought about the boar.

It was a guardian.

He was certain of that much. However, when he'd asked the hunters about natural treasures, he'd gotten no information. There was a clear link between the power of a guardian and its treasure, and if something strong enough to need the protection of something like the unstoppable boar had been found, then the hunters would have heard about it.

So, there was likely a third party at work, though that information didn't help Elijah solve the problem. More, it brought to mind his judgment of the hunters who'd killed the bear near Norcastle. At the time, he'd considered it pointlessly cruel to have slaughtered the guardian. However, after seeing what had happened to the boar, he wasn't so sure. Would the bear have gone mad if he'd awoken to find his treasure gone? Perhaps. And in that case, maybe it was a mercy to have killed him.

In a perfect world, both would have been left alone, but Elijah knew that wasn't realistic. People craved power. In a lot of cases, they needed it to survive. And they would leave no stone unturned in the pursuit of that strength. It was human nature.

Elijah didn't know the solution. His instincts told him to protect natural treasures and their guardians, but he couldn't blame people for looking after their own needs. Perhaps the answer was that there was no one-size-fits-all solution and that he'd need to take each situation as it came.

For most of the night, he pondered the questions plaguing him, but by dawn, nothing had changed. So, he boiled some water before making some coffee. Using his newly enchanted French press for the first time yielded significant results:

You have consumed a Complex-grade beverage. The following benefits will be applied:
+5 Strength, Dexterity, Constitution, and Ethera. +10 Regeneration.
Duration: 37.1 hours.

At first, Elijah thought it was the same notification he'd received each time he drank a cup of his coffee. However, when his focus settled on the last line, he saw the benefit of Lars's work. The duration had increased to more than thirty-seven hours, which was half again as long as it had been before. So, while the benefits were the same—at least in terms of attributes—the fact that they lasted so much longer would be a great boon, especially in the Trial, where he knew he would have to make his supplies stretch a little further than normal.

By the time the hunters arose, Elijah had already finished his coffee and was breaking his fast on some rations he'd brought with him from Argos. The dried meat was tough and gamy, but it had been prepared by a real Cook, so it tasted better than most of what he could prepare for himself. Certainly, it was better than leftover horse.

After the sun rose, Tömörbaatar and the hunters efficiently broke camp, so only an hour later, they were already on their way back to the city. Most rode the remaining horses, but Elijah had no issues keeping up on foot. So, by midafternoon, they found themselves striding back into Khotont.

At first, people looked at them with no small degree of expectation. However, it only took a glance before they realized that the hunt had been unsuccessful. For his part, Tömörbaatar took the attention stoically, asking Elijah to accompany him to the town hall, which Tömörbaatar referred to as the zahiral ger. As it turned out, the building looked little different from any of the others in the city, save that it was slightly larger and stood at five stories tall.

It was there that the hunter reported the results of their expedition to a council made up of three women and two men. They took the news calmly, but when Tömörbaatar explained that he didn't think it was possible to kill the boar, they showed some desperation.

That's when Elijah spoke up. He said, "I think I might have a solution, but I'm not sure if it'll work or not."

That much was true. Elijah had pondered the issue for hours, and though he thought his plan would work, there were no guarantees that he'd read the situation correctly. Still, as he laid out the details of his idea, it was met with some degree of enthusiasm. He ended the explanation with, "And that's pretty much it. I think it will work, but there are no guarantees."

"Do you truly believe you can do this? An Explorer?" one of the women asked. She was old. Probably close to seventy, if Elijah had to guess, with white hair and a face creased with wrinkles.

"Oh. Sorry," Elijah said, remembering he'd left his Ring of Anonymity active. The moment he'd chosen to heal the hunters, he'd thrown aside any notion of keeping his disguise. So, he deactivated it. "My real name is Elijah Hart, and I'm a Druid. You might see my name on the power rankings. Sorry about the deception, but I've found that it's a lot easier to keep my identity secret when I'm traveling."

There was a gasp, but after a couple of them used their skills to identify him, they accepted that his identity was genuine. It helped that Tömörbaatar vouched for his abilities, recounting how he'd already saved lives with his healing spells.

In the end, though, Elijah didn't need their permission or help. His plan only relied on his own abilities. Finally, he asked if there was anyone in town that needed healing. He had ethera to spare, and he'd chosen to balance some of the terrible things he'd done with helping people. And it was rare that nobody needed healing.

"Khotont has been blessed with a number of Healers, but if you would like to take some of that burden, you may do so in our jail," she said. "There are a few dursamj there that most of our people avoid."

Elijah interpreted that word as "outcast," but there seemed to be other connotations there, as well. However, the translation feature that came with the system sometimes lacked nuance, so it didn't give him a firm idea of what to expect. Given that she had used the word to refer to prisoners connected some dots, though.

In any case, Elijah didn't care about social status. So, he agreed to heal the prisoners and was quickly escorted to another nearby building. There, he found a few strong-looking guards who let him and Tömörbaatar inside.

The first thing Elijah noticed was the antiseptic smell. It reminded him of a hospital, where all sorts of horrible odors were covered up by harsh cleaners. The floors were cheap white tile, and the walls were made of painted cinder blocks. But at least everything was clean.

If he was honest with himself, Elijah had expected much worse conditions, but maybe that was his bias showing itself. Regardless, he was soon led down a hall and to the first holding cell. There, he announced his intentions before summoning Healing Rain, which covered the entire cell. The prisoners were morose, but they didn't look as if they'd been ill-treated, though quite a few seemed to be suffering from one ailment or another. Elijah's spell took care of that, and when it completed, he moved on to the next, where he repeated the cast.

Finally, he came to the third and final cell, which only held one prisoner. And unlike the majority of people in the Mongolian town, this man was pale skinned, with thin blond hair and a short, slender frame. That's when Elijah remembered being told about another stranger that had come to town and racked up a gambling debt.

"Oh! Did the Conclave send you to rescue me?" the man asked, his voice brimming with hope. Elijah also heard a German accent. "I assure you, I have executed my duties faithfully! This is just a little hiccup, I swear it."

"Conclave? What's that?" Elijah asked. "And what's your name?"

The man deflated. "Ah. I see. Just leave me here to rot, then. I'll not be bullied!" he said.

"I'm not here to bully you. I'm here to heal you."

"I have no ailments," he said. "But my name is Wilhelm. Perhaps we can come to some accommodation? I can guarantee that, if you help me, the Conclave will pay you back tenfold!"

"Wilhelm, huh?" Elijah echoed. "Well, Will—I've got a lot on my plate here. But if you're still around when I get done with my current task, I just might take you up on that."

Having said what he needed to say, Elijah let the guard escort him back outside. As much as the mention of a Conclave intrigued him, he had no intention of letting himself get distracted. He had a boar to deal with, after all.

67

THE BOAR

That guy's not going to get executed or anything, is he?" asked Elijah, sitting at one of the long tables in the communal dining area. After his first visit, he'd learned that the locals referred to it as zuushny gazar, which fittingly translated to "eating place." However, he'd also heard the word *xopxop* thrown around, which he'd also learned referred to more of a dining experience rather than a place. In this case, the experience centered around cooking various meats—usually involving hot stones—in a communal setting. That description certainly fit what Elijah had experienced, though he was still a little fuzzy about the details.

How the system's translation feature worked was still a bit of a mystery. In some cases, it would translate everything, but in others, it was quite selective, allowing for certain words to come through. The only thing Elijah could think was that the terms it left untranslated had some sort of cultural significance beyond the English meaning, though he wouldn't have been surprised if there was more to it than that. Regardless, he'd resolved to simply take things as they went.

"The gambler? No," replied Tömörbaatar as he speared a hunk of meat with his dagger and dragged it out of the central platter. He took a huge bite, adding, "He will likely be required to work off his debt. It is a shame his class is not physically gifted, or he would be capable of paying it off much more quickly."

"How much does he owe?" asked Elijah. His initial thought was to simply break the man out—assuming his plan with the boar was successful—but that was needlessly confrontational. Instead, he wondered if he could pay the man's debts, then recoup that investment—and then some—when his so-called Conclave paid him back "tenfold." He knew there was risk in that, but something about the pasty man told Elijah that he was important. Or that he could be, given the right circumstances. Plus, he wanted to know more about the organization to which he belonged.

"No more than a gold," Tömörbaatar answered. "Enough to matter, but not enough to kill over. For most people."

Elijah nodded and ate his meal. Upon leaving the jail, he'd fully intended to head out right then, but he'd been persuaded by the grateful hunter to join him for a meal. Mostly, the supper was composed of meat, but there were a few vegetables and mushrooms here and there. More importantly, it had clearly been prepared by someone with a cooking ability, which meant that it tasted much better than anything Elijah could prepare. Even with his new pan—which he still hadn't used—he would only be able to mimic the real thing. So, it truly didn't take much to convince him to share a meal with Tömörbaatar.

However, it wasn't long before he was stuffed, and after saying goodbye to his new friend, Elijah left the zuushny gazar behind. As he did, he caught a few stray glances that lingered a little longer than he would have preferred, but he knew that was because word of his class and level had already begun to spread. That was precisely the sort of attention he'd hoped to avoid, but that really hadn't been possible after what he'd done. Perhaps some people would have been slow on the uptake, but for anyone who was paying attention, his disguise would have been useless in the face of his abilities.

Regardless, after leaving the building behind, he joined the flow of pedestrians and horse-mounted residents as he made his way out of Khotont. The pace was glacial but consistent, so he made it to the gates before the sun had begun to dip toward the horizon. He got more looks—most of concern—as he separated from the parade of pedestrians, left the safety of the city behind, and set off into the grassland alone. After a couple of miles, when he was out of sight, he shifted into the Shape of the Sky and took to the air.

The hunters had seen his flight form, so it wouldn't be long before the entire city knew about the colorful reptilian shape. However, Elijah wasn't willing to flaunt his abilities. Rumors were one thing, but seeing it with their own two eyes would bring more attention than Elijah wanted to endure.

He glided through the air, reveling in the freedom flight gave him. In his other forms—even as a human—he could go most places without issue. But there was something about being capable of flight that felt less restrictive than anything else. In that form, with his wings outstretched, he felt that he could go anywhere, that he could do anything. At times, that freedom made it difficult to focus, but with a mission in mind, Elijah managed it all the same.

After a little less than an hour of flight, during which he kept an eye out for the boar, Elijah reached the site of his previous encounter. The town was no less ruined than when he'd left it behind, but there were a few areas where the destruction was far more recent. It would have been nice if Brand of the Stalker had remained active, but after he'd gotten a couple of miles away from the creature, it had deactivated. So, he followed the trail of destruction to the outer reaches of the town, where he found a distinct path through the grassland.

Mostly, the trail was characterized by trampled grass, but there were also areas where the boar had attacked the ground, ripping through the earth with its tusks and hooves. It was such pointless destruction, but ultimately, it was unsurprising. Elijah had already established that the boar was mad; that it would turn its ire on the prairie itself was well within Elijah's expectations.

Fortunately, that also resulted in an easily followed trail, so Elijah had no issues tracking the mad boar. Gradually, he covered the ground, marveling at how far the beast had gone in such a short amount of time. The miles melted beneath him until, at last, just as the sun had begun to peek over the horizon, he caught sight of the creature.

It had slowed down a little, but periodically, it would randomly charge in one direction, dip its head, and drag its tusks through the soft earth. In those cases, dirt and grass would erupt into a cloud dozens of feet high, and the beast would jerk around, looking this way and that before continuing on its way.

Each time that scene repeated, Elijah felt his heart break.

Certainly, the beast was powerful. And deadly. It needed to be stopped. Yet, seeing that its mind had been so thoroughly broken was nauseating. Even as he watched, Elijah's resolve to end the boar's suffering reestablished itself. He knew it needed to be done, and what's more, he suspected that he was the only person who could make it happen.

As a Druid, it was his responsibility.

However, he also knew that making good on that responsibility would not be easy. The creature was largely invulnerable. He had seen that the first time he'd attacked the beast. So, given that he couldn't even penetrate its hide—much less deal with its immense Strength—he'd had to get creative with his plans.

At first, he'd considered a trap. It was a simple enough idea, and he had a little experience with using traps against creatures more powerful than him. He'd employed that strategy in the Sea of Sorrows as well as against the horde of orcs that had assaulted Ironshore.

But he didn't believe he could build a trap the boar couldn't break out of. It might take the creature days or weeks to do so, but it would eventually dig its way out, putting him right back at square one. So, he considered the trap to be plan B. Hopefully, he wouldn't need it.

Plan A was a little different, and it hinged on his observations having been accurate. Or perhaps the assumptions that followed those observations. Whatever the case, because of the swirling ethera that surrounded the creature, Elijah suspected that its impenetrable hide wasn't the result of an incredibly high Constitution attribute. Certainly, the creature was naturally durable. But Elijah was banking the viability of plan A on the suspicion that much of its invulnerability was based on a skill.

And the thing about skills was that they needed fuel. Whether it consumed ethera or stamina, no ability was free. That was an unassailable fact of the multiverse, and one Elijah was reminded of every time he used Iron Scales. As his attributes increased, he could use the ability more often, but even with that increased power, there were limits. He was banking on the boar's ability functioning according to the same paradigm.

But he couldn't just slap the creature with one of his spells, then lead it on a merry chase. The moment the creature realized that it wasn't in any danger, it would stop using the ability and recover its stamina or ethera. No—Elijah needed to put it in a heightened state.

Fortunately, he had the perfect ability to do just that:

Ability: Debilitating Roar	Let out an enraged bellow that sends all nearby targets fleeing in fear, decreasing their damage by 15%. Increases caster's foot speed by 10%. Only usable when caster is under the influence of Shape of the Guardian. Duration based on Ethera attribute. Current duration: 9.2 seconds. Resistance based on target's Constitution attribute.

When he'd first gotten the skill, Elijah had been a little disappointed with it. However, after using it in Seattle, he'd come around to how useful it was. And in his current situation, he knew it would be ideal.

Assuming that it took hold, at least.

If it did, Elijah would only need to keep the effect active—which would necessitate using quite a lot of his own stamina—until the monster ran out of fuel. Then, it would be vulnerable.

With that plan in mind, Elijah circled until the boar started attacking a lonely tree in the middle of the plain. It rammed the thing, over and over without any hesitation between. Elijah saw his opportunity, so as he dropped from the sky, he shifted into his lamellar-ape form, hitting the ground only a few dozen feet away from the creature. His arrival didn't go unnoticed, and the boar whipped around. For a moment, it was like time slowed. Elijah saw madness in the beast's wild eyes. In the thick foam coating its mouth. In the tension in its every bunched muscle.

Then, the moment passed, and the boar's hooves dug into the soft soil, propelling it forward in a reckless charge. Elijah let out a bellow, embracing Debilitating Roar. The sound hit the creature like a sledgehammer, and it skidded to a stop before its charge could truly begin.

Elijah beat his chest, then charged the beast. For a moment, it looked confused, but only a second after the effects of the ability hit it, the boar whipped around and fled. It moved with the jittery abruptness of a terrified animal, and with its clearly superior Strength, it could cover some serious ground.

Fortunately, Elijah's hesitation to follow only lasted an instant before he loped forward in pursuit. Even more thankfully, the ability included an increase to his foot speed, which was more than valuable against the hard-charging beast. Seven seconds after he'd used the ability the first time, Elijah let loose with another instance of the ability. As he did, he felt himself weaken by a minuscule amount. That was his stamina draining away. It was barely noticeable, but he knew the exhaustible, yet hidden resource was the key to whether or not his plan would work. If his store of stamina held up, then he would win. If not, then he'd be forced to retreat.

So, Elijah remained hot on the creature's heels, bellowing his ability every seven or eight seconds. Eventually, he realized that he wouldn't be capable of keeping it up if he used it that often, so he started to experiment. While the ability-induced fear only lasted a little more than nine seconds, it still took longer for the echoes to fade. For a sane and sapient enemy, it wouldn't have mattered. They would see through it. But with the mad boar? It could scarcely distinguish reality, much less whether its fear was genuine or not. So, even after Elijah let the ability fade, the creature continued to flee, flaring its own protective ability the whole time.

It was a domino effect. Every instance of Debilitating Roar sent it careening further into fearful madness. It went on for hours, and eventually, Elijah only had to reapply the effect every ten minutes or so. The boar's madness took care of the rest.

Then, suddenly, when most of the day was gone, the ethera swirling around the beast winked out. A few steps later, it collapsed in a cloud of dust. The sudden stop shocked Elijah, and he very nearly ran into the fallen boar. Yet, he stopped just in time.

As he circled around, the creature continued to shudder, though it was entirely incapable of rising. It had run itself to exhaustion.

Elijah's plan had worked.

Now, he only needed to follow through with the final act.

68

A DRUID'S DUTY

The mighty boar lay on its side, its chest heaving with panic. Eyes bigger than volleyballs twitched back and forth, evidence of the animal's ongoing terror. Foam collected at the corner of its gaping mouth as it hyperventilated, letting out rumbling snorts with every breath. Laying his hand on the enormous beast's side, Elijah felt its knotted and cramped muscles.

But within the oppressive grip of exhaustion, it couldn't move more than a few inches. Every second or two, tiny collections of diffuse ethera swirled as it attempted to reactivate its protective ability. But there wasn't enough to fuel the skill. That had always been the plan, but there was a distinct difference between what he'd imagined and what he now saw before him.

The terrified and terrifying beast was helpless.

And when Elijah looked at it, he couldn't prevent tears from gathering at the corners of his eyes as his thoughts surrendered to pity and guilt. The first because of how far the creature had fallen. It wasn't difficult to imagine that, before it had lost its treasure, the guardian had been a noble and mighty protector not unlike the panther that had saved Elijah's life so many times. That one event could send it careening into madness, subverting its nature so thoroughly that it was indistinguishable from a monster, was horrifying.

It was also a grim reminder of Elijah's own past.

He hadn't been so different after discovering his sister's death. He'd slaughtered hundreds. Perhaps thousands. And he didn't even have the excuse of madness. He had been fully in control. Or he should have been. Yet, he'd let his anger and grief drive him forward until he became a monster in human—or draconic, given the nature of his transformative shapes—form.

Would someone have been justified in putting him out of his misery?

Maybe. Valoria was a cesspool of all the worst facets of humanity, but did that give him the right to slaughter so many? He wasn't sure. And that retrospective uncertainty fueled his doubts, which had given way to shame. He was too strong to give in to those sorts of impulses. He needed to be better. Under more control. Otherwise, he would end up just like the boar.

The shame of his past mingled with the guilt he felt for effectively torturing the beast before him. Elijah didn't know what people felt under the influence of Debilitating Roar. Was it a formless fear? Or was it more specific? Did it dredge up memories? Or was it completely arcane in nature? He wasn't sure, but regardless of how it presented its effects, the ability had pushed the boar into a place of undiluted terror so potent that, in trying to escape, it had run itself to exhaustion.

He sighed.

There was nothing else to be done. There hadn't been much of a choice. If the beast had been allowed to continue its rampage, thousands of people would have died. What's more, animals—be they guardians, monsters, or normal beasts—could gain experience, as well. So, with every death, it would have grown stronger, making it even more invulnerable.

On top of that, putting the boar out of its misery was the right thing to do. It was necessary. It was just.

It was mercy.

Yet, it was a joyless act. A necessary but repulsive action that could not be avoided.

"I'm sorry it had to be this way," he said. The creature flinched at the sound of his words, but it was too exhausted to do more than tremble a bit. Still, Elijah tensed, as well, ready to spring away at the first sign of recovery.

He knew he was on a timer. With every passing moment, the boar would recover some of its energy. But more than that, Elijah didn't want to prolong the beast's suffering any longer than necessary. So, without further hesitation, he drew the knife he'd gotten from Lars and leaped upon the creature's shoulder. The weapon had been enchanted with a Hunter's skill that was supposed to make it better for dressing animals. Elijah hoped that would be enough to allow it to get through the beast's thick hide.

When he reached the boar's thick neck, Elijah knelt. And without further delay, he reared back and plunged the blade into the creature's bristly hide. It parted the skin but only went an inch deep. That was within Elijah's expectations, and he once again stabbed into the same wound. The dagger bit a little deeper this time, eliciting a trickle of blood. That trickle became a river with the next stab, though Elijah knew it was nothing compared to what flowed through the beast's enormous body. So, he kept at it.

The process was not pretty.

Nor was it heroic.

It was messy and traumatizing, eliciting a stream of tears and coating Elijah in dark-red blood. Yet, he continued. Even if he wanted to, he couldn't stop. Once begun, he had no choice but to keep going. And he did. Over and over, he hacked into the creature's neck until, at last, he found an artery. It spurted pressurized blood in a fountain of red, the intensity of the flood increasing with each pump of the boar's enormous heart.

Only then did Elijah stop.

The mighty boar was already dead. It just hadn't realized it yet. Elijah stood, his cheeks stained with blood and tears.

Even then, he could have saved the beast. A few casts of Touch of Nature, and the bleeding would slow. He could have healed the rest of the damage, though he suspected it would take almost all his ethera. And for a brief moment, he considered it. Perhaps he could heal its mind, too. Maybe he could banish the madness that had gripped it.

But he knew that was a pipe dream.

The beast was too far gone. And the price of failure was too high.

So, climbing down, he circled the boar until he reached its head. Once there, he laid his hand between its eyes and flared One with Nature. Just as had happened with the panther, he formed a connection with the beast. However, unlike the island's guardian, the boar's thoughts—which Elijah could only feel in the form of impressions—had been shattered into a million pieces. None of them were pleasant. Instead, there was loss. Confusion. Fear that had nothing to do with Debilitating Roar. And anger. It all coalesced into something Elijah could only call madness.

There would be no recovery for this beast. Touching its mind was just confirmation of what he had known from the very beginning. But Elijah still maintained the connection, trying to convey calm thoughts to the animal as blood gushed from the wound in its neck.

"It's going to be alright," he said in a soothing voice. "It's over. You can rest now."

The boar didn't hear him. It was too far gone, its mind too broken. The words were as much for Elijah's benefit as to comfort the beast. Minutes passed, and the creature's stamina returned enough for it to briefly resume its shielding ability. However, it lasted only a few moments, and it did nothing for the continued blood loss.

Finally, after half an hour, the boar's eyes glazed over. Its muscles went slack, and its jaw fell open. At last, its struggle was over.

With dried boar's blood covering him, Elijah collapsed to the trampled grassland and spent the next few minutes just staring at the ground. He'd killed so often that he thought himself accustomed to taking lives. That was true in the heat of battle, but executing the boar was different. He knew it would stick with him for years to come.

After a little while, Elijah pushed himself back to his feet and steeled himself for the next step in the process. The boar was the highest-level creature he'd ever seen, which meant that it was a treasure trove of usable materials. Its meat alone was enough to feed a village for months, and that was saying nothing for its durable hide, dense bones, and useful organs.

Some people might've considered harvesting the animal to be distasteful, but Elijah saw it as the height of respect. The Mongolian hunters had reaffirmed that when they'd done the same with their fallen horses. Killing a creature and not using it was wasteful. Honoring the beast by putting its body to use was better.

So, armed with his skinning knife, Elijah went to work. Now that the boar was dead, its hide was a little easier to cut, though he wasn't certain if that was because the boar's Constitution was less efficacious or if the knife, being put to its intended use, was more effective. Either way, easier didn't mean easy, and skinning the beast proved to be the work of an entire day.

Then, he started to butcher the body. Thankfully, Elijah had plenty of experience processing various animals, so his work was efficient, with large hunks of meat being piled onto the overturned hide. Still, the beast was so large that the process took another day. Being in the middle of winter, it was well below freezing, so there was no chance of spoilage.

Next came the bones. Elijah didn't take all of those. Instead, he only took the largest pieces. He didn't know what good they would do, but he felt certain that a crafter like Carmen could make use of the powerfully dense material. And finally, Elijah took the brains and fat.

The process had taken nearly four days, but at last, he was finished. The carcass that was left was a pitiful thing. There was still some meat left. The same was true of some of the less useful organs.

Looking upon it once again made Elijah's eyes water, but he quickly dried them. The deed was finished, and there was nothing else to be done. So, he tied the hide into a huge sack he could carry—the bundle was comically large, but it didn't weigh as much as some of the stones he'd toted. Then, Elijah stripped off his soiled clothes, sprinkled them with some cleansing powder, and set them aside. After that, he summoned Healing Rain and, using his soap, washed the dried blood away.

The shower was cathartic, though without his Cloak of the Iron Bear, he keenly felt the bite of the winter morning. That felt appropriate, as well, almost as if he didn't deserve comfort after such a distasteful act. The idea that he needed to endure a penance was ridiculous. He'd only done what was necessary. Yet, reason and emotions rarely mixed, so he reveled in his tiny punishment.

He didn't wallow in it, though, and once he was clean, Elijah gathered his bundle and heaved the burden upon his back. It was almost enough to overbalance him, but he managed it well enough, using some rope he had in his satchel to facilitate it. Then, he began the long walk back to Khotont.

As he did, he finally allowed himself to acknowledge his reward for killing such a powerful beast.

Congratulations! You have reached level eighty-seven. Attribute points allocated according to your class.

He'd gained three levels, which was confirmation of the boar's might. However, despite the fact that those levels had allowed him to reclaim his place at the top of the power rankings—one level higher than Oscar Ramirez—he had difficulty taking joy in his progress. To distract himself from his guilt, Elijah looked at his status:

Name	Elijah Hart		
Level	87		
Archetype	Druid		
Class	Animist		
Specialization	N/A		
Alignment	N/A		
Strength	131 (93)		
Dexterity	113 (87)		
Constitution	99 (91)		
Ethera	99 (96)		
Regeneration	94 (91)		
Attunement	Nature		
Cultivation Stage: Cultivator			
Body	Core	Mind	Soul
Stone	Hatchling	Quartz	Novice

With his gear and buffs, Elijah's attributes had gotten pretty impressive. However, he was a little annoyed that his Ethera attribute was only one point from reaching triple digits. That was because only one piece of his equipment—the Wolf Totem he'd looted from Thor—added any extra points. By comparison, the rest of his attributes were inflated by buffs and equipment.

He could further enhance those with his forms, but at present, that was unnecessary. So, he remained in his human shape as he trudged across the prairie.

As satisfied as he was with his improved attributes, Elijah was more concerned with the other benefit of passing level eighty-five. He'd gained another opportunity to upgrade an ability, and it was one he'd been waiting on for quite some time.

69

A QUESTION OF PRIORITIES

The winter sun hung high in the expansive blue sky, unobscured by even the wisp of a cloud. A hawk cried overhead, and a cold breeze cut across the grasslands. Elijah didn't feel it. Even without his Cloak of the Iron Bear, which protected him from the cold, he wouldn't have paid much attention to his surroundings. Instead, the whole of his focus was on the notification he'd received after killing the guardian boar. Not only had he reached level eighty-seven, but he'd also gained the opportunity to evolve one of his spells.

He'd done so once before, so he'd been looking forward to upgrading the rest of his spell book. Still, it wasn't as simple as gaining more power. It would be that. But it also represented a choice, and one that he knew would prove difficult. It was that decision that occupied the bulk of his attention. He focused on the notification:

Congratulations! You have achieved the requirements for the evolution of the spell Touch of Nature. Please choose a path:		
Mother's Embrace	Nature's Bloom	Spreading Roots
Through the Mother's embrace, heal yourself far more efficiently than you heal others.	Each cast will plant the seed of regrowth. When that seed sprouts, additional healing will follow.	Each cast will cause an ethereal root to spread to an ally, casting a wide net of rejuvenation.

The options seemed pretty straightforward to Elijah. The first choice would make Touch of Nature more powerful when he cast it on himself, while Nature's Bloom and Spreading Roots would give his heal extra effects. In the case of Nature's Bloom, it seemed like each heal would have a secondary heal associated with it. By contrast, Spreading Roots would have an area-of-effect component.

The question was what sort of power increase he should expect. Each evolution meant that the primary effect of the spell would grow stronger. Every guide he'd read was adamant about that. However, the additional effects were based on his Legacy, which was something of a record of his actions.

Some people would only receive one choice, and in those cases, it was almost always just a mundane increase in power. Often, the name of the spell didn't even change, and it gained no extra effects. Three choices was the maximum number the system would offer, which meant that Elijah had been doing something right in his progression. He'd never made choices based on augmenting his Legacy—in fact, he'd never even heard the word, at least in reference to the system, until quite recently—but it seemed that he'd done so anyway.

Regardless, he had an interesting choice before him.

The first option was clearly the best, so long as he only considered his own needs. Having a potent self-heal would help him survive against tough opponents. Elijah only had to think about Guardian's Renewal to recognize that as a fact. However, it felt wrong to only think of himself. What would happen if Miguel was injured and, because he'd taken Mother's Embrace over the other two options, he perished? What about Carmen or Nerthus? The others he cared about?

He would be emotionally destroyed.

Was a better chance at survival the right decision? Maybe. Then again, without knowing exactly what the difference was, he couldn't be certain. What if it was only ten percent better than the other two? Logic suggested that, because it was more limited, it would be far better, but he simply couldn't be sure.

The other two choices were assuredly better for healing other people, but in different ways. The second, called Nature's Bloom, seemed to specialize in healing a single target, while the third's description implied that it would be good for a large group.

As Elijah trudged through the plains, he discarded the third option. He had yet to encounter a situation where he needed to heal a large group of people quickly. Normally, when he was responsible for that kind of healing, there was no time limit. So, as much as he liked the idea behind the Spreading Roots evolution, he didn't see very many situations where it would be required.

That left the first two.

Mother's Embrace was more than tempting. Normally, he fought alone, and an ability to heal himself more quickly was very attractive. However, he'd survived as long as he had with the old version of Touch of Nature, hadn't he? And he had Guardian's Renewal to pick up the slack.

Besides, couldn't Nature's Bloom serve a similar function, but without the drawback of only really helping himself? Looking at it completely logically—or from his perspective, at least—Elijah's choice seemed clear. After all, his archetype—and to a lesser extent his class—was based on versatility. So, pigeonholing himself by limiting his options was antithetical to the idea behind his archetype.

Plus, he kept thinking of situations where the lives of his loved ones might hinge on his ability to heal them, and in those cases, failure simply wasn't an option. He'd rather put himself in a little more danger than fall short when his family or friends needed him most.

So, without further hesitation, he made his decision. When he chose Nature's Bloom, another notification appeared before his inner eye:

Congratulations! You have chosen to evolve Touch of Nature into Nature's Bloom. Complete the following quest to finalize the evolution:

Accomplish three (3) Feats of Strength (Complete)
Heal one thousand (1,000) people (Complete)
Self-heal from the edge of death (Complete)

Elijah felt the quest complete, which was something of a surprise. Obviously, his previous actions had already satisfied the requirements, which shouldn't have been that shocking. Yet, he had expected to have at least one task to complete, much as he had when he'd evolved Ancestral Circle into Roots of the World Tree. In any case, he checked the new spell's description:

Spell: Nature's Bloom	Harness the power of nature to heal yourself or an ally. Upon the completion of the cast, plant the Seed of Renewal. After twenty seconds, the Seed of Renewal will sprout, resulting in another, less powerful heal. Relative potency of the Seed of Renewal is based on Ethera attribute. Current potency: 35.2% of original cast.

It was better than Elijah had hoped, especially if the base spell—even without the Seed of Renewal—had improved as much as he expected. He wouldn't know for sure until he tested it out, though. That made him a bit nervous—testing a new spell in a tense situation always left him wrought with anxiety—but he couldn't properly gauge the efficacy of the spell until he tried to heal some damage. Perhaps he should find some more people in town to test it on.

Or head back to Argos.

Regardless, Elijah was happy with his choice.

As he continued his trek, Elijah used his spell, but considering he was entirely undamaged, it was difficult to determine its potency. It did help to stave off his fatigue, so that was helpful.

It was near sunset when Khotont came into view, and by the time he reached the formerly Mongolian city, darkness had fallen. Still, he was allowed through the gap in the berm, which actually took a bit of doing, since his bundle was so enormous. With the help of the two guards, he managed to squeeze through, though they were amazed that he was able to carry such a huge burden.

The streets were still packed with people, but the crowd of pedestrians parted easily before him. Some even recognized the hide for what it was, and gasps followed Elijah all the way to the zahiral ger, where he found that only a few administrators were present. When he announced that he had killed the boar that had terrorized the region for weeks, he got their attention. And when he asked to make a deal, someone hurried off to fetch a member of the council.

Soon enough, two council members arrived. Both bore the signs of enormous stress, but they still looked hardy enough. Elijah told them that he'd killed the boar, then proved it by setting his burden down and untying the rope that had kept the collection of meat, bones, and other pieces of the boar together. Thankfully, the cold climate had kept it all preserved.

"I can't use all this meat," he said. "Nor do I want all the bones. So, here's what I'm thinking. I'll take what I want, then you can buy the rest."

Elijah had done a little window shopping the last time he'd been in town, so he knew roughly what that much high-quality meat would be worth. The bones, though, were a mystery, so he decided to treat those like other natural resources he'd seen in his travels. Bone was probably not quite as popular of a material for creating weapons as high-grade metal, but given the power of the boar, it would be very useful for the right crafters.

The negotiation went far better than Elijah expected, and he ended up accepting sixty gold for the materials. In addition, they'd chosen to throw in a bag where he could store his portion of the meat and brains.

"It will keep everything fresh for at least a month," the councilman said. "Up to five hundred pounds. After that, the bag will be no more useful than a normal bag of its size."

"Thanks," Elijah answered. It clearly worked similarly to the bags he'd used before the orc invasion, so he was familiar enough with what to expect.

"Do you need someone to prepare the hide? We have a couple of good Leatherworkers here," the other councilwoman said. She was the same older woman Elijah had seen the first time. "Tsas is nearly strong enough to reach the power rankings."

That was true of half the population, it seemed. There were so many people on the verge of reaching the ladder that the distinction only meant that they were competent. Still, that meant that this Tsas—which the system translated to mean "snow"—was a viable option for his project. However, Elijah intended to prepare the hide himself, much as he had with the bear hide that had become his Cloak of the Iron Bear.

"I'll keep that in mind," he said. "I would also like to free the gambler in your custody."

That decision wasn't made on a whim. Elijah wanted to know more about the man's organization. Was it a powerful group? Or was it only the possessor of an ostentatious name? He intended to find out.

"That . . . can be arranged," she agreed. Likely, her quick agreement meant that he'd accepted less than the meat and bones were worth, but Elijah couldn't take them all with him. So, he'd resolved to only take the best pieces, including most of the fat, the choicest cuts of meat, and the most intact bones.

And, of course, the hide, which was the most useful part for him.

In any case, once the deal was done, he accepted a transfer to his folio, and someone fetched the pack that would keep his portion of the meat fresh. After that, he supervised the loading of the pack while a small army of workers descended upon the rest of the pile of pork.

They'd finished loading it in only a few minutes, and Elijah started rolling the hide up. It only barely fit into his Ghoul-Hide Satchel, but that was alright. He intended to take it back to the Grove soon enough.

Finally, the gambler—Wilhelm—arrived. Elijah shoved the Preservation Pack into the man's hands, saying, "Carry this. You're coming with me."

The pack was filled with five hundred pounds of meat and fat, and even though it cut that weight by a significant amount, it was still quite heavy. And Wilhelm clearly hadn't worked on his physical attributes. He tipped over, with the pack landing on his chest.

Elijah rolled his eyes. "Seriously? Come on, man . . ."

Wilhelm grunted, kicking his legs as he tried to push the pack aside. Elijah took pity on him, reaching down to lift the pack himself. When he was freed, Wilhelm gasped for breath, saying, "I . . . I do not have much Strength . . ."

"Obviously," Elijah muttered. "Follow me."

"Perhaps you didn't see, but night has already fallen," Wilhelm said, pushing himself to his feet. Though he held himself with prim propriety, his stay in the jail had clearly taken its toll. His clothes were torn and dirty, and judging by the odor wafting Elijah's way, his clothes weren't the only thing in need of a good cleaning. Finally, his thin blond hair was in disarray, and he bore a wisp of facial hair that made him look like a teenager who had yet to be taught to shave. "We should stay here. I know a fantastic inn next to the best gambling hall in town. And—"

"No. Come with me or you can go back to jail."

"Um . . ."

Elijah sighed. "I swear I won't hurt you. In fact, I just want to know more about your organization."

"Ah. I see," the man said. Then, he looked at the two guards who'd brought him to the zahiral ger, and his complexion paled. "Right. I think I will take you up on your generous offer."

"Great. Let's go," Elijah said. Then, he bade goodbye to the councilors before striding out of the building. Wilhelm hurried to follow.

70

LEY LINES AND CONCLAVES

The night was cold, and Wilhelm definitely wasn't dressed for it. So, Elijah only led him a couple of miles out of town before he stopped and made camp. There weren't many trees in the steppes, so wood was at a premium. That meant that he was forced to use alternate fuel for his fire. Thankfully, he'd stocked up on coal and dried grass during his previous stint in Khotont. And with his laser-pointer fire starter, it was a breeze to get a nice flame going. Elijah even dragged a couple of collapsable camp chairs from his satchel, completing the cozy scene.

"What happened to your clothes?" he asked as Wilhelm leaned close to the flickering flames. "I'm sure you didn't come here wearing that."

"I . . . I regret to say that I experienced a bit of bad luck," the German man said. His accent wasn't thick, but Elijah had recognized it all the same. "Ah, I miss my coat. It was Simple grade, you know. Waterproof. Very durable. Practically armor in and of itself. Now, who knows where it ended up? If they had just given me a little more credit, I could have won it back. I'm certain of it."

Elijah didn't miss the hint in that statement, but he had no intention of giving Wilhelm any money with which he could gamble. Clearly, the man had a problem, and Elijah wasn't going to contribute to it.

"Here," he said, reaching into his satchel and retrieving a set of warmer clothing and a thick coat he'd used before getting his Cloak of the Iron Bear. They'd been sitting in the bottom of his Ghoul-Hide Satchel since then, forgotten and unused. Wilhelm took the offering with no small degree of gratitude, layering the clothes over his own pitiful outfit—which consisted of a pair of thin pants, a cotton shirt, and a pair of cheap sandals. Elijah also gave him a blanket, admitting, "Probably should have stayed in town."

"It's not too late to return," ventured Wilhelm, clutching the blanket around his shoulders. It was cold enough that his breath misted with each word.

Elijah considered it for a moment, but then he shook his head. "I don't think that's a good idea," he stated. Part of it was that he just didn't like staying in cities anymore. It was a bit of an odd situation. Usually, he looked forward to visiting new settlements, and he loved the idea of sleeping in a bed or enjoying novel foods while meeting new people. However, he'd become increasingly uncomfortable with dense civilization, meaning that after the initial burst of excitement that came with new experiences, he usually found himself wanting to head back into the wilderness where he was much more comfortable.

But the other reason Elijah didn't want to go back into Khotont came down to Wilhelm. The man clearly had a potent gambling problem, and the city's residents were more than willing to take advantage of that. He'd even gambled away his clothing. So, it wasn't a big stretch to think that if Elijah let Wilhelm stay in Khotont for even a day more that the man would end up on the wrong side of more gambling debt.

Elijah didn't so much care about the man's well-being—outside of what normal human compassion dictated—but he did want to know about the so-called Conclave. And if it was an organization of import, perhaps he could garner some goodwill by helping their member.

There were a lot of assumptions at play, but it wasn't as if Elijah had gone out of his way to help the man. His release hadn't cost much, and Elijah hadn't really changed his plans to cater to Wilhelm's comfort. So, if the Conclave turned out to be a grandiose name for a weak organization—or worse, a fabrication on the part of Wilhelm—Elijah wouldn't have lost much.

Still, he was eager to know more, so he broached the subject, saying, "You mentioned a Conclave. What is it? And why are you in the steppes? Are you an Explorer?"

"Sort of," Wilhelm answered noncommittally. "Do you have any food? Water, perhaps? They didn't treat me poorly while I was in custody, but they were not terribly considerate of my needs, either."

Elijah sighed, then reached into his satchel and retrieved a strip of dried meat—it had come from one of the lizards around Seattle—as well as a large tin cup, into which he poured some water from his Endless Canteen. He handed both to the slight man, who took it with no small amount of gratitude. Wilhelm ate with gusto, tearing into his meal with a fervor that suggested he hadn't eaten well in days.

Maybe the Mongolians hadn't treated him as well as Elijah had expected.

Regardless, it wasn't long before Wilhelm answered—around a mouthful of food—saying, "The Conclave of Travel is an organization of Scholars, Sorcerers, and Tradesmen who have begun to delve into the secrets of long-distance travel via teleportation. I am one of the founding members, and my job is to find appropriate locations and establish anchors so that our Ethereal Artificers can create portal locations."

His explanation was laced with pride, and to Elijah, it seemed well deserved. There was already a teleportation feature inherent in the system of Branches scattered throughout the world—and the wider multiverse, he assumed—but those had a significant downside in that using them was incredibly expensive. Elijah was likely one of the richest individuals in the region, and the price of using Branch teleportation even a single time would have bankrupted him a hundred times over.

So, the notion that someone would have taken it upon themselves to create their own teleportation network was unsurprising. According to everything Elijah had learned, that was a common response to the terrible expense of the Branch's version. Still, Elijah hadn't expected it to have gotten very far. After all, Earth was still in its infancy, so he expected it to be quite some time before it caught up to the rest of the multiverse's level of progress.

"How does it work?" Elijah asked.

"How is your grasp of mathematics?" was Wilhelm's responding question. Then, with a grin, he launched into a mathematical explanation that reminded Elijah just how much he hated the subject.

Finally, after a few minutes of Wilhelm's excited recitation of advanced equations, Elijah cut him off, saying, "The basics. I don't need to know the numbers."

"Ah. Right. I sometimes forget that others don't share my . . . enthusiasm for mathematics," he said with an embarrassed smile. "In the simplest terms I can manage, we tap into the world's ambient ley lines. Some people call them roots of the World Tree, but we prefer a more neutral term. Regardless, Earth is covered in a dense web of these ley lines, and usually, the locations where they intersect are places of immense power. Normally, that's where natural treasures appear. My job is to find these places and create anchors so that our Ethereal Researchers and Tradesmen can travel to those locations and establish portal apparatuses."

For a moment, Elijah was speechless. The revelation that they were so close to creating a teleportation network was quite the bombshell, and it left Elijah with a host of questions. But one rose above them all, and he asked, "How many have you found? And how close are you to getting it up and running?"

"Ah, there's the rub," answered Wilhelm. "I'm one of the only people capable of traveling through the wilderness with any reliability. Of course, without my bicycle, I will move more slowly, but my feet were, as they say, made for walking. I will manage to find one at some point."

"One? So you haven't found an intersection yet?" Elijah asked with disappointment. Then, he continued, "You have a bike?"

"I do! My pride and joy. When I was young, I would make up all these apocalyptic scenarios in my head," the man eagerly explained, skipping over the first question. That told Elijah the answer. Wilhelm continued, "Zombie invasions and the like. I loved watching those sorts of films. But over time, I came to see all the mistakes they made. For instance, why does everyone go after automobiles? Why do they want to use motorized transport at all? Bicycles are very common, are suitable for all sorts of terrain, are relatively easy to maintain, and most importantly, only require an able-bodied person to operate. So, the moment the world changed, I found a bicycle shop and took my pick."

"I see," Elijah mused. It made sense, but for his part, Elijah would always prefer his own two feet—or wings, as it happened—over any wheeled contraption. "And that's why you can travel through the wilderness? Is it a special bike? Do you have a class that uses it or something?"

"Oh, no. It is just a normal, albeit high-quality bicycle. I'm an Explorer by archetype, and while my class incorporates some Scholar-type abilities, I remain an Explorer," Wilhelm said. "As I said, my job is to find the ley-line intersections. I couldn't do that very well if I had to worry about monster attacks every few kilometers."

"Have you found many intersections, then?" Elijah asked, returning to his previous question.

Wilhelm sighed. "Regrettably, no. The intersections are difficult for me to perceive, even with my abilities," he admitted. "I can only sense them from a maximum distance of a hundred meters. However, there is hope!" the man said, thrusting his finger into the air. "With every point of Ethera I gain, my detection radius increases by half a meter! I merely need to gain levels in order to accomplish my mission."

"Hmm," Elijah said, one facet of his Quartz Mind whirling with the possibilities. Suddenly, a few things clicked into place. Perhaps the feelings he got when he was looking for places to build his dolmens had nothing to do with the natural treasures he usually found, but rather, it was possible that he could sense the intersecting ley lines. His very first dolmen hadn't been built around a natural treasure, but he had still known precisely where to put it. So, after a moment, he asked, "What if I were to lead you to one of these intersections? What would that be worth to you?"

Wilhelm's eyes lit up. "You know of one?"

"I feel pretty confident that I can find something like you described. So, what kind of a reward are we looking at? Also, how long does it take for your Conclave to build the portal apparatus? You said you're the only one who can travel safely, right?"

"Ah . . . Well . . ."

"What?"

"When I left a few months ago, they had yet to crack the code, so to speak," Wilhelm sighed. "They were close. The math all adds up. However, we are missing the key to bring it all together. If we could see an actual teleportation, I feel certain that we could finish the project. The entire Conclave is working toward earning enough etherium to pay for a teleportation via the Branch so that we can study the process."

Elijah felt a smile spreading across his face. He didn't know if Roots of the World Tree functioned on the same principles as the Branches' teleportation feature, but he was willing to bet they were similar enough to give the Conclave some insight into their own research.

"And what if I could show you a teleportation? What about multiple? Could you do something then?" Elijah asked.

"Are you so wealthy?"

"I get by. But that's not really the point. Do you have the skills necessary to use that information?"

"I do not. But I do have equipment meant to record any spatial anomalies. I've yet to see one, but theoretically, they should exist. With that equipment . . . Ah . . . There's a problem."

"You gambled your equipment away."

"I did."

"I'll get it back," Elijah said. "Now, what do I get if I help you?"

"What do you want?"

Elijah narrowed his eyes. It was a good question. He was capable of traveling very quickly, but a teleportation network would still be very useful, especially considering that his dolmens were limited in number. Hopefully, that would increase when he upgraded his Core—which was still an ongoing process—but he didn't know by how much. If it was only one extra dolmen, then the teleportation network would be far more valuable to him than if it was ten more.

Regardless, it would be helpful.

"Free teleportation once you get your network up and running. Also, I want to dictate where the first apparatus goes," Elijah said. "For that, I'll get your equipment back, and I'll provide a demonstration of teleportation."

Of course, Wilhelm tried to negotiate, but he had no leverage at all. So, he ended up caving to Elijah's demands. With that, the deal was struck, and Elijah resolved to return to Khotont in the morning so he could recover Wilhelm's equipment. Then, he would get to work on holding up his end of the bargain.

71

MULTITASKING

Surprisingly, getting Wilhelm's equipment back wasn't difficult. It helped that word of Elijah's deeds had already spread throughout the city of Khotont, but he suspected that the gambling den let the items go mostly because they had no use for the esoteric equipment. It was bound to Wilhelm, so even if someone else could figure out what it did, no one else could even use the pieces—at least until he was dead. Because of that, Elijah only had to pay a couple of silver etherium to obtain the bundle of items. He also recovered the Explorer's bicycle, which cost a few more coins.

The whole ordeal was completed while Wilhelm slept near the fire. To ensure the man's safety, Elijah had deployed the tent he'd gotten from Lars, and when he got back, he was reassured to find that it had worked as advertised. Only then did Elijah climb inside and allow himself a little rest. He could keep going for quite some time without eating or sleeping, but it was never comfortable. So, the night's rest—even if it was only for a few hours—was definitely beneficial.

The next morning, Elijah awoke just after dawn and quickly boiled some water for his daily cup of coffee. He had no intention of sharing with Wilhelm, though. Coffee was a limited resource, and Elijah knew he'd need the buff it provided when he participated in the Trial of Primacy. Perhaps there would be another harvest before it began, but until he was certain, he intended to preserve his store as much as possible.

Thankfully, he finished the cup before Wilhelm even awoke, so there were no awkward conversations about hospitality. When the Explorer finally did wake up, he was more than surprised to find that his equipment—and, more important to him, his bicycle—was back. He thanked Elijah profusely, and soon enough, they broke camp, smothered the fire, and set off across the prairie.

As he had done outside Argos when he was searching for an appropriate place to build his first dolmen, Elijah followed his instincts. He couldn't perceive ley lines, but he could feel the subtle variations in ambient ethera well enough that, at least subconsciously, he stood a good chance of finding the intersections. Still, it took almost the entire day before he felt something—just a twinge—that guided him toward the east. After that, it was only one more day before he reached the confluence of energy that came from intersecting ley lines.

Or the World Tree's roots, as he preferred to think of them.

"What does your skill tell you?" Elijah asked, glancing at Wilhelm, who'd been riding his bicycle the whole time.

The Explorer closed his eyes, clearly focusing as he said, "This is close. Not ideal, but . . . it is worth marking."

"No."

"What?"

"Not here. I'll help you find another spot," Elijah said. "This one's mine."

"I don't understand," Wilhelm admitted.

"You will."

While it might make some sense for Wilhelm to mark the spot and move on, Elijah had other plans for the location. It might not be strong enough for the Conclave's purposes, but for Elijah, it was more than adequate to power one of his dolmens. And while it was a bit frustrating that it would leave him with only one more potential dolmen—at least until he upgraded his Core—it would give him the ability to bypass the swamp and access Khotont, which was the largest settlement in the expansive steppes.

Hopefully, he wouldn't regret it.

After explaining what he intended to do, he shifted into the Shape of the Sky—which garnered quite a bit of shock from Wilhelm—then set off in search of appropriate materials for the structures. At first, he worried that there would be nothing available. After all, the region wasn't particularly rocky. However, he only had to fly south for a few hours before the territory became a bit hillier. It wasn't a huge change, but it wasn't long after that that Elijah found a lonely butte formation that towered over the surrounding area. Upon further inspection, he found that it was composed of sandstone, limestone, and some sort of igneous rock he didn't recognize.

"Perfect," Elijah said, having shifted back to his human form. He ran a hand along the wall of limestone. It wasn't a high-grade material like the dragonstone, but he didn't need it to be, either. The dolmens drew their power from the ley lines, so the materials were far less of a factor than with other important structures. So, while it was mundane, limestone was indeed perfect for his purposes.

So, he got to work quarrying appropriately sized blocks. Fortunately, it was a far less difficult process than it had been with the dragonstone, so it only took a couple of days—during which he periodically returned to the campsite to check on Wilhelm, who was perfectly content to monitor the ley-line intersection with his equipment. Meanwhile, Elijah quarried the stone he needed, then proceeded to carry it across the plain.

That took a further few days, but that couldn't be helped. The distance between the intended dolmen site and the butte formation was close to a hundred miles, so even with Elijah's travel speed, which was enhanced by Essence of the Wolf, he could only cover the ground so quickly. Thankfully, as he could carry enough limestone for two pieces at a time, he only needed to make fifteen trips.

"How does this work, exactly?" asked Wilhelm once all the stones had been gathered.

Elijah told him, emphasizing that none of it would function properly without his skill. "But the structure of the dolmen affects the quality, though I'm not sure what the result will be," he admitted. "I haven't seen any changes to how my spell works."

"Perhaps it will be part of your Legacy. Or maybe it is improving, but at too slow of a rate for you to observe without specialized equipment," Wilhelm suggested.

Elijah could already see that the Explorer wanted to start running experiments. Apparently, the man had a background as a scientist, though he was a little cagey about precisely what field of study. Elijah could have probably pushed, but he chose not to. If Wilhelm wanted to reveal details about his past, then he had the right to do so on his own schedule.

Regardless, Elijah quickly moved to the next stage of his plan, which had nothing to do with the dolmen. Instead, he intended to multitask by preparing the boar's hide to the best of his abilities. Ideally, he would do so in his Grove, where the ambient ethera was much higher, but he didn't want to take the extra couple of weeks that would require. Hopefully, flooding the area with One with Nature, Healing Rain, and Nature's Bounty would suffice.

So, flaring all three skills, Elijah set about fleshing the enormous hide. The boar had been huge, so the hide was nearly thirty feet wide and about half again as long. That meant that working with the piece was extremely time-consuming and more than a little taxing. Thankfully, Elijah's endurance was nearly inexhaustible, and he filled the time with working on his Core cultivation, as well.

It took an entire day of strenuous work to complete the task of stripping the excess fat, flesh, and membrane from the hide, but when he was done, he felt quite satisfied. The next step was salting the hide in order to dry it out. Fortunately, Elijah had thought ahead and purchased quite a lot of salt in his most recent trip back to Khotont. He put it to good use, generously covering the underside of the piece. He knew that it would take a few days for the salt to dry out the hide, so when he'd finished with that step, he shifted his attention back to the dolmen.

Elijah fell into the work, roughly carving the intended shapes. He went with a cuboid shape, with the heel stones being about ten feet tall and four feet wide. The capstones were a little narrower, but at least as long. By the time Elijah had finished carving the rough shapes, three days had passed, and the boar's hide was completely dry.

So, leaving the dolmen's components behind, he started on the next step, which was to remove the hair. With the bear hide, he hadn't bothered, but for the boar hide, it was necessary for what he intended. Thankfully, he had sufficient knowledge to manage it well enough. Traditionally, soaking the hide in urine was how people loosened the hair from hides, but for a hide so large, that just wasn't possible. So, he chose to employ a slightly more modern approach and used some of his discarded limestone to create lime. Doing so required him to heat the rock to an incredibly high temperature, then mix it with water. That necessitated another trip back to Khotont so he could buy a kiln.

Armed with that, the process went off without a hitch, and he soon had enough lime to do the job. So, he mixed the substance with water, then soaked the hide in a large basin he'd dug. It wasn't perfect, but it worked well enough for Elijah's purposes.

While the hide soaked, he went back to the dolmen, arranging the roughly carved stones into a circle he meticulously laid out. As he did so, he paid attention to the ambient flow of ethera, and he was happy to see that it adjusted to the new structure, flowing in and around it. That inspection told him that the layout wasn't perfect, though, so he spent an extra day arranging the stones in such a way that wouldn't impede the flow of ethera. Unsurprisingly, that meant that the dolmen was a perfect circle.

By that point, the lime solution had done its work loosening the tough hairs, allowing Elijah to remove them. It was monotonous work, but he managed it all the same. And after another day's worth of work, he had finished.

That was when the time came to actually tan the hide.

Using the same method he'd used with the bear skin that had become his Cloak of the Iron Bear, Elijah concocted the tanning solution using the boar's brains and some mineral oil he had acquired in Khotont. As before, it was a tedious process, made even more so by the sheer size of the hide. He'd thought about cutting it to pieces and tanning each one individually, but he felt that would compromise the integrity of the finished product. Perhaps he was only imagining it, but he didn't want to take any chances.

In any case, once he'd applied a generous coating to the huge piece of leather, he went back to the dolmen and started to refine the shapes. Not only did they need to be as perfect as he could manage, but he also intended to add a host of embellishments that, when he got to that step, took the form of relief carvings of the mighty boar.

Back and forth Elijah went, reapplying the tanning solution to the hide and carving the dolmen's components until, at last, he'd finished. Overall, it had taken him over two weeks to complete the entire project, but he felt that it was time well spent. Wilhelm agreed, and he'd filled the hours by taking hundreds of measurements. He had found the process fascinating, and he was almost as eager for the final product as Elijah was.

In the end, Elijah gathered everything he'd used and shoved it in his Ghoul-Hide Satchel. It barely fit, which just told him that he needed to return home sooner rather than later. Once everything was accounted for and camp had been broken, he completed the dolmen by using Roots of the World Tree. The cast took quite some time, but when it finished, he got the expected notification.

Congratulations! You have created a unique structure, Circle of the Boar King.
Overall Grade: Growth (Current: Complex)
Enchantment Grade: D

Then, the next notification came:

Spell: Roots of the World Tree	Empower a dolmen, connecting it to your Grove. Teleport to any circle in your network. Cooldown: Three (3) days. Additional effect: When inside any circle, create a persistent gateway to any other circle. Duration: One (1) minute. Maximum capacity: Four (4) entities. Cooldown: Six (6) days. Possible number of circles dependent on Core cultivation. Current circles: Five (5) (four [4] used).

The name of the circle wasn't surprising, but he was a little disappointed that the enchantment grade was lower than the Circle of Spears. Obviously, Carmen's contribution had helped quite a bit.

As soon as the circle was completed, Wilhelm let out a yelp and stumbled to his backside. "What was that?!" he cried, staring at his equipment.

"My spell."

"Can you do it again?" he demanded.

"Not here. Did your equipment get your measurements?"

"It . . . It will take some time to go through the data, but I think so . . ."

"Awesome. Now, do you want to try it out?"

Predictably, Wilhelm's answer was an enthusiastic affirmative.

72

A THOUSAND MILES IN AN INSTANT

Before Elijah activated the gate, he inspected the other notification he'd received after completing the preparation of the hide.

> **Congratulations! You have created a unique item, Tanned Steel-Skin Boar Leather.**
> **Overall Grade: Complex (Mid)**
> **Enchantment Grade: N/A**

"Why are you smiling?" asked Wilhelm.

"Oh. The hide turned out to be Complex grade," he said. "I was worried that it wouldn't get there because of the low density of ethera around here."

"Low?" Wilhelm asked. "It is higher than anyplace I've ever been."

"You haven't been everywhere," Elijah said, clapping the slim man on his shoulder. Despite the fact that Elijah had withheld most of his Strength, Wilhelm still stumbled a little. The man really hadn't bothered investing in his physical attributes at all. "If you stay out of trouble, I might just show you some new places."

After that, they did one last sweep of the area, just to make sure they hadn't forgotten to gather anything. Elijah had already dismantled the kiln—it was just a clay oven, really—since he didn't have anywhere to put it, and all his other possessions remained safely tucked away in his satchel. The Preservation Pack full of meat hadn't even been opened, save to retrieve the brains Elijah had used to tan the boar's hide. As far as Wilhelm's gear, it was in its own box, which the German man wore on his back where it was secured in place by a pair of leather straps. In short, they hadn't left anything behind other than the large basin Elijah had dug, but that wouldn't have much of an impact on the environment.

So, without further delay, Elijah used Roots of the World Tree, and when he finally finished the cast, a series of vines snaked out of the ground, weaving together until they formed the familiar portal. The interior shimmered with gray light before revealing a view of the Dragon Circle's surroundings.

"After you," Elijah offered, gesturing to the gate. "You wanted to see teleportation? Well, here it is."

Wilhelm was speechless and more than a little frightened. However, his curiosity got the better of him, and he cautiously approached. Then, he reached out to touch the portal, but his hand passed through without issue. After Elijah assured him that it was harmless, the man mustered his courage and stepped through. With a roll of his eyes, Elijah followed.

Other than a slight tremor through his Soul channels and an increase in the ambient ethera, stepping across a thousand miles was a bit anticlimactic. One moment, he was in the frigid steppes, and the next he found himself in the much more temperate climate surrounding Argos.

Wilhelm fell to his knees.

Alarmed, Elijah knelt beside him, asking, "Are you alright?"

"I am . . . I am fine," the man said, looking around in wonder. "This is amazing. It is everything I've ever hoped to achieve."

"Oh," Elijah responded, feeling a little awkward as he stood and stepped back. "I see."

After collecting himself, Wilhelm asked, "Where are we?"

"Near a town called Argos," Elijah answered.

"Greek?"

"Used to be, I guess. It mostly still is, but they've got a decent population of other nationalities now," Elijah explained. "It's a nice town. No gambling."

"I wasn't going to—"

"What you do in this town will reflect on me," Elijah stated. "Don't make me regret bringing you here."

He hadn't intended to threaten the man—not originally, at least. Rather, Elijah had only wanted to make certain that Wilhelm knew the stakes. However, his intentions were irrelevant to what actually came out. He almost apologized but, in the end, thought better of it. If a threatening demeanor kept Wilhelm in line, then results were all that mattered.

After Wilhelm assured Elijah that he would be on his best behavior, the two set off for Argos. It was only after a few hundred feet that Elijah sensed something he didn't expect.

"Stay behind me. Don't speak unless I give you the go-ahead," he ordered, stepping in front of much more vulnerable Wilhelm. There was a camp up ahead. Two people. One heavily armored, and the other—well, Elijah couldn't get a good sense of the second person, indicating that some skill was at play. He couldn't perceive any details about the second figure.

The pair sat on opposite sides of a small fire, with two tents that stood next to one another a few feet away. The area around them indicated that they'd been there for a few days. Maybe as much as a week, judging by the neatly piled refuse nearby.

More concerningly, he sensed that the armored figure was quite strong. She—and it was definitely a woman—radiated a decent amount of power. Less than the boar, but enough to put her on the level of someone like Thor. That put Elijah's hackles up because there were only a few reasons someone like that would be camped so close to his dolmen.

And none of them were good.

For a second, Elijah considered shifting into his draconid form and ambushing them, but in the end, he thought better of it. There was a chance that he was walking into a trap, but he refused to approach every encounter as if the other party intended to attack him.

After telling Wilhelm to head back to the dolmen and giving the German man instructions to flee to Argos if there was trouble, Elijah approached the campsite in his natural form. Even as a human, he could move quite stealthily, so when he stepped into the small clearing, the two people reacted with no small degree of surprise.

The woman shot to her feet, drawing a large sword from a nearby scabbard that she tossed aside as soon the blade was bared. The sword was large enough that it was clearly meant to be sheathed on her back, but being in the camp, she'd likely removed it in the name of comfort. That she hadn't done so with her armor said something about the sort of woman she was. Regardless, the only bit of skin that wasn't covered by shining metal was her face.

She was quite striking with features that marked her as someone of East Asian descent. Her hair was long, though it had been gathered in a bun atop her head, and her complexion was like ivory.

In many ways, the man was the woman's complete opposite. Where she was lithe—even in her armor, which had been made in the European style—the man was quite stocky, with a bit of roundness around the middle. He wore leather armor, a long coat in the same black material, and a matching hat that reminded Elijah of the people from the Magister's Estate tower. He was armed with a crossbow, with a pair of shortswords at his waist. Elijah suspected that he carried many more weapons, though. His complexion was much darker than that of his companion, though he was of the same general ethnicity.

"Hello. Is it presumptuous to think you're waiting for me?" Elijah asked in a mild voice. The assumption was based on the fact that, in all the time he'd spent around Argos, he'd rarely seen other people traipsing about the wilderness, much less camping there for days at a time. Why would they, when Argos was so close? Most people didn't relish spending the night outside, largely because there were so many dangers in the wilds. So, Elijah had come to the conclusion that they were probably waiting for him.

"Are you Elijah Hart?" asked the woman, her voice a little deeper than he'd anticipated. It was still well within the range of femininity, but there was a breathiness to it that was quite unexpected. The other surprise was that she spoke with a posh British accent. Perhaps it was his America-centric upbringing, but he had expected her to have an American accent. Or, failing that, then one from one of the Asian countries.

"Who's asking?" he asked. He'd reengaged his Ring of Anonymity before stepping through the gate, but he didn't think it would do much good. Still, he didn't want to volunteer any information.

"My name is Sadie Song. This is Dat Bao," she answered, sounding like she'd stepped out of a period drama. "We have come seeking help."

"Ah," Elijah said, remembering Isaiah's description of the emissaries who'd visited Seattle looking for help with some sort of situation in Hong Kong. The word *undead* had been thrown around. More, Elijah recognized the woman's name from the power rankings, and he felt certain that, even though he wasn't in the top ten, the man was in the top one hundred.

"What's up, bro? You aren't wearing any shoes," the leather-clad Dat Bao stated. His accent was much closer to Elijah's expectations, but it wasn't very thick.

"I'm aware," Elijah said with a slight smile. "And you're dressed like a character from one of those vampire-hunting video games."

"I know, bro," Dat said, grinning. "I'm a Witch Hunter."

"Dat."

"What? It's not a secret, bro," he said, shrugging his shoulders at Sadie's admonishing glare.

She just shook her head, then turned back to Elijah asking, "You know about our situation?"

"Some of it. Isaiah Roberts up in Seattle told me a little. You have a zombie problem, right?"

"Undead. Zombies . . . are the least of our worries. There are many other types, including vampires. And there are demonic creatures."

Elijah frowned. Nerthus had once mentioned that demons were one of the elder races, on par with dragons. "Are there actual demons there?" he asked, stepping forward. Pointedly, Sadie hadn't sheathed her sword.

She shook her head. "Just beasts. Or the equivalent. The more intelligent undead summon them from hell," she stated. "We typically manage to interrupt those rituals, but we don't have the means to find them all."

Then, she went on to describe the situation in more detail. They had been fighting the undead almost from the very beginning of what she referred to as the apocalypse. Elijah didn't correct her terminology, largely because what she described sounded like it qualified for the label. She went on to explain how they'd managed to fight the undead to a standstill, but added, "We know it won't last. They will keep coming until we conquer the primal realm from which they spawn."

Elijah didn't know that much about primal realms. Certainly, he was aware that they were like more elaborate versions of towers and that they could affect the surrounding areas. However, he hadn't realized that that meant creatures could spill out. Did that mean those creatures were real? Or was there some sort of limiter? Elijah vowed not to speculate until he could do some research on the subject. Perhaps Nerthus would know.

"And you want my help in the primal realm, right?" he asked.

"We do," she said.

"Have you managed to convince anyone else?"

Sadie's face remained impassive, but her shoulders slumped slightly. "No," she admitted. "Most are preparing for the upcoming Trial."

"So am I," Elijah admitted. There was less than four months until the Trial of Primacy, which meant that he was going to be cutting it close with his preparations. Stepping forward, he said, "But I will help. I don't know about the timing or how it's all going to work out, but I can't—"

Sadie took a step back, her face abruptly twisting into a grimace. "Stop."

The sudden change surprised Elijah. He asked, "Seriously? You came here to ask for my help. That won't—"

"You stink of murder," she stated. Elijah could feel her disdain cutting through him like a sharp knife. "How many have you killed? Hundreds? Thousands? Tens of thousands?"

Elijah's expression turned to stone. "It's complicated."

"Answer the question."

"Fine. I'm not sure. Multiple thousands. I don't know after that. It depends on what you're counting."

She took another step back, leveling her sword at him.

"It's going to be like that, then?" Elijah asked. He knew his kill count was quite extensive, especially if creatures like the orcs or tower denizens were included. In the old world, he would have been considered a monster. Perhaps in the new world, as well. But aside from what he'd done to Easton—which still brought up mixed feelings—Elijah was at peace with his actions.

Mostly.

In a pleading tone, Dat addressed his companion: "Bro . . ."

"He is a murderer, Dat."

"We need murderers, Sadie," Dat responded, the playful tone in his voice gone. "We need killers. He can help us. He wants to help us. Let him."

Sadie frowned.

"I do not approve," she said. "But we cannot afford to turn down help."

"Just the ringing endorsement every man wants to hear when he offers to put his life on the line for perfect strangers," he said. Then, the resentment hit home. He'd agreed to help them, and without hesitation. Yet, the woman had the audacity to judge him without even knowing the circumstances. He didn't have to deal with that. So, he added, "You know what? Fuck you. Deal with it on your own."

He wanted to help, but he wasn't in the mood to be talked down to or judged. If that was what they wanted to do, then they could combat their undead invasion without him.

"Fine," she said. "Dat, we—"

"No, bro," he said, reaching out to grab her arm. She tried to flinch away, but his hand was a little too quick. He gave her a pointed look. "This isn't how this was supposed to go."

Some unspoken communication passed between the two, and then Sadie pulled away. Her expression softened, and to Elijah, she said, "I apologize. One of my skills affects my . . . judgment. I am still trying to control it properly. When I sensed the number of people you have . . . slain, I overreacted. Please. Forgive me."

The apology came through metaphorically gritted teeth, but Elijah could well understand how a person's perspective could be skewed by an ability. He'd struggled with that ever since he'd started using One with Nature. Still, he wasn't too keen on helping someone who clearly hated him. The possibility of a betrayal aside, it just didn't make him feel great.

Even so, he forced a smile he didn't really feel, then said, "No biggie. We all make mistakes and threaten people we just met while accusing them of being murderers without knowing any context. It's practically a stereotype, right? In any case, I've got business to take care of in Argos. Meet me at Agatha's inn if you want to discuss it further."

With that, Elijah turned around and strode away, intent on doing exactly what he'd said. Regardless of what happened with the curious pair, he still had things he needed to do, and they wouldn't get done until he went into Argos.

Before he'd taken more than a few steps, he stopped and turned back to the two companions. He said, "Oh. If you ever threaten me again, you'd better be ready for a fight. I won't let it slide next time."

73

SINS

As the infuriating man turned away, Sadie seethed. When she felt ethera start to swirl, she embraced Consecrated Shield. It was an upgrade of the basic Warrior ability, Bulwark, but it was far more powerful.

Ability: Consecrated Shield	Summon a shield of ethera to protect allies. When it breaks, it releases a wave of healing. In addition, that wave will damage unholy creatures.

When she'd upgraded it, she'd only had two options, and the other choice was a much sturdier shield that was nearly impossible to break—at least under normal circumstances. But Sadie had never lacked for defensive measures, so she'd chosen the option that would allow her to better protect her allies as well as combat the unliving monstrosities that had overrun Hong Kong.

Ever since leaving Hong Kong, though, she'd begun to rethink her decision. Against hordes of undead and demonic creatures, Consecrated Shield was a great boon—especially when she was fighting alongside less powerful allies. However, traveling alone in the wider world, it wasn't all that much more useful than its predecessor, Bulwark. Yet, she hoped it would be enough against whatever spell the Druid was casting.

The spell completed after a couple of seconds, and the results were shocking. He didn't direct some deadly ability her way. Instead, he transformed, his body morphing into a winged reptilian creature with bright multicolored scales. That monster launched itself into the air and flew away.

"Dragon," she muttered.

"More of a wyvern, bro," Dat said. She glanced over to see that her companion was staring at the sky—or, rather, the rapidly disappearing shape of the winged monster. "Dragons have four legs. Wyverns are more like birds. Might be an amphiptere, though. Maybe a lindworm. But not a dragon."

"What difference does it make?" Sadie asked, letting her own ability fall away. She hadn't completed the cast, so it wouldn't take much ethera or stamina. That was the problem with her Crusader class. It was a hybrid, and as such, many of her abilities used a combination of ethera and stamina, which meant that her attribute points were more spread out than typical melee combatants.

Even so, she wouldn't have traded it for anything. Without those abilities—regardless of the cost—they would have already lost Hong Kong to the undead. For years, she'd been fighting tooth and nail against those disgusting creatures, and yet, they'd made no real progress. The best they could do was hold the line, and even that stretched her abilities. Without help, she knew that the creatures pouring out of the primal realm would overrun the strongholds Sadie and her family—her clan—had built.

"Well, dragons are kind of a big deal, bro," answered Dat. "Elder race, just like the angels. I don't think we want to start calling wyverns dragons. Seems like it might be offensive."

Sadie's face remained impassive, but her heart skipped a beat. She knew good and well just how powerful the elder races were. The angel Gabriel had revealed that much, as well as the reality that Earth was under the watchful eye of many powerful entities. Was it unrealistic to think that a true dragon was watching? That they might take offense to her mischaracterization of what she had just seen?

"You're right."

"I know, bro. What do you think of him?" Dat asked. "Never seen a shape-shifter before."

"It might be an item," Sadie suggested.

"Nah. That's a spell. Called Shape of the Sky."

Sadie shook her head. With a Ranger archetype, Dat was a capable fighter, but he truly excelled in information gathering. He'd saved thousands of lives—and on more than one occasion—by predicting their enemies' movements. Without him, the defense of Hong Kong would have been doomed before it had even started.

"You used Eye of the Chosen?" she asked. That particular ability allowed Dat to identify a spell, so long as he saw it being cast. It gave him information on the spell's strengths and weaknesses, but at the cost of a relatively long cooldown.

After nodding, he said, "Shape of the Sky. Transforms the caster into an airborne hunter. Not great for combat, but good for travel."

"Interesting," Sadie said. She still didn't like it. If he could transform into a noncombat form that looked like that, it was possible that he could become something much more terrifying.

"What do you want to do, bro?" Dat asked.

"We should head into town," she answered, finally sheathing her sword. As she buckled the strap that held the scabbard on her back, she thought back to their first visit to Argos. It had only been a week before, but it stuck with her, largely because of how normal the city was. The people there were thriving, and as far as she could tell, they hadn't had to resort to tyranny to do it. Based on her travels, that was something of a rarity. Most of the leaders she'd met weren't overtly evil, but in such a dangerous world, personal freedoms were easily sacrificed in the name of security.

Argos hadn't gone down that road. And what's more, the stain of sin didn't pervade the town, much as it had nearly everywhere else.

Ability: Sense of Sin	A passive enhancement that allows the Crusader to sense misdeeds.

In many ways, the presence of that ability—which she couldn't just turn off—was the source of her biggest regret. If she'd known that was what awaited her for choosing the Crusader class, she might have picked something else. It had caused so many problems, and it made being around groups of people especially difficult. After all, who was without sin? Who hadn't committed some misdeed?

It was one thing to know that no person was without sin. Something else entirely to have it shoved in her face every time she met someone new. Normally, it only manifested as a slightly noxious odor, but in some cases, there was a visual component, as well. With Elijah Hart, it looked like he was walking around cloaked in a cloud of smog.

The only reason she hadn't immediately attacked him was because the enhancement—or curse, as she sometimes thought of it—wasn't foolproof. Just because it said that Hart was guilty of murder, that didn't mean he actually was. All it meant was that he was a killer. And it made no determination as to whether or not he was justified, which made it fundamentally useless, as far as she was concerned. The world wasn't black-and-white. Rather, it was composed of shades of gray, whether the ability wanted to acknowledge it or not.

Still, Sadie couldn't help but be influenced by it, and because of her disgust, she had very nearly ruined her chances of getting help from the only person who'd actually agreed to assist her people. Her lapse in self-control was as maddening as it was humiliating. Her parents would have been appalled.

"What do you think of him?" she asked.

"He seems cool," Dat answered with a shrug. "Won't know anything else till we get to know him. But I have a good feeling."

"You always have a good feeling," Sadie said. And it was true. Dat rarely met anyone he didn't immediately like, and when he did find someone who drew his ire, the reasons were obvious. "Do you think he will help us? Do you think he can?"

"That depends on you, bro," Dat responded. "He's stronger than either of us. I've never even met a Druid before, and I think his class is a rare variant. Plus, his cultivation is advanced."

That raised an eyebrow. "More than mine?"

"Yes."

There was no hesitation in Dat's answer, but that didn't tell the whole story. Dat's abilities gave him some insight into a person's cultivation, but it wasn't as if a person's entire status was laid bare.

"How is that possible?" was her next question. She'd thought her cultivation was more advanced than anyone else's. After all, she'd had the benefit of living most of the past four years in close proximity to a primal realm, where ethera density was incredibly thick. "Do you think he has access to another primal realm? Maybe natural treasures?"

"Druids don't use natural treasures like that."

"And you're an expert?"

"I've done research," he answered. "Druids are a weird archetype. They're rare, for one. And they don't consume natural treasures. They protect them. Sure, they'll cultivate around one if they find it in the wild, but they wouldn't destroy one."

"But that would only be marginally better than not using one at all."

"I know, bro. It's crazy. Druids are crazy. At least that's what everybody out there thinks," he said, gesturing vaguely toward the sky. Clearly, he meant it to mean the multiverse.

"So, you think he could beat us?"

Dat shrugged. "Maybe. Better to just not pick a fight for no reason," he said. "That way we don't have to find out."

She didn't respond, but her mind whirled as she tried to get her feelings under control. She hadn't liked Elijah Hart from the very first moment she'd had met him, but that was likely due to Sense of Sin rather than any reasonable judgment. And that disapproval had forced a negative reaction, which had spiraled. Then, he'd threatened her, the implications of which had rankled her pride.

But had he truly done anything to warrant her hatred?

No.

So, she pushed that feeling aside and focused on what was at stake. She couldn't let her own weakness take over. She needed to be strong, or her people would be consumed by the undead menace that plagued Hong Kong.

That meant putting aside her personal feelings and working with the man, even if his very existence made her want to retch.

With that in mind, she and Dat broke their camp, packing everything away before heading toward the nearby town. The walk through the wilderness was oddly pleasant, and no wild beasts attacked them. That had been the case since they'd first arrived, though on the second day, Sadie had caught sight of the largest domestic cat she'd ever encountered. When it watched her, she got the feeling that it was at least part of the reason she hadn't seen any other animal life in the area.

In any case, she and Dat soon reached Argos, but when they arrived, she was surprised to see that the odd temple situated atop a hill on the other side of the town had been lit up with ethereal light.

"I thought that was just another Greek temple," she said to herself. Once, she'd visited the Parthenon in Athens, so she thought the building up ahead was a re-creation of a similar temple. A tourist attraction like the statue of Heracles she'd seen in Argos's main square. But now, she wasn't so sure. The statue at the top—which depicted a victorious female warrior—glowed like a beacon.

After seeing that, she led Dat through the city, but the streets were far less populated than they had been before. Or at least that was the case until they reached the square at the base of the temple's hill. There, Sadie saw a crowd of hundreds of people gathered at the bottom of the stairs.

And atop those stairs was a familiar figure.

"What is he doing?" she asked, taking note of the localized rainstorm that extended almost twenty steps from the top of the stairs. To her senses, it glistened with ethera.

"Healing, bro," Dat said. "I told you—Druids are weird. But they're usually good guys."

"Usually isn't always."

"They can sometimes go full ecoterrorist," said Dat. "I read about one that killed every sapient creature on her planet because they kept killing guardians and stripping the world of natural treasures. So . . . Yeah, bro. Not always, I guess."

"Every sapient creature? How?"

"Plants, bro. Plants. They're everywhere."

Sadie felt a shudder of fear flow up her spine. She didn't think Hart was powerful enough to do that, but it did highlight that, despite not being a full-fledged combat class, Druids were capable of doing a lot of damage.

"But he's healing people. He can't be all bad, right? Reminds me of Niko."

"Yeah," she agreed. Her brother spent every waking hour healing the people of Hong Kong. Part of that was due to necessity, but Niko's personality played a big part, as well. He'd always been selfless, and that trait had only grown stronger after the world had changed.

Channeling a bit of Niko's personality, she started up the steps. She had to shoulder her way through the crowd, but being as how she was obviously powerful and wearing full armor, the gathering parted before her.

"Where are you going?" asked Dat as he tried to keep up.

"Niko's not the only one who can heal," she answered.

74

A SLEEPING SPRYGGENT

Nerthus sat on the branch of the juvenile ancestral tree, basking in the potent life coursing through its limbs. The tree wasn't nearly as powerful as its forebear, but then again, Nerthus had never expected it to be. It was still young, and it hadn't been afforded the same opportunities for growth. Even so, it was maturing well, and now that it had finally connected to its progenitor, Nerthus could at last visit it in person.

However, for once, he was less interested in the tree than in the curious creatures scurrying around its base. Nerthus had never had much opportunity to observe other people. Before he'd come to Earth, he had been barely more than a seedling, and his sapience was almost entirely undeveloped. Of his old life, he mostly only remembered emotions. Warmth. Love. Comfort. And, of course, safety. He had an image of his progenitors, but it was blurry, and at times, he thought that those memories were a figment of his imagination.

So, everything he'd witnessed since awakening inside the ancestral tree that had brought him to Earth had been new for him. More than four and a half years later, the novelty of it all still hadn't worn off. From Elijah's stories, Nerthus knew that the planet was a wild, unforgiving, and violent place. He'd lost count of how many times Elijah had nearly been killed—which would have been a disaster, both emotionally and from a practical standpoint. Until now, though, Nerthus had only known peace.

Certainly, there had been the incident with the Voxx surging out of the tower, but Elijah had dealt with that before it had affected Nerthus or the Grove. The same was true with the invaders who'd come from Ironshore, intent on either vengeance or greed. So, given that, as well as the fact that he'd spent his previous years safe in his progenitors' embrace, Nerthus had lived quite a sheltered life, short though it had been.

Which was why he found the little creatures below him so fascinating.

In most ways, they looked a lot like the dwarves and gnomes who'd skirted the island on their way to the tower. They were tiny, with slightly stubbier proportions and an exuberance for life that surprised Nerthus.

That was on display as they chased one another through the area known as Druid's Park. They laughed and screamed as they ran among giant mushrooms and the vibrant flora that had grown amid the ever-increasingly dense ethera surrounding the juvenile tree. At first, Nerthus thought the little creatures were engaged in a battle, and he'd very nearly intervened. After all, the offshoot of the Grove was no place for fighting. Yet, as he watched, he had come to realize that the aim was not to hurt one another. It was a competition, and one whose rules were nebulous at best.

The tiny people shouted at one another, making up rules as they went, and Nerthus found himself smiling at their antics. They were all so innocent, completely unaware of the issues of the wider world. Elijah had given them that. Without him, the entire city would have been overrun with orcs. Or subjected to the dangers of a surging tower. But with his help, they were now safe. The city prospered. And the Grove remained safe from outside interference.

As he watched, Nerthus channeled Plant Authority:

Ability: Plant Authority	Manipulate plant life to encourage or discourage growth and cause minor mutations.

It was the signature ability of his class, Forest Prince, though he enjoyed various other spells and abilities, as well. Shifting his attention from the children playing—yes, that was the word; he was certain of it—he looked at his list of abilities. Elijah referred to it as a spell book, which Nerthus thought was an apt label:

Archetype: Administrator
A noncombat archetype, proficient with organizational skills that can be used to empower and enhance. Features bonuses to Ethera and Regeneration, as well as memory and calculation speed. Required Aspects: [Scholar], [Memory], [Knowledge]

Abilities	
Ethereal Mind	Passive ability that organizes thoughts, memories, and new information into an easily searchable database.
Serenity of the Forest	Omit all external stimuli in order to improve speed of thought.

Organized Mind	Further improve the organization of the mind.
Plant Authority	Manipulate plant life to encourage or discourage growth and cause minor mutations.
Plant Prosperity	Focus your ethera, creating a perfect environment for plant growth.
Germination	Improve the speed with which plant life will mature.
Rain of Regeneration	Summon a gentle rain that will increase an entity's Regeneration by one hundred (100) points. Only usable in areas with high ethera density.
Class: Forest Prince The Forest Prince is a hybrid class derived from the Sorcerer, Druid, and Administrator archetypes. It is meant to protect nature and nurture growth.	
Establish Realm	Create a bond with the forest over which you will rule. Size of the realm determined by Ethera, stage of Core cultivation, and time. Current size: 20.3 square miles.
Animate Plants	Within your Realm, command plant life to become your minions. Number of minions based on Ethera attribute. Current minions: Six (6).
Empower Guardian	Nurture a guardian beast, empowering them to better protect your forest.
Forest Protector	Greatly improve all attributes, dependent on ethera density. Duration based on strength of the bond. Current duration: 7.9 minutes.

As a spyrggent, Nerthus did not get quite as many abilities as most others. His memories were fuzzy on the subject, but he thought that had something to do with his race's origins. Though even with abilities like Ethereal Mind and Organized Mind, he couldn't quite remember why that would have anything to do with it, and it wasn't as if he could visit a Branch to find out.

Not yet, at least.

Perhaps one day Elijah's Grove would grow large enough to earn an existing Branch. For most Groves, that wasn't an issue. They were collectives populated by not just Druids, but by nature-attuned Warriors, Rangers, Tradesmen, and every other archetype. But Elijah was something of a loner, and it didn't seem likely that would change anytime soon.

But maybe the very children chasing one another around the park would end up with nature attunements. Or Miguel would choose to form a bond with his uncle's Grove. The opportunities to expand would present themselves, Nerthus was certain. He need only wait.

After a few more minutes of watching the children, Nerthus noticed that the person on whom he'd been waiting had arrived in the park. The gnome stayed to the edges, obviously hesitant, but the entire park was within Nerthus's purview. So, he had no issues slipping into the tree, following its widespread roots to a location just a few feet away from the gnome, and rising from the ground.

"Hello, Biggle," he said. "Have you come to agree to my terms?"

The little Alchemist whipped around, startled by Nerthus's sudden appearance. That was gratifying to the spryggent, but Nerthus wasn't certain why it amused him.

"Gods below, you scared me out of my skin!" Biggle said in a squeaky voice. "Don't sneak up on me like that!"

"My apologies," Nerthus said with an acquiescent bow. However, he did allow himself a slight smile that he was sure Biggle wouldn't recognize. When he rose to his full height, his face was once again unreadable. "Do you agree?"

"Nice to see you, too," Biggle grumbled, unshouldering his pack. He reached inside and retrieved a small pouch. "This is what you wanted, right?"

As he asked the question, Nerthus cast his awareness to the seeds in the pouch. "Cascading briar," Nerthus identified them. "Poor specimens, but that is no matter. What of the others?"

"All here," Biggle answered, patting the larger pack. And indeed, Nerthus could feel the wide variety of seeds inside. Some were meant to increase the density of the ambient ethera within the Grove, but others would be foodstuffs to replace the inefficient berry bushes that took up so much room. As much as Elijah liked those fruits, they used an inordinate amount of ethera, at least compared to the effects they provided. There were many other fruits that would provide similar—or better—results while absorbing a fraction of the ambient ethera.

The rest were meant for a project concerning the rest of the island, and they would either provide defensive measures or further raise the density of the local ethera. Nerthus's instincts told him that he'd only barely managed to scratch the surface of what was possible, and from the guides he'd had Miguel or Carmen purchase, he knew it wasn't uncommon for a true Druids' grove to possess an ethera density hundreds of times thicker than the surrounding area. As it was, the island fell far short of that mark, and Nerthus wanted to change that.

Part of that determination was based on his instincts. He wanted the area to thrive. However, it was also because his class—as well as his race—was inextricably tied to the Grove. As it grew stronger, so too would he.

"Good. Then I will allow you to grow your little fungi here," said Nerthus. He had initially planned to destroy the invasive mushrooms, but had instead chosen to use their presence to his advantage. They were even more ethera hungry than the berry bushes, but it wasn't such a big deal outside the true Grove. He could work around it in Druid's Park. "You will leave the pack on the beach before tomorrow morning. Until then . . ."

Nerthus trailed off.

"What is it?" asked Biggle, for once reading the spryggent's expression.

"I must go," Nerthus answered. Then, without warning, he slipped through the ground and into the ancestral tree's roots. Without hesitation, he sped along the ethereal connection between it and its progenitor. He moved far more quickly than normal, but he didn't stop once he reached the Grove. Instead, he raced along the roots of the larger ancestral tree, aiming for the edge of the island.

Because a watercraft he didn't recognize had just come into range.

Guinevere Mcintosh gripped the aluminum edge of the raft, crouching low as they approached the rocky shore of the island. It looked inhospitable, but it was still better than the island that had been her home for the past four and a half years. The mere fact that the local airspace lacked giant predatory birds or monsters was enough to make her feel safer than she'd felt since the world had ended.

Still, the vegetation only a few feet from the shore was as dense as any jungle she had ever seen, and as such, she was well aware of just how many dangers it could hide. That was how the new world worked. Everything—even the flora— was capable of killing them. She'd learned that lesson the hard way.

"What do you think?" she asked, glancing at John.

The man didn't look away from the shore. His appearance was nothing like it'd been when she had first met him. Back then, he was clean-cut, with a square jaw and a face that wouldn't have been out of place in a comic book. Now, he wore a great bushy beard, his hair was long and unkempt, and he bore a large puckered scar that cut diagonally across his face from his right temple all the way to his jaw. In addition, he was missing all but four fingers, and she knew for a fact that he walked with a limp.

Guinevere had plenty of her own scars to show for their hardships, but none were as visible as his. And she was one of the few survivors who had managed to keep all her digits.

"It's land. We don't have much of a choice," John said, finally pulling his gaze from the beach. "The others are depending on us to find help, and this is our only chance."

Indeed, the raft they'd built was barely holding itself together. That wasn't surprising, given the punishment it had endured. John and Guinevere weren't the only ones on board, but they were the only two in any condition to make decisions. Rajesh, Leo, and Ada had been knocked unconscious by some tentacled nightmare they'd encountered on the open ocean. The only reason they hadn't been shipwrecked was because of an enormous dolphin that had attacked the monster. Even then, the damage had been done, and the raft they'd spent so long building had been reduced to little more than flotsam. The ones who'd been stung by those tentacles had slipped into comas from which they'd yet to recover even a week later.

But if there was one thing they were accustomed to, it was hardship. They had learned to endure well past what could be expected of any reasonable human being.

And they would continue to do so because they were survivors.

"Nothing else for it," John said, paddling them forward. Once, the raft had been a true boat, with three banks of oars and the benefit of the most powerful enchantments their Tradesmen could imbue into its hull. But the rough seas and the tentacle monster from the deep had changed that. Guinevere was used to making do, though. It was the same for the rest, as well.

Soon enough, the raft crunched into the pebbly shore. A few hundred yards away, Guinevere saw a huge crab scuttling along, but it hadn't noticed them. It looked fearsome, but her Eyes of the Sentinel ability told her that it was far less dangerous than its size would suggest. Durable, sure. And potentially annoying to kill. But it lacked intelligence and offensive prowess.

Besides, she and the rest of the survivors were used to much deadlier monsters than an overgrown crab. Still, she kept an eye on it as she dismounted the raft. The moment her feet hit dry ground, she wobbled, then stumbled to her knees. They'd been at sea for too long, and the lack of rocking back and forth made her dizzy.

She pulsed Recovery, increasing her Regeneration as she looked around. The forest was thicker than anything she'd ever experienced, but that wasn't saying much, really. She wasn't that well traveled, and before recently, she'd only ever been to her home country of Ireland.

That felt like a lifetime ago, though. She had been so naive. So soft. She barely recognized the woman in her memories.

Once she'd gotten her feet under her, she reached down and helped John to drag the raft fully ashore. However, they'd only just managed it when a rustle in the nearby forest drew her attention. She whipped around, hefting her axe. By that point, it was too late, though.

A creature made of roots and branches burst forth from the trees, roaring in fury. Before Guinevere could react, six ambulatory trees threw themselves from the forest and surrounded them.

She shouted, embracing Flowing Blade as she leaped forward, intending to hack the root monster apart with her rough-bladed machete, but before she could do anything, vines erupted from the forest and snaked around her, John, and the three unconscious bodies. They moved so quickly that she hadn't even had a chance to react.

Then, as if being trussed up wasn't enough, a quartet of deer—one with a giant rack of crystalline antlers—charged through the brush, joining the monstrous trees.

It was then that Guinevere realized that her journey had come to an end. She had been through so much, had endured so many hardships—it was galling that, when she and the others had finally escaped that terrible atoll, they'd meet such an ignominious fate.

75

SURVIVORS

I f you keep making that face, it'll freeze like that," said Elijah, looking up from his meal of seared lamb chops and spanakorizo. The lamb chops were well-seasoned and flavorful, with a hint of lemony zest, but the real star of the meal was the spanakorizo, which was a dish composed of spinach and rice. For Elijah, it was a nice change from the relatively bland dried meat that made up most of the meals he'd eaten while traveling. And while he'd enjoyed the Mongolian fare, he had to admit that there was a special place in his heart—or perhaps his stomach—for Greek food. Especially when it was made by Agatha, who clearly had a potent cooking skill.

But the deliciousness of the meal seemingly had no effect on Sadie Song, who sat across from him. Her food remained largely untouched, and her resting expression seemed to be one of mingled disgust and disdain. The only time it had changed was when she had joined him at the Temple of Virtue, where she'd contributed to healing the people of Argos.

And there were plenty of takers, too. More than Elijah would have expected, if he was honest. Argos had grown, but they were still afflicted with a dearth of Healers. As such, only the most egregious wounds were treated with any regularity. Beyond that, the population had to rely on mundane cures and tonics made by Tradesmen dedicated to alchemy-related fields. Even those were rare, which meant that, unless their illnesses or injuries were life-threatening, the only healing available was what Elijah offered at the temple.

The only issue with that was that he was rapidly becoming something of a folk hero for the people of Argos. It wasn't difficult to understand why, either. With a backdrop of the grandiose Temple of Virtue, he cured their illnesses and mended their injuries without question or demands. In their eyes, that made him a saint.

So, he'd been glad to see that Sadie had chosen to join in, if only because the act shifted some of the attention from him. It was also a little surprising. When Elijah first met her, he'd taken the armor and giant sword to mean that she was a Warrior. However, she was capable of healing, as well, which meant that she was, at the very least, some sort of hybrid, just like him.

That was where the similarities ended, though. Elijah's brand of healing was gentle, and in a lot of ways, it functioned by injecting vitality into a person and letting their body take over, healing via its own natural processes. From the outside looking in, it looked miraculous—and it was—but Elijah knew that it was just a sped-up version of what would normally occur.

Mostly.

But Sadie's healing was very different, involving beams of light descending from above. Elijah wasn't capable of tracking it as well as he could his own healing, but Sadie's spells seemed far closer to miracles than his own.

Still, her spells were no more effective than his. In fact, he suspected that they were a little more limited in efficacy, especially after he'd evolved Touch of Nature into Nature's Bloom, which had performed above expectations. The initial effect was at least twice as powerful as Touch of Nature, and the bloom effect was as advertised, adding a second bout of healing twenty seconds later. However, the best part was that, finally, Elijah could cast the spell from afar. The range was still short—maybe ten feet—but even that small distance was a good deal more convenient than having to lay his hands on someone in order to heal them.

It wasn't all good news, though. With that increased power came an increase in cost, as well. Before, he could cast Touch of Nature almost indefinitely without draining his ethera. But now, Nature's Bloom took so much energy that he could only cast it fifteen times before exhausting the contents of his Core. So, he knew he would need to be judicious with his use of the spell going forward.

Fortunately, Soothe and Healing Rain were still just as efficient as ever, and for the most part, they were sufficient for his purposes. Having Nature's Bloom in his back pocket for when he needed rapid healing was nice, though.

In any case, as eager as he was to test his new spell a little more, he was more concerned with the pair sitting across from him. Barely a moment passed that Sadie wasn't glaring at him, but at least Dat seemed amiable enough.

"What?" she asked, responding to his previous statement.

"That's what my mom used to tell me," Elijah answered. "If you keep making that face, it'll freeze like that. I'm pretty sure she wasn't being serious, but I think the sentiment still applies."

Her jaw flexed, and it was clear that she was grinding her teeth. Elijah's mother would've had something to say about that, too, but in this instance, he chose discretion.

"Bro."

"What?" Sadie asked. If Elijah hadn't already heard her explanation of the situation back in Hong Kong, he might've thought that single word was the extent of her vocabulary.

"We talked about this," Dat said with a sigh. "Be nice."

She glared at him, too.

"I once saw a movie where a guy said that massaging his earlobes and saying *woosah* helped with anger management," Elijah offered. "Maybe do that?"

"Did you just give her advice from *Bad Boys II*?" Dat asked. "Bro. That's my favorite movie, bro!"

"You are an idiot." Sadie sighed, dipping her head and massaging her temples. When she looked up, her face was almost completely impassive. There was still a slight wrinkling of her nose when she looked at Elijah that suggested she'd smelled something off-putting, but it was markedly better. "I apologize for my behavior. I will try to do better."

Elijah gave her his best grin. "Water under the bridge. I'm just—"

Just then, he heard the inn's door open, and a familiar figure strode in. Delilah wore her adventuring getup, which meant that she looked a bit like Wonder Woman, but with a bit more muscle than in the movies. She didn't hesitate to cross the common room, then slide onto the bench next to Elijah.

"I heard you were back in town," she said, putting her hand on his back. "But here you are having dinner with another woman. Color me jealous."

She said it as a joke, but Elijah knew Delilah well enough to recognize that there was more than a little truth to the remark.

"Whoa, bro. Your girlfriend is yoked," Dat said. Then, to Delilah, he asked, "Do you lift? What's your routine?"

"Not my girlfriend," Elijah said. "Just a friend."

"Well, not *just* a friend," Delilah added, shifting closer.

"Right," he said, feeling just how uncomfortable everyone was. "But—"

Suddenly, the facet of Elijah's Mind that was dedicated to monitoring his Locus went off. Normally, he barely even paid attention to it, but he'd long since managed to establish a mindset where he would become aware of any major changes. And strangers landing on the shores of his island definitely qualified for that label. There were five of them. Three men, two women. All but a single man and woman were unconscious, but the two that remained active seemed strong enough to cause trouble.

Anger erupted in Elijah's mind.

He had told them. He had made it abundantly clear that no one was allowed on his island without permission. And yet, there they were, acting as if they belonged. As if his commands didn't matter. They were human, which suggested that they were newcomers to Ironshore. Imports from Norcastle that had come along with the trade deal. He'd expected it to happen eventually, but he'd hoped to avoid what would almost assuredly be an unpleasant situation.

"I have to go," he said, already casting Roots of the World Tree. Thankfully, the function that would return him to his island wasn't on cooldown, which just further emphasized that he needed to be careful with how he used the spell. The worst thing that could happen would be if someone or something invaded his island and he couldn't immediately teleport back.

"What? Why?" demanded Sadie. "I didn't mean to offend you!"

"What's up, bro?"

"Is everything okay?" asked Delilah, clearly intending to help. It was a nice gesture, but Delilah was barely level fifty. Anything that could hurt Elijah would obliterate her, regardless of how combat focused her class was.

"It's fine. I'll be back in a week or so," Elijah said.

Then, without further delay, he finished the casting of his spell and disappeared. Only a moment later, he reappeared in the center of his Grove. As he did, he saw through his Locus that Nerthus had already responded to the intrusion, and in an unexpected way. There were six ambulatory trees already surrounding a makeshift raft, and the people who'd come onshore were wrapped in twisting vines.

Elijah's original plan for a response was to fly to the beach in question, but seeing that Nerthus had the invaders well in hand, he chose to run instead. And given his attributes and Essence of the Wolf, he could cover quite a lot of ground in a hurry. So, he arrived after only a couple of minutes.

"Didn't think you had this in you, buddy," he said, approaching Nerthus. The spryggent had once again grown, reaching a height that exceeded Elijah's own, if only by an inch or so. He glanced at the ambulatory trees. "You have control of those?"

"Of the trees, yes. It is a skill. The guardians, no."

Elijah had noticed the family of deer nearby, but he'd thought nothing of it. They often roamed across the whole island, so he hadn't thought that they were responding to a threat. That they had was a great source of comfort. The two adults could pack quite a punch, which would probably help to dissuade any unwanted visitors.

"Have you spoken to them?" he asked, glancing past the tree line and to the surrounded watercraft. The raft was in an advanced state of disrepair, and it looked like it would fall apart at the first sign of rough seas. The people weren't in much better condition, with three of them being unconscious and the other two looking like they'd just stepped off the set of the movie *Waterworld*.

The woman did spark some degree of recognition, though Elijah wasn't certain why that would be. As far as he could remember, he'd never seen her before in his life. And with her mane of red hair and striking appearance, he thought he would remember someone like that.

Perhaps he was just predisposed to looking at pretty women in a favorable light because the man who'd accompanied her was completely unfamiliar to Elijah. Aside from looking like he needed a trip to the barbershop—or a nice hot shower—the only remarkable thing about him was a long scar that ran diagonally across his face.

And he was missing quite a few fingers, Elijah noted.

There was something else going on. These people didn't look like they'd come looking for a fight, and if they'd originated in Ironshore, then surely they would have used a proper boat, rather than something that looked like it had been assembled from discarded flotsam.

Elijah stepped out of the trees, his staff clicking against the rocky shore as he approached the captive invaders. He asked, "Who are you, and why have you come to my island?"

The woman's eyes widened as she declared, "Please, we need your help!"

The moment she spoke, Elijah remembered a frightened, red-haired woman with an Irish accent. More than four years ago, he'd been seated next to her when the plane had been torn to pieces by a giant bird. He didn't remember her name, though.

"You were on the plane with me, weren't you?" he blurted. Then, he glanced at the scarred man. His memory of that flight was more than a little fuzzy. After all, he'd still been reeling from chemotherapy and preparing himself to die. So, he had missed quite a few details. However, he thought the man tangled in Nerthus's roots could have been the pilot he'd seen upon boarding.

The woman's eyes widened. "Are you another survivor?" she asked.

"I am. I think . . . I think we need to have a little talk," Elijah said. "Nerthus, let them go."

The spryggent didn't respond. Instead, he simply complied. The roots retracted, and the two conscious survivors collapsed to the ground. Elijah didn't immediately approach, but he did summon Healing Rain and cast Soothe on each of the castaways. The healing wouldn't do much for the three unconscious people. They had more issues than a simple heal would fix. Namely, they were starved, dehydrated, and exhausted. But the healing would help.

As those heals took effect, Elijah reached into his Ghoul-Hide Satchel and retrieved a handful of his Grove berries. Then, he offered the little fruits to the conscious couple. They took them eagerly, ingesting them without hesitation, and immediately, they began to recover their lost energy.

Once they looked like they weren't about to keel over, Elijah said, "Now, I think it's time you tell me your story. I'll help however I can."

76

A FAMILIAR FACE

It quickly became apparent that none of the people aboard the boat were in any condition to tell a story. The redheaded woman was mostly healthy, but her demeanor was akin to what Elijah would have expected from a cornered animal. Her eyes darted back and forth, and she tensed at every stray sound. It didn't help that Nerthus's trees were still there. Nor did the presence of the stag help. The other deer had already lost interest, but the giant hart, with its crystalline antlers glowing with moonlight, refused to go anywhere.

So, Elijah said, "You know what? I think we'd all be more comfortable if I took you somewhere a little more civilized."

"W-where?" the woman demanded.

"There's a town a couple of miles that way," Elijah said. "We'll have to go by boat, but . . . Well, they're a lot better equipped to help you and your friends than I am."

"A town?"

"Ironshore. It's new," Elijah explained. "Nerthus, help me with the unconscious ones."

In his absence, Carmen had moved the rowboats to the dock, so that was Elijah's intended destination. The boat in which the castaways had arrived didn't look very seaworthy, and the last thing Elijah wanted to do was rescue a bunch of drowning people in the event their makeshift vessel broke apart.

"What's your name, by the way? I'm sorry that I don't remember, but it was more than four years ago," he said. "A lot has happened since then."

"Guinevere," the redheaded woman answered. "And that's John. The three in the boat are Rajesh, Leo, and Ada."

Those three still hadn't awoken, but Elijah's efforts in healing had at least dragged them away from the brink of death. He would have settled down to do more, but he was more than eager to get them away from his island. It wasn't a place for strangers, and the only way he intended to tolerate their presence was if there was absolutely no other option. If it was a choice between revealing his secrets and letting them die, he would certainly do whatever was necessary to keep them from that fate. But now that they weren't in danger of passing away from exposure—or whatever had knocked them unconscious—he had the option of protecting the knowledge of his Grove.

Besides, after the reception Nerthus had given them, they didn't seem particularly comfortable on the island. Still, it took some convincing to get them to follow him. Elijah understood it—they looked like they'd been through a lot—but, in the end, his help was contingent on them following his lead. If they chose not to—or if they showed violent tendencies—he would do what needed to be done. Fortunately, they were too exhausted to put up much resistance, and soon enough, they were following him along the shore toward the dock.

Elijah had to deal with one of the crabs along the way, but by that point, the crustaceans were so weak—in comparison to him—that he only had to use Snaring Roots to immobilize the creature while they moved on. By the time the spell wore off, the party had gotten far enough away that the intellectually limited crab had forgotten about them.

After only half an hour, the group reached the dock Elijah had had built to accommodate the dragonstone blocks. It was a sturdy thing, much larger than he now needed, and the construction certainly suggested a level of development Guinevere and John hadn't expected. It was surprising enough that it actually took them a few moments to notice Ironshore a couple of miles away.

Often, Elijah took the city's growth for granted. Part of it was that he just didn't care all that much about a few extra buildings or the wall they'd built for protection. However, that attitude was also the result of how gradually it had expanded. Yet, when he thought back to his first visit, when Ironshore had been only a little better than a mining camp, he couldn't help but be impressed by the urbanity now on display.

The average building hadn't grown appreciably larger, but there were a few that towered more than ten stories tall. But the largest difference was the architecture, layout, and the density of development. It looked a lot like an idealized version of Victorian London, though with a lot more trees—at Elijah's insistence—and lacking the pall of smog that such a city might've had in the past. One thing Elijah would say about the changed world—with combustion having been so negatively affected, people had been forced to turn to cleaner forms of energy. In some places like Easton or Argos, that meant using solar and wind power, but in Seattle, they'd incorporated ethera into the mix. Ironshore exclusively used ethera to power lights and the few mechanical devices they habitually used. So, the atmosphere surrounding it was much cleaner than any city of its size would have been before Earth had transformed.

It took some doing to get everyone back in the boat. Clearly, both John and Guinevere had some serious trauma related to the ocean, and the fact that the strait was mostly protected from the true behemoths of the sea did little to assuage those issues. Regardless, the draw of civilization was too great for them to resist, and eventually, they climbed aboard. Once they did, Elijah started rowing.

Which reminded him of how grateful he was that he could now fly. He certainly hadn't missed paddling across the strait.

Regardless, with his attributes, it didn't take very long to cover the distance and arrive at the Ironshore docks. That's when the castaways got their next shock.

"What the hell is going on here?" asked John, staring at a goblin fisherman.

"Is that a . . . little person?" asked Guinevere.

"Oh. Shit. I forgot to tell you that Ironshore was founded by gnomes, dwarves, and goblins," Elijah said. "For the most part, they're decent people who are just trying to survive."

Of course, they didn't take Elijah at his word, and when they climbed onto the docks, they did so with no small degree of caution. Fortunately, another familiar face was in the area.

"Colt!" Elijah half shouted. "I'm so glad you're here."

"What's up, hoss?" asked the cowboy as he sauntered down the dock. He had replaced his missing hand with a solid-metal facsimile. It didn't move—not like Isaiah's mechanical leg—but Colt didn't let that affect him. He was wearing a wide-brimmed hat and his armor, and the dust coating everything suggested that he'd just gotten back to the city. "I was 'bout to head over to the island." He tipped his hat to Guinevere, adding, "Ma'am."

Elijah explained what had happened, and Colt helped him gather the still-unconscious people. A few dwarves pitched in, and soon enough, they were nestled snuggly in the healing house, as the locals referred to it. Elijah couldn't think of it as a hospital, largely because they didn't practice medicine as he knew it. Instead, they were wholly reliant on magical healing and alchemical solutions provided by Biggle's operation.

Once they were settled in—and Guinevere and John were satisfied that they were being cared for—Elijah escorted them to the Imperium, where he rented them a multibedroom suite. The pair were more than a little impressed with the decor, and Elijah wasn't particularly happy about the cost, but he felt the castaways deserved a little pampering after what they'd been through.

When they went upstairs to get cleaned up, Elijah also went to Mari's shop and bought them some basic clothes to replace the rags they were wearing. After that, he had one of the Imperium's employees take the clothes to the suite while Elijah settled in to wait in the lobby.

"Where do you think they've been?" asked Colt, sitting in a chair near Elijah. He leaned forward, his elbows on his knees. "They looked like they've had a pretty rough go of it."

"I don't know," Elijah said truthfully. He hadn't gotten any details, but there was a suspicion tickling the back of his mind. "They were on the same plane as me, though. Ripped apart, like, two seconds after Earth was touched by the World Tree. I guess I was the lucky one, even if it didn't feel like it at the time."

"How many survived?"

Elijah shrugged again. "At least these five, I guess. I don't know any more," he admitted.

"Damn."

"Something like that," Elijah agreed. Afterward, they fell into a comfortable silence. That was one thing he liked about Colt. The man didn't speak unless he had something to say.

Eventually, a much cleaner pair emerged from upstairs. They'd still clearly been through the wringer, but they seemed much more energetic than before. Elijah hoped that a good meal would help them recover, so he took them to a small restaurant that could offer both privacy and generous portions. It wasn't as good as the Stuck Pig, and it certainly wasn't as fancy as what they could've gotten in the Imperium, but it was still better than most.

At first, Guinevere and John were a bit reticent, but once the food started flowing, they loosened up. And eventually, they told him of the events they had experienced over the past four years.

"The plane crashed in the middle of an island," Guinevere said after stuffing herself. "It was a volcanic island surrounded by an enormous atoll. That, in turn, is surrounded by an eternal storm that's larger than any cyclone I've ever heard about. We were in the eye of the storm. But so were the harpies."

Elijah paled as she went on to describe the creatures and explain that, a year before, the harpies had blessedly disappeared, flying through the storm and giving the survivors peace. Until that point, they'd had no choice but to hide in an extensive cave system that was populated by all sorts of dangerous monsters. But compared to the harpies, clashing with the cave monsters was far more preferable.

With the harpies gone, though, they had finally gotten up the courage to leave the caves, and they'd even scavenged enough material to build a boat that they hoped could survive the storm.

"Then, the harpies came back," John said, his voice grave. "We lost almost half our people before we could get back to the caves. That's when we knew we had no choice but to leave. They'd never give us peace. The others—about fifty are left now—are still there, hiding in the caves. We started off with almost two hundred. I don't know how so many survived the crash. But it won't be long until they're all dead."

"That's why we need help," Guinevere said. "Otherwise, they're all going to die."

It was not the explanation Elijah had expected, but after having experienced the wrath of the harpies, he knew just how deadly those creatures could be. He was one of the strongest people in the world, and they'd nearly killed him once before, so he expected that they could rip through normal people without issue.

That the plane-crash survivors had been forced to hide underground was not surprising, given what Elijah knew.

He'd wondered where the harpies had come from as well as where they'd ended up. Now he knew. Or at least he hoped that was the case. The alternative—that there were two flocks of those monsters flying around out there—was enough to send a shiver of fear up his spine.

But he knew he couldn't help. Not immediately, at least. Not only was the Trial of Primacy on the horizon, but he'd already committed to assisting Sadie Song in Hong Kong. And between helping tens of thousands of people and saving fifty, he knew which way he'd go.

More, Elijah had seen the storm Guinevere had referenced. He'd experienced the outskirts, and he knew that he wouldn't easily make it through, even if he chose that route.

As the woman looked at him expectantly, he asked, "How long can they survive underground?"

John was the one to answer. "As long as necessary. They have orders not to go topside unless there's no other choice," the scarred man said. "The caves are dangerous, but it's a danger they know."

"You're not going to help," guessed Guinevere.

"I . . . I can't," Elijah said. "Not immediately, at least. I've encountered those harpies once before. I can't beat them alone. I barely survived last time. I need to get stronger, or I need help. I have plans for both, but they're going to take some time."

"How long?" she demanded.

"The Trial of Primacy is in four months," he said. "Maybe a little less—I sometimes lose track of time."

"It's closer to three," supplied Colt.

"Right. That," Elijah said. "Then, I'm going to help Hong Kong, which has been overrun by undead and demons. Hopefully, that will solve my issues. I'll get stronger, and I'll secure the help of my allies from Hong Kong. Then, we can go after your people."

Guinevere clearly wasn't happy about that, but she held her tongue. By comparison, John seemed a little more understanding, though disappointment was still etched on his scarred face. However, Elijah had been entirely truthful with them. Even if he could help them—which, given the power of the harpy flock, wasn't possible—he still had obligations elsewhere.

It wasn't what either of the two castaways wanted to hear, but it was all Elijah had to offer.

77

COMING OF AGE

Miguel sat in the center of the Grove, his legs crossed as he meditated. A gentle rain fell upon his head, soothing his tired muscles. He had been training for hours, running, swimming, and lifting various rocks before spending even more hours working on his weapons forms. It was an exhausting regimen, but one to which he'd remained committed for weeks.

Because he knew the cost of weakness. He had seen it with his own two eyes. He had felt it as he was rendered helpless by the man who'd kidnapped him and as he'd trekked across the wilderness, completely incapable of contributing his fair share. Certainly, he'd made himself as useful as he could, but he had been severely limited by his age and lack of archetype. But he'd also seen how the Scholars had held the group back, and in the end, that experience had been a formative one for the young man.

He refused to be weak.

And so, without the benefit of his archetype, he'd taken to his uncle's training regimen with the full weight of his commitment, pushing himself well past the point of exhaustion. The only time he rested was when his body gave out, and even then, while Nerthus used his healing skill to assist recovery, Miguel worked on preparing the more esoteric facets of development for the moment when he would eventually awaken his archetype.

At first, meditation had been difficult. When Elijah had tried to guide him, Miguel had only felt a faint whisper from the natural world. However, with Nerthus taking the reins, things had gone much more smoothly. Part of that was the environment. The Grove was thick with ethera, to the point where it had initially felt suffocating. Now, though, Miguel used that dense energy to his advantage. He couldn't really harness it—not to fuel abilities or anything. Nor could he guide it the same way that others could. But living in that environment brought him even closer to nature, affirming his attunement in his mind.

He didn't need a line on a status to tell him that he was nature attuned. He knew it in his heart. Perhaps he always had. Even before the world had changed, he'd been fascinated with animals—what young boy wasn't?—but he'd also spent more time in the wilderness than most of his friends. Both of his mothers thought it was important, and though his experiences hadn't been quite as extensive as his uncle's, it had laid the foundation for who he was. And everything he'd been through since then had built upon that framework to become what he hoped was a strong attunement.

According to Nerthus, they weren't all equal. One person's nature attunement was not the same as another's. It wasn't graded by the system, but it was an undeniable truth of the multiverse. And Miguel's attunement was very strong. Not quite as powerful as Elijah's, but that was expected. Again, based on what the spryggent had said, the power of Elijah's attunement was at the peak of what was possible, which was one of the reasons he'd been so successful in his chosen archetype.

Miguel hoped it would be indicative of his own impending success.

Suddenly, he felt a wet nose nudging against his neck. He tried to ignore it, but that only made it more insistent. Finally, he let out a sigh and opened his eyes to see Trevor gazing at him expectantly. The fawn had grown to the size of a normal doe, and his antlers—crystalline, just like his father's—had begun to grow. At present, they were barely more than a pair of nubs on his head, but one day, they would be just as impressive as Bubba's.

"Fine," Miguel said, reaching into his pocket and retrieving a small pouch that was filled with Grove berries. He'd been on a steady diet of the things since coming to live in the Grove, but he could still only handle about half a berry before being overwhelmed by ethera and passing out. Still, he'd been told that they were good for him, and because even one bite gave him the nutrients of a full meal, he'd continued to eat them most days. It was much easier than having to prepare food or worry about what he wanted, which gave him even more time to train.

He tossed one to the juvenile deer, who snapped it out of the air, then turned a circle in excitement. Sometimes, Trevor reminded Miguel of a puppy, which never failed to bring a smile to his face. The entire family of guardians loved those berries, but Nerthus had wasted no time in training them not to just help themselves. If there was one rule on the island, it was that nobody should encroach on Nerthus's garden. In a lot of ways, the Grove was more his domain than Elijah's.

Miguel took a deep breath, and as he felt the dense ethera permeate his body, he took a moment to appreciate his surroundings. During the journey from Easton to Seattle, he'd often felt that he would never be safe again. Yet, here he was, completely and unequivocally safe from any real danger.

And all he wanted was to run off into the real wilderness and regain that feeling of danger that had once pervaded his life. There was something about spending his days balanced on the edge of a knife that made him feel more alive. Training—especially sparring with Colt or Kurik—went a long way toward filling that void, but it just wasn't the same. He wanted to fight. He wanted to scratch and claw for the smallest advantage that would allow him to survive.

It wasn't the adrenaline he craved. Rather, he wanted to matter. He wanted to make a difference. He wanted power, and not just so he could protect the people he cared about. That was a big part of it, but there was also a need to rise above hardship, to endure what others could not. To stand up against whatever the world could throw at him and come out on top.

In short, he wanted to be challenged. To fight for fighting's sake. And he wanted to win. He needed it, and not just for the confirmation that he was better than the obstacles—be they natural or otherwise—arrayed against him.

That was why Miguel trained so much. He never again wanted to be found wanting. To be too weak to overcome adversity. He knew that wasn't realistic. He couldn't always win. Everyone lost. But that wasn't the point. Striving for that goal was all that really mattered.

Those thoughts were racing through his mind while he scratched the fawn between his eyes. Then, suddenly, words appeared before his inner eye:

Scanning human (Miguel Rodriguez) for aspects. [Nature] aspect found. [Martial] aspect found. [Faith] aspect found. [Exploration] aspect found. Generating class choices . . .

"It's happening . . ."

The aspects were not surprising. He'd expected both of the first two, even if he'd hoped to receive the [Scholar] aspect, as well. If he'd still held out hopes of becoming a Druid like his uncle, they were dashed against the reality of his aspects. Without the [Scholar] aspect, it just wasn't possible.

What surprised Miguel was the [Faith] aspect, mostly because he'd never been particularly religious. He knew that his mother had grown up Catholic, but when she'd left Southern California, she'd also moved away from that religion. By comparison, his other mother had maintained her faith, but she'd kept it mostly to herself, letting Miguel decide his own path. The world had changed before he'd ever had the chance, and as far as he could see, finding God didn't make a lot of sense in the new version of Earth. Others, he knew, disagreed.

So, the addition of the [Faith] aspect was a little shocking. Perhaps it didn't refer to a faith in God or religion, but rather in something else. Like family. Or the Grove. Whatever the case, he didn't think he'd get a proper explanation anytime soon. The Branch's Knowledge Base was apparently difficult to navigate, so he'd need to find a Librarian to search out a guide that might explain it. And that just didn't seem all that important at present.

That thought had just crossed his mind when the next notification appeared:

> You have been awarded four choices of class archetypes. Choose well because this decision will forever affect your path.

Miguel had barely finished reading the message when the next appeared:

Archetype: Warrior
A versatile melee archetype, proficient with most weaponry. Features bonuses to durability, Strength, and learning martial techniques.

Required Aspect:
[Martial]

Sample Class Choices:
{Berserker}, {Guardian}, {Knight}, {Brawler}, {Gladiator}

First Skill:
Heavy Blow

Compatibility: 91%

Close on that description was the next:

Archetype: Explorer
The Explorer is a hybrid between the Ranger and the Warrior, with some traits of various other archetypes. Focuses on experiencing new things and discovering new places. Features bonuses to travel speed, memory, and stealth.

Required Aspects:
[Nature], [Martial], [Exploration]

Sample Class Choices:
{Scout}, {Cartographer}, {Treasure Hunter}

First Skill:
Wanderlust

Compatibility: 74%

Then came:

Archetype: Ranger
The Ranger is a hybrid between the Explorer and Warrior archetypes, with strong ties to both the martial and natural paths. Gives up true mastery of either path in favor of versatility. Features bonuses to durability, Regeneration, and One with Nature.

Required Aspects:
[Nature], [Martial]

Sample Class Choices:
{Predator}, {Tamer}, {Trapper}

First Skill:
Instincts

Compatibility: 91%

And finally, he saw the last option:

Archetype: Priest (H)
The Priest is a hidden archetype only available to those of strong [Faith]. It is a combination of Healer and Tactician, with a focus on leading a group of believers.

Required Aspect:
[Faith]

Sample Class Choices:
{Preacher}, {Inquisitor}, {Ritualist}

First Skill:
Preach

Compatibility: 51%

The only surprise was the final option, Priest, which was apparently a hidden archetype that wasn't part of the foundational twelve. He'd never heard anything about the existence of such an archetype, but it was right there in the notification.

"Did it happen?" came Elijah's voice from behind.

"How did you know?" asked Miguel, glancing back to see his uncle's expect-ant expression.

"I felt a surge of ethera. I didn't know what it was until I realized it was com-ing from you," Elijah answered. "Any surprises?"

"Warrior, Explorer, Ranger, and Priest," Miguel read. "The last one is . . . special. It says it's a hidden archetype."

"Interesting," Elijah said, striding forward and planting himself directly across from Miguel. "Read me the description?"

Miguel did, realizing that Nerthus had come to observe, as well. When he'd finished, Elijah announced that he was going to get Miguel's mother and Colt, cautioning him to wait until everyone was there before he made any decisions.

As Elijah transformed and flew away, Miguel asked Nerthus, "Do you know anything about hidden archetypes?"

"No. I only know of the foundational twelve," Nerthus admitted. "But do not mistake its hidden status for power. No archetype is better than the others. Just different."

Miguel wasn't so sure about that. Scholars were markedly weaker than everyone else, at least from his experience. Sure, he recognized that they had their place in society, but that position was dependent on other people to pro-tect it. Without Warriors and Sorcerers, Scholars were extraordinarily vulner-able. Perhaps that was why he hadn't been offered the archetype. It was fine for others, but he never would have chosen it.

"I won't pick it," Miguel said after thinking about it for a couple of minutes. He had no interest in leading followers, and he certainly didn't like the religious connotations of the terminology used in the description of the Priest archetype.

Otherwise, he was a bit torn. He'd expected to get the Warrior and Ranger archetypes as choices, but the addition of the Explorer option was a small sur-prise. Certainly, the Treasure Hunter class that was used as an example in the description awakened something in him. The idea of being rewarded for expe-riencing new places and things was attractive, as well.

But some of that enthusiasm might've been due to the fact that it was new. He'd never even considered it as an option, while he'd been thinking about the Warrior and Ranger archetypes for months. As a result, the novelty certainly contributed to his excitement.

As he gave it some thought, the others arrived, and they began a discus-sion about his future. Miguel knew that it was ultimately his decision, but he would've been a fool not to consider their more experienced opinions.

Elijah put a lot of stock in how the system interpreted his compatibility, while Carmen was more concerned with how he felt. Meanwhile, Colt mostly kept his input to factual statements about what to expect, clearly not wanting to offer undue influence over whatever choice Miguel might make.

For his part, Miguel's decision came down to two options. The Explorer archetype was interesting and novel, but it only took a few minutes' worth of thought for him to discard it. The Priest archetype he'd immediately pushed aside. That left Warrior or Ranger, both of which had extremely high compatibility. So, the choice was one of preference. Did he want to face his enemies head-on? Or did he want to use subterfuge, range, or circumstances?

When he thought of it like that, the decision was easy.

He chose Warrior.

Notably, it was the same archetype his mother had picked. And it wasn't the one her murderer had chosen. He'd have been a bit deluded to think that those facts hadn't affected his own decision.

He felt an influx of ethera that felt like electricity racing through his body. It wasn't unpleasant, but he could feel the surge of power. More, because of his extensive efforts in meditation, he immediately felt the flow of ethera that would allow him to use abilities and, one day, cast spells.

Then, with a thought, he opened his status for the first time ever:

Name	Miguel Rodriguez		
Level	1		
Archetype	Warrior		
Class	N/A		
Specialization	N/A		
Alignment	N/A		
Strength	8		
Dexterity	8		
Constitution	10		
Ethera	9		
Regeneration	7		
Attunement	Nature		
Cultivation			
Body	Core	Mind	Soul
Unformed	Unformed	Unformed	Unformed

"Which one did you pick?" asked his mother.

"Warrior," he said. Then, he explained his reasoning before reading his status to everyone. His mother seemed a little disappointed—or saddened, perhaps—but she tried to hide it. So, Miguel pretended not to notice. By comparison, Colt and Elijah—and even Nerthus—were all smiles.

"Well, you know what this means, right?" asked a grinning Elijah.

"What?"

"Now, you get to start the real work."

78

ON THE HORIZON

You know we can't just babysit him, right?"

Elijah glanced at Carmen, unsure of how to respond. One thing that had almost immediately become clear after Earth had been touched by the World Tree was that leveling was weird. Some things that seemed like they should have given multiple levels barely gave a trickle of experience, while other actions resulted in a flood of progress. He was aware that there were whole classes dedicated to charting the most efficient leveling paths, but he'd never actually met anyone like that. Probably because Scholars, by their very nature, tended to be quite vulnerable, and the situation on Earth wasn't settled enough to guarantee their safety. As a result, compared to most other archetypes, few Scholars had survived.

Whatever the case, he'd learned that watching over Miguel while he tried to level would result in quite a bit less experience than if the young man acted alone or with a group of similarly leveled people. It brought to mind how slowly he had progressed when he'd first been stranded on the island. Over the first few months, he'd killed dozens of crabs, and while they weren't particularly high level, they should have given much more experience than they had. Except that, the entire time, he'd had the panther watching over him, providing him with a safe environment and ready to step in if it looked like Elijah was going to die.

Maybe.

Elijah wasn't entirely certain how it all worked, and he didn't think that would change anytime soon. All he could do was keep going and hope things became clearer as he gained power. Regardless, it wasn't as if gaining levels had ever been the goal. Sure, he liked the way progression felt. He liked getting stronger. But the vast majority of his choices were based on other factors, and leveling had usually been a by-product of seeking out other goals.

"I know," he said, knowing that Miguel would never progress if he had Elijah as his guardian angel. "It just sucks."

"It does," agreed Carmen, taking a sip of coffee. "I wish he would have chosen something noncombat."

"I don't think he had the option."

"He didn't, but that's my fault, too," Carmen said, glancing at Elijah. "Ever since the world changed, I've let him pursue a future as a fighter. At first, I just looked at it like it was a new sport, like he'd taken up football or something, but with the added bonus of letting him protect himself. Then, everything with Alyssa happened . . ."

"It's not your fault," Elijah said.

"It really is," she argued. "I could have brought him into the forge with me. He might have enjoyed making things. But I was so scared. So focused on everything else. And I just pushed him off to Colt. That sealed it."

"I could see that," Elijah contributed. For better or worse, Colt was invariably cool. He wasn't the most powerful person in the world—far from it—but few children could look at a cowboy samurai and not want to emulate him. That was compounded by the fact that Colt was a good, loyal person who took to the mentor role quite well. It was inevitable that Miguel would end up idolizing him.

Carmen leaned back in the chair and gazed across the Grove toward where Miguel was going through guided meditation with Nerthus. It was the first step in preparing the young man for cultivation, which would take up the next month of his life. Only then would Miguel step out into the world and start leveling. Thankfully, there was a large enough population of children in Ironshore who'd recently come of age that there was an opportunity to form parties. Once they did, they would venture out into the local wilderness and hunt the relatively weak beasts in the region. Then, after they'd gained their classes and established teamwork with a static team, they would be given slots to run the local tower.

Elijah wished he could just take Miguel in and escort him through the tower, but the level difference was far too great, and as a result, Miguel would never survive the run.

"It really is frustrating, isn't it?" he said. The system seemed to want people to rise or fall on their own merits. Sure, there were exceptions. They could load Miguel up with high-grade equipment, but even that wasn't foolproof. If the gear was too powerful, he wouldn't be able to support it. So, the help they could offer was limited, mostly to training and preparation, but that could only go so far.

"More than you can know."

"Are you going to make him some armor? A weapon, maybe?" he asked. Thinking that Miguel would eventually choose to become a Ranger, Elijah had been on the lookout for a good Bowyer, but those plans seemed a bit silly now that the young man had chosen to become a Warrior. "You know I still have the spear you made for Alyssa."

It had been incorporated into the statue back in Argos, but it wouldn't be difficult to replace it.

"No. Leave it where it is. I intend to make something special."

"How's your forge project going?" he asked, changing the subject. They would get nowhere by going in circles about their impotency concerning Miguel's development.

Carmen answered, "It's going. I'm about a third of the way finished with the bricks, but there's a lot more to it than something like the Temple of Virtue."

Then, she went on to describe the process, which involved incorporating the high-grade sun copper and blood tin, as well as their alloys, into the entire building. Moreover, the structure would take on the shape of a series of enchanting runes Carmen had learned via a guide. And finally, she intended to make every smithing tool from those high-grade metals. The project wasn't something that could be finished in a few weeks, so Carmen expected to be working on it for quite some time. Months, at the very least. However, given the high density of the ethera in Ironshore—due to the ancestral tree in Druid's Park—Carmen thought the final result would be quite powerful for both cultivation and for crafting purposes.

"What about you?" she asked.

Elijah just leaned back with a sigh. Sitting on his balcony overlooking the Grove, it was easy to forget how much work he had ahead of him. Three issues demanded his attention, and he didn't know which one he'd focus on first.

There was the situation in Hong Kong. Elijah still intended to help rid the city of undead, but given that the source was a primal realm, he knew it wouldn't be the work of a few days. Instead, it would likely take weeks just to fight their way to the primal realm, then an unpredictable amount of time to conquer it. Likely, it would be a dangerous and deadly monthslong endeavor.

Then, he needed to help the survivors of the plane crash, though that presented a host of issues, as well. The largest problem was reaching the atoll, but Elijah had fought—or run from—the harpies, so he knew precisely how much danger their presence added to the mix. Exterminating those monsters would be at least as difficult as conquering the primal realm in Hong Kong.

And finally, he needed to prepare for the Trial of Primacy. He'd never considered not going, though he suspected that eschewing the Trial was probably the most prudent course. But Elijah knew it was important. He wasn't sure exactly how, but he was certain that it would be a formative experience for Earth's future elites. Not going would cripple his position.

Fortunately, the only time-sensitive issue was the Trial, largely because his most recent visit to a Branch resulted in yet another announcement from the system. It read:

> The Trial of Primacy is ninety-six days away. To assist with preparation and to offer peace of mind for the participants, surges from towers will be halted until the Trial is completed. In addition, forces from primal realms will be quarantined during that time frame.
> Prepare yourselves in peace.

That solved the Hong Kong problem, at least for the time being. And according to John and Guinevere, the crash survivors could survive indefinitely. They'd have to do so underground, but they'd managed it for more than four years, which meant that their plight wasn't nearly as urgent as it seemed at first glance.

"I think I need to get ready for the Trial," Elijah said. "It feels important."

Carmen agreed, though she still refused to participate. According to her, she had more than enough on her plate, what with the construction of the Great Forge, equipping her son with as high-grade gear as he could handle, and satisfying the terms of her obligations to Ironshore. But Elijah knew that much of her reticence was due to simple fatigue. She'd had enough danger for a lifetime, and she wanted nothing more than to remain safe and sound in her smithy.

Elijah understood that sentiment. For many people, challenging towers and fighting powerful monsters seemed like an adventure, but that only lasted until they actually had to confront those dangerous situations. That was usually when they started to see the value in a safer existence.

He wasn't like that, but he recognized that his attitude probably made him a bit of an anomaly. Sure, there were plenty of other people like him, but they were the clear minority. Normal people didn't relish repeatedly risking their lives, even when that path had the potential to lead to immense power.

Regardless, Elijah understood Carmen's perspective. He even agreed that it was probably best for her. But it didn't apply to him.

With that in mind, he itemized his plans for his preparation. The first step was one he'd been working on for quite some time. He knew he was close to progressing his Core to the next stage of development, and the ambient ethera in his cultivation cave had grown so dense that he thought it would be enough to push him over the edge. That was the first—and by far the most important—step, but it wasn't the only one.

He wanted to prepare some more soap. He also needed to commission a Cook to make rations out of the meat he'd gotten from the boar. In addition, he intended to hire a Leatherworker to create some armor. And finally, his preparations for creating a new staff had reached an acceptable point, so he needed to do that, as well.

Once he'd explained all of that to Carmen, she asked, "Have you told the castaways yet?"

Elijah shook his head. He also needed to let Sadie Song know about his plans, and he wanted to help Wilhelm find a powerful intersection of ley lines so the German Explorer—whom he'd left in Argos without an explanation—could take the first steps toward building a teleportation apparatus near Argos. That wasn't quite as important as the other tasks on his list of priorities, but he knew just how beneficial it would be for the city. Perhaps it would one day become something of a trade hub. A crossroads, so to speak.

That was a long way down the road, though. But the first step was easy enough to take, and if Elijah planned everything properly, it would only be the work of a day or so. That was a small price to pay to ensure the prosperity of the people of Argos who'd been so welcoming to him.

And finally, there was a party on the horizon. After all, a young man only came of age one time in his life, and it was an event worthy of celebration. So, with that in mind, Elijah headed to Ironshore to buy some supplies. He didn't intend it to be a citywide carnival like what had happened in Argos at the completion of the Temple of Virtue; instead, he knew Miguel would prefer something with just family and close friends.

Elijah could handle that, but afterward, it would be time to get to work.

79

OVER THE EDGE

I'm never drinking again," Elijah muttered to himself as he lay in his bed of moss. Massaging his temples, he refused to open his eyes. He'd made that mistake once already, and even the gentle light from the glowing flowers on the ceiling was enough to send spikes through his hungover brain. Taking a deep breath, he used Soothe, but even that was only marginally effective. So, he cast Nature's Bloom, and at last, his roiling stomach and the pounding pain behind his eyes subsided. He took a deep breath, then sat up.

He felt gross.

And lethargic, despite his efforts at healing himself.

That was the problem with drinking high-grade liquor. It cut right through his enhanced Constitution, even resisting his healing spells. By any measure, it was a poison—just one whose effects were slightly more enjoyable than most. At least in the moment. The aftereffects were markedly less pleasant. If most people drank what he'd drunk, they would've had to deal with more than simple inebriation. Someone like Miguel would have died in minutes.

Smacking his dry mouth, he reached over to his Endless Canteen and took a sip—an effort to wash the disgusting taste out of his mouth. He was unsuccessful, but with every pulse of Soothe, Elijah felt a bit better. So, he dragged himself out of bed and immediately went to his shower, where he let the scalding water as well as his rejuvenating soap do its work. When he finally stepped from the bathroom, he almost felt human again.

After dressing, he headed into the kitchen, where he immediately got to work on the most important cure for his hangover—coffee. By the time he planted himself in his favorite chair on the balcony and took the first sip, most of the aftereffects of the party had faded. In their place was mingled determination and embarrassment at the night's antics.

There was a reason that, after college, he'd mostly given up on serious drinking. Multiple reasons, in fact. The first was the simple knowledge that it wasn't good for him. Back then, he'd used alcohol—and other inebriants—to mask the lingering issues that had cropped up from his parents' deaths. The responsible and oft-ignored well-adjusted part of him knew that wasn't healthy, so he'd moved on from that phase of his life.

But more importantly, drinking always brought out the worst parts of his personality. Even in the best of times, Elijah was quirky and an acquired taste. When he drank, though? He was much worse, and more than anything, embarrassment loomed large in his memories of those days.

So, it was a bit surprising that he'd gone so hard during Miguel's coming-of-age celebration. He'd refrained from drinking too much while his nephew was still around, but the moment Miguel had wandered off—either to train or sleep—Elijah had started drinking far more heavily.

Thankfully, the rest was a blur. Hopefully, he hadn't made too much of an ass of himself, though he didn't put much stock in that hope.

Over the next half hour, Elijah enjoyed two cups of coffee as he sat back and appreciated the early-morning atmosphere of the Grove. Nerthus was already up and about, working on the garden. He'd expressed to Elijah his plans to rework the Grove, and while Elijah would miss the rows of bushes he'd planted in the very beginning, he'd been convinced of the potential benefits the change could bring. The same was true of the rest of the island, which would be far less cultivated, but still be structured according to Nerthus's plan. According to the spryggent, that would hasten the process of increasing the ethereal density—which Elijah could certainly get behind. Still, he couldn't help but feel a sense of loss when he considered the planned changes.

Perhaps Nerthus would manage to retain the place's wild aura.

In any case, Elijah couldn't afford to add micromanagement of the Grove to his list of tasks. He already had plenty on his plate as it was, so he'd decided to give Nerthus free rein when it came to the Grove and the surrounding island. He trusted the spryggent, after all.

By the time Elijah had finished his coffee, the other residents of the Grove were up and about, though, thankfully, no one was in the mood for socializing. That wasn't surprising, given that, aside from Miguel, they'd all had far too much to drink. Even Nerthus had tried a sip of some sort of liquor Colt had acquired. It had not gone well, with the spyrggent immediately passing out. More distressingly, quite a few of the plants in the area had reacted to the event by quivering out of control.

Fortunately, that had only lasted a couple of minutes until Elijah had healed Nerthus—which sort of defeated the purpose of drinking, but in that situation, he thought that was a good thing.

With those memories in mind, Elijah started on his errands. The first stop was to start the process of creating lye, which only took about half an hour before he was forced to wait while the ash soaked. After that, Elijah flew to Ironshore, where he took Carmen's advice and hired the goblin Leatherworker Gavina. She'd actually gained a few levels since his last conversation with his sister-in-law, so Gavina was the same level as the other Leatherworker in town.

"Are you sure you want me to work with this?" Gavina asked, her voice a bit raspy due to her goblin heritage. She was short, even for her race, with huge bat-like ears and a surprisingly dainty nose. Unlike most goblins, her complexion trended more toward blue than green. She ran her hand along the rolled-up boar hide, adding, "This is better than any material I've ever worked with. I might ruin it."

"There's a lot of leather there," Elijah said. The boar had been enormous, after all. "I'm not saying you should waste it, but maybe you should start with armor padding. I think Carmen's going to be coming to you in the next day or so. Use the excess for that."

"I still don't know . . ."

"And there's enough material for a few attempts. Don't sweat it," Elijah said. "I believe in you."

"You don't even know me."

"Right. Well . . . that's true. But I still believe you can do the job!" he said. "I've heard good things. You're an up-and-comer."

She sighed. "This is a lot of pressure."

"Pressure makes diamonds."

"Actually, it's heat and pressure and—"

"My point is that you've got this," Elijah interrupted.

"You're not going to kill me if I fail, right?" she asked. "I mean to say—I appreciate the work. It's a great opportunity. But there's a chance I'll fail, and I don't want you to eat me if I do. Respectfully. I'd rather just not take the job. But then again, maybe refusing the commission will also get me eaten. I'm in a tight spot, I guess is what I'm saying."

"Eat you?" Elijah asked, his jaw dropping. "I don't eat people!"

"That's not what I heard. Respectfully."

"Respectfully," he echoed, annoyed. "You heard wrong." He shook his head. It almost felt like his hangover was coming back, even though he knew that wasn't possible. "I swear to you—I don't just kill people for that kind of thing. And I don't eat people."

"If you say so . . ."

After that, Elijah managed to persuade the goblin Leatherworker to take on the job, paying her far more than he probably should have. Was it a negotiation tactic, then? Or was she truly frightened? Elijah had no idea, but if it meant being done with the uncomfortable conversation, he had no issues with throwing money at the problem.

In any case, he'd managed to accomplish the first goal. He knew the next step was going to be even more uncomfortable. Still, it had to be done, so he returned to the Imperium and let Guinevere and John know that he wasn't going to be able to help their people anytime soon. He'd already said as much, but he wanted there to be no confusion about his priorities going forward.

Surprisingly, though they were obviously disappointed, they took the news well enough.

So, once all of that was finished, Elijah headed for the next item on his to-do list. He needed to get stronger, and there was only one way to accomplish that goal. He had access to a tower—and it just so happened that there was no one inside at the moment, so it was time he used it.

With that in mind, he headed into the Keledge Tower.

Fortunately, he was intimately aware of the tower's ins and outs, and given that he didn't care about his grade, the run was both brutal and efficient. He killed everything, soaking in the experience as he slaughtered his way through the tower. The tower still scaled to his level, so the enemies inside were powerful enough to give him a challenging fight. However, he knew precisely how to attack each level, so he had few issues with finishing it in only a few days.

And though the combination of escalating experience requirements and the decreasing rewards for running a tower multiple times minimized his gains, Elijah still managed to reach his goal. Level ninety.

Which gave him a new ability:

Ability: Bestial Charge	Charge an opponent. You are shielded from harm while charging. Maximum distance based on Strength. Current distance: 138 feet. Shield efficacy based on Constitution. Only usable while under the influence of Shape of the Guardian.

It wasn't a flashy ability, but it was useful. He'd long hoped for some way to close distance with his opponents—especially in his lamellar-ape form—so it definitely filled a gap in his tool kit. Upon testing Bestial Charge, Elijah had found that it worked precisely as he'd hoped, and though it was a little difficult to control, he felt confident that, once he got the hang of it, it would become a vital part of his tactics.

After he left the tower, he was happy to find that Miguel's efforts in cultivation had proceeded well. The young man still hadn't actually taken the first steps, but according to Nerthus, he was close to that point.

Elijah spent a bit of time making more lye for his soap before using Roots of the World Tree to head back to Argos. Once there, he found a very irritated Sadie Song waiting for him at the Temple of Virtue, where he quickly learned she'd spent most of the past week healing anyone who'd visited.

Upon retreating into one of the rooms they'd set up for more intense healing sessions, he apologized for leaving on such short notice. "I had some issues at home that I needed to take care of," he said. "I panicked a little, and I'm sorry. I hope you'll forgive me."

She responded, "Do I have a choice? We need your help. There's not much we won't put up with if it means you'll assist us in saving Hong Kong."

"About that . . ."

Elijah went on to explain that he wouldn't be able to help until after the Trial of Primacy, which was met with exactly the sort of response he'd expected. Sadie was not happy with him, but given that the situation would get no worse until after the Trial, she wasn't as upset as she might have been. So, she accepted his excuses, saying that she intended to participate in the Trial, as well.

"You seem surprised."

Elijah admitted that he was, adding, "I thought you'd be . . . I don't know . . . I guess I'm not sure what I thought."

"The Trial of Primacy will be a good place to make contact with powerful people," she explained. "Also, I need to be stronger. Already, I feel like I'm being left behind, now that I'm not fighting zombies every day."

It was a surprisingly open moment from her, and Elijah didn't know how to respond to the lack of overt animosity. So, he just nodded, saying, "We all need to get stronger. I don't know what comes after this Trial of Primacy, but I'd be willing to bet things are going to get worse before they get better. We're building toward something. I just don't know what. In any case, I'll do everything I can to help you and Dat during the Trial."

She promised to do the same, and the conversation petered out into awkward silence. Elijah excused himself soon after that and went in search of two people. First was Agatha, whom he hired to prepare his rations. She was the best cook he knew, and what's more, she seemed to like him. So, he wasn't averse to paying her quite a lot of money to create pork jerky from the boar's meat. She was happy to do it, too, saying that it would help her level.

Elijah found his next target in a nearby gambling establishment. Predictably, Wilhelm had used his newfound freedom to embark on a quest to lose whatever money he'd managed to stash away. Elijah had seen the man pocketing a few bits and pieces from the boar, which he'd presumably sold as soon as Elijah's back was turned. Surprisingly, Wilhelm had actually hit a bit of a winning streak, multiplying those few silvers into quite a stockpile of gold. So, he was very upset when Elijah dragged him from the gambling hall and into the wilderness. He was less upset when they found a powerful intersection of ley lines that would serve as an appropriate location for a teleportation apparatus.

So, Wilhelm marked it with an anchor, then activated some sort of ethereal beacon that would guide the construction team there. They couldn't actually build the apparatus yet—they didn't have everything worked out—but Wilhelm hadn't gambled all his time away. Instead, he'd been working on a report based on watching Elijah's Roots of the World Tree spell that he hoped would be the missing link for the teleportation process.

Elijah hoped so, too. His plans to position Argos as a trade hub depended on it.

Either way, that satisfied the last item on his to-do list, so Elijah returned to the Grove so he could embark on the next—and most time intensive—part of his preparations.

He needed to push his Core to the next level of advancement.

That would require him to be at his best, so he spent the next day secluded in his tree house, cycling his Core while eating as many Grove berries as he could handle. That influx of ethera pushed his Core to unprecedented density, which he held in place as he headed toward the cultivation cave.

It wasn't easy. In fact, holding that much ethera still was incredibly painful, and it made him feel like he was on the verge of bursting like an overfilled balloon. Yet, Elijah hoped it would make the next part more effective, so he endured the bloated agony as he swam through the underwater cave. Along the way, he noticed the steadily rising ethereal density until, when he reached the cave itself, it felt almost suffocating. Even though he didn't need to breathe—courtesy of the Ring of Aquatic Travel—Elijah still felt like he was drowning.

It was precisely what he needed, though.

For the past couple of weeks, he had felt like he'd reached the absolute limit of what his Core could handle. Cycling in a normal environment wouldn't do much good anymore. Indeed, even the ethereal density of his Grove was insufficient. Thankfully, though, the ambient ethera of the cave was much thicker.

Hopefully, it would be enough.

So, as he floated in the center of the cave, he closed his eyes and began to cycle. At first, it felt like trying to work out after running a marathon, and it only got more difficult from there. One rotation after another, he stirred his ethera, pulling even more into his Core. It was like trying to mix molasses it was so difficult to move, and in the beginning, he felt that he'd made a mistake, that he wasn't ready.

But Elijah persisted, sinking into the meditative state he'd practiced so often. And though the process didn't get any easier, his persistence paid off by helping him cope with the hardship.

After the first day, Elijah recognized that, as powerfully dense as the ethera in his cultivation cave was, there was a good chance that it wouldn't be enough. The requirements to push his Core to the next level were unreal, telling him that it would be quite some time before anyone else on Earth reached the second stage of Core cultivation.

One day turned into two, and two into three. And by the time the first week had passed, Elijah couldn't help but wonder if he'd allocated enough time to complete the process. He couldn't worry about that, though. Instead, he continued to eat the berries, which wasn't nearly as appetizing as it normally was, given that he got some saltwater along with each bite. They did provide nourishment and, perhaps more importantly, sent even more ethera surging through him.

By the end of the second week, Elijah was nearing the end of his endurance. Or that was what he thought until that week turned into another. Each moment inched him closer to his goal. His Core continued to expand, bit by bit, and despite his exhaustion, he knew he couldn't afford to stop. If he did, he would lose most of his progress, and he didn't relish the notion of starting over. More importantly, he didn't have that kind of time.

So, he continued to cycle his Core, drinking in the ambient ethera along the way. Fortunately, the cave had reached the point where it created a perpetuating cycle of ethereal renewal, and it replaced most of the energy he absorbed.

Finally, at the beginning of Elijah's fourth week of cycling his Core, he felt it shift. Suddenly, it expanded of its own volition. It felt like he was on the verge of exploding, the energy inside of him was so intense. He screamed in pain as it tried to rip him into a thousand pieces.

And then, just as the pain reached a crescendo, everything—his senses as well as his Mind—went dark. It only lasted a moment before his perception returned. He fell to the ground, his body slapping against what felt like cold tile. That's when he opened his eyes.

His jaw dropped as he looked around, but he didn't get a chance to take it all in before a voice drew his attention.

"I thought it would take you longer to reach this point," it intoned. "I suppose congratulations are in order. Welcome to the Empire of Scale, whelp."

80

THE PATH LESS TRAVELED

Elijah couldn't speak.

Instead, his breath caught in his chest as he stared at the woman in front of him. She was gorgeous, though that was the least impactful characteristic on display. Power, closely controlled, swirled around her, nearly overwhelming Elijah, body, mind, and soul. Even his Core went quiet, almost as if it sensed a much greater power and was trying to make itself smaller so it could avoid notice.

Golden hair—and he was close enough to recognize that it was actual gold, and not just gold-colored hair—fell upon her slim shoulders. Tiny, gold, and glittering scales surrounded her eyes like makeup, and slightly larger scales patterned her neck, disappearing beneath the white toga-like garment she wore.

Finally, Elijah regained his voice and asked, "Who are you?"

She smiled slightly. "Your patron," she answered, reaching down to stroke his cheek. "You have done well since being granted the Dragon Core, but it is time for you to take your first step on the path. Until now, you have been aimless. A hatchling without purpose living a life without meaning. That must change, and the first step is one every dragon must take. You will live the tale of the first dragon. If you survive, your Core will evolve to the next stage."

"If I survive?" he asked. Until that moment, he'd expected the evolution of his Core to work similarly to the other aspects of his cultivation. Indeed, everything he'd read suggested as much. Clearly, the reality of his situation was quite different, though. Was it because he had the Core of an elder race?

"A small detail," she said. "We do not have much time. Remember, the dragon endures."

"I don't under—"

Before Elijah could get the rest of his sentence out, his mind once again went black. This time, it lasted much longer than an instant, but he had difficulty marking time. It might've been a minute, but it could have been hours. Regardless, he eventually became aware of his changed surroundings.

And his changed body.

At first, he thought he'd had one of his forms forced upon him, but it only took a few moments to recognize that he was in a completely different body.

He lacked the strength of his guardian form, and he certainly didn't feel the unmatched coordination of his draconid shape.

Then, there was the size to consider.

Looking around at his surroundings, Elijah couldn't avoid the notion that either he was inside a cavern whose size dwarfed any other he'd ever experienced or heard about—not impossible, but unlikely—or he was much smaller than he'd been before. In addition, his Mind felt strangely limited, and it only took him a few more seconds to recognize that he lacked cultivation. He only had one strain of thought instead of nine distinct facets.

Casting his perception inward, he was distraught to find that his ethereal channels were much thinner and far less extensive than they had been before. And finally, his Core was tiny. It was little more than a spark of ethera, barely even noticeable within his torso.

A nearby sound jerked his attention to his left, and he saw a skittering bug. Before he could even process what was happening, he pounced, snapping his jaws around the insect and swallowing it whole.

In his shock, Elijah took a moment to truly take stock of his changed form. He was small. Very, very small. Maybe a foot long at most, and that was including his tail. Looking down at his forelegs, he saw pebbled red scales and a set of wicked claws. So, at least he wasn't completely defenseless, though he knew that if he was forced to fight anything truly strong, he'd be better off fleeing than engaging.

More, a sense of being exposed gripped his Mind, and he followed his instincts that pushed him to find shelter. When he slipped into a crack between a pair of black rocks, the panic in his Mind subsided—only a little, but enough to give him leave to investigate his surroundings.

The cave was enormous, and his small size made it seem like a world unto itself. Moreover, it wasn't unpopulated. As Elijah stuck his serpentine head out of the crevice, he saw dozens of other beasts. Some were large—like the turtle-like creature sitting next to a lava flow—while others were even smaller than him. Trees unlike anything he'd ever seen sprouted here and there, alien in their form as well as their coloring. Distressingly, Elijah also lacked One with Nature, and judging by the fact that he felt no connection to the wildlife, his attunement had disappeared, as well, replaced by animalistic instinct.

Panic once again suffused Elijah's being until he forced himself to remember his patron's description, that he would live the tale of the first dragon. Was that what had happened? Was that whose body he inhabited? It wasn't what he might have expected from his impression of dragons. Every story he'd ever heard—both before and after the World Tree had touched Earth—painted dragons as immensely powerful entities.

Clearly, that wasn't always the case.

Humble origins aside, he couldn't just hide between rocks. His patron—who was obviously a dragon, though in a humanoid form—had said that he needed to live the life of the first dragon. So, he suspected that he would fail this . . . test if he didn't do something.

With that in mind, he crouched low to the ground, then slithered out of the crevice. Almost immediately, a sense of alarm suffused his Mind, and he dashed to the side. Something crashed into the rocky ground beside him, and following instincts whose origin he didn't question, Elijah pounced on his would-be attacker, using his wickedly sharp claws and teeth to rip it to shreds like he was the reptilian equivalent of a honey badger.

As it turned out, the beast that had attacked him was some sort of odd bird, though not of a sort that Elijah had ever seen. Its wings were too large, its body too sleek. And its beak was far too sharp.

Sensing that it wouldn't be smart to stick around the kill site, Elijah took a few bites of the beast's flesh, then raced away. Dodging from one rock to the next, he blended into the landscape, while behind him, more beasts descended upon the slain bird. A fight broke out between two heavily armored creatures, but by that point, Elijah was already gone. Still, the sound of their clash—which was characterized by smashing bodies and deafening growls—followed him as he skated along.

As he did, he examined the feelings in his body. He didn't have spells. Nor did he have skills. There was no spell book, and he didn't have a status. However, he had enough experience with using ethera that he could recognize the framework of a skill within him. It was unlike anything he'd ever used, though, so he had no idea how it worked.

There was something else inside of him, too. A spark of energy he couldn't identify. It was weak, but it was still there, just powerful enough to taunt him with his ignorance. Elijah tried to ignore it as he moved on.

Soon enough, he reached one of the lava flows. It cut through the underground forest of odd trees like it was a river, but as he approached the flow of molten rock, he felt oddly comforted. Following his instincts—they were so powerful that he could scarcely resist them—he dived into the fiery flow.

It was only when he was burrowing through the thick and superheated substance that he realized what he'd done. He'd just dived headfirst into a river of lava. If he'd been back on Earth, perhaps he could have survived by virtue of his high Constitution, but this body didn't have the benefit of enhanced durability. By all rights, he should have melted the moment he got close.

But he didn't.

Instead, he felt empowered, as if the lava was his natural habitat. It was only in retrospect that he realized that, before, he'd been like a fish out of water. Now, he was in his element.

Yet, he couldn't let his guard down, as he discovered when what looked like a giant alligator gar with flames for fins tried to eat him. He darted out of the way just in time to avoid its enormous jaws—or, more appropriately, its mouth full of jagged teeth—then burrowed through the lava to hide in the rocks on the riverbed until the thing lost interest. As it happened, a much larger creature that looked like a bulky hybrid between a crocodile and a manatee bit the gar in half.

Despite the heat permeating his body, Elijah felt a chill race up his spine.

The environment reminded him a little of the Sea of Sorrows or the Primordial Jungle, both of which were floors in the Keledge Tower. They weren't really all that similar to his current location, but the primordial, survival-of-the-fittest aura was close enough to bring those two to mind. It gave Elijah some more insight into the constant conflict that pervaded any natural environment. Every organism had a drive to survive, and that took precedence over everything else. They didn't care about morality. They didn't feel empathy or hate. They battled one another because that was the only way they could meet the conditions of their primary mandate.

Survival was the name of the game, and everything else was irrelevant.

Elijah remained nestled in the rocks at the bottom of the lava flow until the current took the remains of the gar away. The other beast went with it, swimming away without even realizing—or perhaps caring—that he was there. Finally, Elijah slipped from his hiding spot, then burrowed his way through the flow until he reached the other side. It wasn't swimming—not really. The substance was far too dense for that, and the ease with which he moved in the substance defied physics in a way Elijah didn't really want to think about. Either way, he reached the other side easily enough, then climbed free. A few bits of magma clung to his red scales, but they fell away after they cooled.

Creeping through the brush—which, to his eyes, was a mixture of purples, blues, and oranges—Elijah kept moving. He ate a few insects here and there, but he'd been moving for more than an hour before he recognized what drove him.

The ambient ethera in the cavern was already dense, but with every step he took, that density rose. And his instincts pushed him toward the increasingly thick ethera. Was there a source? Maybe.

Elijah needed to find out.

Days passed as he continued to live the life of the small lizard whose body he'd come to inhabit, and in that time, a few things became abundantly clear. First, he was far from weak, and he'd often found that he could stand up to creatures much larger than himself. It was never easy, and there had been more than a few close calls, but he'd even managed to take out beasts three times his size.

The only issue with that was the fact that, aside from the insects, he was just about the smallest creature in the cavern. From his perspective, it felt as if he'd set foot into a world of giants. Everything towered over him, dwarfing his tiny size. That brought with it both advantages and disadvantages. The former, in that he often escaped notice from the much larger beasts. The latter because, if they knew he was there, he had very little defense except running and hiding.

It was a valuable learning experience. Of late, Elijah had adopted some bad habits, most stemming from the fact that he was the highest-level person in the world. That had led him to believe he was more powerful than anything he encountered. It wasn't true, as he'd discovered with his recent confrontation with the boar, but habits weren't easy to discard.

He'd been in need of a reality check, and his time as a lizard was perfect for that, even if he felt like he was balanced on the edge of a cliff, just waiting for something to splatter him like a bug.

Regardless, as he crossed the subterranean jungle, Elijah's own experiences from his first couple of years after Earth's transformation combined with the lizard's natural instincts to keep him out of harm's way. More than once, he was forced to traverse more lava flows, but those instances were more comforting than not, even if those rivers of molten rock were home to some of the most powerful creatures.

Finally, though, Elijah reached his destination when he arrived at the edge of an enormous crater. For the first time, he could look up and see the sky through the huge mouth of the cave. Predictably, it was not a sky he recognized. Instead of seeing a starry expanse populated by a single moon, Elijah saw colorful bands that it took him a moment to recognize as planetary rings.

More concerningly, he also saw huge shapes flitting about the sky. Some dwarfed even the massive cave, casting everything in shadow for a few seconds before they flew away.

But Elijah was more interested in what lay at the center of the crater. It was a flower the size of a cottage. A lotus, if he wasn't mistaken, and it was wreathed in orange flame. Clearly, he'd found the source of the increased ethera.

Unfortunately, Elijah wasn't the only one because the entire surface of the crater was packed full of every sort of beast he'd seen since beginning his trek across the large cavern.

He hissed in annoyance as he began to ponder just how he was going to get closer to that flower.

81

CUNNING

Elijah crouched on the tree limb, using his long tail for balance as he watched the creature down below. At the most basic level, it looked a little like a rhinoceros, though with scales instead of a thick leathery hide. It also had seven horns jutting from its densely armored head and a series of spikes flowing down its spine.

So, perhaps it was more like a dinosaur than a rhino.

Either way, it didn't matter. The creature was precisely what he'd been looking for over the past few days. Its suitability for his plan was based on three things. First, it wasn't just huge. The thing was the size of a brontosaurus, with a stout, low-slung body that would make it a nightmare to fight. Second, it was incredibly territorial, and Elijah had watched it slaughter more than a couple of other beasts that had wandered nearby. It had also chased a sleek wolflike creature for more than a mile.

And finally, it swirled with ethera strongly enough that Elijah could feel it, even in his much less sensitive form. That told him that it was powerful—perhaps even more so than all the creatures in the crater, which was perfect for his plan.

The idea was simple enough. He wanted to pick a fight with the enormous creature, then lead it on a merry chase into the crater, where he hoped the other beasts would respond to the newcomer with violent intentions. A fight would ensue, and if everything went according to his plans, they would finish each other off.

However, simple didn't mean easy, and the anticipation kept Elijah glued to the branch. That monster was large enough that even a glancing blow would flatten him. There would be no margin of error. No room for mistakes. He would have to be perfect.

To that end, he'd already mapped out his path. The crater was more than a mile away, which was an incredible distance for his small form. Still, he'd practiced running back and forth so often that he knew he could make the trip without missing a beat. The only variable was the giant beast's reaction.

In the back of his mind, Elijah knew that he was driven by instinct as much as by his own brain. He was reliving a real event, and as such, the whole experience was on the rails. That didn't remove the danger, though. He could still die. And he could certainly fail. But the path to victory seemed clear.

It was an odd feeling, knowing that he was in control, yet not, and rather than trying to grow accustomed to it, Elijah had chosen to simply accept it, then move on. Already, he'd spent days on this endeavor, and aside from not wanting to spend any longer than absolutely necessary, his ever-more-insistent instincts told him that he was on the clock.

So, without further hesitation, he leaped from the branch, landing on the rhino lizard's armored head. A second later, and he was burying his claws into one of the thing's many eyes. The orbs were larger even than Elijah's entire body, but they were curiously vulnerable. His claws bit deep, and an eruption of vitreous gel coated his body. Yet, even as the creature bucked and trumpeted its ire, Elijah moved on to the next eye.

Then the next after that.

In all, he savaged four eyes before leaping free and racing away. Predictably, the beast followed, driven by the pain of the attack as well as its territorial nature. Elijah leaped from one fallen branch to the next, dipping in and out of various depressions as the beast stomped its way through the forest, plowing through trees, uprooting them as it went. Apparently, Elijah had compromised the beast's depth perception, and so, it found it difficult to avoid trees it would have otherwise dodged.

That was the only reason he stayed ahead of it, confirming that his instincts had put him on the right path.

On and on he raced, and the mile or so he had to travel felt like ten times that. Still, when he finally reached the crater, he knew that his task was just beginning. He skidded down the slope, aiming for the hiding place he'd found the day before. Just as Elijah slid under the rock and into the small space underneath, his enormous pursuer thundered out of the forest and, without hesitation, barreled into the mass of beasts surrounding the flower.

The enraged creature spared nothing in its path, ripping into them with its horns as it completely forgot about the pest that had started it all. The other animals didn't go down without a fight, and they dished out hundreds of wounds in the space of a few minutes. But where they could only barely get through its thick armor, the rhinosaur killed with every twitch of its head.

It was a massacre, but not one without cost.

Elijah crouched in his hiding place, thankful for his tiny size, as the beast rampaged through the crater.

Of course, it was not the only powerful monster in the area. Far from it. The closer it came to the flower, the stronger its opponents were. And given the sheer numbers arrayed against it, its wounds soon grew more numerous and far more grievous. Still, it fought on, well past the point where it would even consider retreat.

Besides, it was a king of the forest. Running away had never been an option.

The battle raged on for hours as one beast after another fell until, at last, there were only three left. Predictably, the rhino lizard was one of the survivors. It was barely capable of remaining upright, but as it stood over the other survivor—a beast that looked like a *Tyrannosaurus rex*, but with fur instead of scales—it let out a roar of victory.

Just as it speared its opponent through the chest, the third survivor—Elijah—struck. Once again, he went for the vulnerable eyes, tearing the remaining four orbs to pieces before the creature could even react.

Then, he bounded free, feeling ethera gathering in his chest. He had felt the skill since the very beginning, but it had taken him quite some time to figure out how it worked. Now, he knew. He felt it. He only needed to push things a little more before he could activate it.

The beast reacted predictably, swinging its great armored head like a spiked battering ram. Elijah leaped over the first attack, twisting in the air before landing lightly. The power built a little more.

But it wasn't enough.

A second attack came whistling toward him. This time, he flattened himself to the ground, then vaulted over a third attack. The fourth came straight at him like a spear intent on piercing his heart. So, Elijah twisted away, narrowly avoiding having his body obliterated.

On and on it went. The blinded creature tried to trample him. It attempted to spear him. It kept aiming one sweeping attack after another at him. If Elijah had had a moment to consider it, he would have been impressed by the beast's unerring aim. However, he had no chance to think about anything but avoiding the next attack. And with each avoided blow, Elijah felt the power build a little more.

Then, finally, it was like a switch had flipped inside his mind.

The skill was ready.

And what's more, he could feel what it would do. The power of a dragon welled up within him, and when he released it, it was just as devastating as he could have hoped. His mouth yawned open, and a gout of pure red flame erupted from his throat. It was so hot that it blistered his own forked tongue, and yet, it continued to pour out, hotter with every passing second.

The fire gouged into the beast's face, carving a blistering gash from one side to another. It reeled in obvious agony, but Elijah kept going, embracing the skill to the fullest extent of his abilities. Red turned white, and the flames graduated to a new level of destruction. Instead of blistering and burning, they simply obliterated anything in their way.

The ability only lasted a few seconds before Elijah's tiny store of ethera was spent, but in that time, the fire had burned a hole right through the king of the cavern. Elijah had been aiming for its brain, but the stream of fire had gone far past that, melting through its skull and digging through its body, boiling its internal organs along the way.

It tried to step forward, but all it could do was collapse.

Elijah stared at it for a long few seconds, shocked at the power he'd brought to bear. Before that moment, he'd wondered how such a small lizard could have ever been linked to a dragon.

Now, he understood.

He swayed drunkenly as he struggled to remain upright. Using the skill had pushed him well past the point of exhaustion. But still, he staggered toward the lotus. It pulsed with thick ethera, promising power and, Elijah hoped, recovery. Besides, it was his prize, wasn't it? He'd engineered the deaths of every beast in the crater. By all rights, he deserved his reward.

Even as those thoughts danced in his mind, Elijah put one foot before the other. Only a hundred or so yards separated him from the lotus, but that short distance felt like a thousand miles. He continued forward, feeling his body breaking down with every step. He'd gone too far. He had pushed himself too much.

But he would not be defeated.

He couldn't let himself give in.

He would claim his treasure.

Gradually, he staggered forward, and after what felt like an eternity, Elijah reached the lotus. He could feel the power wafting off of it, nearly strong enough to destroy him just as surely as the backlash from his skill had. It didn't matter.

It was his.

Reward? Trophy? Treasure? Or salvation? Maybe it was all four. Regardless, every one of Elijah's instincts told him to climb to the top of the lotus. There, he would finally be able to rest.

So, he did, using his sharp claws to dig into the plant's rubbery stalk. His body was tiny. He barely weighed more than a few pounds. But it felt like he had the weight of the world on his back.

He could feel his scales sloughing off, revealing blistered flesh. He ignored it. He was in so much pain that it had long since lost meaning. There was power within him, though. A bright sun had bloomed stronger with every step. He'd felt it inside of him, and that feeling drove him just as surely as his instincts.

Finally, he reached the blue petals. The fire burned him, yet the pain was nothing compared to the agony already coursing through him. Or that was what he told himself. In reality, he was on the verge of surrendering to unconsciousness. If he'd been in control, he would have. But his instincts had taken over, and he had become a passenger in his own body.

It didn't matter.

He wanted the same thing his instincts wanted.

He only had to hold on. To endure. To persist. So, that was what he did, and after a few moments, it felt like he was watching himself from afar. He finally saw the lizard's body. It resembled a salamander, though with a crested mane and fire dancing along its scales.

He watched. He felt. The duality of his existence was difficult to track. He was Elijah, a witness. But he was also the salamander, driven forward by instinct and fate as it embarked on a task that would change the multiverse.

At last, the little lizard crested the petal and tumbled forth, passing the collection of stamens and coming to rest on the carpel. For a moment, Elijah thought that it—no, he—had died. But with a twitch, it rolled back to its feet. Then, miraculously, it released the power within it.

Though it did not send out a large gout of superheated flame. Instead, the power came out the other end, taking the form of a large golden egg. Only once the egg had pushed free did the lizard finally give in to death.

For a few seconds, Elijah felt as if he was hovering over the entire scene, and he watched as the world sped up. His heart caught in his throat when the egg hatched, but instead of another salamander, the first dragon was born.

That's when Elijah's mind went blank, and after a couple of moments, he once again appeared on the cold tiles within the Empire of Scale.

His patron knelt beside him as he wept, her warm hand on his back. He knew he'd just seen something quite profound. The beginning of real power. But all he could think about was the salamander's sacrifice. Its suffering. Its perseverance. It might not have been a dragon, but it had certainly possessed the spirit of one. Going forward, he could only hope to emulate its example.

82

PATH OF DRAGONS

Elijah lay on the cold floor, overcome with emotion as the memory of what he'd just seen—of what he had just experienced—engulfed his thoughts.

"It truly is overwhelming, is it not?" came a voice from above. Elijah recognized it as coming from his patron—the beautiful woman who'd greeted him before he'd been thrust into another life. "I still remember when I saw it. Tens of thousands of years, and that memory is still as fresh as it was when I was a hatchling."

Her voice was wistful. Motherly. Comforting in a way Elijah couldn't quite articulate. After a moment, he felt her standing over him. Heat radiated from her body, far hotter than a person should be. Finally, he looked up to see her smiling face, and he reveled in her approval. In that instant, Elijah wanted nothing more than to please the dragon woman.

That feeling passed quickly, but the echoes remained long after, influencing his thoughts like nothing else could.

"Arise. We haven't much time."

Elijah pushed himself to all fours, then rose to his feet. Glancing down, he realized that he looked the same as he had before being pushed into that memory. The same could be said of the dragon woman that was his patron, though even if nothing had changed about her appearance, to Elijah, she looked even more striking than ever before. It was as if, until that very moment, he'd never seen true beauty, and now that he had, nothing else could compare. He wanted to drop to his knees and worship her like that goddess she clearly was.

And he didn't like that one bit.

"Stop doing that," he muttered.

"What?" she asked innocently.

"Whatever you're doing to my mind," he answered. "I don't like it. So, stop." Belatedly, he added, "Please."

That brought a studious gaze followed by a tinkling laugh. A second later, the enchantment of her presence faded. After it did, Elijah could still tell that she was gorgeous, and in a way that defied the notion of imperfection. However, it was a distant thing. Alien in its flawlessness. He'd once thought the same about elves, but in comparison, they were warm and approachable.

"Most whelps have difficulty seeing through my Presence," she said with another smile. "I am pleased that you managed it. I knew you were special the moment you completed the quest and saved my daughter."

"Sara? Wait . . . You're . . ."

Elijah was loath to admit it, but he'd actually forgotten the name of the dragon who'd given him the quest that had changed his life. Saraalinisa was far more memorable in his mind, largely because he'd actually met her. By contrast, her mother, who'd given Elijah the quest, was just a line on a notification.

"I am Kirlissa, third elder of the Golden Flight," she announced. "And your patron."

"I don't understand what's going on. Why am I here?" Elijah asked.

"You are not here, strictly speaking," she explained. "Your spirit is. Each step you take on the Path of Dragons will be progressively more physical. In addition, you will gain more control over the memories until, in the end, you will write the story yourself."

Elijah nodded, though he wasn't entirely sure what she meant, save that he was having some sort of out-of-body experience. "Was this a test, then?"

"In a sense," she answered. "It is also necessary for each dragon to understand our history. Without the context of our origin, dragons tend to grow . . . arrogant. When I feel myself becoming overbearing, I remember that my race began with a simple fire salamander."

"I see," Elijah lied.

"No. You do not. But you are no true dragon—not yet—so your lack of perspective is forgivable," she said, her smile widening slightly. It was the sort of expression a mother would bestow upon a troublesome child who'd somehow managed to make her proud. It made Elijah want to squirm away.

"How did the salamander do it?" he asked. He suspected the dragon wouldn't reveal much more about his circumstances, so he chose to move on to the purpose of the entire vision. "I felt her falling apart after using that fire-breathing ability. She shouldn't have made it to the top of the lotus. And when she got there, she just laid an egg and died? How was it fertilized? How did the baby dragon survive?"

"So many questions," Kirlissa said. "The answer to most is that we do not know. The Mother of Dragons was an enigmatic creature, and the Dream was pieced together from thousands of scattered sources. We have no insight into why she sought the Fire Lotus. Nor do we know how the egg was fertilized. The first dragon's path is lost to time. The only thing we know for certain is that it survived and thrived, and our race was born. Some of our most talented Scholars suppose that the egg was fertilized by the Fire Lotus itself, giving birth to a creature of mingled magic and flesh, though other factions refute that claim. Wars have been fought over the details."

Elijah could understand that. On Earth, people killed one another over religion all the time, and the origin of dragons seemed like the same sort of thing. So, Elijah decided to push his curiosity aside and focus on what really mattered.

"What will happen next?" he asked, glancing around at his surroundings. He stood in the center of a grand hall that was lined with white marble pillars capped with gold. In the distance, he saw a massive throne that stood before an even larger pile of treasure. Elijah could feel ethera wafting from the collected mass of gold etherium, and he even saw quite a few coins that were probably platinum.

It was the dragon's hoard.

"In a moment, you will return to your body and complete your cultivation. Most of it is finished, but you still need to push your Core to the next stage," she explained. "It will be painful, but if you could endure the origin of dragons, you are more than capable of withstanding the transition from the first stage to the second."

"And after that?" he asked. "Am I going to grow scales or something?"

She laughed again. "No," she answered. "Not unless you wish to, and not until much later in the cultivation process. You have taken the first step on the Path of Dragons, but you have a long way to go before you can truly call yourself one of us. That is how it is with dragonkin like yourself."

Her face turned serious. "I will warn you now. There are those in the Empire of Scale who will treat you as lesser because you are not a natural dragon. These . . . people are wrong. If you reach the right stage of cultivation, you will be as much a dragon as anyone in the empire," she explained. "Perhaps more so. Until then, you will need to remain on guard for those who would look down on you for your humble origins."

Elijah sighed. "Dragon racism," he muttered. "Great."

"Do not worry yourself. You will not soon reach the empire, and by the time you do, I will have prepared the way," she said. "You did not hatch from one of my eggs, but you are still one of my children. And I will brook no disrespect against my family. My protection will only go so far, though. You must learn to fly on your own merit."

"I will," Elijah said. And he meant it, too. He would take any help he was offered, but he'd been on his own for long enough that he was more than comfortable with that.

"I believe you," said Kirlissa, reaching out to stroke his cheek. Her touch felt like being hit by a tiny bolt of lightning. "I am forbidden from giving too much information concerning what is coming. Even I am subordinate to the system. However, I will offer you this advice. Do not underestimate the benefits of conquering primal realms. The fate of your world will depend on it."

"How—"

Elijah never got the chance to finish his question. Instead, his mind once again went blank, which lasted for a few moments before he once again found himself within his cultivation cave. All around him, the water roiled with kinetic energy as well as ethera, and his Core felt as if it was going to burst. It had grown far larger than before he'd been whisked away, and the ethera inside had become much denser, reaching the point where it felt like he held a bowling ball in his chest.

He grabbed the ethera, wresting it under control. Agony erupted inside of him as the Core grew larger with every passing second. He clamped down on it, compressing it with every ounce of resolve he possessed. At first, it barely responded, but after a few agonizing moments, it reacted to his will.

Enduring the pain of so much power rushing through him, Elijah focused on the final step he needed to take before progressing to the next stage. Leveraging every facet of his Quartz Mind, he took hold of the ethera raging throughout his body and forced it all into his Core. However, he didn't do it without direction. Instead, he used that ethera to progressively, layer by layer, reinforce the structure of the Core.

Adding each layer felt like moving a mountain.

But he persisted in his efforts, and he endured the agony.

Minute by minute, he shoved more ethera into the Core's structure until he felt like it was on the verge of going supernova.

Without the advanced stage of his cultivation, Elijah never would have managed it. His Mind let him control the flows of ethera while quarantining the pain into its own facet. Meanwhile, if his Quartz Mind gave him the ability to control it all, then his Novice Soul provided the means by which that control could be exerted. Without those reinforced channels, the process would have backed up.

Ethera was the source of everything, but too much of even a good thing was tantamount to poison. The immense flow of energy racing through him was no different, and it required significant durability to withstand so much ethera. That was where the Body of Stone came into play. Without reaching the second stage of Body cultivation, the powerful flows of energy would have dissolved the flesh from his bones.

Even with the advantage of his cultivation, Elijah struggled to endure the power of progressing his Core. That, he'd learned, was one of the issues with something like a Dragon Core. It was far more powerful than other, more normal Cores, but that power came at a cost. One of those was that it often had special requirements attached to its progression. Elijah had just experienced that for himself, and he expected those conditions would only grow more onerous with each step he took on the so-called Path of Dragons. In addition, even when those requirements were met, actually progressing a special Core required far more effort and ethera. Doing so before advancing the other aspects of cultivation was generally viewed as suicidal.

Fortunately, Elijah's Body, Mind, and Soul had already reached the second stage, which gave him just enough of an edge to manage his powerful Core. Still, it was as exhausting as it was agonizing, but he endured until, at last, his Dragon Core started to absorb every last drop of ethera in the area. At first, he tried to corral it, but it quickly became apparent that the process had progressed far beyond his ability to control it. He could only endure and hope that he'd done enough.

Power on a level he'd never experienced raced into the vortices in his Mind, scorching its way through the pathways of his Soul and into his bloated Core. Even as the ambient ethera flooded into him, the surrounding water evaporated. As he fell to the cave's floor, the flora and fauna disintegrated, providing even more fuel for the transition. Elijah barely noticed it. Instead, the whole of his attention was on the expanding globe of power at the center of his being.

He leveraged every last ounce of his willpower into compressing it. One heave after another, it shrank, and inch by inch, relief flooded Elijah's Mind, Body, and Soul. Then, just as his exhaustion bypassed the boundaries of what he could endure, the process completed, and he received a notification:

Congratulations! Your Dragon Core has reached the Whelp stage.

Just before Elijah's body gave out, he let out a dry chuckle. Whelp. It sounded almost derogatory, and it didn't indicate the level of power he'd just felt racing through his body. But before he could contemplate the irony of that name any further, he lost consciousness.

83

FINAL PREPARATIONS

Elijah awoke to the sensation of something nibbling on his toe. At first, he barely even noticed it, but then consciousness fully took hold, and he jerked his foot away. The moment he moved, the fish darted away, frightened by the sudden motion. Elijah blinked his eyes open, and his memories came flooding back.

At some point, seawater had come rushing back into the cave, so he found himself floating just above the cave's floor. The last phase of pushing his Dragon Core to the Whelp stage had killed everything within the cavern, but enough time had passed that a few fish had come to investigate. In addition, a couple of tiny strands of kelp had managed to take hold, telling Elijah that at least a few days had passed while he was unconscious.

Otherwise, he had no idea how much time had elapsed since he'd begun the process of taking the next step in his Core cultivation. He remembered that, even before reliving the tale of the birth of the first dragon, he'd spent almost a month cycling. So, given that he'd spent at least a few more days unconscious, he felt impatient to determine precisely how much time had passed.

With that in mind, he swam to the cave's exit and pushed himself through the tunnel until he reached open water. Normally, he would have taken a few hours to repopulate the cave, but for now, he needed to take stock of his situation. Before isolating himself in the cultivation cave, he'd had about three months left before the Trial of Primacy began, so he knew he didn't have much room for error.

Kicking to the surface, he leaped free of the water, then cast Shape of the Sky, transforming in midair. He flapped his wings, gaining altitude before racing across the sky toward his grove. He landed in a small open space Nerthus had created as a bit of a landing pad, then called out for his spyggent friend.

Nerthus appeared after only a few moments, and Elijah asked, "How long have I been gone?"

"Forty-eight days," Nerthus answered.

Elijah frowned. That meant he only had about six weeks left before the Trial of Primacy. He thought that would be enough time, but there was a small chance that he'd have to make some cuts to his schedule. Originally, he'd intended to run the tower a few more times in the hopes of gaining a couple more levels. However, with how much time his Core cultivation had required, that just wouldn't be possible. So, he'd have to be satisfied with being level ninety. After having reached the second stage in every aspect of his cultivation, he hoped that would be enough.

"You reached the second stage," Nerthus said. "Congratulations. Many people consider that the true beginning of cultivation."

That made some sense. It had certainly been much more difficult than taking the first step, though Elijah had no real context for what that first stage of Core cultivation usually looked like. After all, he'd accomplished it via the completion of a Kirlissa's quest, so he'd never experienced doing it on his own. However, he expected that it would have been much easier than what he'd just put himself through.

"I think I have enough time," he said, rubbing his bearded chin. "It's going to be close, though."

"If I may offer a suggestion?" Nerthus ventured.

"Sure."

"Perhaps a nice meal and a shower will help," he said.

"Are you saying that I stink?"

"Like a dead fish," Nerthus answered without hesitation.

"Ouch," Elijah muttered. "Message received."

After that, he asked about Miguel's progress, and to Elijah's surprise, he discovered that his nephew had already reached the first stage in everything but his Core cultivation. On top of that, he was well on his way to preparing himself to take that step, as well. Most of it was due to Nerthus's help. Much as he'd done for Elijah, Nerthus had sacrificed a good deal of his own power to ease Miguel's cultivation. It wouldn't have been possible if the young man hadn't possessed a strong nature attunement, and according to the spryggent, his race—or others like them—often performed similar functions in the communities that grew around Druid groves. Seemingly, Nerthus regarded it as part of his duty, and though Elijah worried about the spyrggent overextending himself, he elected to trust his judgment.

Other than that, Nerthus let him know that his plans for the garden were well underway. Soon, he would replace the Grove-berry bushes with better alternatives, and the defenses he'd begun to grow had already taken root and were thriving. In short, everything was going according to plan.

So, it was with a slightly lighter heart that Elijah retreated to his tree house to follow Nerthus's advice. He wasn't certain which was more beneficial—the shower or the meal—but, when he finally emerged, he was ready to finish his preparations for the Trial of Primacy.

The first step was to complete his soapmaking project. He wasn't sure if it truly had lasting effects, but he'd grown used to the jolt of energy he received when using it. The notion of going without while he was in the Trial was an unattractive one, so he made enough soap to last him for more than a year.

After that, he headed into Ironshore and visited a couple of shops. His first stop was Biggle's laboratory, where he picked up a few sacks of cleansing powder. Then, he visited the Tailor Mari, who sold him a few new outfits. They were cut in the same style he was used to, but they had the benefit of having a durability enchantment that would hopefully preserve them during the Trial.

He also visited the general store, where he stocked up on odds and ends that he thought might prove useful. None of it was of graded quality, but things like rope, bandages, and waterproof bedding didn't need to be, either.

Finally, he found himself in Gavina's workshop. To his surprise, the little goblin Leatherworker was actually happy to see him, which was a huge departure from their previous meeting.

"Thank goodness you came back," she greeted him, relief in her voice. "Having that armor here put a target on my back."

"Huh?"

"It's mid-Complex!" she practically shouted. "Do you know what people would do for that kind of armor? And it's the whole set, too! I'm surprised someone hasn't already killed me for it!"

"Do you really think somebody would do that?" Elijah asked skeptically. Ironshore probably had some criminal element—every settlement of any size did—but he'd heard nothing of open murder.

"I don't know! Maybe," Gavina answered with exasperation. "I'm not strong enough to fight them if they did, though. Better that you take it now."

After that, she shoved a large bundle into his hands. It was heavier than Elijah had expected, though given the materials, he should have anticipated it.

"I need a description of what it does."

The goblin Leatherworker rolled her eyes and massaged her forehead. "Ugh. Of course you do. Here," she said, handing him a piece of paper. "That's what it is. Now go! Before someone attacks!"

Elijah didn't think it was reasonable to expect an attack, but he got the sense that Gavina was the paranoid sort. She'd been worried about him killing her during their first meeting, but it seemed she'd graduated to suspecting an external threat. Still, there might've been some merit to her suspicions, especially if the armor was as high-quality as she'd said.

Before he left, Elijah took a look at the description on the piece of paper:

> **Armor of the Boar King (Set)**
>
> Composed of nine (9) pieces (bracers [2], gauntlets [2], chest guard, pants, foot wraps [2], headband). Total attribute bonuses (from individual pieces):
>
> **+15 Strength**
> **+25 Dexterity**
> **+15 Constitution**
> **+10 Ethera**
> **+20 Regeneration**
>
> When wearing the entire set, gain the ability Bulwark of the Boar King: Wrap the wearer in an impenetrable shield. Duration: Thirty (30) seconds. Cooldown: Fifteen (15) days.

"This is . . . This is amazing," Elijah said. But then he saw a problem. "These foot wraps . . ."

"Don't worry about it. I noticed that you walk around barefoot like a savage, so I figured there must be some reason," Gavina said. "Those foot wraps don't really cover much of the foot. I think they should be fine for your . . . whatever it is that keeps you from wearing shoes. And don't tell me. Nobody can torture information out of me if I don't know it!"

Elijah just shook his head at the little Leatherworker's enthusiastic paranoia. There was nothing he could do about it, though, so he just paid what he owed and left the shop behind. However, he did stop by Ramik's office to ask the mayor if he could periodically send someone by Gavina's shop to ensure that she was okay.

"I will, but you should know that this is nothing new for Gavina," Ramik said, sipping a cup of tea while he sat behind his desk. "She is a talented Leatherworker, but she came from a city ruled by an authoritarian regime. Her paranoia is well-earned, and despite my insistence that she doesn't have to worry about those things anymore, old habits are difficult to discard."

"It would still give me some peace of mind if you'd keep an eye on her. If you can't, I understand. I'll just get Colt to do it."

"No—it's fine. It will be no trouble to send someone by every few days," Ramik stated.

After that, Elijah asked if anyone else from Ironshore intended to participate in the Trial of Primacy, and Ramik answered, "We are sending one team. Kurik is leading it."

"Can you afford to lose him? Or anyone else, for that matter?" Elijah asked.

"He's the only combatant. The others are Tradesmen or Merchants. We intend to use this Trial to make some trade alliances," Ramik announced. "Our mine has proved quite productive, but that potential is being squandered by the fact that we only have one trading partner. Hopefully, this Trial will give us a chance to make some connections."

That was a bit of a surprise for Elijah, but he supposed it made sense. So far, he'd thought of the Trial of Primacy as a test of combat potential, but there was nothing to suggest that it wouldn't offer opportunities for noncombat archetypes, as well. With that in mind, he offered to help the team from Ironshore in whatever way he could, though he wasn't certain what form that help might take.

After that, his meeting with Ramik ended, and he returned to his Grove. By that point, night had fallen, and with it came Carmen, who let him know everything that had been going on during his time in the cultivation cave. Apparently, Miguel was itching to level, but he'd so far agreed to forgo doing so until he'd reached the first stage of every aspect of cultivation.

"He doesn't like it, though," Carmen admitted.

"Have you finished his equipment?"

She shook her head. "Still a work in progress. The problem is that he can't really use Complex-grade items. They're too powerful. So, I have to find a way to make something weaker, which means that I can't use the best materials. I'll figure it out before he starts leveling, though."

"I'm sure," Elijah said. "Is there anything I can do?"

"No," she admitted. "What about you? Is everything ready?"

"Not yet. I still have one project left before I go, and it's going to take a while. I don't know if I'll have enough time to finish."

"Then you'd better get started, right?" she asked. "What's the project?"

"New staff," Elijah said. "The Dragon-Touched Staff is nice, and I'll keep it as a backup, but it doesn't really do much for my damage or healing."

The staff gave him a lot of attributes, including increasing the efficacy of his buffs by five points each, but he was more interested in direct enhancements to his abilities. And besides, he had the freedom to swing for the fences. If he failed, he still had the Dragon-Touched Staff to fall back on.

"Can I help?" Carmen asked.

Elijah shook his head. "I think I get better results if I do it all myself," he said. "But I'll let you know if that changes."

"Fair enough."

With that, the conversation moved on to other things—like local gossip. None of it was really all that interesting to Elijah, but he listened as Carmen explained who was courting whom, which families were feuding, and what she expected to come from the Norcastle alliance going forward. The discussion seemed comfortably normal, which was all Elijah really wanted.

Because tomorrow, he would start the final project before he embarked upon the Trial of Primacy. Given that, a little normalcy was precisely what he needed.

84

MASTERPIECE

Elijah stood in front of the tree, unsure about his plan. In his head, it all made sense, but now that he was looking at the thing, he doubted it. Not the viability of the intended product—he felt certain he could do something worthwhile—but, rather, his doubts centered on whether or not he had the right to destroy something so vibrant. He wasn't so deluded that he equated killing a tree to murdering a person, but there were notes of that line of thinking in his mind.

It would be so easy to ignore them, but he was a Druid, wasn't he? Didn't that mean he had a duty not to do that?

"This is acceptable," said Nerthus.

"Huh?" asked Elijah turning to see the spryggent standing behind him. "What do you mean?"

"I can sense your doubt. These trees were created for this purpose. There is no shame in using them," he stated. Indeed, Elijah had asked Nerthus to grow the trees to his specifications, using acorns from the trees that ringed the Grove. They'd marked the original boundaries of his Ancestral Circle, and as such, they were infused with more potential than any other trees on his island—excepting the ancestral tree itself. And their progeny was almost as special. "If it still worries you, know that this will not kill them. So long as their roots remain, they will grow once again."

Elijah sighed. That was true, too. Still, his doubts persisted. He'd once grown angry just looking at the deforestation associated with Ironshore, and now he couldn't help but feel like he was on the verge of doing the same thing. It should have disgusted him. And yet, it didn't.

And that was worrying, largely because it signified that he wasn't really sure what being a Druid meant. Maybe the answer was that it didn't mean anything. Perhaps all the influences he thought he'd felt in the past few years were in his head.

That frightened him.

But the reality was that, the moment he'd asked Nerthus to nurture the trees, he'd become committed to using them. Because if he didn't, Nerthus would doubtless rip them up by the roots just because they didn't follow the pattern he wanted the Grove to follow.

So, without further delay, he knelt before the trees and got to work cutting them down. The trio had grown around one another, their white-barked trunks inextricably intertwined and nurtured on a steady diet of ethera. As a result, they pulsed with energy that exceeded that of any other tree in his Grove— again, excepting the ancestral tree at its center.

The trunks themselves weren't large, only reaching diameters of a few inches. Yet, they were harder than they had any right to be, so it took Elijah nearly an hour to fell them. When he finally did, he saw the thin blue veins running through them, linking each of the three trunks in a way he didn't truly understand.

But he knew enough that he could work with it.

The trees were somewhere between being saplings and reaching maturity, so they were around eight feet tall. That would be enough for Elijah to work with. So, once he had them in hand, he headed to a spot within the Grove that Nerthus had made for him. The spryggent was nothing if not anal about what grew within the Grove, so given that Elijah meant to consistently flare One with Nature as well as Nature's Bounty, he'd made a place just for that.

Settling in, Elijah got to work.

The first step was to remove the limbs, which he set aside for later. One day, he'd use them to create lye, which he hoped would make for better soap. But for now, he only wanted them out of the way.

Gradually, Elijah kept working, stripping the bark, then sanding the inter-twined trees smooth. Altogether, they were more than six inches in diameter, so he had a lot of work ahead of him to pare them down to size.

Days passed as Elijah sanded and whittled, eventually coming up with a straight white staff that was about two inches thick and six feet long. Thank-fully, he didn't have to go through the effort of straightening the shaft, so the next step was carving it. Using a series of small knives and files he'd bought for that purpose, Elijah did just that.

Along the way, he lost track of time, though on more than one occasion, he took breaks to either repopulate the cultivation cave or help Miguel with his training. Eventually, Miguel took the next step in cultivation, attaining what Nerthus referred to as a Guardian Core. It wasn't as powerful as Elijah's Dragon Core, but it was one of the best paths Miguel could hope to take without getting outside help from an elder race. After that, Miguel headed to the mainland to begin his leveling process.

Meanwhile, Carmen kept at it with the Great Forge, throwing herself into her work in order to distract herself from the fact that Miguel was going off into the wilderness where he would be forced to risk his life. That wasn't what any mother wanted to deal with, but knowing that she couldn't stop it, she had chosen to focus on her tasks. Judging by the conversations she and Elijah shared during that time, it didn't work.

Day by day, Elijah's staff took shape. He didn't dare think too much about what he was carving, but he couldn't ignore the designs that took hold at the end of his knives. Still, he did everything he could to keep his influence out of it. It was better to let the process dictate what it would be.

In the end, it took five weeks for Elijah to finish the carving, and even then, he thought he'd rushed it. If he'd had another couple of months, he would have not only been much more meticulous in his efforts, but he would have further infused it with his ethera.

Still, he was happy with the design.

The staff was straight, ending up at a little less than two inches thick. The design made it look like a Celtic weave, which bared the glowing ethereal veins. At the top was a coiled dragon, with an intricately carved head that was as detailed a piece as any Elijah had ever created.

But the staff wasn't finished.

He still needed to seal it.

Fortunately, he had plenty of wax from Nerthus's apiary, so after cutting it with some mineral oil he'd bought in Ironshore, he went to work sealing the staff. The process wasn't a short one, and it required him to leave the staff for as much as twenty-four hours while each coat of the sealant soaked in and dried. During those times, he finalized his preparations for the Trial.

He visited Argos to collect his pork jerky, and while he was there, he met with Sadie and Dat. They both had been occupied with their own preparations, but Elijah was surprised to find that Sadie had spent quite a lot of time healing people at the Temple of Virtue.

He also stopped by to talk to Delilah, where he learned that both she and Isaak intended to participate in the Trial, as well. Elijah didn't much care for that, but he knew better than to try to talk them out of it. As it turned out, Atticus was going, too, though he made it clear that he had no intention of fighting.

"If things get rough, I'll be out of there in a hurry, my friend," he assured Elijah, clapping him on the shoulder with a laugh.

Soon enough, though, Elijah had done all there was to do. He had all the supplies he could carry, and he'd even broken in his new armor. All that was left was to complete the staff, but even as the day of the Trial crept closer, Elijah refused to shortchange the project.

It was only on the day before the Trial was supposed to commence that he finally finished it, getting the following notification:

NICHOLAS SEARCY

Congratulations! You have created a unique item, Staff of the First
Dragon. This item will serve to enhance all spells by significant degree.
Overall Grade: Complex (High)
Enchantment Grade: C

Elijah pumped his fist in celebration. The staff had turned out better than he
could have hoped, though he still wasn't certain what it would do exactly. He'd
need someone to analyze it for that. Thankfully, he knew a dwarven Tailor who
had an item that would allow for just that. So, he took on the Shape of the Sky
and flew to Ironshore. He landed in the middle of the street outside Mari's shop,
which caused a bit of a ruckus. He was too excited to worry about that, though,
and he quickly hurried inside.

Of course, Mari wasn't one to be rushed, and she glared at him with disapproval before agreeing to let him borrow her analysis apparatus. Once she did,
Elijah wasted no time before holding up the small piece of what looked like
ordinary glass and channeling some ethera through it.

That was when he got a little more information:

Staff of the First Dragon

A staff created by the Druid Elijah Hart from the trunk of a juvenile
ancestral tree. It is infused with his ethera, binding it to him the
moment it was created.

+20 Strength, Dexterity, Constitution, Ethera, and Regeneration

Effect: Enhances all spells by 25%.

Effect: Increases the effective radius of One with Nature by 70%.

Ability: Rejuvenation—Use stored ethera to fuel a single cast of Soothe.
Cooldown: One (1) day. Usable in all forms.

It was beyond anything Elijah could've hoped to create, and as he read one
benefit after another, he very nearly dropped Mari's analysis glass. The attribute
bonuses alone were extremely powerful, but then it also increased the effect
of all his spells by twenty-five percent? And it more than doubled the radius
of One with Nature? And that ability? It was a perfect addition to his tool kit.

"Thank you," he said to Mari, handing the glass back to her.

"I hope you got good news. That Trial sounds a bit dodgy. Mark my words—
people are going to die in there," she said. "And for what it's worth, I hope it isn't you."

"Really? I didn't think you cared about me at all."

"Of course I do. You're my best customer," she said. "Now, get out of my shop. You're scaring everyone off."

"Aw. I'm touched," he replied with a grin. But at her glare, he quickly ducked out of the building.

After that, Elijah made the rounds, saying goodbye to everyone he was close to in town. That included Ramik, Carisa, Biggle, and even Gavina—who wouldn't even answer her door. Instead, she just pretended like she didn't hear his knock, even going so far as to innocently whistle.

Finally, he bought a veritable feast from the Stuck Pig, which he brought back to the Grove for the evening meal. That night, he and his family—including Nerthus and Colt—had something of a going-away party. Miguel had already progressed to level eight, so he would be getting his class within a couple of weeks, which was the source of some excitement. The possibilities dominated their discussion for quite some time as Miguel animatedly detailed everything he'd been doing since being let off his leash. He clearly took quite a bit of joy in the retelling, though Carmen didn't seem too enthused to hear that her son had been risking his life.

In Elijah's case, he wasn't certain how he felt. On the one hand, it was good that Miguel was gaining enough power to protect himself, but Elijah would have been lying if he said he wasn't worried about his nephew. In the end, he could only trust that the young man would be smart about the risks he took.

Before Elijah knew it, everyone had gone to bed, leaving only him and Nerthus sitting in the Grove.

"You'll take care of things while I'm gone, right?" he asked.

"I will," Nerthus assured him. "Anyone who comes to this island with malice in their hearts will rue the day they chose their path."

Elijah believed the spryggent.

So, without further ado, he retreated to his tree house, where he checked and rechecked his supplies. He didn't intend to leave anything behind, so he spent hours going through his lists.

He didn't bother sleeping that night. Instead, when dawn came, he gathered his Ghoul-Hide Satchel, said his final goodbyes to Carmen, Miguel, and Nerthus, then headed toward the Branch in Ironshore.

There, he waited alongside Kurik, a few Tradesmen and Merchants he didn't know, as well as Nia and Robolo. The latter two couldn't meet Elijah's gaze, probably because they remembered what had happened the last time they had grouped up with him. Hopefully, this time would be better.

The timer ticked down until, at last, the Branch began to glow. Then, a notification flashed before Elijah's inner eye:

> **You have been invited to attend the Trial of Primacy. Please report to your local Branch of the World Tree if you would like to participate. Invite expires in twelve (12) minutes.**

Elijah wasted no time before placing his hand on the Branch. The moment his fingers made contact, his senses went dark as he was whisked away to the Trial of Primacy.

85

THE BEST OF THE BEST

Sadie Song stared at the Branch, waiting for the seconds to tick away until she could enter the Trial of Primacy. Even though everything pointed to it being the right decision, she still felt guilty about her choice to attend. There was a niggling thought in the back of her mind that she should have simply gone home. After all, with the corrupted forces of the primal realm having been quarantined, the survivors of Hong Kong would have a perfect opportunity to solidify their grip on the region and retake lost territory. She should have been spearheading that instead of preparing to participate in some sort of contest.

"You okay, bro?" asked Dat, standing on her right side. She glanced toward her friend, seeing that he'd taken the impending Trial very seriously. He'd spent weeks in preparation, buying useful items and plenty of supplies. Most of those supplies were nestled snuggly inside the backpack he'd been awarded for conquering the local tower with a few friends he'd made in town.

That was the thing about Dat, and the trait that made Sadie more than a little envious. He'd always been good at making friends. Part of that was due to his easygoing demeanor, but it could also be chalked up to his nonjudgmental nature. He accepted people as they were, even going so far as to show enthusiasm about their interests.

Sadie had never been able to do that.

Charitably, she could have been called cold, but there were less generous labels that had been thrown her way, many of which were quite vulgar. It had been that way since childhood, and things had only gotten worse after she'd grown up and acquired her class. She wanted to be different. She'd tried to be like Dat. But her attempts at connecting with other people usually came off awkward or condescending, neither of which were endearing qualities.

But at least she had Dat. And her family, though she wasn't sure how much the latter actually liked her. Her family loved her, certainly, but even Niko avoided her unless they pursued mutual goals.

Most of all, though, keeping her company were Sadie's obligations. Others could worry about friendship and being liked. She concerned herself with more important things—like survival. Even if they often called her unflattering names, she would still save as many people as she could.

For her part, she'd spent most of her time in Argos at the Temple of Virtue. It was a comforting place with dense ethera—probably due to the natural treasure that grew at its center—but, more importantly, it gave her the opportunity to help people. Because, for all her cold demeanor, that was what she really wanted out of life. Every step she'd taken had been in pursuit of that goal, and standing before that temple and healing people was the purest expression of those desires.

Unfortunately, she hadn't received the same sort of adulation as that infuriating Druid. When he visited Argos, it was like a parade. And the worst part was that he didn't even notice it. Nor did he seem to care. By comparison, she'd only gotten looks of suspicion and begrudging acceptance of the help she offered.

And it bothered her more than she wanted to admit.

"I'm fine," she lied, shifting her own pack on her shoulder. It was smaller than Dat's, but because of the spatial enchantment, it held even more supplies. But even if she lost it, she felt confident that she could survive with nothing but the enormous sword on her back. The weapon—which she'd received as a reward from a system task associated with the primal realm—was called the Sword of the Morning, and it had been her constant companion for the past year. By comparison, her armor—called Silverine Battle Gear—had been crafted by her clan's most advanced Blacksmith from the best materials they could find, and the results had been a revelation.

Hopefully, it would be enough to protect her. She didn't fear death, but if she fell, Hong Kong would be destroyed. Thousands of lives would be lost. And the undead scourge would spread across the world.

Pushing that pressure from her mind, she glanced back at the others who would participate in the Trial. One of them was a Merchant, while the tall woman who'd latched on to Elijah Hart led a group of fighters. The odd one out was a pretty young man with curly hair. Despite his slight frame and bookish demeanor, he was the only one who felt strong enough to threaten her.

Suddenly, the Branch lit up with blue ethera, and she received a notification informing her that the Trial was ready. So, she reached out and touched the closest crystalline limb, and a moment later, her mind went dark. The last thing she thought was that she hoped she had made the right decision.

Benedict Emerson tried to ignore the agonized moans of all the people around him. Why couldn't they simply remain silent and accept their doom? They were already dead. Their fates had been established the moment they had attacked him, and they had been sealed when they had been impaled by Ritual Spike.

Spell: Ritual Spike	Summon a spear that erupts from the ground to impale a victim. Functions in conjunction with Ritual Circle to channel powerful flows of ethera into a summoning spell.

He glanced up, seeing a perfect circle of black spikes, onto which the bandits had been impaled. Thirteen of them, in fact. An ideal number for his new ritual. One for each of the foundational twelve, then another to represent all the hidden powers of the multiverse. Ten more bodies lay in a nearby heap, discarded and forgotten.

The spikes had been arranged equidistant from one another, and they surrounded four chained imps. They chattered excitedly, completely uncomprehending of what was coming. That was the issue with the demonlings. They weren't completely stupid, but Benedict would describe them more as cunning than intelligent. Whatever the case, the moment he'd evolved Summon Demonling into Summon Malicious Guard, he had chosen to sacrifice them.

Spell: Summon Malicious Guard	Using an empowered summoning circle, summon a tier-2 fel servant and bind the creature to your will. Cooldown based on Ethera attribute. Current cooldown: 18.6 days.

The description hadn't changed much from its previous incarnation, but the ritual's requirements were quite a bit steeper. Not only did those conditions necessitate using Ritual Spike, but they also included sacrificing his previously summoned servants. That was okay, though. Imps were useful, but Benedict believed that one powerful servant would be better than four weaker demonlings.

He'd been quite upset when he'd discovered that four was his current limit. He had plenty of ethera to support more, but that didn't seem to matter. More than once, he'd found himself wishing he'd refused Thakon's offer and continued on as a necromancer. Of course, that only lasted a few moments—long enough for the self-pity to give way to the realization of his increased power—but, in his weaker moments, he found himself railing at the circumstances.

He had adjusted, though. Where he'd once specialized in controlling a great horde of zombies, he would now focus on enslaving the strongest minions he could summon. Quality over quantity—a tenet he could get behind.

Gradually, Benedict completed his ritual circle. After six months, his mastery had become instinctive. He'd always had an eye for detail, and that perfectionism was evident when he stood up and looked at the ritual circle he'd drawn with his victims' blood. He dismissed his ritual dagger, then stepped out of the bloody circle.

Once he did, he took a moment to glance around at his surroundings. He'd stumbled upon the town while seeking a tower to challenge, and to his dismay, they'd reacted poorly to his arrival. It was the same all over the world. Bandits and malcontents all. It wasn't surprising. Benedict had always known that the world was full of bullies. He'd felt their wrath often enough, especially in his youth. The only difference was that now he had the ability to resist.

He'd exercised that ability without hesitation, and the results were all around him. There might've been a few survivors hiding in the town, but his imps had been thorough enough in their quest of extermination. The only issue was that, when they killed without his input, Benedict only received a fraction of the experience.

A small price to pay, but an annoying one.

Regardless, the reward for the imps' efforts was that they were given the chance to fuel his latest summoning. They should have been happy to serve such an undertaking. They weren't, though. Instead, as they began to realize what was happening, they filled the air with their inane chatter, begging him to reconsider. Ungrateful creatures. Hopefully, the malicious guard would be better.

He pulled his attention away from the smoking ruins of the town and focused on the circle. Then, he used Empower Summoning Circle, shoving ethera into the ritual. The blood with which he'd drawn the runes lit up with glimmering power.

Then, finally, he cast Summon Malicious Guard.

The ritual spikes flared with blinding light as they drained not just ethera, but also vital energy from the thirteen impaled villains. That power rushed into the circle and to the chained imps. They exploded into a rainbow of light, cutting off their incessant screeching. Finally, the atmosphere ripped apart, revealing a world of fire and brimstone.

A huge creature stepped through. All glistening black muscle and horns, it looked like a proper demon. It was a quadruped, looking like the unholiest of centaurs, though instead of the body of a horse, the origin of the bottom half was clearly that of a predator, with raking claws, armored plates, and a forked tail. What would have been a human half on a centaur came from a hulking primate, though one with thick rhinoceros-like skin instead of fur. A crown of six horns decorated its tusked simian face.

It roared, shaking the very foundations of the town's still-smoldering buildings.

And Benedict smiled.

Yes—quality over quantity was the right strategy.

"Master," it rumbled, bowing its head.

Before Benedict could respond, he received a notification:

> **You have been invited to attend the Trial of Primacy. Please report to your local Branch of the World Tree if you would like to participate. Invite expires in twelve (12) minutes.**

"Oh," he mused. "That was today?"

He'd totally forgotten about the system's little competition. Though he had to admit that such a Trial might be a perfect proving ground for his newly summoned malicious guard. And as luck would have it, the town he'd so fortuitously visited played host to a Branch.

So, without giving it too much thought, he gestured for his minion to follow as he stepped past the bodies and headed toward the Branch.

Oscar Ramirez was confused.

But that was nothing new. He couldn't count how many times he'd dragged himself out of the struggle to survive and found a new setting. Usually, that meant different variations of the wilderness—or the ruins of civilization—but, in this case, he was standing outside of a functional town.

Nearby were the companions who'd been with him since the very beginning. One of them—Escobar—barked.

"I know," he grunted, glancing at the Chihuahua. He wore a spiked collar, but even though Oscar knew just how powerful the little dog was, Escobar looked no different than in the beginning. Of course, that wasn't the case with all the rest. Seven dogs, mostly stray mutts who'd been brought to the shelter where Oscar had once worked, each one bigger and stronger than any dog had been before the world had changed. Oscar had seen them take down enormous monsters, ripping through them without issue.

He'd done plenty of killing, as well, using the abilities he'd gained from his Pack Leader class to empower, heal, and direct his companions.

But none of them were even close to as strong as little Escobar.

Oscar turned his attention back to the town. It was surrounded by a large wall, which was guarded by a trio of sentries. In his experience, towns were places to be avoided. That was why he spent so much time in the wilderness.

At least that was what he told himself in his more lucid moments. The forests were wild and dangerous places, but he felt more at home away from so-called civilization. Happier, even though it was usually a difficult life filled with violence. But that was what survival meant.

He'd learned that within hours of the world's transformation, when a giant ratlike creature had invaded the animal shelter where he used to work. He'd narrowly managed to survive with the help of his companions, but most of the other animals—as well as his coworkers—had been killed. Since then, he'd encountered one deadly hardship after another, but with the assistance of his pack, he'd overcome them all.

Now, though, he had a choice to make.

The nearby town played host to a Branch. Normally, he didn't care about those curious crystalline trees. He preferred the wilderness, after all. But the Trial of Primacy was important. He wasn't sure why. He just knew it was.

Escobar agreed, an opinion he made known with another series of yapping barks.

Oscar sighed. "I know," he repeated. "We need to go into town." He turned to his other companions and said, "Be on your best behavior."

Two of them—Jackson and Sophie, both of whom were rottweiler mixes—snorted. Freddy let out an excited bark. And Jojo—a tiny shih tzu who could move too fast for Oscar to even track—wagged her tail. The rest took the order stoically, just staring at him with undiluted trust.

With that, Oscar strode forward. He had to force himself to move like the person he'd once been. In the wilderness, he'd gotten into the habit of moving like a wild predator, and pushing those learned tendencies aside was more difficult than he had expected. Still, he managed all the same.

When he reached the guards, they were understandably alarmed by the pack of dogs following him. However, he put on his most soothing voice—the one he used when the members of his pack were upset about something—as he said, "They're with me. Don't worry. They don't bite or anything."

Thankfully, his companions were far more amenable to civilization than he was, and they put on quite a show of wagging tails as they charmed the sentries. It was odd, knowing that the animals were better with people than he was. That had probably always been the case, but increasingly, Oscar found it difficult to remember what his life was like before the world's transformation. That should have been a little alarming, but he found it easier to accept everything that had happened if he didn't have to think about all of that.

Regardless, once the guards had fallen under the dogs' spell, they let him through, even telling him where to find the Branch. He made his way there without delay, though he did buy his companions some meat from a street vendor. Over the past few years, he'd earned a lot of coins, which he didn't hesitate to use to make his pack happy.

Soon enough, he reached the Branch, and it was just in time, too. Almost as soon as he entered the building, he received a notification telling him that the Trial had begun. There were a few people waiting to enter, just like him, and one by one, they touched the Branch and disappeared.

When it came to Oscar's turn, he directed the members of his pack to touch the Branch, and they too disappeared. Escobar was the last to go, and when he did, a deep sense of sorrow enveloped Oscar. He hated being alone. So, he didn't waste any time before touching the Branch, as well.

And when he did, he was whisked away to the Trial.

Emperor Yloa K'hnam sat on his throne, one set of arms folded in front of his muscular chest as the other gripped the armrests. The ostentatious chair had been carved from the bone of his first Deific conquest—a leviathan that had descended upon his city with ill intent—but it had lost much of its inherent power.

It was the same with the entire realm, which the system had dubbed the Last Bastion of the Fallen. It was a fitting name, but when Yloa considered it, cracks spread across the armrest. Even with the shackles imposed by the system, his Strength was monumental, and his anger was even more powerful.

Woe be unto those who chose to participate in this sham of a Trial.

Primacy? He almost laughed at the ill-fitting word. They were fuel. A means for Yloa to drag his people back to relevance. That was what the system had promised.

> Excised world has been temporarily reconnected to the World Tree. To make this connection permanent, slay the participants in the Trial of Primacy before they complete the event. Acceptance of this task is contingent on the application of Shackles that will reduce your power to that of a peak Mortal.

Yloa had accepted without question. His world had long since been excised from the World Tree. It was only through his valiant efforts that they'd managed to resist falling under the influence of the abyss.

But now, they had a chance to rejoin the World Tree. And he only had to kill a few thousand people to do so. It was a gift. A reward for his long dedication to ensuring the survival of his people. Resisting the Ravener had not been easy. Even now, he could feel the great entity pressing against the quarantine instituted by the system. It would find no weaknesses, but its nature dictated that it would never stop trying.

Just as Yloa would never cease in his attempts to save his people. They had already sacrificed so much, and that was before the excision. Now, they had a chance for redemption.

And he wouldn't let them squander it.

As those thoughts flitted through his mind, he felt thousands of surges of power. They were like pinpricks in his mind, each one representing another invader into his world. They were all so pitiful. So weak. If it weren't for the Shackles, he could have destroyed them without ever leaving his throne. With those system-imposed restraints, he would need to be a little more hands-on, though.

Or his people would.

Turning to his adviser, he said, "Ready the hunters. Our visitors have arrived."

The woman nodded, her ivory skin glistening in the ethereal light of the throne room. "As you say, emperor."

ABOUT THE AUTHOR

Nicholas Searcy is the author of Death: Genesis, Mistrunner, and Path of Dragons, originally released on Royal Road. He enjoys writing, reading, spending time with family, sports, and, of course, a good cup of coffee.

⧉ **Podium**

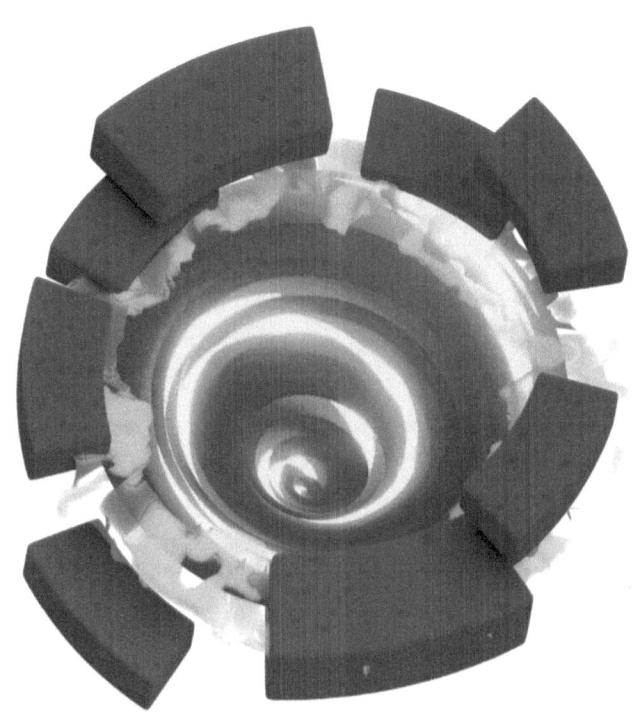

RESPAWN YOUR CURIOSITY
follow us on our socials

 podiumentertainment.com

 @podiumentertainment

 /podiumentertainment

 @podium_ent

 @podiumentertainment

CHAPTER EIGHTY-EIGHT

The break is now over! Let the fourth round of the Foundation Establishment battles begin!"

Finally, a real challenge! None of those squishy robed weaklings. It's time to see who the real dual cultivator is around here!

Zack was bouncing on his feet as he waited in the arena for his next opponent. This was it—the battle he had been waiting for.

But Zack looked almost scrawny in comparison when he stood across from the giant of a man that Ashton was.

Despite this, he eyed Ashton hungrily as the White Tiger disciple landed in the arena with a thud that seemed to shake the very earth itself. Zack had to crane his neck back just to meet Ashton's eyes!

"I've had an eye on you even before the tournament started, big guy," Zack declared. "You're the only one here who seems like they can give me a real workout."

Ashton's stoic expression morphed into one of faint surprise.

"You . . . were watching me?" He blinked slowly. "My apologies, but I do not remember you."

It was true—the White Tiger disciple hadn't paid attention to any of the other battles besides his own. In his mind, none of the other competitors seemed worth his time or effort.

Zack threw his head back and laughed. "Well, after we're done here today, I guarantee you won't forget me ever again!" He slammed a fist against his chest. "So, get those Tiger claws ready, 'cause I'm gonna give you the fight of your life!"

Ashton considered Zack for a moment before dipping his head in acknowledgement.

"You have spirit. I look forward to exchanging techniques."

Elder Fred raised a hand. "Fighters ready? Then . . . begin!"

In perfect sync, both cultivators shot towards each other like loosed arrows. Zack reared back a crackling fist, Ashton mirroring his motions in reverse. Thunderclap met Earthquake as their knuckles collided.

A visible shockwave of rippling air erupted outwards from the point of impact.

For a brief instant, surprise flashed through Ashton's normally stoic gaze. Though smaller in frame, Zack matched his strength and then some. He had not anticipated the Black Rose disciple possessing such a powerful physique beneath his robes.

Impressive.

"You're . . . a fellow dual cultivator?"

A wide grin split Zack's face, knowing he had shaken the immovable giant. "Not bad, huh? Bet you weren't expecting another freak like me!" Zack laughed. "While everyone else wastes time on pretty light shows, you and I put in real work!"

He flexed an arm, veins bulging. "Cultivating the body takes serious dedication. No shortcuts, only blood, sweat, and pain!"

Ashton gave a solemn nod. This junior's physical cultivation was clearly exceptional. Strength recognized strength. "Your body refinement exceeds my expectations. However . . ."

Seamlessly, Ashton flowed into another attack, this time adding an open palm elemental strike alongside his fist.

". . . there is more to dual cultivation than simply possessing two arts," he continued. "True mastery lies in synergizing their power as one."

But Zack merely cackled, unfazed. "Is that all you've got? Then let me show you how it's done!"

With a burst of qi, massive wings crackling with electricity unfurled from his back. Flapping the Thunder Wings once, Zack propelled himself backwards right as Ashton's deadly combination neared. The White Tiger disciple's attacks sliced through empty air.

Before Ashton could react, Zack's palm thrust out, a vortex of lightning spiraling within. "Thunderclap Palm!"

The lightning vortex erupted forward, crashing squarely into Ashton's side. The giant's bulky frame flew through the air, crashing down heavily near the arena's edge. The spectators winced.

But Zack didn't let up for a second, pressing his momentary advantage. Sucking in a deep breath, he let out a roar.

"Dragon Roar of the Thunderous Sky!"

As the cry left Zack's lips, a visible shockwave of sound and electricity surged outwards, tearing across the arena straight at Ashton.

Still struggling to rise, Ashton quickly crossed his arms. But the Thunder Roar smashed into him like a raging tsunami. A groan slipped past Ashton's clenched teeth as the thunder energy racked his body.

Up in the stands, Astrid frowned, her eyes narrowing. This Black Rose upstart was proving unexpectedly troublesome for her student. His mastery over lightning techniques combined with dual body and spirit cultivation made him a difficult matchup.

Perhaps it was time to change tactics . . .

"You alive in there, big guy? I'm just getting warmed up!" Zack cocked his head, squinting through the cloud of dust.

In response, an earth-shaking roar echoed from the debris. A massive shape erupted forth, scattering rubble in all directions.

Towering over fifteen feet high, a white tiger now stood in Ashton's place. Muscles rippled beneath its skin as the beast lowered its head, baring its razor-sharp fangs.

"Guess that's a yes!" Zack laughed. Even transformed, the guy was a man of few words. He always respected someone who let their actions speak for themselves.

With a ground-trembling bound, the white tiger pounced, swiping both paws down towards Zack in a hammer blow. Zack barely leaped aside in time, the crushing force pulverizing the arena floor where he'd stood moments before.

Not letting up, Ashton spun, lashing out with a flick of his powerful tail. Caught off guard, Zack took a direct hit to the chest, the heavy blow launching him halfway across the ring. He tumbled roughly before skidding to a stop in the dirt.

"Ugh, cheap shot," Zack grunted. He really needed to watch that tail. It was already difficult enough to keep track of four deadly limbs!

The tiger reared back its head and unleashed an earth-shaking roar, laced with sonic vibrations.

The arena trembled under the sound assault. Zack clutched his ears in pain, coordination thrown off. Seizing the opening, Ashton pounced forward, claws swiping towards Zack's torso.

Zack barely managed to ignite his lightning wings again and lurch out of the way. But the very tip of one claw still grazed his side, drawing a red line across his robes.

Twisting in midair, Zack fired off several Thunderclap Palms in quick succession, forcing the white tiger back momentarily. But his head was still spinning from the disorienting roar.

Capitalizing on his dazed state, Ashton charged forward again. This time his claws found their mark, smashing Zack out of the air and flattening him against the arena floor.

Pinning Zack under one massive paw, the white tiger bared its saber-like fangs, ready to crunch down on his head.

This is bad. I need to pull myself together quick or I'm about to become kitty chow.

"Celestial Lightning Tribulation!"

At the last possible second, thunder rumbled as a blinding lightning bolt crashed down from the sky directly onto Zack.

The electricity coursed through his body, using him as a conduit before blasting upwards into Ashton.

Howling in surprise and pain, the white tiger recoiled from the unexpected counter. Zack crawled to his feet, clothes smoking but otherwise unharmed. He wiped a trickle of blood from his mouth.

"You're one tough bastard, I'll give you that." Zack grinned fiercely. "But playtime's over now. Time to break out the big guns!"

Zack drew his sword and settled into a high guard stance, blade angled back parallel to his shoulder.

"You're pretty tough to put down, I'll give you that." He pointed the sword tip towards the pacing tiger. "But let's see how you handle my Void Piercer technique!"

The tiger's ears flattened back against its skull. Crouching low, it prepared to pounce yet again. But this time, Zack didn't wait for it to attack.

With a slash of his sword, he used Void Piercer to warp space and pierce through the very air itself to strike at his opponent.

Caught by surprise, the white tiger stumbled. It coughed, vomiting a mouthful of blood. The big cat swayed on its feet, not understanding why it was injured despite not seeing an attack. With a final groan, it toppled over face-first, reverting fully back to human form as he lost consciousness.

Elder Fred descended, quickly examining Ashton before raising a hand. "Victory to Zack of the Black Rose Sect!"

A stunned silence gripped the crowd for several heartbeats before erupting into excited chatter. How spectacular! What a comeback! The Black Rose disciple's strength and wits were simply too much, even for one of the White Tiger's elites.

Up in the stands, Caelum's eyes had narrowed when Zack unleashed his final sword technique. He knew his junior brother had some skill, but that strike had incorporated profound spatial manipulation—the hallmark of a high-level Heaven Ranked technique!

It seems I underestimated just how rapidly Zack's swordsmanship has progressed, Caelum mused. *At this rate, he may indeed surpass me in that area.* The thought gave Caelum pause, though not from jealousy. Only satisfaction that his junior brother was advancing so quickly under their master's guidance.

Among the other elders, Zack's performance also earned nods of appreciation and murmurs of praise.

Even the Heaven's Light First Elder, Zofia, seemed grudgingly impressed despite her dislike of demonic cultivators.

Beside her, Astrid tightened her jaw, though she held back any obvious outrage at her disciple's defeat. Ashton had lost fair and square. And there was one thing that the White Tiger Sect respected: strength.

"That Black Rose boy is clearly exceptional," she muttered. "His combat instinct and adaptability are commendable. Few can withstand Ashton's onslaught once enraged."

"Such marvelous use of space-based techniques!" Leontius applauded. "And at his young age too. Remarkable, truly remarkable!"

Zofia's lips pressed together in a thin line. That the Black Rose Sect had somehow produced such a monstrous talent was concerning. She would need to reevaluate their threat level.

"Yes, Zack has grown substantially under my tutelage," Slifer cut in, maintaining his humble façade. "In fact, all my disciples have blossomed beautifully." He waved a hand as if brushing aside praise. "But raw talent requires careful nurturing. They all still have far to go."

Beside him, Vowron said nothing, merely staring down at Zack with an inscrutable gaze. Though his handsome features betrayed no reaction, an intense glint simmered behind his eyes.

Oblivious to the elders' comments, Zack whooped loudly down in the ring, pumping a fist in the air.

"Now that's what I'm talking about! You really made me work for it, big guy."

He stood over Ashton's unconscious body, grinning widely. "I gotta say, that was the best fight I've had in ages. You even forced me to pull out one of my trump cards!"

Zack leaned down and slapped Ashton heartily on one meaty shoulder.

"Rest up and let's have a rematch sometime. I'll show you a few more of my super-secret techniques! Can't have you thinking that sword move was my only trick."

With that, he made his way back up into the Black Rose stands, accepting back slaps and praise from his sect brothers and sisters.

After ordering the medical team to carry the unconscious Ashton away for treatment, Elder Fred raised his voice. "The next match is . . ."

Just then, Slifer received a spiritual transmission from Morvran.

"Supreme Elder, Kalin and I have discovered something important relating to the Sealed Realm. Please meet us at your quarters when you have a chance."

Though Slifer kept his expression neutral, inwardly his thoughts raced.

What had they found? Ugh, no use speculating. Best to go find out now.

Smoothly excusing himself from the other elders, Slifer made his way out of the stands. However, as he departed, Slifer noticed Vowron watching him with narrowed eyes.

No matter—dealing with that old vulture can come later. For now, Slifer put the issue from his mind as he headed for his quarters . . .

CHAPTER EIGHTY-NINE

Slifer arrived at his private quarters, glancing around with the Insight skill before entering to make sure he wasn't followed. Inside, Morvran and Kalin, were already waiting for him.

"Well?" Slifer asked as he closed the door behind him. "What did you find out?"

Morvran stepped forward first, clearing his throat. "Master, my men report that there seems to have been some kind of internal conflict within the Black Death Sect a few months back. Details are scarce, but it appears to have been quite serious—they say some of the grand elders were even killed."

Slifer's eyes narrowed slightly. For Origin Realm cultivators to have been killed, this conflict was no minor spat. "The Black Death Sect has always been ruthless towards its own members, but for elders to turn on each other to that degree is . . . unusual."

"That's about all I was able to gather for now." Morvran spread his hands. "The Black Death Sect has kept a tight lid on whatever went down. My men are still digging, but . . ."

He trailed off with a shrug. Information from a secretive demonic sect was difficult to come by at the best of times.

"I reached out to my contact in the Immortal Realm." Kalin spoke up. "He confirmed that the Black Death Sect's representative, who regularly relayed messages between the sect and the Black Tree Sect, has gone silent in recent weeks." He paused before continuing. "It's likely he's dead."

Slifer's lips thinned, mind racing over the implications. For a matter to be kept hidden even from the Immortal Realm overseers . . . what in the world had happened in the Black Death Sect?

"Were there any sightings of Nascent Soul Realm cultivators from the Black Death Sect entering our borders?" he asked Morvran sharply. Information was critical right now.

Morvran shook his head. "None that we could uncover. If they sent anyone this way, they did so in secret."

"And the Black Heart Sect Master?" Slifer continued. "Have you learned anything more about his sudden disappearance?"

Again, Morvran gave a negative reply. "Vanished without a trace as far as we can tell. Like he just blinked out of existence one day. No signs of a struggle. My men are still investigating."

Slifer slowly paced the room, mind churning. The timing was too close to be coincidence. The Black Death Sect's internal conflict, the Black Heart Sect Master's disappearance, Vowron's casual reaction to the Inter-Sect Tournament. There had to be a connection.

What in the blazes are you up to, Vowron? Slifer thought. If there was some grand scheme relating to the Sealed Realm between the two demonic sects, why had the Black Rose Sect been excluded? They were supposed to be allies . . . well allies against the righteous sects. *Unless the target is the Black Rose Sect itself . . .*

A tense silence fell over the room as all three men contemplated the implications of everything they had learned . . . or rather, hadn't learned.

Finally, Slifer let out a slow breath and straightened, hands clasped behind his back.

"Keep digging, both of you," Slifer commanded. "I want answers."

The two subordinates bowed.

"Here is what we'll do for now . . ." Slifer began laying out his plans.

When Slifer returned to the arena stands, the final match of the fourth round was just concluding. He slid back into his seat next to the other supreme elders with a polite nod.

"Apologies for my absence, fellow elders. Sect business, you understand."

Supreme Elder Leontius gave him an understanding nod. "Think nothing of it. We are aware how busy your duties must keep you with the sect master away." His gaze took on a hint of admiration. "Oh, and congratulations, it seems all of your disciples have progressed into the fifth round."

"Ah, yes." Slifer laughed. "They've done quite well for themselves, haven't they?"

Slifer was not particularly surprised—he'd been receiving regular updates from the System on his disciples' victories.

I wouldn't ignore the 300 Karmic Credits I get from each win, and that's without the one hundred percent loyalty multiplier!

Supreme Elder Zofia, on the other hand, wore a perpetual frown whenever looking Slifer's way. "Hmph. Too convenient that all your disciples ended up in the finals."

Slifer resisted the urge to roll his eyes. Clearly the old crow still hadn't gotten over her grudge regarding the beating she took when they first met. Best not to indulge her bitterness.

Just then, Elder Fred's voice rang out. "The break is now over! We will begin the final elimination round shortly. The five victors from each division will earn the right to enter the Sealed Realm!"

A buzz of excitement ran through the crowd. Up in the stands, Slifer leaned forward. This was the crucial moment. For his plans to proceed, all his disciples needed to secure slots for the Sealed Realm.

"Let the final round commence!" Fred shouted.

Nomed walked into the arena as his name was called out to fight a disciple named Cilasis.

Seeing that his final opponent was a Black Death disciple, Nomed sighed with relief. As an Early Foundation Establishment cultivator, it wasn't easy defeating Peak Foundation Establishment cultivators one after another, no matter how easy Nomed made it seem.

But at least this battle would be different . . .

Cilasis clasped his hands and gave Nomed a slight bow of the head. Nomed returned the greeting.

"Begin!"

Immediately, Cilasis rushed forward, long sleeves rippling as his arms moved in a flurry of strikes. Rather than counter with any techniques, Nomed met the assault head-on, exchanging blows in a dizzying hand-to-hand exchange.

Up in the stands, Supreme Elder Astrid turned to Slifer with an arched brow. "I was not aware you had another body cultivation disciple, Elder Slifer. The boy matches Cilasis strike for strike."

Slifer blinked, then quickly covered his own confusion with a laugh. "Oh yes, young Nomed is quite gifted! I encourage pursuit of all avenues of cultivation."

Inwardly, his thoughts raced. *Nomed had no body cultivation whatsoever, according to his status window. How in the world is he keeping up with a demon in close quarters then?*

The longer the bout dragged on, the more Slifer's suspicions grew. To him, it almost seemed as though the two disciples were . . . cooperating. Nomed would attack, Cilasis would dodge, creating openings for Nomed to safely disengage whenever necessary.

It almost seems like a badly choreographed dance . . .

After a few more flurry of blows, Cilasis abruptly pulled back, shifting stances.

Nomed smiled, taking the opportunity Cilasis had given him to disengage. With some space between them now, Nomed activated one of his spiritual techniques.

"Divine Ray Annihilation!"

Beams of blazing divine light burst from Nomed's hands, scorching towards Cilasis. The Black Death disciple quickly crossed his arms, defending against the attack, but the force still sent him skidding backwards several feet.

An Early Foundation Establishment cultivator shouldn't have been able to push back a Peak Foundation Establishment opponent so fiercely. But Nomed's light techniques gave him an edge when battling a demon.

Seeing yet another light technique performed by a Black Rose disciple, Zofia clicked her tongue in annoyance. "How does a demonic sect have access to so many light techniques? Those cultivators ought to stick to their gloomy shadows where they belong."

She probably would have insinuated the techniques were stolen from the corpses of her sect's disciples, if not for the fact these particular light arts were unfamiliar to her.

Just where exactly did Slifer's disciples pick up such unusual cultivation methods? The Black Rose Sect seems almost . . . too versatile. Zofia's eyes narrowed suspiciously.

In the Black Rose stands, Nomed's friend, Dusty, was on his feet yelling encouragement with his mouth full of food.

"Yeah, Nomed! Smash his face in!" the pudgy boy hollered, pumping his fist. Crumbs spilled down his dirty robes.

Nomed's lips twitched in amusement at his friend's antics. He gave a slight shake of his head. *No, I can't overdo it,* he thought. *The goal isn't to seriously injure Cilasis after all.*

Crouching down, Nomed placed one palm flat against the arena floor. Golden light instantly sparked from his hand, spreading outwards until the entire stage glowed with celestial runes.

"Demi-Divine Territory!" Nomed called out.

Seeing the domain-like technique, Slifer's eyes narrowed. Nomed's cultivation method relied on a higher being's power, one of the pros of using such an unreliable cultivation method was that it gave users the chance to use techniques that were beyond their cultivation level.

I still don't know what that boy's cultivation plan is, the being that gives the power can just as easily take it away. Slifer shook his head. From the looks of things, his disciple Nomed was craftier than he let on.

Before Slifer could contemplate further, Nomed pointed a finger at Cilasis. A blinding lance of light shot forward, crossing the distance between them in an instant.

Caught off guard, Cilasis barely managed to twist aside, the beam grazing his shoulder and tearing a gash in his robes. The demonic disciple hissed in pain, forced on the retreat now as more lances of light shot towards him in quick succession.

Weaving between the attacks, Cilasis suddenly changed direction and charged right at Nomed. But before he could reach his opponent, a wall of light flashed into existence, blocking his path. Cilasis slammed against the barrier at full speed, bouncing back from the heavy impact.

"My domain, my rules," Nomed stated calmly.

With a flick of his sleeve, glowing chains manifested around Cilasis, wrapping tightly around his limbs and torso. Try as he might, the demonic disciple could not break free, the holy light suppressing his strength.

However, to Slifer, the Black Death disciple's exaggerated look of "panic" was quite unconvincing.

"I-I forfeit!"

Elder Fred blinked in surprise at the sudden concession, but quickly recovered and raised his arm. "Victory to Nomed of the Black Rose Sect!"

Nomed smiled and let out a soft sigh of relief as cheers erupted from the Black Rose pavilion. His goal had been accomplished—he had secured a spot to enter the Sealed Realm.

"Congratulations on another victory, Supreme Elder. That boy . . . I can say for certain he has a bright future. Now, if only I had your luck with disciples." Leontius sighed.

"I agree. The boy shows great maturity for one so young, unlike some of your other disciples," Astrid added, lifting an eyebrow.

Slifer smiled graciously, nodding in acknowledgement of their praise. But inwardly, his thoughts were already racing ahead.

Ding!
Your Disciple Nomed Won
350 Karmic Credits Gained

And no, his thoughts weren't fixated on his credits.

They were focused on the battle he had just witnessed. That match had been odd. The way Cilasis created openings for Nomed, how he just let himself get caught . . . it was almost like he was throwing the fight on purpose.

But why would a Black Death disciple allow a Black Rose disciple to secure a spot in the Sealed Realm? What was really going on here?

The questions churned endlessly in Slifer's mind, even as the next match started. He had an inkling that whatever was transpiring likely tied back to the scheme Vowron seemed to be orchestrating.

Slifer's eyes unconsciously drifted towards the Black Death Sect Master seated beside him. But as usual, Vowron's expression remained unreadable.

With so few pieces of the puzzle, Slifer could only speculate and strategize for now.

But one thing was certain—he needed to keep an even closer eye on Nomed going forward. The boy clearly had an agenda of his own. And until Slifer figured out what that agenda was, young Nomed needed to be monitored.

"*Morvran, there's one other thing I'd like you to do . . .*"

* * *

"Caelum of Black Rose Sect versus Lucian of Heavenly Light Sect!"

Caelum calmly walked into the arena. The Heavenly Light disciple, a nervous-looking young man, gulped at the sight of the undefeated swordsman. This fight would not last long.

As expected, Lucian could do little but defend desperately against Caelum's elegant but ruthless swordplay. Within minutes, Bloodthorn had slipped past his guard and rested lightly against his neck.

"I . . . I yield."

Caelum nodded and stepped back, flicking blood from his sword before sheathing it smoothly. Another easy victory.

The matches continued quickly. Hughie faced off against a bulky teen from Black Heart Sect who specialized in earth techniques. But for once, the big oaf didn't just rely on brawling.

He calmly analyzed his opponent's moves before using his transformations to counter effectively. Though the other disciple landed some solid blows that left Hughie a little bloody, in the end Hughie's tenacity won out. His opponent surrendered after nearly being crushed by Hughie's giant toad form.

"Ha! Did you see that, gramps?" Hughie grinned, reverting back to human form. "I totally dominated that guy!"

"For once, you actually used your brain amidst all that brawling." Li Fenghao harrumphed. "Perhaps you are finally learning strategy, boy."

Hughie laughed and gave the ring a cocky thumbs-up, though internally, he was pleased by the rare praise from the grumpy immortal spirit.

Next up was Dentos, who was pitted against a nervous-looking youth wearing a Black Rose badge—one of the Disciplinary Hall members.

"Um, er, I forfeit!" the boy squeaked out, trembling at the prospect of facing his eccentric boss.

Dentos sighed, another opportunity to wow the supreme elder missed.

The second to last match of the Foundation Establishment bracket saw William against a White Tiger disciple. The young master was clearly reaching his limit—face pale and breathing ragged by the end. But through sheer determination, the scrappy youth had clawed his way to victory. Slifer had briefly wondered what motivated the young master to push himself that far.

Now, only two matches remained—Zack versus Caitlyn, and Amelia versus Ironius. The vampire-looking girl and the dark-haired youth were both Black Death disciples, and something in their predatory gazes during previous rounds told Slifer they would not be throwing their matches like Cilasis had.

No, these two wanted blood.

"Zack of the Black Rose Sect versus Caitlyn of the Black Death Sect!" Elder Fred roared.

Slifer's avatar calmly landed in the arena across from the pale girl.

"Aw, you were hoping to get a go at me during the first stage, weren't you?" Zack grinned. "Well, better late than never!"

Caitlyn said nothing, merely staring back like he was worth less than the dirt beneath her shoes.

Zack's smile didn't waver, but behind it, his thoughts grew wary. This girl wasn't just here to compete—she wanted him dead. He could see the murderous intent clearly now. Things could get troublesome if he wasn't careful.

It's fine, the fish has taken the bait. Now, all I have to do is reel it in . . .

"Begin!"

CHAPTER NINETY

The girl rushed forward to engage Zack in hand-to-hand combat, just as he had antici-pated. As a dual cultivator proficient in both spiritual and body techniques, Zack was not afraid to face a demon in close quarters.

Their initial exchanges were fairly evenly matched, neither able to gain a clear advantage as they traded blows. Zack utilized his quick footwork and agility to avoid the girl's vicious strikes, while looking for openings to counterattack.

"Not bad, little bat," Zack quipped, deflecting a palm aimed at his chest. "But you'll have to try harder than that!"

The pale-skinned girl said nothing in response, her expression remaining cold and blank.

Suddenly, her next palm strike was wreathed in coils of sinister-looking black qi. Zack's eyes narrowed as he barely sidestepped the attack, the corrosive miasma leaving a hissing trail along his sleeve. He countered with a Thunderclap Palm aimed at her shoulder, but the girl nimbly darted backwards, avoiding the blow.

Zack eyed the death qi coming off her palm with a frown. Getting hit by that would be bad news. He felt a phantom pain spike in his shoulder at the thought.

Unlike the other Black Death disciples who had refrained from openly using their spiri-tual techniques during the tournament, this girl clearly had exceptional control over her qi, enabling her to utilize spiritual techniques without fully revealing her identity as a demon.

Zack had already suspected as much from their brief clash during the first stage of the tournament. It seemed this vampire bat was not merely here to compete, but to kill specific targets—with him being at the top of her list.

As for why that was, he still had no clue.

Caitlyn suddenly launched a long-range death qi attack, firing a spear of swirling miasma straight at Zack's heart.

"Whoa, easy there!" he yelped, lightning wings bursting from his back as he took to the air, narrowly avoiding the strike. The death spear dissolved a chunk of arena floor where it landed.

Zack appeared behind the girl in a flash, palm cocked back. "Thunderclap Palm!"

She spun around, meeting his attack with a death qi palm of her own. Their qi collided in an explosion of lightning and miasma, both combatants skidding backwards from the force.

Okay, time to kick things up a notch! Zack thought. "Dragon Roar of the Thunderous Sky!"

Soundwaves and lightning bolts surged towards the death cultivator. She crossed her arms, black qi coalescing to form a shield that managed to blunt the force of the technique. Still, the attack clearly staggered her.

Not wasting the opening, Zack instantly flickered behind the girl in a flash of golden light.

"Sunrise Slash!"

His sword carved a blazing trail aimed at her back. Sensing the danger, the girl spun around, grabbing a hold of the sword with a claw of death qi.

"Aww, man, I liked that sword!" Zack clicked his tongue as the corrosive energy began eating away at his weapon. Before it could spread, he released his grip, allowing the dissolved sword to fall to the ground with a metallic clang.

That had been a little too close for comfort. He couldn't afford to take many direct hits from those death claws.

The Black Death disciple pressed her advantage, unleashing several more ranged death attacks that forced Zack on the defensive. He zipped around the arena using his lightning movement techniques, but the miasma barrage was relentless.

Then with a cold smirk, the girl made a pulling motion with her hands, condensing and shaping the scattered death qi into an enormous, black spectral dragon. It hovered above her, jaws gaping wide as it prepared to swallow Zack whole.

"Oh shi—" was all Zack had time to utter before the monstrosity pounced.

The death dragon struck the arena with earth-shaking force, blooming into an enormous cloud of swirling miasma that obscured everything from view.

The audience members murmured nervously, wondering about the battle's outcome. Had that devastating attack landed on Zack? If so, then he was certainly dead.

Up in the stands, the elders were not so easily fooled. Their spiritual sense pierced the veil of death qi with ease.

"Hmph. That's the end of that match," Supreme Elder Astrid scoffed.

"I didn't expect a Foundation Establishment cultivator to have such a trump card," Zofia's eyes narrowed at Slifer.

"A technique at the Nascent Soul Realm." Leontius sighed, glancing between Vowron and Slifer's impassive faces.

When the death cloud settled, Zack was nowhere to be seen. Caitlyn nodded in satisfaction. The annoying gnat was finally dead. His arrogance had left him completely unprepared for the full power of her techniques. After all, it was rare for a Foundation Establishment cultivator to attack with the power of the Peak Core Formation Realm!

Suddenly, the girl froze. A subtle sound behind her was the only warning before her head detached cleanly from her shoulders, bouncing along the ground with hollow thuds.

Behind her headless body stood Zack, wearing a smoky gray armor and holding a black greatsword. His eyes were hard and cold.

"You shouldn't have underestimated me," he whispered as the Nascent Soul Armor dissipated.

For a brief moment, the arena was dead silent. Then cheers erupted from the Black Rose disciples, celebrating their sect brother's victory.

"The winner is Zack of the Black Rose Sect!" Elder Fred roared over the crowd.

Zack's shoulders relaxed slightly as he flicked blood from his blade. Glancing up at the supreme elders' booth, he exchanged a brief look with the Main Body.

During the first stage of the tournament, he had played things cautiously to avoid being ganged up on. But for these one-on-one battles, he knew he had to eliminate any serious threats.

The special interest towards him and the Main Body from the girl and her companion had been obvious. They needed to be dealt with, so he had decided to fool around to lower their guard. It usually worked for those protagonists, so he figured it'd work for him too.

And that it did!

Still, as he shook his head and gave a wry smile, Zack had to admit he enjoyed playing the obnoxious, goofy protagonist a bit more than he should have.

As the Black Rose Sect members rushed forward to remove the corpse from the arena, Vowron made a subtle motion with his hand. Caitlyn's lifeless body and severed head silently flew through the air into his outstretched palm before being stored away into his storage ring.

The other elders gave him bemused looks at this action, but he offered no explanation.

Turning to Slifer, Vowron stated. "That death was unnecessary, Elder Slifer."

Before Slifer could respond, Zofia intervened with a scoff. "You had no issues when disciples of other sects were killed during this tournament." She gave Vowron a pointed stare. "Why the concern now, I wonder?"

Vowron's eyes narrowed slightly but he did not bother to respond.

Ding!
Your Avatar Zack Won

Slifer continued to stare at his avatar. He had instructed Zack to finish her, though it had hardly required much convincing.

With the Black Death Sect's suspicious activities, it seemed wise to get rid of any dangerous elements among their members when the opportunity presented itself. Even if she was only a Foundation Establishment, it never hurt to be too careful in the world of cultivation.

If only we could have interrogated her, but knowing these types of people, we wouldn't get anything out of it. Maybe I should buy a soul-searching technique, even if it is demonic, it'd be worth it . . .

"The final match of the Inter-Sect Tournament," Elder Fred announced. "Amelia of the Black Rose Sect versus Ironius of the Black Death Sect! Competitors, take your positions!"

The two disciples stepped into the arena, sizing each other up. Amelia gave her opponent a predatory smile, licking her lips. Ironius stared back impassively.

"Begin!" Fred shouted.

Amelia inclined her head in an exaggerated mocking bow. "I hope you'll prove more entertaining than that worm I just disposed of."

Ironius said nothing, settling into a combat stance.

With a smirk, Amelia brought out her black dagger. "Not much of a talker? Doesn't matter, it's the quiet ones that squeal the most."

She dashed forward, feinting high before sweeping the dagger at Ironius's midsection. He reacted instantly, pivoting on one foot as her blade narrowly grazed his robes. Not sparing a moment, his leg snapped out in a brutal roundhouse kick.

Amelia flipped backwards, the heel of his boot missing her chin by inches. Ironius pressed the attack, closing the gap with a flurry of palms strikes.

Light on her feet, Amelia ducked and wove between the blows. She caught his wrist as it shot past her shoulder, angling the dagger for his neck. But quicker than she could react, his other hand came up, grabbing her elbow and stopping her strike cold.

"Tch." Clicking her tongue in annoyance, Amelia dissolved into a wisp of purple smoke, reappearing a few feet away.

Slifer sighed softly from his seat in the stands. This matchup did not bode well for his disciple. Styles made fights after all, and Ironius was the worst possible opponent for a soul cultivator like Amelia.

As a demon, Ironius possessed far greater natural soul strength compared to a human at the same cultivation level. Not to mention his mastery of physical techniques and powerful physique. Trying to overcome such advantages with her soul attacks alone would be an uphill battle.

Still, he had faith that Amelia could pull through. She was a pseudo-protagonist, even if her sadistic tendencies could be rather . . . troublesome at times.

Down below, Amelia circled her opponent slowly. "Not bad. But let's see how you handle this!"

With a pulse of her qi, purple wings unfurled from her back. Ironius narrowed his eyes, dropping into a lower stance.

In a blur, Amelia shot forward, afterimages trailing behind her. She zigzagged around Ironius, dagger striking out from all angles too fast to properly track.

But somehow, the Black Death disciple managed to counter every blow. Swaying and twisting his body like a reed in the wind, Ironius avoided or deflected each strike.

Amelia's smirk slipped. Flitting backwards, she dragged her tongue along the dagger. "Soul Shockwave!"

Rippling waves of violet qi cascaded off the blade, barreling towards Ironius. Crossing his arms, he weathered the direct hit. The soul attack forced him back a step, but otherwise left him unharmed.

"What?" Amelia stared, dumbfounded. That was one of her strongest techniques! How could this nobody endure it so easily? Just what was his soul made of?

Just as I expected, a direct soul attack failed to significantly harm the demon. Slifer shook his head. This just might be the first loss for one of his disciples . . .

Wasting no time, Ironius shot forward like an arrow. Amelia barely raised her dagger in time to parry a hook punch aimed at her head. The force still sent her skidding backwards.

With a surge of desperation, Amelia melted into smoke once more. She reappeared above Ironius, condensing qi into her palms.

"Twin Soul Lances!"

A brace of glowing purple spears flew from her hands. But Ironius displayed uncanny reflexes, twisting and swaying impossibly to avoid both projectiles.

Capitalizing on her distraction, Ironius lunged upwards and seized Amelia's ankle before she could flee. Whipping her down viciously, he drove her into the earth like a sledgehammer.

The impact knocked the wind from Amelia's lungs, leaving her stunned. Ironius pressed his advantage, stomping a heel down towards her face. At the last second, she regained her senses and rolled away. The blow gouged a hole in the arena floor where her head had just been.

Stumbling to her feet, Amelia backed away hastily. This guy was reading all her moves and manhandling her like she was an amateur!

"Don't get cocky just yet." Amelia gnashed her teeth angrily. "I'm just getting started!"

Her beautiful features began morphing, skin paling as she activated her Ghoul Transformation. Smoky wings extended from her back once more, except this time lined with sharp spikes. Her speed and power doubled instantly.

Ironius narrowed his eyes, widening his stance.

Like a violet comet, Amelia shot straight for his chest. But at the last second, she dissolved into smoke, reforming poised at his back for a sneak attack.

"Too slow!" she hissed as she struck with her claws.

Spinning rapidly to avoid the blow, Ironius lashed out with a back kick, his heel catching Amelia right in the stomach.

All the air expelled from her lungs at once. The arena tiles cracked under her as she was driven into the ground like a nail.

Before she could rise, Ironius's foot came down hard on her back, pinning her. He grabbed one of her wings, ignoring the spikes digging into his palm. Slowly he began twisting it at an unnatural angle.

Amelia bit her tongue, holding back a scream as the joints in her wing wrenched and popped. Thrashing violently, she tried to dissolve into smoke to escape, but Ironius just applied more pressure.

Up in the stands, Slifer rubbed his chin as he observed Amelia getting utterly demolished down below.

"Hmm . . . this one-sided thrashing is a bit *unfortunate*," Vowron murmured. "But your disciple does tend to play with her food. I suppose turnabout is fair play."

The Black Death Sect Master wore a faint, satisfied smile as he watched the battle unfold. One of Slifer's pets had just arrogantly slain his disciple, Caitlyn. Now it was only right that he repay the humiliation.

"Savage creatures," Zofia muttered. "This is the true face of demonic cultivators on full display. No restraint or honor, only mindless brutality."

Beside her, Leontius frowned. "It does seem . . . excessive," he said carefully. "The match is clearly decided, there's no need to drag it out like this . . ."

Slifer stayed silent, though a muscle ticked in his jaw. Amelia liked dealing out pain, but how much could she take herself? This was the perfect test of character for her. Either she would break, or she would find a way to overcome. Still, he tensed, ready to intervene if things went too far.

Just when it seemed the wing joint would pop, a desperate idea flashed through Amelia's mind. Focusing inwards, she recalled all the spiritual energy bringing her wing back into her core.

The sudden loss of reinforcement caused the wing to dissipate into smoke, allowing her to slip free from Ironius's grip, and she immediately scrambled away.

Panting harshly, Amelia eyed Ironius with apprehension. She really didn't know what to do next, never before had she been so thoroughly dominated.

Scowling, she poured all of her remaining qi into her dagger. The blade released a purple glow.

"I'll crush you!" she screamed, charging recklessly. Every scrap of speed she could muster went into this final attack.

But Ironius evaded it almost casually before countering with a devastating combo. A knee to the gut doubled Amelia over. An elbow to the back of the neck sent her sprawling face down.

Before she could rise, Ironius's foot slammed down on the back of her skull, grinding her cheek into the ground.

Amelia thrashed and scratched at the ground, but she was pinned helplessly. Ironius stared down at her coldly, as if contemplating how to end this.

Up in the stands, Slifer nodded to himself. *This is definitely a harsh lesson for Amelia, but a necessary one. She'll emerge stronger for it. What doesn't kill you makes you stronger, after all! Or severely maims you. Either way, character development!*

He glanced over at the other Black Rose disciples. Caelum watched impassively, though a glint of understanding showed in his eyes. As Amelia's senior brother, he had long been forced to tolerate her cruel games. This was overdue karma.

Hughie gripped the railing in anger, his body trembling. Every fiber of his being wanted to leap down there and beat Ironius to a bloody pulp for daring to harm his junior sister!

These protagonists need to have better self-control. Slifer made a mental note to have a chat later about anger issues.

Dentos shook his head at the gruesome scene. Efficient battling was the way. No point in dragging things out.

Fenlock simply looked sickened as he watched Amelia being thrashed so brutally. Though no fan of senseless violence himself, he knew the world of cultivation was often cruel. Still, this seemed excessive.

That's enough for now, any more and this guy might really kill her, Slifer thought as Ironius picked Amelia up by the neck, his hands slowly tightened their grip . . .

Ding!
Alert!
Your Disciple Amelia Is in Mortal Danger
Save Her
Reward: 1000 Karmic Credits
Failure: Death of a Disciple

To think I got more credits for her losing . . .

A subtle motion from Slifer drew Elder Fred's attention. The elder's own eyes widened in understanding.

"The match is over, victory to Ironius of the Black Death Sect!" he announced hurriedly before Ironius could continue.

Disappointment flashed briefly in Vowron's eyes. He was surprised that a demonic cultivator that had reached the Ascendant Realm would intervene to save a disciple's life . . . how strange. No matter. The humiliation dealt today was enough.

With some reluctance, the Black Death disciple released Amelia and stepped back.

Amelia crawled to her feet, features returned to normal but no less ugly for the hate and humiliation twisting them.

"This . . . this isn't over . . ." she hissed before limping off stage.

Ironius watched her walk off before making his own exit. The blank mask never slipped from his face. Throughout the battle, he had never said a word. After all, his words were wasted on lower beings.

Throughout the spectator stands, discussions were still ongoing regarding the shocking fight. But soon enough, Elder Fred descended to the arena once more.

"This is the end of the Inter-Sect Tournament!" he announced. "Will the winners of both divisions come onto the stage . . ."

CHAPTER NINETY-ONE

The crowd roared with excitement as the ten winners stood on the grand stage.

In the Core Formation division stood Caelum, Dentos, Hughie, Ironius, and Ziven. Caelum watched the crowd calmly, while Hughie grinned and played up to the attention. Dentos's eyes darted around rapidly, every so often his gaze would fall on Slifer before quickly moving on. Ironius stared straight ahead, face an emotionless mask. Ziven had a small smirk on his face, drinking in the cheers.

The winners of the Foundation Establishment division were Zack, Nomed, William, Maria, and Arva.

Up in the elders' booth, Zofia eyed the Black Rose disciples on stage. "My, isn't this a fascinating turn of events?" She chuckled. "I seem to recall in all the past tournaments, the Black Rose disciples were lucky to even qualify, much less dominate the finals."

Zofia turned, regarding Slifer with a lofty gaze. "Yet, now in your sect's first time hosting, your people suddenly overrun the top ranks. How very . . . convenient."

"It's simple, Supreme Elder Zofia. Our standards for selection have risen while yours seem to have fallen." Slifer paused, smirking. "Perhaps if you spent less time nitpicking the tournament format and more whipping your disciples into shape, the results wouldn't sting quite so much."

Supreme Elder Astrid cut in before Zofia could retort. "It seems the Heaven's Light Sect only sing praises when they are on the winning side. Once the tables turn, all we hear are complaints and excuses."

Zofia scowled but held her tongue. She had hoped the other elders would agree with her, allowing her to put pressure on the Black Rose Sect. *This many demonic cultivators just didn't deserve to enter the Sealed Realm!*

Down below, Zack studied his fellow disciples. The two female cultivators, Maria and Arva, seemed distinctly average based on their tournament performances. Nothing for him to worry about.

No, the real threats here were the Core Formation monsters like that emotionless Ironius, and especially that smug pretty boy Ziven who kept throwing the Main Body dirty looks.

Speaking of Ziven, the arrogant Son of Heaven glanced up at the Heavenly Light Sect's private booth, smirking as he noticed a particular blonde-haired youth.

Arkan, the so-called Legacy Disciple, sat slumped in his seat, eyes hollow and broken as he stared at the stage.

Ziven shook his head in disappointment. He had expected more from the Legacy Disciple. The so-called genius had utterly embarrassed himself against that lunatic Dentos. So much for living up to his hype.

Ziven's expression turned serious as he regarded the Black Rose disciples. In particular, Caelum and Dentos concerned him most as potential obstacles. He would need to be cautious of them in the Sealed Realm, as both seemed difficult opponents.

His gaze drifted to the supreme elder of the Black Rose Sect—he pictured the old demon's look of shock when none of his precious disciples returned alive. Oh, how he would savor that moment!

"Congratulations to the victors!" Elder Fred's voice boomed, interrupting Ziven's fantasies. "Remember to rest up tonight, as tomorrow the supreme elders will open the gateway into the Sealed Realm. I wish you all good fortune on your journey!"

With those words still ringing in the air, the disciples bowed before making their exit. The tournament was done. Now the real trial began.

Back at Slifer's compound, Slifer sat with his disciples to offer some praise and advice before the big day.

He started with Caelum, his top disciple. "Caelum, you have done me proud as always. Stay vigilant and remember to take care of your juniors in the Sealed Realm."

"Thank you, Master. I'll make sure nothing happens to them." Caelum dipped his head.

Hearing that he had made Slifer proud gave him a fuzzy feeling in his chest; he wasn't used to his master complimenting him.

Slifer turned next to Hughie, his expression growing stern. "As for you, while I applaud the . . . unconventional route to victory, such luck won't hold forever. Take things seriously in the Sealed Realm unless you fancy an early death."

The young man shrugged sheepishly under his master's scrutiny. "Hey, hey, no worries! I'll be careful . . . probably."

With a resigned sigh, Slifer faced his avatar Zack. "And that advice goes double for you. I know your strength, but do not get complacent."

Zack nodded along absently. Of course, the Main Body had to put on this show for appearances. Once inside the Sealed Realm, he would be all business. And like the Main Body repeatedly reminded him, the priority was making sure he came out of this alive.

After all, he was just starting to enjoy life—no need to cut it short so soon!

When Slifer's eyes fell upon Nomed, the supreme elder paused thoughtfully. According to Morvran's reports, the child was a complete enigma. An orphan with no known family or history, who, when growing up in the village, would mysteriously disappear for days on end, only to reappear out of the blue. Highly suspicious behavior that suggested the boy's background was not simple.

Clearing his throat, Slifer addressed the orphan. "Nomed, you performed remarkably well, especially for one so . . . inexperienced. I did not expect you to not only reach the finals, but win. It seems even I underestimated your talent."

"Thank you, Master. It was all thanks to your teachings," Nomed replied with a humble bow.

But his respectful tone and measured words rang hollow to Slifer's ears. Clearly the boy held no true loyalty. A spy perhaps? Either way, the kid had earned his slot to the Sealed Realm. It would bring up too many questions if Slifer were to forcefully take it away.

Zack will keep a close eye on you in there, and if it comes to it . . . eliminate you.

The last thing Slifer wanted to do was kill one of his own disciples, but could a traitor truly be considered a disciple?

Shaking his head, Slifer turned to his only female disciple. The girl kept her head low, hair obscuring her face after the day's humiliating defeat.

"The rest of you are dismissed for now," Slifer said at last. "Amelia, stay a moment."

After the other disciples had shuffled out, Amelia finally lifted her head. Her porcelain features were drawn and sullen, full lips pressed thin.

"You're disappointed," Slifer said after a moment. It wasn't a question.

"How could I not be?" Amelia burst out angrily. "I was made a complete fool! In front of everyone, no less. Worst of all, by that . . . that nobody from the Black Death Sect," she spat the name like a curse.

"So, your pride is wounded," Slifer concluded.

Amelia bit her lip, clearly fighting back a snippy retort. Eventually she murmured, "I just . . . don't understand how I could lose so badly. I've never . . ."

"Never suffered a defeat before," Slifer finished gently. "And it's for that very reason this experience will benefit you greatly."

Seeing Amelia's skeptical look, he went on. "You have always enjoyed tormenting your enemies. Humiliating them physically and mentally before moving in for the kill. I've warned you many times of the dangers of such arrogance. And today, you finally received a taste of your own medicine."

Amelia winced but didn't deny his words.

"The path of cultivation is a harsh one. Loss, pain, humiliation—all disciples must endure these trials at some point." Slifer's expression softened. "The question is, will you let this crush you? Or will you learn from it and grow stronger?"

"Master, you've been . . . humiliated before?" Amelia asked, her eyes widening. She had never expected that her master, the supreme elder of the Black Rose Sect, had been publicly beaten to a pulp.

Me? I get humiliated enough by the System as it is. Slifer shook his head. *I'd rather die than have some arrogant young master slap me around.*

As much as he loved to blame the System for its . . . strange attitude towards him, he had to admit it did a good job at protecting him.

But that's only because it seems to need me for this "destroy all evil" mission.

A long silence followed as Amelia waited for her master to reply.

"Your Senior Brother Tyrus leaving was enough humiliation for a dozen lifetimes," Slifer murmured, trying to give her the impression that it took a lot out of him to admit that.

It was technically true, the original seemed to have been driven crazy by his eldest disciple's departure.

Why else would the old fool chase after him when he had just failed his Origin Realm breakthrough?

Amelia nodded slowly, digesting her master's words. When she finally spoke, her voice was almost a whisper. "You're right, Master. I've been too prideful. Toying with my opponents, laughing at their pain . . . I realize I can't continue on like that." She took a deep breath. "I . . . I will try to change."

"That is all I ask," Slifer said, feeling a small glow of satisfaction.

Ding!
Your Disciple Amelia Has Experienced Significant Character Growth
Reward: 1000 Karmic Credits
Your Disciple Amelia's Loyalty Has Increased By 10%

Slifer nodded to himself. It seemed the System truly valued him nurturing his disciples' character and integrity. He was more than happy to oblige if it meant more Karmic Credits.

Speaking of rewards . . . A sly glint entered Slifer's eyes. "You know, it just so happens I have something that will lift your spirits."

Amelia lifted her head warily, skepticism written clearly across her face.

Grinning, Slifer announced, "You will take the final slot to enter the Sealed Realm!"

"What?" Amelia's head jerked up in shock. In her misery, she had forgotten that her master held one reserve slot. "But, Master, not only did I lose but I was humiliated. I . . . I don't deserve it."

"Nonsense." Slifer waved dismissively. "It was my plan all along to award the reserve slot should one of you unexpectedly fail to qualify. Consider it a second chance to prove yourself."

In truth, Slifer knew the Sealed Realm offered greater opportunities to earn Karmic Credits than remaining outside. But Amelia didn't need to know that.

"Th-thank you, Master!" Amelia stammered. "I swear I'll bring you back something from the Sealed Realm!"

I'm counting on it . . .

The Great Wolf tavern was bustling with activity. Patrons laughed and slammed down cups. The air smelled of roasted meat, spilled ale, and tobacco smoke.

In one corner, a group of musicians played a lively tune on lute, fiddle, and drum.

The noise softened for a moment as the front door banged open.

A young man in black robes strode in, his handsome features set in a scowl. The tavern's conversations stuttered to a halt as all eyes turned towards this new arrival. They could sense the aura of power radiating from him—this was no ordinary customer.

The youth marched right up to the bar, where an old man was filling tankards from the tap. He slammed down a golden coin on the counter.

"Clear this place out for the next few hours," he ordered the gaping owner. With a flick of his sleeve, the gold coin floated into the man's hand.

"Of course, Young Master! Right away!" The owner bowed repeatedly, clutching the coin tightly. This amount of money would cover his establishment's expenses for a month. Not to mention, it wasn't worth risking his life by angering an immortal cultivator over something so trivial.

"Sorry folks, we're closing early tonight! Finish your drinks and be on your way now!" the owner said as he began ushering patrons outside.

"Ah, come on, I just got my ale!"

"You can't kick us out without any bloody warning!"

"Hey, I wasn't finished!"

The owner waved his hands desperately. "I'm real sorry, but you all need to clear out immediately!" He jerked his head meaningfully at the glowering disciple.

Finally, understanding dawned in the patrons' eyes. Their protests died away as they sensed the dangerous atmosphere. With many backwards glances and muttered curses, the crowd began funneling towards the exit.

But a large, burly man in particular seemed intent on staying behind.

"Bah! These so-called immortals think they own the damn place," he grumbled loudly.

"I paid good coin for my drink and I ain't leavin' till it's finished!" He demonstratively gulped down his ale, dripping foam through his bushy whiskers. Then he belched thunderously in the direction of the black-robed youth.

His friends paled and edged away. "Erwin, you fool, are you trying to get us killed? Let's get out of here!"

But Erwin refused to budge, staring challengingly at the disciple with bloodshot eyes.

The black-robed youth's features remained impassive. He glanced at the tavern owner, who was wringing his hands anxiously.

The black-robed youth sighed, then suddenly appeared before the drunkard in a blur of motion. "I believe it's time for you to leave."

Before anyone could react, his hand lashed out faster than the eye could follow, delivering a slap to the brute's face. The man was launched sideways, crashing through tables and chairs before slamming into the far wall. He slumped to the floor, unconscious.

A hushed silence descended on the tavern. The remaining patrons scrambled over each other in their haste to flee out the doors. In seconds, the tavern was empty.

The young man sighed, nudging a broken chair with his foot. "Just look at this mess. Now I have to tidy up before the others arrive."

The tavern owner stood frozen, unsure whether he should try offering assistance or flee for his life. In the end, he decided to run.

The disciple gathered up the debris strewn around the tavern with surprising meticulousness, arranging the remaining furniture neatly. Within a few minutes, the common room was again presentable.

At that moment the entrance creaked open.

Jin's eyes widened as they settled on the new arrival—it was Lucious, the sect leader's disciple!

"Greetings, Senior Brother!"

Lucious glanced around the vacant tavern before settling his gaze on Jin. "Yes, this should work well enough if things get . . . messy."

Jin shuddered at the implication but nodded in agreement. A meeting between the top cultivators of the younger generation could easily get heated.

"Now, prepare us some tea."

"Yes, Young Master!" Jin scurried away, sending a tea service flying through the air onto an intact table. Hands shaking, he carefully poured steaming tea into two ceramic cups.

Lucious picked his up, blowing gently before taking a sip.

Jin shifted anxiously from foot to foot. Not only would this be the first gathering between the top disciples of the younger generation from the major sects, but also the first and only time they would enter the Sealed Realm.

Noticing his discomfort, Lucious inclined his head slightly. "You may take your leave. Do not let anyone else enter until I say so."

"Of course, Young Master!" Jin retreated hastily out the front door.

Alone now, Lucious settled in to wait, absently swirling the tea leaves at the bottom of his cup. He needed his mind clear for the meeting, this would be his first time meeting some of them.

The creak of the door opening snapped Lucious from his thoughts.

He glanced up as the number one Core Formation disciple from the Pure Soul

Sect—Celestia—entered the tavern. Her golden hair swayed behind her as she walked towards him.

"Greetings, Brother Lucious," she said politely, if somewhat reservedly.

"Sister Celestia," Lucious inclined his head. "I'm pleased you accepted my invitation."

Her answering smile didn't reach her eyes. "If it was Brother Lucious himself, then how could I refuse?"

Lucious nodded. "Have a seat."

Celestia settled down on a chair across from Lucious. An awkward silence descended on them as neither seemed inclined to continue the conversation.

After a few minutes, the door creaked open again and a tall, muscular woman with snow-white hair strode in. Her icy blue eyes scanned the room before settling on Lucious and Celestia.

"Sister Larissa, please sit down."

"So, I'm not the first . . . pity." Larissa completely ignored Lucious as she sat down, focusing her attention on Celestia. "Hello, Sister Celestia."

"Sister Larissa, it has been too long! I believe the last time we met was at the Zhongyuan Festival, a year ago?" Celestia smiled back warmly. "I'm glad to see you well."

"Hmph. Save the pleasantries," Larissa said bluntly, though not unkindly. "I've no patience for that today."

Before Celestia could respond, the door swung open again and in came the Black Heart Sect's Horocus. He was a young man with a pale complexion and piercing red eyes.

As Horocus approached, Lucious noticed faint tension in the man's shoulders and the way his smile seemed forced. With his sect leader missing, it was no wonder Horocus seemed on edge.

"Hello there, friends," Horocus said, taking a seat. "Quite a rare gathering we have here." His eyes darted around the group, as if expecting an attack at any moment.

"Just two more and we'll be ready to begin," Lucious replied. Right on cue, the door opened, and a handsome, silver-haired youth strode in, smiling brightly.

"Apologies for my tardiness, friends," Raphael laughed. "I hope I didn't keep you waiting too long?"

"Not at all, we only just arrived ourselves," Celestia replied whilst the others nodded.

Lucious noticed Raphael's smile falter briefly when he scanned the room, clearly having expected to be the last arrival. *Trying to assert dominance by being fashionably late? How droll.*

As Raphael sat down, the five disciples simply observed one another, silently taking stock.

The tension in the room was palpable.

Horocus spoke up. "It seems Arcavious won't be joining us. I haven't been able to contact him . . . I don't think he's interested in whatever this meeting is about."

Not surprised that the reclusive Black Death genius decided not to attend, Lucious cleared his throat.

"Shall we get down to business then?" At their nods, he continued, "As you know, we all plan to enter the Sealed Realm tomorrow. I called this meeting so we may . . . discuss arrangements, for how to handle things inside."

"Spare me your slick words." Larissa snorted. "There's nothing to understand in the Sealed Realm beyond the obvious—take what you want by any means necessary."

They were all too prideful in their own abilities to team up with even members of their own sect so why would they be interested in working with each other?

"In theory, yes, that is how things are usually done there." Lucious turned to her. "But why waste time fighting amongst ourselves and giving others the chance to take the spoils from under our noses?"

Larissa's eyes narrowed but she stayed silent.

"You make a reasonable case, Brother Lucious," Celestia chimed in. "What arrangement did you have in mind?"

Inwardly, Lucious smiled. The Pure Soul disciple's reaction was predictable—spineless and eager to avoid conflict. As if reading his thoughts, Larissa shot Celestia a disgusted look.

"It's simple. We divide the Sealed Realm into five territories, one for each of us," Lucious explained. "Give your word that you won't cross into another's territory, and they shall extend the same courtesy."

Raphael tapped his fingers on the table. "And if one territory proves less . . . bountiful than the rest?" He posed the question innocently, but his meaning was clear: he would never accept less than the lion's share.

"The Sealed Realm is vast," Lucious countered calmly. "I doubt that will be an issue. Unless you're afraid you can't hold your own portion?"

Raphael's eyes narrowed; he wasn't worried about the disciples who had earned their slot through competing in the Inter-Sect Tournament. No, the only cultivators he had to be wary of were those sitting here beside him.

"A sensible proposal," Horocus agreed.

But Larissa looked anything but convinced, turning on Horocus with a sneer. "Look at you, scurrying to make a truce the moment your master disappears. How pathetic."

Horocus flushed but he held his tongue. Larissa was known to be crude and provocative.

"Enough." Celestia's gentle voice cut through the tension. "I also agree to this arrangement."

All eyes turned to Raphael and Larissa.

Raphael gave an exaggerated sigh. "Well, I was hoping we could settle this through outright battle to determine who was the strongest between us . . . but I suppose this could work as well." He paused, meeting each of their eyes. "Oh, and I'll be taking the central region."

Lucious nodded, having expected as much from the arrogant Heavenly Light disciple.

Larissa growled, unsatisfied, but gave a terse nod. "North region for me then."

In the end, Lucious claimed the eastern quarter for himself. Horocus took the west, and Celestia the south.

With the territories divided up, Lucious clasped his hands together. "It's decided then. We enter the Sealed Realm as . . . allies." His tone sounded sincere, but inwardly, a cold smile tugged at Lucious's lips.

There would be no honoring of boundaries within the Sealed Realm, regardless of what promises exchanged hands today. Even Celestia and Larissa would not be so naïve as to fully trust each other's word.

No, this meeting accomplished its true purpose: to know the starting location of his "allies" and to gain a better understanding of them.

Horocus was a paranoid mess who could easily be manipulated.

Raphael, like any other Heavenly Light Sect disciple, had an ego problem.

Larissa was quick to anger and could be lured to her death.

And Celestia . . . well, the peacemaker lived up to her reputation, willing to compromise to avoid conflict.

Now, if he were to reach the Nascent Soul Realm first, he would be able to hunt his fellow Legacy Disciples one by one, starting with the most arrogant one first of course.

But to break through before them, I need to keep them distracted . . .

And that was where the newbies came into play. Oh yes, he'd had his eyes on the supreme elder's disciples for a while now.

Whilst he didn't expect any of them to actually defeat the Legacy Disciples, he felt they would be able to keep them entertained until he was ready.

Now, time to introduce myself as the benevolent senior brother . . .

CHAPTER NINETY-TWO

The crowds roared with excitement, the stands packed full of disciples. Today was the opening of the Sealed Realm, and everyone wanted to witness this momentous event.

"Can you believe it's finally happening?" a female disciple gushed to her friends. "We're so lucky to be here! I can die happy now!"

"Speak for yourself." One of her friends elbowed her side lightly. "I plan on living a good long while! But you're right, today will certainly be one to remember."

In the row behind them, two male disciples were having a heated debate.

"That Ziven is supposed to be really impressive. Do you think he has a shot against the big names in there?"

His friend gave him an incredulous look. "Ziven might be crazy talented for his age, but he's still just a junior compared to the Legacy Disciples. Pitting geniuses against each other is one thing, but . . . this is a whole different level."

Before the argument could continue, a sudden commotion from the arena caught their attention.

"Look, someone's arrived!" a sharp-eyed disciple exclaimed.

All eyes turned towards the arena gates as a figure strolled casually into view.

"It's him! The Son of Heaven!" A voice rang out excitedly as people recognized Ziven's striking profile and piercing green eyes.

Ziven paused to give the audience a small smile and nod before moving to stand at the center of the arena. The smile didn't reach his eyes though, which remained hard chips of jade, betraying his tightly leashed killing intent.

Those that entered the Sealed Realm at the Core Formation Realm typically exited as an Origin Realm expert. It was exceptionally rare for anyone to reach the Ascendant Realm; however, Ziven had no choice, only by breaking through to the Ascendant Realm would he have a chance at getting revenge.

Xander . . . I'll make sure that demonic scum pays, Ziven promised.

One by one, the qualifying disciples filed into the arena. When all ten disciples had gathered, the hushed conversations took on an uneasy tone. The general consensus was that despite their impressive showings so far, these disciples were simply out of their depth against true elites.

Right on cue, a collected gasp echoed through the stands. All eyes turned once more towards the arena entrance.

"Look, it's Brother Lucious!" a female disciple squealed. Unlike with Ziven, the excitement in her voice was genuine.

The number one Black Rose disciple strode into view, midnight robes swaying gracefully with each step. As Lucious approached the other Black Rose disciples, his handsome features settled into an easy smile. He gave Caelum, Hughie, and the rest polite nods.

"Hello there, juniors," Lucious said warmly as he took up position beside them. "I know things can get dangerous in there. As your Senior Brother, please know that you can rely on me."

His sincere tone and comforting words took the crowd by surprise. A demonic cultivator showing such care? It was unheard of!

"So handsome and so kind too!" one girl cooed under her breath. "Why can't the disciples from our Heavenly Light Sect be more like him? They just too arrogant!"

Next to arrive was the Black Heart Sect's number one disciple, Horocus. The red-eyed youth wore a tense, wary expression as he silently took his place.

The other top disciples appeared in short order—Larissa, Celestia, and finally Raphael, pride of the Heavenly Light Sect.

If the crowd was excited by Lucious's arrival, then they were absolutely frenzied at the sight of Raphael. After all, he represented the undisputed strongest sect amongst the younger generation.

Raphael paused beside Ziven, placing a hand on his shoulder. "Well done on making it here, Junior. I'm pleased to see such promising youths from our sect."

Ziven wanted to slap away that condescending hand but managed a stiff nod instead. The time for talking was over. Only strength would matter in the Sealed Realm.

At last, it was time for the guest of honor—the supreme elders themselves. Excitement reached a fever pitch throughout the arena stands as disciples clamored for the best view of these legendary figures.

First to arrive was Astrid, supreme elder of the White Tiger Sect. With a roar, an enormous white tiger descended from the heavens, its passenger seated calmly on top of its head. The disciples marveled at the incredible sight.

"Amazing! That tiger has to be at least thirty meters long!"

"No way, it's got to be bigger. Fifty meters at least!"

Next arrived Leontius, supreme elder of the Pure Soul Sect, descending gently on a floating cloud. Compared to Astrid's dramatic entrance, his subtle arrival elicited fewer reactions.

"The Pure Soul Sect always favors grace over intimidation."

"But don't underestimate Elder Leontius because of that . . ."

Right on cue, a piercing shaft of radiance split the heavens as Zofia, supreme elder of the Heaven's Light Sect, descended amidst a corona of blazing light. Many disciples cried out, forced to turn their eyes away from the blinding brilliance.

"Such dazzling glory! As expected of the number one righteous sect."

"Elder Zofia's strength is said to be second only to the sect leader's . . ."

In contrast, the reaction was more muted when Vowron emerged, riding a creepy chariot pulled by skeletal horses. They could always trust the Black Death Sect to make a morbid entrance.

Yet all other arrivals were forgotten when an earth-shaking draconic roar resounded across the city. All heads turned upwards as the massive form of Val descended from the heavens, flames spewing dramatically around her. The dragon landed with an impact that shook the arena itself.

As she shrank down into the tiny, cat-sized form, excited chatter broke out amongst the disciples once more.

"Did you see that entrance? Much better than just riding some big cat!"

"Yeah it gave me goosebumps!"

"That dragon fire was insane! I could feel the heat from here!"

"Val is just the cutest! I want a mini dragon pet too!"

Val lapped up the chorus of praise, turning to Slifer with a toothy grin. "Master, did you see that? They loved it!"

Slifer chuckled, patting her head. "Of course, my little Val. You're the star of the show!"

Satisfied, she scurried to his shoulder, draping herself across it like a scaly scarf.

He then met the gaze of his fellow supreme elders. "Shall we begin?" At their nods, he retrieved the golden keys from his robe that would unlock this sacred realm. Each supreme elder contributed their key to the collection.

With a flick of his wrist, Slifer sent the keys spinning skyward. Halfway up they collided in a dazzling cascade of light, merging and expanding until a single massive key now hung suspended before them.

Slowly, the colossal key began rotating in place, faster and faster as space itself warped and stretched around it. A resonating hum filled the air as a tiny pinprick of light appeared that rapidly tore itself wider.

Within moments, the air had ripped open entirely, revealing a swirling portal of darkness—the gateway leading into the Sealed Realm!

At an unspoken signal, the five elite Legacy Disciples stepped forward as one and paused before the portal.

"Try not to die before I can crush you myself," Larissa remarked to Celestia, though her tone held a hint of wry humor rather than true malice.

Celestia's answering smile was polite, if a little strained. "Take care as well, Sister."

With no more words wasted, the top disciples dissolved into the void one by one until only darkness remained.

Now the tournament victors stepped up to take their turn.

Hughie was practically vibrating with excitement. "This is it, guys! Our time to shine."

Beside him, Zack kept his true feelings carefully concealed. But across the portal, his eyes briefly met Slifer's own. One curt nod was exchanged between the Main Body and his avatar—nothing more needed to be said.

Nomed was the last to approach. For just a moment, his eyes darted towards Vowron. But the movement was so brief none noticed. A heartbeat later, the boy too had vanished into the Sealed Realm.

Just as the portal was beginning to constrict on itself, Slifer stepped forward to retrieve the key. But before his fingers could close around it, his entire body abruptly locked up, muscles seizing and refusing to budge no matter how fiercely his mind strained against the paralysis!

Beside him, the other supreme elders seemed frozen in place as well.

"Leave now, quickly!" Slifer urgently communicated to Val through their spiritual bond.

The little dragon shook her head. "And abandon you, Master? Never! I can help you fight!"

"Go, Val! Be with the others—that is how you can best help me now."

Seeing the uncharacteristic sternness in her master's eyes, Val hesitated only a moment longer before spreading her wings and flying away.

Slifer heard dark laughter, then Vowron walked slowly into his field of vision. "So sorry for the delay, friends," the Black Death Sect Leader said, smiling coldly. "It seems a few more of my disciples wish to enter the festivities after all."

With a laugh, Vowron's aura swelled explosively. In the span of a few breaths, his strength had already exceeded the Ascendant Realm.

"Half . . . Immortal Realm!" Zofia spat in disbelief. "Your cultivation . . . how is this possible?!"

"Come now, Supreme Elder, surely a cunning woman like yourself would have sensed if something was amiss before today?" Vowron purred as he circled the paralyzed elders like a shark.

"Unfortunately, you simply aren't as clever as you believe. But don't feel too bad." The Black Death Master chuckled as he withdrew a small black cube, etched with pulsating red runes. "A gift from a mutual friend in the Immortal Realm. He certainly has taken a liking to me. And this delightful toy creates a stasis field that can restrain any cultivator below the Immortal Realm."

Understanding mixed with fury flashed in the elders' eyes.

The smile never leaving his face, Vowron cocked one finger. Responding to his summons, black-clad disciples bearing the insignia of the Black Death Sect began dropping into the arena from the spectator stands.

"You didn't think I would pass up this rare chance, did you?" Vowron smirked. "The flower must seize its moment while the garden lies unguarded."

With that, the death disciples rushed headlong towards the still-open portal leading into the Sealed Realm. But before they could approach it, more figures appeared in their path— led by none other than Morvran!

"I'm afraid this is as far as you'll go," Slifer's trusted supporter declared. Behind him, other Black Rose members fanned out, preparing to fight the invaders.

Slifer had warned him that Vowron would likely make a move when the portal opened. He had instructed Morvran to tell the grand elders to be prepared.

Even as the first clashes broke out across the arena floor, more powerful auras from both sides joined the fray. Like ripples in a pond, the combat quickly expanded outwards to engulf the entire coliseum.

Amidst the chaos, Fenlock leapt into action. Unleashing furious screams amplified by his sound cultivation, he caught a group of Black Death Nascent Soul cultivators off guard. They clamped hands over their ears in agony, only to find themselves cut down ruthlessly by Morvran's men.

With an earth-shaking roar, Val suddenly reappeared in her massive form. The dragon dove into the enemy ranks, claws and fangs shredding all in her path.

Several Black Death cultivators screamed as they were snatched up in her jaws, crushed and devoured in seconds. Others tried to fight back only to be blasted by scorching flames.

Yet despite the Black Rose members' efforts, the Black Death cultivators continued to press forward with fanatical determination.

For each one killed, two more seemed to take their place.

Trapped behind their barriers, the supreme elders could only watch helplessly as their disciples fought and fell before their eyes.

"Damn you, Vowron!" Zofia screeched. "I'll see your sect destroyed for this!"

"Now, now, no need for such hostility," Vowron chided mockingly. "Not that it matters anymore . . ."

> *Ding!*
> New Task: Save the Supreme Elders
> Reward: 5,000 Karmic Credits for Each Elder You Save

Slifer released a sigh as he saw the task notification pop up in his vision. A part of him had briefly considered just letting Vowron kill the other supreme elders—it would certainly weaken the major sects. However, if the elders were to all perish here in Black Rose territory with Slifer as the only survivor . . . well, the backlash would be immense.

His thoughts were interrupted by Vowron's expression twisting into a sneer. "I believe I'll start with you, Slifer."

Slifer's eyes widened in surprise as Vowron's own flashed red, his body morphing into an emaciated, lich-like form. With astounding speed, the Death Sect Leader conjured a bone spear caked in swirling black energy and hurled it straight towards Slifer's heart.

The spear passed harmlessly through Slifer's body, embedding itself into the arena wall behind. The other elders didn't even flinch, already aware of Slifer's space technique.

"A space cultivator," Vowron hissed in understanding. "An amusing trick, but it only delays the inevitable."

After circling for a little while, he noticed Slifer's form become corporal, and darted forward, bony claws reaching towards Slifer's throat.

And in that instant, a massive green cauldron materialized between them!

Caught by surprise, Vowron was unable to stop his momentum in time. An irresistible force latched onto his body, dragging the Death Sect Leader towards the open cauldron.

"What is this?!" Vowron shrieked, struggling in vain against the pull.

With a final scream, he was swallowed by the ancient artifact.

A heavy thud sounded as the lid slammed shut over the opening. Faint banging could be heard coming from within as the cauldron quickly vanished into Slifer's storage ring.

At the same moment, the supreme elders found themselves able to move once more, the stasis field broken. Zofia's eyes were wide with disbelief as she turned on Slifer.

"You . . . you're an alchemist as well?" she demanded.

Slifer let out a laugh. "I dabble from time to time."

The elders exchanged dubious looks. That had clearly been no ordinary pill cauldron, but an immortal-grade treasure! No mere dabbler would possess such a tool.

Seeing their skepticism, Slifer sighed internally. In truth, the cauldron was something he brought recently from the Shop—he'd felt the need for alternate sources of income, and in the novels alchemists always ended up rich. Besides, few dared provoke someone with the backing of countless pill-hungry cultivators. Should anyone be foolish enough to try . . . well, they'd quickly come to regret it.

> *Ding!*
> Reward: 15,000 Karmic Credits

"You have my gratitude for saving us, Brother Slifer," Leontius said with a respectful bow.

Astrid nodded firmly in agreement. "We are in your debt."

Zofia's eye twitched, but she too offered grudging thanks.

Slifer waved off their words hurriedly, turning his focus back to the collapsing portal. With a flick of his sleeve, he summoned the golden key back into his hand. The gateway winked out of existence, sealing off access to the interior plane.

Slifer watched as the supreme elders took to the air, flaring their cultivation bases. The disciples below instantly froze at the overwhelming pressure.

"Take the invaders captive!" Slifer ordered. "Morvran, have them sent to the dungeons for interrogation."

"At once, Master!" The pudgy man bowed before racing off to relay the commands.

As the death cultists were being chained and led away, Morvran paused to report back. "Master, I'm afraid a handful managed to slip past us into the portal before it closed."

Slifer frowned, glancing at the other elders. Too many unscheduled entrants could potentially destabilize the delicate balance of energies within the pocket realm.

Typical xianxia complication, Slifer mused. *What better way to end the first book than by trapping the protagonists in a collapsing world?*

EPILOGUE

Under a demonic tree sat a young woman wearing red robes. She was looking up at the sky, wondering why her love had not responded to any of her letters.

A maid rushed over. "My lady, I'm afraid I have news—"

"This had better involve my Darius, or I have no interest." The young woman cut her off as she examined her long, pointed black nails.

The maid hesitated. "It does, my lady. I'm afraid it's rather . . . unfortunate news."

The young woman's gaze snapped to the maid, eyes flashing dangerously. "Speak, worm."

The maid flinched. "Y-your lover . . . he is dead, my lady."

Silence descended. The words hung heavy in the air as the young lady stared.

"W-what?"

"Darius . . . he is dead," the maid repeated nervously. "Killed in a cultivator battle in the Mortal Realm, or so I heard."

The young woman was silent for a long moment. When she finally spoke, her voice was a chilling whisper. "If my love is dead, then so are you."

As she uttered the words, her eyes turned red. The maid's own eyes glazed over, entranced. "Yes, my lady, I am dead," she said dully.

Turning, she began walking straight towards the tree.

The twisted branches of the demonic tree suddenly whipped down and coiled around the maid's body. She made no sound as they lifted her high and stuffed her directly into the trunk.

The tree shuddered in ecstasy as it hungrily devoured its meal.

The young lady turned away, the red light in her eyes dimming back to cold black orbs.

"I will find whoever took you from me, my love," she whispered. "And I will paint the Mortal Realms crimson with their blood."

ABOUT THE AUTHOR

Kalzara is the author of the Demonic Sect Elder series, originally released on Royal Road. He is an avid reader of LitRPG and cultivation novels so it was only a matter of time before he decided to write one of his own.

≋ Podium

RESPAWN YOUR CURIOSITY

follow us on our socials

 podiumentertainment.com

 @podiumentertainment

 /podiumentertainment

 @podium_ent

 @podiumentertainment

www.ingramcontent.com/pod-product-compliance
Lightning Source LLC
Chambersburg PA
CBHW031056130726
47906CB00008B/388